Thomas Beddoes

Alexander's expedition down the Hydaspes & the Indus to the Indian ocean

Alexander's expedition down the Hydaspes & the Indus to the

Indian ocean

Thomas Beddoes

Alexander's expedition down the Hydaspes & the Indus to the Indian ocean

ISBN/EAN: 9783742845184

Manufactured in Europe, USA, Canada, Australia, Japa

Cover: Foto ©Andreas Hilbeck / pixelio.de

Manufactured and distributed by brebook publishing software
(www.brebook.com)

Thomas Beddoes

Alexander's expedition down the Hydaspes & the Indus to the Indian ocean

THOMAS GARNETT, M.D.

Published Jan 1, 1803, by the Executors, for the benefit of his orphan Children.

POPULAR LECTURES

ON

ZOONOMIA,

OR

THE LAWS OF ANIMAL LIFE,

IN

HEALTH AND DISEASE.

BY THOMAS GARNETT, M.D.

MEMBER OF THE ROYAL COLLEGE OF PHYSICIANS, LONDON; OF THE ROYAL IRISH ACADEMY; OF THE ROYAL MEDICAL SOCIETY OF EDINBURGH; HONORARY MEMBER OF THE BOARD OF AGRICULTURE; FELLOW OF THE LINNEAN SOCIETY; MEMBER OF THE MEDICAL SOCIETY, LONDON; AND OF THE LITERARY AND PHILOSOPHICAL SOCIETY OF MANCHESTER; &c. &c.

FORMERLY PROFESSOR OF NATURAL PHILOSOPHY AND CHEMISTRY IN THE ROYAL INSTITUTION OF GREAT BRITAIN.

LONDON:

FROM THE PRESS OF THE ROYAL INSTITUTION OF GREAT BRITAIN: W. SAVAGE, PRINTER. PUBLISHED FOR THE BENEFIT OF THE AUTHOR'S CHILDREN BY HIS EXECUTORS. TO BE HAD OF MR. NICHOLSON, SOHO SQUARE, MR. PRICE, WESTMINSTER LIBRARY, JERMYN STREET, AND OF ALL THE BOOKSELLERS.

1804.

TO THE RIGHT HONOURABLE, AND HONOURABLE,

THE MANAGERS OF THE ROYAL INSTITUTION OF GREAT

BRITAIN,

THESE LECTURES,

COMPOSED BY A MAN, WHO, IN HIS LIFE TIME, WAS

HONOURED BY THEIR SELECTION,

AS THEIR FIRST LECTURER;

AND WHOSE INFANT FAMILY HAVE SINCE EXPERIENCED

THEIR BENEVOLENCE AND PROTECTION,

ARE, WITH PERMISSION, DEDICATED,

BY THE TRUSTEES OF THE SUBSCRIPTION,

IN FAVOUR OF THOSE ORPHANS.

CONTENTS.

CONTENTS.

CONTENTS.

THE LIFE OF THE AUTHOR.

Dr. Garnett was born at Casterton, near Kirkby Lonsdale, Westmoreland, on the 21st of April, 1766. During the first fifteen years of his life, he remained with his parents, and was instructed by them in the precepts of the established church of England, from which he drew that scheme of virtue, by which every action of his future life was to be governed. The only school education he received during these early years, was at Barbon, a small village near his native place, to which his father had removed the year after he was born. The school was of so little consequence, that its master changed not less than three times during the space of seven or eight years, and the whole instruction he received, was comprehended in the rudiments of the English grammar, a small portion of Latin, and a little French, together with the general principles of arithmetic. His bodily constitution was from the beginning weak and susceptible; he was unequal to joining in the boisterous amusements of his companions, while from the liveliness of his disposition he could not remain a moment idle. To these circumstances we are, perhaps, to attribute the uncommon progress he made in every branch of knowledge to which he afterwards applied himself.

Whilst a schoolboy, the susceptibility of his mind, and a diffidence of character connected with it, caused him to associate very little with his schoolfellows: he dreaded the displeasure of his preceptor, as the greatest misfortune which could befal him The

moment he arrived at home, he set about preparing his lesson for
the next day; and as soon as this was accomplished, he amused
himself by contriving small pieces of mechanism, which he exhibited with conscious satisfaction to his friends. His temper was
warm and enthusiastic; whatever came within the narrow circle of
his early knowledge he would attempt to imitate. He saw no difficulties before hand, nor was he discouraged when he met with them.
At the early age of eleven years, he had somewhere seen a dial
and a quadrant, and was able to imitate these instruments, nay,
with the assistance of the latter, and the small knowledge of
arithmetic and trigonometry, which he had then obtained, he
formally marched out with his younger brother, and rudely attempted to measure the height of a mountain behind his father's
house. When he was nearly fifteen years of age, he was, at his
earnest desire, put apprentice to the celebrated mathematician,
Mr. Dawson, of Sedbergh, who was at that time a surgeon and
apothecary. This situation was peculiarly advantageous to him,
on account of the great mathematical knowledge of his master,
by whom he was instructed in the different branches of this
science; and, notwithstanding his constant employment in necessary business, his ardent pursuit of professional information,
and his extreme youth, in the course of four years, he became
well acquainted with mechanics, hydrostatics, optics, and astro-
nomy. He afterwards applied himself with energy to the study
of chemistry, and other subjects, with which it was thought ex-
pedient that he should be acquainted, previously to attending
the medical lectures in the University of Edinburgh. Strongly
impressed with a sense of the value of time, he was indefatigable
in the pursuit of knowledge: by a concurrence of fortunate circumstances, his talents had become so flexible, that he succeeded
almost equally well in every subject to which he applied himself;
but of chemistry he was particularly fond, and from this time it
became his favourite study.

During the four years of his apprenticeship, his conduct was in every respect highly commendable; he was assiduous, he was virtuous. His pursuit after general knowledge was restrained to one object only at a time; he had advanced far in the abstruse sciences; his inclination for study was increased: when in the year 1785, he went to Edinburgh with a degree of scientific knowledge, seldom attained by young men beginning the study of medicine. He became a member of the Medical and Physical Societies, where he soon made himself conspicuous, and of the latter of which, he was afterwards president.

Well acquainted with the first principles of natural philosophy, he had considerable advantages over his contemporaries; and his superiority was soon acknowledged. He was not, however, on this account inclined to remit his industry; he attended the lectures of the ablest professors of the day, and more particularly those of Dr. Black, with the most scrupulous punctuality, and endeavoured to elucidate his subject by every collateral information he could obtain. He avoided almost all society; and it is said, he never allowed himself, at this time, more than four hours sleep out of the twenty four. The famous Dr. Brown was then delivering lectures on his new theory of medicine. Dr. Garnett, fired with the enthusiasm of this noted teacher, and struck with the conformity of his theory to the general laws of nature, became one of the most zealous advocates of his doctrine; and from this period, he took, during the remainder of his life, every opportunity of supporting it.

During two summers he returned to Mr. Dawson at Sedbergh, passing the intervening winters in Edinburgh: about this time he wrote the essay, which, in the year 1797, he published under the title of a Lecture on Health, which very neatly and perspicuously explains the fundamental parts of the Brunonian theory of medicine: in September 1788, he published his inaugural dissertation de Visu, and obtained the degree of M. D.

Very soon afterwards he went to London, to pursue his professional studies, which he continued to do with the greatest perseverance: he attended with unceasing diligence the lectures of the most eminent lecturers, and he sought practical knowledge in the chief hospitals of the metropolis with the most ardent zeal; so that whilst he gained information to himself, he set an impressive example to his contemporary medical students, who in the delusive pursuits of a great city, are too apt to neglect the objects their parents had in view in sending them to the capital. Having finished his studies in London, Dr. Garnett, in 1789, returned to his parents. At the time he left London, he had lost none of his ardour; still he continued indefatigable and observant. He had been flattered and respected by his fellow students, and praised by his seniors; and his previous success animated him with the strongest expectation of future advancement. At this time, it is supposed, he wrote the justly admired Treatise on Optics, which is in the Encyclopaedia Britannica. Soon after his establishment as a physician, at Bradford, in Yorkshire, which took place in the year 1790, he began to give private lectures on philosophy and chemistry. He wrote his treatise on the Horley Green Spa; and in a short time, gained a deserved character of ingenuity and skill as a chemist, a physician, and a benevolent member of society. Bradford did not afford scope for his practice as a physician, equal to the sanguine expectations he had formed; and he was induced to change his situation.

In the year 1791, therefore, he removed to Knaresborough, intending to reside at that place during the winter, and at Harrowgate during the summer. This plan he put in execution till the year 1794; his reputation rapidly increased, and his future prospects appeared cheering and bright. He continued to apply himself very closely to chemistry, which was now decidedly his most pleasant and interesting study. He endeavoured to apply his various knowledge to practical purposes, and in many instances was peculiarly successful. No sooner had he arrived at Knaresborough, than anxious to investigate every thing in the neighbourhood, which could at all affect the health of the inhabitants, he began to analyse the Crescent Water at Harrowgate; which he did, with all the accuracy a subject so difficult could admit of; and in 1791, he published his treatise upon it. The same spirit led him, in 1792, to analyse the other mineral waters at the same place of fashionable and general resort, the detail of which he published in the same year. These publications became generally read, and gained him a very extensive reputation. The late Dr. Withering, whose knowledge on these subjects could not be disputed, before he had seen his general analysis of the Harrowgate Waters, said, that " excepting only the few examples given us by Bergman, the analysis of the Crescent Waters was one of the neatest and most satisfactory accounts he had ever read of any mineral water." But his exertions were not confined to professional and scientific pursuits: laudably desirous of advancing knowledge amongst every branch of the community, he formed the plan of a subscription library, which has, since 1791, been of great convenience and utility to the inhabitants of Knaresborough. Far from joining in the opinion which has so much prevailed in modern times, that it was sufficient to aim at general utility, he lost no opportunity of doing good to every member of society. He greatly promoted and encouraged the making of the pleasure grounds and building on the rock, called Fort Montague; and he instructed and assisted the poor man, who is called the Governor, to institute a bank, and to print and issue small bills of the value of a few halfpence, in imitation of the notes of the country bankers, but drawn and signed with a reference of humour to the fort, the flag, the hill, and the cannon. These notes, the nobility and gentry, who during the Harrowgate season crowd to visit this remarkable place, take in exchange for their silver, and by these means the governor, who is a man of gentle and inoffensive manners, has been enabled, with the assistance of his loom, to support himself and a numerous family, and to ameliorate their condition, by giving education to his children.

No station in life escaped his benevolent attentions. In order to benefit John Metcalf, who is perhaps more generally known by the name of Blind Jack of Knaresborough, he assisted him to publish an account of the very singular and remarkable occurrences of his life, during a long series of years, under the heavy affliction of total blindness; by the sale of which, this venerable old man derived a considerable contribution towards his subsistence.

Whilst at Harrowgate, Dr. Garnett obtained the patronage and protection of the Earl of Rosslyn, then Lord Loughborough, who in the year 1794 built a house for him, which for the future Dr. Garnett meant should be his only residence; it was not long however before he discovered that his situation at Harrowgate was but ill calculated to forward his liberal and extended views. At this place he had small opportunities of attaching himself to his favourite sciences; in the winter months he was without literary society, and it was not for his ardent spirit to remain inactive. About this time also, he formed the idea of going to America, where he thought he might live both honourably and profitably as a teacher of chemistry and natural philosophy. All these circumstances were floating in his mind, when in the year 1794, about the end of July, at the instance of a medical friend, who resided in London, he received as boarders into his house, which was kept by his sister, Miss Catharine Grace Cleveland, daughter of the late Mr. Cleveland, of Salisbury Square, Fleet Street, who was recommended to the use of the Harrowgate waters, together with her friend Miss Worboys. To all who were acquainted with the prepossessing exterior of Dr. Garnett, the liveliness of his conversation, the urbanity of his manners, and his general desire of communicating knowledge to whomever he saw desirous of gaining information, it will be no surprise, that a mutual attachment grew up between him and his inmate, Miss Cleveland, a young lady possessing, in all respects, a mind similar to his own, and who must have felt a natural gratification in the zeal with which the company of the person, on whom she had placed her affections, was sought by all ranks resorting to this fashionable watering place, where every one thought himself most fortunate who sat nearest to him at the table, and where he enlivened the circle around him with his conversation, which was not only instructive, but playfully gay, and entertaining, ever striving to amuse, and always successful in his attempts. The Doctor now began to project plans of happiness, which he had only before held in idea. Previous to his visitors leaving Harrowgate, which was towards the latter end of December, he communicated to Miss Cleveland his intention of going to America. At first she hesitated about accompanying him; but finding his resolution fixed, she at length consented. From this time, till the beginning of March 1795, he continued deliberating upon and maturing his plan. He now departed from Harrowgate, and followed the object of his affection to her mother's residence at Hare Hatch, Berks. He was married to her on the 16th of March, and a fortnight afterwards returned to Harrowgate, to dispose of the lease of his house, and his furniture. Having again joined his wife, he then went to London, where he purchased apparatus for his lectures, and after visiting his parents, he proceeded to Liverpool, in order to obtain a passage to America.

Whilst he was thus waiting for the opportunity of a vessel to transport him across the Atlantic, he was solicited by the medical gentlemen at Liverpool, to unpack his apparatus, and give a public course of lectures on chemistry and experimental philosophy. At all times desirous of diffusing the knowledge he had acquired, and eager to fulfil the wishes of his friends, he complied with their request, and entered upon a plan, which in the end completely overturned the scheme he had for several months been contemplating with such ardent hopes of happiness and prosperity. No sooner had he been prevailed upon, than he set about getting every thing ready for his lectures, and after a single week's preparation; he commenced his course. The deep interest he took in his subject, the anxiety he showed to make himself understood, and the enthusiastic hope he constantly expressed of the advancement of science, had a remarkable effect upon his audience; and his lectures were received with the most flattering marks of attention, and excited the most general applause and satisfaction. In a short time, he received a pressing invitation from the most eminent characters at Manchester, to repeat his course in that town. This invitation he accepted, and, encouraged by the success he had just experienced, he postponed the idea of leaving his country. He arrived at Manchester about the middle of January 1796, and began his lectures on the 22nd of that month. Before his arrival, not less than sixty subscribers had put down their names, the more strongly to induce him to comply with their wishes, and many more had promised to do it, as soon as his proposals were published. Notwithstanding he was thus led to expect a large audience, and had procured apartments, which he imagined would be sufficiently spacious for their reception, he was obliged, for want of room, to change them not less than three times during one course. With such success did the career of his philosophical teaching begin, and with such extreme attention and respect was he every where received, that he used afterwards to mention this period, as not only the most profitable, but the most happy of his life. On the 24th of February, his wife was brought to bed of a daughter, the eldest of the two orphans who have now to lament the death of so valuable a parent, to deplore the loss of that independence which his exertions were certain to have raised them, and to rely on a generous public for protection, in testimony of the virtues and merit of their father.

After this time Dr. Garnett repeated nearly the same course of lectures at Warrington and at Lancaster; to both which places he was followed by the same success.

Whilst he was in this manner exerting himself for the general diffusion of knowledge, his fame spread with the delight and instruction he had every where communicated to his audience. The inhabitants of Birmingham wished to have the advantage of his lectures; and he also received a most pressing invitation from Dublin, where a very large subscription had already been formed. It was his intention to have accepted of the latter invitation, but previous to his departure for Ireland (from whence he had even yet some thoughts of emigrating to America) he was informed of the vacancy of the professorship in Anderson's Institution, at Glasgow, by his friend the late Dr. Easton of Manchester, who strongly urged him to become a candidate. As this situation must inevitably destroy all his future prospects, he for a long time hesitated; but Dr. Easton having informed the Managers of the Institution, that there was a possibility of their obtaining a professor, so eminently qualified as Dr. Garnett, they, after making further inquiry concerning him, offered it to him in so handsome a manner, that, although the situation was by no means likely to be productive of so much emolument as the plan of life he had lately been pursuing, he yielded to their proposal, strengthened as it was by the earnest solicitation of Mrs. Garnett, who felt considerable apprehension at the thoughts of going to America, and consented to accept of the professorship.

He began his lectures at Glasgow in November 1796, and a short account of them may be found in his Tour to the Highlands, vol. ii. p. 196. The peculiar clearness with which he was wont to explain the most difficult parts of science, together with the simplicity of the terms he employed, rendered his lectures particularly acceptable to those who had not been initiated in the technical terms, generally used on such occasions. Every thing he delivered might easily be understood by those who had not previously attended to the subject; and of consequence, all who had been disgusted, or frightened by the difficulties they had before met with, or imagined, were eager to receive his instructions; and the audience he obtained, was much more numerous, than either the trustees, or himself, had deemed probable.

When the session was completed, he repaired to Liverpool for the purpose of fulfilling a promise he had formerly given to his friends, to repeat his course of lectures in that town. Mrs. Garnett, in the mean time, remained at Kirkby Lonsdale, where he joined her as soon as his lectures were finished. He spent the latter part of the summer chiefly in botanical pursuits, and returned to Glasgow in the autumn, when he made known his intention of practising as a physician. Fortune continued to favour him, his reputation increased, and he rapidly advanced towards the first professional situation in Glasgow.

In July 1798, he began his Tour to the Highlands, an account of which he published in 1800, and having returned to his duties in the Institution, the success of his lectures suffered no interruption, but whilst he was reaping the benefit due to his industry and his talents, his happiness received a blow, which was irrecoverable, by the loss of his wife, who died in child birth, December the 25th 1798: the infant was preserved. The sentiments of Dr. Garnett on this occasion will be best expressed in his own words, in a letter to Mr. Ort, of Bury in Lancashire.

" Glasgow, January 1st. 1799.

" Oh my dear cousin, little did I expect that I should begin the new year with telling you that I am now deprived of all earthly comforts; yes, the dear companion of my studies, the friend of my heart, the partner of my bosom, is now a piece of cold clay. The senseless earth is closed on that form which was so lately animated by every virtue; and whose only wish was to make me happy.

"Is there any thing, which can now afford me any consolation? Yes, she is not lost, but gone before: but still it is hard to have all our schemes of happiness wrecked: when our bark was within sight of port, when we were promising ourselves more than common felicity, it struck upon a rock: my only treasure went to the bottom, and I am cast ashore, friendless, and deprived of every comfort. My poor, dear love had been as well as usual during the two or three last months, and even on the dreadful evening (christmas eve) she spoke with pleasure of the approaching event. My spirits were elevated to so uncommon a pitch, by the birth of a lovely daughter, that they were by no means prepared for the succeeding scene; and they have been so overwhelmed, that I sometimes hope it may be a dream, out of which I wish to awake. The little infant is well, and I have called it Catharine, a name which must ever be dear to me, and which I wish to be able to apply to some object whom I love; for though it caused the death of my hopes, it is dear to me, as being the last precious relic of her, whom every body who knew her esteemed, and I loved. I must now bid adieu to every comfort, and live only for the sweet babes. Oh! 'tis hard, very hard.

"To Mr. Ort, Bury,   "THOMAS GARNETT."
Lancashire.

The affliction Dr. Garnett experienced on the death of his wife, was never recovered. On all occasions of anxiety which were multiplied upon him, by reason of his exquisite sensibility, he longed for the consolation her society used to afford him; and although his susceptibility to the action of external causes, would not allow him to remain in continued and unalterable gloom and melancholy, yet in solitude, and on the slightest accident, his distress returned, and he despaired of the possibility of ever retrieving his lost happiness. Had it not been for his philosophical pursuits, and the duties of his extensive practice, which kept him almost constantly engaged, it may be doubted, whether he could at this time have sustained the load of sorrow with which he was oppressed.

The circumstances which remain to be mentioned are few. From the death of his wife, Dr. Garnett may be considered as unfortunate; for although a fair prospect opened before him, a series of occurrences took place, which neither his state of mind, nor his constitutional firmness enabled him to support.

At the time of the formation of the Royal Institution of Great Britain, in London, Count Rumford wrote to Dr. Garnett, to whom he was then an entire stranger, inquiring into the nature and economy of Anderson's Institution, Glasgow; the plan of the lectures given, &c. &c.; and after hinting at the opportunities of acquiring reputation in London, he finally proposed that Dr. Garnett should become lecturer of the new Institution. With this proposal, arduous as was the task, to deliver a course of lectures on almost every branch of human attainment, Dr. Garnett complied, relying on his acquirements, and the tried excellence of his nature; and conscious that no difficulty could resist the indefatigable exertions which on other occasions he had so successfully applied. Flattered by the honour and respect he conceived to be paid to his abilities and qualifications; pleased with the prospect of more rapidly accumulating an independence for himself and his children; and animated with the hope of meeting with more frequent opportunities of gratifying his thirst after knowledge, his spirits were again roused, and he looked forward to new objects of interest in the advancement of his favourite pursuits. In the enthusiasm of the moment, he was known to say, that he considered his connexion with the Royal Institution, from which the country had a right to expect so much, as one of the most fortunate occurrences of his life. On the 15th October 1799, he informed a special meeting of the Managers of Anderson's Institution, of his appointment to the Professorship of Philosophy, Chemistry, and Mechanics, in the Royal Institution of Great Britain, and on that account requested permission to resign his situation. The resignation of a man, whom all loved and revered, was reluctantly, though, as tending to his personal advancement, and the promotion of science, unanimously accepted by the meeting ; he was congratulated on his new appointment, and thanked for the unremitting attention he had paid to the interests of Anderson's Institution, ever since he had been connected with it. As an instance of the high esteem in which he was held by the trustees, it may be observed, that his successor, Dr. Birkbeck, was elected by a very great majority of votes, principally on account of his recommendation. In November, he pursued his journey to London, leaving his children at Kirkby Lonsdale, under the care of Miss Worboys. This lady, whose friendship for Mrs. Garnett had induced her to become almost her constant companion, and had even determined her to go with her friend to America, if the Doctor had put his intentions in execution; soon after the death of Mrs. Garnett, had pledged herself, never to desert the children, so long as she could be of any use to them. How faithfully she observes this obligation, all who know her must acknowledge ; nor can we, without increased anxiety, reflect upon the situation the poor orphans must have been in without her protection.

Dr. Garnett was received by the Managers of the Royal Institution with attention, civility, and respect. During the winter, the lecture room was crowded with persons of the first distinction and fashion, as well as by those who had individually contributed much to the promotion of science ; and although the northern accent, which Dr. Garnett still retained

in a slight degree, rendered his voice somewhat inharmonious
to an audience in London, his modest and unaffected manner
of delivering his opinions, his familiar, and at the same time
elegant language, rendered him the object of almost universal kindness and approbation.

The exertions of the winter had in some measure injured his
health, and a degree of uncertainty that he saw in his prospects,
tended greatly to depress his spirits. He determined, however,
to keep his situation at the Institution, in order that he might
at a more convenient time be justified to himself in resigning it.
In the summer of 1800, he visited his children in Westmoreland ; but his anxiety of mind was not diminished, nor consequently his health improved, by this relaxation from active
employment. He walked over the same ground, and viewed
the same prospects that he had formerly enjoyed in the company of his wife. He had not resolution to check the impressions as they arose ; and thus, instead of being solaced by
the beauties which surrounded him, he gave the reins to his melancholy fancy, which, unchecked by any other remembrance,
dwelt only on the affection and the virtues of her, whose loss he
had ever to deplore; the want of whose society he imagined to be
the chief source of his misery. Towards the end of autumn,
he returned to the Institution, and in the winter, recommenced
his duties as professor. The effect produced upon his lecturing
by these and other irritating circumstances was remarkable.
Debility of body, as well as uneasiness of mind, incapacitated
him for that ardent and energetic pursuit of knowledge, by
which he had been so eminently distinguished. His spirited,
and at the same time modest method of delivery was changed
into one languid and hesitating, that, during this period, occasioned an erroneous judgment to be formed of his abilities as
a man of science, and a teacher, by such of his audience as were
unacquainted with the cause, or the intrinsic value and merit of the

man. At the close of the season, his determination of retiring from the Institution was fixed; and he presented to the Managers his resignation.

It was well known to Dr. Garnett's particular friends, that during the early part of this session, he determined to withdraw himself from the Institution ; but the success and advancement of the establishment, which he sanguinely hoped would stand unrivalled in the universe, was so intimately connected with the affections of his mind, that he resolved to forego every personal consideration, rather than risk an inconvenience to the Institution, by ceasing to deliver his lectures in the middle of a course ; liberally considering, that the Managers, after the business of the season was over, would have time and opportunity before the ensuing session, to fill the professor's chair with talents competent to the arduous undertaking; a circumstance the Managers afterwards so eminently profited by, with the highest credit to themselves, and advantage to the public, in the nomination of the gentlemen who now fill the situation held by Dr. Garnett, and who discharge its important duties with the most distinguished abilities.

The transactions of the last winter almost completely served to undermine the small strength of constitution he had left ; he was constantly harrassed by complaints in the organs of digestion ; head ache deprived him of the power of application ; his countenance assumed a sallow complexion ; the eye which had beamed with animation, retired within its socket, deprived of lustre ; melancholy conceptions filled his imagination more habitually, and were excited by slighter causes ; at times, they altogether deprived him of the power of exertion ; and while he lamented their effect, the contemplation of themselves rendered him the more their prey. At this time, a gloomy day, or the smallest disappointment, gave him inconceivable distress ; but he was not altogether incapable of temporary relief, and the few moments of pleasure he seemed to enjoy, would have given reason to believe, that he might once more have recovered, and have long continued to be the delight and instructor of his friends. A more close observation would at the same time have justified the supposition, that the strong and painful emotions of mind he had suffered, had already induced disorders of the bodily system, which were irrecoverable. Before Doctor Garnett had left his situation at Glasgow, he had determined to practice as a physician in London; but from this he was restrained, during the time he was at the Royal Institution. To his former intention he now determined to apply himself, and in addition to the attempt, by giving private lectures, to assure himself of that independency, of which his unfortunate destiny, though with every reasonable expectation before him, had hitherto deprived him.

With this intention, he purchased the lease of a house in Great Marlborough Street; and in the summer of 1801, built a lecture room. He brought his family to town, and once more looked forward with hope. The flattering success he soon met with, and a short residence at Harrowgate in the autumn, contributed to afford a temporary renovation of health and spirits; it was, however, but a short and delusive gleam of prosperity which now dawned upon him; for, confiding too much in his newly increased strength, he exerted himself to a much greater degree than prudence would have suggested. In the course of the following winter, he delivered not less than eight courses of lectures; two on chemistry, two on experimental philosophy, a private course on the same subject, one on mineralogy, and the course to which this sketch is prefixed, which he also delivered in an apartment at Tom's Coffee house, for the convenience of medical students, and others, in the city. Besides these, he commenced two courses on botany, one at Brompton, and the other at his own house; but a return of ill health prevented his concluding them. It was not to be expected, that a constitution so impaired and debilitated, could long support this continued labour of composition and recitation; accordingly he became affected with a consequent disorder, which rapidly exhausted his strength; and, being unable to employ the only probable means of recovering it, he became more incapable of exertion. His spirits however were roused, and he ceased not to use every means of increasing his practice. In the spring of 1802, the office of physician to the St. Mary le Bonne Dispensary happened to be vacant, and he became a candidate; he was more than commonly anxious to obtain this situation. It seemed to him, as if his future good or ill fortune depended altogether upon the event of his canvass, he spared no effort to ensure his success; and accordingly was appointed to the situation in May. His life now drew near a close. Little was he calculated to bear the accumulated labours, and extreme fatigue, to which he was daily exposed. Any benefit which might have resulted from constant and well regulated occupation was frustrated; for whilst he still suffered from the vividness of his conception, representing to him in mournful colours the occurrences of his past life, he became liable to other evils, not less injurious and destructive. The practice of medicine requires both vigorous health of body and firmness of mind. Dr. Garnett, now greatly weakened in body, and not exempt from anxiety of mind, became more and more susceptible to the action of morbific matter. It was not long before he received the contagion of typhous fever, whilst attending a patient, belonging to that very dispensary of which he had been so anxious to become physician. He laboured under the disorder for two or three weeks, and died the 28th of June, 1802; and was buried in the new burial ground of the parish of St. James, Westminster.

Thus was lost to society a man, the ornament of his country, and the general friend of humanity. In his personal attachments, he was warm and zealous. In his religion he was sincere, yet liberal to the professors of contrary doctrines. In his political principles, he saw no end, but the general good of mankind ; and, conscious of the infirmity of human judgment, he never failed to make allowances for error. As a philosopher, and a man of science, he was candid, ingenuous, and open to conviction ; he never dealt in mystery, or pretended to any secret in art ; he was always ready in explanation, and desirous of assisting every person willing to acquire knowledge. Virtue was the basis of all his actions ; science never possessed a fairer fabric, nor did society ever sustain a greater loss.

LECTURES ON ZOONOMIA.

LECTURE I.

INTRODUCTION

1 AM well aware of the difficulties attending the proper composition of a popular course of lectures on the animal economy, which must be essentially different from those generally delivered in the schools of medicine; because it professes to explain the structure and functions of the living body, to those who are supposed to be unacquainted with the usual preliminary and collateral branches of knowledge. It must be obvious to every one, that it can be by no means an easy task to give in a few lectures, a perspicuous view of so extensive a subject; but I trust that the consideration of this difficulty will readily extend to me your indulgence.

That such a course, if properly conducted, must be interesting, needs scarcely to be observed; for the more we examine the structure and functions of the human body, the more we admire the excellence of the workmanship, and beauty of contrivance, which presents itself in every part, and which continually shows the hand of omniscience. The most ingenious of human inventions, when compared with the animal frame, indicate a poverty of contrivance which cannot fail to humble the pretensions of the sons of men.

Surely then there are few who will not feel a desire to become acquainted with subjects so interesting.

But there is another point of view which will place the utility of such inquiries in a still stronger light. We shall afterwards see, that our life is continually supported by the action of a number of substances, by which the body is surrounded, and which are taken into the stomach for its nourishment. On the due action of these depends the pleasant performance of the different functions, or the state of health; without which, riches, honours, and every other gratification, become joyless and insipid.

By understanding the manner in which these powers act, or, in other words, by becoming acquainted with the principles of physiology, we shall be enabled to regulate them, so as, in a great measure, to guard against the numerous ills that flesh is heir to: for it is universally agreed, that by far the greatest part of the diseases to which mankind are subject, have been brought on by intemperance, imprudence, and the neglect of precautions, which often arises from carelessness, but much oftener from ignorance of those precautions.

Physiological ignorance is, undoubtedly, the most abundant source of our sufferings; every person accustomed to the sick must have heard them deplore their ignorance of the necessary consequences of those practises, by which their health has been destroyed: and when men shall be deeply convinced, that the eternal laws of nature have connected pain and decrepitude with one mode of life, and health and vigour with another, they will avoid the former and adhere to the latter.

It is strange, however, to observe that the generality of

mankind do not seem to bestow a single thought on the preservation of their health, till it is too late to reap any benefit from their conviction; so that we may say of health, as we do of time, we take no notice of it but by its loss; and feel the value of it when we can no longer think of it but with retrospect and regret.

When we take a view of the human frame, and see how admirably each part is contrived for the performance of its different functions, and even for repairing its own injuries, we might at first sight imagine, that such a structure, unless destroyed by external force, should continue for ever in vigour, and in health: and it is by mournful experience alone that we are convinced of the contrary. The strongest constitution, which never experienced the qualms of sickness, or the torture of disease, and which seems to bid defiance to the enemies of health that surround it, is not proof against the attacks of age. Even in the midst of life we are in death; how many of us have contemplated with admiration the graceful motion of the female form; the eye sparkling with intelligence; the countenance enlivened by wit, or animated by feeling: a single instant is sufficient to dispel the charm: often without apparent cause, sensation and motion cease at once; the body loses its warmth, the eyes their lustre, and the lips and cheeks become livid. These, as Cuvier observes, are but preludes to changes still more hideous. The colour passes successively to a blue, a green, and a black; the flesh absorbs moisture, and while one part of it escapes in pestilential exhalations, the remaining part falls down into a putrid liquid mass. In a short time no part of the body remains, but a few earthy and saline principles; its other elements being dispersed through air, or carried off by water, to form new combinations, and afford food for other animals.

The human body has been defined to be a machine composed of bones and muscles, with their proper appendages, for the purpose of motion, at the instance of its intelligent principle. From this principle, nerves, or instruments of sensation, are likewise detached to the various parts of the body, for such information as may be necessary to determine it to those motions of the body, which may conduce to the happiness of the former, and the preservation of both.

It may perhaps be objected to this definition, that the body consists of other parts besides bones, muscles, and nerves; this is undoubtedly true; but, if we examine more minutely, we shall find that all the other parts, as well as functions of the body, seem only to be subservient to the purposes I have mentioned. For, in the first place, the muscles which are necessary to the motions of the body, are, from the nature of their constitution, subject to continual waste; to repair which waste, some of the other functions have been contrived.

Secondly, most of the other parts and functions of the body, are either necessary to the action of the muscles, or to the operation of the intelligent principle, or both.

Lastly, from the sensibility, and delicate structure, of the muscles and nerves, they require to be defended from external injuries: this is done by membranes, and other contrivances, fitted for the purpose.

To see this more clearly, we shall examine a little more particularly how each of the functions is subservient to the muscular and nervous systems. For this purpose it may be observed, 1st. that'the stomach and digestive faculties serve to assimilate the food, or convert it into matter proper to repair the continual waste of solids and fluids. The circulation of the blood besides being absolutely necessary, as we shall afterwards see, to the action of the muscles, distributes the nourishment, thus assimilated and prepared by the stomach, to all parts of the body The different glands separate liquors from the blood, for useful, but still for subservient purposes. Thus the salivary glands, stomach, pancreas, and liver, separate juices necessary to the proper digestion and assimilation of the food. The kidneys serve to strain off from the blood the useless and superfluous water, salts, &c. which if allowed to remain in the body would be very injurious to it.

We shall afterwards see, that the nerves are not only instruments of sensation, but the origin of motion; it being immediately by their means that the muscles are moved. A certain degree of heat is necessary to keep the blood fluid, and also to the action of the nerves; without either of which, no motion could be performed. Respiration or breathing is so necessary to life, that it cannot exist, even a few minutes, without the exercise of that function; and yet we shall afterwards see, that the ultimate end of respiration is to keep the body in a proper state, for the purposes of muscular motion and sensation.

The skin serves like a sheath to defend the body from injuries; the skull serves the same purpose to the brain, which is the origin of the nerves. The different membranes separate the fibres, muscles, nerves, and various organs of the body, from each other. Hence we see that there is no im-

propriety, in calling the human body a machine composed
of bones and muscles, with their proper appendages, for the
purpose of motion, at the instance of its intelligent principle.

In order to show more clearly how each part is subservient to these ends, I shall give a short account of the structure of the human body, but I must premise, that the nature of this course will prevent my entering minutely into
anatomical detail. All that can be done is, to give such a
general outline of anatomy and physiology, as will furnish
individuals with so much knowledge of themselves, as may
enable them to guard against habitual sickness.

Among the solid parts of the human frame the bones
stand conspicuous. Their use is, to give firmness and shape
to the body. Some of them likewise serve as armour, or defence, to guard important parts; thus the skull is admirably
contrived to defend the brain; and the spine or backbone is
designed, not only to strengthen the body, but to shield that
continuation of the brain, called the spinal marrow, from
whence originate great numbers of nerves, which pass through
convenient openings of this bone, and are distributed to various parts of the body In the structure of this, as well as
every other part, the wisdom of the Creator is manifest. Had
it been a single bone, the loins must have been inflexible; to
avoid which, it consists of a number of small bones, articulated
or joined together with great exactness, which are strengthened by compact ligaments. Hence it becomes capable of
various inflections, without injuring the nerves, or diminishing
that strength which is so much required.

The whole system of bones, or skeleton, is constructed of

several parts, of different shapes and sizes, joining with one another in various manners, and so knit together, as best to answer to the motions which the occasions of the animal may require.

These bones serve as levers for the muscles to act on; which last serve as mechanical powers, to give the machine various motions, at the command of the will.

The muscles are fleshy fibres, attached by their extremities to the bones. When the fibres shorten themselves, the two parts into which the muscle is inserted are brought nearer; and, by this simple contrivance, all the motions of animals are performed, and their bodies carried from one place to another.

Joints are provided with muscles for performing the motions for which they are adapted; every muscle pulling the bone, to which it is attached, in its own particular direction. Hence the muscles may be considered as so many moving forces, as was before hinted; and their strength, the distance of their insertion from the centre of motion, the length of the lever to which they are attached, and the weight connected with it, determine the duration and velocity of the motions which they produce. Upon these different circumstances depend the different kinds of motion performed by various animals, such as the force of their leap, the extent of their flight, the rapidity of their course, and their address in catching their prey.

Most of the muscles act upon the bones, so as to produce the effects of a lever of the third kind, as it is termed by mechanics, where the power acts between the centre of motion and the weight; hence it has a mechanical disadvantage; as

an instance of this, the muscle which bends the forearm, is
inserted about one eighth or one tenth of the distance from
the centre of motion that the hand is, where the weight or
resistance is applied; hence the muscle must exert a force
eight or ten times greater than the weight to be raised. But
this disadvantage is amply compensated by making the limbs
move with greater velocity; besides, if room had been given
for the muscles to act with greater advantage, the limbs
must have been exceedingly deformed and unwieldy *.

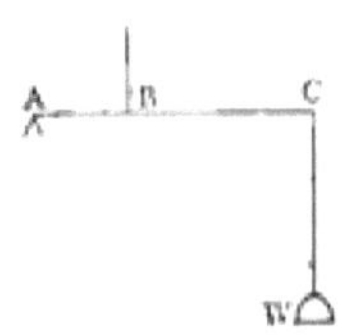

* Suppose AC to be a lever, held in equilibrio by
the force B and weight W, then the whole momentum exerted at B must be equal to that at W, but
the forces will be different. For $B \times AC = W \times AB$,
and if $AC = 10AB$, then a force equal to ten times
the weight to be raised must be exerted by the muscle. Hence we see, that in the actions of muscles
there is a loss of power, from their insertions being
nearer the fulcrum than the weight. For example, suppose the deltoid muscle
to act and raise a weight of 55℔. : the weight of the arm is 5℔., and the distance of its insertion is only $\frac{1}{3}$ of the arms length, hence the force exerted must
be $(55 + 5) \times 3 = 180$℔.

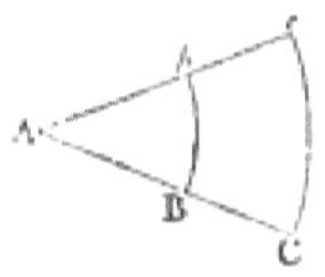

But by this contrivance we gain a greater extent
of motion, and also a greater velocity, and both with
less contraction. Let A be the centre of motion, or
articulation; B the insertion of a muscle, and AC
the length of the lever or bone; then, by a contraction only equal to Bb, C is carried through Cc, which
is to Bb as AC to AB. It is obvious also, that the
velocity is greater, since C moves to c in the same time as B to b.

A loss of power is likewise occasioned by the obliquity of the muscular action, and the oblique direction of the fibres.

For, in this case, there is a compound of two forces, and a consequent loss of
power; for the forces are proportioned to the two sides of a parallelogram, but
the effects produced are proportioned only to the diagonal.

The muscles, in general, at least those which serve for voluntary motion, are balanced by antagonists, by means of which they are kept beyond their natural stretch. When one of two antagonists is contracted by the will, the other relaxes in order to give it play; or at least becomes overpowered by the contraction of the first. Also when one of such muscles happens to be paralytic, the other being no longer balanced, or kept on the stretch, immediately contracts to its natural length, and remains in that situation. The part to which it is fixed will, of course, be affected accordingly. If one of the muscles which move the mouth sideways be destroyed, the other immediately contracting, draws the mouth awry; and in that situation it remains. The same may be observed of the leg, the arm, and other parts. Some muscles assist one another in their action, while others have different actions; according to their shapes, the course of their fibres, and the structure of the parts they move.

According to the shape and nature of the bones to be moved, and of the motions to be performed, the muscles are either long, or short; slender, or bulky; straight, or round. Where a great motion is required, as in the leg, or arm, the muscles are long; where a small motion is necessary, they are short; for a strong motion they are thick, and for a weak one slender.

Some of the muscles are fastened to, and move bones; others cartilages, and others again other muscles, as may best suit the intention to be answered.

With respect to the bones, some are solid and flattened; others hollow and cylindrical. Every cylindrical bone is hollow, or has a cavity containing a great number of cells, filled with an oily marrow. Each of these cells is lined with a fine membrane, which forms the marrow. On this membrane, the blood vessels are spread, which enter the bones obliquely, and generally near their middle; from some branches of these vessels the marrow is secreted; while others enter the internal substance of the bones for their nourishment; and the reason why they enter the bones obliquely is, that they may not weaken them by dividing too many fibres in the same place.

The bones being made hollow, their strength is greatly increased without any addition to their weight; for if they had been formed of the same quantity of matter without any cavities, they would have been much weaker; their strength to resist breaking transversely being proportionate to their diameters, as is evident from mechanics.

All the bones, excepting so much of the teeth as are out of the sockets, and those parts of other bones which are covered with cartilages, are surrounded by a fine membrane, which on the skull is called pericranium, but in other parts periosteum. This membrane serves for the muscles to slide easily upon, and to hinder them from being lacerated by the hardness and roughness of the bones.

But though the apparatus which I have been describing is admirably contrived for the performance of motion; it would continue for ever inactive, if not animated by the nervous system.

The brain is the seat of the intelligent principle: from this organ, white, soft, and medullary threads, called nerves, are sent off to different parts of the body: some of them proceed immediately from the brain to their destined places, while the greater number, united together, perforate the skull, and enter the cavity of the backbone, forming what we call the spinal marrow, which may be regarded as a continuation of the brain. Portions of the spinal marrow pass through different apertures to all parts of the body.

We are not conscious of the impression of external objects on our body, unless there be a free communication of nerves, between the place where the impression is made and the brain. If a nerve be divided, or have a ligature put round it, sensation is intercepted.

There is perhaps only one sense which is common to all classes of animals, and which exists over every part of the surface of the body; I mean the sense of touch. The seat of this sense is in the extremities of the nerves distributed over the skin; and by means of it we ascertain the resistance of bodies, their figure, and their temperature.

The other senses have been thought to be only more refined modifications of the sense of touch; and the organs of each are placed near the brain on the external surface of the head. The sense of sight, for instance, is seated in the eye; the hearing in the ear; the smell in the internal membrane of the nose; and the taste in the tongue.

The light; the pulses, or vibrations of the air; the effluvia floating in the atmosphere; saline particles, or particles which are soluble in water or saliva, are the substances which act upon these four senses; and the organs which transmit their action to the nerves, are admirably adapted to the respective nature of each. The eye presents to the light a succession of transparent lenses to refract its rays; the ear opposes to the air membranes, fluids, and bones, well fitted to transmit its vibrations; the nostrils, while they afford a passage to the air in its way to the lungs, intercept any odorous particles which it contains, and the tongue is provided with spongy papillae to imbibe the sapid liquors which are the objects of taste.

It is by these organs that we become acquainted with what passes around us; by these we know that a material world exists. We may however observe, that the nervous system, besides making us acquainted with external things, gives us notice of many changes that take place within our own body Internal pain warns us of the presence of disease; and the disagreeable sensations of hunger, thirst, and fatigue, are signs of the body standing in need of refreshment or repose.

Concerning the manner in which we become acquainted with external things, by means of the senses, we know nothing. Many hypotheses have been offered to explain this: none of them however are the result of experiment and observation. Many philosophers have supposed the universe to be filled with an extremely subtile fluid, which they have termed ethereal; and this hypothesis has been sanctioned by the illustrious authority of Newton. He however merely offered it in the modest form of a query, for the attention of other philosophers; little thinking that it would be made use of to explain phenomena which they did not understand. His query about a subtile elastic fluid pervading the universe, and giving motion and activity to inert masses of matter, and thereby causing the phenomena of attraction, gravitation, and many other appearances in nature, was immediately laid hold of by his followers, as a fact sufficiently supported, because it seemed to have the sanction of so great an authority.

This hypothesis was made use of to explain a great number of phenomena, and the physiologists, whose theories were generally influenced by the prevailing philosophy, eagerly laid hold of it to explain the phenomena of sensation, and muscular motion. When an impression was made upon any part of the external surface of the body, whether it was occasioned by heat, or mechanical impulse, they supposed, that the ether in the extremities of the nerves was set in motion. This motion, from the energy of the ether, is communicated along the nerves to the brain, and there produces such a change as occasions a consciousness of the original impression, and a reference in the mind to the place where it was made. Next they supposed, that the action of the will caused a motion of the ether to be instantly propagated along the nerves that terminate in the fibres of the muscles, which stimulated them to contraction.

Other philosophers imagined, that a tremulous motion was excited in the nerves themselves, by the action of external impulses, like the motions excited in the string of a harp. These motions they supposed to be propagated along the nerves of sense, to the brain, and from thence along the motory nerves, to the muscles.

Before they attempted this explanation of the phenomena, they should have proved the existence of such a fluid, or at least brought forward such circumstances, as rendered its existence credible. But supposing we grant them the hypothesis, it will, in my opinion, not avail much; for it is not easy to conceive how the motion of a subtile fluid, or the vibration of a nerve, can cause sensation.

Nor are the internal senses, as they are generally called,

namely, memory, and imagination, any better explained on this supposition; for we cannot conceive how this nervous fluid is stored up and propelled by the will.

After all, I think we must confess, that this subject is still enveloped in obscurity. One observation is worth making, namely, that our sensations have not the smallest resemblance to the substance or impression, which causes them; thus the sensation occasioned by the smell of camphor, possseses not the smallest resemblance to small particles of camphor floating in the atmosphere; a sensation of pain has no similitude whatever to the point of a sword which occasions it; nor has the sensation of sound any resemblance to waves or tremors in the air. In our present state of knowledge, therefore, all that we can say, is, that nature has so formed us, that when an impression is made on any of the organs of sense, it causes a sensation, which forces us to believe in the existence of an external object, though we cannot see any connexion between the sensation and the object which produces it.

But though philosophers were certainly blameable for assuming an unknown cause, to account for various phenomena, yet later experiments would seem to prove that even the conjectures of Newton were not founded on slight grounds. His idea that the diamond was inflammable, has been confirmed by various experiments: and that there exists in nature a subtile fluid, capable of pervading with ease the densest bodies, the phenomena of electricity would seem to show, and some late experiments render it by no means improbable, that this fluid or influence, acts a conspicuous part in the nervous system. That it exists in great quantity in animal bodies, is evident on gently rubbing the back of a cat in the dark ; and it would seem that, in some instances, it may be given out or secreted by the nerves. We shall afterwards see that the seat of vision is a delicate expansion of a large nerve which comes from the brain, and is spread out on the bottom of the eye; and flashes of light, or a kind of sparkling, is often seen to dart from the eyes of persons in high health, and possessed of much nervous energy. These luminous flashes are very apparent in the dark in some animals; such as the lion, the lynx, and the cat; and it is difficult to account for this appearance unless we suppose it electrical.

The experiments of Galvani and others, have however proved beyond all doubt, that this fluid, when applied to the nerves and muscles, is capable of exciting various sensations and motions. To produce this fluid by the application of two metals, it is necessary that one of them should be in such a situation, as to be easily oxidable, while the other is prevented from oxidation. If a piece of zinc be put into water, no change will take place; but if a piece of silver be put along with it, the zinc will immediately oxidate, by decomposing the water, and a current of electricity will pass through the silver. If the upper and under surfaces of the tongue be coated with two different metals, one of which is easily oxidable, and these be brought into contact, a sensation is produced resembling taste, which takes place suddenly, like a slight electrical shock. This taste may likewise be produced by applying one part of the metals to the tongue and the other to any part of the body deprived of the cuticle, and bringing them in contact.

The sensation of light may be produced in various ways;

such as by applying one metal between the gum and the upper lip, and the other under the tongue; or by putting a silver probe up one of the nostrils, and a piece of zinc upon the tongue; a sensation resembling a very strong flash of light is perceived in the corresponding eye, at the instant of contact.

But the experiments which tend most strongly to prove what I have hinted, are made in the following manner. Lay bare a portion of a great nerve leading to any muscle or limb of an animal, for instance, the leg of a frog separated from the body. Touch the bared nerve with a piece of zinc, and the muscle with a piece of silver, and strong contractions take place the instant these metals are brought into contact. The same effect may be produced by placing a piece of silver on a larger piece of zinc, and puting a worm or a leech on the silver; in moving about, the instant it touches the zinc it is thrown into strong convulsions.

These phenomena have been clearly proved to be electrical; for by a number of pieces of these metals, properly disposed, strong shocks can be given, the electrometer can be affected, a Leyden vial charged, the electric spark seen, and combustible bodies inflamed.

Some animals likewise possess the power of accumulating this influence in a great degree; for instanc the torpedo, and electrical eel, which will both give strong shocks; and if the circuit have a small interruption a spark may be seen, as was shown by Mr. Walsh. On dissecting these fish, Mr. Hunter found an organ very similar to the pile of Volta; it consists of numerous membranaceous columns, filled with plates or pellicles, in the form of thin disks, separated from each other by small intervals, which intervals contain a fluid substance ; this organ, like the pile of Volta, is capable of giving repeated shocks, even when surrounded by water.

It is not absolutely necessary to use two metals to produce the galvanic phenomena; for if one side of a metal be made to oxidate, while the other is prevented from oxidation, these appearances will still be produced. It is not indeed necessary to use any metal; for a piece of charcoal, oxidated in the same way, produces galvanism; so does fresh muscular fibre, and perhaps any substance capable of oxidation. The most striking circumstance in galvanism, is, that it accompanies oxidation, and is perhaps never produced without it. But oxidation is always going on in the body by means of respiration and the circulation of the blood. We shall afterwards find reason to believe, that the oxygen, received from the atmosphere by the lungs, is the cause of animal heat, and probably of animal irritability ; and it is perhaps not unreasonable to suppose, that the nervous influence or electricity may be separated by the brain, and sent along the nerves, which seem the most powerful conductors of it, to stimulate the muscles to action.

What the nature of the electric fluid is, we are ignorant; some galvanic experiments have led me to suppose that it may be hydrogen, which when combined with caloric appears in the form of gas, but when pure, or perhaps in a different state, may be capable of passing through solid bodies in the form of electricity.

Having given this short view of the human body, considered as a machine composed of bones, muscles, and nerves, I shall proceed to state the different subjects which I shall consider

in this course. It is extremely difficult to begin a course like
this; for we must either enter abruptly into the middle, or
the outset must be in some measure tedious and dry. I have
chosen however rather to hazard the latter appellation, with
respect to this lecture, than to enter more abruptly into the
subject, in order to make it more entertaining. As we proceed, I trust you will feel an increasing interest in the subject:
and, I think I may venture to promise, that this will be found
the least entertaining lecture in the course. The subject
will be illustrated by experiments, in order to render the deductions more striking.

I shall next proceed to consider the phenomena of respiration, and animal heat; after which I shall explain the circulation of the blood; and the phenomena of digestion and
nutrition. I shall then examine, more minutely than has
been done in this lecture, the connexion of man with the
external world, which will lead to a discussion of the different senses; vision, hearing, smelling, tasting, and feeling.

When these subjects have been discussed as fully as our
time will allow, I shall examine, at considerable length, the
manner in which the powers that support life, which have
been improperly called by physiologists, the nonnaturals,
act upon the body. This will naturally lead to a fuller
explanation of the system which I have attempted to defend,
in my lecture on health. And, after I have fully explained
the laws by which the irritable principle is regulated, I shall
proceed to show, how those variations from the healthy state,
called diseases, are produced; I shall point out the difference
that exists between the debility which is brought on by the
diminished action of the powers which support life, and that

which results from their too powerful action; I shall then inquire into the nature of diseases of increased excitement; and after having shown how the undue action of the powers which support life, operates in producing disease, I shall endeavour to lay down such rules for the preservation of health, as are the result of reasoning on these subjects, and are also confirmed by experience.

LECTURE II.

In the last lecture I took a short view of the human body, as a moving machine, regulated by the will. We shall now proceed to examine some of its functions more particularly

I need not tell any of my audience, how necessary air is to the living body; for every person knows that we cannot live when excluded from this fluid; but, before we can understand the manner in which it acts on the body, we must become acquainted with some of its properties.

That the air is a fluid, consisting of such particles as have little or no cohesion, and which slide easily among each other, and yield to the slightest force, is evident from the ease with which animals breathe it, and move through it. Indeed from its being transparent, and therefore invisible, as well as from its extreme tenuity, and the ease with which bodies move through it, people will scarcely believe that they are living at the bottom of an aerial ocean, like fishes at the bottom of the sea. We become, however, very sensible of it, when it flows rapidly in streams or currents, so as to form what is called a wind, which will sometimes act so violently as to tear up the strongest trees by the roots, and blow down to the ground the best and firmest buildings.

Some may still be inclined to ask, what is this air in which we are said to live? We see nothing; we feel nothing; we find ourselves at liberty to move about in any direction, without any hindrance. Whence then comes the assertion, that we are surrounded by a fluid, called air? When we pour water out of a vessel, it appears to be empty ; for our senses do not inform us that any thing occupies the place of the water, for instance, when we pour water out of a vial. But this operation is exactly similar to pouring out mercury from a vial in a jar of water, the water gets in and supplies the place of the mercury; so does the air which supplies the place of the water; and this air will prevent water from rising, or filling a vessel which contains it.

Hence we see that air possesses similar appearances of impenetrability with other matter: for it excludes bodies from the space which itself occupies.

Air being therefore material must have weight; and we shall accordingly find, that a quart of it weighs about fifteen grains. But a quart of water weighs about two pounds; this fluid therefore is nearly a thousand times heavier than air.

But though air is so much lighter than water, yet, because it extends to a considerable height above the surface of the earth, it is evident, that it must press strongly on the surfaces of bodies. It is thought to extend nearly fifty miles above the surface of the earth, and must therefore press heavily on this surface. This may be evinced by different experiments, performed by means of the air pump.

Another property of the air, by which it is distinguished from most other fluids, is its elasticity. It may be compressed into a less space than it naturally occupies, and when the compressing force is removed, it expands to its former bulk, by its spring or elasticity. Indeed it is always compressed into less space than it would naturally occupy, by the weight of the superincumbent air.

The trachea, or windpipe, commences at the further end of the mouth, between the root of the tongue, and the passage into the stomach: its upper part is termed the larynx; it forms the projection in the fore part of the neck, which is more prominent in the male than the female: its opening is called the glottis, and is covered with a small valve, or lid, called the epiglottis, which is open while we breathe, but shuts when we swallow any thing, to prevent its getting into the lungs: sometimes, however, particularly when we attempt to speak at the time we swallow, a small portion of our food or drink gets into the larynx, and excites violent coughing until it is thrown back again.

The windpipe is composed of cartilaginous rings, covered with membrane, which keep it open: after having run downwards for the space of a few inches, it divides into two great branches, each of which is subdivided into a vast number of ramifications, ultimately terminating in little vesicles, which, when distended with air, make up the greatest part of the bulk of the lungs.

The cavity in which the lungs are contained is called the thorax, or chest: and is bounded by the ribs, and backbone or spine, and separated from the abdomen by a muscular membrane, called the diaphragm. The thorax, by the action of the diaphragm and intercostal muscles, is alternately enlarged and diminished. Suppose then the thorax to be in its least state; if it become larger, a vacuum will be formed, into which the external air will descend by its weight, filling and distending the vesicles of the lungs.

The thorax, thus dilated, is brought back to its former magnitude, principally by the relaxation of the muscles, which distended it, and the natural elasticity of the parts, aided by the contraction of the abdominal muscles; the thorax being thus diminished, a quantity of air is expelled from the lungs. The muscles which distend the thorax beginning again to act, the air reenters; and this alternate dilatation and contraction, is called respiration. The entrance of the air into the lungs, is termed inspiration, and its expulsion, expiration.

To form a more accurate idea of the manner in which respiration is performed, let us suppose this room to be filled with water. On enlarging the thorax, in the manner before mentioned, the water by its weight would rush in, and fill the newly formed void ; and, upon the diminution of the capacity of the thorax, a part of this water would be expelled. Just in the same manner the air will alternately enter and be expelled from the lungs by this alternate dilatation and contraction of the thorax.

Respiration is a function of such consequence, that death follows if it is suspended for a few minutes only. By means of this function the blood is elaborated, and rendered fit to nourish the body ; by means of it the system is, most probably, supplied with irritability ; by means of it the nervous energy is, most likely, conveyed into the body, to be expended in sensation, and muscular motion. It appears, likewise, that in this way, animals are supplied with that heat which preserves their temperatures nearly the same, whatever may be the temperatures of surrounding bodies.

If any number of inanimate bodies, possessed of different degrees of heat, be placed near each other, the heat will begin to pass from the hotter bodies to the colder, till there be an equilibrium of temperature. But this is by no means the case with respect to animated matter; for whatever be the degree of heat peculiar to individual animals, they preserve it, nearly unchanged, in every temperature, provided the temperature be not altogether incompatible with life or health. Thus, we find, from experiments that have been made, that the human body is not only capable of supporting, in certain circumstances, without any material change in its temperature, a degree of heat considerably above that at which water boils; but it likewise maintains its usual temperature, whilst the surrounding medium is several degrees below frost.

It is evident, therefore, that animals neither receive their heat from the bodies which surround them, nor suffer, from the influence of external circumstances, any material alterations in that heat which is peculiar to their nature. These general facts are confirmed and elucidated by many accurate and well authenticated observations, which show, that the degree of heat in the same genus and species of the more perfect animals, continues uniformly the same, whether they be surrounded by mountains of snow, in the neighbourhood of the pole, or exposed to a vertical sun, in the sultry regions of the torrid zone.

This stability and uniformity of animal heat, under such a disparity of external circumstances, and so vast a latitude in the temperature of the ambient air, prove, beyond doubt, that the living body is furnished with a peculiar mechanism, or power of generating, supporting, and regulating its own temperature; and that this is so wisely adapted to the circumstances of its economy, or so dependent upon them, that, whatever be 'the temperature of the atmosphere, it will have very little influence either in diminishing or increasing that of the animal.

In order that we may see how this effect is produced, we must examine the chemical properties of the air. Previously to this, however, it will be necessary to point out briefly how bodies are affected, with respect to heat, when they change their form.

When a body passes from a state of solidity to that of fluidity, it absorbs a quantity of heat, which becomes chemically combined with it, and insensible to the touch or the thermometer; in the same manner, when it passes from a fluid state to that of vapour or gas, it combines with a still larger quantity of heat, which remains latent in it, so long as it continues in the state of gas, but when it returns to the liquid or solid state, it gives out the heat which was combined with it, which, being set at liberty, flows into the surrounding bodies, and augments their temperature.

This is evinced by the conversion of ice into water, and of water into steam ; and by the return of steam into water. It is evinced likewise by the evaporation of ether, and by numberless other experiments.

Modern chemistry has shown that the atmosphere is not a homogeneous fluid, but consists of two elastic fluids, endowed with opposite and different properties.

If a combustible body, for instance a candle, be confined in a given quantity of atmospheric air, it will burn only for a certain time; after it is extinguished, if another combustible

body be lighted and immersed in the same air, it will not burn,
but will immediately be extinguished.

It has been proved by chemical experiments, that in this
instance, the combustible body absorbs that portion of the
air which is fitted for combustion, but produces no change
on that which is unfit: so that, according to this, the air of the
atmosphere consists of two elastic fluids, one of which is capable of supporting combustion, and the other not; and that
they exist in the proportion of one part of the former to three
of the latter nearly

These two parts may be separated from each other, and experiments made with them.

Many metals, and particularly manganese, when exposed
to the atmosphere, attract the combustible air from it,
without touching the other; and it may be procured from
these metals by the application of heat, in very great purity

Because this air is essential to the formation of acids, it
has been called by chemists the acidifying principle, or oxygen gas.

On plunging a combustible body into the remaining air, it
is instantly extinguished; an animal in the same situation
is immediately deprived of life: from this latter circumstance
this air has been called azote, or azotic gas. If we take three
parts of azote and one of oxygen, and mix them together,
we shall form an air in every respect similar to that of the
atmosphere.

If I plunge a piece of iron, previously heated, into oxygen
gas, it will burn with great brilliancy, the gas will be diminished in quantity, and the iron augmented in weight, and

this increase of weight in the metal will be in proportion to the oxygen which has disappeared: at the same time a great quantity of heat is given out. This is the heat which was combined with the oxygen in the state of gas, and which now becomes free, when the oxygen becomes solid and joins with the iron.

The same phenomena take place when phosphorus is burned in oxygen gas; the gas becomes diminished, the phosphorus increased, in weight, and converted into an acid, and a great quantity of heat is given out. The same is the case when charcoal is burned in this gas. In short, in every instance of combustion, the oxygen combines with the combustible body, and at the same time gives out its heat, which supported it in the form of gas. This is the case of the combustion of coal in a common fire, as well as in other cases of combustion; the heat comes from the air, and not from the coal.

When we examine the phenomena of respiration with attention, we shall find them very analogous to those of combustion. A candle will not burn in an exhausted receiver; an animal in the same situation ceases to live.

When a candle is confined in a given quantity of atmospheric air, it will burn only for a certain length of time. On examining the air in which it has been burned, the oxygen is found to be all extracted, nothing remaining but azotic gas, and a quantity of carbonic acid gas, produced by the union of the charcoal of the candle with the oxygen of the atmospheric air.

In the same manner, if an animal be confined in a given quantity of atmospheric air, it will live only a short time; on examining the air in which it has ceased to live, it will be found to have lost its oxygen: what remains being a mixture of azotic and carbonic acid gases.

When a candle is enclosed in a given quantity of pure oxygen gas, it will burn four times as long as in the same quantity of atmospheric air.

In the same manner it has been proved, that an animal will be four times as long in consuming a given quantity of pure oxygen gas, as in rendering unfit for respiration the same quantity of atmospheric air.

Here then we observe a striking similarity between combustion and animal respiration. The ancients seem to have had a more accurate idea of respiration than most of the philosophers who followed them. They supposed that the air contained a principle proper for the support and nourishment of life, which they called pabulum vitae. This idea, which was unconnected with any hypothesis, was followed by systems destitute of foundation. Sometimes it was thought that the air in the lungs incessantly acted as a stimulus or spur to drive on the circulation; sometimes the lungs were considered in the light of a pair of bellows, or fan, to cool the body, which was supposed to be heated by a thousand imaginary causes: and when philosophers were convinced, by experiments, that the bulk of the air was diminished by respiration, they explained it by saying, that the air had lost its spring.

Modern chemistry however enables us to explain the phenomena of respiration in a satisfactory manner.

In order to see this, we shall proceed to examine the changes produced by respiration; firstly, on the air, and secondly, on the blood.

The air which has served for respiration, is found to contain a mixture of azotic and carbonic acid gas, with a small quantity of oxygen gas; and a considerable quantity of water is thrown off from the lungs, in the form of vapour, during respiration.

From a variety of facts, it appears that oxygen gas is decomposed in the lungs during respiration; a part of it unites, as we shall afterwards see, with the iron contained in the blood, and converts it into an oxid; another and greater portion unites with the carbon, brought by the venous blood from all parts of the body to the lungs, and thus forms carbonic acid gas; while another portion of the oxygen unites with the hydrogen, brought in the same manner by the blood, and forms water. Thus then we are able to account for the different products of respiration.

Hence we see, that the explanation of animal heat follows as a simple and beautiful corollary from the theory of combustion; and we may consider respiration as an operation in which oxygen gas is continually passing from the gaseous to the concrete state; it will therefore give out at every instant the heat which it held in combination, and this heat, being conveyed by the circulation of the blood to all parts of the body, is a constant source of heat to the animal.

These facts likewise enable us to explain the reason, why an animal preserves the same temperature, notwithstanding the various changes which occur in the temperature of the surrounding atmosphere. In winter the air is condensed by the cold, the lungs therefore receive a greater quantity of oxygen in the same bulk, and the heat extricated will be proportionally increased. In summer, on the contrary, the air being rarefied by the heat, a less quantity of oxygen will be received by the lungs during each inspiration, and consequently the heat which is extricated must be less.

For the same reason, in northern latitudes, the heat extricated by respiration will be much greater than in the southern. By this simple and beautiful contrivance, nature has moderated the extremes of climate, and enabled the human body to bear vicissitudes which would otherwise destroy it.

Of all the phenomena of the animal body, there is none at first sight more remarkable, than that which animals possess of resisting the extremes of temperature.

The heat of the body, as has already been observed, continues at the same degree, though the temperature of the atmosphere be sometimes considerably hotter, at other times considerably colder, than the animal body: so that man is able to live, and to preserve the temperature of health, on the burning sands of Africa, and on the frozen plains of Siberia.

The alterations of temperature which the human body has been known to bear, without any fatal or even bad effects, are not less than 400° or 500° of Fahrenheit. The natural heat of the human body is 96° or 97° In the West Indies, the heat of the atmosphere is often 98° or 99°, and sometimes rises even to 126°, or 30° above the temperature of the human body, notwithstanding which, a thermometer put in the mouth points to 96° or 97°. The inhabitants of the hot regions of Surinam support, without inconvenience, the heat of their climate. We are assured that in Senegal, about the latitude of 17°, the thermometer in the shade generally stands at 108°, without any fatal effects to men or animals. The Russians often live in places heated by stoves to 108° or 109°, and some philosophers in this country, by way of experiment, remained a considerable time in a room heated above the boiling point of water.

On the other hand, an equal excess of cold seems to have no greater effect in altering the degree of heat proper to animal bodies. Delisle has observed a cold in Siberia 70° below the zero of Fahrenheit's scale, notwithstanding which animals lived. Gmelin has seen the inhabitants of Jeniseisk under the 58th degree of northern latitude, sustaining a degree of cold, which in January became so severe, that the spirit in the thermometer was 126° below the freezing point. Professor Pallas in Siberia, and our countrymen at Hudson's Bay, have experienced a degree of cold almost equal to this. All these facts tend to prove, that the heat of animals continues without alteration in very different temperatures. Hence it is evident that they must be able to produce a greater degree of heat, when surrounded by a cold medium; and on the contrary, that they must effect a diminution of the heat, when the surrounding medium is very hot.

All these circumstances may be accounted for, by the principles we have laid down ; the decomposition of oxygen in the lungs.

There have not been wanting, however, some very eminent physiologists, who have contended that animal heat is produced chiefly by the nerves. They have brought forward in proof of this the well known fact, that when the spinal marrow is injured, the temperature of the body generally becomes diminished; and that in a paralytic limb the heat is less than ordinary, though the strength and velocity of the pulse remain the same. These facts, and others of a similar nature, have induced them to believe, that the nervous system is the chief cause and essential organ of heat; and they have adduced similar arguments, to prove that nutrition is performed by the nerves, for a limb which is paralytic from an injury of the nerves, wastes, though the circulation continues.   The truth is, that the nerves exert their influence upon these, and all other functions of the body, and modify their action.   The liver secretes bile, but if the nerves leading to it be destroyed, the secretion of bile will cease; but who will say, that the bile is secreted by the nerves?   The nitric acid will dissolve metals, and this solution will go on more quickly if heat be applied; but surely the nitric acid is the solvent, the heat being only an aiding cause.

But though the human body has been so wisely constructed, as to bear, without inconvenience, a considerable variation of temperature; yet this latitude has its limits, which depend upon the capability of extricating heat from the atmosphere. There must be a limit below which the diminution of heat takes place faster than its production.   If this be continued, or increased, the heat of the animal must diminish, the functions lose their energy, and an insuperable inclination to sleep is felt, in which if the sufferer indulge, he will be sure to wake no more.

This is confirmed by what happened to Sir Joseph Banks and his party on the heights of Terra del Fuego. Dr. Solander, who had more than once crossed the mountains which divide Sweden from Norway, well knew that extreme cold produces an irresistible torpor and sleepiness, he therefore conjured the company to keep always in motion, whatever exertion it might require, and however great might be their inclination to rest. Whoever sits down, says he, will sleep; and whoever sleeps will wake no more. Thus, at once admonished and alarmed, they set forward; but, while they were still upon the naked rocks, the cold was so intense, as to produce the effects which had been so much dreaded. Dr. Solander himself was the first who found the inclination against which he had warned others, irresistible; and insisted on being suffered to lie down. Sir Joseph entreated and remonstrated in vain; he lay down upon the ground, though it was covered with snow; and it was with great difficulty that his friend kept him from sleeping. One of his black servants also began to linger, having suffered from the cold in the same manner as the Doctor. Partly by persuasion, and partly by force, they were got forwards; soon however they both declared that they would go no further. Sir Joseph had recourse again to entreaty and expostulation, but these produced no effect: when the black was told, that if he did not go on, he would shortly be frozen to death; he answered, that he desired nothing so much as to lie down and die. The Doctor did not so explicitly renounce his life, but said, he would go on, if they would first allow him to take some sleep, though he had before told them, that to sleep was to perish. They both in a few minutes fell into a profound sleep, and after five minutes Sir Joseph Banks happily succeeded in waking Dr. Solander, who had almost lost the use of his limbs; the muscles were so shrunk, that his shoes fell from his feet; but every attempt to recal the unfortunate black to life proved unsuccessful.

As the circulation of the blood is the means by which the heat produced is conveyed to all parts of the body; and as it is a function of the highest importance, I shall, in the next lecture, proceed to the consideration of it.

LECTURE III.

CIRCULATION OF THE BLOOD.

Two kinds of motion may be distinguished in the animal economy; the one voluntary, or under the command of the will, which takes place at certain intervals, but may be stopped at pleasure. The other kind of motion is called involuntary, as not depending on the will, but going on constantly, without interruption, both when we sleep and when we wake.

Of the first kind is the motion of the limbs, of which I have already spoken in general terms; the object of which is, to change the situation of the animal, and carry it where the will directs.

Among the involuntary motions, the most remarkable is the circulation of the blood, which I shall proceed to consider in this lecture.

There is one motion, however, which claims a middle place between the voluntary and involuntary; I mean respiration. This action is so far under the command of the will, that it may be suspended, increased, or diminished in strength and frequency: but we can only suspend it for a very short time; and it goes on regularly during sleep, and in general, even when we are awake, without the intervention of the will; its continuation being always necessary, as we have already seen, to support life.

The motion of the fluids in the living body is regulated by very different laws, from those which govern the motion of ordinary fluids, that depend upon their gravity and fluidity: these last have a general centre of gravitation to which they incessantly tend. Their motion is from above downwards, when not prevented by any obstacles; and when they meet with obstruction, they either stop till the obstacle is removed, or escape where they find the least resistance. When they have reached the lowest situations, they remain at rest, unless acted upon by some internal impulse, which again puts them in motion.

But the motion of the fluids in an animal body, is less uniform, constant, and regular; it takes place upwards as well as downwards, and overcomes numerous obstacles; it carries the blood from the interior parts of the body to the surface, and from the surface back again to the internal parts; it forces it from the left side of the body to the right, and with such rapidity that not a particle of the fluid remains an instant in the same place.

The principal organ concerned in the circulation of the blood, is the heart; which is a hollow muscle, of a conical figure, with two cavities, called ventricles; this organ is situated in the thorax or chest; its apex or point is inclined downwards and to the left side, where it is received in a cavity of the left lobe of the lungs.

At the basis of the heart on each side are situated two cavities, called auricles, to receive the blood: and these contracting, force the blood into the ventricles, which are two cavities in the heart, separated from each other by a strong muscular partition. The cavity which is situated on the right side of the heart, is called the right ventricle, and that on the left the left ventricle. From the right ventricle of the heart issues a large artery, called the pulmonary artery, which goes to the lungs, and is there divided and subdivided into a vast number of branches, the extremities of which are too small to be visible. These ultimate ramifications unite again into larger branches; these again into branches still larger, and so continually, till at last they form four tubes, called the pulmonary veins, which are inserted into the left auricle of the heart,

From the left ventricle of the heart there issues another large artery, called the aorta, which, in its passage, sends off branches to the heart, arms, legs, head, and every other part of the body. These branches, in the course of their progress, are divided and subdivided into innumerable minute ramifications, the last of which are invisible. These small ramifications unite again into branches continually larger and larger, till they form two great tubes, called the venae cavae; which large veins are inserted into the right auricle of the heart; where a vein, termed the coronary vein of the heart, which returns the blood from the heart itself, also terminates.

From what has been said, it will be evident, that strictly speaking, there are only two arteries and seven veins in the body; one pulmonary artery, which carries the blood from the right ventricle of the heart to the lungs, and four pulmonary veins, which bring it back again; then the aorta or large artery, which carries the blood from the left ventricle of the heart to all parts of the body; the two venae cavae, and the coronary vein of the heart, which bring it back again.

At the beginning of both arteries, where they leave the heart, are placed valves, which allow the blood to flow freely from the heart into the arteries, but which prevent its return to the heart. There are likewise valves between the auricles and ventricles, which permit the blood to flow from the former into the latter, but prevent its return into the auricles. The veins are likewise furnished with valves, which allow the blood to flow from their minute branches along the larger towards the heart, but prevent its returning to these minute branches.

The blood being brought back from all parts of the body into the right auricle of the heart, distends this cavity, and thus causes it to contract; this auricle, by contracting, forces the blood into the right ventricle; this muscular cavity being distended and irritated by the blood, contracts, and propels the blood through the pulmonary artery into the lungs: from hence it is brought back by the pulmonary veins, to the left auricle of the heart, by whose contraction it is forced into the left ventricle. The contraction of this ventricle propels the blood, with great force, into the aorta, through the innumerable ramifications of which, it is carried to every part of the body, and brought back by veins, which accompany these arterial ramifications, and form the venae cavae, which conduct the blood into the right auricle of the heart, from whence it is again sent into the right ventricle, which sends it through the pulmonary artery, to the lungs; the pulmonary veins bring it back again to the heart, from whence it is propelled through the aorta, to all parts of the body: thus running a perpetual round, called the circulation of the blood.

Thus then we see, that the circulation consists of two circles or stages, one through the lungs, which may be called the

pulmonary, or lesser circle, and the other through all parts of
the body, which may be termed the aortal, or greater circle.

That the blood circulates in this manner, is evident, from
the valves placed at the origin of the arteries, and in the
large branches of the veins, which prevent the return of the
blood to the heart, in any other manner than that I have
described. This is likewise evident, in the common operation of blood letting: when the arm is tied, the vein swells
below the ligature, instead of above, and we do not make
the opening above the ligature, or on the side next the
heart. If the vein were opened above the ligature, it would
not bleed. For it only swells next the hand, which shows
that the blood does not flow into the vein downwards from
the heart, but upwards from the hand.

If the ligature be too tight, the blood will not flow through
the opening in the vein. The reason of this, is, that the
artery is compressed, in this case, as well as the vein; and
as the veins derive their blood from the arteries, it follows
that if the blood's motion be obstructed in the latter, none
can flow from them into the former: when we wish to open
an artery, the orifice must be made above the ligature.

Another proof of the circulation being performed in this
manner, is derived from microscopic observations, on the
transparent parts of animals, in which the blood can be
seen to move towards the extremities, along the arteries,
and return by the veins.

The blood, however, does not flow out of the heart into
the arteries in a continued stream, but by jets, or pulses;
when the ventricles are filled with blood from the auricles,
this blood stimulates them, and thereby causes them to con-

tract; by such contraction, they force the blood, which they contain, into the arteries; this contraction is called the systole of the heart. As soon as they have finished their contraction, they relax, till they are again filled with blood from the auricles, and this state of relaxation of the heart, is called the diastole.

This causes the pulsation or beating of the heart. The arteries must, of course, have a similar pulsation, the blood being driven into them only by starts; and accordingly we find it in the artery of the wrist; this beating we call the pulse; the like may also be observed in the arteries of the temples, and other parts of the body. The veins, however, have no pulsation, for the blood flowing on, in an uninterrupted course, from smaller tubes to wider, its pulse becomes entirely destroyed.

The different cavities of the heart do not contract at the same time; but the two auricles contract together, the ventricles being at that time in a state of relaxation; these ventricles then contract together, while the auricles become relaxed.

Both the arteries and veins may be compared to a tree, whose trunk is divided into large branches; these are subdivided into smaller, the smaller again into others still smaller; and we may observe, likewise, that the sum of the capacities of the branches, which arise from any trunk, is always greater than the capacity of the trunk.

The minutest branches of the arteries, being reflected, become veins, or else they enter veins that are already formed, by anastomosis, as it is called; the small veins continually receiving others, become, like a river, gradually larger, till they form the venae cavae, which conduct the blood to the heart.

Anatomical injections prove, that the last branches of the arteries terminate in the beginning of veins ; but it is the opinion of many celebrated physiologists, that the arteries carry the blood to the different parts of the body to nourish them, and that the veins commence by open mouths, which absorb or suck up what is superfluous, and return it back to the heart.

From what has been said, it must be evident that there is a considerable resemblance between the circulation of the blood in the animal body, and the circulation of the aqueous fluid on the surface of the globe. In the latter case the water is raised from the ocean, by the heat of the sun, and poured down upon the dry land, in minute drops, for the nourishment and economy of its different parts. What is superfluous is collected into little rills; these meeting with others, form brooks ; the union of which produce rivers, that conduct the water to its original source, from which it is again circulated.

In the same manner, the blood is sent by the heart to different parts of the body, for the nourishment and economy of its different parts ; what is superfluous is brought back by veins, which, continually uniting, form those large trunks, which convey the vital fluid to the heart.

The blood does not circulate, however, in the manner which I have mentioned, in all parts of the body ; for that which is carried by arteries to the viscera, serving for digestion, such as the stomach, bowels, mesentery, omentum, and spleen, is collected by small veins which unite into a large trunk called the vena portarum ; this vein enters the liver, and is subdivided in it like an artery, distributing through the liver a great quantity of blood, from which the bile is secreted: and, having served this purpose, the blood is collected by small veins; these unite and form the hepatic vein, which pours the blood into the vena cava, to be conducted to the heart.

The reason of this deviation, is probably, to diminish the velocity of the blood in the liver, for the secretion of the bile; which could not have been effected by means of an artery

The force which impels the blood, is, first, the contraction of the heart, which propels the blood into the arteries with great velocity; but this is not the only force concerned in keeping up the circulation; this is evident, from the diminished heat, and weakened pulse, in a paralytic limb, which ought not to take place, if the blood were propelled merely by the action of the heart.

The arteries are possessed of an elastic and muscular power, by means of which they contract when they are distended or stimulated. It is however by the muscular power alone, that they assist in propelling the blood; for the elasticity of their coats can serve no other purpose than preserving the mean diameter of the vessel. If we suppose the arteries to be dilated by the blood, poured into them by the heart, they will, by their contraction, as elastic tubes, undoubtedly propel the blood: but supposing them to be perfectly elastic, the force of the heart will be just as much diminished in dilating them as the force of the blood is increased by their contraction. We are not however acquainted with any sub-

stance perfectly elastic, or which restores itself with a force
equal to that with which it was distended: hence the elastic
power of the arteries will subtract from, instead of adding to,
the power of the heart. It is evident, therefore, that it must
be by the muscular power of the arteries, which causes them
to contract like the heart, that they propel the blood.

That such is the case, appears from the muscular structure
of the arteries observed by anatomists; as also from the
effects of mechanical irritation of their coats, which causes
them to contract; this is likewise evident from the inflammation produced by the application of stimulating substances
to particular parts; for instance, cantharides and mustard.
It appears likewise, from the secretion in some parts being
preternaturally increased, while the motion of the general
mass of the blood continues unaltered.

The contraction of the arteries always propels the blood
towards the extreme parts of the body: this must necessarily happen, because the valves at the origin of the arteries prevent its return to the heart, it must therefore move in
the direction in which it finds least resistance.

If it were not for this muscular power of the arteries, the
force of the heart would not alone be able to propel the
blood to the extreme parts of the body, and overcome the
different kinds of resistance it has to encounter. Among the
causes that lessen the velocity of the blood, may be mentioned the increasing area of the artery; for it was before
observed, that the sum of the cavities of the branches from
any trunk exceeded the cavity of the trunk: and from
the principles of hydrostatics, the velocities of fluids, propelled by the same force, in tubes of different diameters, are

inversely as the squares of the diameters, so that in a tube of double the diameter, the velocity will only be one fourth ; in one of the triple, only one ninth : and since the arteries may be looked upon as conical, it is evident that the velocity of the blood must be diminished from this cause.

The curvilinear course of the arteries likewise gives considerable resistance ; for at every bending the blood loses part of its momentum against the sides ; and this loss is evidently proportioned to the magnitude of the angle, at which the branch goes off. Convolutions are frequently made, in order to diminish the force of the blood in particular organs; this is especially the case with the carotid artery before it enters the brain.

The angles which the ramifications of the arteries make, are greater or more obtuse nearer the heart, and more acute as the distance increases ; by which means the velocity of the blood is rendered more equal in different parts.

The anastomosing or union of different branches of arteries, likewise retards the velocity of the blood, the particles of which, from different vessels, impinging, disturb each other's motion, and produce a compound force, in which there is always a loss of velocity: and it is evident, from the composition of forces, that this loss must be proportioned to the obliquity of the angle at which the vessels unite.

The adhesion of the blood to the sides of the vessels, likewise causes a loss of velocity in the minuter branches, which may be owing to a chemical affinity : the viscidity or imperfect fluidity of the blood is another retarding cause. All these causes united, would render it impossible for the heart to propel the blood with the velocity with which it moves in the very minute branches of the arteries, if these arteries were not endowed with a living muscular power like the heart, by which they contract and propel their contents.

In the veins, the motion of the blood is occasioned partly by the vis a tergo, and partly by the contraction of the neighbouring muscles, which press upon the veins; and these veins being furnished with valves, the return of the blood towards the arteries is prevented; it must therefore move towards the heart.

That the contraction of the muscles of the body tends very much to promote the circulation of the blood, is evident, from the increase of the circulation from exercise, and likewise from the languid motion of the blood in sedentary persons, and those given to indolence. Hence we may account for the different diseases to which such persons are subject, and know how to apply the proper remedies. Hence likewise, we see the reason why rest is so absolutely necessary in acute and inflammatory diseases, where the momentum of the blood is already too great.

It has been doubted by anatomists, whether the veins were possessed with muscular power; but this seems now to be confirmed. Haller found the vena cava near the heart to contract on the application of stimulants, though he could see no muscular fibres; these, however, have been discovered by succeeding anatomists.

The magnitude of the veins is always greater than that of the corresponding arteries; hence the velocity of the blood must be less in the veins; and hence likewise we may account for their want of pulsation; for the action of the heart upon the arteries is at first very great ; but as we recede from the heart, this effect becomes less perceptible ; the arterial tube increases both in size and muscularity, in proportion to its distance from the source of circulation. The powers of the heart are spent in overcoming the different resistances which I have noticed, before the blood enters the veins ; hence the blood will flow uniformly in these last.

The blood is subject in the veins to retarding causes, similar to those which operate in the arteries, but perhaps not in an equal degree ; for the flexures are less frequent in the veins than in the arteries.   As the capacity of the arterial tube increases with its distance from the heart, the velocity, from this cause, as has already been observed, is continually diminished; but a contrary effect takes place in the veins ; for the different branches uniting, form trunks, whose capacities are smaller than the sums of the capacities of the branches, hence the velocity of the blood in the veins will increase as it approaches the heart.

Another retarding cause may be mentioned, namely, gravity, which acts more on the venous than the arterial system. The effects of gravity on the veins may be exemplified, by a ring being pulled off the finger with ease when the hand is elevated ; also by the swellings of the feet that occur in relaxed habits, which swellings increase towards night, and subside in the morning, after the body has been in a horizontal posture for some hours.

In weak persons, the frequency of the pulse is increased by an erect posture, which may probably depend on gravity ; as we know, from the observations of Macdonald and others, that an erect posture will make a difference of 15 or 20 beats in a minute. The experiments alluded to, were made by gently raising a person fastened to a board, where there being no muscular exertion, respiration would not be increased ; so that the whole effect was probably owing to gravity accelerating the column of arterial blood.

The inverted posture produces a still more remarkable effect in accelerating the pulse, than the erect, for it sometimes causes it to beat 10 or 12 times more in the former case than in the latter.

While we are on this subject, it may not be improper to take notice of the effects of swinging on the circulation, which have been found by Dr. Carmichael Smyth, and others, to diminish the strength and velocity to such a degree, as to bring on fainting. These effects have never been satisfactorily accounted for ; but they would seem to admit of an easy explanation on mechanical principles : they are undoubtedly owing, at least in a great measure, to the centrifugal force acquired by the blood.

By a centrifugal force, I mean, the tendency which revolving bodies have to fly off from the centre, which arises from their tendency to move in a straight line, agreeably to the laws of motion. Hence a tumbler of water may be whirled in a circle vertically without spilling it ; the centrifugal force pushing the water against the bottom of the tumbler. In the same manner when the human body is made to revolve vertically in the arch of a circle, this centrifugal force will propel the blood from the head and heart towards he extremities; hence the circulation of the blood will be weakened, and the energy of the brain diminished. The contrary, however, will take place on a horizontal swing, as I have frequently observed, both on myself and others; for the centrifugal force in this case will propel the blood from the extremities towards the head.

It has been already observed, that the pulsations of the artery which we feel at the wrist, are occasioned by its alternate dilatations and contractions, which vary according to the strength and regularity of the circulation, which is liable to be affected by the smallest changes in the state of health. Hence physicians make use of the pulse as a criterion whereby to judge of the health of the body. And we may observe that there are few more certain characteristics of the state of the body than the pulse; yet the conclusions that have been drawn from it have often been erroneous; and this has arisen from trusting to observation without the aid of reason.

That we may better understand the phenomena of the pulse, I shall lay down the following postulata. 1st. It is now generally believed, that every part of the arterial system is endowed with irritability, or a power of contracting on the application of a stimulus, and that the blood acting on this contractibility, if the term may be allowed, causes contraction ; and that the alternate relaxation and contraction gives the phenomenon pulsation. 2d. The greater the action of the stimulus of the blood, the greater will be the contraction, that is, the nearer will the sides of the artery approach towards the axis. 3d. That the velocity with which a muscular fibre, in a state of debility, contracts, is at least equal to that with which a fibre in a state of strength contracts, is a fact generally allowed by physiologists.

We shall afterwards see, that a deficient action of stimulus on the vessels may arise, either directly from diminishing the quantity of blood contained in them, or indirectly, from the application of too great a stimulant power, which has diminished the capability of contracting inherent in the vessels.

From these postulata, it will be evident, that the greater the action of the arteries, that is, the more powerful their contraction, the longer will be the intervals between the pulsations.

For the velocity being at least equal in debility and in strength, the times between the pulsations will be proportioned to the approach of the sides of the artery towards its axis: but the approach of the sides towards the axis is greater when the arteries are in a state of vigour than when debilitated; consequently the intervals between the pulsations will be greater when the arteries are in a state of vigour than when debilitated.

Hence it is evident, that a frequency of pulse must generally indicate a diminished action or debility; while a moderate slowness indicates a vigorous or just action.

Hence likewise the opinion of increased action, which has been supposed to take place in fevers, because a frequent pulse was observed, must be false, because the frequency arises from a directly opposite state, and indicates a diminished action of the vascular system.

In a sound and adult man the frequency of the pulse is about seventy beats in a minute; and in an infant, within the first five or six months, the pulse is seldom less than one hundred and twenty, and diminishes in frequency as the child grows older. But though seventy beats in the minute may be taken as a general standard; yet in persons of irritable constitutions the frequency is greater than this, and many, who are in the prime of life, have the pulse only between fifty and sixty.

It is generally observed, that the pulse is slower in the morning, that it increases in frequency till noon, after dinner it again becomes slow, and in the evening its frequency returns, which increases till midnight.

These phenomena may be rationally explained on the principles just laid down. When we rise in the morning, the contractibility being abundant, the stimulus of the blood produces a greater effect, the pulse becomes slow, and the contractions strong; it becomes more frequent, however, till dinner time, from a diminished contractibility; after dinner, from the addition of the stimulus of food and chyle, it again decreases in frequency, and becomes slow till the evening, when its frequency returns, because the contractibility becomes exhausted: and this frequency continues till the vital power have been recruited by sleep.

By the same principles it is easy to explain the quickness of the pulse in infancy, its gradual decrease till maturity, its slowness and strength during the meridian of life, and the return of its frequency during the decline.

Having now described the phenomena of the circulation, it will be proper to examine the changes produced by this function on the blood; and, in the first place, it may be observed, that the blood which returns by the vena cava to the heart, is of a dark colour inclining to purple; while that which passes from the left ventricle into the arteries, is of a bright vermilion hue. The blood which is found in the pulmonary artery has the same dark purple colour with that in the vena cava, while that in the pulmonary vein resembles the aortal blood in its brightness. Hence it would appear, that the blood, during its passage through the lungs, has its colour changed from a dark purple to a bright vermilion, in which state it is brought by the pulmonary vein to the left auricle of the heart; this auricle, contracting, expels the blood into the corresponding ventricle, by whose action, and that of the arteries, it is distributed to all parts of the body. When it returns, however, by the veins, it is found to have lost its fine bright colour. It would appear, therefore, that the blood obtains its red colour during its passage through the lungs, and becomes deprived of it during its circulation through the rest of the body

That the blood contains iron, may be proved by various experiments: if a quantity of blood be exposed to a red heat in a crucible, the greatest part will be volatilised and burnt; but a quantity of brown ashes will be left behind, which will be attracted by the magnet. If diluted sulphuric acid be poured on these ashes, a considerable portion of them will dissolve; if into this solution we drop tincture of galls, a black precipitate will take place, or if we use prussiate of potash, a precipitate of prussian blue will be formed. These facts prove, beyond doubt, that a quantity of iron exists in the blood.

I shall not now particularly inquire how it comes there: it may partly be taken into the blood along with the vegetable and animal food, which is received into the stomach; for the greatest part of the animal and vegetable substances, which we receive as food, contain a greater or less quantity of iron. Or it may be partly formed by the animal powers, as would appear from the following circumstance. The analysis of an egg, before incubation, affords not the least vestige of iron, but as soon as the chick exists, though it has been perfectly shut up from all external communication, if the egg be burnt, the ashes will be attracted by the magnet.

But, however we may suppose the blood to obtain its iron, it certainly does contain it; if the coagulable lymph and serum of the blood be carefully freed from the red particles, by repeated washing, the strictest analysis will not discover in either of them a particle of iron, while the red globules thus separated will be found to contain a considerable quantity of this metal.

That the red colour of the blood depends upon iron, appears likewise from the experiments of Menghini, which show, that the blood of persons who have been taking chalybeate medicines for some time, is much more florid that it is naturally; the same is agreeable to my own observation. A late analysis, by Fourcroy, has likewise proved, that the red colour of the blood resides in the iron ; but, though the red colour of the blood may reside in the iron which it contains, we shall find that this colour is likewise connected with oxidation.

If the dark coloured blood, drawn from the veins, be put under a vessel containing oxygen gas, its surface will immediately become florid, while the bulk of the gas will be diminished. Mr. Hewson enclosed a portion of a vein between two ligatures, and injected into it a quantity of oxygen gas ; the blood, which was before dark coloured, instantly assumed the hue of arterial blood. Thuvenal put

a quantity of arterial blood under the receiver of an air
pump; on exhausting the air it became of the dark colour
of venous blood; on readmitting the air, it became again
florid. He put it under a receiver filled with oxygen gas,
and found the florid colour much increased.

Dr. Priestley exposed the blood of a sheep successively
to oxygen gas, atmospheric air, and carbonic acid gas; and
found, that in oxygen gas its colour became very florid,
less so in atmospheric air, and in carbonic acid gas it became quite black. He filled a bladder with venous blood,
and exposed it to oxygen gas; the surface in contact with
the bladder immediately became florid, while the interior
parts remained dark coloured.

All these facts prove, that the red colour which the blood
acquires in the lungs, is owing to the oxygen, which probably combines with it, and the last mentioned fact shows,
that oxygen will act on the blood, even though a membrane
similar to the bladder, be interposed between them.

The same effect, probably, takes place in the lungs; the
blood is circulated through that organ by a number of fine
capillary arteries; and it is probable that the oxygen acts
upon the blood through the membranes of these arteries,
in the same manner that it does through the bladder.

In short, it seems likely, that the blood, during its circulation through the lungs, becomes combined with oxygen;
that this oxidated blood, on its return to the heart, is circulated by the arteries to all parts of the body; and that,
during this circulation, its oxygen combines with the hydrogen and carbon of the blood, and perhaps with those parts
of the body with which it comes into contact; it is therefore

brought back to the heart, by the veins, of a dark colour, and deprived of the greatest part of its oxygen.

This is the most probable theory, in the present state of our knowledge; it was proposed by Lavoisier, who imagines the focus of heat, or fireplace to warm the body, to be in the lungs: others, however, have thought it more consonant to facts, to suppose, that, instead of the oxygen uniting with carbon and hydrogen in the lungs, and there giving out its heat, the oxygen is absorbed by the blood, and unites with these substances during the circulation, so that heat is produced in every part of the body; and this doctrine seems certainly supported by several facts and experiments.

The circulation of the blood, though so simple and beautiful a function, was unknown to the ancient physicians, and was first demonstrated by our countryman, Harvey: when he first published his account of this discovery, he met with the treatment which is generally experienced by those who enlighten and improve the comfort of their fellow creatures, by valuable discoveries. The novelty and merit of this discovery drew upon him the envy of most of his contemporaries in Europe, who accordingly opposed him with all their power; and some universities even went so far, as to refuse the honours of medicine to those students, who had the audacity to defend this doctrine; but afterwards, when they could not argue against truth and conviction, they attempted to rob him of the discovery, and asserted that many of the ancient physicians, and particularly Hippocrates, were acquainted with it. Posterity, however, who can alone review subjects of controversy without prejudice, have done ample justice to his memory.

LECTURE IV

DIGESTION, NUTRITION, &c.

The human body, by the various actions to which it is subject, and the various functions which it performs, becomes, in a short time, exhausted; the fluids become dissipated, the solids wasted, while both are continually tending towards putrefaction. Notwithstanding which, the body still continues to perform its proper functions, often for a considerable length of time; some contrivance, therefore, was necessary to guard against these accelerators of its destruction. There are two ways in which the living body may be preserved; the one by assimilating nutritious substances, to repair the loss of different parts; the other to collect, in secretory organs, the humours secreted from these substances.

We are admonished of the necessity of receiving substances into the body, to repair the continual waste, by the appetites of hunger and thirst. For the stomach being gradually emptied of its contents, and the body, in some degree, exhausted by exercise, we experience a disagreeable sensation in the region of the stomach, accompanied by a desire to eat, at first slight, but gradually increasing, and at last growing intolerable, unless it be satisfied.

When the fluid parts have been much dissipated, or when we have taken, by the mouth, any dry food, or acrid substance, we experience a sensation of heat in the fauces, and at the same time a great desire of swallowing liquids. The former sensation is called hunger, and the latter thirst.

From the back part of the mouth passes a tube, called the oesophagus or gullet, its upper end is wide and open, spread behind the tongue to receive the masticated aliment: the lower part of this pipe, after it has passed through the thorax, and pierced the diaphragm, enters the stomach, which is a membranous bag, situated under the left side of the dia- phragm: its figure nearly resembles the pouch of a bagpipe, the left end being most capacious; the upper side is concave, and the lower convex: it has two orifices, both on its upper part; the left, which is a continuation of the oesophagus, and through which the food passes into the stomach, is named cardia; and the right, through which the food is conveyed out of the stomach, is called pylorus: within this last orifice is a circular valve, which, in some degree, prevents the re- turn of the aliment into the stomach.

From the pylorus, or right orifice of the stomach, arise the intestines, or bowels, which consist of a long and large tube, making several circumvolutions, in the cavity of the abdomen ; this tube is about five or six times as long as the body to which it belongs. Though it is one continued pipe, it has been divided, by anatomists, into six parts, three small, three large. The three small intestines are the duodenum, the jejunum, and the ileum: the duodenum commences at the pylorus, and is continued into the jejunum, which is so called from its being generally found empty: the ileum is only a prolongation of the jejunum, and terminates in the first of

the great intestines, called the caecum. The other great guts
are the colon and the rectum.

The whole of what has been described is only a production of the same tube, beginning at the oesophagus. It is called by anatomists the intestinal canal, or prima via, because it is the first passage of the food. It has circular muscular fibres, which give it a power of contracting when irritated by distension; and this urges forward the food which is contained in it. This occasions a worm like motion of the whole intestines, which is called their peristaltic motion.

The mesentery is a membrane beginning loosely on the loins, and thence extending to all the intestines; which it preserves from twisting by their peristaltic motion. It serves also to sustain all the vessels going to and from the intestines, namely the arteries, veins, lacteals, and nerves; it also contains several glands, called, from their situation, mesenteric glands.

The lacteal vessels consist of a vast number of fine pellucid tubes, which arise by open mouths from the intestines, and proceeding thence through the mesentery, they frequently unite, and form fewer and larger vessels, which pass through the mesenteric glands, into a common receptacle or bag, called the receptacle of the chyle. The use of these vessels is to absorb the fluid part of the digested aliment, called chyle, and convey it into the receptacle of the chyle, that it may be thence carried through the thoracic duct into the blood.

The receptacle of the chyle is a membranous bag, about two thirds of an inch long, and one third of an inch wide, at ts superior part it is contracted into a slender membranous pipe, called the thoracic duct, because its course is principally through the thorax; it passes between the aorta and the vena azygos, then obliquely over the oesophagus, and great curvature of the aorta, and continuing its course towards the internal jugular vein, it enters the left subclavian vein on its superior part.

There are several other viscera besides those I have described, which are subservient to digestion; among these may be mentioned the liver, gall bladder, and pancreas. The liver is the largest gland in the body, and is situated immediately under the diaphragm, principally on the right side. Its blood vessels that compose it as a gland, are the branches of the vena portarum, which, as I mentioned in the last lecture, enters the liver and distributes its blood like an artery. F om this blood the liver secretes the bile, which is conveyed by the hepatic duct, towards the intestines: before this duct reaches the intestines, it is joined by another, coming from the gall bladder: these two ducts uniting, form a common duct, which enters the duodenum obliquely, about four inches below the pylorus of the stomach.

The gall bladder, which is a receptacle of bile, is situated between the stomach and the liver; and the bile which comes from the liver, along the hepatic duct, partly passes into the duodenum, and partly along the cystic duct into the gall bladder. When the stomach is full, it presses on the gall bladder, which will squeeze out the bile into the duodenum at the time when it is most wanted.

The bile is a thick bitter fluid, of a yellowish green colour, composed chiefly of soda and animal oil, forming a soap; and it is most probably in consequence of this saponaceous property that it assists digestion, by causing the different parts of the food to unite together by intermediate affinity. When the bile is prevented from flowing into the intestines, by any obstruction in the ducts, digestion is badly performed, costiveness takes place, and the excrements are of a white colour, from being deprived of the bile. This fluid, stagnating in the gall bladder, is absorbed by the lymphatics, and carried into the blood, communicating to the whole surface of the body a yellow tinge, and other symptoms of jaundice.

The jaundice therefore is occasioned by an obstruction to the passage of the bile into the intestines, and its subsequent absorption into the blood: this obstruction may be caused either by concretions of the bile, called gall stones, or by a greater viscidity of the fluid, or by a spasm, or paralysis of the biliary ducts.

The pancreas, or sweet bread, is a large gland lying across the upper and back part of the abdomen, near the duodenum. It has a short excretory duct, about half as wide as a crow quill, which enters the duodenum at the same place where the bile duct enters it.

The food being received into the mouth, is there masticated or broken down, by the teeth, and impregnated with saliva, which is pressed out of the salivary glands, by the motions of the jaw and the muscles of the mouth. It then descends, through the oesophagus, into the stomach, where it becomes digested, and, in a great measure, dissolved, by the gastric juice, which is secreted by the arteries of the stomach. It is then pushed through the pylorus, or right orifice of the stomach into the duodenum, where it becomes mixed with the bile from the gall bladder and liver, and the pancreatic juice from the pancreas. These fluids seem to complete the digestion : after this, the food is continually moved forwards by the peristaltic motion of the intestines.

The chyle, or thin and milky part of the aliment, being absorbed by the lacteals, which rise, by open mouths, from the intestines, is carried into the receptacle of the chyle, and from thence the thoracic duct carries it to the subclavian vein, where it mixes with the blood, and passes with it to the heart.

The food of animals is derived from the animal or vegetable kingdoms. There are some animals which eat only vegetables, while others live only on animal substances. The number and form of the teeth, and the structure of the stomach, and bowels, determine whether an animal be herbivorous, or carnivorous. The first class have a considerable number of grinders, or dentes molares ; and the intestines are much more long and bulky ; in the second class, the cutting teeth are predominant, and the intestines are much shorter.

Man seems to form an intermediate link between these two classes : his teeth, and the structure of the intestines, show, that he may subsist both on vegetable and animal food ; and, in fact, he is best nourished by a proper mixture of both. This appears from those people who live solely on vegetables, as the Gentoo tribes, and those who subsist solely on animals, as the fish eaters of the northern latitudes, being a feebler generation than those of this country, who exist on a proper mixture of both. A due proportion, therefore, of the two kinds of nourishment, seems undoubtedly the best.

Having taken a general view of the course of the aliment into the blood, I shall now examine more particularly, how each part of the organs concerned in digestion, or connected with that function, contributes to that end.

The food being received into the mouth, undergoes various preparations, which fit it for those changes it is afterwards to undergo. By the teeth the parts of it are divided and ground, softened and liquified by the saliva, and properly compressed by the action of the tongue and mastication.

The mouth, in most animals, is armed with very hard substances, which, by the motion of the lower jaw, are brought strongly into contact. Those parts of the teeth which are above the sockets, are not simply bony, they are much harder than the bones, and possess the property of resisting putrefaction, as long as this hard crust continues to cover them. The teeth are divided into three classes : 1st. The cutting teeth, which are sharp and thin, and which serve to cut or divide the food : 2nd. The canine teeth, which serve to tear it into pieces still smaller : 3rd. The grinders, which present large and uneven surfaces, and actually grind the substance already broken down by the other teeth. Birds, whom nature has deprived of teeth, have a strong muscular stomach, called the gizzard, which serves the purposes of teeth, and they even take into the stomach small pieces of grit, to assist in grinding to a powder the grain that they have swallowed.

Among those parts of the mouth which contribute to the preparation of the food, we must reckon the numerous glands which secrete saliva, and which have therefore been called salivary glands. The saliva is a saponaceous liquor, destitute of taste or smell, which is squeezed out from these glands, and mixed with the food during mastication. In the mouth, therefore, the food becomes first broken down by the teeth, impregnated with saliva, and reduced to a soft pasty substance, capable of passing with these, through the oesophagus, into the stomach. It is here that it undergoes the change, which is particularly termed digestion.

Digestion comprehends two classes of phenomena, distinct from each other: 1st. Physical and chemical: 2nd. Organic and vital. The object of the first, is to bring the alimentary substances to such a state as is necessary, that they may be capable of the new combinations into which they are to enter, to obtain the animal character. The object of the second is, to produce those combinations which some have thought to be very different from those produced by simple chemical attractions.

The physical and chemical phenomena of digestion, relate chiefly, 1st. To the action of heat; 2ndly To the dissolution of the alimentary substances. The heat of the animal is such, as is well fitted to promote solution.

That digestion is performed by solution, is evident, from several experiments, particularly those made by Dr. Stevens, who enclosed different alimentary substances in hollow spheres of silver, pierced with small holes. These were swallowed, and after remaining some time in the stomach, the contents were found dissolved. The great agent of solution is the gastric juice, which possesses a very strong solvent power. This juice is secreted by the arteries of the stomach ; it may be collected in considerable quantity, by causing an animal that has been fasting for some time, to swallow small hollow spheres, or tubes of metal filled with sponge.

This liquid does not act indiscriminately upon all substances: for if grains of corn be put into a perforated tube, and a granivorous bird be made to swallow it, the corn will remain the usual time in the stomach without alteration; whereas if the husk of the grain be previously taken off, the whole of it will be dissolved. There are many substances likewise which pass unaltered through the intestines of animals, and consequently are not acted upon by the gastric juice. This is the case frequently with grains of oats, when they have been swallowed by horses entire, with their husks on. This is the case likewise with the seeds of apples and other fruits, when swallowed entire by man; yet if these substances have been previously ground by the teeth, they will be digested. It would appear therefore, that it is chiefly the husk or outside of these substances which resists the action of the gastric juice.

This juice is not the same in all animals; for many animals cannot digest the food on which others live. Thus sheep live wholly on vegetables, and if they are made to feed on animals, their stomachs will not digest them: others again, as the eagle, feed wholly on animal substances, and cannot digest vegetables.

The accounts of the experiments made on gastric juice are very various: sometimes it has been found of an acid nature, at other times not. The experiments of Spallanzani show, however, that this acidity is not owing to the gastric juice, but to the food. The result of his experiments, which have been very numerous, prove, that the gastric juice is naturally neither acid nor alkaline. No conclusion, however, can be drawn from these experiments made out of the stomach, with respect to the nature of the gastric juice; nor do the analyses which have been made of it throw any light on its mode of action. But, from the experiments which have been made on digestion, in the stomach, particularly by Spallanzani, the following facts have been established.

The gastric juice attacks the surfaces of bodies, and combines chemically with their particles. It operates with more energy and rapidity, the more the food is divided, and its action increased by a warm temperature. By the action of digestion, the food is not merely reduced to very minute parts, but its chemical properties become changed; its sensible properties are destroyed, and it acquires new and very different ones. This juice does not act as a ferment; so far from it, it is a powerful antiseptic, and even restores flesh which is already putrid.

When the alimentary substances have continued a sufficient time in the stomach, they are pushed into the intestines, where they become mixed with the bile and pancreatic juice, as was before observed. What changes are caused by these substances, we have yet to learn; but there is no doubt, that they serve some important purposes. By the peristaltic motion of the bowels, the alimentary matters thus changed are carried along, and applied to the mouths of the lacteal vessels, which open into the intestines, like a sponge, and by some power, not well understood, absorb that part which is fitted for assimilation, while the remainder is rejected as an excrement.

The lacteal vessels are furnished with valves, which allow a free passage to the chyle from the intestines, but prevent its return. The most inexplicable thing in this operation, is the power which these vessels possess of selecting from the intestinal mass, those substances which are proper for nutrition, and rejecting those which are not.

These lacteal vessels, as was before observed, pass through the mesentery, and their contents seem to undergo some important change in the mesenteric glands. The chyle which passes through vessels, appears to be an oily liquor, less animalised than milk, and its particles seem to be held in solution by the intermedium of a mucilaginous principle. It is conveyed along the thoracic duct in the manner already described, and enters the blood slowly, and, as it were, drop by drop, by the subclavian vein; in this way it becomes intimately mixed with the blood, and combining with oxygen in the lungs, it acquires a fibrous character, and becomes fit to nourish the body.

We have now seen how the process of digestion is performed, at least, so far as we are acquainted with it, and how its products are conveyed into the blood. But to what purposes the blood is employed, which is formed with so much care, we have yet to discover. It seems to answer two purposes. The parts of which the body is composed, namely, bones, muscles, ligaments, membranes, &c. are continually changing: in youth they are increasing in size and strength, and in mature age they are continually acting, and, consequently, continually liable to waste and decay. They are often exposed to accidents, which render them unfit for performing their various functions; and even when no such accidents happen, it seems necessary for the health of the system that they should be perpetually renewed. Materials must therefore be provided for repairing, increasing, or renewing all the various organs of the body. The bones require phosphate of lime, and gelatine, the muscles fibrine, and the cartilages and membranes albumen; and accordingly we find all these substances contained in the blood, from whence they are drawn, as from a storehouse, whenever they are wanted. The process by which these different parts of the blood become various parts of the body is called assimilation.

Over the nature of assimilation the thickest darkness still hangs; all that we know for certain is, that there are some conditions necessary to its action, without which it cannot take place. These are, 1. A sound and uninterrupted state of the nerves. 2. A sound state of the blood vessels. 3. A certain degree of tone or vigour in the vessels of the part.

There remains yet to be noticed another set of vessels, connected with the circulating and nutritive systems, called lymphatics. These vessels are very minute, and filled with a transparent fluid: they rise by open mouths in every cavity of the body, as well as from every part of the surface, and the course of those from the lower extremities, and indeed from most of the lower parts of the body, is towards the thoracic duct, which they enter at the same time with the lacteal vessels already described. They are furnished,

9

like the lacteals, with numerous valves, which prevent their contents from returning towards their extremities.

The minute arteries in every part of the body exhale a colourless fluid, for lubricating the different parts, and other important purposes ; and the lymphatic vessels absorb the superfluous quantity of this fluid, and convey it back to the blood.

It must be evident therefore, that, if the lymphatics in any cavity become debilitated, or by any other means be prevented from absorbing this exhaled fluid, an accumulation of it will take place: the same will happen, if the exhaling arteries be debilitated, so as to allow a greater quantity of fluid to escape than the absorbents can take up. When the balance between exhalation and absorption is destroyed, by either or both of these means, a dropsy will be the consequence.

Before we finish the subject of digestion, I shall take a short view of some of the morbid affections, attending this important function of the animal economy.

A deficiency of appetite may arise, either from an affection of the stomach, or a morbid state of the body: for there is such a sympathy between the stomach and the rest of the system, that the first is very seldom disordered, without communicating more or less disorder to the system : nor can the system become deranged and the stomach remain sound.

A want of appetite may arise from overloading the stomach, whereby its digestive powers will be weakened. And this may be occasioned in two ways. First, by taking food of the common quality in too great quantity, which will certainly weaken the powers of the stomach. An excellent rule, and one which if more attended to, would prevent the dreadful consequences of indigestion, is always to rise from the table with some remains of appetite. This is a rule applicable to every constitution, but particularly to the sedentary and debilitated.

The second way in which the stomach may be debilitated, is by taking food too highly stimulating or seasoned; and this even produces much worse effects than an over dose with respect to quantity. The tone of the stomach is destroyed, and a crude unassimiláted chyle is absorbed by the lacteals, and carried into the blood, contaminating its whole mass. Made dishes, enriched with hot sauces, stimulate infinitely more than plain food, and bring on diseases of the worst kind; such as gout, apoplexy, and paralysis. " For my part," says an elegant writer, " when I behold a fashionable table set out in all its magnificence, I fancy I see gouts, and dropsies, fevers, and lethargies, with other innumerable distempers, lying in ambuscade among the dishes. "

All times of the day are not equally fitted for the reception of nourishment. That digestion may be well performed, the functions of the stomach and of the body must be in full vigour. The early part of the day therefore is the proper time for taking nutriment; and, in my opinion, the principal meal should not be taken after two or three o'clock, and there should always be a sufficient time between each meal to enable the stomach to digest its contents. I need not remark how very different this is from the common practice of jumbling two or three meals together, and at a time of

the day likewise when the system is overloaded. The breakfast at sunrise, the noontide repast and the twilight pillow,
which distinguished the days of Elizabeth, are now changed for the evening breakfast, and the midnight dinner.
The evening is by no means the proper time to take much
nourishment; for the powers of the system, and particularly of the stomach, are then almost exhausted, and the
food will be but half digested.　Besides, the addition of fresh
chyle to the blood, together with the stimulus of food acting
on the stomach, always prevents sleep, or renders it confused and disturbed, and instead of having our worn out
spirits recruited, by what is emphatically called by Shake-
speare, " the chief nourisher in life's feast," and rising in
the morning fresh and vigorous, we become heavy and stupid,
and feel the whole system relaxed.

It is by no means uncommon, for a physician to have patients, chiefly among people of fashion and fortune, who
complain of being hot and restless all night, and having a
bad taste in the mouth in the morning.　On examination,
I have found that, at least in nineteen cases out of twenty,
this has arisen from their having overloaded their stomachs,
and particularly from eating hot suppers; nor do I recollect
a single instance of a complaint of this kind in any person
not in the habit of eating such suppers.

The immoderate use of spirituous and fermented liquors, is
still more destructive of the digestive powers of the stomach;
but this will be better understood, when we have examined
the laws by which external powers act upon the body　The
remarks I have made could not, however, I think, have come
in better, than immediately after our examination of the

structure of the digestive organs, as the impropriety of intemperance, with respect to food, is thus rendered more evident.

The appetite becomes deficient from want of exercise, independently of the other causes that have been mentioned. Of all the various modes of preserving health, and preventing diseases, there is none more efficacious than exercise; it quickens the motion of the fluids, strengthens the solids, causes a more perfect sanguification in the lungs, and, in short, gives strength and vigour to every function of the body. Hence it is, that the Author of nature has made exercise absolutely necessary to the greater part of mankind for obtaining means of existence. Had not exercise been absolutely necessary for our well being, says the elegant Addison, nature would not have made the body so proper for it, by giving such an activity to the limbs, and such a pliancy to every part, as necessarily produce those compressions, extensions, contortions, dilatations, and all other kinds of motion, as are necessary for the preservation of such a system of tubes and glands.

We may, indeed, observe, that nature has never given limbs to any animal, without intending that they should be used. To fish she has given fins, and to the fowls of the air wings, which are incessantly used in swimming and flying; and if she had destined mankind to be eternally dragged about by horses, her provident economy would surely have denied them legs.

The appetite becomes deficient on the commencement of many diseases, but this is to be looked upon here rather as a salutary than as a morbid symptom, and as a proof that nature refuses the load, which she can neither digest nor bear with impunity.

In healthy people the appetite is various, some requiring more food than others; but it sometimes becomes praeternaturally great, and then may be regarded as a morbid symptom. The appetite may be praeternaturally increased, either by an unusual secretion of the gastric juice, which acts upon the coats of the stomach, or by any acrimony, either generated in, or received into the stomach, or, lastly, by habit, for people undoubtedly may gradually accustom themselves to take more food than is necessary.

The appetite sometimes becomes depraved, and a person thus affected, feels a desire to eat substances that are by no means nutritious, or even esculent: this often depends on a debilitated state of the whole system. There are some instances, however, in which this depravity of the appetite is salutary; for example, the great desire which some persons, whose stomachs abound with acid, have for eating chalk, and other absorbent earths: likewise, the desire which scorbutic patients have for grass, and other fresh vegetables. Appetites of this kind, if moderately indulged in, are salutary, rather than hurtful.

The appetite for liquids as well as solids is sometimes observed to be deficient, and sometimes too great. The former can scarcely be considered as a morbid symptom, provided the digestion and health be otherwise good. But when along with diminished thirst, the fauces and tongue are dry, this deficiency may be regarded as a morbid and dangerous symptom.

A more common morbid symptom, however, is too great

thirst, which may arise from a deficiency of fluids in the body, produced by violent exercise, perspiration, too great a flow of urine, or too great an evacuation of the intestines. A praeternatural thirst may likewise arise from any acrid substance received into the stomach, which our provident mother, nature, teaches us to correct by dilution; this is the case with respect to salted meats, or those highly seasoned with pepper. It may arise also from the stomach being overloaded with unconcocted aliment, or from a suppressed or diminished secretion of the salivary liquors in the mouth, which may arise from fever, spasm, or affections of the mind; an increased thirst may likewise take place, from a derivation or determination of the fluids to other parts of the body; of this, dropsy affords an example. Indeed, various causes may concur to increase the thirst; this is the case in most fevers, where great thirst is occasioned by the dissipation of the fluids of the body by heat, as well as by the diminished secretion of the salivary humours which should moisten the mouth; to which may be added, the heat and diminished concoctive powers of the stomach.

From what has been said, we can easily understand, why praeternatural thirst may sometimes be a necessary instinct of nature, at other times, an unnecessary craving; why acids, acescent fruits, and weak fermented liquors quench thirst more powerfully than pure water; and, lastly, why thirst, in some instances, may be relieved by emetics, when it has resisted other remedies.

There is no organ of the body whose functions are so easily deranged as those of the stomach; and these derangements prove a very fertile source of disease; they ought, therefore, carefully to be guarded against; and it is fortunate for us that we have this generally in our power, if we would but avail ourselves of it : for most of the derangements proceed from the improper use of food and drink, and a neglect of exercise. Indeed, when we examine, we shall find but a short list in the long catalogue of human diseases, which it is not in our power to guard against and prevent : and which surely will be guarded against, when their causes are known, and consequences understood.

Among the diseases arising from a disordered state of the stomach and indigestion, may be enumerated the following; great oppression and anxiety, pain in the region of the stomach, with acid eructations, nausea, vomiting, the bowels sometimes costive, sometimes too loose, but seldom regular, depression of spirits, and all the long list, commonly, but very improperly, termed nervous complaints, deficient nutrition, and consequently general weakness, a relaxed state of the solids, too great a tenuity of the fluids, headach, vertigo, and many other complaints, too numerous to mention here.

The greatest misfortune, and which indeed arises from a want of physiological knowledge, is, that people labouring under these disorders, imagine they may be cured by the reception of drugs into the stomach, and thus they are induced to receive into that organ, half the contents of an apothecary's shop. There is no doubt that these complaints may oftentimes be alleviated, and the cure assisted, by medicines : thus, when the stomach is overloaded, this may be removed by an emetic; the same complaint of the bowels may be removed by a cathartic; and when the stomach is debilitated, we are acquainted with some substances which will give it vigour, such as iron, the Peruvian bark, and several kinds of bitters. These however, when used alone, afford but temporary relief; and unless the cause which induced the disease be removed, it will afterwards return with redoubled violence. When the stomach, for instance, is debilitated by want of exercise, I would ask, is there an article in the whole materia medica, that can cure the complaints of sedentary people, unless proper exercise at the same time be taken? With exercise tonic remedies will undoubtedly accelerate the cure, but without it, they will only make bad worse.

Again, when the stomach is debilitated by the use of improper food, or the abuse of fermented or spirituous liquors, I would say to any one who pretended to cure me of these complaints, without my making a total change in the manner of living, that he either was ignorant of the matter, or intended to deceive me.

In many cases the change of food must be strictly observed and persevered in for a long time before a cure can be effected. In some instances where the powers of the stomach were too weak to prevent the food from undergoing perhaps both a vinous and acetous fermentation, and where, in consequence of the disengagement of gas and the formation of acid, the most excruciating pains were felt, the most dreadful sickness experienced, and all the symptoms of indigestion present in the most aggravated state; after almost every article in the materia medica, generally employed, had been tried without success, I have cured the patient merely by prohibiting food

10

subject to fermentation, such as vegetables, and enjoining a strict use of animal food alone.

In short, wherever the cause of a disease can be ascertained, the grand and simple secret in the cure, is the careful removal of that cause.

LECTURE V

OF THE SENSES IN GENERAL.

In this lecture, I propose to take a view of the connexion of man with the external world, and shall endeavour to point out the manner in which he becomes acquainted with external objects, by means of the faculties called senses.

A human creature is an animal endowed with understanding, and reason; a being composed of an organized body, and a rational mind.

With respect to his body, he is pretty similar to other animals, having similar organs, powers, and wants. All animals have a body composed of several parts, and, though these may differ from the structure of the human body in some circumstances, to accommodate it to peculiar habits and wants of the animal, still there is a great similarity in the general structure.

The human body is feeble at its commencement, increases gradually in its progress by the help of nourishment and exercise, till it arrives at a certain period, when it appears in full vigour; from this time it insensibly declines to old age, which conducts it at length to dissolution. This is the ordinary course of human life, unless it happen to be abridged either by disease or accident.

With regard to his reasoning faculties, or mind, man is eminently distinguished from other animals.   It is by this noble part that he thinks, and is capable of forming just ideas of the different objects that surround him: of comparing them together; of inferring from known principles unknown truths; of passing a solid judgment on the mutual agreement of things, as well as on the relations they bear to him; of deliberating on what is proper or improper to be done; and of determining how to act.   The mind recollects what is past, joins it with the present, and extends its views to futurity. It is capable of penetrating into the causes of events, and discovering the connexion that exists between them.

Governed by invariable laws, which connect him with all the beings, whether animate or inanimate, among which he exists, man has certain relations of convenience, and inconvenience, arising from the particular constitution of the surrounding objects, as well as of his own body.   These external objects possess qualities which may be useful or prejudicial to him ; and his interest requires, that he should be capable of ascertaining and appreciating these properties.

It is by sensation, or feeling, that the knowledge of external objects is obtained.   The faculty of feeling, modified in every organ, perceives those qualities for which the peculiar structure of the organ is fitted ; and all the various sensations of sound, colour, taste, smell, resistance, and temperature, find appropriate organs by which they are perceived, without mixing with, or confounding each other. External objects, therefore, act upon the parts of the body endowed with feeling, and their action is diversified in such a manner, as to give us a great number of sensations, which appear to have no resemblance to each other, and which

make us acquainted with the various properties of surrounding objects.

It would not, however, have been sufficient for man,
merely to have possessed this power of perceiving the different properties of the objects which surround him : it was
necessary likewise, that he should be possessed of motion,
that he might be able to approach or avoid them, to seize or
repulse them, as it suited his convenience or advantage.
By the extreme mobility of his limbs, he is able to move
his body, and transport it from place to place ; to bring
external objects nearer to him, to remove them to a greater
distance, and to place them in such situations and such
circumstances, as may enable them to act on each other,
and produce the changes which he wishes.

The human body, therefore, may be regarded as a machine composed (besides the moving parts which have formerly been noticed) of divers organs upon which external objects
act, and produce those impressions which convince us of
their presence, and make us acquainted with their properties.
These impressions are transmitted to the sentient principle,
or mind ; and the faculty we possess of perceiving these impressions has been called by physiologists, sensibility.

Sensation has generally been defined by metaphysicians
to be a change in the mind, of which we are conscious,
caused by a correspondent change in the state of the body.
This definition, however, leaves the matter where they found
it, and throws no light whatever on the nature of sensation;
nor can we say any thing more concerning it, than that, when
the organs are in a sound state, certain sensations are per-

ceived, which force us to believe in the existence of external objects, though there is no similarity whatever, nor any necessary connexion, that we can perceive, between the sensation and the object which caused it.

All the different degrees of sensation may be reduced to two kinds: pleasant and painful. The nature of these two primitive modes of sensation, is as little known to us as their different species: all that can be said, is, that the general laws by which the body is governed, are such, that pleasure is generally connected with those impressions which tend to its preservation, and pain with those which cause its destruction.

In a general point of view, sensibility may be regarded as an essential property of every part of the living body, disposing each part to perform those functions, the object of which is to preserve the life of the animal. Sensibility presides over the most necessary functions, and watches carefully over the health of the body: she directs the choice of the air proper for respiration, and also of alimentary substances ; the mechanism of the secretions is likewise placed under her power ; and in the same way that the eye perceives colours, and the ear sounds, so every animated and living part is fitted to receive impressions from the objects appropriated to it.

That every part of the animal is endowed with sensibility, is evident from a variety of facts, particularly from the action which follows when a muscle taken out of the animal body is irritated by any stimulus: this is evident, by a variety of facts mentioned by .Whytt, Boerhaave, and others, which show, that parts recently taken from the animal body retain a portion of sensibility, which continues to animate them, and render them capable of action for a considerable time.

The primary organ of sensation appears to be the brain, its continuation in the form of medulla oblongata and spinal marrow, and the various nerves proceeding from these ; and it seems now generally agreed, that unless there be a free communication of nerves between the part where the impression is made, and the brain, no sensation will take place ; for instance, if the nerves be cut or compressed.

In a sound body, sensation is caused, whenever a change takes place in the state of the nervous power, whether that change be produced by an external, or an internal cause. The former kind of sensation is said to arise from impression or impulse, the latter from consciousness.

Every impression or impulse is not, however, equally calculated to produce sensation ; for this purpose, a middle degree of impulse appears the best. An impulse considerably less produces no sensation, and one more violent may cause pain, but no proper sensation denoting the presence or properties of external objects. Thus too small a degree of light makes no impression on the optic nerve ; and if the object be too strongly illuminated, the eye is pained, but has no proper idea of the figure or colour of the object. In the same way, if the vibrations which give us an idea of sound, be either too quick or too slow, we shall not obtain this idea. When the vibration is too quick, a very disagreeable and irritating sensation is perceived, as for instance, in the whetting of a saw : and on the other hand, when the vibrations are too slow, they will not produce a tone or sound.

This might be proved of all the senses, and shows, that a certain degree of impression is necessary to produce perfect sensation.

There is another circumstance likewise requisite to produce sensation : it is not enough, that the impression should be of the proper strength ; it is necessary likewise, that it should remain for some time, otherwise no sensation will be produced. There are many bodies whose magnitude is amply sufficient to be perceived by the eye ; yet, by reason of their great velocity, the impulse they make on any part of the retina is so short, that they are not visible. This is proved by our not perceiving the motions of cannon and musket balls, and many other kinds of motion. On this principle depends the art of conjuration, or legerdemain ; the fundamental maxim of those who practise them, is, that the motion is too quick for sight.

If the impulse be of a proper degree, and be continued for a sufficient length of time, the impression made by it will not immediately vanish with the impulse which caused it, but will remain for a time proportioned to the strength of the impulse. This, with respect to sight, is proved by whirling a firebrand in a circular manner, by which the impression of a circle is caused, instead of a moving point : and, with respect to hearing, it may be observed, that when children run with a stick quickly along railing, or when a drum is beaten quickly, the idea of a continued sound is produced, because the impression remains some time : for it is evident, that the sounds produced in succession are perfectly distinct and insulated.

Sensation likewise depends, in a great measure, on the

state of the mind, and on the degree of attention which it gives. For if we are engaged in attention to any object, we are insensible of the impressions made upon us by others, though they are sufficiently strong to affect us at other times. Thus, when our attention is fixed strongly upon any particular object, we become insensible of the various noises that surround us, though these may be sometimes very loud. On the contrary, if our attention be upon the watch, we can perceive slight, and almost neglected impressions, while those of greater magnitude become insensible. The ticking of a clock becomes insensible to us from repetition, but if we attend to it, we become easily sensible of it, though at the same time we become insensible of much stronger impressions, such as the rattling of coaches in the streets.

The attention depends in some degree on the will, but is generally given to those impressions which are particularly strong, new, pleasant, or disagreeable; in short, to those which particularly affect the mind. Hence it is, that things which are new, produce the most vivid impressions, which gradually grow fainter, and at last become imperceptible.

There is one circumstance respecting sensation, which will probably account for our only perceiving those impressions to which the mind attends: and this is, that the mind is incapable of perceiving more than one impression at a time: the more accurately we examine this, the greater reason we shall have to think it true; but the mind can turn its attention so quickly, from one object to another, that at first sight, we are led to believe, that we are able to attend to several at the same time.

But though the mind cannot perceive or attend to various

11

sensations at the same time, yet if two or more of these are capable of uniting in such a manner as to produce a compound sensation, this may be perceived by the mind.

This compound sensation may be produced either by impressions made at the same instant, or succeeding each other so quickly, that the second takes place before the first has vanished.

As an instance of the first, we may mention musical chords, or the sounds produced by the union of two or more tones at the same time. We have another instance likewise in odours or smells; if two or more perfumes be mixed together, a compound odour will be perceived, different from any of them.

As an instance of the latter, if a paper painted of various colours be made to revolve rapidly in a circle, a compound colour, different from any of them, will be perceived. These observations apply particularly to the senses we have mentioned, and likewise to taste: but the sensations afforded us by touch do not seem capable of being compounded in this manner.

There are many things necessary to perfect sensation, besides those that have been mentioned. The degree and perfection of sensation will depend much on the mind, and will be continually altered by delirium, torpor, sleep, and other circumstances; much likewise depends on the state of the organs with respect to preceding impressions; for if any organ of sense have been subjected to a strong impression, it will become nearly insensible of those which are weaker.

Of this innumerable instances may be given: an eye which has been subjected to a strong light, becomes insensible of a weaker: and on the contrary, if the organs of sense have been deprived of their accustomed impressions for some time, they are affected by very slight ones. Hence it is, that when a person goes from daylight into a darkened room, he can at first see nothing; by degrees however he begins to have an imperfect perception of the different objects, and if he remain long enough, he will see them with tolerable distinctness, though the quantity of light be the same as when he entered the room, when they were invisible to him.

Sensation often arises from internal causes, without any external impulse. To this source may be referred consciousness, memory, imagination, volition, and other affections of the mind. These are called the internal senses. The senses, whether internal or external, have never been accurately reduced to classes, orders, or genera; the external indeed are generally referred to five orders ; namely, seeing, hearing, smelling, tasting, and feeling, or touch. With respect to the four first, the few qualities of external bodies which each perceives may be easily reduced to classes, each of which may be referred to its peculiar organ of sensation, because each organ is so constituted, that it can only be affected by one class of properties; thus the eye can only be affected by light; the ear by the vibrations of the air, and so of the rest.

The same organ, whatever be its state, or whatever be the degree of impulse, always gives to the mind a similar sensation; nor is it possible, by any means we are acquainted with, to communicate the sensation peculiar to one organ by means of another. Thus we are incapable, for instance, of hearing with our eyes, and seeing with our ears: nor have we any reason to believe that similar impressions produce dissimilar sensations in different people. The pleasure, however, as well as the pain and disgust, accompanying different sensations, differ very greatly in different persons, and even in the same person at different times; for the sensations which sometimes afford us pleasure, at other times produce disgust.

Habit has a powerful influence in modifying the pleasures of sensation, without producing any change in the sensation itself, or in the external qualities suggested by it. Habit, for instance, will never cause a person to mistake gentian or quassia for sugar, but it may induce an appetite or liking for what is bitter, and a disgust for what is sweet. No person perhaps was originally delighted with the taste of opium or tobacco, they must at first be highly disgusting to most people; but custom not only reconciles the taste tó them, but they become grateful, and even necessary.

Almost every species of sensation becomes grateful or otherwise, according to the force of the impression; for there is no sensation so pleasant, but, that, by increasing its intensity, it will become ungrateful, and at length intolerable. And, on the contrary, there are many which on account of their force are naturally unpleasant, but become, when diminished, highly pleasant. The softest and sweetest sounds may be increased to such a degree as to be extremely unpleasant: and when we are in the steeple of a church, the noise of a peal of bells stuns and confounds our senses, while at a distance their effect is very pleasant. The smell of musk likewise at a distance, and in small quantity, is pleasant; but when brought near, or in large quantity, it becomes highly disagreable. The same may be observed with respect to the objects of the other senses.

For a similar reason, many sensations which are at first pleasing, cease to delight by frequent repetition; though the impression remains the same. This is so well known that illustrations are unnecessary. Those who are economical of their pleasures, or who wish them to be permanent, must not repeat them too frequently. In music, a constant repetition of the sweetest and fullest chords, cloys the ear; while a judicious mixture of them with tones less harmonious will be long relished. Those who are best acquainted with the human heart need not be told, that this observation is not confined to music.

On the same principle likewise we can account for the pleasure afforded by objects that are new; and why variety is the source of so many pleasures; why we gradually wish for an increase in the force of the impression in proportion to its continuance.

The pleasures of the senses are confined within narrow limits, and can neither be much increased nor too often repeated, without being destructive of themselves: thus we are admonished by nature, that our constitutions were not formed to bear the continual pleasures of sense; for the too free use of any of them, is not only destructive of itself, but induces those painful and languid sensations so often complained of by the voluptuary, and which not unfrequently produce a state of mind that prompts to suicide.

As the transition from pleasure to pain is natural, so the remission of pain, particularly if it is great, becomes a source of pleasure. There is much truth, therefore, in the beautiful allegory of Socrates, who tells us, that Pleasure and Pain were sisters, who, however, met with a very different reception by mankind on their visit to the earth ; the former being universally courted, while the latter was carefully avoided : on this account, Pain petitioned Jupiter, who decreed that they should not be parted; and that whoever embraced the one, obtained also the other.

There is a great diversity with respect to the duration of the pleasures of the different senses : some of the senses become soon fatigued, and lose the power of distinguishing accurately their different objects : others, on the contrary, remain perfect a long time. Thus smell and taste are soon satiated ; hearing more slowly ; while, of all the external senses, the objects of sight please us the longest. We may, however, prolong the pleasures of sense by varying them properly, and by a proper mixture of objects or circumstances which are indifferent, and afford less delight. But the very constitution of our nature limits our enjoyments, and points out the impossibility of perpetual pleasures in this state of our existence. To a person who is thirsty, water is delicious nectar ; to one who is hungry, every kind of food is agreeable, and even its smell pleasant ; to a person who is hot and feverish, the cool air is highly refreshing. But to the same persons in different circumstances, the same things are not only indifferent, but even disgusting ; for instance, a person cannot bear the sight or smell of food, after having satiated himself with it, and perpetual feasting will cloy the appetite of the keenest epicure.

I shall conclude this account of the general laws of sensation, by a short recapitulation of those laws.

And, in the first place, it may be observed, that the energy or force of any sensation, is proportioned to the degree of attention given by the mind to the external object which causes it.

Secondly, A repetition of sensations diminishes their energy, and at last nearly destroys it; but this energy is restored by rest, or the absence of these sensations.

Thirdly, The mind cannot attend to two impressions at the same time: so that two sensations never act with the same force at the same instant; the stronger generally overcoming the weaker. The mind, however, can attend to the weaker sensation, in such a manner, as to overpower the stronger, or to render it insensible.

Having fully considered the general laws of sensation, I shall now proceed to examine those proper to each sense; and in this examination, two objects will engage our attention. 1. The structure of the organ which receives and transmits the impulse to the mind. 2. The qualities or properties of external bodies, particularly those by which they are fitted to excite sensation.

The first sense that we shall examine is touch, which, of all the external senses, is the most simple, as well as the most generally diffused. By means of this sense, we are capable of perceiving various qualities and properties of bodies, such as hardness, softness, roughness, smoothness, temperature, magnitude, figure, distance, pressure, and weight; this sense is seldom depraved; because the bodies, whose properties are examined by it, are applied immediately to the extremities of the nerves, without the intervention of any medium liable to be deranged, as is the case with the eye, and ear.

The organ of touch is seated chiefly in the skin, but different parts of this covering possess different degrees of sensibility. The skin consists of three parts. 1. The cutis vera, or true skin, which covers the greatest part of the surface of the body. When the skin is examined by a microscope, we find it composed of an infinite number of papillae, or small eminencies, which seem to be the extremities of nerves, each of which is accompanied by an artery and a vein, so that when the vessels of the skin are injected, the whole appears red. 2. Immediately over the true skin, and filling up its various inequalities, lies a mucous reticulated substance, which has been called by Malpighi, who first described it, rete mucosum. The real skin is white in the inhabitants of every climate; but the rete mucosum is of various colours, being white in Europeans, olive in Asiatics, black in Africans, and copper coloured in Americans. This variety depends chiefly on the degree of light and heat; for, if we were to take a globe, and paint a portion of it with the colour of the inhabitants of corresponding latitudes, we should have an uniform gradation of shade, deepening from the pole to the equator.

The diversity of colour depends upon the bleaching power of the oxygen, which, in temperate climates, combines more completely with the carbonaceous matter deposited in the rete mucosum; while, in hotter climates, the oxygen is kept in a gaseous state by the heat and light, and has less tendency to unite with the carbonaceous matter. In proof of this, the skins of Africans may be rendered white by exposure to the oxygneated muriatic acid.

Over the rete mucosum is spread a fine transparent membrane, called the cuticle, or scarf skin, which defends the organ of feeling from the action of the air, and other things which would irritate it too powerfully. In some parts of the body this membrane is very thick, as in the soles of the feet, and palms of the hands; and this thickness is much increased by use and pressure.

In general, the thinner the cuticle is, the more acute is the sense of touch. This sense is very acute and delicate about the ends of the fingers, where we have the most need of it; but in the lips, mouth, and tongue, it is still more delicate; a galvanic or electrical shock being felt by the tongue, when it is impossible for us to perceive it by the fingers.

This sense, like the others, becomes more exquisite when its organ is defended from the action of external bodies; it is on this account that the cuticle becomes so sensible under the end of the nail, which defends it from the action of external objects; and when part of the nail is taken away, we can scarcely bear to touch any thing with this newly exposed part of the skin.

When we place our fingers upon the surface of any body, the first sensation we experience is that of resistance, after which the other properties are perceived in a natural order; such as heat or cold, moisture or dryness, motion or rest, distance, and figure or shape.

With respect to the diseases of this sense, it is very seldom that it becomes too acute over the whole body; though it frequently does so in particular parts, which may arise from the cuticle being too thin or abraded, or from an inflamed state of the part.

It however becomes sometimes obtuse, and indeed almost abolished over the whole body; and this takes place from compression of the brain, and various affections of the nervous power. This diminution is called anaesthesia. The touch becomes deficient, and indeed almost abolished, when the cuticle is injured by the frequent application of hot bodies, or acrid substances: thus the cuticle of the hands of blacksmiths and glassblowers is generally so hard and horny, that they can take up and grasp in their hand pieces of redhot iron with impunity.

We generally refer pain to this sense, though it may arise from too violent an impress on made upon any of the organs of sense.

Pain is an unpleasant sensation, which the mind refers to some part of the body, and very accurately, if any part of the surface is affected, but less so, if it arises from the affection of an internal part. The sensation of pain may arise from any thing which tends to injure the structure of the body, whether that be internal or external; so that it serves as a monitor to put us on our guard, and to induce us to remove any thing which might be injurious to us. This sensation is produced by any thing which punctures, cuts, tears, distends, compresses, bruises, corrodes, burns, or violently stimulates any part of the body.

A moderate degree of pain in any part excites the action of the whole body; a greater quantity of blood and nervous energy is determined to the part. A still greater degree of pain brings on inflammation and its consequences, and if it be intense, it will bring on fever, convulsions, delirium, fainting, and even death.

The endurance of pain depends much on the strength of mind possessed by the patient, which, in some instances, is

such, that the most violent pains are patiently endured;
while in other instances, the slightest can scarcely be born.

It is a curious circumstance, that a moderate degree of
pain, when unaccompanied by fever, often tends to render
the understanding more clear, lively, and active. This is
confirmed by the experience of people labouring under gout.
We have an account of a man who possessed very ordinary
powers of understanding, but who exhibited the strongest
marks of intelligence and genius in consequence of a severe
blow on the head; but that he lost these powers when he
recovered from the effects of the blow. Pechlin mentions a
young man, who during a complaint originating from worms,
possessed an astonishing memory and lively imagination,
both of which he nearly lost by being cured. Haller mentions a man who was able see in the night, while his eyes
were inflamed, but lost this power as he got well. All these
facts show, that a certain action or energy is necessary for
the performance of any of the functions of the body or mind;
and whatever increases this action will, within certain limits,
increase those functions.

Feeling is by far the most useful, extensive, and important
of the senses, and may be said indeed to be the basis of
them all. Vision would be of very little use to us, if it were
not aided by the sense of feeling; we shall afterwards see that
the same observation may be applied to the other senses. In
short, it is to this sense that we are indebted, either immediately or indirectly, for by far the greatest part of our
knowledge; for without it we should not be able to procure
any idea with respect to the magnitude, distance, shape,

heat, hardness or softness, asperity or smoothness of bodies ; indeed, if we were deprived of this sense, it is difficult to say whether we should have any idea of the existence of any external bodies ; on the contrary, it seems probable that we should not.

LECTURE VI.

TASTE AND SMELL.

From the sense of touch we proceed naturally to that of taste, for there seems to be less difference between these two senses than between any of the others. The sense of taste appears to be seated chiefly in the tongue; for any sweet substance, such as sugar, applied to any other part of the mouth, scarcely excites the least sensation of taste. The same may be observed with respect to any other sapid body, which, unless it is strongly acrid or irritating, produces no effect on any other part than the tongue; but if it is possessed of much acrimony, it then not only affects the palate, and uvula, but even the oesophagus.

The tongue is a muscular substance, placed in the mouth, connected by one end with the adjacent bones and cartilages, while the other end remains free, and easily moveable. The tongue is furnished, particularly on its upper surface, with innumerable nervous papillae, which are much larger than those I described as belonging to the skin. These papillae are of a conical figure, and extremely sensible, forming, without doubt, the true organ of taste; other papillae are found between them, which are partly conical, 'and partly cylindrical.

Over the papillae of the tongue is spread a single mucous,

and semipellucid covering, which adheres firmly to them, and serves the purpose of a cuticle.

Under these papillae are spread the muscles which make up the fleshy part of the tongue: these are extremely numerous, and by their means the tongue possesses the power of performing a great variety of motions with surprising velocity.

The arteries leading to the tongue are extremely numerous; and, when injected with a red fluid, the whole substance appears of a beautiful red.

The tongue is likewise furnished with a large supply of nerves, some of which undoubtedly serve to supply its muscles with nervous energy, while others terminate in the papillae, and form the proper organ of taste: this office seems to be performed by the third branch of the fifth pair of nerves. The papillae, before described, are formed or composed of a number of small nerves, arteries, and veins, firmly united together by cellular substance. These papillae are excited to action by the application of any sapid body; in consequence of which they receive a greater supply of blood, become enlarged, and vastly more sensible.

The structure of the tongue differs in different animals, which likewise possess corresponding differences with respect to taste. In those quadrupeds, in which it is armed with sharp points, the sense of taste is by no means acute. The same is the case with birds and reptiles, whose tongues are very dry and rough.

In a former lecture I took notice of a liquor which is secreted by the glands of the mouth and neighbouring parts, which is called saliva. This liquor acts an important part in the production of taste; it does not differ much from water,

excepting by containing a quantity of mucilage ; and nothing is sapid, or capable of affecting the sense of taste, unless
it is in some degree soluble in this liquor. Hence earthy
substances, which are nearly insoluble, have little or no taste.

It is not, however, sufficient that the substance be possessed of solubility alone; it is necessary likewise that it should
be possessed of saline properties, or, at least, of a kind of
acrimony, which renders it capable of stimulating the nervous
papillae. Hence it is that those substances which are less
·saline, and less acrid than the saliva, have no taste.

We are capable of distinguishing various kinds of taste,
but some of them with less accuracy than others. Among
the different kinds of taste, the following have been considered by Haller, and some other physiologists, as primitive :
sweet, sour, bitter, and saline. The others have been thought
to be compounded of these ; for the sense of taste, as well
as sight and hearing, is capable of perceiving compound
impressions. To these primitive tastes, Boerhaave added
alkaline, spirituous, aromatic, and some others. Of these,
in different proportions, all the varieties of tastes, which are
extremely numerous, are composed.

Some tastes are pleasant and agreeable, others disagreeable, and scarcely tolerable : there is, however, a great diversity in this respect experienced by different persons ; for the
same taste, which is highly grateful to some, is extremely unpleasant to others.

But the most pleasant tastes, agreeably to the general
laws of sensation, which I described in the last lecture, become gradually less pleasant, and at last disgusting ; while,
on the contrary, the most disagreeable savours, such as to-

bacco, opium, and assafoetida, become, by custom, not only tolerable, but highly agreeable.

Nature designed this difference of tastes that we might know and distinguish such foods as are salutary ; for we may in general observe, that no kind of food which is healthy, and affords proper nutriment to the body, is disagreeable to the taste ; nor are any that are ill tasted proper for our nourishment. Those substances, therefore, which possess strong or disagreeable savours, and which, in general, possess a power of producing great changes on our constitution, are to be ranked as medicines, and only to be used when the constitution is deranged ; whereas, in general, those which are pleasant, or mild tasted, are proper for nourishing the body We are therefore excited or prompted to receive nourishment by the pleasant smell or taste of the food; but the avidity with which we take it depends much on the state of the stomach, and likewise on a certain inanition or emptiness ; for the coarsest food is grateful to those who are hungry, and whose digestion is good ; whereas, to those who have lately eaten, or whose digestive powers are impaired, the most delicate food affords little pleasure. While we are eating, the saliva flows into the mouth more copiously, which excites a more acute sensation of taste. This flow of saliva is likewise frequently excited by the smell or sight of substances agreeable to the taste, which causes an appetite, or desire of eating, similar to that caused by an accumulation of gastric juice in the stomach.

In brute animals, who have not, like ourselves, the advantage of learning from each other by instruction, the faculty of taste is much more acute, by which they are admonished to abstain from noxious or unhealthy food. This sense, for the same reason, is more acute in savages than in those who live in civiilsed society, which, whatever perfection it gives to the reasoning faculties of man, certainly diminishes the acuteness of all our senses, partly by affording fewer inducements to exercise them, and partly by our manner of living, and by the application of substances to the organs of sense, which tend to vitiate them, and render them depraved.

Taste is modified by age, temperament, habit, and disease; and in this it obeys the general laws of sensation. Children are pleased with the taste of what is sweet, and little stimulating; as we advance in years the taste of more stimulating substances becomes agreeable to us; so that we are admonished by this sense to take into the stomach the kind of nourishment fitted to each period of life. We often, however, counteract this salutary monitor by depraving our sense of taste, by the too free use of vinous or spirituous liquors, which so far deadens the sense of taste, that sweet substances become unpleasant, and nothing but acrid and stimulating things can make an impression on our diminished and vitiated sense of taste.

This sense, as well as others, is liable to be diseased. In order that the sense may be perfect, it is necessary that the membrane which envelopes the nervous papillae of the tongue, and serves as a cuticle, should neither be too thick nor too thin, too dry nor too moist. It is necessary likewise that the qualities of the saliva be natural; for alterations in the nature of this liquor affect very much the sense of taste; if it is bitter, which sometimes happens in bilious complaints, all kinds of food have a bitter taste; if it is sweet, the food has a faint

13

and unpleasant flavour; and if it is acid, the food too tastes
sour.

This sense is seldom observed to be too acute, unless from
a vitiated state of the cuticle, or membrane, which covers
the tongue: if this has been abraded or ulcerated, then the
substances applied to the tongue are more sensibly tasted; in
many instances, however, they do not produce an increased
sensation of taste, but only of pain.

The sense of taste, as well as of touch, may become deficient, from various affections of the brain and nerves; this,
however, is not often the case. Some persons have naturally
a diminished sense of taste, and this generally accompanies
a diminished sense of smell. This sense is frequently diminished in sensibility from a deficiency of saliva, as well as
of the proper moisture of the tongue. Hence, in many
diseases, it becomes defective, such as fevers, colds, and the
like; both from a want of the proper degree of moisture,
and from defect of appetite, which, as was before observed,
is necessary to the sense of taste.

The sense of taste is often diminished by a thickened
mucous covering of the tongue, which prevents the application of substances to its nervous papillae. This mucous
covering arises from a disordered state of the stomach, as
well as from several other affections of the body: hence physicians inspect the tongue, that they may be able to judge of
the general state of the body; and next to the pulse, it is
undoubtedly the best criterion that we have, as it not only
points out the nature and degree of several fevers, but likewise, in many instances, the degree of danger to be apprehended.

Having examined the sense of taste, I shall now proceed to consider that of smell ; the use of which, like taste, is to enable us to distinguish unwholesome from salutary food : indeed, by this sense, we are taught to avoid what is prejudicial before it reaches the sense of taste, to which it might be very injurious ; and thus we are enabled to avoid any thing which has a putrid tendency, which, if received into the stomach, would taint the whole mass of fluids, and bring on speedy dissolution.

The seat of this sense is a soft pulpy membrane, full of pores, and small vessels, which lines the whole internal cavity of the nose. On this membrane are distributed abundance of soft nerves, which arise chiefly from an expansion of the first pair of nerves coming from the brain. This membrane is likewise plentifully supplied with arteries; so that by means of this nervous and arterial apparatus, this membrane is possessed of very great sensibility; but the nerves of the nose being almost naked, require a defence from the air, which is continually drawn through the nostrils into the lungs, and forced out again by respiration. Nature has therefore supplied this part with a thick insipid mucus, very fluid at its first separation, but gradually thickening, as it combines with oxygen, into a dry crust, approaching often to a membranous matter. This mucus is poured out, or exhaled, by the numerous minute arteries of the nostrils, and serves to keep the nervous apparatus moist, and in a proper state for receiving impressions, as well as to prevent the violent effects which might arise from the stimulus of the air and other bodies. The sense of smell is the most acute about the middle of the septum of the nose, where the nervous membrane which I have described is thicker and softer, than in the cavities more deeply situated, where it is less nervous and vascular. These parts are not however destitute of the sense.

As taste proceeds from the action of the soluble parts of bodies on the nervous papillae of the tongue, so smell is occasioned by minute and volatile particles flying off from bodies, which become mixed with the air, and drawn up with it into the nostrils, where these small particles stimulate or act upon the nerves before described, and produce the sensation which we call smelling.

The air therefore, being loaded with the subtile and invisible effluvia of bodies, is, by the powers of respiration, drawn through the nose, so as to apply these particles to the almost naked olfactory nerves, which, as was before observed, excites the sense of smelling. When we wish to smell accurately, we shut the mouth, open the nostrils as wide as possible, and making a strong inhalation, draw up a greater number of these volatile particles, than could be drawn up by the common action of respiration, by which means the olfactory nerves are more stimulated, and produce a stronger sensation.

In order that this sense may be enjoyed in perfection, it is necessary that the organ of smell be in a proper state or condition to receive impressions, and that the odorous bodies be likewise in a proper state. With respect to the first, it is necessary that the state of the nerves be sound, and particularly that they be kept in a proper state with respect to moisture.

With regard to the odorous bodies, it is necessary, first, that their minute particles should be disengaged, either by heat, friction, fermentation, or other means capable of decomposing those bodies which are the subjects of smell: secondly, that they may be capable of assuming the vaporous or gaseous state, by combining with caloric, or at any rate, that they should remain for a certain time dissolved or suspended in the air: thirdly, that they should not meet with any substance in their way to the nostrils, which is capable of neutralising them, or altering their properties by its chemical action.

Notwithstanding all the pains which physiologists have taken to detect the nature of odorous bodies, they have met with but little success. They are so extremely minute as to escape the other senses, and we can only say that they must be composed of particles in an extreme state of division and subtilty, because very small quantities of odorous matter exhale a sufficient quantity of particles to fill a large space. A grain of camphor, musk, or amber exhales an odour which penetrates every part of a large apartment, and which remains for a long time.

There is perhaps no substance in nature which is absolutely incapable of being changed from a solid state into that of a fluid or gas, by combining with caloric; though different substances require very different quantities of heat to produce those effects. Those which are with difficulty converted into fluids or gases, are termed fixed, while those which are easily changed are called volatile; though these are only terms of comparison, for there is probably no body which is absolutely fixed, or incapable of being reduced to vapour by the application of a sufficient degree of heat.

The odorous property is probably as general as that of being convertible into gas. There is perhaps no body so hard, compact, and apparently inodorous, as to be absolutely incapable of exciting smell by proper methods: two pieces of flint rubbed together, produce a very perceptible smell. Metals which appear nearly inodorous, excite a sensation of smell by friction, particularly lead, tin, iron, and copper. Even gold, antimony, bismuth, and arsenic, under particular circumstances, give out peculiar and powerful odours. The odour of arsenic in its metallic state, and in a state of vapour, resembles that of garlic. The chief means of developing the odorous principles are friction, heat, electricity, fermentation, solution, and mixture. The effect of mixture is very remarkable in the case of lime and muriate of ammoniac, neither of which, before mixture, has any perceptible odour.

There is perhaps then no body which is perfectly inodorous, or entirely destitute of smell: for those which have been generally accounted such, may be rendered odorous by some of the methods I have mentioned.

Several naturalists and physiologists, such as Haller, Linneus, and Lorri, have attempted to reduce the different kinds of odours to classes, but without any great success; for we are by no means so well acquainted with the physical nature of the odorous particles, as we are with that of light, sound, and the objects of touch; and till we do obtain a knowledge of these circumstances, which perhaps we never shall, it will be in vain to attempt any accurate classification. The division of them into odours peculiar to the different kingdoms, is very inaccurate; for the odour of musk, which is thought to be peculiarly an animal odour, is developed in the solution of gold by some mineral solvents; it is perceptible in the leaves of the geranium moschatum, and some other ve-

getables. The smell of garlic is possessed by many vegetables, by arsenic, and by toads. The violet smell is perceived in some salts, and in the urine of persons who have
taken turpentine. The same may be observed with respect
to several other odours.

As taste keeps guard, or watches over the passage by
which food enters the body, so smell is placed as a sentinel
at the entrance of the air passsage, and prevents any thing
noxious from being received into the lungs by this passage,
which is always open. Besides, by this sense, we are invited
or induced, to eat salutary food, and to avoid such as is corrupted, putrid, or rancid. The influence of the sense of
smell on the animal machine is still more extensive: when a
substance which powerfully affects the olfactory nerves is
applied to the nostrils, it excites, in a wonderful manner,
the whole nervous system, and produces greater effects in an
instant, than the most powerful cordials or stimulants received by the mouth would produce in a considerable space
of time. Hence in syncope or fainting, in order to restore
the action of the body, we apply volatile alkali, or other
strong odorous substances, to the nostrils, and with the greatest effect. It may indeed for some time supply the place,
and produce the effects, of solid nutriment usually received
into the stomach We are told that Democritus supported
his expiring life, and retarded, for three days, the hour of
death, by inhaling the smell of hot bread, when he could
not take nutriment by the stomach. Bacon likewise gives
us an account of a man who lived a considerable time without meat or drink, and who appeared to be nourished by
the odour of different plants, among which were garlic,

onions, and others which had a powerful smell. In short, the stimulus which active and pleasant odours give to the nerves, seems to animate the whole frame; and to increase all the senses, internal and external.

The perfection of the organ of smell is different in different animals; some possessing it very acutely; others on the contrary having scarcely any sense of smell. We may in general observe that this sense is much more acute in many quadrupeds than in a man: and in them the organ is much more extensive: in man, from the shape of the head, little opportunity is given for extending this organ, without greatly disfiguring the face. In the dog, the horse, and many other quadrupeds, the upper jaw being large, and full of cavities, much more extension is given to the membrane which is the organ of smell, which in some animals is beautifully plaited, in order to give it more surface. Hence a dog is capable of following game, or of tracing his master in a crowd, or in a road where it could not be done by the mere track. Nay, we are told of a pickpocket being discovered in a crowd, by a dog who was seeking its master, and who was directed to the man by the pocket handkerchief of his master, which the pickpocket had stolen. In dogs the sense of smell must be uncommonly delicate, to enable them to distinguish the way their master has gone in a crowded city.

The habit of living in society, however, deadens this sense in man as well as taste; for we have the advantage of learning the properties of bodies from each other by instruction, and have therefore less occasion to exercise this sense; and the less any sense is exercised, the less acute will it become: hence it is, that those whom necessity does not oblige to to exercise their senses and mental faculties, and who have nothing to do but lounge about, and consume the fruits of the earth, become half blind, half deaf, and, in general, have great deficiency in the sense of smell. The use of spirituous liquors, and particularly of tobacco in the form of snuff, serves likewise in a remarkable manner to deaden this sense.

Savages, however, who are continually obliged to exercise all their senses, have this, as well as others, in very great perfection. Their smell is so delicate and perfect, that it approaches to that of dogs. Soemmering and Blumenbach indeed assert, that in Africans and Americans the nostrils are more extended, and the cavities in the bones lined with the olfactory membrane much larger than in Europeans.

I have already observed the powerful effects which some odours have upon the nervous system. There are some which agreeably excite it, and produce a pleasant and active state of the mind, while others, on the contrary, produce the most terrible convulsions, and even fainting. Those particular antipathies with respect to smells, arise sometimes from something in the original constitution of the body, with which we are unacquainted, but generally from the senses having been powerfully and unpleasantly affected by certain odours at an early period of life. The latter may often be cured by resolution and perseverance, but the former cannot.

The sense of smell sometimes becomes too acute, either from a vitiated state of the organ itself, which is not often the case; or from an increased sensibility or irritability of the whole nervous system, which is observed in hysteria, phrenitis, and some fevers.

This sense is however more often found deficient; and this

may arise from a fault in the brain or nerves, which may either proceed from external violence, or from internal causes. A defect of smell often arises from a vitiated state of the organ itself; for instance, if the nervous membrane is too dry, or covered with a thick mucus; of both of which we have an example in catarrh or common cold, where, at the beginning, the nostrils feel unusually dry, but as the disease advances, the pituitary membrane becomes covered with a thick mucus: in both states, the sense of smell is in general deficient, and sometimes nearly abolished.

This sense is sometimes depraved, and smells are perceived when no odorous substance is present; or odours are perceived to arise from substances, which are very different from those which we perceive in a sound state.

There are many diseases likewise of the nose, and neighbouring parts, which cause a depraved sensation; such as ulcers, cancer, caries; a diseased state of the mouth, teeth, throat, or lungs; or a vitiated state of the stomach, which sometimes exhales a vapour similar to that of sulphureted hydrogen. This sense likewise sometimes becomes depraved from a diseased state of the brain and nerves.

LECTURE VII.

SOUND AND HEARING.

Having in the last lecture examined the senses of taste and smell, I now proceed to that of hearing. As the sense of smell enables us to distinguish the small particles of matter which fly off from the surfaces of bodies, and float in the air, so that of hearing makes us acquainted with the elastic tremors or impulses of the air itself.

The sense of hearing opens to us a wide field of pleasure, and though it is less extensive in its range than that of sight, yet it frequently surmounts obstacles that are impervious to the eye, and communicates information of the utmost importance, which would otherwise escape from and be lost to the mind.

Sound arises from a vibratory or tremulous motion produced by a stroke on a sounding body, which motion that body communicates to the surrounding medium, which carries the impression forwards to the ear, and there produces its sensation. In other words, sound is the sensation arising from the impression made by a sonorous body upon the air or some other medium, and carried along by either fluid to the ear.

Three things are necessary to the production of sound; first, a sonorous body to give the impression; secondly, a medium or vehicle to convey this impression; thirdly, an organ of sense or ear to perceive it. Each of these I shall separately examine.

Strictly speaking, sonorous bodies are those whose sounds are distinct, of some duration, and which may be compared with each other, such as those of a bell or a musical string, and not such as give a confused noise, like that made by a stone falling on the pavement. To be sonorous, a body must be elastic, so that the tremors exerted by it in the air may be continued for some time: it must be a body whose parts are capable of a vibratory motion when forcibly struck.

All hard bodies, when struck return more or less of a sound; but those which are destitute of elasticity, give no repetition of the sound; the noise is at once produced and dies; while other bodies, which are more elastic and capable of vibration, repeat the sounds produced several times successively. These last are said to have a tone; the others are not allowed to have any. If we wish to give nonelastic bodies a tone, it will be necessary to make them continue their sound, by repeating our blows quickly upon them. This will effectually give them a tone; and an unmusical instrument has often by this means a fine effect in concerts. The effects of a drum depend upon this principle. Gold, silver, copper, and iron, which are elastic metals, are sonorous; but lead, which possesses scarcely any elasticity, produces little or no tone. Tin, which in itself has very little more sound than lead, highly improves the tone of copper when mixed with it. Bell metal is formed of ten parts of copper, and one of tin. Each of these is ductile when separate, though tin is only so in a small degree, yet they form when united a substance almost as brittle as glass, and highly elastic. So curious is the power of tin in this respect, that even the vapour of it, when in fusion, will give brittleness to gold and silver, the most ductile of all metals. Sonorous bodies may be divided into three classes; first, bells of various figures and magnitudes: of these such as are formed of glass have the most pure and elegant tones, glass being very elastic, and its sound very powerful; secondly, pipes of wood or metal; thirdly, strings formed either of metallic or animal substances. The sounds given by strings are more grave or more acute according to the thickness, length, and tension of the strings.

Air is universally allowed to be the ordinary medium of sound, or the medium by which sounds are propagated from sonorous bodies, and communicated to the ear. This may be shown by an experiment with the air pump; also with the condenser.

But though air is the general vehicle of sound, yet sound will go where no air can convey it; thus the scratching of a pin at the end of a long piece of timber may be heard by an ear applied at the other end, though it could not be heard at the same distance through the air. On this account it is that sentinels are accustomed to lay their ears to the ground, by which means they can often discover the approach of cavalry, at a much greater distance than they can see them.

For the same reason two stones being struck together under water, may be heard at a much greater distance by an ear placed under water likewise, than it can be heard through the air. Dr. Franklin, who several times made this experiment, thinks that he has heard it at a greater distance than a mile. This shows that water is better adapted to convey sound than air.

When an elastic body is struck, that body, or some part of it, is made to vibrate. This is evident to sense in the string of a violin or harpsichord, for we may perceive by the eye, or feel by the hand, the trembling of the strings, when by striking they are made to sound. If a bell be struck by a clapper on the inside, the bell is made to vibrate. The base, of the bell, is a circle, but it has been found that by striking any part of this circle on the inside, that part flies out, so that the diameter which passes through this part of the base will be longer than the other diameter. The base, by the stroke, is changed into an ellipse or oval, whose longer axis passes through the part against which the clapper is struck. The elasticity of the bell restores the figure of the base, and makes that part which was forced out of its place, return back to its former situation, from which the same principle throws it out again ; so that the circular figure of the bell will be again changed to an ellipse, only now the shorter axis will pass through the part which was first struck.

The same stroke, which makes the bell vibrate, occasions the sound, and as the vibrations decay, the sound grows weaker. We may be convinced by our senses that the parts of the bell are in a vibratory motion while it sounds. If we lay the hand gently on it, we shall easily feel this tremulous motion, and even be able to stop it, or if small pieces of paper be put upon the bell, its vibrations will put them in motion.

These vibrations in the sounding body will cause undulations or waves in the air ; and, as the motions of one fluid may often be illustrated by those of another, the invisible motions of the air have been properly enough compared to the visible waves of water produced by throwing a stone therein. These waves spread themselves in all directions in concentric circles, whose common centre is the spot where the stone fell, and when they strike against a bank or other obstacle, they return in the contrary direction to the place from whence they proceeded. Sound in like manner expands in every direction, and the extent of its progress is in proportion to the impulse on the vibrating chord or bell.

Such is the yielding nature of fluids, that when other waves are generated near the first waves, and others again near these, they will perform their vibrations among each other without interruption: those that are coming back will pass by those that are going forwards, or even through them, without interruption: for instance, if we throw a stone into a pond, and immediately after that, another, and then a third, we shall perceive that their respective circles will proceed without interruption, and strike the banks in regular succession.

The atmosphere in the same manner possesses the faculty of conveying sounds in the most rapid succession or combination, as distinctly as they were produced. It possesses the power not only of receiving and propagating simple and compound vibrations in direct lines from the voice, or an instrument, but of retaining and repeating sounds with equal fidelity after repeated reflection and reverberation, as is evident from the sound of a French horn among hills.

Newton was the first who attempted to demonstrate that the waves or pulses of the air are propagated in all directions round a sounding body, and that during their

progress and regress they are twice accelerated and twice
retarded, according to the law of a pendulum vibrating in
a cycloid. These propositions are the foundation of almost
all our reasoning concerning sound. When sonorous bodies
are struck, they, by their vibration, excite waves in the air,
similar to those caused by a stone thrown into water; some
parts of these waves entering the ear, produce in us that
sensation which we call sound. How these pulsations act
upon the auditory nerve, to produce sound, we know not,
as we see no necessary connexion between the pulses and
the sensation, nor the least resemblance between them; but
we can trace their progress to a certain extent, which I shall
now endeavour to do.

The external part of the ear is called the auricle, or outward
ear, which is a cartilaginous funnel, connected to the bones
of the temple, by means of cellular substance, and likewise
by its own proper ligaments and muscles. This cartilage is
of a very compound figure, being a kind of oval, marked with
spirals standing up, and hollows interposed, to which other hollows and ridges correspond on the opposite side. The outer
eminence is called helix. Within the body of the cartilage
arises a forked eminence called antihelix, which terminates
in a small and short tongue called antitragus. The remaining
part of the ear, called the concha or shell, is anteriorly hollow,
but posteriorly convex, growing gradually deeper; with a
crooked line or ridge running along its middle, which is immediately joined to the meatus auditorius, or entrance into
the ear; before which stands a round moveable appendix,
which serves as a defence, called tragus.

Against this funnel of the ear the sonorous waves strike,

and its different parts are most admirably contrived to reflect them all into the meatus auditorius : if it would not occupy too much time, it might be shown, that all these curves and spirals are contrived in the best manner possible, and with a most perfect knowledge of the geometry of sounds, to reflect the sonorous pulses accurately, and in the greatest possible quantity, into the ear.

This external part of the ear is differently formed in different animals ; and admirably suited to their various situations and habits. In man it is close to the head, but so formed as to collect the various pulses with great accuracy ; in other animals it is more simple, where less accuracy is required, but it is, in general, much larger, having the appearance of an oblong funnel; and this gives them a greater delicacy of hearing, which was necessary for them.

In animals which are defenceless and timid, and which are constantly obliged to seek their safety in flight, the opening of this funnel is placed behind, that they may better hear the noises behind them. This is particularly instanced in the hare. Beasts of prey have this opening before, that they may more easily discover their prey; as the lion and tiger. Those that feed on birds have the opening directed upwards, as the fox; and it is inclined downwards in animals, such as the weasel, which seek their prey on the earth.

To this external part of the ear, which I have described, is connected the meatus auditorius, or passage to the internal ear, which is somewhat of a compressed cylindrical figure, lessening as it bends inwards: a considerable part of it is bony, and it is bent towards the middle. Across this passage, at its inner extremity, is stretched a thin membrane,

15

called membrana tympani. Upon the surface of this membrane, the sonorous waves, which have been directed inwards by the external ear, strike, and cause it to vibrate like the membrane of a drum. This membrane is stretched over a cavity in the bone, called the os petrosum, which cavity is called the tympanum, or drum of the ear, which is of a rounded figure, divided in its middle by a promontory, and continued backwards to the cells of the mastoid bone. Besides this continuation of the tympanum into the mastoid cells, it has a free communication with the mouth, by means of a tube I shall soon describe.

Within this cavity of the tympanum are placed four small bones, which facilitate the hearing: the first is the malleus or hammer, so called from its shape: the upper part of its round head rests upon the concavity of the tympanum, from whence the handle is extended down, along the membrane of the tympanum; this bone has several muscles, which move it in different directions, and cause it to stretch or brace the membrana tympani, when we wish to hear with accuracy.

Connected with the malleus is another small bone, called the incus, or anvil, which is connected with another, called the stapes, or stirrup, from its shape. These two bones are connected by a small oval shaped bone, called os orbiculare, placed between them: the whole forming a little chain of bones.

The stapes, or stirrup, has its end of an oval shape, which fits a small hole called fenestra ovalis, in that part of the ear called the labyrinth, or innermost chamber of the ear.

The labyrinth consists of three parts; first, the vestibule, which is a round cavity in a hard part of the os petrosum;

secondly, the semicircular canals, so called from their shape, which however is not exactly semicircular; thirdly, the cochlea, which is a beautifully convoluted canal, like the shell of a snail. This part has a round cavity called fenestra rotunda, which is covered with a thin elastic membrane, and looks into the tympanum.

The vestibule, semicircular canals, and cochlea, the whole of which is called the labyrinth, form one cavity, which is filled with a very limpid fluid resembling water, and the whole lined with a fine delicate membrane, upon which the auditory nerve is expanded, like the retina upon the vitreous humour of the eye. This beautiful apparatus was only lately discovered by an Italian physician, Scarpa. The auditory nerve is a portion of the seventh pair, which is called the portio mollis or soft portion.

There is one part of the ear still to be described, namely, the Eustachian tube, so called from Eustachius, the anatomist, who first described it. This tube opens by a wide elliptical aperture into the tympanum behind the membrane; the other end, which gradually grows wider, opens into the cavity of the mouth. By this canal the inspired air enters the tympanum to be changed and renewed, it likewise serves some important purpose in hearing, with the nature of which we are yet unacquainted. It is certain that we can hear through this passage, for if a watch be put into the mouth, and the ears stopped, its ticking may be distinctly heard; and in several instances of deafness, this tube has been found completely blocked up.

The waves, which have been described as propagated in the air, in all directions from the sounding body, enter the external cartilaginous part of the ear, which, as has before been observed, is admirably fitted for collecting and condensing them. As soon as these pulses excite tremors in the membrane of the tympanum, its muscles stretch and brace it, whence it becomes more powerfully affected by these impulses. It is on this account that we hear sounds more distinctly when we attend to them, the membrane being then stretched.

A tremulous motion, being excited in this membrane, is communicated to the malleus annexed to it, which communicates it to the incus, by which it is propagated through the the os orbiculare to the stapes, which imparts this tremulous motion through the foramen ovale to the fluid contained in the labyrinth. This tremor is impressed by the waves excited in this fluid, on every part of the auditory nerve in the labyrinth. The use of the foramen rotundum or round hole, before described, is probably the same as that of the hole in the side of a drum; it allows the fluid in the labyrinth to be compressed, otherwise it could not vibrate.

If the organization is sound, and tremors are communicated to the auditory nerve, they are in some way or other conveyed to the mind, but in what manner we cannot tell. Nature has hid the machinery by which she connects material and immaterial things entirely from our view, and if we try to investigate them, we are soon bewildered in the regions of hypothesis.

Tremors may however be communicated to the auditory nerve in a different manner from what I have described. If a watch be put between the teeth, and the ear stopped, tremors will be communicated to the teeth, by them to the bones of the upper jaw, and by these to the auditory nerve. In this way a person born deaf, and having no power of hearing through the medium of the air, may become sensible of the pleasures of music.

That sound may be propagated by vibrations, independent of pulses of the air, is evident from the experiment with the string and poker.

There is, strictly speaking, no such thing existing as sound; it being only a sensation of the mind, caused by tremors of the air, or vibrations of the sounding body.

In order to understand more clearly how pulses, or waves are caused by the vibration of bodies, and the manner in which vibrating bodies are affected, I shall just enumerate some of the properties of pendulums, which however I shall not stop to demonstrate here, as that would consume much time.

When two pendulums vibrate which are exactly of the same length, their vibrations are performed in equal times; if they set out together to describe equal arcs, they will agree together in their motions, and the vibrations will be perform-ed in equal times.

But if one of these pendulums be four times as long as the other, the vibrations of the longer will be twice as slow as those of the shorter; the number of vibrations being as the square roots of their lengths.

A pendulum is fixed to one point, but a musical string is extended between two points, and in its vibrations may be compared to a double pendulum vibrating in a very small arc, hence we see how strings of different lengths may agree in their motions after the manner of pendulums; but we must observe that it is not necessary to quadruple the length of a musical string, in order to make the time of vibration twice as long; it will be sufficient merely to double it.   We know that from whatever height a pendulum falls on one side, to the same height will it rise on the other.   In the same manner will an elastic string continue to vibrate from one side to the other for some time, till its motion be destroyed by the resistance of the air, and friction about its fixed points, and each of its small vibrations, like those of a pendulum, will, for the same reason, be performed in times exactly equal to each other.

Thus we gain from the analogy between a pendulum and a musical string, a more adequate conception of a subject which was never understood till this analogy was discovered. It explains to us why every musical string preserves the same pitch from the beginning to the end of its vibration, or as long as it can be distinguished by the ear; and why the pitch remains still unvaried whether the sound is loud or soft, and all this because the vibrations of the same pendulum whether they are longer or shorter, when compared among themselves, are found to be all performed in equal times till the pendulum be at rest, the difference of the space, which is moved over, compensating for the slowness of the motion till its decay.

To illustrate this subject still further, suppose we have a piece of catgut stretched between two pins; I lay hold of it in the middle and pull it sideways; I let it go, and you will observe that it first straightens itself or returns to its original position.   This depends on the elasticity of its particles, which tend to reunite when they have been separated by an external force, just in the same way that the particles of a piece of caoutchouc or Indian rubber attract each other when pulled asunder; and this force not only enables the string to restore itself to its former situation, but will carry it nearly to an equal distance on the other side, just in the same manner as a ball falling down an inclined plane will rise nearly to the same height up another, or a pendulum will rise nearly to the height from which it fell.

In this way will a string move backwards and forwards, till friction and the resistance of the air have destroyed the velocity which it acquired by the force of elasticity.

It is obvious that when a string is thus let fly from the finger, whatever be its own motion, such will also be the motion of the particles of the air which fly before it: the air will be driven forwards, and by that means condensed. When this condensed air expands itself, it will expand not only towards the string, but as its elasticity acts in all directions, it will also expand itself forwards and condense the air that is beyond it, this last condensed air, by its expansion, will produce the same effect on the air that lies still further forwards, and thus the motion produced in the air, by the vibration of the elastic string, is constantly carried forwards and conveyed to the ear.

It will be proper however to observe, that these pulses are sometimes produced without any such vibration of the sounding body, as we find it in musical strings and bells. In these cases we have to discover by what cause these condensations or pulses may be produced without any apparent vibrations in what is considered as the sounding body. We have two or three instances of this kind; one in wind instruments, such as the flute or organ pipe; another in the discharge of a gun.

In an organ, or flute, the air, which is driven through the pipe, strikes against the edge of the lips of the instrument in its passage, and by being accumulated there, is condensed, and this condensation produces waves or pulses in the air.

When a gun is discharged, a great quantity of air is produced, by the firing of the gunpowder, which being violently propelled from the piece, condenses the air that encompasses the space where the expansion happens; for whatever is driven out from the space where the expansion is made will be forcibly driven into the space all around it. This condensation forms the first pulse, and as this, by its elasticity, expands again, pulses of the same sort will be produced and propagated forwards.

There is likewise another curious instance of the production of sound, when a tube is held over a stream of inflamed hydrogen gas issuing out of a capillary tube in a bottle.

Sounding bodies propagate their motions on all sides, directly forwards, by successive condensations and rarefactions, so that sound is driven in all directions, backwards and forwards, upwards and downwards, and on every side; the pulses go on succeeding each other like circles in disturbed water.

Sounds differ from each other both with respect to their tone and intensity: in respect to their tone, they are distinguished into grave and acute: in respect to their intensity, they are distinguished into loud and low, or strong and weak. The tone of a sound depends on the velocity with which the vibrations are performed, for the greater the number of vibrations in a given time, the more acute will be the tone, and on the contrary, the smaller the number, the more grave it will be.   The tone of a sound is not altered by the distance of the ear from the sounding body; but the intensity or strength of any sound depends on the force with which the waves of the air strike the ear; and this force is different at different distances; so that a sound which is very loud when we are near the body that produces it, will be weaker if we are further from it, though its tone will suffer no alteration; and the distance may be so great that we cannot hear it at all.   It has been demonstrated, that the intensity of sound at different distances from the sounding body is inversely as the square of the distance.

Sound moves with the same velocity at all distances from the sounding body, otherwise it would not produce the same tone at all distances.   Sounds of different tones likewise move with the same velocity   This is evident from a peal of bells being heard in the same order in which they are rung, whether we are near, or at a distance.

It is likewise found that sounds of the same tone but of different intensities are propagated with the same velocity. A low sound cannot indeed be heard so far as a loud one; but sounds, whether low or loud, will be conveyed in an equal time to any equal distance at which they can both be heard.   The report of a cannon does not move faster, or pass over a given space sooner, than the sound of a musical string.

The principal cause of the decay of sound is the want of perfect elasticity in the air: whence it happens that every subsequent particle has not the entire motion of the preceding particle communicated to it, as is the case with equal and perfectly elastic bodies; consequently the further the motion

16

is propagated, the more will the velocity with which the
particles move be diminished; the condensation of the air
will be diminished also, and consequently its effect on the
ear. That the want of perfect elasticity in the air is the
principal cause of the decay of sound, appears from this,
that sounds are perceived more distinctly when the north
and easterly winds prevail, at which time the air is dry and
dense, as appears from the hygrometer and barometer;
and, of course, the air in this state must be more elastic, for
the vapours diffused through the atmosphere, unless dilated
by intense heat, diminish the spring of the air.

That sound is not propagated to all distances instantane-
ously, but requires a sensible time for its passage from one
place to another, is evident from the discharge of a gun at a
distance; for the report is not heard till some time after the
flash is seen. Light moves much more swiftly than sound; it
comes from the sun in eight minutes, which is at the rate of
74,420 leagues in a second ; so that the velocity of light may
be considered as instantaneous, at any distance on the earth;
and, as sound takes up a considerable time in its passage, the
interval between the flash and the report of the gun shows
the space it passes over in a given time, which is found to be
1142 feet in a second; so that if three seconds elapse between the time when we see the flash and hear the report of
the gun, it must be distant 1142 yards.

From experiments that have been made at different times,
by various philosophers, we may collect the following results.
First, That the mean velocity of sound is a mile in about 4½
seconds, or 1142 feet in a second of time.   Secondly, That all
sounds, whether they be weak or strong, have the same velo-

city. Thirdly, That sound moves over equal spaces in equal times, from the beginning to the end.

The tone of a musical string, or a bell, appears continu-ous. This depends upon a law of sensation, formerly men-tioned, namely, that impressions made upon any of the or-gans of sense do not immediately vanish, but remain some time; and we hear sound continuous from these vibrations, for the same reason that we hear it continuous when we draw a stick quickly along a rail, or a quill along the teeth of a comb; the vibrations succeed each other so quickly that we hear the succeeding before the effect of the preceding is worn off; though it must be evident that the impression produced by each pulse or wave of the air is perfectly distinct and insu-lated.

The act of combining sounds in such a manner as to be agreeable to the ear, is called music. This art is usually di-vided into melody and harmony. An agreeable succession of sounds is called melody; but when two or more sounds are produced together, and afford an agreeable sensation, the effect is called harmony. When two sounds are produced together, and afford pleasure to the sense of hearing, the ef-fect is called a concord; but when the sensation produced is harsh or disagreeable, it is called a discord. These different effects seem to depend upon the coincidence of the vibra-tions of the two strings, and consequently on the coincidence of the pulses which they excite in the air. When the strings are equally stretched, and of the same length and thickness, their vibrations will always coincide, and they produce a sound so similar to each other, that it is called unison, which is the most perfect concord. When one string is only half

the length of the other, the vibrations coincide at every second vibration of the shorter string: this produces a compound sound, which is more agreeable to the ear than any
other, except the unison: this note, when compared with the
tone produced by the longer string, is called the octave to
it, because the interval between the two notes is so divided by
musicians that from one to the other they reckon eight different tones.

If the strings be of the length, two and three, the coincidence of the pulses will happen less frequently, viz. at every
third vibration of the shorter string, and the concord will be
less perfect. This forms what is called a fifth. The less frequent the coincidence of the vibrations, the less perfect will
be the concord, or the less pleasure will it afford to the mind;
till the vibrations coincide so seldom, that the sound produced by both strings at once is harsh and disagreeable, and
is called a discord.

The effects of music upon the mind, the power by which it
moves the heart, touches the passions, and excites sometimes
the highest pleasure, and sometimes the deepest melancholy,
depend upon melody. By a simple melody the ignorant are
affected as well as those skilled in music. The pleasures
arising from harmony or a combination of sounds are acquired rather than natural. Its pleasures are the result of
experience and knowledge in music; music affords a source
of innocent and inexhaustible pleasure, but its effects are
different on different persons: some are enthusiastically fond
of it, while others hear the sweetest airs with a listlessness
bordering upon indifference. This has been supposed to
depend on a musical ear, which is not given by nature to all.

The cause of this difference is by no means evident. It does not depend on the delicacy of the sense of hearing, for there are some persons half deaf, who have the greatest relish for music; while others who have a very acute sense of hearing have no relish for music. In some instances I think a musical ear has been acquired where it did not seem originally to exist.

The force of sound is increased by the reflection of many bodies, particularly such as are hard or elastic, which receive the waves or pulses of the air and reflect them back again; these reflected pulses, striking the ear along with the original, strengthen the original sound. Hence it is, that the voice of a speaker is louder, and more distinctly heard, in a room than in the open air. I said that these reflected sounds entered the ear at the same time with the original: this however is not strictly the case, for they must enter the ear after the original, because the sound has a greater space to move over: but they enter the ear so quickly after the original that our sense cannot distinguish the difference. If however the reflecting body should be placed at such a distance, that the reflected sound should enter the ear some considerable or sensible time after the original, an echo or distinct sound would be heard.

It appears from experiment that the ear of an experienced musician can only distinguish such sounds as follow each other at the rate of nine or ten in a second, or any lower rate; and therefore that we may have a distinct perception of the direct and reflected sound, there should at least be an interval of $\frac{1}{9}$ of a second; but in this time sound passes over one hundred and twenty seven feet, and consequently, unless the space between the sounding body and the reflecting surface, added to that between the reflecting surface and the ear, be greater than one hundred and twenty seven feet, no echo will be heard, because the reflected sound will enter the ear so soon after the original, that the difference cannot be distinguished; and therefore it will only serve to augment the original sound.

From what has been said, it is evident, in order that a person may hear the echo of his own voice, that he should stand at least sixty three, or sixty four feet from the reflecting obstacle, so that the sound may have time to move over at least one hundred and twenty seven feet before it come to his ear, otherwise he could not distinguish it from the original sound.

But though the first reflected pulses may produce no echo, both on account of their being too few in number, and too rapid in their return to the ear; yet it must be evident that the reflecting surface may be so formed, that the pulses, which come to the ear after two or more reflections, may, after having passed over one hundred and twenty seven feet or more, arrive at the ear in sufficient numbers to produce an echo, though the distance of the reflecting surface from the ear be less than the limit of echoes. This is instanced by the echoes that we hear in several caves or caverns.

The sense of hearing is more apt to be vitiated or diseased than any of the other senses, which indeed is not surprising, when we consider that its organ is complex, consisting of many minute parts, which are apt to be deranged.

It sometimes becomes too acute, and this may arise either from too great an irritability of the whole nervous system, which often occurs in hysteria, also in phrenitis, and some fevers; or from an inflamed state of the ear itself.

The sense of hearing becomes diminished, and often entirely abolished; and this may arise from various causes, such as an original defect in the external ear, or the meatus auditorius, or both; the meatus auditorius is often blocked up with wax or other substances, which being removed, the hearing becomes perfect. Deafness may likewise arise from a rigidity of the membrane of the tympanum, from its being erodedor ruptured, or from an obstruction of the Eustachian tube. It may likewise arise from a paralysis or torpor of the auditory nerve, or from some diseased state of the labyrinth, or from a vitiated state of the brain and nerves. There is a kind of nervous deafness which comes on suddenly, and often leaves the patient as suddenly.

There are various instances, however, in which the membane of the tympanum has been lacerated or destroyed, without a total loss of the sense of hearing, or indeed any great diminution of it. A consideration of these circumstances induced Mr. Astley Cooper to think of perforating it, in cases of deafness arising from a permanent obstruction of the Eustachian tube, and he has often performed this operation with great success. Of this he has given an account in the last part of the Philosophical Transactions. This operation ought however only to be performed in case of the closure of the Eustachian tube. Cases of this kind may be distinguished by the following criteria. If a person on blowing the nose violently, feel a swelling in the ear, from the membrane of the tympanum being forced outwards, the tube is open; and though the tube be closed, if the beating of a watch placed between the teeth, or pressed against the side of the head, cannot be heard, the operation cannot relieve, as the sensibility of the auditory nerve must have been destroyed. In a closed Eustachian tube, there is no noise in the head, like that accompanying nervous deafness.

There is one species of deafness, which occurs very frequently, and happens generally to old persons, though sometimes to the delicate and irritable in the earlier periods of life. Anxiety and distress of mind have been known to produce it. Its approach is generally gradual, the patient hears better at one time than at another; a cloudy day, a warm room, agitated spirits, or the operation of fear, will produce a considerable diminution in the powers of the organ. In the open air the hearing is better than in a confined situation; in a noisy, than in a quiet society; in a coach when it is in motion, than when it is still. A pulsation is often felt in the ear; a noise resembling sometimes the roaring of the sea, and at others the ringing of distant bells is heard. This deafness generally begins with a diminished secretion of the wax of the ear, which the patient attributes to cold. It may be cured, particularly at its commencement, by the application of such stimulants as are capable of exciting a discharge from the ceruminous glands; for which purpose they should be introduced into the meatus auditorius.

In some cases of this kind, where the auditory nerve has been in some degree torpid, or rather perhaps where there has been a kind of paralysis, or want of action, in the muscles which brace the membrane of the tympanum, and keep the chain of bones in their proper state; a person has not been able to hear, except during a considerable noise. Willis mentions the case of a person who could only hear when a drum was beaten near her; and we are told of a woman who could not hear a word except when the sound of a drum was near, in which case she could hear perfectly well. When she married, her husband hired a drummer for his servant. In instances of this kind the noise probably excites the action of the torpid muscles, which then put the apparatus in a proper condition to hear.

LECTURE VIII.

VISION.

In order to understand properly the theory of vision, it will be necessary to premise an anatomical description of the eye; but I shall content myself with as short a one as will suffice to explain the effects it produces on the rays of light, so as to produce the distinct vision of an object.

The shape of the eye is nearly spherical; it is composed of several coats or tunics, one within another; and is filled with transparent humours of different densities.

The proper coats of the eye are reckoned five in number; viz. the sclerotica, cornea, choroides, iris or uvea, and the retina.

After the tunica conjunctiva, or adnata, (a membrane, which, having lined the eyelids in the manner of a cuticle, surrounds the anterior part of the globe) is removed, we perceive a white, firm, membrane, called the sclerotica, which takes its rise from that part of the globe where the optic nerve enters, and surrounds the whole eye, except a little in the fore part; which fore part has a membrane, immediately to be described, called the cornea. The tunica sclerotica, viewed through the conjunctiva, forms what is called the white of the eye. Some anatomists have supposed that this coat is a continuation of the dura mater, which surrounds the optic nerve; but later observations have shown this opinion to be ill founded. The tunica sclerotica consists of two layers, which are with difficulty separated.

The next coat is the cornea, so called from its resemblance to transparent horn; it arises where the sclerotic coat ends, and forms the fore part of the eye. The cornea is a segment of a lesser sphere than the rest of the eye, and consequently makes it more prominent on the fore part: it is transparent, and firmly connected by its edges to the sclerotica.

Immediately adherent to the sclerotica, within, is the choroides, which takes its rise from that part of the eye where the optic nerve enters, and accompanies the sclerotica to the place where it is joined to the cornea; here it is very closely connected to the sclerotica, where it forms that annulus, called ligamentum ciliare; then leaving the sclerotic coat, it is turned inwards, and surrounds the crystalline lens; but as this circle, where it embraces the crystalline, is much narrower than where the membrane leaves the sclerotic coat, it becomes beautifully corrugated, which folds or corrugations have been, by the more ancient anatomists, improperly called ciliary processes.

To the same part of the choroid coat, where the ciliary ligament begins, is fixed a moveable and curious membrane, called the iris; this membrane has a perforation in the middle, called the pupil, for the admission of the rays of light. The iris is composed of two kinds of fibres: those of the one sort tend, like the radii of a circle, towards its centre, and the others form a number of concentric circles round the same centre. The pupil is of no constant magnitude, for when a very lu-

minous object is viewed, the circular fibres of the iris contract, and diminish its orifice; and, on the contrary, when
objects are dark and obscure, those fibres relax, and suffer
the pupil to enlarge, in order to admit a greater quantity of
light into the eye: it is thought that the radial fibres also
assist in enlarging the pupil. The iris is variously coloured
in different persons, but according to no certain rule; though
in general, they who have light hair, and a fair complexion,
have the iris blue or grey; and, on the contrary, they whose
hair and complexion are dark, have the iris of a deep brown:
but whether this difference in colour occasions any difference
in the sense, is not yet discovered. In the human eye the
whole choroid coat, and even the interior surface of the iris
or uvea, is lined with a black mucus: this mucus, or as it is
called, pigmentum, is darkest in young persons, and becomes
more light coloured as we advance in years. In many animals, but more particularly those which catch their prey in
the night, this pigmentum is of a bright colour: its use will
appear afterwards.

The last, and innermost coat of the eye, is the retina, it
differs much from the abovementioned coats, being very
delicate and tender. It is nothing but an expansion of the
medullary part of the optic nerve, which is inserted into each
eye, nearer the nose, and a little higher, than the axis. This
coat has been thought by many to end where the choroides,
going inwards, towards the axis of the eye, forms the ciliary
ligament; Dr. Monro thinks that it is not continued so far,
and we cannot see with what advantage it could have been
continued to the ciliary ligament, since none of the rays of
light, passing through the pupil, could fall upon that part

of it. In the middle of the optic nerve is found the branch of an artery, from the internal carotid, which is diffused and ramified in a beautiful manner along the retina. From this artery, a small branch goes through the middle of the vitreous humour, and giving off branches on every side, expands itself upon the capsule of the crystalline lens.

We shall now consider the humours of the eye, which are three in number, the aqueous, the crystalline, and the vitreous; all transparent, and in general colourless; but of different densities.

The aqueous humour, so called from its resemblance to water, fills up all the space between the cornea and the crystalline humour. It is partly before and partly behind the uvea, and is divided by that membrane into two parts, which are called the chambers of the aqueous humour; which chambers communicate with each other by means of the pupil.

The next humour is the crystalline; it is situated between the aqueous and vitreous humours, and is connected to the choroid coat by the ciliary ligament: it is not the least of all the humours, as has been generally supposed, the aqueous and it being of equal weights; but its substance is more firm and solid than that of the other humours: its figure is that of a double convex lens; but the fore part next the pupil is not so convex as its other side, which is contiguous to the vitreous humour; the diameter of the sphere, of which its anterior segment is a part, being in general about seven or eight lines, whereas the diameter of the sphere, of which its posterior segment forms a portion, is commonly only about five or six lines. It is covered with a fine transparent capsule, which is called arachnoides. This humour is situated exactly behind the pupil, but not in the centre of the eye, as was supposed by Vesalius, being a good deal nearer its forepart. The convexity of its posterior surface is received into an equal concavity of the vitreous humour. It is not of an equal density throughout, but is much more hard and dense towards its centre than externally, the reason of which will appear hereafter. Till we arrive at about our thirtieth year, this humour continues perfectly transparent, and colourless; about that time it generally has a little tinge of yellow, and this colour increases with age.

The third humour of the eye, is the vitreous; it is the largest of all the humours, filling up the whole of that part of the eye which lies behind the crystalline humour. It is thicker than the aqueous, but thinner than the crystalline humour; on its back part is spread the retina, and in the middle of its fore part is a small cavity, in which the whole posterior surface of the crystalline lens lies; this humour is also enclosed in a very fine capsule, called tunica vitrea; this capsule at the edge of the crystalline humour is divided into two membranes, of which the one is continued over the whole anterior surface of the vitreous humour, and lines that cavity into which the back part of the crystalline is received; the other passes over the crystalline humour, and covers all its fore part, by which means these two humours are closely connected together. The weights of the aqueous, crystalline, and vitreous humours in a human eye, are, according to the accurate Petit, at a medium, to each other, as 1,1, and 25.

It was thought necessary to premise this general description of the structure of the eye, in order that what we are going to add in the remaining part of this Lecture may be the more easily comprehended. A more distinct idea will perhaps be had from a contemplation of the following figure, which represents the section of an eye by a vertical plane passing through its centre.

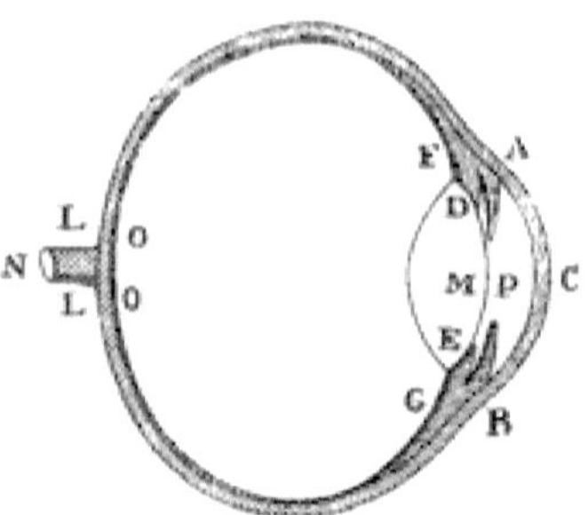

EXPLANATION.

NOO represents the optic nerve.

The outmost line ALLB represents the sclerotic coat, and the part ACB the transparent cornea.

The line ALLB, immediately within the former, represents the choroides; the part APB is the iris or uvea, in which the hole at P is the pupil.

The line FOOG is the retina.

The cavity ACBEMDA is the aqueous humour.

DE is the crystalline lens or humour.

The space DFOOGE, lying behind the crystalline, represents the vitreous humour.

BE and AD is the ligamentum ciliare.

Nature and Properties of Light.

After this short description of the human eye, I shall next proceed to take notice of some of the properties of light; but shall confine myself to such as are absolutely necessary for

explaining the phenomena of vision, as far as that can be
done from optical principles.

1. It is, I believe, generally at present agreed, that light
consists of exceedingly small particles of matter, projected
with great velocity in all directions from the luminous or radiant body. This hypothesis, to which no solid objection has
yet been made, appears to be more simple than any other;
and is so consistent with all the phenomena yet observed,
that we have great reason to think it true: however, as it is
not absolutely and directly demonstrated, it may have been
wrong in optical writers to have given this hypothesis (for it
can only be called a hypothesis) as a definition of light.

2. The space through which light passes is, by opticians,
called a medium, and it is observed, that, when light passes
through a medium, either absolutely void, or containing matter of an uniform density, and of the same kind, it always
proceeds in straight lines.

3. Those rays of light which come directly from a luminous
body to the eye, only give us a perception of light; but when
they fall upon other bodies, and are from them reflected to
the eye, they give us an idea or perception of those bodies.

4. When a ray of light passes out of one medium into
another of different density, it is bent out of its course, and is
said to be refracted. We must, however, except those rays
which fall in a direction perpendicular to the surface of the
refracting medium; as the refractive force acts in the same
direction in which those rays move, they will not be turned
out of their course, but proceed in the same direction they
had before they entered the refracting medium. When a
ray passes out of a rarer into a denser medium, it will be

refracted, or bent towards a line which is perpendicular to
the surface which separates the media at the point where it
falls; but when it passes out of a denser into a rarer medium,
it will be bent from the perpendicular.

5. Whenever the rays, which come from all the points of
any object, meet again in so many points, after they have
been made to converge by refraction, there they will form
the picture of the object, distinct, and of the same colours, but inverted. This is beautifully demonstrated by a
common optical instrument, the camera obscura. If a double
convex lens, be placed in the hole of a window shutter in a
dark room, and a sheet of white paper be placed at a certain
distance behind the lens; a beautiful, but inverted picture
of the external objects will be formed: but if the paper be
held nearer, or more remote than this distance, so that the
rays from each point shall not meet at the paper, but be-
twixt it and the lens, or beyond the paper, the picture will be
indistinct and confused.

Of the Manner in which Vision is performed.

From the just mentioned properties of light, and the description we have given of the eye, it will not be difficult to
explain the theory of vision, so far as it depends upon optical
principles. For the eye may, with great propriety, be compared to a camera obscura; the rays which flow from external objects, and enter the eye, painting an inverted picture
of those objects on the retina: if you carefully dissect from
the bottom of an eye, newly taken out of the head of an
animal, a small portion of the tunica sclerotica and choroides,

and place this eye in a hole made in the window shutter of a dark chamber, so that the bottom of the eye may be towards you; the pictures or images of external objects will be painted on the retina in lively colours, but inverted.

In order to see how the several parts of the eye contribute to produce this effect, let us follow the rays proceeding from a luminous point, and see what will happen to them from the beforementioned properties of light.

Since the rays of light flow from every visible point of a body in every direction, some of them, issuing from this point, will fall upon the cornea, and, entering a medium of greater density, will be refracted towards the perpendicular, and as they fall upon a convex spherical surface, nearly in a parallel state, the pupil being so extremely small, it is evident, from the principles of optics, that they will be made to converge: those which fall very obliquely will either be reflected, or falling upon the uvea, or pigmentum nigrum, which covers the ciliary ligaments, will be suffocated, and prevented from entering the internal parts of the eye: those which fall more directly, as was before said, become converging, in which state they fall upon the anterior surface of the crystalline humour, which, having a greater refracting power than the aqueous humour, and its surface being convex, will cause them to converge still more, in which state they will fall upon the posterior surface of the crystalline, or anterior surface of the vitreous humour; which having a less refractive power than the crystalline, they will be refracted from the perpendicular: but, as they fall upon a concave surface, it is evident, from the principles of optics, that they will be made to converge still more: in which state they will go on to the retina, and if the eye is well formed, the refraction of these several humours will be just sufficient to bring them to a point or focus on the retina.

The same thing will happen to rays flowing from every other visible point of the object: the rays which flow from every point will be collected into a corresponding point on the retina, and, consequently, will paint the image of that object inverted ; the rays coming from the superior part of any object, being collected on the inferior part of the retina, and vice versa, as is manifest from the principles of optics.

If the rays are accurately, or very nearly, collected into a focus on the retina, distinct vision will be produced; but if they be made to converge to a point before or beyond the retina, the object will be seen indistinctly ; this is proved by holding a convex or concave glass before the eye of a good sighted person: in the former case, the rays will be made to converge to a point before they arrive at the retina, and in the latter, to a point beyond it.   In these cases, it is plain that the rays which flow from a point in the object, will not form a point, but a circular spot, upon the retina, and these various circles intermixing with other, will render the image very indistinct. This is well illustrated by the camera obscura, where if you hold the paper nearer or more remote than the focal distance of the lens, the picture will be indistinct.

So far then, in the theory of vision, are we led by the principles of optics, and we can with certainty, by their assistance, affirm, that if the eye is sound, and the image of an object distinctly painted upon the retina, it will be seen distinctly, erect, and of its proper colours: so far we can proceed on safe and sure grounds, but if we venture further, we shall find ourselves bewildered in the regions of hypothesis and fancy. The machinery by which nature connects the material and immaterial world is hidden from our view; in most cases we must be satisfied with knowing that there are such connexions, and that these connexions invariably follow each other, without our being able to discover the chain that goes between them. It is to such connexions that we give the name of laws of nature; and when we say that one thing produces another by a law of nature, this signifies no more, than that one thing, which is called the cause, is constantly and invariably followed by another, which we call the effect, and that we know not how they are connected. But there seems a natural propensity in the mind of man, to endeavour to account for every phenomenon that falls under his view, which has given rise to a number of absurd and romantic conjectures in almost every branch of science. From this source has risen the vibration of the fibres of the optic nerve, or the undulation of a subtile ether, or animal spirits, by which attempts have been made to explain the theory of vision; but all of them are absurd and hypothetical.

Kepler was the first who had any distinct notion of the formation of the pictures of objects on the bottom of the eye; this discovery he published about the year 1600. Joannes Baptista Porta had indeed got some rude notion of it prior to the time of Kepler, but as he knew nothing of the refraction made by the humours of the eye, his doctrine was lame and defective, for he imagines that the images are painted on the surface of the crystalline humour.

The disputes concerning the theory of vision had very much divided the ancient philosophers; some of them imagining that vision was caused by the reception of rays into the eye; while a great many others thought it more agreeable to nature, that certain emanations, which they called visual rays, should flow from the eye to the object.

We shall now inquire more particularly how each part of the eye is peculiarly fitted to produce distinct vision. Though the eye is composed of different humours, yet one might have been sufficient to collect the rays into a focus, and form the picture of an object upon the retina. By the experiments of the accurate Dr. Robertson, it appears that there is less difference in the density, as well as in the refracting power of the humours, than has been generally thought: by weighing them in a hydrostatic balance, he found that the specific gravities of the aqueous and vitreous humours were very nearly equal, each being nearly equal to that of water: and that the specific gravity of the crystalline did not exceed the specific gravity of the other humours in a greater proportion than that of about 11 to 10. Hence it would seem to follow, that the crystalline is not of such great use in bringing the rays together, and thereby forming the pictures of objects on the retina, as has been commonly thought by optical writers; for though in shape it resembles a double convex lens, and is, on that account, fitted to make the rays converge; yet, be cause it is situated between two humours nearly of the same refractive power with itself, it will alter the direction of the light but a little. From this, the reason is evident why the sight continues after the operation for the cataract, in which the crystalline is depressed, or extracted, and why a glass of small convexity is sufficient to supply the little refraction wanting, occasioned by the loss of this humour. But without doubt, several important purposes are effected by this construction of the eye; which could not have been attained if it had been composed of one humour only. Some of those purposes seem sufficiently evident to us; for instance, by placing the aqueous humour before the crystalline, and partly before the pupil, and making the cornea convex, a greater quantity of light is made to enter the eye than could otherwise have done without enlarging the size of the pupil : the light will also enter in a less diverging state than it could have done if the pupil had been enlarged, and consequently be more accurately collected to a focus on the retina; for a perfect eye can only collect such rays to a focus on that membrane, as pass through the pupil nearly in a state of parallelism.

Another, and perhaps a principal advantage derived from the different humours in the eye, is, probably, to prevent that confusion arising from colour, which is the consequence of the different degrees of refrangibility of the rays of light. From the experiments of Mr. Dollond, it appears, though contrary to the opinion of Newton, and most other optical writers, that different kinds of matter differ extremely with respect to the divergency of colour produced by equal refractions: so that a lens may be contrived, composed of media of different dispersing powers, which will form the image of any object free of colour; this discovery Mr. Dollond has applied to the improvement of telescopes, with great success. It is by no means improbable, that nature has, for the same purpose, placed the crystalline lens betwen two media of different densities, and, probably, different dispersing powers, so that an achromatic image, free from the prismatic colours, will be formed on the retina. Indeed we find a conjecture of this kind, so long since as Dr. David Gregory's time, he says, in speaking of the imperfection of telescopes, " Quòd si ob difficultates physicas, in speculis idoneis torno elaborandis, et poliendis, etiamnum lentibus uti oporteat, fortassis media diversae densitatis ad lentem objectivam componendam adhibere utile foret, ut à naturâ factum observamus in oculo, ubi crystallinus humor (fere ejusdem cum vitro virtutis ad radios lucis refringendos) aqueo et vitreo (aquae quoad refractionem hand absimilibus) conjungitur, ad imaginem quam distinctè fieri poterit, à naturâ nihil frustra moliente, in oculi fundo depingendam."

In describing the eye, I observed, that the crystalline humour was not every where of the same consistence, being much more hard and dense towards its centre, than externally: in the human eye, it is soft on the edges, and gradually increases in density as it approaches the centre: the reason of this construction is evident, at least we know of one use which it will serve; for, from the principles of optics, it is plain that the rays which fall at a distance from the axis of the crystalline, by reason of their greater obliquity, if the humour were of the same density in all its parts, would be more refracted than those which fall near its axis, so that they would meet at different distances behind the crystalline humour; those which pass towards its extremity, nearer, and those near its axis, at a greater distance, and could not be united at the same point on the retina, which would render vision indistinct; though the indistinctness arising from this cause, is only about the $\frac{1}{5500}$ part of that which arises from the different refrangibility of the rays of light, as Sir Isaac Newton has demonstrated. Nature has, however, contrived a remedy for this also, by making the crystalline humour more dense and solid near its centre, that the rays of light which fall near its axis, may have their refraction increased, so as to meet at the same point with those which fall at a distance from its axis.

Of the manner in which the Eye conforms itself in order to see distinctly at different Distances.

It has been much disputed in what manner the eye conforms itself to see distinctly at different distances; for it is evident, that, without some change, the rays which flow from objects at different distances, could not be collected into a focus at the same point, and, consequently, though the eye might see distinctly at one distance, it could not at another.

This subject has given rise to a variety of opinions, but few of them are satisfactory; and though several of them might explain the phenomena of vision, at different distances, yet it is by no means proved that those supposed changes do take place in the eye. I shall content myself with just mentioning the principal opinions on this subject, without engaging in a controversy, which has for a long time employed the ingenuity of philosophers to little purpose.

Some are of opinion, that the whole globe of the eye changes its figure; becoming more oblong when objects are near, and more flat when they are removed to a greater distance; and this change in the figure of the eye is differently explained by different authors; some maintain that it is rendered oblong by the joint contraction of the two oblique muscles : others think that the four straight muscles acting together, compress the sides of the globe, and by this compression, reduce it to an oblong figure, when objects are near; and that, by its natural elasticity, it recovers its former figure when these muscles cease to act. Others again think that when these four straight muscles act together, they render the eye flat by pulling it inwards, and pressing the bottom of it against the fat; and that it is reduced to its former figure, either by the joint contraction of the two oblique muscles, or by the inherent elasticity of its parts, which exerts itself when the muscles cease to act.

That, if such a change should take place in the eye, it would produce distinct vision, will be readily granted; but that such a one does not take place, at least in any of these ways, is, in my opinion, very certain. Dr. Porterfield thinks that the crystalline lens has a motion by means of the ligamentum ciliare, by which the distance between it and the retina is increased or diminished, according to the different distances of objects. The ligamentum ciliare, he says, is an organ, the structure and disposition of which excellently qualify it for changing the situation of the crystalline, and removing it to a greater distance from the retina, when objects are too near for us; for that, when it contracts, it will not only draw the crystalline forwards, but will also compress the vitreous humour, lying behind it, so that it must press upon the crystalline, and push it from the retina. Although this hypothesis will, in a great measure, account for distinct vision at different distances, yet it could only be of use where the rays enter the eye with a certain degree of divergency, while, however we are sure, that in looking at very distant objects which are at different distances from us, the eye undergoes a change. But a sufficient objection to Dr. Porterfield's hypothesis is, that it is by no means proved that the crystalline lens can be moved in the manner he supposes, or that the ligamentum ciliare is possessed of muscular fibres; on the contrary some eminent anatomists deny that they are.

We shall now take a view of the opinion of M. de la Hire, who considered this subject, as well as almost every other relating to vision, with the closest attention; he maintains, that, in order to view objects distinctly at different distances, there is no alteration but in the size of the pupil, which is well known to contract and dilate itself according to the quantity of light flowing from the object we look at, being most contracted in the strongest light, and most dilated when the light is weakest; and consequently will contract when an object is held near the eye, and dilate as it is removed, because in the first case the quantity of light entering the eye is much greater than in the last. That this contraction of the pupil will have the effect of rendering vision distinct, especially when objects are within the furthest limits of distinct vision, will plainly appear, if we consider the cause of indistinct vision. Dr. Jurin has shown, that objects may be seen with sufficient distinctness, though the pencils of rays issuing from the points of them do not unite precisely in another point on the retina, but instead thereof, if they form a circle which does not exceed a certain magnitude, distinct vision will be produced; the circle formed by these rays on the retina he calls the circle of dissipation. The pupil will, by contracting, not only diminish the circles of dissipation, and thereby help to produce distinct vision, but will also prevent so great a quantity

of light from falling near the circumferences of those circles;
and Dr. Jurin has shown, that, if the light on the outer side
of the circles of dissipation is diminished, the remainder will
scarce affect the sense. In both these ways, the contraction
of the pupil has a tendency to diminish the circles of dissipation, and, consequently, to produce distinct vision. This
is likewise confirmed by experiment, for when an object is
placed so near, that the pupil cannot be so much contracted
as is necessary for distinct vision, the same end may be obtained by means of an artificial pupil: for, if a small hole is
made in a card, a very near object may be viewed through it
with the greatest ease and distinctness. Also, if a person
have his back turned towards a window, and hold a book
so near his eyes as not to be able to read, if he turn his face
to the light, he will find, that he will be able to read it very
distinctly; which is owing to the contraction of the pupil by
means of the light.

M. Le Roi, a member of the Royal Academy of Mont-
pelier, has attempted to defend the opinion of M. de la Hire,
and, indeed, it seems, of all others, the best supported by
facts; but perhaps it may not account so well for vision at
great distances. It is likewise rendered more probable by
viewing the pictures of external objects, formed in a dark
chamber, by rays coming through a hole in the window shutter; those pictures will be rendered distinct, by dilating, or contracting the aperture, without the assistance of a lens, accordingly as the object is more or less distant; those who have
had the crystalline lens depressed, or extracted, by means of
one glass can see objects pretty distinctly at different distances.
These, and several other arguments that might be brought,

tend to prove that the eye accommodates itself to view objects distinctly at different distances, chiefly by means of the motion of the pupil; and though this does not explain the phenomenon so satisfactorily as we could wish, yet it is certain, that it has a share in it; we are however certain, that, in whatever manner it may be produced, the eye has a power of accommodating itself to view objects distinctly enough at several different distances.

Concerning the Seat of Vision.

No subject has been more canvassed than that concerning what is improperly called the seat of vision. In early times, the crystalline lens was thought to be best qualified for this office; but this substance, though situated in the middle of the eye, which Baptista Porta thought to be the proper centre of observation, had universally given place to the better founded pretensions of the retina: and, from the time of Kepler, few ventured to dispute its claim to that office, till M. Mariotte was led, from some curious circumstances, to think that vision was not performed by the retina, but by the choroid coat. Having often observed in the dissections of men, as well as of brutes, that the optic nerve is not inserted exactly opposite to the pupil, that is, in the place where the picture of the objects upon which we look directly, is made: and that in man it is somewhat higher, and on the side towards the nose, he had the curiosity to examine the reason of this structure, by throwing the image of an object on this part of the eye. In order to do this, he fastened on a dark wall, about the height of his eyes, a small round paper, to serve for a fixed point of sight; and he fastened such another paper on the right hand, at the distance of about two feet, but rather lower than the former, so that light issuing from it, might strike the optic nerve of his right eye, while the left was kept shut. He then placed himself over against the former paper, and drew back by degrees, keeping his right eye fixed, and very steady upon it, and when he had retired about ten feet, he found that the second paper entirely disappeared. This, he says, could not be imputed to the oblique position of the second paper, with respect to his eye, because he could see more remote objects on the same side. This experiment he repeated by varying the distances of the paper and his eye. He also made it with his left eye, while the right eye was kept shut, the second paper being fastened on the left side of the point of sight; so that by the situation of the parts of the eye, it could not be doubted that this defect of vision is in the place where the optic nerve enters, where only the choroides isdeficient.

From this he concludes, that the defect of vision is owing to the want of the choroid coat, and, consequently, that this coat is the proper organ of vision. A variety of other arguments in favour of the choroides occurred to him, particularly he observed that the retina is transparent, which he thought could only enable it to transmit the rays further, and he could not persuade himself that any substance could be considered as being the termination of the pencils, and the proper seat of vision, at which the rays are not stopped in their progress.

Mr. Pequet, in answer to Mariotte's observation, says,

that the retina is very imperfectly transparent, resembling oiled paper, or horn: and, besides, that its whiteness demonstrates that it is sufficiently opaque for stopping the rays of light as much as is necessary for vision: whereas, if vision be performed by means of those rays which are transmitted through such a substance as the retina, it must be very indistinct.

Notwithstanding the plausibility of this opinion of M. Mariotte, and the number of celebrated men who joined him in it, I must confess, that none of their arguments, though very ingenious, have been able to make me a convert to that opinion.

If we argue from the analogy of the other senses, in all of which the nerves form the proper seat of sensation, we shall be induced to give judgment in favour of the retina. And this argument from analogy is much strengthened, by considering that the retina is a large nervous apparatus, immediately exposed to the impressions of light; whereas the choroides receives but a slender supply of nerves, and seems no more fitted for the organ of vision than any other part of the body. But facts are not wanting which make still more in favour of the retina. It appears from observations made upon the sea calf and porcupine, that these animals have their optic nerves inserted in the axis of the eye, directly opposite the pupil, which renders it very improbable that the defect in sight, where the optic nerves enter, can be owing to the want of the choroides in that place; for were this true, then in those creatures which have the optic nerves inserted in the axis of the eye, and which by consequence do directly receive on the extremity of the nerve the pictures of objects, all objects would become invisible to which their eyes are turned, because the choroides is wanting in that place where the image falls; but this is contrary to experience.

M. Le Cat, though he strenuously supports Mariotte's opinion, takes notice of a circumstance, which, if he had properly considered it, might have led him to a contrary conclusion: from a beautiful experiment he obtains data, which enable him with considerable accuracy to determine the size of the insensible spot in his eye, which he finds to be about $\frac{1}{10}$ or $\frac{1}{12}$ of an inch in diameter, and consequently only about $\frac{1}{4}$ or $\frac{1}{5}$ of the diameter of the optic nerve, that nerve being about $\frac{1}{2}$ of an inch in diameter. I find that in my eye likewise, the diameter of the insensible spot is about $\frac{1}{12}$ of an inch, or something less. Whence it is evident that vision exists where the choroid coat is not present, and consequently that the choroid coat is not the organ of vision.

It is probably owing to the hardness and callosity of the retina where the nerve enters, that we have this defect of sight, as it has not yet acquired that softness and delicacy which is necessary for receiving such slight impressions as those of the rays of light, and this conjecture is rendered still more probable by an observation of M. Pequet, who tells us, that a bright and luminous object, such as a candle, does not absolutely disappear, but one may see its light, though faint. This not only shows that the defect of sight is not owing to a want of the choroides, but also that the retina is not altogether insensible where the nerve enters. These circumstances, in my opinion, render it certain, that the retina, and not the choroid coat, is the organ of vision.

Of our seeing Objects erect by inverted Images.

Another question concerning vision, which has very much perplexed philosophers, is this; how comes it that we see objects erect, when it is well known that their images or pictures on the retina are inverted? The sagacious Kepler, who first made this discovery, was the first that endeavoured to explain the cause of it.

The reason he gives for our seeing objects erect, is this, that as the rays from different points of an object cross each other before they fall on the retina, we conclude that the impulse we feel upon the lower part of the retina comes from above; and that the impulse we feel from the higher part, comes from below. Des Cartes afterwards gave the same solution of this phenomenon, and illustrated it by the judgment we form of the position of objects which we feel with our arms crossed, or with two sticks that cross each other. But this solution is by no means satisfactory: first, because it supposes our seeing objects erect to be a deduction from reason, drawn from certain premises, whereas it seems to be an immediate perception; and secondly, because all the premises from which this conclusion is supposed to be drawn, are absolutely unknown to far the greater part of mankind, and yet they all see objects erect.

Bishop Berkeley, who justly rejects this solution, gives another, founded on his own principles, in which he is followed by Dr. Smith. This ingenious writer thinks that the ideas of sight are altogether unlike those of touch; and since the notions we have of an object by these different senses, have no similitude, we can learn only by experience how one sense will be affected, by what, in a certain manner, affects the other. Thus, finding from experience, that an object in an erect position, affects the eye in one manner, and that the same object in an inverted position, affects it in another, we learn to judge, by the manner in which the eye is affected, whether the object is erect or inverted. But it is evident that Bishop Berkeley proceeds upon a capital mistake, in supposing that there is no resemblance between the extension, figure, and position, which we see, and that which we perceive by touch. It may be further observed, that Bishop Berkeley's system, with regard to material things, must have made him see this question, in a very different light from that in which it appears to those who do not adopt his system.

In order to give a satisfactory answer to this question, we must first examine some of the laws of nature, which take place in vision; for by these the phenomena of vision must be regulated.

It is now, I believe, pretty well established, as a law of nature, that we see every point of an object in the direction of a right line, which passes from the picture of that point on the retina, through the centre of the eye. This beautiful law is proved by a very copious induction of facts; the facts upon which it is founded are taken from some curious experiments of Scheiner, in his Fundamenta Optices. They are confirmed by Dr. Porterfield, and well illustrated by Dr. Reid. The seeing objects erect by inverted images is a necessary consequence of this law of nature: for from thence it is evident that the point of the object whose picture is

lowest on the retina, must be seen in the highest direction
from the eye ; and that the picture which is on the right side
of the retina, must be seen on the left.

Of seeing Objects single with two Eyes.

That we should have two pictures of an object, and yet
see it single, has long been looked upon as a curious circumstance by philosophers: and of consequence, many attempts
have been made to account for it, few of which, however,
are satisfactory.

As it would take up too much time to give a view of all
the opinions on this subject, I shall pass over the opinions
of Galen, Gassendus, Baptista Porta, Rohault, and others,
which do not deserve a serious refutation ; and shall content
myself with making a few observations on the hypothesis of
Bishop Berkeley.

But it seems the most proper way of proceeding, first of
all to consider the phenomena of single and double vision, in
order, if possible, to discover some general principle to which
they lead, and of which they are necessary consequences;
and, for the sake of perspicuity, we shall premise the following definition.

When a small object is seen single with both eyes, those
points on the two retinas on which the pictures of the object
fall, may be called corresponding points: and when the object
is seen double, we shall call such points, non-corresponding
points.

Now we find that in sound and perfect eyes, when the
axes of both are directed to one point, an object placed in

that point is seen single; and in this case, the two pictures which show the object single, are painted on the centres of the retinas. Hence, the centres of the two retinas correspond.

Other objects at the same distance from the eyes, as that to which their axes are directed, do also appear single: and in this case, it is evident to those who understand the principles of optics, that the pictures of an object to which the eyes are not directed, but which is at the same distance as that to which they are directed, fall both on the same side of the centre, that is, both to the right, or both to the left, and both at the same distance from the centre. Hence it is plain, that points in the retina, which are similarly situated with respect to the centres, are corresponding points.

An object which is much nearer, or much more distant from the eyes, than that to which their axes are directed, appears double. In this case, it will easily appear, that the pictures of the object which is seen double, do not fall upon points which are similarly situated. From these facts, we are led to the following conclusion, viz. that the points of the two retinas, which are similarly situated with respect to the centres, correspond with each other, and that the points which are dissimilarly situated, do not correspond. The truth of this general conclusion is founded upon a a very full induction, which is all the evidence we can have for a fact of this nature.

The next thing that seems to merit our attention, is, to inquire, whether this correspondence between certain points of the two retinas which is necessary to single vision, is the effect of custom, or an original property of the human eyes.

We have a strong argument in favour of its being an original property, from the habit we get of directing our eyes accurately to an object; we get this habit by finding it necessary for perfect and distinct vision; because thereby, the two images of the object falling upon corresponding points, the eyes assist each other in vision, and the object is seen better by both eyes together, than by one: but when the eyes are not accurately directed, the two images of the object fall upon points which do not correspond, whereby the sight of the one eye disturbs that of the other. Hence it is not unreasonable to conclude, that this correspondence between certain points of the retina is prior to the habits we acquire in vision: and, consequently, natural and original.

We have all acquired the habit of directing our eyes in one particular manner, which causes single vision ; now if the Author of Nature had ordained that we should see objects single, only when our eyes are thus directed, there is an obvious reason why all mankind should agree in the habit of directing them in this manner; but, if single vision were the effect of custom, any other habit of directing the eyes would have answered the purpose; we therefore, on this supposition, can give no reason why this particular habit should be so universal.

Bishop Berkeley maintains a contrary opinion, and thinks that our seeing objects single with both eyes, as well as our seeing them erect, by inverted images, depends upon custom. In this he is followed by Dr Smith, who observes, that the question, why we see objects single with both eyes, is of the same nature with this, why we hear sounds single with both ears; and that the same answer will serve for both; whence he concludes, that as the second of these phenomena is the effect of custom, so also is the first. But I think, that the questions are not so much of the same sort, as that the same answer will serve for both; and, moreover, that our hearing single with both ears is not the effect of custom. No person will doubt that things which are produced by custom, may be undone by disuse, or by a contrary custom. On the other hand, it is a strong argument, that an effect is not owing to custom, but to the constitution of nature, when a contrary custom, long continued, is found neither to change nor weaken it. Now it appears, that from the time we are able to observe the phenomena of single and double vision, custom makes no change in them, every thing which at first appeared double, appearing so still in the same circumstances. Dr. Smith has adduced some facts in favour of his opinion, which, though curious, seem by no means decisive. But in the famous case of the young man couched by Mr. Cheselden, after having had cataracts in both his eyes till his thirteenth year, it appears that he saw objects single from the time he began to see with both eyes. And the three young gentlemen mentioned by Dr. Reid, who had squinted, as far as he could learn, from infancy, as soon as they learned to direct both eyes to an object, saw it single.

In these cases it is evident that the centres of the retina corresponded originally, for Mr. Cheselden's young man had never seen at all before he was couched, and the other three had never been accustomed to direct the axes of both eyes to the same point. These facts render it probable, that this correspondence is not the effect of custom, but of fixed and immutable laws of nature.

With regard to the cause of this correspondence, many

theories have been proposed, but as none of them can be
looked on in any other light than as probable conjectures, I
think it would be to little purpose to notice them. That of
the illustrious Newton is the most ingenious of any, and
though it has more the appearance of truth than any other,
that great man has proposed it under the modest form of
a query.

Having given a short account of the principal phenomena
of vision, I proceed next to treat of some of the diseases to
which this sense is subject, I shall first take notice of the
deformity called squinting.

Of Squinting.

Though this is a subject which well deserves our particular
attention, yet having spoken of such a variety of subjects
in the preceding part of this lecture, I have not time for
many observations on this. I shall just mention the principal opinions, concerning the cause of this deformity, and point
out that which seems to me most probable. This subject
is certainly very worthy the attention of the physician, as
it is a case concerning which he may often be consulted, and
which it may be sometimes in his power to cure.

A person is said to squint, when the axes of both his eyes
are not directed to the same object.

This defect consists in the wrong direction of one of the
eyes only. I have never met with an instance in which both
eyes had a wrong direction, neither have I seen one accurately described by any author.

The generality of writers on this subject have supposed this

defect to proceed from a disease of, or want of proper correspondence in, the muscles of the eyes, which not acting in proper
concert with one another, as in persons free from this blemish, are not able to point both eyes to the same object.
But this, I think, is very seldom the cause, for when the
other eye is shut, the distorted eye can be moved by the
action of its muscles, in all possible directions, as freely as
that of any other person, which shows that it is not owing to
a defect in the muscles, neither is it owing to a want of correspondence in the muscles of both eyes ; for when both eyes
are open, and the undistorted eye is moved in any direction
whatever, the other always accompanies it, and is turned the
same way at the same instant of time.

I shall next take notice of the hypothesis of M. de la Hire,
who supposes, that in the generality of mankind, that part
of the retina which is seated in and about the axis of the
eye, is of a more delicate sense and perception than what
the rest of the coat is endowed with; and therefore we direct
both axes to the same object, chiefly in order to receive the
picture on that part of the retina which can best perceive it;
but in persons who squint, he conceives the most sensible
part of the retina of one eye, not to be placed in the axis,
but at some distance from it: and that, therefore, this more
sensible part of the retina is turned towards the object, to
which the other eye is directed, and thus causes squinting.
This ingenious hypothesis has been followed by Dr. Boerhaave, and many other eminent physicians. If it be true,
then if the sound eye be shut, and the distorted eye alone be
used to look at an object, it must still be as much distorted
as before, for the same reason: but the contrary is true in

fact; for if you desire such a person to close his other eye
and look at you with that which is usually distorted, he will
immediately turn the axis of it directly towards you.　If
you bid him open the undistorted eye, and look at you with
both eyes, you will find the axis of this last pointed at you
and the other turned away, and drawn close to the nose, or
perhaps to the upper eye lid.　From these facts, and some
others mentioned by Dr. Jurin, I think we may conclude
that this defect is seldom, if ever, occasioned by such a
preternatural make of the eye, as M. de la Hire supposed.

From the most accurate observations it will appear, that
by far the most common cause of squinting, is a defect in
the distorted eye.　Dr. Reid examined above twenty people
that squinted, and found in all of them a defect in the sight
of one eye: M. Buffon likewise, from a great number of
observations, has found that the true and original cause of
this blemish, is an inequality in the goodness, or in the limits of distinct vision, in the two eyes.　Dr. Porterfield says
this is generally the case with people who squint; and I have
found it so in all that I have had an opportunity of examining.

With regard to the nature of this defect, the distorted
eye is sometimes more convex, and sometimes more flat,
than the sound one; sometimes it does not depend upon
the convexity, but upon a weakness, or some other affection,
of the retina, of the nature of which we are ignorant.

It will be easy to conceive how this inequality of goodness
in the two eyes, when in a certain degree, must necessarily
occasion squinting, and that this blemish is not a bad habit, but a necessary one, which the person is obliged to

learn, in order to see with advantage. When the eyes are equally good, an object will appear more distinct and clear when viewed with both eyes than with only one; but the difference is very little. The ingenious Dr. Jurin, who has made some beautiful experiments to ascertain this point, has shown, that when the eyes are equal in goodness, we see more distinctly with both than with one, by about one thirteenth part only But M. Buffon has found that when the eyes are unequal, the case will be quite different. A small degree of inequality will make the object, when seen with the better eye alone, appear equally bright or clear, as when seen with both eyes; a little greater inequality will make the object appear less distinct when seen with both eyes, than when it is seen with the stronger eye alone; and a still greater inequality will render the object, when seen with both eyes, so confused, that in order to see it distinctly, one will be obliged to turn aside the weak eye, and put it into a situation where it cannot disturb the sight of the other. The truth of this may be easily proved by experiment. Let a person take a convex lens, and hold it about half an inch before one of his eyes; he will, by these means, render them very unequal. and if he attempt to read with both eyes, he will perceive a confusion in the letters, caused by this inequality; which confusion will disappear as soon as he shuts the eye which is covered with the lens, and looks only with the other.

Squinting is a necessary consequence of this inequality in the goodness of the two eyes; for a person whose eyes are to a certain degree unequal, finds that, when he looks at an object, he sees it very indistinctly; every conformation, or change of direction of his eyes which lessens the evil, will be agreeable; and he will acquire a habit of turning his eye towards the nose, not for the sake of seeing better with it, but in order to avoid, as much as possible, seeing at all with the distorted eye; for which purpose it will be drawn either under the upper eye lid, so that the pupil may be entirely or partially covered; or directly towards the nose, in which case the image of the object will fall at a distance from the axis of the eye: and it is a fact well known to philosophers, that we never naturally attend to an image which is at a distance from the axis; so that in this situation it will give little disturbance to the sight of the other.

It is easy to show that a squinting person very seldom, if ever, sees an object with the distorted eye. Indeed in above forty cases that I have examined, I found that when I placed an opaque body between the undistorted eye and the object, it immediately disappeared, nor were they able to see it at all, till they directed the axis of the distorted eye to the object. I find the same observation made by Dr. Reid and M. Buffon.

M. Buffon takes notice of a fact which I have often observed; viz. that many persons have their eyes very unequal without squinting.

When the difference is very considerable, the weak eye does not turn aside, because it can see almost nothing, and therefore cannot disturb the vision of the good eye. Also, when the inequality is but small, the weak eye will not turn aside, as it affords very little disturbance to the sight of the other: when the inequality consists in the difference of convexity, or difference of the limits of distinct vision, having the limits of distinct vision in each eye given, it may be calculated with some degree of accuracy what degree of inequality is necessary to produce squinting. It seems then that there are certain limits with regard to the inequality of the eyes, necessary to produce this deformity; and that if the inequality be either greater or less than these limits, the person will not squint.

Having now endeavoured to show what is the most common cause of squinting, I shall briefly attempt to point out those cases in which we may expect to effect a cure, and afterwards give a very short account of the most likely methods of doing it.

We cannot have great hopes of success, when there is a very great defect in the distorted eye. When the eyes are of different convexities, there is no other way of removing the deformity, than by bringing them to an equality by means of glasses, and then the person would only look straight when he used spectacles. When this defect is owing to a weakness in the distorted eye, it may sometimes be cured: M. Buffon observes that a weak eye acquires strength by exercise, and that many persons, whose squinting he had thought to be incurable, on account of the inequality of their eyes, having covered their good eye for a few minutes only, and consequently being obliged to exercise their bad one for that short time, were themselves surprised at the strength it had acquired, and on measuring their view afterwards, he found it to be more extended, and judged the squinting to be curable. In order therefore to judge with any certainty of the possibility of a cure, it ought always to be tried whether the distorted eye will grow better by exercise; if it does not, we can have little hopes of success; but when the eyes do not differ much in goodness, and it is found that the distorted eye acquires strength by exercise, a cure may then be attempted: and the best way of doing it, (according to M. Buffon) is to cover the good eye for some time, for, in this condition, the distorted eye will be obliged to act, and turn itself towards objects, which by degrees will become natural to it.

When the eyes are nearly brought to an equality by exercise, but cannot both be directed to the same point, Dr. Jurin's method may be practised, which is as follows.

If the person is of such an age, as to be capable of observing directions, place him directly before you, and let him close the undistorted eye, and look at you with the other; when you find the axis of this fixed directly upon you, bid him endeavour to keep it in that situation, and open the other eye; you will now see the distorted eye turn away from you towards his nose, and the axis of the other will be pointed towards you, but with patience and repeated trials he will, by degrees, be able to keep the distorted eye fixed upon you, at least for some time after the other is opened, and when you have brought him to keep the axis of both eyes fixed upon you, as you stand directly before him, it will be time to change his posture, and set him, first a little to one side of you, and then to the other, and so practise the same thing. And when, in all these situations, he can perfectly and readily turn the axes of both eyes towards you, the cure is effected. An adult person may practise all this before a mirror, without a director, though not so easily as with one: but the older he is, the more patience will be necessary.

With regard to the success of this method, M. Buffon says, that having communicated his scheme to several persons, and, among others, to M. Bernard de Jussieu, he had the satisfaction to find his opinion confirmed by an experiment of that gentleman, which is related by Mr. Allen, in his Synopsis Universae Medicinae. Dr. Jurin tells us that he had attempted a cure in this manner with flattering hopes of success, but was interrupted by the young gentleman's falling ill of the small pox, of which he died. Dr. Reid likewise tried it with success on three young gentlemen, and had brought them to look straight when they were upon their guard. Upon the whole this seems by much the most rational method of attempting to cure the deformity.

The only remaining morbid affections of the eye which I shall take notice of in this lecture, are two, which produce the indistinct vision of an object, by directly opposite means. The first is caused by the cornea, and crystalline, or either of them, being too convex, or the distance between the retina and crystalline being too great. It is evident, that from any of these causes, or all combined, the distinct picture of an object, at an ordinary distance, will fall before the retina, and therefore the picture on the retina itself must be confused, which will render the vision confused and indistinct; whence, in order to see things distinctly, people whose eyes are so formed are obliged to bring the object very near their eyes; by which means the rays fall upon the eye in a more diverging state, so that a distinct picture will be formed on the retina, by which the object will be distinctly seen: from the circumstance of such persons being obliged to hold objects near their eyes, in order to see them distinctly, they are called short sighted.

If a short sighted person look at an object through a small hole made in a card, he will be able to see even remote objects, with tolerable distinctness, for this lessens the circles of dissipation on the retina, and thus lessens the confusion in the picture. For the same purpose, we commonly observe short sighted people, when they wish to see distant objects more distinctly, almost shut their eye lids: and it is from this, says Dr. Porterfield, that short sighted persons were anciently called myopes.

The sight of myopes is remedied by a concave lens of proper concavity, which, by increasing the divergency of the rays, causes them to be united into a focus on the retina: and they do not require different glasses for different distances, for, if they have a lens which will make them see distinctly at the distance most commonly used by other persons, for example, at the distance at which persons whose eyes are good generally read, they will, by the help of the same glass, be able to see distinctly at all the distances at which good sighted people can see distinctly: for the cause of shortsightedness, is not a want of power to vary the conformation of the eye, but is owing to the whole quantity of refraction being too great for the distance of the retina from the cornea.

The other defect to be mentioned, is of an opposite nature, and persons labouring under it are called long sighted, or presbytae: it is caused by the cornea and crystalline, or either of them, being too flat in proportion to the distance between the crystalline and retina : whence it follows, that the rays which come from an object at an ordinary distance, will not be sufficiently refracted, and, consequently, will not meet at the retina, but beyond it, which will render the picture on the retina confused, and vision indistinct. Whence, in order to read, such persons are obliged to remove the book to a great distance, which lessens the divergency of the rays falling on the eye, and makes them converge to a focus sooner, so as to paint a distinct image on the retina.

The presbytical eye is remedied by a convex lens of proper convexity, which makes the rays converge to a focus sooner, and thus causes distinct vision : the sight of such persons is even more benefited by a convex lens, than that of myopes by a concave one ; for a convex lens not only makes the picture of the object on the retina distinct, but also more bright, by causing a greater quantity of light to enter the pupil ; while a concave one, at the same time that it renders vision distinct, diminishes the quantity of light.

Long sighted persons commonly become more so as they advance in years, owing to a waste of the humours of the eye; and even many people whose sight was very good in their youth, cannot see without spectacles when they grow old. The same waste in the humours of the eye, is the reason why shortsighted persons commonly become less so as they advance in years; so that many who were short-sighted in their youth, come to see very distinctly when they grow old. Dr. Smith seems to doubt this, and thinks that it is rather a hypothesis than a matter of fact. I have however myself seen several instances in confirmation of it; and it is very natural to suppose, that since short and long sight depend upon directly opposite causes, and since the latter is increased by age, the former must be diminished by it.

LECTURE IX.

THE LAWS OF ANIMAL LIFE.

In the preceding lectures I have taken a view, first of the general structure and functions of the living body, and next of the different organs called senses, by means of which we become acquainted with external objects. I shall next endeavour to show that, through the medium of these different senses, external objects affect us in a still different manner, and by their different action, keep us alive : for the human body is not an automaton; its life, and its different actions, depend continually on impressions made upon it by external objects. When the action of these ceases, either from their being withdrawn, or from the organization necessary to perceive them, being deranged or injured, the body becomes a piece of dead matter; becomes obedient to the common laws of chemical attraction, and is decomposed into its pristine elements, which, uniting with caloric, form gases ; which gases, being carried about in the atmosphere, or dissolved in water, are absorbed by plants, and contribute to their nourishment. These are devoured by animals, which in their turn die, and are decompounded; thus, in the living world, as well as in the inanimate, every thing is subject to change, and to be renewed perpetually

    " Look nature through, 'tis revolution all,

    All change, no death; day follows night; and night,

The dying day; stars rise, and set, and rise;
Earth takes th example; see the summer gay,
With her green chaplet, and ambrosial flowers,
Droops into pallid autumn; winter gray,
Horrid with frost, and turbulent with storm,
Blows autumn and his golden fruits away,
Then melts into the spring; soft spring with breath
Favonian, from warm chambers of the south
Recals the first.   All to reflourish, fades;
As in a wheel, all sinks to reascend."

The subject on which we are entering is of the utmost
importance; for, by pointing out the manner in which life is
supported and modified by the action of external powers,
it discovers to us the true and only means of promoting
health and longevity; for the action of these powers is generally within our own direction; and if the action of heat,
food, air, and exercise, were properly regulated, we should
have little to fear from the attacks of diseases.

When we examine the human body, the most curious and
unaccountable circumstance that we observe, is its life, or
its power of motion, sensation, and thought: for though the
structure of the different parts which we have examined
must excite our admiration and wonder, each part being
admirably fitted for the performance of its different functions,
yet without the breath of life, all these beautiful contrivances
would have been useless.   We have seen that the structure
of the eye indicates in its contriver, the most consummate
skill in optics; and of the ear the most perfect knowledge of
sounds; yet if sensibility had not being given to the nerves

which administer to these organs, the pulses of the air might have been communicated to the fluid in the labyrinth, and the rays of light might have formed images in the retina, without our being, in the smallest degree, conscious of their existence.

Though our efforts to discover the nature of life have hitherto been, and perhaps always will be, unsuccessful, yet we can, by a careful induction, or observation of facts, discover the laws by which it is governed, with respect to the action of external objects. This is what I shall now attempt to do.

The first observation which strikes us, is that of the very different effects that are produced when inanimate bodies act on each other, and when they exert their action on living matter.

When dead matter acts upon dead or inanimate matter, the only effects we perceive are mechanical, or chemical; that is, either motion, or the decomposition and new combination of their parts. If one ball strikes another, it communicates to it a certain quantity of motion, this is called mechanical action; and if a quantity of salt, or sugar, be put into water, the particles of salt, or sugar, will separate from each other, and join themselves to the particles of the water; these substances in these instances are said to act chemically on each other, and in all cases whatever, in which inanimate or dead bodies act on each other, the effects produced are motion, or chemical attraction; for though there may appear to be other species of action which sometimes take place, such as electric and magnetic attraction and repulsion, yet these are usually referred to the head of mechanical action or attraction.

But when dead matter acts upon those bodies we call

living, the effects produced are much different. There are many animals which pass the winter in a torpid state which has all the appearance of death; and they would continue in that state, if deprived of the influence of heat; now heat if applied to dead matter, will only produce motion, or chemical combination: in fluids it produces motions by occasioning a change in their specific gravity; and we know that it is one of the most powerful agents in chemical combination and decomposition; but these are the only effects it produces when it acts upon dead matter. But let us examine its effects when applied to living organized bodies. Bring a snake or other torpid animal into a moderately warm room, and observe what will be the consequence. After a short time the animal begins to move, to open its eyes and mouth; and when it has been subject to the action of heat for a longer time, it crawls about in search of food, and performs all the functions of life.

Here then, dead matter, when applied to the living body, produces the living functions, sense and motion: for if the heat had not been applied, the animal would have continued senseless, and apparently lifeless.

In more perfect animals, the effects produced by the action of dead matter upon them, are more numerous, and are different in different living systems; but are in general the following; sense and motion in almost all animals, and in many the power of thinking, and other affections of the mind.

The powers, or dead matters, which by their action produce these functions, are chiefly heat, food, and air. The proof that these powers do produce the living functions is in my opinion very satisfactory, for when their action is suspended, the living functions cease. If we take away, for instance, heat, air, and food, from animals, they soon become dead matter. This is as strong a proof that these matters are the cause of the functions, as that heat is the cause of the expansion of bodies, when we find that by withdrawing it the expansion ceases. Indeed it is not necessary that an animal should be deprived of all these powers to put a stop to the living functions; if any one of them is taken away, the body sooner or later becomes dead matter: it is found by experience, that if a man is deprived of air, he dies in about three or four minutes; for instance, if he is immersed under water: if he is deprived of heat, or in other words is exposed to a very severe degree of cold, he likewise soon dies; or if he is deprived of food, his death is equally certain, though more slow; it is sufficiently evident then that the living functions are owing to the action of these external powers upon the body

What I have here said is not confined to animals, but the living functions of vegetables are likewise caused by the action of dead matter upon them. The powers, which by their actions produce the living functions of vegetables, are principally heat, moisture, light, and air.

From what has been said, it clearly follows, that living bodies must have some property different from dead matter, which renders them capable of being acted on by these external powers, so as to produce the living functions; for if they had not, it is evident that the only effects which these powers could produce, would be mechanical, or chemical.

Though we know not exactly in what this property consists, or in what manner it is acted on, yet we see that when bodies are possessed of it, they become capable of being acted on by external powers, so as to produce the living functions.

We may call this property, with Haller, irritability, or, with Brown, excitability; or we may use vital principle, or any other term, could we find one more appropriate. I shall use the term excitability, as perhaps the least liable to exception, and in using this term, it is necessary to mention that I mean only to express a fact, without the smallest intention of pointing out the nature of that property which distinguishes living from dead matter; and in this we have the illustrious example of Newton, who called that property which causes bodies in certain situations to approach each other, gravitation, without in the least hinting at its nature. Yet though he knew not what gravitation was, he investigated the laws by which bodies were acted on by it, and thus solved a number of phenomena which were before inexplicable: in the same manner, though we are ignorant of the nature of excitability, or of the property which distinguishes living from dead matter, we can investigate the laws by which dead matter acts upon living bodies through this medium. We know not what magnetic attraction is, yet we can investigate its laws: the same may be observed with respect to electricity. If ever we should obtain a knowledge of the nature of this property, it would make no alteration in the laws which we had before discovered.

Before we proceed to the investigation of the laws by which the living principle or excitability is acted on, it will be first necessary to define some terms, which I shall have occasion to use, to avoid circumlocution: and here it may not be improper to observe, that most of our errors in reasoning have arisen from want of strict attention to this circumstance, the accurate definition of those terms which we use in our reasoning. We may use what terms we please, provided we accurately define them, and adhere strictly to the definition. On this depends the excellence and certainty of the mathematical sciences. The terms are few, and accurately defined; and in their different chains of reasoning mathematic ans adhere with the most scrupulous strictness to the original definition of the terms. If the same method were made use of in reasoning on other subjects, they would approach to the mathematics in simplicity and in truth, and the science of medicine in particular would be stripped of the heaps of learned rubbish which now encumber it, and would appear in true and native simplicity Such is the method I propose to follow: I am certain of the rectitude of the plan; of the success of the reasoning it does not become me to judge.

When the excitability is in such a state as to be very susceptible of the action of external powers, I shall call it abundant or accumulated; but when it is found in a state not very capable of receiving their action, I say it is deficient or exhausted. Let no one however suppose that by these terms I mean to hint in the least at the nature of the excitability. I do not mean by them that it is really at one time increased in quantity or magnitude, and at another time diminished: its abstract nature is by no means attempted to be investigated. These or similar terms the poverty or imperfection of language obliges us to use. We know nothing of the nature of the excitability or vital principle, and by the terms here used I mean only to say, that the excitability is sometimes easily acted on by the external powers, and then I call it abundant or accumulated; at other times the living body is with more difficulty excited, and then I say the vital principle or excitability, whatever it may be, is deficient or exhausted.

On examination we shall find the laws by which external powers act on living bodies to be the following.

First, when the powerful action of the exciting powers ceases for some time, the excitability accumulates, or becomes more capable of receiving their action, and is more powerfully affected by them.

If we examine separately the different exciting powers which act on the body, we shall find abundant confirmation of this law   Besides the exciting powers which act on the body, which I mentioned ; viz. heat, food, and air, there are several others, such as light, sound, odorous substances, &c. which will be examined in their proper places. These powers, acting by a certain impulse, and producing a vigorous action of the body, are called stimulants, and life we shall find to be the effect of these and other stimulants acting on the excitability.

The stimulus of light, though its influence in this respect is feeble, when compared with some other external powers, yet has its proportion of force. This stimulus acts upon the body through the medium of the organ of vision.   Its influence on the animal spirits strongly demonstrates its connexion with animal life, and hence we find a cheerful and depressed state of mind in many people, and more especially in invalids, to be intimately connected with the presence or absence of the sun. Indeed to be convinced of the effects of light we have only to examine its influence on vegetables. Some of them lose their colour when deprived of it, many of them discover a partiality to it in the direction of their flowers; and all of them perspire oxygen gas only when exposed to it; nay it would seem that organization, sensation, spontaneous motion, and life, exist only at the surface of the earth, and in places exposed to light. Without light nature is lifeless, inanimate, and torpid.

Let us now examine if the action of light upon the body is subject to the law that has been mentioned. If a person be kept in darkness for some time, and then be brought into a room in which there is only an ordinary degree of light, it will be almost too oppressive for him, and will appear excessively bright; and if he have been kept for a considerable time in a very dark place, the sensation will be very painful. In this case, while the retina or optic nerve was deprived of light, its excitability accumulated, or became more easily affected by light: for if a person go out of one room into another, which has an equal degree of light, he will perceive no effect.

You may convince yourselves of the truth of this law, by a very simple experiment; shut your eyes, and cover them for a minute or two with your hand, and endeavour not to think of the light, or what you are doing; then open them, and the daylight will for a short time appear brighter.

If you look attentively at a window for about two minutes, then cast your eyes upon a sheet of white paper, the shape of the window frames will be perfectly visible upon the paper; those parts which express the wood work appearing brighter than the other parts. The parts of the optic nerve on which the image of the frame falls, are covered by the wood work from the action of the light; the excitability of these parts will therefore accumulate; and the parts of the paper which fall upon them must of course appear brighter.

If a person be brought out of a dark room where he has been confined, into a field covered with snow, when the sun shines, it has been known to affect him so much as to deprive him of sight altogether.

This law is well exemplified when we come into a dark room in the day time. At first we can see nothing; but with the absence of light the excitability accumulates, and we begin to have an imperfect glimpse of the objects around us; after a while the excitability of the retina is so far accumulated, and we become so sensible of the feeble light reflected from the surfaces of bodies, that we can discern their shapes, and sometimes even their colours.

Let us next consider what happens with respect to heat, which is a uniform and active stimulus in promoting life. The extensive influence of heat upon animal life is evident from its decay and suspension during winter, in certain animals, and from its revival upon the approach and action of the vernal sun.

If this stimulus is for some time abstracted from the whole body, or from any part, the excitability accumulates, or, in other words, if the body has been for some time exposed to cold, it is more liable to be affected by heat afterwards applied. Of this also you may be convinced by an easy experiment. Put one of your hands into cold water, and then put both into water which is considerably warm: the hand which has been in the cold water will feel much warmer than the other. If you handle some snow in one hand while you keep the other in the bosom, that it may be of the same heat with the body, and then bring both within the same distance of the fire, the heat will affect the cold hand infinitely more than the warm one. This is a circumstance of the utmost importance, and ought always to be carefully attended to. When a person has been exposed to a severe degree of cold for some time, he ought to be cautious how he comes near a fire, for his excitability will be so much accumulated that the heat will act very violently, often producing a great degree of inflammation, and even sometimes of mortification. This is a very common cause of chilblains, and other similar inflammations. When the hands, or any other parts of the body, have been exposed to a violent cold, they ought first to be put in cold water, or even rubbed with snow, and exposed to warmth in the gentlest manner possible.

The same law regulates the action of food, or matters taken into the stomach: if a person have for some time been deprived of food, or have taken it in small quantity, whether it be meat or drink, or if he have taken it of a less stimulating quality, he will find that when he returns to his ordinary mode of life it will have more effect upon him than before he lived abstemiously.

Persons who have been shut up in a coal work, from the falling in of the pit, and have had nothing to eat for two or three days, have been as much intoxicated by a bason of broth, as a person in common circumstances with two or three bottles of wine.

This circumstance was particularly evident among the poor sailors who were in the boat with Captain Bligh after the mutiny. The Captain was sent by government to convey some plants of the bread fruit tree from Otaheite to the West Indies : soon after he left Otaheite the crew mutinied, and put the captain and most of the officers, with some of the men, on board the ship's boat, with a very short allowance of provisions, and particularly of liquors, for they had only six quarts of rum, and six bottles of wine, for nineteen people, who were driven by storms about the south sea, exposed to wet and cold all the time, for nearly a month; each man was allowed only a teaspoonful of rum a day, but this teaspoonful refreshed the poor men, benumbed as they were with cold, and faint with hunger, more than twenty times the quantity would have done those who were warm and well fed; and had it not been for the spirit having such power to act upon men in their condition, they never could have outlived the hardships they experienced. All these facts, and many others which might be brought forward, establish, beyond dispute, the truth of the law I mentioned; viz. that when the powerful action of the exciting powers ceases for some time, the excitability accumulates, or becomes more capable of receiving their actions, and is more powerfully affected by them.

When the legs or arms have for some time been exposed to cold, the slightest exertion, or even the stimulus of a gentle heat, throws the muscles into an inordinate action or cramp.   The glow of the skin, in coming out of a cold bath, may be explained on the same principle.   The heat of the skin is diminished by the conducting power of the water, in consequence of which the excitability of the cutaneous vessels accumulates; and the same degree of heat afterwards applied, excites these now more irritable vessels to a great degree of action.

On this principle depends the supposed stimulant or tonic powers of cold, the nature of whose action has been much mistaken by physicians and physiologists.   Heat is allowed to be a very powerful stimulus; but cold is only a diminution of heat; how then can cold act as a stimulus?   In my opinion it never does; but its effects may be explained by the general law which we have been investigating.   When a lesser stimulus than usual has been applied to the body, the excitability accumulates, and is then affected by a stimulus even less than that which, before this accumulation, produced no effect whatever.   The cold only renders the body more subject to the action of heat afterwards applied, by allowing the excitability to be accumulated.   No person, I believe, ever brought on an inflammation, or inflammatory complaint, by exposure to cold, however long might have been that exposure, or however great the cold; but if a person have been out in the cold air, and afterwards come into a warm room, an inflammatory complaint will most probably be the consequence.

Indeed coming out of the cold air into a moderately warm room generally produces a lively and continued warmth in the parts that have been exposed.

The second general law is, that when the exciting powers

have acted with violence for a considerable time, the excitability becomes exhausted, or less fit to be acted on; and this we shall be able to prove by a similar induction.

Let us first examine the effects of light upon the eye: when it has acted violently for some time on the optic nerve, it diminishes the excitability of that nerve, and renders it incapable of being affected by a quantity of light, that would at other times affect it. When we have been walking out in the snow, if we come into a room, we shall scarcely be able to see any thing for some minutes.

If you look stedfastly at a candle for a minute or two, you will with difficulty discern the letters of a book which you were before reading distinctly. When our eyes have been exposed to the dazzling blaze of phosphorus in oxygen gas, we can scarcely see any thing for some time afterwards, and if we look at the sun, the excitability of the optic nerve is so overpowered by the strong stimulus of his light, that nothing can be seen distinctly for a considerable time. If we look at the setting sun, or any other luminous object of a small size, so as not greatly to fatigue the eye, this part of the retina becomes less sensible to smaller quantities of light; hence when the eyes are turned on other less luminous parts of the sky, a dark spot is seen resembling the shape of the sun, or other luminous object on which our eyes have been fixed.

On this account it is that we are some time before we can distinguish objects in an obscure room, after coming from broad daylight, as I observed before.

We shall next consider the action of heat. Suppose water to be heated to 90°, if one hand be put into it, it will appear warm; but if the other hand be immersed in water heated to 120°, and then put into the water heated to 90°, that water will appear cold, though it will still feel warm to the other hand: for the excitability of the hand has been exhausted, by the greater stimulus of heat, to such a degree as to be insensible of a less stimulus.

Before we go into a warm bath, the temperature of the air may seem very warm and pleasant to the body, even though exposed naked to it; but after we have remained for some time in the warm bath, we feel the air, when we come out, very cool and chilling, though it is of the same temperature as before; for the hot water exhausts the excitability of the vessels of the skin, and renders them less capable of being affected by a smaller degree of heat. Thus we see that the effects of the hot and cold bath are different and opposite; the one debilitates by stimulating, and the other produces stimulant or tonic effects by debilitating. This seeming paradox may, however, be easily explained by the principles we have laid down; and though the hot and cold bath produce such different effects, yet it is only the same fluid, with a small variation in the degree of temperature; but these effects depend on the temperature of our body being such, that a small decrease of it will produce an accumulation of excitability, while a small increase will exhaust it.

I shall next proceed to examine the effects of the substances taken into the stomach; and as the effects of spirituous and vinous liquors are a little more remarkable than those of food, I shall first begin with them.

A person who is not accustomed to take these liquors, will be intoxicated by a quantity that will produce no effect upon one who has been some time accustomed to take them; and when a person has used himself to these stimulants for some time, the ordinary powers which in common support life, will not have their proper effects upon him, because his excitability has been, in some measure, exhausted by these stimulants.

The same holds good with respect to tobacco and opium; a person accustomed to take opium, or smoke tobacco, will not be affected by a quantity that would completely intoxicate one not used to them, because the excitability has been so far exhausted by the use of those stimulants, that it cannot be acted on by a smaller quantity.

That tobacco or opium act in the same manner as wine or spirits, scarce needs any illustration. In Turkey they intoxicate themselves with opium, in the same way that people in this country do with wine and spirits; and those who have been accustomed to take this drug for a considerable time, feel languid and depressed when they are deprived of it for some time; they repair to the opium houses, as our dram drinkers do to the gin shops in the morning, sullen, dejected, and silent; in an hour or two, however, they are all hilarity. This shows the effects of opium to be stimulant. Tobacco intoxicates those who are not accustomed to it, and in those who are, it produces a serene and composed state of mind by its stimulating effects. Like opium and fermented liquors it exhausts the excitability, and leaves the person dejected, and all his senses blunted, when its stimulant effects are over.

That what is more properly called food acts in the same way as the substances I have just examined, is evident from the fact which I mentioned some time ago, that persons whose excitability has been accumulated, by their being deprived of food for some days, have been intoxicated by a bason of broth.

These facts, with innumerable others which will easily suggest themselves, prove, beyond doubt, the truth of the second law, namely, that when the exciting powers have acted violently, or for a considerable time, the excitability is exhausted, or less fit to be acted on.

Besides the stimulants which I have mentioned, there are several others which act upon the body, many of which will hereafter be considered: but all act according to this law; when their action has been suspended or diminished, the excitability of the organ on which they act becomes accumulated, or more easily affected by their subsequent action; and, on the contrary, when their action has been violent, or long continued, the excitability becomes exhausted, or less fit to receive their actions.

Among the stimulants acting on the body, we may mention sound, which has an extensive influence on human life. I need not mention here its numerous natural, or artificial sources, as that has been fully done in a preceding lecture. The effect of music, in stimulating and producing a state of mind approaching to intoxication, is universally known. Indeed the influence of certain sounds in stimulating, and thereby increasing, the powers of life, cannot be denied. Fear produces debility, which has a tendency to death. Sound obviates this debility, and restores to the system its natural degree of excitement. The schoolboy and the clown

24

invigorate their trembling limbs, by whistling, or singing, as they pass by a country churchyard, and the soldier feels his departing courage recalled in the onset of a battle, by the " spirit stirring drum."

Intoxication is generally attended with a higher degree of life or excitement than is natural. Now sound will produce this effect with a very moderate portion of fermented liquor; hence we find persons much more easily intoxicated and highly excited at public entertainments, where there is music and loud talking, than in private companies, where no auxiliary stimulus is added to that of wine.

Persons who are destitute of hearing and seeing, possess life in a more languid state than other people; which is, in a great degree, owing to the want of the stimulus of light and noise.

Odours have likewise a very sensible effect in promoting animal life. The effects of these will appear obvious in the sudden revival of life, which they produce, in cases of fainting. The smell of a few drops of hartshorn, or even a burnt feather, has frequently, in a few minutes, restored the system from a state of weakness, bordering upon death, to an equable and regular degree of excitement.

All these different stimuli undoubtedly produce the greatest effects upon their proper organs; thus the effect of light is most powerful on the eye; that of sound on the ear; that of food on the stomach, &c. But their effects are not confined to these organs, but extended over the whole body. The excitability exists, one and indivisible, over the whole system;

we may call it sensibility, or feeling, to enable us to understand the subject.   Every organ, or indeed the whole body,
is endowed with this property in a greater or less degree,
so that the effects produced by any stimulus, though they
are more powerful on the part where they are applied, affect the whole system : odours afford an instance of this;
and the prick of a pin in the finger, produces excitement, or
a stimulant effect, over the whole body.

From what has been said, it must be evident that life is
the effect of a number of external powers, constantly acting
on the body, through the medium of that property which
we call excitability; that it cannot exist independent of the
action of these stimuli ; when they are withdrawn, though the
excitability does not instantly vanish, there is no life, no
motion, but the semblance of death. Life, therefore, is constantly supported by, and depends constantly on, the action
of external powers on the excitability: without excitability
these stimulants would produce no effect, and whatever may
be the nature of the excitability, or however abundant it
may be, still, without the action of external powers, no life
is produced.

From what has been said, we may see the reason why
life is in a languid state in the morning : It acquires vigour
by the gradual and successive application of stimuli in the
forenoon: It is in its most perfect state about midday,
and remains stationary for some hours : From the diminution or exhaustion of the excitability, it lessens in the evening, and becomes more languid at bed time; when, from
defect of excitability, the usual exciting powers will no

longer produce their effect, a torpid state ensues, which we call sleep, during which, the exciting powers cannot act upon us; and this diminution of their action allows the excitability to accumulate; and, to use the words of Dr. Armstrong,

" Ere morn the tonic, irritable nerves
Feel the fresh impulse, and awake the soul."

LECTURE X.

THE LAWS OF ANIMAL LIFE, CONTINUED.

In the last lecture I began to investigate the laws by which living bodies are governed, and the effects produced by the different exciting powers, which support life, upon the excitability, or vital principle. The facts which we examined led us to two conclusions, which, when properly applied, we shall find will explain most of the phenomena of life, both in health, and in disease. The conclusions alluded to, are these: when the exciting powers have acted more feebly, or weakly, than usual, for some time; or when their action is withdrawn, the excitability accumulates, and becomes more powerfully affected by their subsequent action. And, on the contrary, when the action of these powers has been exerted with violence, or for a considerable time, the excitability becomes exhausted, and less fit to receive their actions.

A number of facts were mentioned in proof of these conclusions, and a great number more might have been brought forwards, could it have served any other purpose than to have taken up our time, which I hope may be better employed.

This exhaustion of the excitability, by stimulants, may either be final, or temporary. We see animals, while the exciting powers continue to act, at first appear in their greatest vigour, then gradually decay, and at last come into that state, in which, from the long continued action of the exciting powers, the excitability is entirely exhausted, and death takes place.

We likewise see vegetables in the spring, while the exciting powers have acted on them moderately, and for a short time, arrayed in their verdant robes, and adorned with flowers of many mingling hues; but as the exciting powers, which support their life, continue to be applied, and some of them, for instance heat, as the summer advances, become increased, they first lose their verdure, then grow brown, and at the end of summer cease to live: because their excitability is exhausted by the long continued action of the exciting powers: and this does not happen merely in consequence of the heat of the summer decreasing, for they grow brown, and die, even in a greater degree of heat than that which in spring made them grow luxuriantly. In some of the finest days of autumn, in which the sun acts with more power than in the spring, the vegetable tribe droop, in consequence of this exhausted state of their excitability, which renders them nearly insensible of the action, even of a powerful stimulus.

These are examples of the final or irreparable exhaustion of the excitability; but we find also that it may be exhausted for a time, and accumulated again. Though the eye has been so dazzled by the splendour of light, that it cannot see an object moderately illuminated, yet if it be shut for some time, the excitability of the optic nerve will accumulate again, and we shall again be capable of seeing with an ordinary light.

We find also that we are not always equally capable of performing the functions of life. When we have been engaged in any exertion, either mental or corporeal, for some hours only, we find ourselves languid and fatigued, and unfit to pursue our labours much longer.

If in this state several of the exciting powers are withdrawn, particularly light and noise, and if we are laid in a posture which does not require much muscular exertion, we soon fall into that state which nature intended for the accumulation of the excitability, and which we call sleep. In this state many of the exciting powers cannot act upon us, unless applied with some violence, for we are insensible to their moderate action. A moderate degree of light, or a moderate noise, does not affect us, and the power of thinking, which very much exhausts the excitability, is in a great measure suspended. When the action of these powers has been suspended for six or eight hours, the excitability is again capable of being acted on, and we rise fresh and vigorous, and fit to engage in our occupations.

Sleep then is the method which nature has provided to repair the exhausted constitution, and restore the vital energy. Without its refreshing aid, our worn out habits would scarcely be able to drag on a few days, or at most, a few weeks, before the vital spring would be quite run down: how properly therefore has our great poet called sleep " the chief nourisher in life's feast!"

From the internal sensations, often excited, it is natural to conclude, that the nerves of sense are not torpid during sleep, but that they are only precluded from the perception of external objects, by the external organs being in some

way or other rendered unfit to transmit to them the impulses
of bodies during the suspension of the power of volition;
thus the eyelids are closed, in sleep, to prevent the impulse
of light from acting on the optic nerve; and it is very probable that the drum of the ear is not stretched; it seems
likewise reasonable to conclude, that something similar
happens to the external apparatus of all our organs of sense,
which may make them unfit for their office of perception
during sleep.

The more violently the exciting powers have acted, the
sooner is sleep brought on, because the excitability is sooner exhausted, and therefore sooner requires the means of
renewing it: and, on the contrary, the more weakly these
powers have acted, the less are we inclined to sleep. Instances of the first are, excess of exercise, strong liquors,
or study; and of the latter, an under or deficient proportion
of these.

A person who has been daily accustomed to much exercise, whether mental or corporeal, if he omit it, will find
little or no inclination to sleep; this state may however be
induced by taking some diffusible stimulus, as a little spirits
and water, or opium, which seem to act entirely by exhausting the excitability, to that degree which is compatible with
sleep, and, when the stimulant effect of these substances are
over, the person soon falls into that state.

But though the excitability may have been sufficiently exhausted, and the action of external powers considerably
moderated, yet there are some things within ourselves, which
often stimulate violently, and prevent sleep, such as pain,
thirst, and strong passions and emotions of the mind. These

all tend to drive away sleep, by their vehement stimulating effect, which still has power to rouse the excitability to action, though it has been considerably exhausted. The best method of inducing sleep, in these cases, is to endeavour to withdraw the mind from these impressions, particularly from uneasy emotions, by employing it on something that makes a less impression, and which does not require much exertion, or produce too much commotion ; such as counting to a thousand, or counting drops of water which fall slowly; by listening to the humming of bees, or the murmuring of a rivulet. Virgil describes a situation fitted to induce sleep, most beautifully, in the following words.

> " Fortunate senex, hic inter flumina nota,
> Et fontes sacros, frigus captabis opacum.
> Hinc tibi, quae semper vicino ab limite sepes
> Hyblaeis apibus florem depasta salicti,
> Saepe levi somnum suadebit inire susurro."

In infancy much sleep is required; the excitability, being then extremely abundant, is soon exhausted by external stimulants, and therefore soon requires renewing or accumulating; on this account, during the first five or six months of their life, children require this mode of renewing their exhausted excitability several times in the day: as they advance in years, and as this excess of excitability is exhausted by the application of stimulants, less sleep is required: in the prime of life least of all is necessary. There is great difference however, in this respect, in different constitutions. Some persons are sufficiently refreshed by three or four hours sleep, while others require eight or ten hours. More however depends, in my opinion, on the mode of living. Those who indulge in the use of spirituous or fermented liquors, which exhaust the excitability to a great degree, require much more sleep than those who are content with the crystal stream. The latter never feel themselves stupid or heavy after dinner, but are immediately fit to engage in study or business. As age advances, more sleep is again required; and the excitability at last becomes so far exhausted, and the system so torpid, that the greatest portion of gradually expiring life is spent in sleep.

Temperance and exercise are the most conducive to sound healthy sleep, hence the peasant is rewarded, for his toil and frugal mode of life, with a blessing, which is seldom enjoyed by those whom wealth renders indolent and luxurious. The poor in the country enjoy sound and sweet sleep: forced by necessity to labour, their excitability becomes exhausted in a proper and natural manner, and they retire to rest early in the evening. Their sleep is generally sound, and early in the morning they find themselves recruited, and in a state fit to resume their daily labour. The blooming complexion, strength, and activity, of these hardy children of labour, who recruit their wearied limbs on pallets of straw, form a striking contrast with the pallid and sickly visage, and debilitated constitution of the luxurious and wealthy, who convert night into day, and court repose in vain on beds of down. Nature undoubtedly intended that we should be awake, and follow our occupations, whether of pleasure or business, during the cheering light of day, and take repose when the sun withdraws his rays. All other animals, and even vege-

tables, obey the command of nature: man alone is refractory;
but nature's laws are never violated with impunity. Dr.
Mackenzie very properly observes, that those who sleep long
in the morning, and sit up all the night, injure the constitution without gaining time: and those who do this merely
in compliance with fashion, ought not to repine at a fashionable state of bad health.

From what has been said, it is evident that, in order to
enjoy sound sleep, our chambers should be free from noise,
dark, and moderately cold; because the stimulant effects of
noise, light, and heat, prevent the accumulation of excitability:
and as we shall afterwards see that this accumulation depends
on free respiration, and the introduction of oxygen by that
means into the system, our bed rooms ought to be large and
airy, and, in general, the beds should not be surrounded by
curtains. We may from this likewise see the reason why it
is so desirable to sleep in the country, even though we are
obliged to spend the day in town.

These observations on sleep have however led me a little
from the direct road; but I thought they could not be better introduced than here. I shall now return to the subject
of our more immediate inquiry.

By induction we have discovered two of the principal laws
by which living bodies are governed: the first is, that when
the ordinary powers which support life have been suspended,
or their action has been lessened for a time, the excitability, or vital principle, accumulates, or becomes more fit to
receive their actions; and secondly, when these powers have
acted violently, or for a considerable time, the excitability
is exhausted, or becomes less fit to receive their actions.

There are therefore three states in which living bodies exist.
First, a state of accumulated excitability. Secondly, a state
of exhausted excitability Thirdly, when the excitability is
in such a state as to produce the strongest and most healthy
actions, when acted upon by the external powers.

From what has been said, it must be evident that life depends continually on the action of external powers on the
excitability, and that by their continued action, if they be
properly regulated, the excitability will be gradually, and
insensibly exhausted, and life will be resigned into the hands
of him who gave it, without a struggle, and without a
groan.

We see then that nature operates in supporting the living
part of the creation, by laws as simple and beautiful as those
by which the animated world is governed. In the latter
we see the order and harmony which is observed by the
planets, and their satellites, in their revolution round the
great source of heat and light ;

> " —————— — ——— all combin'd
> And ruled unerring, by that Single Power,
> Which draws the stone projected, to the ground.

In the animated part of the creation, we observe those
beautiful phenomena which are exhibited by an almost infinite variety of individuals ; all depending upon, and produced by one simple law ; the acting of external powers upon
their excitability

I cannot express my admiration of the wisdom of the
Creator better than in the words of Thomson.

" O unprofuse magnificence divine!
O wisdom truly perfect! thus to call
From a few causes such a scheme of life;
Effects so various, beautiful, and great."

Life then, or those functions which we call living, are the effects of certain exciting powers acting on the excitability, or property distinguishing living from dead matter. When these effects, viz. the functions, flow easily, pleasantly, and completely, from the action of these powers, they indicate that state which we call health.

We may therefore, as we before hinted, distinguish three states of the irritable fibre, or three different degrees of excitability, of which the living body is susceptible.

1. The state of health which is peculiar to each individual, and which has been called by Haller, and other physiologists, the tone of the fibre. This is produced by a middle degree of stimulus acting upon a middle degree of excitability: and the effect produced by this action, we call excitement.

2. The state of accumulation, produced by the absence or diminished action of the accustomed stimuli.

3. The state of exhaustion, produced by the too powerful action of stimuli; and this may be produced either by the too powerful, or long continued action of the common stimulants which support life, such as food, air, heat, and exercise; or it may be caused by an application of stimulants, which act more powerfully on the excitability, and which exhaust it more quickly, such as wine, spirits, and opium, musk, camphor, and various other articles used in medicines.

The state of health, or tone, if we use that term, consists therefore in a certain quantity or energy of excitability necessary to its preservation. To maintain this state, the action of the stimuli should be strong enough to carry off from the body the surplus of this irritable principle. To obtain this end, a certain equilibrium is necessary between the excitability and the stimuli applied, or the sum of all the stimuli acting upon it must be always nearly equal, and sufficient to prevent an excess of excitability, but not so strong as to carry off more than this excess. It is in this equilibrium between the acting stimuli and the excitability, that the health, or tone of the living body consists.

When the sum of the stimuli, acting on the body, is so small, as not to carry off the excess of excitability, it accumulates, and diseases of irritability are produced. Of this nature are those diseases to which the poor are often subject, and which will be particularly considered hereafter.

When the sum of the stimuli acting on the body, is too great, it is deprived not only of the excess of excitability, but also of some portion of the irritable principle necessary for the tone of the body: or, to speak more distinctly, the body loses more excitability than it receives, and of course must, in a short time, be in a state of exhaustion. This gives rise to diseases which afflict drinkers, or those who indulge in any kind of intemperance, or persons born in climates where the temperature is moderate, but who emigrate to those which are much warmer.

Thus we have endeavoured, after the example of Dr. Brown, to ascertain the cause of the healthy state, before the causes of diseases were investigated; and though this is contrary to the general practice, yet it must be evident to every one, that unless we are acquainted with the causes of good health, it will be impossible for us to form any estimate of those variations from that state, called diseases: hence it is that a number of diseases, which have been brought on merely by the undue action of the exciting powers, such as gout, rheumatism, and the numerous trains of nervous complaints, which were by no means understood, may be easily and satisfactorily explained, and as easily cured, by restoring the proper action of these powers, and bringing the excitability to its proper state. As this theory, therefore, is so important, not only in respect to the preservation of health, which nearly concerns every individual, but to the cure of diseases, which is the province of the physician, I have endeavoured to explain it as fully and minutely as possible; to make it still plainer we may perhaps make use of the following illustration.

Suppose a fire to be made in a grate or furnace, filled with a kind of fuel not very combustible, and which could only be kept burning by means of a machine, containing several tubes placed before it, and constantly pouring streams of air into it. Suppose also a pipe to be fixed in the back of the chimney, through which a constant supply of fresh fuel is gradually let down into the grate, to repair the waste occasioned by the combustion kept up by the air machine.

The grate will represent the human body; the fuel in it the life or excitability, and the tube behind, supplying fresh fuel, will denote the power of all living systems, constantly to regenerate or produce excitability; the air machine, consisting of several tubes, may denote the various stimuli applied to the excitability of the body; the flame produced in consequence of that application, represents life : the product of the exciting powers acting upon the excitability

Here we see, that flame, like life, is drawn forth from fuel by the constant application of streams of air, poured into it from the different tubes of the machine. When the quantity of air poured in through these different tubes is sufficient to consume the fuel as it is supplied, a constant and regular flame will be produced: but if we suppose that some of them are stopped, or that they do not supply a sufficient quantity of air, then the fuel will accumulate, and the flame will be languid and smothered, but liable to break out with violence, when the usual quantity of air is supplied.

On the contrary, if we suppose a greater quantity of air to rush through the tubes, then the fuel will be consumed or exhausted faster than it is supplied ; and in order therefore to reduce the combustion to the proper degree, the quantity of air supplied must be diminished, and the quantity of fuel increased.

If we suppose one of the tubes, instead of common air, to supply oxygen gas, it will represent the action of wine, spirits, ether, opium, and other powerful stimulants upon the body: a bright and vivid flame will be produced, which however will only be of short duration, for the fuel will be consumed faster than it is supplied, and a state of exhaustion will take place.

We may carry this illustration still further, and suppose that the air tubes exhaust the fuel every day faster than it can be supplied, then it will be necessary at night to stop up some of the tubes, so that the expense of fuel may be less than its supply, in order to make up for the deficiency. When this is made up, the tubes may in the morning be opened, and the combustion carried on during the day as usual. This will illustrate the nature of sleep. In speaking of this subject, it was observed, that the more violently the exciting powers have acted, the sooner is sleep brought on; because the excitability is sooner exhausted. In the same way the more the air rushes through the tubes, the sooner will the fuel be consumed, and want replenishing. When the exciting powers have acted feebly, a person feels no inclination to sleep, because the excitability is not exhausted to the proper degree, and therefore does not want accumulating. But any diffusible stimulus, as spirits, or opium, will soon exhaust it to the proper degree.

In the same way, if the air have not passed rapidly through the tubes, the fuel will not be exhausted: but it may be brought to a proper degree of exhaustion by the application of oxygen gas.

When the air which nourishes the flame is so regulated, that it consumes the fuel as it is supplied, but no faster, a clear and steady flame will be kept up, which will go on as long as the fuel lasts, or the grate resists the action of the fire: but at last when the fuel, which we do not suppose inexhaustible, is burnt out, the fire must cease.

In the same manner, if the different exciting powers which support life were properly regulated, all the functions of the body would be properly performed, and we should pass our life in a state of health, seldom known to any but savages, and brute animals not under the dominion of man, who regulate these powers merely by the necessities of nature.

When air is applied in too great quantity, and especially if some of the tubes convey oxygen gas, then a violent combustion and flame is excited, which will, in all probability, consume or burn out the furnace or grate, or if it do not, it will burn out the fuel, and thus exhaust itself.

In like manner, if the stimulants which support life be made to act too powerfully, and particularly if any powerful stimulus, not natural to the body, such as wine or spirits, be taken in too great quantity, a violent inflammatory action will be the consequence, which may destroy the human machine: but if it do not, it will exhaust the excitability, and thus bring on great debility.

This analogy might be pursued further, but my intention was solely to illustrate some of the outlines of our theory, by a comparison which may facilitate the conception of the manner in which external powers act on living bodies. The different powers which support life, and without whose action we are unable to exist, such as heat, food, air, &c. have been very improperly called nonnaturals, a term which is much more applicable to those substances which we are daily in the habit of receiving into the system, which excite it to undue actions, and which nature never intended we should receive; such as spirituous and fermented liquors, and high seasoned foods. In the preceding illustration, I have spoken of a tube, as constantly pouring in fresh fuel, because it was not easy otherwise to convey a familiar idea of the power which all living systems possess of renewing their excitability, when exhausted. The excitability is an unknown somewhat, subject to peculiar laws, some of which we have examined, but whose different states we are obliged to describe, though, perhaps, inaccurately, by terms borrowed from the qualities of material substances.

Though Dr. Brown very properly declined entering into the consideration of the nature of excitability, or the manner in which it is produced, the discoveries which have been made in chemistry since his time, have thrown great light on the subject, and it is now rendered highly probable that the excitability or vital principle, is communicated to the body by the circulation, and is intimately connected with the process of oxidation.

Many circumstances would tend to show, that a strict connexion exists between the reception of oxygen into the body, and the vital principle.

When an animal has been killed by depriving it of oxygen gas, the heart and other muscles, and indeed the whole system, will be found completely to have lost its excitability. This is not the case when an animal is killed in a different manner. When an animal is shot, or killed in the common manner, by bleeding to death, if the heart be taken out, it will contract for some hours, on the application of stimulants. But this is not the case with an animal that has been drowned, or killed by immersion in carbonic acid, azotic, or hydrogenous gases; in these last instances, the heart either does not contract at all, or very feebly, on the application of the strongest stimulants.

We have already seen that oxygen unites with the blood in the lungs, during respiration: by the circulation of the blood it is distributed to every part of the system, and we shall find, that in proportion to its abundance is the excitability of the body. In proof of this, I shall relate some facts and experiments.

Dr. Girtanner injected a quantity of very pure oxygen gas into the jugular vein of a dog: the animal raised terrible outcries, breathed very quickly, and with great difficulty: by little and little his limbs became hard and stiff, he fell asleep, and died in the course of a few minutes afterwards. It ought here to be observed, that any of the gases, or almost any fluid, however mild, when thus suddenly introduced into the circulating system, generally, and speedily, occasions death.

On opening the chest, the heart was found more irritable than ordinary, and its external contractions and dilatations continued for more than an hour: the right auricle of the heart, which usually contains black venous blood, contained, as well as the right ventricle, a quantity of blood of a bright vermilion colour; and all the muscles of the body were found to be more than usually irritable. This experiment not only proves that the vermilion colour of the blood proceeds from oxygen, but likewise seems to show, that oxygen is the cause of excitability.

A quantity of azotic gas, which had been exposed for some time to the contact of lime water, in order to separate any carbonic acid gas it might contain, was injected into the jugular vein of a dog. The animal died in twenty seconds. Upon opening the chest, the heart was found filled with black and coagulated blood: this organ, and most of the muscles had nearly lost the whole of their irritability, for they contracted but very weakly, on the application of the strongest stimulants.

A quantity of carbonic acid gas was injected into the jugular vein of a dog: the animal became sleepy, and died in about a quarter of an hour: the heart was found filled with black and coagulated blood, and had lost the whole of its irritability; neither it, nor any of the muscles producing any contractions, upon the application of stimulants.

Humboldt likewise mentions a curious fact, which tends strongly to confirm this idea. When the excitability of the limb of a frog had been so far exhausted, by the application of zinc and silver, that it would produce no more contractions, on moistening it with oxygenated muriatic acid, the contractions were renewed.

After the excitability of the sensitive plant (mimosa pudica) had been so far exhausted, by irritation, that it ceased to contract, when further irritated, I restored this excitability, and brought it to a very high degree of irritability, by moistening the earth in which it grew with oxygenated muriatic acid. Seeds likewise vegetate more quickly when moistened with this acid, than when they are not.

In short, we shall find, first, that every thing which increases the quantity of oxygen in organized bodies, increases at the same time their excitability

Secondly, That whatever diminishes the quantity of oxygen, diminishes the excitability

The excitability of animals, made to breathe oxygen gas, or to take the oxygenated muriate of potash, or acid fruits, is very much increased.

On the contrary, when persons have inspired carbonic acid, or azotic gas, or have taken into the system substances which have a strong affinity for oxygen, and therefore tend

to abstract it, such as hydrogen, and spirits, the excitability
becomes very much diminished.

When we sleep, in consequence of the excitability being
exhausted, the breathing becomes free, and a great quantity
of oxygen is received by the lungs, and combined with the
blood, while very little of it becomes exhausted by the actions of the body, for none, excepting those which are called
involuntary motions, are carried on during sound sleep: so
that in a few hours the body recovers the excitability which
it had lost: it is again sensible of the impressions of external
objects, and with the return of light we wake.

These facts afford satisfactory proofs that the excitability
of the body is proportioned to the oxygen which it receives:
but in what manner it produces this state of susceptibility,
and how it is exhausted by stimulants, we have yet to learn.

The following theory may perhaps throw some light upon
the subject.   I propose it, however, merely as an hypothesis,
for we have no direct proofs of it, but it seems to account for
many phenomena.

It is now well known, that while the limb of an animal
possesses excitability, the smallest quantity of electricity sent
along the principal nerve leading to it, produces contractions
similar to those produced by the will.   This is instanced in
the common galvanic experiment with the limb of a frog,
which I had formerly occasion to show

From the effects produced, when a stream of electricity is
sent through water, I think it not improbable that hydrogen
and electricity may be identical.   When a piece of zinc and
silver are connected together, and the zinc is put in a situation to decompose water, and oxidate, a current of hydro-

gen gas will separate from the silver wire, provided this be immersed under water; but when it is not, a current of electricity passes, which is sensible to the electrometer.

Now there appears no greater improbability in the supposition that hydrogen, in a certain state, may be capable of passing through metals, and animal substances, in the form of electricity, and that when it comes in contact with water, which is not so good a conductor, it may combine with caloric, and form hydrogen gas, in which state it becomes incapable of passing through the conductors of electricity: I say there appears no greater improbability in this, than that caloric should sometimes be in such a state, that it will pass through metals, and animal substances, which conduct it, and at other times, as when combined with oxygen or hydrogen, it should form gases, and be then incapable of passing through these conductors of heat. Galvanic effects may be produced by the oxidation of fresh muscular fibre without the aid of metals, and contractions have been thus produced in the limb of an animal; and we have already noticed, that when this contraction ceases, it may be restored, by moistening the limb with oxygenated muriatic acid.

The excitability of the body may, most probably, be conveyed by respiration, and the circulation of the blood, which tend continually to oxidate the different parts: and hydrogen or electricity may be secreted by the brain, and sent along the nerves, which are such good conductors of it, and by uniting with the oxygen of the muscle, may cause it to contract; but as the oxygen will, by this union, be diminished, if the contractions be often repeated, the excitability will thus be expended faster than it can be supplied by the circulation, and will become exhausted. But will facts bear us out in this explanation? To see this, we must examine the chemical nature of the substances which produce the greatest action, and the greatest exhaustion of the vital principle: namely, those which produce intoxication.

Fermented liquors differ from water, in containing carbon and more hydrogen; these produce intoxication: but pure spirits, which contain still more hydrogen, produce a still higher degree of intoxication, and consequent exhaustion of the excitability. Ether, which appears to be little more than condensed hydrogen, probably kept in a liquid state by union with a small quantity of carbon, and which easily expands by caloric into a gas, which very much resembles hydrogen gas, produces a still greater degree of intoxication: so that we see the action produced by different substances, as well as the exhaustion of excitability which follows, is proportioned to the quantity of hydrogen they contain.

There is another circumstance which seems to strengthen this idea. The intoxicating powers of spirits are diminished by the addition of vegetable acids, or substances which contain oxygen, which will counteract the effects of the hydrogen. Thus it is known that the same quantity of spirit, made into punch, will not produce either the same ebriety, or the same subsequent exhaustion, as when simply mixed with water.

Recollect however that I propose this only as a hypothesis: its truth may be confirmed by future observations and experiments, or it may be refuted by them: but it is certainly capable of explaining many of the phenomena, which is one of the conditions required by Newton's first rule of philosophizing.

Heat, and light, and other stimuli, may perhaps exhaust the excitability, by facilitating the combination of oxygen in the fibres with the hydrogen and carbon in the blood.

There are several substances which cause a diminution or exhaustion of the excitability, without producing any previous increased excitement. These substances have by physicians been called sedatives: and though the existence of such bodies is denied by Dr. Brown, yet we are constrained to admit them; nor do their effects seem incapable of being explained on the principle laid down, especially if we call in the aid of chemistry.

Any substance which is capable of combining rapidly with oxygen, and diminishing its quantity, will be a sedative. But the action of some of the animal and vegetable poisons is difficult to explain in the present state of our knowledge; such very minute portions of these produce great exhaustion of the excitability, and even death, that we can scarcely explain their action on the supposition that they combine with the oxygen. They may perhaps act as ferments, and occasion throughout the whole system a new and rapid combination of oxygen with the hydrogenous, carbonic, and perhaps azotic parts of the blood and fluids, and even of the solids, which will speedily destroy the excitability, and even the organization.

Many of the vegetable narcotics, though they will destroy life when given in considerable doses, yet when exhibited in less quantities become very powerful remedies, particularly in cases where the excitability is accumulated, in consequence of which violent spasms and inordinate actions take place, which are very quickly calmed by opium, camphor, musk, asafoetida, ether, &c. medicines that occasion a speedy exhaustion of the excitability. In diseases of exhaustion, however, these remedies are improper. The indication here is to accumulate the irritability, by the introduction of oxygen, and by the diminution of the action of the stimulants which support life. In this idea too I dissent from Dr. Brown, who taught that diseases of exhaustion are to be cured by stimulants, a little less powerful than those which produced the disease. This subject will however be more fully discussed hereafter.

This doctrine of animal life, which I have been attempting to illustrate, and render familiar, exhibits a new view of the manner in which it is constantly supported. It discovers to us the true means of promoting health and longevity, by proportioning the number and force of stimuli to the age, climate, situation, habits, and temperament, of the human body. It leads us to a knowledge of the causes of diseases: these we shall find consist either in an excessive or preternatural excitement in the whole or part of the human body, accompanied generally with irregular motions, and induced by natural or artificial stimuli, or in a diminished excitement or debility in the whole, or in part. It likewise teaches us that the natural and only efficacious cure of these diseases depends on the abstraction of stimuli, from the whole, or from a part of the body, when the excitement is in excess: and in the increase of their number and force when the contrary takes place.

The light which the discoveries of Galvani, and others who

have followed his steps, begin to throw on physiology, pro-
mises, when aided by the principles of chemistry, and the
knowledge of the laws of life, to produce all the advantages
that would result from a perfect knowledge of the animal
functions.

From what has been said, it does not seem improbable
that muscular contraction may depend upon the combination of oxygen with hydrogen and azote, in consequence of a sort of explosion or discharge produced by nervous electricity. According to this hypothesis, animal motion, at least that of animals analagous to man, would be
produced by a beautiful pneumatic structure. This hypothesis, though not perhaps at this moment capable of strict
demonstration, seems extremely probable, it being coun-
tenanced by every observation and experiment yet made on
the subject. It accounts likewise for the perpetual necessity of inhaling oxygen, and enables us to trace the changes
which this substance undergoes, from the moment it is received into the system, till the moment it is expelled. By
the lungs it is imparted to the blood; by the blood to the
muscular fibres; in these, during their contraction, it combines with the hydrogen, and perhaps carbon and azote, to
form water and various salts; which are taken up by the
absorbents, and afterwards exhaled or excreted. We know
the necessity of oxygen to muscular motion, and likewise
that this motion languishes when there is a deficiency of
the principle, as in sea scurvy. Thus a boundless region
of discovery seems to be opening to our view: the science
of philosophy, which began with remote objects, now pro-
mises to unfold to us the more difficult and more interest-

ing knowledge of ourselves. Should this kind of knowledge ever become a part of general education, then the
causes of many diseases being known, and the manner in
which the external powers, with which we are surrounded,
act upon us, a great improvement not only in health, but
in morality must be the consequence.

With respect to its influence on the science of medicine,
we may observe that, from the time of Hippocrates till almost the present day, medicine has not deserved the name
of a science but, as he called it, of a conjectural art. At present however, by the application of the laws of life, and of
the new chemistry, there is beginning to appear in physiology
and pathology, something like the simplicity and certainty of
truth. In proportion as the laws of animal nature come to be
ascertained, the study of them will excite more general attention, and will ultimately prove the most popular, as well
as the most curious and interesting branch of philosophy.

This must be productive of beneficial consequences to
society, since these truths, once impressed upon the mind
by conviction, will operate as moral motives, by which
the sum of disease and human' misery cannot fail to be
greatly diminished.

LECTURE XI.

OF THE NATURE AND CAUSES OF DISEASES.

In the two last lectures I have attempted to investigate the laws of life. I now proceed to the most important part of our course, and for which all the preceding lectures were intended to prepare us; I mean the application of the laws of life to explain the nature and causes of diseases, and the methods of curing them, which must always be imperfect, and conjectural, unless the nature of the diseases themselves be well understood.

We have already seen that life is constantly supported by the action of the external powers which surround us, and that if the action of these powers be properly regulated, and at the same time no other powers be suffered to act on the body, we shall enjoy perfect health, but if, on the contrary, the exciting powers which support life, act either too feebly or too powerfully, then the functions will not be performed with precision and vigour, but irregularly; the mind and body will become deranged, and death will often take place many years before the natural period at which that event might be expected.

As health is the greatest blessing which man can enjoy, it is natural to think, that in the early ages of society, when men began to lose sight of the dictates of nature, and feel the torture of disease, they would regard with gratitude those who had contributed towards their relief, and that they would place their physicians among their heroes and their gods. In the early ages, however, diseases would be very few, for it would not be till civilisation had made considerable progress, that such unnatural modes of life as conduce to their production, would take place.

As the first professors of physic knew nothing of the animal economy, and little of the theory of diseases, it is evident that whatever they did, must have been in consequence of mere random trials. Indeed it is impossible that this or any other art could originate in any other manner. Accordingly history informs us that the ancient nations used to expose their sick in temples, and by the sides of highways, that they might receive the advice of every one that passed.

It would take up too much time to pursue the history of medicine from this rude origin, through all its changes and revolutions, till the present time: let it therefore suffice to say, that after various theories had been invented and overturned, and after one age had destroyed the labours of another, though different branches of the healing art, and particularly anatomy, had been enriched with valuable discoveries, still a rational theory was wanting; there was nothing to guide the practitioner in his way, and we may truly say that till the laws of life, which I have been endeavouring to illustrate, were investigated by Dr. Brown, medicine could boast of no theory which had a title to be called philosophical.

The theories of Stahl, Boerhaave, and Cullen, have passed away, and are almost forgotten, but this, which is founded on nature, and on fact, will, like the Newtonian philosophy, last for ever. It has already influenced the practice of medicine, and is taught in almost all the schools of Europe and America.   In this country it seems to have had less attention paid to it than it deserved, because its influence was counteracted by the arrogance and profligacy of its author, as if the grossness of a man's manner affected the conclusiveness of his arguments; but this influence did not extend beyond Britain, while the light of his theory illuminated the opposite hemisphere. And when the manner in which he was persecuted is recollected, the liberal mind will allow something to the deep consciousness of neglected merit.

A circumstance much in favour of this doctrine is, that those who understand its principles thoroughly, are guided by it in their practice with a certainty and success before unknown. I say those who understand its principles, for these were not perfectly understood even by the author himself. He first saw with his mind's eye the grand outline of the system, from which, for want of proper reflection, he often drew wrong deductions, and which he often applied improperly. But whatever errors Brown may have committed in the application of his system, and however short his doctrines may fall of a perfect system of medicine, we may venture to predict that the grand outlines will remain unshaken.

From what has been already shown, it must be evident that if the just degree of excitement could be kept up, mankind would enjoy continual health. But it is difficult, if not impossible, to regulate the action of the exciting powers in this equable manner, and if their action is increased, the first effect they produce on the functions is to increase them, and the next is, to render them disturbed or uneasy; or, in other words, to bring on diseases of increased action, or what have been called inflammatory or phlogistic, both of which terms are improper, as they convey false ideas, and are connected with erroneous theories: Dr Brown has given the name of sthenic to these diseases, from their consisting in increased strength or action, and this is certainly a more appropriate term. On the contrary, when the action of the exciting powers is diminished more than is natural, the functions become languid and disturbed, and by a still further decrease of the action of these powers, they become irregular and inordinate. This state of the body, which is opposite to the former, Dr. Brown has denominated asthenic.

But the stimulant powers may act so powerfully, and exhaust the excitability to such a degree, that they may overstep the bounds of sthenic or inflammatory disease and bring on debility. Debility may therefore arise either from the stimuli acting too weakly, or from a deficient excitability, while the stimulus is not deficient. Debility produced in the former manner is called direct debility, and in the latter indirect debility.

To explain this more clearly, let us take a common instance. If a person by any means be deprived of the proper quantity of food, he will feel himself enfeebled, and the functions will gradually grow more and more languid, and at last become irregular, and be performed with pain. This state is called direct debility. Here is excitability enough, and even too much, for it has accumulated by the subtraction of a stimulus; but here is a deficiency of excitement from defect of stimulus.

If now we suppose that a person, in good health, begins to take a greater quantity of food than usual, and adds a quantity of wine, all the functions will at first be increased in vigour, but at last they will be irregularly performed, and inflammation, with other symptoms of too great excitement, will be the consequence. This state is called sthenic diathesis or disease. But if the stimulant power be pushed still further, the excitability will become gradually exhausted, till at last there will be too little to produce the healthy actions, even though there may be plenty of stimulus. This state of asthenic diathesis is called indirect debility, because it is not produced by directly subtracting the powers which support life, but indirectly, by over stimulating. An instance of this latter state is afforded by that debility which is the consequence of intoxication.

There is a state however between perfect health and disease, which is called predisposition; and in which, though the functions are undisturbed, the slightest cause will bring on disease. Strictly speaking, there is perhaps only one point, or one degree of excitement, at which the health is perfect: the first alterations from this point, on either side, are scarcely perceptible, but if the morbid causes be continued, the functions will become gradually more and more disturbed, till at last they become so uneasy or painful that they are termed disease.

In order to render what has been said still more plain, it may be proper to make use of an illustration by means of numbers: we must recollect however that it is merely for the sake of illustration, for we have not data to enable us to reduce either the excitability, or excitement, or stimulus, to numerical calculation; if we could do this, the science of medicine would be perfect, and we could cure diseases as easily as we could perform any chemical or philosophical experiment. A very principal object however is to understand the nature of predisposition, and the kind of diathesis, whether sthenic or asthenic, to which it inclines: this not only throws light on the nature of the disease, but affords us the only means of preventing it. When a slight uneasiness or predisposition is felt, it is almost impossible to say from our feelings whether it leads to a sthenic or an asthenic state: here we must be guided chiefly by the exciting powers. If we find that these have acted too powerfully; that is, if we have lived freely, been exposed to heat, and perhaps indulged in some of the unnatural stimuli, such as wine and spirits; and particularly if we previously to the present time perceived the functions to go on with more vigour, our spirits and strength greater, before we experienced the slight disturbance of which we complain, we are verging towards sthenic or inflammatory disease, and therefore to prevent the disease we ought immediately to diminish the action of the exciting powers; the quantity of food ought to be diminished, wine and other liquors abstained from, heat carefully avoided; and even the quantity of blood in the circulating system diminished, if the habit is full and the pulse strong.

On the contrary, if the exciting powers have acted more feebly than is natural; that is, if we have lived on a less nourishing diet, or have taken it in less quantity; if we have been long exposed to cold, without alternating with heat, and other debilitating causes; and if at the same time we find the vigour of the functions diminished, though they are not yet become much disturbed, we are verging towards asthenic disease. To prevent which, we must take a more nutritious diet, and join a portion of wine, and perhaps take some tonic medicines. This however ought to be done gradually, for fear of exhausting the excitability, which in these cases is morbidly accumulated.

It must be evident that the great difficulty here is to determine the nature of the predisposition; for if we make a mistake, instead of preventing, we shall accelerate the disease. For instance, the first slight disturbance of the functions which rises from a sthenic state, often resembles those verging towards a state of debility or asthenia. I have seen various instances arising from plethora, or a sthenic state, where the patient complained of depression of spirits, and inability to move ; and, in short, from his own account was labouring under asthenic diathesis: but by inquiring carefully into the action of the exciting causes, examining minutely the state of the pulse and of the functions, I have been convinced that the depression of spirits which he felt, and other symptoms of weakness, depended on fullness, and they have been quickly removed by lowering the diet, administering a laxative, or taking a little blood : whereas if, apprehending from the symptoms that he had laboured under debility, I had ordered him a more generous diet and tonic remedies, an inflammatory disease would have been the consequence, which might have terminated in death.

I have seen various instances where patients have complained of this unusual depression, and inability to move: they have shown me prescriptions in which the stimulant or tonic plan was recommended, but instead of any alleviation the symptoms had become worse from their use. This hint was generally sufficient, for if the disease of predisposition had been asthenic, cordials and tonics ought to have relieved it: if, on inquiry, I found the exciting powers had acted too powerfully, I then, without hesitation, had recourse to the debilitating plan, and with the greatest certainty of success. Before I viewed diseases and their causes in this way, I must confess that I often felt great hesitation in practice; and judging merely from symptoms, which are frequently very fallacious, the operation of a remedy often disappointed me, and I could not pretend to predict the event with the certainty that I now can. This observation is of the greatest consequence in the cure both of predisposition and of disease. Though excitement regulates all the phenomena of life, yet the symptoms of diseases which either its excess or deficiency produces, do not of themselves lead to any proper judgment respecting it. On the contrary their fallacious appearance has proved the source of infinite error.

As excitement both depends on exciting powers and excitability, it is evident that when a middle degree of stimulus acts upon a middle degree of excitability, the most perfect effect will be produced. This point, could we ascertain it, might be called the point of health. For the sake of illustration, we may suppose that the greatest excitability of which the living body is capable is 80 degrees: this may be supposed to be the excitability possessed by the body at the commencement of its life, because no part has then been wasted or exhausted by the action of stimuli. Now, if we suppose a scale of excitability to be formed, and

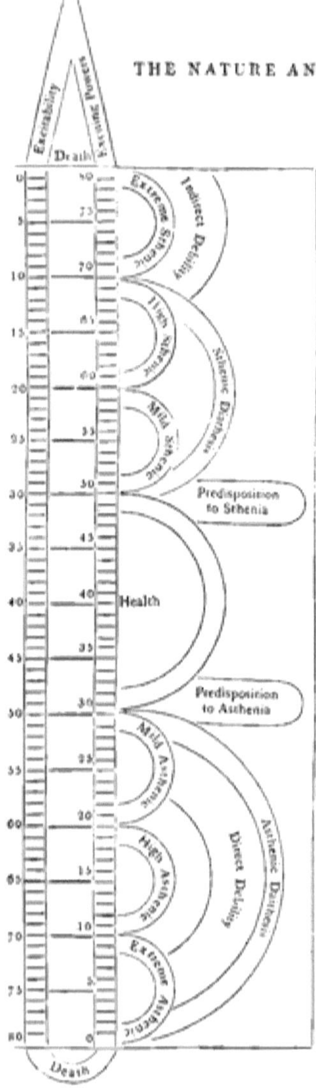

divided into 80 equal parts or degrees, the excitability will be wasted or exhausted in proportion to the application of stimuli, from the beginning to the end of the scale. One degree of exciting power applied takes of one degree off excitability, and every subsequent degree impairs the excitability in proportion to its degree of force. Thus a degree of stimulus or exciting power equal to 10 will reduce the excitability to 70, 20 to 60, 30 to 50, 40 to 40, 50 to 30, 60 to 20, 70 to 10, 80 to 0; and, on the contrary, the subtraction of stimulant power will allow the excitability to accumulate.

The range of good health is ranked from 30 to 50 degrees in the scale; for perfect health, which consists in the middle point only, or at 40 degrees, rarely occurs; in consequence of the variation of the stimuli to which man is continually exposed, such as meat and drink, heat, exercise, and the emotions of the mind, the excitement commonly fluctuates between 30 and 50 degrees, and yet no particular disturbance of the functions takes place. But when at these points, 30 or 50, predisposition commences, the slightest debilitating cause in the former case, and the slightest stimulating cause in the latter, brings on disease, in which the functions begin to be disturbed in various ways, and this disturbance is always in proportion to the hurting powers which have produced the disease, and the delicacy or importance of the part affected.

The effect produced on the excitability by any stimulus, must evidently be in a ratio compounded of the degree of excitability and the force of the stimulus. The same stimulus will produce greater contractions upon a fibre that is more irritable than upon one which possesses less irritability; and the irritability or excitability of the fibre being given, or remaining the same, the contraction will be in proportion to the strength of the stimulus. Hence it is evident, that the effect or excitement must be in a ratio compounded of the exciting powers and excitability.

Sthenic diathesis and disease is caused by the operation of different exciting powers, which produce too great a degree of excitement in the system: this at first increases all the functions, and, when increased, produces a disturbance and inordinate action of them, which is communicated to the whole body. In diseases of this kind there is often an appearance of debility, but this is extremely fallacious, and arises from the disturbed state of the different functions. Hence it is evidently of the utmost consequence to ascertain carefully whether this debility is real, or the effect of asthenic disease: or whether it is owing to the disturbance of the functions by over stimulating, and in this case fallacious; for should a sthenic disease be treated by stimulants and cordials, the effect would be an aggravation of all the symptoms, and a much higher degree of disease.

Asthenic diathesis and disease is brought on by the excitement of the system being diminished: and this may proceed either from a diminution of common stimulant powers, while the excitability is sufficiently abundant, or it may proceed from an exhausted excitability, while the stimulus is sufficiently abundant. The former is called direct, and the latter indirect debility. The exciting causes therefore of asthenic disease, first impair the functions, then occasion a disturbed or inordinate action of them, giving many of them a false appearance; some of them, for instance, appear to be increased, for in hysteria and epilepsy, which are both diseases of debility, the action of the muscles seems to be preternaturally increased; but this depends chiefly on the accumulated excitability, which gives such a degree of irritability to the system, that the smallest irritation, whether external, such as heat, exercise, &c. or internal, as emotions of the mind, excite a strong spasmodic action, which brings on the symptoms of epilepsy and hysteria. This inordinate action however soon exhausts the morbid excitability, and thus suspends itself, a sleep often follows, from which the patient wakes with only a general sense of languor and debility: but as the same cause still remains, the excitability of the body again becomes morbidly accumulated, and thus the slightest stimulus produces a recurrence of the fit, and the tendency to return will increase with its recurrence, so that at last the slightest imaginable cause will produce it, on account of the power of habit and association.

Gout likewise appears like a sthenic disease, and an inflammation takes place, which resembles pleurisy or peripneumony; but this symptom is fallacious, for it depends on debility, and is only to be cured by means, which in pleurisy and peripneumony, would produce death.

Hence it must be evident that those phenomena of diseases, which we call symptoms, are generally fallacious; but this may be owing to our imperfect knowledge of the animal economy, so that we are not able to explain or understand the manner in which they are produced: we ought however carefully to guard against being misled by them in practice. The great difficulty is to distinguish the nature of the disease, whether it is sthenic or asthenic, or whether it depends on too great excitement, or on debility; for this being once clearly ascertained, we proceed with certainty in our mode of treatment, instead of the random practice, which must be the consequence of not taking a proper view of the laws of life, and the causes of diseases.

The nature of the disease may be generally ascertained, by attending to the habits of the patient, and the manner in which he has lived, as well as to the state of the pulse; but in cases where these circumstances do not render it clear, it may be ascertained, beyond a doubt, by a trifling degree of stimulus, as, for instance, by any cordial, as a little wine or spirits. If the disease be of an inflammatory or sthenic kind, the symptoms will be aggravated, and the cordial will not produce its usual pleasant effects on the system; but on the contrary, if the nature of the disease be asthenic, then the usual pleasant effects of the cordial will be perceived, and the pain and other symptoms will be alleviated. This trial, which is soon made, and without danger, will determine our plan of cure, and we can then proceed with the most perfect certainty. Thus you will see that this view we have taken leads to a very different and much more rational plan of practice than is generally followed, in which the most judicious physicians confess that they have no clue to guide them ; and complain that the science of medicine consists merely in a number of insulated facts, not connected by any theory: that they merely prescribe a remedy because they have seen it of use in an apparently similar state, but that they have no certainty of its producing a similar effect in the cases in which they prescribe it. This all depends on trusting to the fallacious appearance of symptoms, and not having taken a proper view of the laws of life, or the manner in which the exciting powers act on living bodies.

After these observations on the diagnosis, or the method of distinguishing the nature of diseases, I shall proceed to consider more particularly the nature of sthenic diseases, and the methods of curing them, which will occupy the remainder of our time this evening.

The powers or causes, which by their action produce inflammatory or sthenic diseases, are, first, heat, which is a very frequent cause, particularly when it succeeds cold; for the cold accumulates the excitability, and then renders the whole body, or a part, more liable to be affected by the heat afterwards applied. In this way is produced rheumatism, catarrh, or, as it is commonly called, a cold, and peripneumony.

29

These complaints have been often attributed to cold, but I believe that there never was a well attested instance where cold alone, without being either followed by heat or some other stimulus, produced a real sthenic, or inflammatory disease. This is not merely a distinction, it is a circumstance of the utmost importance, because it influences the mode of practice to be pursued. Heat is one of the exciting or stimulant powers which support life, and one of the most powerful of these stimulants; but cold is only a diminution of it: how then can this produce a sthenic state, or a state of too high excitement? The blood is one of the exciting powers, which, by its continual circulation supports life; but surely if we abstracted a quantity of this fluid from the body, no person will be bold enough to say, that we by that means should produce an inflammatory disease. Cold renders the body more liable to be affected by heat, or any other stimulus applied, but does not of itself produce any stimulant or inflammatory effects.

To see more clearly the manner in which cold acts, let us inquire how it produces or contributes towards the production of catarrh. When we go into the cold air, at every respiration we take a quantity of it into the lungs, which brushes over the surface of the mucous membrane that lines the nostrils and trachea, and thus, robbing them of their heat, allows the excitability to accumulate. But we feel no fever, no sense of tightness or stuffing, nor any other symptom of catarrh, so long as we continue in the cold. If however we afterwards go into a warm room, and particularly near a fire, we receive by the act of respiration the warm air into those very parts which have been previously exposed to cold, and whose excitability is consequently accumulated. The first effect we perceive is a glow of the parts, which is by no means unpleasant, this however increases; and, in the course of half an hour or an hour, a sense of dryness and huskiness comes on, with a sensation of stuffing in the nostrils, and a tendency to a short dry cough: often likewise, if the exposure to cold has been considerable, and the heat afterwards applied great and sudden, we experience a shivering, and other symptoms of fever. These symptoms are all increased by taking into the stomach any liquid that is either of warm temperature or stimulating quality, or particularly both; we spend a restless night, and awake with all the symptoms of a catarrh, or cold, as it is improperly called. For it is evidently an inflammatory fever, and can be speedily cured by the debilitating plan, and particularly by keeping in a moderately cool place, where the temperature is equable, and not subject to alternations of heat and cold.

But how easily might this complaint have been avoided, were the person subject to it acquainted with its real nature, and the manner in which it is brought on. When we come out of a very cold atmosphere, we should not at first go into a room that has a fire in it; or, if this cannot be well avoided, we should keep for a considerable time at as great a distance from the fire as possible, that the accumulated excitability may be gradually exhausted by the moderate and gentle action of heat; and then we may bear the heat of the fire without any danger; but above all, we should refrain from taking warm or strong liquors while we are hot. In confirmation of this opinion, numerous instances might be brought, where catarrh was cured merely by exposure to cold.

When a part of the body only has been exposed to the action of cold, and the rest kept heated; if, for instance, a person in a warm room has been sitting so that a current of air, coming through a broken window, has fallen upon any part of the body, that part will soon be affected with an inflammation, or what is called a rheumatic affection. In this case, the excitability of the part exposed to the action of the cold, becomes accumulated, and the warm blood, rushing through it, from every other part of the body, excites an inflammation.

Thus catarrh and rheumatism are inflammatory complaints, or depend on too great a degree of excitement, and are to be cured by lowering the excitement, or diminishing the action of the exciting powers; by bleeding, purging, low diet, and particularly keeping in a moderately cool place; and these complaints will be as speedily and certainly cured by these methods, properly and judiciously persevered in, as a slight cut or wound will be healed by what surgeons call the first intention.

There are complaints which resemble these, but whose nature, however, is very different, and which require a very different mode of treatment. After a part has been long affected with rheumatic inflammation the excitability of the muscular fibres becomes so far exhausted, that a state of indirect debility takes place, and an inflammation, accompanied with pain and redness, which is very different from that I formerly described, as it depends upon a debilitated or relaxed state of the parts, instead of too great a degree of excitement. This instance shows strongly the fallacy of symptoms; but it may be readily distinguished from the inflammatory rheumatism, by attention to the effects of the exciting causes. The inflammatory rheumatism is aggravated by heat, hence it is more violent in bed than at any other time. The latter complaint, however, is greatly relieved by heat: the warm bath alleviates all the symptoms; so does a warm bed. It is evident that these diseases, though attended by the same symptoms, are as opposite, and require as different modes of treatment as an inflammation of the brain, and a dropsy The inflammatory state has been called the acute rheumatism, and the other, the chronic rheumatism; I would, however, prefer the terms sthenic and asthenic rheumatism.

In the same manner, there is a catarrh, which is liable to afflict persons who have often been subject to an inflammatory cold, particularly persons advanced in years; and this depends on a state of indirect debility of the parts, the excitability of which has been exhausted by frequent and violent inflammatory affections. This complaint, which I would call asthenic catarrh, requires directly opposite treatment from the inflammatory or sthenic catarrh. The latter is aggravated by heat, but relieved by a cool temperature. Warm air is peculiarly grateful to those who are afflicted with the former, and if they go into a cool temperature, they are immediately seized with cough, and expectoration; for the disease being a disease of debility, the withdrawing the stimulus of heat, must increase it. The excitability of the parts is so far exhausted, that it requires a stimulus even more than natural to keep them in tone: hence persons labouring under asthenic catarrh, and some species of asthma, which are only varieties of this disease, find themselves best when exposed to a warm temperature, but on the heat being diminished, and consequently the parts relaxed, the cough and difficulty of breathing immediately come on.

Having examined the effect of heat, in producing inflammatory or sthenic disease, I now proceed to the consideration of the other powers. Of the articles of diet, the only food in danger of being too stimulant, is perhaps flesh or land animal food, used in too great quantity, particularly when seasoned, a preparation which adds much to its stimulant power. Spirituous and vinous liquors, let them be ever so weak or much diluted, stimulate more quickly, and more readily than seasoned food, and their stimulus is in proportion to the quantity of alcohol which they contain. These substances, when conjoined with rich food, must bring on a predisposition to sthenic disease, in almost any constitution, particularly in the young and healthy, and, in many instances, those diseases actually take place; or should this not be the case, should the person avoid, or escape the effects of inflammatory diseases, the excitability will be exhausted, and diseases of indirect debility, such as gout, apoplexy, indigestion, palsy, &c. will take place.

These stimulants are never necessary to a good constitution, and their effects will always, sooner or later, be experienced: for though a person with a good constitution may continue for years to indulge in the pleasures of the bottle, or the luxuries of the table, depend upon it that a continuance of them will sap the vigour of the strongest constitution that ever existed.

As nothing contributes more to the health of the body than moderate and frequently repeated exercise, which rouses

the muscles to contraction, and promotes the circulation of
the blood in the veins towards the heart : it thus produces
excitement; but an excess of it will produce sthenic diathesis;
and, if carried to great excess, it will produce a state of indirect debility, or exhausted excitability

When any, or all of these exciting powers act too strongly
on the body, the first effect they produce is a preternatural
acuteness of all the senses ; the motions, both voluntary and
involuntary, are performed with vigour, and there is an
acuteness of genius and intellectual power. In short, every
part of the body seems in a state of complete vigour and
strength ; that this is the case with the heart and arteries,
appears from the strong and firm pulse ; in the stomach it
is shown by the appetite; and, in the extreme parts, by the
ruddy colour and complexion. In short, every appearance
marks vigour of the body, and abundance of blood. Could
the body be kept in this state, nothing could be more
to be desired; this, however, is impossible ; the excitement, though still within the bounds of health, has over-
stepped the point of good health, and is verging fast to predisposition to sthenic disease; so that, to secure a permanent
state of health, it is always better to keep the excitement
rather under the middle point, or 40°, than above it. During
the predisposition to sthenic disease, which is produced by
the longer continued, or increased action of these powers,
no symptoms of disease appear; but shortly after, disturbed
sleep, depressed spirits, languor, a sense of fulness, heaviness,
particularly after eating, show that this sthenic state cannot be further increased with impunity. The least increase
of sthenic diathesis now brings on a disturbance of the func-

tions, or actual disease ; the commencement of which is generally a shivering, and a sense of cold ; thirst and heat
succeed ; and then generally a pain in some part, either external or internal : costiveness generally attends this state,
the urine is clear, and secreted in small quantity ; memory
and imagination become diminished, and there is generally
less appetite for food.

In peripneumony, inflammatory sore throat, and acute
rheumatism, there is an inflamed condition of the lungs, of
the parts about the throat, or of the muscles of the extremities: this shows that the excitement here is greater than in
other parts of the body; but it is still increased or too great
in every part, only those parts which give the peculiar character to the disease are more affected than other parts of
the body, by being more exposed to the exciting causes:
thus, if a person be in perfect health, or a little below, he
will not be easily affected by any of the exciting causes
of sthenic disease, unless their application be very violent ;
he will go into a warm room out of the cold air, and
feel no other effect than a pleasant glow: but if, by high
living, or other means, he is brought near the point of
predisposition to sthenic disease, then the slightest additional stimulus will bring it on, and if the throat has been
exposed to the application of cold, and the person comes
afterwards into a heated room, an inflammation of the parts
about the throat, or an inflammatory sore throat, accompanied by a sthenic diathesis of the whole system, will be the
consequence. This cannot be cured by merely diminishing
the excitement of the part, while the excitement of the whole
system remains: if we apply leeches to the throat in this

state, to diminish the quantity of blood, we only debilitate the vessels, while fresh quantities of blood are poured into them from the too full vessels of the body; even if we could thus remove the sthenic diathesis of the part, we should go but a little way towards removing the inflammatory disease, which universally pervades the system.

The mode to be pursued therefore is, to take a quantity of blood from the body, by opening a vein; to keep the body cool, by remaining in a room where the temperature is at temperate, or a little below; by abstaining from animal food, and from spirituous or fermented liquors; and by the exhibition of purgatives, or at least of laxatives. Then leeches or blisters applied to the part affected will produce a good effect; and even stimulant applications to the inflamed part may be advantageous; for a topical inflammation, as we shall afterwards have occasion to see, depends on a debilitated state of the minute vessels of the part, while at the same time the action of the whole system is increased.

Besides the energy of the exciting hurtful powers, which I have mentioned, there is in the parts which undergo the inflammation, a greater sensibility, or an accumulated excitability; by which it happens that some are more affected than the rest. To this we may add, that whatsoever part may have been injured by inflammation, that part in every future sthenic attack is in more danger of being inflamed than the rest. Hence inflammatory sore throat, rheumatism, and some other complaints of the kind, when once they have supervened, are very apt to recur.

Among the sthenic or inflammatory diseases may be enumerated rheumatism, catarrh, cynanche, or sore throat, scarlet fever, inflammations of the brain, stomach, lungs, &c. &c.

Many of the contagious diseases, particularly small pox and measles, produce a sthenic state, and are to be cured, or their action moderated, by the debilitating plan which has been pointed out; and particularly by a moderate, constant, and equable diminution of temperature. Hence the violence of these diseases is greater when they attack a person already predisposed to sthenic diathesis, but much more mild when the excitement is rather under par.

LECTURE XII.

ON INFLAMMATION AND ASTHENIC DISEASES.

The last lecture was taken up chiefly with an account of sthenic diseases, or those depending on too great a degree of excitement, and which have been generally, but improperly, called inflammatory or phlogistic. In that lecture I attempted to show, that when the natural exciting powers, which support life, act with too much power, or particularly if we employ any stimulants not natural to the body, the functions both of body and mind become increased in vigour; but if the exciting causes are continued and increased, the functions become disturbed, and their action becomes painful and distressing.   This state, which is called sthenic diathesis, is often accompanied by a redness, swelling, pain, and increased heat of some particular part: these symptoms constitute what is usually termed an inflammation of the part.

The method of cure in sthenic diseases was shown to be, by reducing or moderating the action of the exciting powers; by keeping the body cool; abstaining from high seasoned, and, in general, from animal food; by the use of purgatives, and in many cases by diminishing the quantity of blood in the body. I mentioned likewise, that it would be but of little use to attempt to subdue the excitement of the inflamed part, unless the excitement of the whole system was previously diminished; but that after a general bloodletting, stimulant remedies applied to the inflamed part, might be employed with success. This is strictly agreeable to experience, but at first sight seems so very contrary to the principles that have been advanced, that I shall endeavour to explain the phenomena of inflammation, which do not seem to be in general well understood.

All kinds of inflammation agree, in being attended with redness, increased temperature, pain, and swelling; but they vary according to the situation and texture of the part affected. All parts of the body, excepting the cuticle, nails, hardest part of the teeth, and hair, are subject to inflammation.

Among the causes of these complaints, may be enumerated too full a diet, particularly too free a use of fermented liquors, and whatever increases the impetus of the blood towards the part, as mechanical and chemical irritation, and sudden changes of temperature, particularly from cold to heat.

To explain the nature of inflammation, it may be observed, that such is the wise constitution of the animal body, that whatever injures it, excites motions calculated to correct or expel the offending cause. Thus if an irritating substance is received into the stomach, it excites vomiting; if into the lungs, a violent fit of coughing is excited, and if into the nostrils, sneezing is the consequence. In such cases we can readily trace the motions excited, and the manner in which they act; but cannot trace the manner in which the offending cause excites these motions.

Now if it can be shown that inflammation, like vomiting and coughing, is an effort of the system to remove an offending cause, and if we can trace every step of this operation, with the exception of the changes induced on the nervous system, we shall understand the nature of inflammation as completely as that of any function of the body

The circumstance the most difficult to explain, is the increased redness of the part affected, which can only depend on an increased quantity of blood in the vessels. This has been supposed to depend upon an increased action of the vessels of the part; but that this is not the case, must be evident from what was said when we were speaking of the circulation of the blood. It was shown, that the circulation could not be carried on by the mere force of elasticity alone; this force, were it perfect, would produce no effect; but as there is no body with which we are acquainted that is perfectly elastic; so the coats of the arteries are very far from being so, hence their effect as elastic tubes will be to diminish the force of the heart, instead of adding to it; for a certain quantity of this force will be spent in distending the vessels, which, were they perfectly elastic, would be restored to them, but as this is not the case, this force is by no means restored. Indeed a variety of considerations, observations, and experiments, tend to prove, that the vessels are endowed with a power very different from elasticity, which differs only in degree from that of the heart; in short, they are possessed of muscular power.

After each contraction of the muscular coat, the elastic will act as its antagonist, and enlarge the diameter, till the vessel arrive at a mean degree of dilatation, but after this there is no further power of distention inherent in the vessel. The action of the elastic coat ceases; and no one will assert that a muscular fibre has power to distend itself.

The only power by which the vessel can be further distended, is the vis a tergo: after the vessel arrives at its mean degree of dilatation, both the elastic and muscular coats act as antagonists to the vis a tergo, or force which propels the blood into, and thus tends further to dilate the vessel. If then the vis a tergo become greater than in health, the powers of resistance inherent in the vessels remaining the same; or if the latter be weakened, the vis a tergo, or propelling force, remaining the same, the vessel must suffer a morbid degree of dilatation. These appear to be the only circumstances under which a vessel can suffer such dilatation.

But if, while the powers of the vessels remain the same, the vis a tergo, or propelling force, be diminished, or the propelling force remaining the same, the power of the vessels become increased; then an opposite condition or state of the vessels, viz. a preternatural diminution of their area, will take place.

In the one case the distending force bears too great a proportion to the resisting force; and preternatural distention is the consequence. In the other the resisting force bears too great a proportion to the distending force, and preternatural contraction is the consequence.

It is not necessary that the vessels should be in a state of greater debility than in health, in order that an inflammation or distention may take place: it is only necessary that the proportion which their action bears to the propelling force be less than in health. If the propelling force remain the same, the vessels must be in a state of debility before an inflammation can take place; but if the propelling force be increased by a fullness of the vessels and sthenic diathesis, inflammation may take place, although the vessels of the part act as powerfully as in health, or more so.   But after inflammation has taken place, as the vessels are preternaturally distended, they must also be debilitated.

The degree of inflammation is not however proportioned to the debility of the minute vessels of an inflamed part, but to the diminished proportion of their power to the propelling force.

When, therefore, inflammation arises from an increased action of the arterial system, or an increased propelling force, while the force of the capillaries or minute vessels remains the same, it constitutes what is called an active inflammation, and is to be cured by general bleedings, and then by gentle applications of tonics to the part, to increase its action; but when it arises from a debility of the minute vessels, without any increase of the propelling force, it forms what is known by the name of passive inflammation; in which general bleeding is not required, but the application of stimulants and tonics to the inflamed part to enable the vessels to recover their lost tone, and restore the balance between their action and the vis a tergo.   From what has been said, it must be evident, that if inflammation depend on the diminished proportion of the power of the capillaries to the propelling force, it will be more apt to supervene under the three following circumstances.

1. In a state of plethora, because then all the vessels are over distended, and consequently any cause tending fur-

ther to distend them, whether it be a cause which debilitates them, or increases the propelling force, will be more
felt than in health.

2. In a state of general debility, because the vital powers
in any part are more readily destroyed than in health.

3. In a state of general excitement, because then the
propelling force is every where strong, and consequently apt
to occasion distention of the vessels, wherever any degree of
debility occurs. These are the states of the system which
are found to predispose to inflammation. In the first and
last, the inflammation is generally of that kind, which is
termed active: the propelling force is considerable, and the
larger arteries are readily excited to increased action. In the
second state the inflammation is of the passive kind.

This is not merely a useless physiological disquisition;
it is of the greatest use in directing our practice; and teaches
us that, in passive inflammation, which has all the symptoms
of active, and therefore shows in a striking point of view
the fallacy of symptoms, we shall not succeed by applying
leeches, and other debilitating means, to the inflamed part;
on the contrary, we shall aggravate the complaint; and the
cure must be effected by stimulants applied to the part.

As an instance of this kind of inflammation, I may mention that kind of ophthalmia or inflammation of the eyes,
which is of long standing, and which not only resists the
powers of leeches and blisters, but is increased by them.
I have frequently been consulted by patients, who had for
months been under the debilitating plan, without any benefit; and who have been relieved almost instantly by the
application of electricity and a stimulating lotion, which re-

stored the tone of the debilitated vessels of the sclerotic coat, and enabled them to expel their overcharged contents; and the balance between their action and the propelling force being restored, the inflammation disappeared.

Indeed the effects of electricity in these kinds of inflammations are wonderful: it seems to act almost by a charm, so quickly does the inflammation subside; but when we understand the nature of this kind of inflammation, it is nothing but what we might expect from its action.

I have been thus minute on the subject of inflammation, because the theory of it, which I have attempted to defend, differs considerably from the commonly received opinions. I shall now proceed to consider the nature of asthenic diseases.

From what has been already said, it must be evident that the causes of diseases which we have assigned, are very different from those delivered by physicians who preceded Dr. Brown. Some physicians imagined that diseases were caused by a change in the qualities of the fluids, which became sometimes acid, and sometimese alkaline; or on a change of figure of the particles of the blood: some imagined diseases to be owing to a rational principle, which they called the vis medicatrix naturae, which governed the actions of the body, and excited fever or commotion in the system to remove any hurtful cause, or expel any morbid matter, which might have insinuated itself into the body. Others supposed many diseases to arise from a constriction of the extreme vessels by cold; or from a spasm of them, which was a contrivance of the vis medicatrix, to rouse the action of the heart and arteries to remove the debility induced.

31

We have seen, however, that health and diseases are the same state, and depending upon the same cause; viz. excitement, but differing in degree; and that the powers producing both are the same, sometimes acting with a proper degree of force: at other times either with too much, or too little.

We shall now examine how the diminished actions of the different exciting powers produce asthenic disease; and we shall take them in the same order as when we were speaking of sthenic diseases. It must be recollected however that an asthenic state, or a state of debility, may be produced in two ways. First, by directly diminishing the action of the exciting powers. Secondly, by exhausting the excitability, by a strong or long continued stimulant action. The former state is called direct debility, and the latter indirect debility This is not merely a distinction without a difference, the body is in very different states, under these two different forms of disease. In the former case, the excitability is abundant, and highly susceptible of the action of stimulants. In the latter, it is exhausted, and the body has very little susceptibility.

Cold, or a diminution of heat, carried beyond a certain degree, is unfriendly to all animals. Dr. Beddoes has shown very clearly in his Hygeia, that it is the cause of a great many diseases which take place at boarding schools, and that it there gives origin to a great number of diseases that afterwards arise, and, indeed, not unfrequently ruins the constitution. It produces relaxation of the vessels, asthenic or passive inflammation, and even gangrene. He has shown that in most schools children are afflicted with chilblains from this cause; this is a case of passive inflammation, but is only a symptom of the general debility induced, which shows itself afterwards by the production of other symptoms. Hence it is necessary for the preservation of health, that the temperature of school rooms should always be kept equable, and regulated by means of a thermometer. It should not exceed 50 degrees, nor should it be allowed to fall much below it. If precautions of this kind are thought to be necessary, and practised with uncommon attention, in places where vegetables are reared, surely they ought not to be neglected in those seminaries where the human species are to be brought to maturity, and a good constitution established.

But though I have no doubt whatever, that this equable temperature would prevent a number of diseases, which originate in too low a temperature, yet I am far from wishing to have it thought that I would not induce a hardy state of the constitution, which would enable it to bear the vicissitudes to which it must be exposed in its journey through life, by every means in my power. Hardiness is the most enviable of all the attributes of animal nature, and can neither be acquired, nor recovered when it is lost, but upon certain terms, to which many people submit with reluctance, because they must give up many indulgences and gratifications with which it is utterly inconsistent.

One of the causes that chiefly contributes to reduce persons living in affluence below the standard of hardiness, is the dependence they place on a considerable degree of external warmth, for preserving a comfortable state of sensation. From what has been said again and again in some of the latest of these lectures, it must be evident that continued warmth renders the living system less capable of being excited to strong, healthy, and pleasant action: heat in excess, whether it may be excess of duration or intensity, constantly debilitates, by exhausting the excitability of the system, and thus producing a state of indirect debility. Every muscle steeped in a heated medium, whether of air or water, loses much of its contractibility A heart kept in heated air, or put in hot water, will not contract on the application of a stimulus; even the limb of a frog, when heated in this manner, ceases to move on the application of the galvanic exciters. Every nerve grows languid, and when it does become excited, it acquires a disposition to throw the moving fibres, with which it is connected, into starts, twitchings, and other irregular convulsive motions. Though therefore nothing can more contribute to the health of the body than a moderate and well regulated temperature, about 48 or 50 degrees, sometimes for a short interval a little lower, when exercise is taken at the same time, yet when we consider the life led by persons of fashion, we should hope that it proceeded from ignorance of these consequences; so diametrically opposite is it to the dictates of nature and reason.

Instead of rising from table after dinner, and availing themselves of the cooling and refreshing qualities of the air, even in the finest seasons, when every thing which pure and simple nature can offer, invites them abroad, they do every thing they can, as Dr. Beddoes observes, to add to the overstimulating operation of a full and hearty dinner. After taking strong wine with their food, they sit in rooms rendered progressively warmer, all the afternoon, by the presence of company, by the increase of fires, and for more than half the year, by the early closing of the shutters, and letting down of the window curtains.   After a short interval, tea and coffee succeed; liquors stimulating both by their inherent qualities, and by virtue of the temperature at which they are often drank. And that nothing may be wanting to their pernicious effect, they are frequently taken in the very 'stew and squeeze of a fashionable mob.   The season of sleep succeeds, and to crown the adventures of the evening, the bed room is fastened close, and made stifling by a fire: and though the robust may not quickly feel the effects of this mode of life, with the feeble it is quite otherwise.   These, as they usually manage, rarely pass a few hours of sleep without feverishness and uneasy dreams; both of which contribute to their finding themselves by far more spent and spiritless in the morning, than after their evening fit of forced excitement, instead of having their spirits and strength recruited by the " chief nourisher in life's feast," Perhaps they drink tea before rising, and indulge in a morning nap; this weakens much more than the greatest muscular exertion they would be capable of supporting for an equal time.   For the sleep at this time is almost invariably disturbed, and attended by a heat of the skin.   The reason of this must be evident to every one who has attended these lectures.

The effect of sleep is to accumulate the excitability, or render it more sensible to the effects of any stimulants applied.   This takes place in every constitution, and much more in the more delicate: hence the heat of the bed, and of the tea, acts so powerfully on the surface, as, in general, to produce great perspiration, or, at any rate, great languor and debility.

Let me ask, can any one, who lives in this manner, expect to enjoy good health? With as great probability might we expect, that when we plunged a thermometer into hot water, the mercury would not rise, or when we applied a lighted match to gunpowder, it would not explode. The laws of nature are constant and uniform, and the same, or similar causes, both in the animate and inanimate world, are always productive of the same, or similar effects.

The cure of these complaints is at least obvious, if not easy. It consists in deserting crowded and heated rooms, at least for part of the time they have been usually occupied; in abstaining from strong wines; in keeping the bed rooms moderately cool; and retiring to rest at a proper hour.

With respect to the effects of nutriment, in producing asthenic diseases, we may observe, that all watery vegetable food, too sparing a use of animal food, as also meat which is too salt, and deprived of its nutritious juices by keeping, when more nutritious matter is at the same time withheld, constantly weaken, and thereby tend to produce asthenic diseases. Hence would appear to arise that remarkable imbecility of body and mind which distinguishes the Gentoos. Hence arise the diseases with which the poor are every where afflicted; hence scrofula, epilepsy, and the whole band of asthenic diseases.

But intemperance in eating and drinking, or taking nutritious and highly stimulant substances too freely, will, infallibly, bring on asthenic disease, or a state of indirect debility, by exhausting the excitability; and it must be observed, that this species of debility is much worse to cure than the direct kind; for in the latter we have abundance of excitability, and a variety of stimuli, by which we can exhaust it to the proper degree, and thus bring about the healthy state; whereas, in indirect debility, the vital principle or excitability is deficient; and we have not the means of reproducing it, at pleasure, absolutely under our command. Besides, the subtraction of stimulants, which is one of the most certain means we have of accumulating excitability, if carried to a great extent, in diseases of indirect debility, would produce death, before the system had power to reproduce the lost or exhausted excitability. Hence the cure, in these two kinds of debility, must be very different: in cases of direct debility, as in epilepsy, we must begin with gentle stimulants, and increase them with the greatest caution, till the healthy state is established: we must, however, guard most carefully against over doing it; for, if we should once overstep the bounds of excitement, and convert the direct into indirect debility, we shall have a disease to combat, in which we have both a want of excitement and of exciting power.

In cases of violent indirect debility, as, for instance, in gout, when it affects the stomach: it would be wrong to withdraw the stimulus, for the excitability is in such an exhausted state as to produce no action, or very imperfect and diseased, from the effect of the common exciting powers; we must, therefore, here apply a stimulus greater than natural, to bring on a vigorous and healthy action, and this stimulus we should gradually diminish, in order to allow the excitability to accumulate, by which the healthy state will be gradually restored.

This method was very judiciously recommended, by a very

eminent physician, in the case of a Highland chieftain, who had brought on dreadful symptoms of indigestion by the use of whisky, of which he drank a large silver cup full five or six times in the day   The doctor did not merely say, diminish the quantity of spirits gradually, for that simple advice would not have been followed; but he advised him to drink the cup the same number of times full, but each morning to melt into it as much wax as would receive the impression of the family seal. This direction, which had something magical in it in the mind of the chieftain, was punctually obeyed.   In a few months the cup was filled with wax, and would hold no more spirits; but it had thus been gradually diminished, and the patient was cured.

This reminds me of a number of cases, which had been brought on by drinking porter, and other stimulant liquors, without knowing the taste of water. In many of these cases if a moderate quantity of water were drank every day they would be cured; but you would find few who would follow such plain and simple directions. How then must a physician proceed? Why, as is generally done by the most judicious: they direct their patients to Bath or Buxton, and there advise them to swallow a certain quantity of water every day, which they do most scrupulously, and, of course, return home cured.

As causes of asthenic disease, we must not omit the undue exercise of the intellectual functions. Thinking is a powerful exciting cause, and produces effects similar to those of intoxication. None of the exciting powers have more influence upon our activity, than the exercise of the intellectual powers, as well as passion and emotion. Homer,

the great observer and copyist of nature, observes of the
hero, whom he gives for a pattern of eloquence, that, upon
his first address, before he had got into his train of thought,
he was awkward in every motion, and in his whole attitude;
he looked down upon the ground, and his hands hung straight
along his sides, as if they had lost the power of motion; and
his whole appearance was a picture of torpidity.   But when
he had once fairly entered upon his subject, his eyes were
all on fire, his limbs all motion, grace, and energy.

Hence, as the exercise of the intellectual functions evidently
stimulates, an excess of thinking must bring on indirect debility, by exhausting the excitability   But though we do
meet with instances of indirect debility arising from this
source, it must be confessed that they much oftener arise
from the use of very different stimulants.

As excessive exercise of the intellectual powers will bring
on indirect debility, so the deficient, weak, or vacant state
of mind, which is unable to carry on a train of thinking, will
produce direct debility   Indeed this debility often occurs
to those whose minds have been all their life actively engaged in business, but who have at last retired to enjoy
themselves, without having a cultivated mind fit for retirement.   They become languid, inert, and low spirited, for
want of the stimulus of mental exertion; and in many cases
cannot be completely restored to health, till they are again
engaged in their usual occupations.

Violent passions of the mind, such as great anger, keen
grief, or immoderate joy, often go to such an extent as to
exhaust the excitability, and bring on diseases of indirect de-

bility.   Hence both epilepsy and apoplexy have been the consequences of violent passion.

On the contrary, when there is a deficiency of exciting passion, as in melancholy, fear, despair, &c. which are only lower degrees or diminutions of joy, assurance, and hope, in the same way that cold is a diminution of heat, this produces a state of direct debility. The immediate consequences observable are, loss of appetite, loathing of food, sickness of the stomach, vomiting, pain of the stomach, colic, and even low fevers.

The effect of impure air, or air containing too small a proportion of oxygen, is likewise a very powerful cause of debility.

In short, when any or several of these causes, which have been mentioned, act upon the body, asthenic diseases are the consequence.

Asthenic diseases, as has frequently been hinted, may be divided into two classes, those of direct debility, and those of indirect debility.

Among the diseases of direct debility may be enumerated dyspepsia, hypochondriasis, hysteric complaints, epilepsy, bleeding of the nose, spitting and other effusions of blood, cholera morbus, chorea, rickets, scrofula, scurvy, diabetes, dropsy, worms, diarrhoea, asthma, cramp, intermittent fevers.

Among those of indirect debility, or which are produced by over stimulating, which exhausts the excitability, may be enumerated, gout, apoplexy, palsy, jaundice, and chronic inflammation of the liver, violent indigestion, confluent small pox, typhous fever, and probably the plague, dysentery, putrid sore throat, tetanus.

Diseases, therefore, according to this system, may be divided into two classes. First, general diseases, which commence with an affection of the whole system, and which must be accounted general, though some part may be more affected than the rest. Secondly, local diseases, which originate in a part, and which are to be regarded as local, though they may sometimes in their progress affect the whole system, like universal diseases: still however they are to be cured by remedies, applied not to the whole system, but to the part affected only.

A pleurisy or peripneumony, for instance, is a general disease, though the chief seat of the symptoms seems confined to a portion of the thorax: but the affection of this part, though it may be somewhat greater than that of any other equal part, is vastly less than the affection or diathesis diffused over the whole body. The exciting or hurtful causes which produce these diseases, by no means exert their whole power upon a small portion of the superficial vessels of the lungs, and leave the rest untouched; on the contrary, they affect every part of the system, and the whole body partakes of the morbid change. Indeed the general or universal affection; viz. a sense of heaviness and fullness, uneasy sleep, and other symptoms of increased excitement, are commonly perceived some time before the pain of the thorax becomes sensible. The remedies which remove the disease ; viz. venesection, abstaining from animal food, and every mode of debilitating, do not exert their whole efficacy on an inflamed portion of the lungs; for by removing the affection of the lungs we should go but a little way towards removing the disease.

Among local diseases we may enumerate wounds, or solutions of the continuity of the part, bruises, fractures, inflammations from local irritation, &c. Hence it is evident that the treatment of general diseases is the province of the physician; and of local ones of the surgeon. But there are some general diseases which are apt to degenerate into local, and therefore require the attention both of the physician and the surgeon. Among these we may reckon suppuration and gangrene, sphacelus, and some others.

The first class, or general diseases, may be divided into two orders; sthenic, and asthenic. The asthenic order may be subdivided into two genera; viz. diseases of direct debility, and diseases of indirect debility; for debility, according to the system I am explaining, is that relaxed or atonic state of the system which accompanies a deficient action of the stimulant or exciting powers; and this deficient action may arise immediately from the partial or too sparing application of the exciting powers; the excitability or capacity of the system to receive their actions, being unaffected or sufficiently abundant; or it may arise from the excitability being exhausted, by the violent or long continued action of the exciting powers.

This arrangement of diseases, which naturally follows from the fundamental principles of the doctrine, and which is guided by the state and degree of excitement, is widely different from that of former nosologists, who have arranged or classed them according to symptoms, which have already been shown to be fallacious; and which method of arrangement brings together diseases the most opposite in their nature, and separates those most nearly allied.   This is evident in every part of the nosology of Sauvages and Cullen.   In the genus cynanche of the latter, are placed the common sthenic or inflammatory sore throat, or cynanche tonsillaris, and the putrid or gangrenous sore throat, the cynanche maligna: the former is a sthenic disease; the latter one of the greatest debility ; yet they have the same generic name.

The mode of classing diseases which I have adopted, after the example of Dr. Brown, is the consequence of first taking a view of the nature of life, and the manner in which it is supported; and from thence observing how those variations from the healthy state, called diseases, are produced; and this is certainly the proper plan; for, as every effect will be produced with more accuracy, whilst its cause is acting in a proper degree, it is certainly right to begin by drawing our general propositions from the healthy state; by which means we avoid being misled by those false appearances which the living system puts on, during a morbid state; and though the contrary has been the general practice of nosologists and pathologists, I must confess it appears to me like beginning where the end should be; for to lay down rules for restoring health, and begin by observing the phenomena of disease, is like building a house, and beginning with the roof.

In the last lecture I pointed out the general method of curing sthenic diseases: I shall now proceed to the cure of asthenic, and shall begin with those depending on direct debility, as in these diseases the excitability is morbidly accumulated, and consequently more liable to be overpowered by the action of a stimulus, we must, therefore, at first, apply very gentle stimulants, increasing them by degrees, till the excitement be arrived at the healthy state.

In cases of indirect debility, the excitability is so far exhausted as not to be sufficiently acted on by the ordinary powers which support life; we must therefore employ, at first, pretty strong stimulants, to keep up such a degree of action as is necessary to preserve life ; we should, however, be careful not to overdo it ; for our intention here, in giving these stimuli, is only to keep up life, while the cure must depend upon the accumulation of the excitability. That this may take place, therefore, we must gradually lessen the quantity of stimulus, till the excitability become capable of being sufficiently acted on by the exciting powers, when the cure will be effected.

There is, however, an important point, with respect to the cure of diseases of exhausted excitability, which could not be known to Dr. Brown; and this depends on the fact which was formerly pointed out; viz. that the degree of excitability was in proportion to the oxydation of the system.   On this account I have given the oxygenated muriate of potash in typhus, which is a disease of diminished excitability, in more than one hundred cases, without the loss of one, a success which has attended no other mode of practice in this disease, if we except, perhaps, the affusion of cold water, as described by Dr. Currie, the effects of which are wonderful, but which can only be applied at the commencement of the disease.   In all diseases of indirect debility, therefore, it is proper to attempt the introduction of oxygen into the system, by the oxygenated muriate of potash, acid fruits, nitre, &c.   I do not think that the inhaling of oxygen gas for a few minutes in the day can do much good; but free ventilation of apartments, and gentle exercise in the open air, are highly useful.

In either case of debility, we should by no means rely on the action of medicines alone; for though there are a variety of stimulants which will produce excitement, yet this is only temporary, we must therefore endeavour, by nutritious substances, to fill the vessels with blood, and employ all the natural exciting powers in due proportion as soon as possible.

But in the cure of either sthenic or asthenic diseases we shall seldom succeed by the use of one remedy only: for since no stimulus exerts its effects equally on all parts of the body, but always acts more powerfully on some part than on others, we cannot by the use of one remedy alone obtain an equal increase or diminution of excitement.

There are few diseases however in which the excitement is equally increased or diminished over the body; some part being generally more affected than the rest; and this inequality produces the various phenomena or forms of disease; indeed no disease but increase or diminution of strength would take place, on the supposition that an equal increase or diminution of excitement all over the body, were produced by the hurtful powers causing the disease.

From what has been said, it necessarily follows, that every stimulus will not be equally efficacious in curing every form of disease; which is sufficiently confirmed by experience. Hence there may be some ground for the appellation of specifics, as some medicines may act more powerfully upon the part which is the principal seat of the disease, than others do.

In the cure of diseases we ought always to attend to two things most carefully: first, to employ the proper kinds of powers, and then not to overdo them, so as to convert either diathesis into the other; and by passing over the line of health, instead of the intended cure, to substitute one disease instead of another, and thereby bring life itself into danger.

LECTURE XIII.

ON THE GOUT.

There is no disease, with which the human race is afflicted, whose nature has been more mistaken than that which is to form the subject of our present consideration. It has been regarded by most practitioners as a salutary effort of the body to expel some hurtful cause, and restore health; and therefore has been looked upon as desirable to the patient. To attempt to cure it, therefore, would have been wrong, had it been curable; but it has likewise been looked upon as beyond the reach of medicine, or perfectly incurable; and, on both these accounts, after having tried a variety of drugs, without any good effect, the physicians have at last abandoned their patients, to the care of patience and flannel, which, if the constitution be not very much shattered, will often see them through the disease.

But that it is a salutary disease I deny; and I affirm, that it restores health in no other way, than the indigestion of a habitual dram drinker would be relieved by a disease in the throat, which would, for a time, prevent his swallowing any more liquor; the consequence would be, that his digestive powers would recover their tone, and he would, after a few weeks, feel himself better.

In the same way the pain and fever, which attend gout,

and at the same time the inability to move, with the weakened
stomach, and bad appetite, prevent the continuance of the
mode of life which brought on the disease; and thus, a truce
being obtained, the exhausted excitability of the body is
allowed to accumulate, and the constitution, of course, feels
itself renovated.

Were the disease to be viewed in this light, it is probable
that many patients might in future desist from their former
mode of life, which brought on the disease; and we might
venture to promise them, if they did, that they would have
no return of the complaint.   But the misfortune is, they
think the gout has restored their constitution, and that therefore they may return to their old mode of living with impunity: in consequence of which, after a few months more,
the excitability is again exhausted; symptoms of indigestion
come on, and the stimulant mode of living is increased, with
a view to bring on the disease, which is to cure these symptoms.   In this way, each time, a greater and greater degree
of indirect debility is induced, and at last the system becomes
so enfeebled, that the asthenic inflammation is not confined
to the extremities, but attacks the head, the stomach, the
lungs, and often puts a period to the existence of the patient,
which has for some time been miserable.

Besides, the idea, that the gout is incurable, is a false, and
a very dangerous doctrine; this is very far from being the
case, and I am firmly persuaded, not only from the nature
of the disease, but from experience, that it may always be
cured, if taken in time, and proper directions be followed.
If, by the cure of gout be meant the administration of some
pill, some powder, or some potion, which shall drive away

the complaint, I firmly believe, that it never was, nor ever will be cured. Indeed, it is astonishing that such an idea should have ever entered the mind of any person, who has any knowledge of nature, or particularly of the human frame; for, if the gout is a disease of indirect debility, and the effect of intemperance, as will be shown by and by, then a medicine to cure it must be something to enable a man to bear the daily effects of intemperance, during his future life, unhurt by the gout, or any other disease ; that is, it must be something given now, that will take away the effects of a future cause: as well might a medicine be given to prevent a man breaking his leg, or his arm, seven years hence.

But no rational physician, or surgeon, would give a medicine with this view, in such a case as I have supposed; on the contrary, he would caution his patient against mounting precipices, scaling walls, or bringing himself again into a situation, such as produced the accident; and if he took his advice, he would, in all probability, escape a broken limb in future.

In the same way a rational physician would advise a person recovering from gout, to abstain totally and entirely from the course of life which brought it on; and this being complied with, we might venture to predict, with as much certainty in the one case as in the other, that he would in future escape it.

What I have frequently endeavoured to inculcate in the course of these lectures, always appears to me of the utmost importance: I mean, the general diffusion of physiological knowledge, or a knowledge of the human frame; this knowledge ought to form a part of general education, and is, in my opinion, as necessary for a person to learn as writing, or accounts, or any other branch of education; for if it is necessary that a young man should learn these, that he may be able to take care of his affairs, it surely can be no less necessary, that he should learn to take care of his health; for to enjoy good health, as a celebrated practical philosopher observes, is better than to command the world.

If knowledge of this kind were generally diffused, people would cease to imagine that the human constitution was so badly contrived, that a state of general health could be overset by every trifle; for instance, by a little cold; or that the recovery of it lay concealed in a few drops, or a pill. Did they better understand the nature of chronic diseases, and the causes which produce them, they could not be so unreasonable as to think, that they might live as they chose with impunity; or did they know any thing of medicine, they would soon be convinced, that though fits of pain have been relieved, and sickness cured, for a time, the reestablishment of health depends on very different powers and principles. Those who are acquainted with the nature and functions of the living body, well know, that health is not to be established by drugs; but that if it can be restored, it must be by nicely adjusting the action of the exciting powers to the state of the constitution, and the excitability; and thus gently and gradually calling forth the powers of the body to act for themselves. And though I believe that most general diseases will admit of a cure, yet I am confident, that no invalid was ever made a healthy man by the mere power of drugs. If this is a truth, should it not be universally known? If it were, there would undoubtedly be an end of quackery, for all quack medicines, from the balm of Gilead, to the botanical syrup, are supposed to cure diseases, or at least asserted to do so, in this mysterious manner.

Dr. Cullen, in his Nosology, gives us the following definition of the gout.

" Morbus haereditarius, oriens sine causa externa evidente, sed praeeunte plerumque ventriculi affectione insolita; pyrexia ; dolor ad articulum, et plerumque pedis pollici, certe pedum et manuum juncturis, potissimum infestus; per intervalla revertens, et saepe cum ventriculi et internarum partium affectionibus alternans."

Now, though this definition comprises a tolerably good general character of the disease, it contains some notions, depending on the prejudice of hypothesis, which, on a careful examination, ought not, I think, to be admitted.

In the first place, I would deny, that the gout, considered as a diseased state of the system, is hereditary. This may perhaps excite some degree of surprise; and, " I had it from my father," is in the mouth of a great majority of gouty patients.

If the diseased state of the system, which occurs in gout, were hereditary, it would necessarily be transmitted from father to son; and no man, whose father had it, could possibly be free from it. There are, however, many instances to the contrary. Our parents undoubtedly give us constitutions similar to their own, and there is no doubt, that if we live in the same manner in which they did, we shall have the same diseases. This, however, by no means proves the disease to be hereditary.

We shall hereafter see, that the gout is a disease of indirect debility, brought on by a long continued use of high
seasoned food and fermented liquors. There is no doubt
that particular constitutions are more liable to be affected
by this mode of living than others; and if my father's constitution be such, I, who probably resemble him in constitution, shall in all probability be like him, subject to the
gout, provided I live in the same way; this however by
no means proves the disease to be hereditary. The sons of
the rich, indeed, who succeed to their fathers estate, generally succeed also to his gout, while those who are excluded from the former, are also exempted from the latter,
and for very obvious reasons, unless they acquire it by
their own merit.

So that though the son of a gouty parent may have a
constitution predisposing to the gout; that is, more liable
to be affected by causes, which produce this disease, still,
if he regulate the stimuli to the state of his excitability,
he will remain exempt from it.

This distinction is of much greater importance than is
generally imagined; for if a person firmly believes that the
gout, as a disease, is hereditary, what will be his conduct?
My father had the gout, says he, therefore I must have it;
well, what cannot be avoided, must be endured; let me
then enjoy a short life, but a merry one: he therefore aban-
dons himself to a luxurious mode of life, and, if the gout be
the consequence, which most probably it will, he accuses his
stars, and his ancestors, instead of his own misconduct.

On the contrary, if a person be convinced that he has
received from his ancestors a constitution liable to be

overpowered by the use of high seasoned food, and fermented liquors, and excited into gouty action, what will be his conduct? Surely, if he reason at all, it must be in this way: my father was dreadfully afflicted with the gout; I have frequently witnessed his sufferings with the deepest concern. But is not my constitution, which resembles his, liable to be affected in the same manner, by similar causes? To avoid his sufferings, therefore, I must be very temperate; more so than those who have not the hereditary propensity; for the exciting powers, which would only keep them in health, would, if applied to me, infallibly bring on the gout. In consequence of this reasoning, he adopts a temperate mode of living, and avoids the disease.

From this you must be convinced, that it is not a matter of small moment to determine, whether the gout is hereditary, and consequently unavoidable, or not. The next part of Dr. Cullen's definition is " oriens sine causa evidente". This too, I can have little hesitation to pronounce erroneous. The cause of gout, namely, the use of highly seasoned food, and the use of fermented liquors, with, in general, a luxurious, and indolent mode of living, are quite evident enough in most gouty cases, and are amply sufficient to produce the disease.

There is another part of the definition, likewise, to which I would object, as it gives a false idea of the nature of the disease, and therefore causes the preventative plan to be pursued with less confidence. I mean that part where he says " per intervalla revertens."

That the gout, when once cured, is apt to return, if the mode of life which brought it on be not abandoned, no one

will deny; nay, the fits will increase in violence, because
the constitution gets more and more debilitated. This,
however, is not peculiar to the gout, but common to most
diseases.

In describing a broken leg, it would surely be wrong to
say, that it is a disease which returns at intervals, after being
cured; yet, it will return as infallibly as the gout, if a person
take the same kind of leap, or expose himself to the same
accidents as those which brought it on. Let those, therefore,
who wish to avoid a return of the gout, totally change their
mode of living: otherwise, if the attacks return, let them
blame themselves, and not the nature of the complaint.

These observations were thought necessary, with a view
to do away some prejudices, which very much retarded our
inquiries into the nature and cure of this disease. I shall
now proceed to give an account of the symptoms by which
it is usually attended.

The gout generally attacks the male sex ; but it sometimes,
though more rarely, attacks also the female, particularly those
of robust and full habits. It does not generally make its
appearance, till the period of greatest strength and vigour
is past ; for instance, about the fortieth year; but, in some
cases, where the exciting causes have been powerfully applied, or where the hereditary predisposition is very strong,
it attacks much earlier; such cases are, however, comparatively rare, and can, in general, be easily accounted for.

This disease is seldom known to attack persons employed
in constant bodily labour, and who live temperately ; and
is totally unknown to those who use no wine or other fermented liquors.

If then a person of a full strong habit have for several years accustomed himself to full diet of animal food, and a regular use of wine, and malt liquor, though he may for a long time find that he can perform all the functions with vigour, his strength will at last fail : the mind and body become affected with a degree of torpor and languor for which he cannot account, and the functions of the stomach become more or less disturbed. The appetite becomes diminished, and flatulency, and other symptoms of indigestion are felt. These symptoms take place for several days, and sometimes for several weeks before the fit comes on ; but often, on the day immediately preceding it, the appetite becomes greater than usual.

In this state, if the person have fatigued himself by violent exercise, or if he have exposed the extremities to cold, or if his mind have been particularly affected by any anxiety, or distressing event ; or in short, if any directly debilitating cause have been applied, the fit will often follow. It sometimes comes on in the evening, but more commonly, about two or three o'clock in the morning ; the pain is felt in one foot, most commonly in the ball or first joint of the great toe ; but sometimes in the instep, or other parts of the foot. With the coming on of this pain there is generally more or less of a cold shivering, which as the pain increases, gradually ceases, and is succeeded by heat, which often continues as long as the pain; from the first attack the pain becomes by degrees more violent, and continues in this state, with great restlessness of the whole body, till next midnight, after which it gradually remits, and after the disease has continued for twenty four hours from the commencement of the first attack, it of-

ten ceases, and with the coming on of a gentle perspiration allows the patient to fall asleep. The patient on coming out
of this sleep in the morning finds the part affected with some
degree of redness and swelling, which, after having continued for some days, gradually abate.

Still however, after a fit has come on in this manner, although the violence of the pain after twenty four hours, by
the excitement that it produces, cures itself, and is considerably abated, the patient is seldom entirely relieved from it.
For several days he has every evening a return of considerable pain and fever, which continue with more or less violence till morning. This return is owing to the exhaustion
of the excitability by the stimuli of the day, and its remission
is caused by the accumulation of the excitability, by sleep.

After having continued in this manner for several days, the
disease often goes off, and generally leaves the person in
much better health, and enjoying greater alacrity in the
functions of both body and mind, than he had for some time
experienced. This is owing to the general excitement produced
by the pain, which removes the great torpor and debility
which preceded the fit ; and from the inability to take exercise or food, the excitability accumulates again. This is the
true explanation : it does not depend on any morbid matter,
which the gout hunts from its lurking places, drives to a joint,
and thence out of the body, as has been imagined by many.

At first the attacks of the disease are confined to one foot
only : afterwards both feet become affected, though seldom
at the same time ; but when the inflammation appears in
one, it generally disappears in the other, and as the disease
continues to recur, it not only affects both feet at once, but

is felt in the other joints, especially those in the upper and lower extremities, so that there is scarcely a joint in the body that is not on one occasion or other affected. After frequent attacks, the pains are commonly less violent than they were at first, the joints lose their strength and flexibility, and often become so stiff as to be deprived of all motion.

Concretions of a chalky or calcarious nature are likewise formed upon the outside of the joints. This arises from an inability of the capillary vessels, which ought to secrete the calcarious matter, and deposite it in the bones, to perform their office, from debility : hence by sympathy other vessels ta ke up the matter and deposite it in a wrong place. These concretions, though at first fluid, become at last dry, and firm : they effervesce with acids, and are totally, or in a great measure, soluble in them.

After this short description of the gout, when it occurs in its regular form, as it is called, I shall now proceed to inquire how the exciting causes produce this disease, and what is the state of the body under which it occurs.

The gout seldom occurs but in those who have for several years lived upon a full diet of animal food, often highly seasoned, and at the same time been in the habit of taking daily, or at least very constantly, a greater or less quantity of fermented liquors, either in the form of wine, or malt liquor, or both. The affection of the limb has all the appearance of an active inflammation : the part becomes swelled, hot, red, and intolerably painful. It is this circumstance which has misled practitioners, who have supposed it a case of sthenic, or active inflammation : not only the appearance, but the causes which produced it, induced them to think so; hence they were naturally led to employ the debilitating plan : a little time and observation would, however, be sufficient to convince them of its inefficacy. They would find that the application of leeches to the part, and of the lancet to the arm, instead of subduing the inflammation, would increase it : or if it did not, that the pain often attacked some internal part, which was ascribed to a translation of the morbific matter from one part to another, but which is merely owing to an increased debility : a little attentive observation would convince practitioners, however mysterious it might seem to them, that this violent inflammation was not to be cured by debilitating : on the contrary, they would see cases, in which the patient, though contrarily to the strict orders of his physicians, could not forego his old habits ; but would take his wine as usual, or in greater quantity, after a few days abstinence ; and this abstinence having in some degree accumulated the excitability, he would find himself much relieved by wine, and would exultingly tell them, that they were mistaken. Circumstances of this kind seem to have staggered their faith a little, but still the idea of active inflammation which they believed was visible, and almost palpable, dwelt so upon their minds, that they were but half convinced. The favourite idea of increased action of the vessels of the part had so interwoven itself with every other, that we find it never lost sight of, in the indications of cure. Hence, though bleeding is not now generally practised with the lancet, yet leeches are often applied ; but the most usual plan is to consign the patient to patience and flannel ; strictly forbidding wine, or fermented liquors. As an exception to this general mode, it is however observed, by some practitioners, that when the stomach is weak, and when the patient has been much accustomed to the use of strong liquors, a little animal food, and even wine, may be allowable, and even necessary.

Thus has an erroneous view of the disease been the cause of an inert practice, which wavers between the suggestions of a favourite hypothesis, and the conviction of facts.

On inquiry, however, we shall find none of the increased vigour in the system, which has been suspected, nor increased action in the part more particularly affected; on the contrary, the whole body is in a state of indirect debility, or exhausted excitability, and the part more particularly affected, in a state of asthenic inflammation.

If the gout were of a sthenic or inflammatory nature, might we not ask, why the causes which produce it, do not produce it in the meridian of life, when they produce their greatest effect, and when real sthenic diseases are most apt to occur? or, why the symptoms of the inflammation, like all other real sthenic inflammations, are not relieved by the debilitating plan? The contrary, however, points out to us clearly the nature of the disease: the gout is not a sthenic disease, or a disease of strength: it does not depend upon increased vigour of the constitution, and plethora, but is manifestly asthenic, like all the rest of the asthenic diseases. The mode of living is such as brings on indirect debility, or exhaustion of the excitability, such as the use of rich and highly seasoned food, and a daily use of fermented liquors. These at first certainly produce vigour, or strength, and will be the cause of sthenic diseases; but they are generally taken in such a manner, that, though they produce a degree of excitement above the point of health, still they only approach the line of sthenic disease, without in general falling into it. They continue, however, to exhaust the excitability, and by the time that the vigour of the body begins naturally to decline, the system of a person who has lived in this manner is unusually torpid ; all the blood vessels, which have hitherto been distended with rich blood, begin to lose their tone, from their excitability having been exhausted by the use of these powerful stimulants ; but this torpor is particularly and first experienced in those parts which have been more immediately subject to the action of the exciting causes; viz. the stomach and bowels: symptoms of indigestion occur, and the excitability of these organs having been almost entirely exhausted by the violent action of the stimulants applied, cannot now be roused to any healthy action ; the food is not properly digested, but runs into a kind of fermentation, which causes an extrication of gas: this distends the stomach and bowels, and produces pains, uneasy eructations, and all the distressing symptoms of indigestion. Nor is this in the least surprising, when we consider that many people who have brought on complaints of this kind, have been in the habit of eating heartily of rich and highly seasoned animal food, and of drinking from a pint to a bottle of wine, and perhaps a quantity of malt liquor, almost every day of their lives for years. This mode is sufficient to wear out the powers of the stomach, were it three times as capacious as it is, and of the constitution, were it ten times as strong.

When a torpor, or state of exhausted excitability, of the whole system, has been induced in this manner, and symptoms of indigestion produced, any directly debilitating

cause applied to the extremities, adding to the indirect debility, causes a total torpor, or inactivity of the minute vessels of the part, and thus totally destroys the balance between the propelling and resisting force; hence the
vessels will be morbidly distended with blood, a swelling
and redness will take place, and an asthenic inflammation,
produced in the way which I fully pointed out in the last
lecture, will be established. Hence the pain, and other
symptoms, which accompany a fit of the gout. Hence likewise we see, why debilitating powers applied to the part will
not reduce the inflammation ; and why a warmth, which ag-
gravates every really sthenic inflammatory affection, is so
comfortable in this.

Almost any debilitating cause, when the system has been
brought by intemperance to the torpid state, which I have
described, will bring on a fit of the gout, but nothing more
certainly than cold or moisture : hence if a person have his
feet chilled or wet, he will be almost certain to have an attack.

Hence we see that the asthenic inflammation is not the
disease, but merely a symptom of it ; and like other symptoms, fallacious in its appearance ; the disease is a state of
indirect debility, to which our attention ought to be
directed.

When this inflammation is violent, and accompanied with
great pain, after several hours continuance, it excites the action of the minute vessels, enables them to propel the blood,
by which they are morbidly distended, and restores the balance between the resisting and the propelling force ; and
thus the inflammatory appearances will for a time subside,
but the torpor of the whole system remaining, and the debi-

lity of the vessels returning, when their excitement, which
was the consequence of their action, has ceased, another asthenic inflammation will take place, which will again cure
itself as before ; so that during a paroxysm, several remis-
sions will take place, as was mentioned in the description of
the disease. As, during the paroxysm, the pain causes a considerable degree of excitement over the whole system, the
action of the stomach and other parts is roused by it ;
during the fit likewise, little nutriment is taken, so that by
the action of the stomach and bowels, they get rid of their
load ; rest likewise assists to accumulate the excitability, so
that from all these causes together, the body becomes restored to a state of vigour, which, compared with its former
torpidity, makes the patient imagine that this friendly disease
has restored him to a state of unusual health, and even renovated the powers of his constitution. Under this mistaken
idea, he does not, when the fit leaves him, abandon the mode
of life, which brought on the disease ; highly seasoned food,
and the usual quantity of wine, are again resorted to : after a
time the torpor of the system, and symptoms of indigestion
return, and he again hopes that his friend the gout will come
and cure him.

By a continuance of this plan, the inflammation again appears ; but the system having become more torpid, the inflammatory action is by no means so great as it was before :
if it has power to restore the equilibrium between the resistance and propelling force, and thus cure itself, this effect is
entirely confined to the inflamed part. The other foot labouring under similar torpor, or debility, now feels the effects of the propelling force, and an inflammation takes place

in it, which having cured itself in the same manner, and the torpor of the foot first affected being returned, or even greater than it was before, on account of the previous excitement ; the inflammation again attacks this foot, and thus the gout is supposed to emigrate from one limb to another. The gout, as a disease of general debility, however, remains the same ; and it is only these symptoms, which form but a small part of the disease, that vary according to circumstances.

If, during an asthenic inflammation of the lower, or upper extremities, the torpor and debility of the whole system increase, then the force of the circulation, or propelling force, being diminished, the symptoms of inflammation will suddenly disappear ; but as great debility now prevails, the stomach will be apt to be affected with cramps or convulsions, or an asthenic inflammation of some internal part will take place: for, though the propelling force is not sufficient to overdistend the debilitated vessels of the extremities, it will distend those of the internal parts nearer the heart, which are now debilitated.

In this case, it has been generally, but absurdly imagined, that the gout is translated, or recedes from the extremities to some internal part: the term of retrocedent gout has therefore been applied to occurrences of this nature. From the explanation which has been given, it is evident, that this term is improper. The general debility being increased, the propelling force becomes unable to produce an inflammation of the extremities, and this is the reason why it disappears. The disease, however, is not at all altered in its nature by this variation of symptoms. It is still the same, by whatever name it may be called.

It sometimes happens, that after full living, the stomach becomes particularly affected, and the patient is troubled with flatulency, indigestion, loss of appetite, eructations, nausea, and vomiting, with great dejection of spirits, pain and giddiness of the head, disturbed recollection, or muddiness of intellect, as it is termed, with all the symptoms, which usually precede a regular fit of the gout, yet no inflammatory affection of the joints is produced. This state has been absurdly enough called the atonic gout, as if there were a gout accompanied with vigour and sthenic diathesis: but the absence of inflammation in the extremities may depend on two causes. First, the powers producing the disease, may have debilitated the stomach and first passages, while the vessels of the extremities are not particularly debilitated, and the resisting force is able to counterbalance the propelling force: in this case, no morbid degree of distention or inflammation of the extreme vessels can take place. Secondly, the general debility may be such, and the power of the circulation so much diminished, that, though the extreme vessels may be debilitated, no inflammation, or preternatural distention will take place.

Hence, we see, that this is still the same disease; but that physicians have erred in their explanation of the symptoms, by regarding that as the principal part of the disease, which is only a symptom.

We have seen then, that by the theory which has been unfolded, all the symptoms of this hitherto mysterious disease are plainly and naturally explained. We shall next see if the only method of cure which experience warrants, cannot be explained upon the same principles.

If, on entering on this part of the subject, any one should expect that I should furnish him with a receipt, consisting of certain drugs, which swallowed, will cause this terrible disease to disappear, and health to take its place, he would be very much mistaken ; for, can any person in his senses suppose that a disease, which he has been almost his whole life in contracting, and an exhausted state of the excitability, which has been gradually brought on by years of intemperance, can be dispersed by a pill, a powder, or a julep? Or, if the symptoms could be relieved by medicine, which they often may, can he suppose, that they will not return, if the same mode of living, which first brought them on, be continued ?

I shall, however, proceed to give some directions, which if rigidly persevered in, will not only afford relief in the fit, but will prevent its return with such violence, and at last totally eradicate it, provided the constitution be not completely exhausted, and almost every joint stiffened with calcarious concretions.

The inflammation of the extremities may at any time be relieved by means of electricity, or by stimulant embrocations applied to the part, and this without any danger whatever of throwing the complaint on some more vital part, as has generally been imagined. If I were to apply any debilitating means to the part, I should then probably relieve the pain ; but, by debilitating the whole system, should cause an attack of the stomach, or some other internal part, as has

been already explained ; but by a stimulant application to
the inflamed part I run no such risk. The inflammation is of
the asthenic kind, depending upon a debility of the small
vessels, whereby they do not afford sufficient resistance to
the propelling force, and therefore become morbidly distended, or inflamed, as it is termed, though this term is certainly improper, even in a metaphorical view : but a stimulant application to the part excites the debilitated vessels to action ; their contraction diminishes the morbid
quantity of blood ; and the balance between the propelling
and resisting forces being restored, the inflammation of course
ceases.   This is not a mere deduction, a priori, from the theory of inflammation, which I have delivered ; it is the result of
repeated experience.   I have seen several very violent gouty
inflammations very speedily removed by electricity.   Small
sparks should be drawn from the part affected, at first
through flannel, and increased as the patient can bear them :
sparks alone are necessary ;   recourse need never be had to
shocks.   But though we thus remove a very painful part of
the disease, yet still a formidable debility remains, and unless this be removed, the inflammation will be apt to return.
In endeavouring to remove this general debility, we must recollect, that it is of the indirect kind, or depends upon an
exhausted state of the excitability ; our great object therefore, is to allow the excitability to accumulate.   But this
accumulation depends as well upon the proper action of
the different functions, as upon the withdrawing of stimulants : we ought therefore to guard carefully against costiveness, by which the proper action of the stomach and bowels
is very much injured : but we must use warm laxatives.

An infusion of senna and rhubarb in proof spirits, made still stronger by aromatics, has always seemed to me to answer the purpose best, and this should be taken of a temperature rather above blood warm ; for instance, about 100 degrees. This is particularly necessary, when the gout attacks the stomach, and I have several times seen a severe attack of it removed in half an hour, by a tincture of this kind. Indeed, the most violent attacks of the stomach may be relieved ; and are only to be relieved by spirits, ether, and opium.

It is on this organ, that the hurtful powers have produced their greatest effect ; for to it they are immediately applied. It is by no means surprising, that the constant application of highly seasoned foods, with fermented and spirituous liquors, should at last wear out the vital principle of this organ. Indeed it is often so far exhausted, that the most terrible cramps and convulsions take place, which would soon end in its total extinction, unless it were roused to somewhat like a proper action by the most powerful stimulants. Still, however, their effect is but temporary.

With respect to a regular fit, after the inflammation of the extremities has been subdued by the means I have mentioned, a generous, but not full diet should be used. A person who has been for a long time accustomed to wine, cannot easily be deprived of it at once ; but he should drink Madeira, and those wines, which neither contain much carbonic acid, nor deposite much tartar. His food should be of the plainest kind, and generally boiled, instead of roast. The great thing is to keep the spirits and excitement rather under par, but not to let the patient sink too low. In this way, the exhausted excitability will gradually accumulate, and the healthy state be reestablished. When this is once effected, the gout may be prevented in future with the greatest certainty, if the patient will have resolution. The whole secret consists in abstaining, in toto, from alcohol, in every form, however disguised, or however diluted. He must not take it, either in the form of liqueurs, cordials, wine, or even small beer.

I believe there never was an instance of a person having the gout, who totally abstained from every form of alcohol, however he might live in other respects; and I doubt very much, if ever the gout returned after a person had abstained from fermented or spirituous liquors for two years.

Temperance in eating, and exercise, are, no doubt, powerful auxiliaries, and tend very much to promote health; but still they will not secure a person from a return of the gout, without this precaution. There seems something in alcohol, which peculiarly brings on this state of the constitution, and without it, it would seem that gout could not be produced. Here then is an effectual method of curing the gout, which will no more return, if this method be strictly persevered in, than the smallpox will attack the constitution after inoculation.

During the fit therefore, I would say, nearly in the words of Dr. Darwin, Drink no malt liquor on any account. Let the beverage at dinner consist of two glasses of Madeira, diluted with three half pints of water ; on no account whatever drink any more wine or spirituous liquors in the course of the day. Eat meat constantly at dinner, without any seasoning, but with any kind of tender vegetables, that are found to agree. When the fit is removed, use the warm bath twice a week, an hour before going to bed, at about 93°, or 94° of heat. Keep the body open by means of lenitive electuary and rhubarb ; for there is an objection to the tincture I mentioned, as containing alcohol. Use constant, gentle exercise ; but never so violent as to bring on great fatigue. The grand secret, however, in the cure, as has been already observed, but which cannot be too often inculcated, is to abstain, in toto, from every thing that contains alcohol.

In short, though in acute diseases medicines are highly useful, a chronic disease can never be cured, and the healthy state reestablished, by them alone. To effect a cure in such cases, we must reform our mode of life, change our bad habits into good ones ; and then, if we have patience to wait the slow operations of nature, we shall have no reason to regret our former luxuries.

LECTURE XIV

NERVOUS COMPLAINTS, &c.

In this lecture I propose to take a view of some of those affections, which have been commonly, but improperly known by the appellation of nervous complaints, because it has been supposed by many that they are owing to a deranged state of the nerves, which, however, is by no means the case ; for I hope to be able to make it appear, that these symptoms arise from a general affection of the excitement of the system. In short, by far the greater number of these complaints, arise from such a state of the excitement as approaches predisposition, or perhaps ranges between predisposition and disease, but does not in general actually reach disease ; or rather, it is a state of the excitement, so far departing from the point of perfect health, that the functions are not performed with that alacrity, or vigour, which ought to take place ; but labour under that disturbed and uneasy action, which, though it cannot be called actual disease, yet deviates considerably from the point of perfect health.

This is a new view of these diseases, but the more I have examined it, the more I am convinced that it is just. Indeed, the name, nervous; has generally been given to an

assemblage of symptoms, which the physicians did not understand ; and when the patient relates a history of symptoms, and expects that his physician shall inform him of the
name, and nature of his complaint, he generally receives for
answer, that his complaints are nervous, or bilious ; terms
which convey no distinct ideas, but which serve to satisfy
the patient, and to conceal the ignorance of the physician,
or spare him the labour of thinking.

Indeed, the idea of nervous diseases, which I have
already pointed at, is not only new, but could only
have arisen from such a view as we have been taking of
the states of excitement and excitability. This view will
not only lead us to form a more just idea of the manner in
which these diseases originate, but will point out a distinction of them into two classes, of the utmost use in practice,
but which distinction has totally escaped the attention of
practitioners ; for though these complaints have been generally thought to arise from a lowness of the nervous
energy, or some kind of debility, or weakness of the nervous system, and, on this account, the stimulant and cordial
plan of cure has been recommended, I am convinced, from
observation, that nearly one half of them, if not more,
originate from a state of the excitement verging towards
sthenic disease ; and in these cases, this general mode of
treatment must be highly improper.

It has been already shown, that when the common exciting powers which support life, act in such a manner, that a
middle degree of exciting power, acts upon a middle degree
of excitability, the most perfect state of the system, or a
state of perfect health, takes place : it is, however, seldom

in our power so to proportion the state of excitement and
excitability to each other.   The action of the exciting powers
is continually varying in strength ; and the excitability, from
a variety of stimulants, and other circumstances, which are
not entirely under our direction, is sometimes more, and
sometimes less abundant, than this middle degree.   There
is, however, a considerable latitude, on each side the point
of health, within which the excitement may vary, and yet
no disease, nor any disturbance of the functions may take
place : but this has its limits, beyond which if the excitement be brought, on either side, it is evident that an uneasy
or unpleasant exercise of the functions must take place.
There is not, however, any precise line or boundary between this state, and that in which the functions begin to be
disturbed ; on the contrary, the law of continuity and gradation seems to extend throughout every part of nature.
This departure from the healthy state, and approach to disease, in which what has been called the nervous state consists, is gradual and scarcely perceptible ; but is apt to be
produced by any circumstances, which lead the excitement
beyond its proper limits.

Nervous complaints may therefore be divided, like all
other diseases, into two classes.   First, those in which the
excitement is increased, or in which it verges to, or has actually reached, the point of predisposition to sthenic disease;
Secondly, those in which the excitement is diminished, or in
which it verges towards asthenic disease.   This last class, as
has been done before, may be subdivided into two orders.
The first will comprise those diseases in which the excitability is sufficiently abundant, or even accumulated, but

where the excitement is deficient from a want of energy in the exciting powers. In the second, there has been no deficiency in the action of the exciting powers; but on the contrary, probably for a considerable time, some of the diffusible stimuli not natural to life have been applied; in this case, the excitability has become exhausted, and a proper degree of excitement cannot be produced by the action of the common exciting powers.

No diseases show so clearly the fallacy of trusting to symptoms, as those of the former class. I have met with innumerable cases of this kind, in which, if you were to trust to the patients own description, they laboured under considerable debility; and had it not been for the particular attention I paid to my own case, I should not probably have suspected that a directly opposite state of the system may produce these symptoms.

From inheriting a good constitution, and being brought up in the country in a hardy manner, I am so much predisposed to the sthenic state, that I may consider the state of my excitement, as generally, indeed almost always, above the point of health; and unless I live in the most temperate, and even abstemious manner, the excitement is extremely liable to overstep the bounds of predisposition, and fall into sthenic disease. I have had several attacks of this kind of disease; and indeed, I never remember to have laboured under any disease of debility, or diminished excitement.

Health, according to the view we have taken of it, may be compared to a musical string, tuned to a certain pitch, or note; and though perhaps in the great bulk of mankind, either from the manner of living, or from other circumstances,

the excitement is a little below, and requires to be screwed
up to the healthy pitch, yet there are others where it is apt
to get constantly above, and where it requires letting down
to this pitch ; my constitution is one of these : but I have
this consolation, that if I can for a few years ward off the
fatal effects of some acute sthenic diseases, this tendency to
sthenic diathesis will gradually wear off, and I may probably enjoy a state of good health, at a time, when most
constitutions of an opposite cast begin to give way.
Whenever I have for some time lived rather fully, though by
no means intemperately, after having for some days, or
perhaps some weeks experienced an unusually good flow of
spirits, and taken exercise with pleasure, I begin, first of all,
to have disturbed sleep, I find myself inclined to sleep in the
morning, as if I had not been refreshed by the night's sleep ;
my spirits become low, and I am apt to look upon the gloomy
side of every thing I undertake or do.   I feel a general sense
of languor and debility, and am ready, as I have heard
many patients labouring under the same state exclaim, to
sink into the earth.   From the slightest causes, I am apt to
apprehend the most serious evils, and my temper becomes
irritable, and scarcely to be pleased with any thing.   If in
this state, I take exercise, I soon feel myself fatigued ; a
disagreeable stupor comes on, without, however, the least
degree of perspiration, and I feel an inability to move.

At first, I used to imagine these to be symptoms of debility, or diminished excitement, nor was it till after several
ineffectual trials to relieve them by the tonic, or stimulant
plan, that I was convinced of my mistake.   This plan always
caused an aggravation of every symptom, and if I persevered

in it, an inflammatory disease was sure to be the consequence. Indeed, I might have suspected this, from considering, that these symptoms had been brought on by full
living, and preceded by good spirits ; but my mind had received such a prejudice from the writings of medical men,
who had uniformly described these as a train of nervous
symptoms, as they called them, depending on a debilitated
state of the nervous system, that I was blind to conviction,
till repeated disappointment from the stimulating plan, convinced me I must be wrong. The only alternative therefore,
was a contrary plan, and the immediate relief I experienced,
was a proof that I had detected the real nature of the
complaint. Since that time, I can at any time prevent
these unpleasant symptoms, by an abstemious course of life,
and remove them, when they have come on, by the debilitating plan ; which, instead of weakening, gives additional
elasticity and strength to the fibres, and alacrity to the
spirits. I have described the symptoms in one case, as this
will serve as a general description. We may add, that persons labouring under this kind of predisposition, are particularly attentive to the state of their own health, and to
every change of feeling in their bodies ; and from every uneasy sensation, perhaps of the slightest kind, they apprehend great danger, and even death itself. In cases of this
kind, the bowels are generally costive, and the spirits of the
patient are very apt to be affected by changes in the wea-
ther, particularly by a fall of the barometer. How the diminution of atmospheric pressure acts in increasing the
symptoms, we perhaps do not know ; but its effects are experienced almost universally.

It is evident, that the only mode of cure in cases of this kind is extreme temperance : animal food should be taken sparingly, and wine and spirits in general totally abstained from. The bowels should be kept open by any mild neutral salt. I have generally found magnesia and lemonade to agree remarkably well in such cases. Exercise on horseback, is also particularly useful; bark, bitters, and the fetid and antispasmodic medicines, which are generally prescribed in such cases, are extremely hurtful.

This view of nervous complaints is, I may venture to say, as new as it is just. It has never been imagined, that any of them depended upon too great excitement ; on the contrary, they have been universally considered as originating in debility, and of course, tonics were prescribed, which, though they produced the greatest benefit in the other class of nervous complaints, in these they occasioned the most serious evils, and often brought on real inflammatory diseases, or even diseases of indirect debility, as I have repeatedly seen.

These cases cannot at first sight, however, be easily distinguished from those of the opposite class ; the symptoms being nearly alike, and the patient complaining of languor, debility, and extreme depression of spirits in both. But by attending carefully to the effects produced by the exciting powers, they may in general be distinguished. A patient of this kind will tell you, that he does not feel pleasant effects from wine, or spirituous liquors ; instead of exhilaration, his spirits become depressed by them ; whereas, in the contrary state, he finds almost instant relief. By attending to circumstances of this kind, the nature of the complaint may in general be ascertained.

Highly seasoned, and strongly stimulant foods should in the sthenic hypochondriasis, if it may be so called, be avoided; but the most mischievous agent of all, and which contributes to bring on the greater number of these complaints, is wine. This, I believe, produces more diseases, than all other causes put together. Every person is ready to allow, that wine taken to excess is hurtful, because he sees immediate evils follow : but the distant effects, which require more attentive observation to perceive, very few see, and believe ; and, judging from pleasant and agreeable feelings, they say that a little wine is wholesome, and good for every one ; and accordingly take it every day, and even give it to their children ; thus debauching their natural taste in the earliest infancy, and teaching them to relish what will injure their constitutions; but which, if properly abstained from, would prove one of the most valuable cordial medicines we possess.

The idea that wine or spirituous liquors assist digestion, is false. Those who are acquainted with chemistry, know that food is hardened, and rendered less digestible by these means ; and the stimulus, which wine gives to the stomach, is not necessary, excepting to those who have exhausted the excitability of that organ, by the excessive use of strong liquors. In these, the stomach can scarcely be excited to action, without the assistance of such a stimulus. If the food wants diluting, water is the best diluent. Water is the only liquor that nature knows, or has provided for animals; and whatever nature gives us, is, we may depend upon it, the best, and safest for us. Wine ought to be reserved as a cordial in sickness, and in old age; and a most salutary remedy would it prove, did we not exhaust its power by daily use.

I am sensible that I am treading on delicate ground, but I am determined to speak my sentiments with plainness and sincerity, since the health and welfare of thousands are concerned. Most persons have so indulged themselves in this pernicious habit of drinking wine, that they imagine they cannot live without a little every day; they think that their very existence depends upon it, and that their stomachs require it. Similar arguments may be brought in favour of every other bad habit. Though, at first, the violence we do to nature makes her revolt; in a little time she submits, and is not only reconciled, but grows fond of the habit; and we think it necessary to our existence: neither the flavour of wine, of opium, of snuff, or of tobacco, are naturally agreeable to us: on the contrary, they are highly unpleasant at first; but by the force of habit they become pleasant.

It is, however, the business of rational beings to distinguish carefully, between the real wants of nature, and the artificial calls of habit; and when we find that the last begin to injure us, we ought to use the most persevering efforts to break the enchantment of bad customs; and though it cost us some uneasy sensations at first, we must learn to bear them patiently; a little time will reward us for our forbearance, by a reestablishment of health and spirits.

I shall now proceed to examine the opposite class of nervous complaints: or such as do really depend on debility, or an asthenic state of the system. These may be divided into two orders ; viz. those of direct, and those of indirect debility.   I shall first consider those of direct debility

Though these complaints originate from a deficiency of stimulus, yet it is very seldom from a deficiency of the common stimulant powers. The only people, who in general labour under this deficiency of the common stimulants, are the poor ; they are seldom troubled with nervous complaints; their daily exercise, and constant attention to procure common necessaries, prevent their feeling what so grievously afflicts the rich and luxurious. These complaints arise chiefly from a deficiency of mental stimuli. The most common cause of them, and whose effects are the most difficult to remove, is to be looked for in the mind.

The passions and emotions, when exercised with moderation, and kept within proper bounds, are the sources of life and activity; without these precious affections, we should be reduced to a kind of vegetation, equally removed from pleasure and from pain. For want of these elastic springs, the animal spirits lose their regularity and play ; life becomes a lethargic sleep, and we fall into indifference and languor.

If then the passions are so necessary to the support of the health of the body, when in a proper degree, can we expect, that when they are inordinate or excessive, or even deficient, we shall escape with impunity ? tumultuous passions are like torrents, which overflow their bounds, and tear up every thing before them; and mournful experience convinces us, that these effects of the mind are easily communicated to the body We ought, therefore, to be particularly on our guard against their seduction.

> " 'Tis the great art of life to manage well
>   The restless mind."

It is particularly in their infancy, if it may be so called, that we ought to be upon our guard against their seduction ; they are then soothing and insidious ; but if we suffer them to gain strength, and establish their empire, reason, obscured and overcome, rests in a shameful dependence upon the senses ; her light becomes too faint to be seen, and her voice too feeble to be heard ; and the soul, hurried on by an impulse to which no obstacle is presented, communicates to the body its languor and debility. The passions, by which the body is chiefly affected, are, joy, grief, hope, fear, love, hatred, and anger. Any others may be reduced to some of these, or are compounded of them. The pleasurable passions produce strong excitement of the body, while the depressing passions diminish the excitement ; indeed it would seem that grief is only a diminution of joy, as cold is of heat ; when this passion exists in a proper degree, then we feel no particular exhilarating sensation, but our spirits and health are good : we cannot doubt, however, that we are excited by a pleasant sensation, though we are unable to perceive it. In the same manner, when heat acts moderately, or is about the degree we call temperate, we do not perceive its effects on the body, though there can be no doubt, that the body is under the influence of its stimulus, and powerfully excited by it ; for when it is diminished, or cold applied, we feel a deficiency of excitement, and become afterwards more sensible of heat afterwards applied.

The same takes place with respect to joy and grief, and proves, I think, clearly, that the one is only a diminution of the other, and that they are not different passions. When the body has been exposed to severe cold, the excitability becomes so much accumulated with respect to heat, that if it be afterwards applied too powerfully, a violent action, with a rapid exhaustion of the excitability, which ends in mortification, or death of the part, will take place. We should therefore apply heat in the gentlest manner possible, and gradually exhaust the morbidly accumulated excitability.

In the same manner, when the body has been under the influence of violent grief, any sudden joy has been known to overpower the system, and even produce instant death. We have an instance in history, of a mother being plunged into the extreme of grief, on being informed that her son was slain in battle; but when news was brought her, that he was alive, and well, the effect upon her spirits was such, as to bring on instant death. This event ought to have been unfolded to her in the most gradual manner; she should have been told, for instance, that he was severely wounded; but that it was not certain he was dead; then that there was a report he was living, which should have been gradually confirmed, as she could bear it. The same observations may be made, with respect to hope and fear, or despair; the former is an exciting passion, the latter, a depressing one; but the one is only a lower degree of the other; for a moderate degree of hope produces a pleasant state of serenity of the mind, and contributes to the health of the body; but a diminution of it weakens; and a great degree of despair so accumulates the excitability of the system, as to render it liable to be overpowered by any sudden hope or joy afterwards applied. What proves that joy and hope act by stimulating, and grief and despair by withdrawing stimulant action from the body, is, that the former exhaust excitability, while the latter accumulate it. Joy, for instance, does not render the system more liable to be affected by hope, but the reverse; and the same may be said of hope. In the same way, heat does not render the body more liable to be affected by food, but the reverse. Both these are stimulants, and exhaust the excitability. But after heat has been applied, if it be followed by cold, a great degree of languor or weakness will take place; because we have here a direct debility, added to indirect debility. In the same way, grief succeeding joy, or despair succeeding hope, produce a greater degree of dejection, both of mind and body, than if they had not been preceded by these stimulant passions; because here, direct debility is added to indirect. The excitability is first exhausted, and then the stimulus is withdrawn.

We see then, that the passions of the mind act as stimulants to the body, that, when in a proper degree, they tend to preserve it in health; but when their action is either too powerful, or too small, they produce the same effects as the other powers. We should therefore naturally expect, that when there is a deficient action of this kind of mental stimulus, or when the mind is under the influence of the depressing passions, a predisposition to diseases of direct debility would take place, and even these diseases be produced. Accordingly we find a numerous class of nervous complaints originating from these causes. Indeed, the undue action of the mental stimulants, produces more quick alterations in the state of the excitement, than that of the other exciting powers. Violent grief, or vexation, will immediately suspend the powers of the stomach. If we suppose a person in the best health, and highest good humour, sitting down to dinner with his friends, if he suddenly receives any afflicting news, his appetite is instantly gone, he cannot swallow a morsel. If the same thing happens after he has made a hearty dinner, the action of the stomach is suddenly suspended, and the whole process of digestion stopped, and what he has eaten, lies a most oppressive load. But this is not all : the whole circulation of the blood becomes disturbed ; the contraction and dilatation of the heart become irregular ; it flutters, and palpitates ; hence all the secretions become irregular, some of the glands acting too powerfully, others not at all ; hence the increased action of the kidneys, and hence a burst of tears ; hysterical affections, epilepsy, and syncope, frequently succeed, in which every muscle of the body becomes convulsed. Indeed, many terrible diseases originate from this source, which were formerly ascribed to witchcraft, and the possession of devils.

In slower, more silent, but longer continued grief, the effects are similar, but not so violent. The functions of the stomach are more gently disturbed, its juices vitiated ; and acidity, and other symptoms of indigestion, will show themselves. Hence no bland and nutritive chyle is conveyed into the blood ; whence emaciation and general debility must follow ; and the patient will at last die, as it is said, of a broken heart.

Besides the disturbed state of the stomach, and bad digestion, there can be no sleep in this state of mind ; for,

> " Sleep, like the world, his ready visit pays,
> Where fortune smiles ; the wretched he forsakes ;
> Swift on his downy pinion flies from woe,
> And lights on lids unsullied with a tear."

Hence the animal spirits will not be recruited, nor the worn out organs restored to vigour.

The minds of patients labouring under this division of nervous diseases, are likewise in general filled with over anxiety concerning their health ; attentive to every feeling, they find, in trifles light as air, strong confirmations of their apprehensions.

It is evident, that in these cases, a state of direct debility prevails, attended with a morbidly accumulated excitability ; hence, those remedies afford relief, which produce a quick exhaustion of this principle, and thus blunt the feelings, and lull the mind into some degree of forgetfulness of its woes. Hence opium, tobacco, and the fetid gums are often resorted to ; and in the hands of a judicious practitioner, they will afford great relief, provided he carefully watch the patient, and prevent their abuse ; for, if left to the discretion of the patient, he finds that kind of relief which he has long wished for; his moderation knows no bounds, and he is apt to take them in such a manner, as to add indirect debility, to direct, and thus bring on a state of exhausted excitability, while there is still a diminished state of mental stimulants. This will cause his spirits to be more depressed than ever ; he will therefore increase the dose, whether it be of opium, tobacco, or spirituous liquors, and thus he will be hurried on, adding fuel to the flame, till his exhausted excitability becomes irrecoverable, and he ends his days in a miserable state of imbecility, if not by suicide. Hence, though some of these narcotic stimulants, which exhaust the excitability, and blunt the feelings, may be employed with advantage, in order to prepare the mind for those changes, which the physician wishes to produce, they should be used with the greatest caution, and never left in any degree to the discretion of the patient. The cure, however, depends chiefly on regulating the state of the mind, or interrupting the attention of the patient; and diverting it, if possible, to other objects than his own feeling.

Whatever aversion to application of any kind we may meet with in patients of this class, we may be assured that nothing is more pernicious to them than absolute idleness, or a vacancy from all earnest pursuit.

The occupations of business suitable to their circumstances, and situations in life, if neither attended with emotion, anxiety, nor fatigue, are always to be advised to such patients; but occupations which are objects of anxiety, and more particularly such as are exposed to accidental interruptions, disappointments, and failures, are very improper for patients of this class.

To such patients exercise in the open air is of the utmost consequence. Of all the various methods of preserving health and preventing diseases, which nature has suggested, there is none more efficacious than exercise. It puts the fluids all in motion, strengthens the solids, promotes digestion, and perspiration, and occasions the decomposition of a larger quantity of air in the lungs, and thus not only more heat, but more vital energy is supplied to the body; and of all the various modes of exercise, none conduces so much to the health of the body, as riding on horseback: it is not attended with the fatigue of walking, and the free air is more enjoyed in this way, than by any other mode of exercise. The system of the vena portarum, which collects the blood from the abdominal viscera, and circulates it through the liver, is likewise rendered more active, by this kind of exercise, than by any other, and thus a torpid state, not only of the bowels, but of this system of vessels, and the biliary system, is prevented.

When a patient of this class, however, goes out for the sake of exercise only, it does not in general produce so good an effect, as might be expected ; for he is continually brooding over the state of his health : there is no new object to arrest his attention, and he is constantly reminded of the cause of his riding. Exercise will therefore be most effectual when employed in the pursuit of a journey, where a succession of pleasant scenes are likely to present themselves, and new objects arise, which call forth his attention. A journey likewise withdraws the patient from many objects of uneasiness and care, which might present themselves at home.

With respect to medicines, costiveness, which often attends these diseases, ought to be carefully avoided, by some mild laxative. Calcined magnesia, and lemonade, have always seemed to me to answer the purpose ; but the most effectual method is to acquire a regular habit, which may be done by perseverance, and strict attention.

Chalybeate waters have been frequently tried, and may in general be recommended with success, particularly, as the amusement and exercise generally accompanying the use of these waters, aid the tonic powers of the iron. The bark may likewise be exhibited with advantage.

There is yet another class of nervous diseases which we have to notice, which are by no means uncommon ; yet they have, like the first class, escaped the attention of writers on this subject, and of medical practitioners in general :

I mean those where the system is in a state of torpor, or exhausted excitability.

This state of the system may be brought on by various causes, but principally by the long continued use of opium, tobacco, or fermented liquors.

When these substances, which are powerful stimulants, have been taken for some time, they bring on a state of the system so torpid, that the usual exciting powers, and the usual occurrences, which in general produce pleasant sensations, do not occasion a sufficient degree of excitement, in those whose excitability is thus exhausted. They therefore feel continual languor and listlessness, unless when under the influence of the stimulus which brought on the exhaustion. Every scene, however beautiful, is beheld with indifference by such patients, and the degree of ennui they feel is insupportable: this makes them have recourse to the stimulus which has exhausted their excitability, which in some degree removes this languor for a time; but it returns with redoubled strength, and redoubled horror, when the stimulant effect is over: and as this repetition exhausts the excitability more and more, the stimulus is repeated in greater quantity, and thus the disease increases to a most alarming degree.

There is no way of curing this state of nervous torpor, but by leaving off the stimuli which caused the exhaustion; and if the patient have resolution to do this for a few weeks, though, at first, he will, no doubt, find his spirits a little depressed, he will ultimately overcome the habit, and will be rewarded by alacrity of spirits, such as he never experiences under the most powerful action of artificial stimulants.

I must not, however, forget to notice, that there is a nervous state, or ennui, originating from a wrong direction of mental exertion, which exhausts the excitability to a great degree, and brings on a state of depression scarcely to be born.

When a person has by habit made his mind constantly dependent on dissipation, on gaming, and on frivolous, but not inactive pursuits, in order to produce pleasurable sensations, and at the same time neglected that culture of the understanding which will enable him to retire into himself with pleasure, and receive more enjoyment from the exercise of this cultivated understanding than he does in the most noisy, or fashionable circle of dissipation: I say, when there is this vacancy of mind, whenever it is not engaged in such pursuits as I have mentioned, a languor and weariness is experienced, which is intolerable, and which prompts the person so circumstanced, to fly continually to the only scenes which interest his mind. Hence, the passion for gaming, in which the anxiety attending it causes an interest in the mind, which takes off the dreadful languor experienced, when it is not thus employed.

It is owing to wealth, admitting of indolence, and yielding to the pursuit of transitory and unsatisfying amusements, or to that of exhausting pleasures only, that the present times exhibit to us so many instances of persons suffering under this state: it is a state totally unknown to the poor, who labour for their daily bread, and to those whose minds are actively employed in study or business. It can only be cured by cultivating the understanding, and applying to some art or science, which will engage and interest

the attention.   I have received the thanks of many for recommending the study of philosophy, and particularly of
chemistry, to their attention.   This affords a rational and
interesting pursuit, which, if entered into with ardour, and
if the person actually works, or makes experiments himself,
he will soon experience an enjoyment and an interest, such
as he never experienced at the gaming table, or at any
other place of fashionable amusement.   Nay, I will venture
to say, that all elegant amusements will be enjoyed with
much greater relish by one who employs himself in some
rational pursuit, and only resorts to such amusements as a
relaxation, than by one who makes these amusements a business.

From the view we have taken of these complaints, it is evident, that they are like other general diseases of the sthenic,
or asthenic kind; they seem to constitute a state of the
body between predisposition and disease; and they differ
from most diseases in this, that in most complaints the increase, or diminution of the excitement is unequal in different parts of the body, and this gives rise to the different
forms of disease ; but in nervous complaints the excitement
seems much more equably affected in different parts. These
complaints, as we have seen, may be divided into three
classes; sthenic; those of accumulated excitability ; and
those of exhausted excitability: but though they are evidently distinguishable in this manner, and require different
modes of cure, I have never seen any account of more than
one kind in any medical writer : the same remedies were pre-
cribed for all, however different they might be.

Though medicines may relieve complaints of this kind,

and particularly those of the second class, yet from what
has been said, it must be evident, that much more may be
done by regulating the action of the common exciting
powers. Indeed, this is the case in most chronic diseases.
Exercise and temperance will do infinitely more than medicine. By their means, most diseases may be overcome ;
but without them we may administer drugs as long as we
please.

Voltaire sets this advice, which I have frequently inculcated, in so strong a light, that it may perhaps carry more
conviction than any thing I can say. Ogul was a voluptuary, ambitious of nothing but good living : he thought that
God had sent him into the world for no other purpose than
to eat and drink : his physician, who had but little credit with him, when he had a good digestion, governed him
with despotic sway, when he had eaten too much.

On feeling himself much and seriously indisposed by indolence and intemperance, he requested to know what he
was to do, and the doctor ordered him to eat a basilisk,
stewed in rose water, which he asserted would effect a complete cure. His slaves searched in vain for a basilisk.; at
last they met with Zadig, who was introduced to this
mighty lord, and spoke to him in the following terms.

" May immortal health descend from Heaven to bless all
thy days ! I am a physician ; at the report of thy indisposi-
tion, I flew to thy castle, and have now brought thee a
basilisk, stewed in rose water. But, my lord, the basilisk
is not to be eaten ; all its virtue must enter through thy
pores. I have enclosed it in a little ball, blown up and covered with a fine skin. Thou must strike this ball, with all

thy might, and I must strike it back for a considerable time: and by observing this regimen for a few days, thou wilt see the effects of my art." The first day Ogul was out of breath, and thought he should have died with fatigue; the second he was less fatigued, and slept better. In eight days he recovered all the strength, all the health, all the agility and cheerfulness of his most agreeable years. Zadig then said unto him, " there is no such thing in nature as a basilisk; but thou hast taken exercise, and been temperate, and hast recovered thy health." In the same manner I say, that temperance and exercise are the two great preservers of health, and restorers of it when it is lost; and that the art of reconciling intemperance and health is as chimerical, as washing the Ethiopian white.

It will easily be perceived that the system of animal life which I have investigated, may be applied to all other general diseases, as well as the gout and those called nervous: I have merely given a view of these by way of specimen of its application.

Should these lectures contribute in any degree to lessen the future sufferings of my hearers, or any of their friends, I shall not have delivered them in vain. To be assured of this, would be the greatest pleasure that I could receive.

THE END.

From the Press of the Royal Institution of Great Britain,
Albemarle Street, London: W. Savage, Printer.

INDEX.

LIST OF SUBSCRIBERS.

	£.	s.
A.		
Henry Ainslie, M. D.	10	10
James Peter Auriol, Esq. P. R. I.	5	5
James Acheson, Esq. *Oaks, Londonderry*	1	1
W. Dacre Adams, Esq.	1	1
Miss Adams	1	1
Mr. Adams, *Optician*	5	5
————— Addington, Esq.	1	1
Mr. Thomas Addison, *Preston*	2	2
Mrs. Addison	2	2
John Aikin, M. D.	1	1
Mr. Arthur Aikin	1	1
Charles R. Aikin, Esq. *Surgeon*	1	1
William Alers, Esq.	2	2
Dr. Alexander, *Hallifax*	2	2
Henry Alexander, Esq.	1	1
E. Alexander, M. D. *Leicester*	1	1
William Allen, Esq. F. L. S.	2	2
Robert Anderson, Esq.	1	1
Dr. Anderson	1	1
Dr. Anderson, *Hammersmith*	1	1
A. Apsley, Esq.	1	1
Mr. D. Archer, *Bath*	1	1
Mr. J. T. Armiger	1	1
Nicholas Ashton, Esq. *Liverpool*	1	1
Mr. Thomas Aston	1	1
Abram Atkins, Esq.	3	3
William James Atkinson, Esq.	3	3
Mr. Accum	10	10
Mr. Noah Ayton	1	1

	£.	s.
B.		
Rt.Hon.Sir Joseph Banks, Bart. K.B. Pr. R.S. F.A.S. P.R.I. F.L.S.	10	10
SirC.W.RouseBoughton,Bart.P.R.I.	1	1
Sir William Blizard, F.R.S. F.A.S.	2	2
Mr. B. *Lancaster*	1	1
Dr. Babington, *Physician to Guy's Hospital.*	3	3
Miss Bacon	1	1
Miss Mary Bacon	1	1
John Bailey, Esq.	1	1
Andrew Bain, M. D.	5	5
John Baker, Esq.	10	10
William Baker, Esq.	10	10
Mr. Joseph Ball	1	1
Rev. Edward Balme	1	1
Mr. Ransford	1	1
Rev. John Banks, P. R. I. *Boston, Lincoln,*	1	1
Mr. Banks, *Leeds*	1	1
Charles Baratty, Esq. F. A. S.	1	1
Robert Barclay Esq. *Southwark* P R. I. F. L. S.	1	1
Mr. William Barclay	1	1
R. J. Barlow, Esq.	3	3
Dr. Barrow	1	1
Rev. William Barton, *Whalley*	1	1
Mr. Barton	1	1
Thomas Baskerfeild, Esq. F. A. S.	1	1
Jacob Bath, Esq. *Surgeon, 66th Reg.*	1	1
Robert Batty, M.D. P.R.I. F.L.S.	5	5

	£.	s.
Mr. Charles Baumer	1	1
E. Baxley, Esq. *St. Petersburg*	1 11	6
Mr. John Baynes	1	1
Mr. Beckett	1	1
Hugh Bell, Esq.	1	1
William Bell, Esq. *St. Petersburg*	1 11	6
Mr. Bell	5	5
Christopher K. Bellew, Esq.	2	2
Rev. N. Benezer, *Swaffham*	1	1
Nathaniel Barnardiston, Esq.	1	1
Thomas Bernard, Esq. P R. I.	5	5
W. Berwick, Esq. *St. Petersburg*	1 11	6
Richard Best, Jun. Esq.	1	1
Henry Bickersteth, Esq. *Kirkby Lonsdale*	2	2
Henry Bickersteth, Jun. Esq. *Kirkby Lonsdale*	1	1
Mr. John Bickersteth	2	2
Mr. E. Bickersteth	1	1
T. Bigge, Esq. *Newcastle upon Tyne*	1	1
Mr. George Biggin	1	1
W. Bindsale, Esq. *Pickering, Surgeon*		
Charles Binney, Esq.	1	1
Joseph Birch, Esq. M. P.	3	3
Dr. Birkbeck	5	5
Morris Birkbeck, Jun. Esq. *Wanborough, Surry*	1	1
Thomas Blacker, Esq. P. R. I.	5	5
Mr. Blades	1	1
Alexander Blair, Esq. P. R. I.	5	5
William Blair, Esq.	3	3
Dr. Blake, *Taunton*	1	1
Dr. Blane	5	5
Mr. Henry Blatch, *Surgeon*	1	1
Ditto, *2nd Subscription*	4	4
Ralph Blegborough, M. D. P. R. I.	2	2
John Bliss, Esq.	1	1
Robert Blundell, Esq.	1	1
Samuel Boddington, Esq. P. R. I.	1	1

	£.	s.
George Bodley, Esq.	1	1
Thomas Bodley, Esq.	1	1
John Bolton, Esq.	1	1
Dr. Bolton	5	5
Thomson Bonar, Esq. P. R. I.	10	10
George Booth, Esq.	2	2
John Bostock, M. D.	2	2
Josiah Boydell, Esq.	3	3
Daniel Braithwaite, Esq. F. R. S. F. A. S.	5	5
Miss Braithwaite	2	2
Mr. James Braithwaite	1	1
——Brande, Esq.	1	1
Joseph Brandreth, M. D.	5	5
Mr. Brandreth, *Surgeon*	3	3
Mr. Brandreth, *Attorney*	2	2
Messrs. Brash and Reid, *Glasgow*	2	2
John Breare, Esq.	1	1
Martin Bree, Esq.	1	1
J. H. Brehmer, Esq. *St. Petersburg*	1 11	6
Brentford Book Society	1	1
William Bridgman, Esq. P. R. I. F. L. S.	1	1
Mr. Richard Briggs	2	2
Mrs. Richard Briggs	1	1
Lowbridge Bright, Esq. *Bristol*		
British Library, *St Petersburg*	1	1
Theodore Henry Broadhead, Esq. F. A. S. P. R. I.	2	2
Messrs. Broderip	5	5
James Brogden, Esq. M. P.	3	3
Mr. E. Brook	1	1
Joshua Brooks, Esq. *Lecturer on Anatomy, Surgery, &c.*	5	5
James Brown, Esq. *Leeds*	1	1
J. Brown, M. D. *Islington*	1	1
Mr. Brown	1	1
——Bryant, Esq. *Lynn Regis, Surgeon*	1	1

	£.	s.
Dr. Buchan	1	1
Rev. Gilbert Buchanan, LL. D.		
Rector of Woodmanstow, Surry	1	1
Mr. Buchenson, *Surgeon*	1	1
Buckingham Book Society	1	1
George Buckle, Esq.	2	2
William Buckley, Esq.	1	1
Mr. Henry Budd	1	1
Mr. John Buddle	1	1
Mr. J. Buncomb, *Taunton, Somerset.*	1	1
Mr. A. S. Burkitt, *Chemist* 3	5	6
Charles Burney, LL. D. F. R. S.		
F. A. S. P. R. I. *Greenwich*	1	1
Robert Burns, Esq.	1	1
Mrs. Butts	1	1

C.

	£.	s.
Sir John Chetwode, Bart.	1	1
Henry Cavendish, Esq. F. R. S.		
F. A. S. P. R. I.	10	10
Thomas Coutts, Esq. P. R. I.	10	10
Mr. John Callow	1	1
Dr. Alexander Campbell, *Secretary*		
to the Medical Board, Calcutta		
Dr. Campbell, *Lancaster*	1	1
Colonel James Campbell	1	1
Mr. Card	1	1
Anthony Carlisle, Esq. F. L. S.	1	1
Mr. John Carpenter, Senr. *Lyme*		
J. C. Carpue, Esq.	2	2
George Carr, Esq. *St. Petersburg* 1	11	6
Thomas W. Carr, Esq. P. R. I.	1	1
Mr. W. Cary	1	1
William Cass, Esq.	1	1
Dr. Cassels, *Lancaster*	1	1
D. Cassidy, Esq.	1	1
John Cates, Esq.	1	1
H. Cayley, Esq. *St. Petersburg* 1	11	6
William Chamberlain, Esq.	1	1

	£.	s.
L. B. Chateauneauf, Esq.	1	1
Chester Public Library	1	1
Henry Chevalier, Esq. F. L. S.	2	2
Mrs. Chevalier	1	1
James Chew, M. D. *Blackburn*	1	1
Mr. Christian, *Attorney*	1	1
————Clapham, Esq. *Thorney Abbey, Surgeon*	1	1
John Clarke, Esq.	1	1
J. Calvert Clarke, Esq.	5	5
Ralph Clarke, Esq.	1	1
Richard Hull Clarke, Esq. *Devon.*	1	1
Mr. John Clay	1	1
S. P. Cockerell, Esq. P. R. I.	2	2
Miss Codrington	2	2
Mr. John Cohen	1	1
Mr. Collier	1	1
Mr. Coltman, *Surgeon*	2	2
Mr. Colton	1	1
Mr. Cooke	1	1
B. Coombe, Esq.	2	2
Astley Cooper, Esq. F. R. S.	5	5
Rev. Stuart Corbett		
Adam Cottam, Esq. *Whalley, near Blackburn*	1	1
Mr. Cotter, *Godstone, Surry*	1	1
Mr. Cotter	1	1
John Cowan, Esq.	1	1
Theodore Cox, Esq.	2	2
John Craig, Esq. *Glasgow*	1	1
Mr. Cregg	1	1
Thomas Creser, Esq.	1	1
William Cresswell, Esq.	1	1
Alexander Crichton, M.D. F.R.S.		
F. L. S.	2	2
Mr. Crigg	1	1
George Crooke, Esq.		
Hugh Cross, Esq.	2	2
C. Cuppage, Esq.	1	1

	£.	s.
Mr. William Cuppage	2	2
James Currie, M. D. F. R. S. Physician to Guy's Hospital	2	2
————Currie M. D.	5	5
————Cuthbert	1 11	6
Mr. John Cuthbertson	1 11	6

D.

	£.	s.
Sir George Duckett, Bart. P. R. I.	1	1
Peter Denys, Esq. P. R. I.	10	10
Lady C. Denys	5	5
George William Denys, Esq. P. R. I.	5	5
David Dale, Esq.	5	5
J. P. Dale, Esq.	5	5
Thomas Dale, M. D.	1	1
Mr. Daniel Dale	5	5
Mr. Daltera, *Attorney*	1	1
Mr. Darbyshire	1	1
Mr. Davie, *St Thomas's Hospital*	1	1
Dr. Davies, *Bath*	1	1
Dr. Davison, *Harewood*		
Humphry Davy, Esq. F. R. S.	5	5
Mr. Joseph Dawson	1	1
Thomas Dawson, Esq. *Surgeon*	1	1
Mr. Thomas Dawson	1	1
Mr. Dawson	2	2
Thomas Day, Esq. P. R. I.	5	5
Miss Day	2	2
Mrs. Delamore	1	1
Thomas Denison, Esq.	1	1
R. Dennison, M. D. and F. A. S.	2	2
Osbert Denton, Esq. *Chelsea*	10	0
Mrs. Denton	10	0
Miss Denton	5	0
Mr. Benjamin Devaynes	1	1
N. Devy, Esq.	1	1
Charles Dibdin, Esq.	5	5
William Dick, Esq.	1	1
W Dickson, LL. D. *Clipstone St.*	2	2

	£.	s.
Charles Dilly, Esq.	2	2
Mr. William Dinsley, *Leeds*	1	1
————Doig, Esq.	1	1
Mr. Doig	1	1
George Dominicus, Esq.	2	2
Rev. Thomas Donald, *Anthorne, Cumberland*	1	1
Andrew Douglas, Esq. F. R. S. P. R. I.	5	5
Mr. James Dove	1	1
Henry Downer, Esq.	1	1
Mr. Drewe	1	1
F. Duboulay, Esq.	1	1
Dr. Andrew Duncan, *Edinburgh*		
Dr. Andrew Duncan, Jun. *Do.*		
Mrs. Dunlop, *Hammersmith*	1	1
Miss Dunlop, *Hammersmith*	1	1
James Dupre, Esq. P. R. I.	1	1

E.

	£.	s.
Marquis of Exeter, F.R.S. F.A.S.	5	5
Marchioness of Exeter	5	5
The Earl of Egremont, F. R. S. F. A. S. P. R. I.	10	10
Sir H. C. Englefield, Bart. F.R.S. F. A. S. P. R. I.	3	3
Sir James Earle	2	2
Hon. William Elphinstone	1	1
R. G. Ealand, Esq.	1	1
Willis Earle, Esq.	2	2
————Eccles, Esq. *Clithero*	1	1
D. B. Plantagenet Eccleston, Esq.	1	1
Library of the University of Edinburgh		
Mr. Edmondson, *Surgeon, Lancaster*	1	1
Mr. Richard Elgar	1	1
George Ellis, Esq. F.R.S. F.A.S. P. R. I.	1	1

	£. s.
John Fullerton Elphinstone, Esq.	
East Lodge, Enfield	1 1
Alexander Erskine, Esq. F. L. S.	1 1
George Erving, Esq.	1 1
John Esdaile. Esq. P. R. I.	1 1
Isaac Espinasse, Esq.	2 2
William Etty, Esq.	1 1
Mr. Evans	1 1

F

	£. s.
Col. the Hon.T. W. Fermor, P.R.I.	10 10
James Fallofeild, Esq. P. R. I.	2 2
Vere Fane, Esq.	1 1
Thomas Farquhar, Esq.	1 1
Robert Farquhar, Esq. *Rochester*	1 1
Mr. Faulder	1 1
W. Fawkes, Esq. *Farnley, near Leeds*	3 3
John Feltham, Esq.	2 2
Richard Firmin, Esq.	3 3
Mr. M. Fitzgerald	1 1
Lewis Flannagan, Esq.	2 2
Arch. Fletcher, *Advocate, Glasgow*	2 2
Caleb Fletcher, Esq.	2 2
Mr. Benjamin Flockton	
———— Forbes, Esq.	1 1
Henry Fock, Esq. *St. Petersburg*	1 11 6
Mr. Ford, *Pimlico*	1 1
———— Ford, Esq.	2 2
R. Forrester, Esq. *St. Petersburg*	1 11 6
B. M. Forster, Esq.	1 1
Rev. Edward Forster, F.R.S. F.A.S. P. R. I.	1 1
Thomas Foster, Esq.	1 1
Thomas Fothergill, Esq.	2 2
John Foulks, Esq.	2 2
Joseph Fox, Esq.	2 2
Rev. M. Foxcroft	1 1
James Fraser, Esq. P. R. I.	1 1
F. Freelong, Esq.	1 1

	£. s.
———— French, Esq.	1 1
A Friend	2 2
A friend, W. M.	1 1
A friend, J. C.	1 1
A friend, T. K.	2 2
A friend, E.	4 4
A friend, T.	10 0
A friend. J. G.	5 5
A friend, A.	2 2
A friend, H. W. by Mr. Lawson	1 1
A friend, W. W.	1 1
A friend, I. A. W.	1 1
A friend, I. S.	1 1
A friend, A. B.	2 2
A friend, I. B.	5 5
A friend, W. D.	2 2
A friend, D. D.	2 2
A friend, J. L. Esq.	3 3
A friend, E. A.	1 1
A friend, I. S.	1 1
A friend, I. B.	1 1
A friend, M. W.	1 1
A friend, M. B.	5 0
A friend, I. A. W.	1 1
A friend, E. D.	1 1
A friend, J. D.	1 1
A friend, J. P. D.	1 1
A friend, S. B. D.	4 4
A friend, S. D.	5 5
A friend, Mr. B.	1 1
A friend, Mr. B.	1 1
A friend, S. E. D.	1 1
A friend, S. F. D.	1 1
A friend, S. M. D.	1 1
A friend, I.T. by Mr. I. J. Armiger	1 1
A friend, by Dr. Batty	3 3
A friend, I. H. D. by Dr. Batty	3 3
A friend, by D. Braithwaite, Esq.	3 3
A friend, by Miss Braithwaite	2 2

	£.	s.
Thomas Harrison, Esq.	1	1
Mr. Joseph Harrison, *Bury*	3	3
Mr. William Harrison, *Manchester*	1	1
Harrowgate Book Club	1	1
Enoch Harvey, Esq. *Liverpool*	2	2
Joseph Haskins, Esq. P.R.I.	3	3
William Huskisson, Esq.	1	1
Charles Hatchett, Esq. F. R. S. F. L. S. P. R. I.	10	10
Dr. Hawes, (W. H. S.)	1	1
Mr. B. Hawes	1	1
Richard Haworth, Esq.	2	2
Mr. Joseph Hawthorne, *Reading*	1	1
Thomas Hay, Esq.	1	1
———— Haygarth, M. D. *Bath*	2	2
William Headington, Esq.	1	1
John Heath, M.D. *Fakenham, Nor.*	1	1
Mr. Richard Heathfield	1	1
Mr. Henbest	2	2
William Henderson, Esq.	2	2
Messrs. Thomas and William Henry	5	5
Messrs. T. and W. Henry	5	5
Benjamin Arthur Heywood, Esq.	2	2
B. A. Heywood, Esq.	2	2
Mr. Hicks, *Surgeon*	1	1
Dr. Higgins	2	2
John Benton Higgon, Esq.	1	1
Henry Hinckley, Esq.	2	2
John Hinckley, Esq. P. R. I.	2	2
Elias Hocker, Esq. *Brook House, Devon.*	1	1
Hoddesdon Book Society	2	2
Mrs. Hodge	1	1
Henry Hodgson, Esq.	1	1
Rev. Dr. Hodgson, *Market Rasen, Lincolnshire*	1	1
Charles Holford, Esq. *Hampstead*	1	1
Mr. W. Holland	1	1
Edward Holme, M. D.	2	2
Mr. Jacob Holme	1	1
Everard Home, Esq. F.R.S. P.R.I.	5	5
Mr. Hommey, *Military Academy, Woolwich*	1	1
Mr. Hooke, *Optician*, P. R. I.	2	2
Dr. Hooper, F. L. S.	5	5
Dr. Thomas C. Hope, *Edinburgh*		
Rev. J. J. Hornsby	1	1
Mr. J. D. Hose, Jun.	1	1
Mr. Houseman	1	1
Luke Howard, Esq.	3	3
S. R. Howard, Esq.	1	1
T. M. Hubert, Esq.	1	1
Henry Hughs, Esq.	3	3
Richard Hughes, Esq.	5	5
Hull Subscription Library	1	1
John Hull, M. D.	2	2
Dr. Hull	2	2
Dr. Hulme	2	2
N. Hulme, M.D. F.R.S. and F.A.S.	3	3
Mr. N. Hume	3	3
Mr. J. Hume	1	1
Mrs. Hunt	3	3
Robert Hunter, Esq. *Kew*	1	1
Dr. Hunter, *York*		
Mr. John Hustler	1	1
Walter Hutton, Esq.	2	2
Mr. Hutton, *Sheffield*		

J

	£.	s.	
G. Jackson, Esq. *St. Petersburg*	1 11	6	
Mr. Jackson, *Lancaster*	1	1	
Miss Sarah Jackson	1	1	
William James, Esq.	1	1	
Thomas I'anson, Esq.	2	2	
———— Jaques, M. D. *Harrowgate*	2	2	
———— Jardine, M. D.	2	2	
George Jeffery, Esq.	1	1	
Edward Jenner, M.D. F.R.S. F.L.S.	10	10	

	£.	s.
Edward Jenings, Esq. *Kensington*	1	1
William Ingham, Esq. *Newcastle upon Tyne*	2	2
Rt. Innes, Esq. *Newcastle upon Tyne*	1	1
Edward Johnson, Esq. *Mile End*	1	1
Christopher Johnson, Esq.	1	1
R. Johnson, Esq.	1	1
———— Jones, Esq. *Chelsea*	1	1
W. Jones, Esq. *St. Petersburg*	1 11	6
Thomas Jones, Esq. *Llandisilleo Hall, Oswestry*	1	1
Mr. John Jones, *Surgeon*	2	2
Stephen Jones, Esq.	1	1
Gibbs Walker Jordan, Esq. F.R.S.	3	3
Major Jourdan	1	1
Rev. J. Joyce	1	1
Thomas Irving, Esq.	2	2
Thomas Irwin, Esq.	1	1
Mr. Ives, *Surgeon, Chertsey*		

K

	£.	s.
The Hon. George Knox, F. R. S.	10	10
Frederick Kanmacher, Esq. P.R.I. F. L. S.	1	1
Mr. B. A. Keck, *Leeds*		
Miss Keene	2	2
Mr. P. Kelly	1	1
Dr. E. Kentish, *Bristol*		
Mr. Jonathan Key	1	1
T. King, Esq. *Carshalton, Surry*	1	1
James King, Esq.	2	2
J. King, Esq. *Finsthwaite, Kendal*	1	1
Messrs. Knipe and Mower	2	2
Kirkby Lonsdale Book Club	1	1
John Knox, Esq.	1	1
William Knox, Esq.	1	1

L

	£.	s.
Right Hon. Lady Lyttelton	3	3
Sir James Lake, Bart.	1	1
George Lackington, Esq.	2	2
Mr. W. Laforest	2	2
H. Lamatte, Esq.	1	1
Mrs. Lappan	1	1
Samuel Lawford, Esq. P.R.I. *Peckham*	1	1
Thomas Wright Lawford, Esq.	1	1
Mr. Samuel Lawford, jun.	1	1
Johnson Lawson, Esq. P. R. I.	5	5
Henry Lawson, Esq.	5	5
Rev. G. Lawson	1	1
James Inglish Lawson, Esq.	1	1
William Leake, Esq.	2	2
Mr. Joseph Leay	1	1
Mr. William Leay	1	1
Rev. Francis Lee	2	2
John Leeds, Esq. *Chelsea*	1	1
James Leighton, Esq.	2	2
Dr. Lempriere	1	1
J. Lestourgeon, Esq.	1	1
Thomas Lewis, Esq. P. R. I.	2	2
William Lewis, Esq. F. L. S.	5	5
Mr. Lewthwaite	1	1
Library of the Sheffield Infirmary		
Henry Lider, Esq. *Stilton*	1	1
John Lightbody, Esq. *Liverpool*	5	5
A. S. Lillingston, Esq. *Lyne*	1	1
Lincoln Medical Society		
Literary Fund	30	0
Literary Society at Newcastle	2	2
Mr. Littlewood	1	1
Liverpool Library	1	1
John Lloyd, Esq. *Baskail Lodge, Yorkshire*	1	1
H. E. Lloyd, Esq.	1	1
Mr. James Long, *Optician*	3	3
C. Lormar, Esq. *Bath*	1	1
Mr. R. Low, *Surgeon*	1	1

	£.	s.
James Lowe, Esq.	2	2
Mrs. W. Lowry	5	5
Captain John Lucas	1	1
Mr. Lucas	2	2
James Ludlam, Esq. *Homerton*	1	1
Mr. Lumley	1	1
William Luxmoore, Esq. P.R.I.	1	1
T. Luxmoore, Esq.	1	1
Lynn Subscription Library	1	1
John Lyon, M. D.	3	3

M

	£.	s.
Right Hon. Lord Muncaster		
John Mac Arthur, Esq. P. R. I.	1	1
John McCartney, M. D.	2	2
A. McCausland, Esq. *St. Petersburg*	1 11	6
Angus McDonald, Esq.	2	2
Angus McDonald, M. D.	1	1
Dr. Macdonald, *Taunton, Somerset.*	1	1
Duncan Macfarlane, Esq.	5	5
George McIntosh, Esq.	4	4
Dr. McIntosh	2	2
Mr. Mackender	1	1
Alexander McLeay, Esq.	1	1
Mr. Maddon, jun.	1	1
John Mair, Esq.	2	2
Mr. Malcolm	1	1
F H. Maltz, jun. Esq. *Hamburgh*	1	1
Alexander Marcet, M. D. P. R. I. *Assistant Physician to Guy's Hospital*	2	2
Charles Marsh, Esq. F. A. S. P. R. I.	1	1
Dr. Marshal	1	1
Mr. William Marshall	1	1
William Maud, Esq.	1	1
P. W. Mayow, Esq.	1	1
W. W. Mayow, Esq.	1	1

	£.	s.
Samuel Mellish, Esq. P R. I.	1	1
W. Menish, Esq. P. R. I. *Bromley, Kent*	2	2
Richard Meux, jun. Esq.	5	5
John Middleton, Esq.	1	1
John Milford, Esq.	2	2
James Millar, Esq. *College, Glasgow*	1	1
Captain Millar	1	1
Miss Millar	1	1
———— Miller, Esq. *Peterborough, Surgeon*	1	1
James Milne, *College, Glasgow*	2	2
Charles Minier, Esq.	2	2
William Minier, Esq.	2	2
Mr. Minchell, *Surgeon*	3	3
Ed. Moberly, Esq. *St. Petersburg*	1 11	6
Mr. Mogg	1	1
Dr. Alex. Monro, Sen. *Edinburgh*		
Matthew Montagu, Esq. F. R. S.	1	1
Charles Montague, Esq. *Surgeon*	1	1
Robert Monteith, Esq.	1	1
John Monteith, Esq.	1	1
Robert Montgomerie, Esq.	1	1
G. Morgan, Esq. *Norfolk, Virginia*	5	0
Mr. Joseph Morgan	1	1
William Morley, jun. Esq. P. R. I.	1	1
John Morris, Esq.	2	2
Mr. James Moss	1	1
P. S. Munn, Esq.	1	1
Sir John Chardin Musgrave, Bart.	1	1

N

	£.	s.
Edward Nairne, Esq. F R. S. P R. I.	5	5
Rev. Archdeacon Nares, F. A. S.	2	2
Mr. Charles Newby	2	2
Mr. J. Nicholas	1	1
George Nicholson, Esq. *Ponehaill, near Ludlow*	1	1

	£.	s.
Mr. Francis Nicholson, *Artist, Sowers Town*	2	2
Mrs. William Nicholson	5	5
Mrs. Norman, *Chelsea*	1	1
William Norris, Esq.	2	2
Henry Norris, Esq. *Davy-Hulme-Hall, near Manchester*	5	5
Mr. Norris	5	5
William North, Esq.	1	1
Thomas Northmore, Esq.	5	5
Messrs. Norton and Son, *Bristol*		

O

	£.	s.
James Ogilvy, Esq.	1	1
Edward Ogle, Esq.	1	1
Henry Okey, Esq.	1	1
Mr. Oliver	1	1
Mr. Serjeant Onslow	1	1
Rev. Richard Ormerod, *Kensington*	1	1
Alexander Oswald, Esq.	5	5
R. Oswin, Esq.	2	2
Mr. Otley	1	1
————Owen, Esq.	10	10

P

	£.	s.
Royal College of Physicians	20	0
The Earl of Pomfret, P. R. I.	10	10
Sir William Pepperell, Bart.	2	2
Sir Christopher Pegge, Knt. *Regius Professor of Physic, Oxford*		
Philip Palmer, Esq.	5	5
Felix Palmer, Esq.	3	3
Mrs. Palmer	3	3
Executors of Mrs. Palmer	10	0
Thomas Park, Esq. F. A. S.	1	1
Mr. Park, *Surgeon*	3	3
Mr. J. C. Parker	5	5
Thomas Parker, Esq.	5	5
Mr. Robert Parker	1	1

	£.	s.
G. Parkinson, Esq.	3	3
————Parkinson, Esq. *Clitheroe*	1	1
Dr. Parkinson, *Lancaster*	1	1
John Parry, Esq.	5	5
John Pattison, Esq.	7	7
Mrs. Paulin, *Chelsea*	1	1
William Payne, Esq. *Bradford*	1	1
Thomas Paytherus, Esq.	2	2
John Peake, Esq. *Battersea*	1	1
C. Pears, Esq. F. L. S.	2	2
Rev. William Pearson, P. R. I.	3	3
William Pearson	3	3
Thomas Pearson, Esq.	1	1
William Scott Peckham, Esq.	1	1
Edmund Peckover, Esq. *Bradford*	1	1
W. H. Pepys, Esq.	5	5
W. H. Pepys, jun. Esq. P. R. I.	5	5
Edmund Pepys, Esq.	1	1
Thomas Perceval, M. D. F. R. S. F. A. S.	2	2
Dr. Percival	2	2
Mr. B. D. Perkins	1	1
W. Perrin, Esq.	2	2
James Perry, Esq. P. R. I.	3	3
Louis Hayes Petit, Esq. F. A. S.	2	2
Mr. C. H. Pfeifel	1	1
Rev. W. G. Philips, P. R. I.	1	1
William Phillips, Esq.	1	1
Mr. R. Phillips, *Bookseller*	5	5
Mr. Richard Phillips	1	1
Mrs. Charles Phillott, *Bath*	1	1
Johnson Phillott, Esq. *Bath*	1	1
Philosophical Society, *Hythe, Kent*	1	1
Physical Society, *Guy's Hospital*	6	6
Library of the College of Physicians, *Edinburgh*		
J. K. Picard, Esq. *Summergang's House, near Hull*	2	2
Charles Preschell, Esq. P. R. I.	2	2

	£.	s.
Gillery Pigott, Esq.	2	2
T. Pilkington, Esq, *Bewdley, Surgeon*	1	1
William Pilkington, Esq.	2	2
Mrs. Pilkington	1	1
William Pim, Esq.	2	2
I. Pinchard, Esq. *Taunton*	1	1
Dr. Pinckard	2	2
Thomas Pitt, Esq. F. A. S. P. R. I.	2	2
William Plasted, Esq. *Chelsea*	1	1
———— Pocock, Esq.	1	1
Plymouth Literary Society	1	1
R. Podmore, Esq.	1	1
Mr. William Pollard, *Bradford*	1	1
Thomas C. Porter, Esq.	1	1
Portsmouth Book Society	2	2
The Rev. Josiah Pratt, F. A. S.	1	1
J. Prescott, Esq. *St. Petersburg* 1	11	6
The Rev. I. Preston, *Flasby Hall, Yorkshire*	1	1
Joseph Price, Esq.	1	1
Rev. William Price, *Bath*	1	1
Benjamin Price, Esq.	1	1
Mr. Joseph Priestly, *Bradford*	1	1
Mr. Prince	1	1
Mr. Pritt	1	1
Mr. Pullen	1	1
T. Pulley, Esq.	1	1

R

	£.	s.
The Royal Institution of Great Britain	50	0
Earl of Radnor, F. R. S. F. A. S.	4	0
Hon. Dr. Francis Rigby, *Jamaica*		
The Hon. Mrs. Rollo	2	2
Rev. Thomas Rackett, F.R.S. F.A.S. P.R.I. F.L.S.	1	1
Mrs. Rackett	1	1
Miss Rackett	0 10	6

	£.	s.
Richard Radford, Esq.	1	1
Rev. Dr. Raine, F. R. S. F. A. S.	2	2
Richard Raley, Esq. *Clare Hall, Cambridge*	1	1
George Ranking, Esq. P. R. I.	2	2
John Ranking, Esq. *St. Petersburg* 1	11	6
Mr. Rathbone	5	5
Thomas Rawson, jun. Esq.	2	2
Mr. W. L. Reay, *Surgeon*	2	2
Rev. Dr. Rees, F. R. S.	1	1
Joshua Reeve, Esq. P. R. I.	5	5
T. R. Reid, Esq.	1	1
James Remnant, Esq.	2	2
Thomas Renwick, M. D.	3	3
George Reveley, Esq.	1	1
S. W. Reynolds, Esq.	2	2
Dr. Reynolds, F. R. S. F. A. S.	2	2
D. Ricardo, Esq.	1	1
Mr. Rich, *Fryston, Yorkshire*	5	0
Mrs. Richards	5	5
Isaac Ried, Esq.	1	1
J. Ring, Esq.	2	2
John Risdon, Esq. *Peckham*	1	1
Mr. Rittson, *Lancaster, Surgeon*	1	1
Thomas Roberts, Esq.	1	1
James Robertson, Esq.	1	1
Arthur Robinson, Esq.	1	1
Mr. Robinson, *York*	1	1
———— Robinson, Esq.	1	1
Jonathan Rogers, M. D.	3	3
Dr. Rogerson	2	2
John Rollo, M. D.	1	1
Thomas Rolph, Esq. *Peckham*	1	1
Samuel Romilly, Esq.	2	2
William Rosco, Esq.	3	3
Dr. Rowley	5	5
———— Rowley, M. D.	5	5
J. Rowlat, Esq. *St. Petersburg* 1	11	6

	£.	s.
Edward Rudge, Esq. F. L. S.	1	1
Rev. Joshua Ruddock, A. M.	2	2
Mr. L. T. Rupp	2	2
Mr. Rupp	2	2
T. Rutt, Esq.	1	1
John Rutter, M. D.	2	2

S

	£.	s.
Earl Stanhope, F. R. S. P. R. I.	1	1
Sir Richard Joseph Sullivan, Bart. F. R. S. F. A. S. P. R. I.	5	5
Sir John St. Aubyn, Bart.		
Mr. William Salter	1	1
Dr. Satterley, *Tunbridge Wells*	1	1
George Saunders, Esq. F. A. S.	1	1
Thomas Scott, Esq.	1	1
Mrs. P. Scott	2	0
Mr. G. M. Sears	1	1
John Semple, Esq.	2	2
Miss Senior, *Sittingbourne*	1	1
Thomas Serjeant, Esq.	1	1
Dr. Serney, *Boston, Lincolnshire*	1	1
Henry Settree, Esq.	1	1
Mr. Edmund Shadwick	1	1
George Grinley Sharpe, Esq. *Peckham, Surgeon*	1	1
Mr. Shaw, *Surgeon*	2	2
Townley Rigby Shawe, Esq. *Preston*	1	1
Miss Shee	1	1
Miss E. Shee	1	1
Miss J. Shee	1	1
Miss H. Shee	1	1
Library of Sheffield Infirmary		
W Shepherd, Esq.	1	1
Stephen Shute, Esq.	1	1
Mr. William Silver, *Portsmouth*	1	1
Richard Simmons, Esq. *Surgeon*	2	2
Mr. John Simmons	1	1
Mr. Thomas Simpkin	1	1

	£.	s.
Mr. John Simpson	1	1
Mr. Robert Sampson, jun.	1	1
Samuel Everingham Sketchley, Esq.	1	1
Mr. Alexander Sketchley	1	1
Mr. Alexander Sketchley, *Clapham*	1	1
———Slade, Esq.	1	1
R. Smales, Esq.	1	1
Rev. Mr. Smirnove	1	1
John Stafford Smith, Esq.	1	1
J. R. Smith, Esq.	5	5
Nathan Smith, Esq.	1	1
———Smith, Esq. *Lancaster, Surgeon*	1	1
James Smith, Jun. Esq. *Glasgow*	2	2
Dr. Smith	1	1
Rev. Thomas Jenyns Smith, *Dulwich*	1	1
Mr. Egerton Smith	1	1
Mr. Frederick Smith	1	1
Mr. Smithson, *Heath, Wakefield*	2	2
Society for the Encouragement of Arts, Manufactures, and Commerce	5	5
Samuel Solly, Esq. P. R. I.	2	2
Archibald Sorley, Esq.	2	2
James Sowerby, Esq. *Lambeth*	1	1
John Spence, Esq. *Greenock*	3	3
Knight Spencer, Esq.	2	2
———Spencer, Esq. *Surgeon*	2	2
John Spencer, Esq.	2	2
John Sperling, Esq.	1	1
M. Spratt, Esq.	1	1
William Stainstreet, Esq.	3	3
William Stanniforth, Esq. *Sheffield, Surgeon*		
Rev. T. Starkie, A. M. *Blackburn*	1	1
S. F Statham, Esq. *Arnold, Notting.*	1	1
Mr. William Standley, *Bradford*	1	1
Mr. Thomas Steel	1	1
J. Steers, Esq.	1	1

	£.	s.
Francis Stephens, Esq.	1	1
Mr. J. Stephenson	1	1
Rev. W. Stevens	1	1
William Stodart, Esq. P. R. I.	5	5
Mr. James Stodart, P. R. I.	5	5
Mr. M. Stodart	1	1
Miss Strickland, *Boynton*		
Sunderland Subscription Library	1	1
John Swale, Esq.	1	1
Mr. Swan	1	1
Mr. Sydenham, *no Book*	1	1
Godfrey Sykes, Esq.	1	1

T

	£.	s.
Peter Tahourdin, Esq.	1	1
John Tate, jun. Esq.	1	1
C. H. Tatham, Esq.	1	1
B. Tayle, Esq.	1	1
John Taylor, Esq.	3	3
James Taylor, Esq.	2	2
R. S. Taylor, Esq.	1	1
Mr. I. Taylor, *Gomersall*		
Arthur Tegart, Esq.	1	1
Dr. Temple	5	5
Mrs. Tennant	2	2
Mr. Frederick Thackerey, *Emanuel College, Cambridge*	1	1
H. L. Thomas, Esq.	1	1
Robert Thompson, Esq. F. A. S.	2	2
Robert Thompson, jun. Esq.	1	1
Mrs. Thompson	2	2
John P Thompson, Esq.	1	1
Messrs. Thomson and Son, *Manchester*	1	1
Robert Thornton, Esq. M.P. F.A.S. P. R. I.	5	5
Samuel Thornton, Esq. F. A. S. P. R. I.	1	1

	£.	s.
Samuel Thornton, Esq.	1	1
Robert John Thornton, M. D.	1	1
Anthony Thorp, Esq. *York*	1	1
William Hall Timbrel, Esq.	1	1
Mr. Cornelius Tongue	1	1
John Townshend, Esq. *Chelsea*	5	5
John Townsend, Esq. *Wandsworth*	5	5
Samuel Turner, Esq.	2	2
Thomas Turner, M. D.	2	2
Sharon Turner, Esq. F. A. S.	1	1
Dawson Turner, Esq. F. A. S.	2	2
J. Turton, Esq.	1	1
Thomas Tyndall, Esq. *Bristol*		

U

	£.	s.
Peter Vere, Esq. F. A. S.	1	1
Mr. Underwood	1	1
James Upton, Esq.	1	1
J. Upton, Esq.	1	1
T. Upward, Esq.	2	2
Miss S. Vranken, *Bristol*		
Gordon Urquhart, Esq.	1	1

W

	£.	s.
Sir William E. Welby, Bart.	2	2
Honourable J. S. Wortley, P R. I.	1	1
M. F Wagstaff, Esq.	1	1
Daniel Walker, Esq.	1	1
Samuel Walker, Esq. *Masbrough*		
Mr. J. Walker	1	1
Mr. Joseph Walker	1	1
Martin Wall, M. D. *Clinical Professor, Oxford*		
T. Walshman, M. D. *Physician to the Western and Surry Dispensaries, and President of the Physical Society*	1	1
John Walter, Esq. *Pimlico*	1	1

	£.	s.
D. Walters, Esq.	1	1
Olaus Warberg, Esq. *Copenhagen*	1	1
Mrs. Ward, *Hampstead*	1	1
Gilbert Wardlaw, Esq. *Glasgow*	1	1
James Ware, Esq. F. R. S. F. A. S.	5	5
Rev. John Ware, *York*		
John Warren, Esq. P. R. I.	1	1
Mr. Watkins	2	2
Mr. Watson	2	2
W. H. Watts, Esq.	5	5
David Pike Watts, Esq. P. R. I.	2	2
Mrs. Wawn	1	1
Rev. George Wearing, *Whalley*	1	1
Mr. James Weatherby	1	1
Mr. Matthew Wedeson	1	1
J. Wedgwood, Esq. P. R. I.	1	1
J. C. Weguelin, Esq.	2	2
Mr. J. Welbank	1	1
William Earle Welby, Esq. *Carlton*		
House, Nottinghamshire	3	3
Richard Earle Welby, Esq.	2	2
George Welch, Esq.	1	1
Mrs. Welch	2	2
Thomas West, Esq. *Bath*	1	1
Mrs. West	5	5
Westminster Library	1	1
Lawson Whalley, Esq. *Lancaster*	1	1
Lawson Whalley, Esq. *Lancaster*	1	1
The Rev. John Wheeler	1	1
Samuel Whitbread, Esq. M. P.	3	3
Edward White, Esq.	1	1
Rev. Samuel White	1	1
Mrs. White, *Bury St. Edmunds*	2	2
Miss White	1	1
Rev. Walter Whiter	1	1
Robert Whitfield, Esq. *Surgeon*	1	1
William Whittington, Esq.	5	5
Miss Whittington	3	3
Miss E. Whittington	2	2
Edward Athenry Whyte, Esq. *Dub-*		
lin	1	1
Rev. Thomas Wigan	1	1
Mr. John Wiglesworth	1	1
Lieut. Col. Wilder	1	1
Mr. Wilkes	1	1
Thomas Willan, Esq.	5	5
Mrs. Willan	5	5
John Willan, Esq.	5	5
John Williams, Esq. *Caermarthen,*		
Surgeon	1	1
———— Williams, Esq.	1	1
Mr. William Henry Williams, *Caius*		
College, Cambridge	1	1
Dr. A. F. M. Willich	1	1
Dr. Robert Willis	5	5
H. W. C. Wilson, Esq.	2	2
James Wilson, Esq.	2	2
Dr. Wilson	2	2
Rev. Thomas Wilson, *Clitheroe*	1	1
Miss Winckworth	1	1
Joseph Windham, Esq. F. R. S.		
F. L. S.	2	2
Alexander Wood, Esq. *Edinburgh,*		
Surgeon		
R. Wood, Esq.	1	1
Robert Wood, Esq. *Tamworth*	1	1
William Wood, Esq. *Hackney*	1	1
Mr. James Wood	1	1
Samuel Woods, Esq.	3	3
Mr. Henry Worboys	1	1
Mr. John Worboys	1	1
Peter Wright, Esq. P. R. I.	2	2
Mr. James Wright, *Liverpool*	2	2
Dr. Wright	1	1
Mr. Wright, *Optician*	1	1
William Wynch, Esq. P. R. I	2	2

	£.	s.
W. Wynch, Esq. *2nd Subscription*	1	1

Y

	£.	s.
Joseph Yallowley, Esq.	1	1
Rev. John Yates	3	3
Matthew Yatman, Esq. F. A. S.	1	1

	£.	s.
Dr. Yelloly	2	2
J. W. Yonge, Esq.	2	2
Thomas Young, M.D. For. Sec. R.S. F. L.S.	5	5
G. Young, Esq.	1	1
William Younge, M. D. *Sheffield*		

From the Press of the Royal Institution of Great Britain,
Albemarle Street, London: William Savage, Printer.

ADDENDA.

<table>
<tr><td colspan="3">A</td><td>£.</td><td>s.</td></tr>
<tr><td>The Right Hon. Lord Altamont</td><td></td><td></td><td>1</td><td>1</td></tr>
<tr><td>Nicholas Ashton, Esq.</td><td></td><td></td><td>5</td><td>5</td></tr>
<tr><td>J. J. Angerstein, Esq.</td><td></td><td></td><td>10</td><td>10</td></tr>
<tr><td>Mr. James Asperne</td><td></td><td></td><td>1</td><td>1</td></tr>
<tr><td>J. B. Austin, Esq.</td><td></td><td></td><td>1</td><td>1</td></tr>
<tr><td>Mr. Abernethey</td><td></td><td></td><td>5</td><td>5</td></tr>
</table>

A

	£.	s.
The Right Hon. Lord Altamont	1	1
Nicholas Ashton, Esq.	5	5
J. J. Angerstein, Esq.	10	10
Mr. James Asperne	1	1
J. B. Austin, Esq.	1	1
Mr. Abernethey	5	5

B

	£.	s.
Scrope Bernard, Esq.	1	1
C. F. Barnwell, Esq.	1	1
Rev. Dr. Balward	1	1
Rev. T. Browne	5	5
Rev. B. Bridge	1	1
Rev. T. Brooke	1	1
W. S. Bruere, Esq.	1	1
J. D. Borton, Esq.	1	1
William Breese, Esq.	2	2
Mr. Bradner	1	1
James Bureau, Esq.	3	3
Mrs. Mary Bowyer	1	1
Rev. G. Butler	1	1
Rev. J. Brown	1	1
Mr. Bryant	1	1
John Butts, Esq.	1	1
Mr. Bruce Boswell	1	1

C

	£.	s.
James Collins, Esq.	1	1
William Cass, Esq.	2	2
M. Da Costa	1	1
F. Carter, Esq.	1	1
Rev. T. Cautley	1	1
G. Caldwell, Esq.	1	1
Rev. T. Clarkson	1	1
E. D. Clarke, Esq.	1	1
T. M. Cripps, Esq.	1	1
Rev. B. Chapman	1	1

D

	£.	s.
The Lord Bishop of Durham	10	10
P. Denys, Esq.	4	4
Rev. F. Drake	1	1
J. Dearman, Esq. *Champion Hill*	1	1
M. Dobson, Esq.	1	1
Dr. Denman	2	2
Mr. Durham	2	0
Rev. Dr. Dealtry	1	1
Martyn Davy, M. D.	1	1
Philip Derbishire, Esq.	1	1

E

	£.	s.
Sir James Esdaile	1	1
Dr. G. B. Eaton	1	1

F

	£.	s.
John Fuller, Esq.	1	1
Edward Foster, Esq.	1	1
Edward Foster, jun. Esq.	1	1
John Fellowes, Esq.	1	1
A friend, W. H. S. by Mr. Cuppage	1	1
A friend	5	5
A friend, S. B.	2	2
A friend, R. R.	1	1
A friend, C. A. Esq.	1	1

G

	£.	s.
Stephen Gaselee, Esq.	2	2
W. B. Garlike, M. D.	2	2
D. Garnett, Esq.	1	1
Mrs. Garnett	1	1
J. R. Gladdow, Esq.	1	1

H

	£.	s.
The Hon. Major Henniker	1	1
J. Hall, Esq.	1	1
———— Hill, Esq.	2	2
Richard Hussey, Esq.	2	2
Mark Huish, jun. Esq.	1	1
Nathaniel Hubbins, Esq.	1	1
Dr. Heberden	2	2
T. Holmes, Esq.	1	1
John Holkyard, Esq. *Surgeon*	1	1
Professor Harwood	2	2
E. Hibgame, Esq.	1	1
T. P Hackhouse, Esq.	1	1
B. Harvey, Esq.	1	1
Rev. T. Holden	1	1
Rev. Mr. Holme	1	1
William Hutton, Esq.	1	1
Dr. Halliday	2	2
Thomas Halliday, Esq.	1	1

	£.	s.
William Holden, Esq.	1	1
————Van Hoorst, Esq.	1	1

J

	£.	s.
Rev. T. Jones	1	1
Mr. S. Jones	1	1

K

	£.	s.
L. Knight, Esq.	1	1
Rev. J. Kenrick	1	1

L

	£.	s.
Sir John Leggart, Bart.	1	1
William Lewis, Esq.	1	1
A. S. Lillingstone, Esq.	2	2
Dr. Latham	5	5

M

	£.	s.
Basil Montague, Esq.	1	1
James Mackintosh, Esq.	1	1
H. Mayers, Esq.	1	1
Lieutenant Col. McDonald	1	1
M. Marshall, Esq.	1	1
Rev. Mr. Maule	1	1
Rev. Mr. Manning	1	1
Rev. W. Miller	1	1
Dr. John William Minier	2	2
Mr. Miller	1	1
Mr. Marshall	1	1

N

	£.	s.
Richard Nixon, Esq.	1	1
George Norman, Esq.	3	3
————Nottage, Esq.	2	2
Mr. Richard Nicholls	1	1

O

	£.	s.
Benjamin Oakley, Esq.	1	1
Rev. W. Otter	1	1

	£. s.
P	
Hon. Mr. Pakenham	1 1
N. Palmer, Esq.	1 1
Dr. David Pitcairn	5 5
Dr. Pennington	1 1
The Rev. G. Pollen	10 10
St. Peter's College	6 6
R	
W. Robinson, Esq.	1 1
William Rathbone, Esq.	5 5
Rev. H. R. Rouney	1 1
Rev. Mr. Renouard	1 1
Mr. Rawlins	1 1
S	
A. Smith, Esq.	2 2
James Skirrow, Esq.	1 1
Dr. Sloper	5 5
John Simpson, M. D.	1 1
Rev. Mr. Simeon	1 1
Rev. J. Satterthwaite	1 1

	£. s.
T	
The Right Hon. John Trevor	2 2
Rev. Dr. Towitt	1 1
Mr. Thomas Teasdale	1 1
V	
Rev. T. Vickers	1 1
W	
M. S. Wakefield, Esq.	1 1
Thomas Wilson, Esq.	2 2
R. S. Wells, Esq.	1 1
William White, Esq.	1 1
Joseph Walker, Esq.	1 1
John Welbank, Esq.	1 1
Rev. J. Wood	1 1
Rev. Mr. Wheatear	1 1
Rev. J. Walker	1 1
Mrs. Ward	1 1
Y	
J. A. Young, Esq.	2 2
Dr. Young	1 1

LONDON: Sold by J. MURRAY, No. 32, Fleet-Street; and JAMES PHILLIPS,
George-Yard, Lombard-Street.
M,DCC,XCII.

(iii)

ADVERTISEMENT.

THE peculiar irritability of minds, employed in the cultivation of the fine arts, has been long obferved and fatisfactorily explained. Of this tormenting quality, the offspring and companion of Vanity, the votaries of verfe are known to have their full allotment. So important do the tranfactions of their underftandings appear in their own eyes, that they often indulge us with an account of the accident, which ftruck the firft fpark from their imagination; and then regularly proceed to inform us how by degrees, under the flattering encouragement of friends, and the accumulation of materials, it was cherifhed into a blaze, fit to be exhibited to the public eye. Nor is Statius the only verfifier, who has been at the pains to tell us how foon a number of indifferent lines may be ftrung together.

One may frequently obferve much the fame fort of Vanity in thofe, whom experience has not yet taught, how little men are difpofed to fympathize with their equals in the ordinary occurrences of life. Children, for inftance, often attempt to excite an intereft in their own favour by a recital of their efcapes from danger or difeafe. But the ftratagem feldom fucceeds. They find among their play-fellows many who have equally fuffered from fevers and broken bones. Nor is it now fo uncommon to be a writer of verfe or profe, that any one fhould think it worth his while to tell how he became one. And, if ever there could have been hopes of propitiating the reader by thefe confidential communications, it is to be feared that the charm has long fince loft its power.

In fpite of confiderations fo difcouraging, I think it neceffary to mention in a few words the occafion of the following lines. They originated in a ftratagem, which, if not entirely innocent, can be charged only with the guilt of prefumption. In order to impofe upon a few of their common acquaintance, the writer, in a few paffages at leaft, attempted to affume the ftyle of the moft elegant of modern poets; and thought he was encouraged, by fome degree of fuccefs, to extend his defign, he cannot build much hope upon fo flender a foundation. He is too fenfible of the difference between a hafty recital and a cool perufal, and between the effect of the fame compofition in manufcript and in print: nor can he forget the power of an

A 2

illuftrious

illuſtrious name to difarm cenfure. But perhaps even by profeſſing fo far a defign to imitate, he ſhall not efcape the charge of plagiarifm. For, are there not imitations of older poets? Some he knows there are; and there are poſſibly others of which he is ignorant. Having formerly, like other young perfons, delighted in works of imagination, he paſſed a long interval with little intercourfe with the favourites of his youth, and cannot now always diſtinguiſh between the fuggeſtions of memory and invention.

Having never written twice as many lines as the following pages contain, he is not a little furprized to find himfelf an artificer in rhime. To this confeſſion or apology, he begs leave to add, that the following verfes were not only written, but nearly printed before the appearance of *the Œconomy of Vegetation* and the third edition of *the Loves of the Plants*; a fact of which he could eafily produce evidence, if it were neceſſary. He could not therefore tranfplant any of the Graces with which the more recent productions of this great poet and philofopher abound. Neither would he have attempted it, for imitation carried too far, becomes contemptibly puerile.

The intelligent critic will probably cenfure the profufion of notes. They were chiefly written with a view to diffufe more widely a knowledge of old and new Hindoo literature, which although fufficiently familiar to the learned, is but juſt reaching the circle of ordinary readers. When the imagination is once enamoured of any object, no pains will be fpared to inveſtigate it thoroughly: and upon this principle a perfon who poſſeſſes, like the author of the Botanic Garden, a ſtore of images and a command of language, fufficient to conſtitute a poet, may entitle himfelf to public gratitude, by offering to thofe, who feel oppreſſed by the burden of life, fome engaging purfuit, and he may add a new intereſt to the exiſtence of others.— If it were wiſhed that a boy ſhould apply himfelf earneſtly to the ſtudy of Engliſh hiſtory, it might be proper, among other indirect inducements, to carry him to the reprefentation of fome of Shakefpeare's plays. It is excited Fancy that has worked fo many miracles in art and fcience; and one may lament, both for the fake of knowledge and humanity, that fome attention is not paid to this truth in education. —For feveral of the fentiments in the annexed *obfervations* the author will not offer a vain apology. He forefees that they will be warmly difapproved. But it is an happy circumſtance in the conſtitution of the human mind, that we can find in truth, or, if you pleafe, in deliberate opinions, a compenfation for that antipathy which the avowal often excites. The antients have faid, and the moderns have re-

peated

peated, that Virtue to be loved, needs only to be seen. The history of mankind shews that the exact contrary holds with regard to Truth. No art can so set her off that she shall not, on her first appearance, excite almost universal abhorrence. It is well for us, that she improves upon acquaintance !

Something will occur in the notes concerning the character of Alexander, which has so often been an object of contemplation to the Philosopher and Historian : and I might quote from Mr. Barthelemi's admired work an elaborate portrait of my Hero. But I think he may be delineated in a very narrow compass, and of him, as of other great men, I should think it sufficient to say that his mind was discriminated by *exquisite sensibility*. By whatever object they were touched, the springs of his nature bent deeply inwards, but they immediately rebounded with equal energy into action. Hence one may explain his passionate excesses ; that independance of mind, which would not blindly submit even to an Aristotle ; and those extraordinary projects by which he sometimes aspired to praise according to the false standard of excellence then established, as well as those equally magnificent designs, which exceeded the comprehension of his age. Thus, His genius was doubtless, great. But his birth and times determined its mode of exertion.

It is, in my opinion, nothing extraordinary, that so young a man should form such mighty enterprizes. Youth has always been the season of enlarged conceptions and great discoveries. Even in the severer sciences it might be shewn by a large induction of particulars that the youthful faculties are best calculated to form original and just combinations. The history of Newton, Locke, Boerhaave, Linnæus, Lavoisier with that of almost all other great discoverers, and founders of sciences and systems proves that the most noble and most beneficial discoveries have been made, and the largest comprehension of thought displayed, by men that had not yet attained the middle of life ; and frequently by those who were only not boys. Great political changes also have been commonly effected in the world by young men, or at least in consequence of plans framed early in life.—Without attending to the course of our own thoughts, we may easily be led, when we hear of the different faculties of the mind, to imagine that these faculties are fixed to different parts of the mind, as the organs of sense are to different parts of the head : and we may conceive our several faculties to be in vigour at different periods of life. So much misapprehension do arbitrary distinctions and illusive metaphors occasion ! A little reflection, however, will easily convince us of the unity of the intellectual principle : We shall be sensible.

ble that its different operations, as they are called, are carried on almost at the same inftant, or follow each other in the moft rapid fucceffion, and are for ever intermingling. A mind, vigourous in imagining, is alfo vigourous in judging. Probably in the moft abftrufe refearches of fcience as much imagination is exerted as in the higheft flights of poetry; and in the latter we judge and compare as much as in the former. It feems too, perfectly indifferent to the power, by which we combine ideas, what fort of ideas it has to combine; and I will venture at the rifque of ridicule, to conjecture that, had the circumftances of their lives been mutually exchanged, Homer might have been the greateft of geometricians, and Newton the chief of poets.—Some favourites of Nature indeed long retain the vigour of their faculties as we fee fome perfons long retaining the moft obvious attributes of youth. But perhaps many of thofe productions which have been exhibited to the public eye at a mature or an advanced age, were planned and partly executed at an early period of life. Nor is there any occafion to fuppofe that the decay of the intellectual organ is other than very gradual like that of the moving and fentient parts of our frame; and perhaps when we come to be well acquainted with the laws of human nature, even the flow progrefs of intellectual decay may be retarded. If it be objected that the Judgment muft improve by exercife and the accumulation of materials, (and this is equally true of the Imagination) it fhould be remembered that many minds are thoroughly well difciplined by reflection at the age of five-and-twenty or thirty, and even earlier. And if this advantage is at prefent confined to a few, where does the fault lie, but in thofe inftitutions, which by every direct and indirect means, counteract the defigns of creative wifdom, and check the improvement of the individual, and, by confequence, of the fpecies?

Thefe reflections will not, I hope, be fo mifunderftood as if all young men were afferted to be fuperior, in their intellectual powers, to all their feniors: I only affign a few, out of many reafons, which biography and pfychology prefent, for fuppofing the *acme* of mental, to be nearly contemporary with that of corporeal vigour. They may animate the induftry, without increafing the prefumption, of youth. In a larger treatife fomething might be added to their precifion, with little limitation of their extent. They will, in the mean time, be very differently received by readers of different ages.

The engravings in the following pages will be praifed or excufed when it is known that they are the performance of an uneducated and uninftructed artift, if fuch an application be not a profanation of the term, in a remote village. All the affiftance he received was from the example of Mr. Bewick's moft mafterly engravings on wood. The defigns would have been better, if he could have made himfelf more perfectly acquainted with the *coftume* of Nature in India.—The firft may give thofe who have not feen Mr. Rennel's maps, an idea of the *Sunderbunds*.—The fecond was fuggefted by one of Mr. Daniel's views of Calcutta, which the engraver had not before him. Vegetation is the great enemy of buildings in India; and this view fhews with what vigour Nature carries on her eternal war againft Art in that fultry climate.—That in p. 1. refers to lines 69—72;—the Pagoda at the end of the verfes is not one of the celebrated edifices of that name. It is from Calcutta.— A French work on the religious ceremonies of all nations furnifhed the engraving in p. 49. The brutalized Faquir in front, is, I believe, faithfully copied.—The Tiger (p. 64.) bears Indian rockets on his back.—The triple figure is an Hindoo Deity. It is taken from Mr. Niebbuhr, who copied it from the wonderful antient fculptures in the excavations of the ifle Elephanta.

In fpite of fome deficiences in the typographical apparatus, and fome unfavourable circumftances befides, the following pages are not ill printed. The *compofitor* was a young woman in the fame village. I know not if women be commonly engaged in printing, but their nimble and delicate fingers feem extremely well adapted to the office of compofitor; and it will be readily granted that employment for females is among the greateft defiderata of fociety.

(viii)

A R G U M E N T.

NOW the new Lord of Persia's wide domain
Down fierce Hydaspes seeks the Indian Main;

Alexander's expedition. After his defeat at Arbela, the feeble Darius was feized by a party of his own Satraps and Officers. Beſſus, who was at the head of the confpiracy, aſſumed the title of King of Perfia, took the name of Artaxerxes and feems to have made preparations for oppofing Alexander. The fpeed and vigilance however of the Grecian General fruſtrated his defigns; and the confpirators, finding themfelves fo hard preſſed that they could not carry off the captive monarch, murdered him, and flying left his body behind. This atrocious act ferved but to ſtimulate Alexander. It is pleafing to trace him, as he is hurried along by a generous

B

High

High on the leading prow the Conqueror ſtands,

Eyes purer ſkies, and marks diverging ſtrands.

indignation in purſuit of the aſſaſſins, firſt in an Eaſterly and then in a Northern
direction, through the heart of Aſia. Bazaernes was delivered up by the Indians on
the weſt of the Indus and executed. The fear of being purſued into their deſerts
induced the Scythians to ſend the head of Spitamenes; Satibazzanes was killed in
battle. And it was in vain that Beſſus croſſed the great ridge of Hindoo Kho, the
Indian Caucaſus, laid waſte the country at the foot of the mountains, and burned
the boats in which he had tranſported himſelf and his followers acroſs the Oxus.
The indefatigable avenger of Darius followed cloſe upon his footſteps. He was
ſeized by Ptolemy not far from the banks of the Jaxartes or Sihon. At the ſight
of Beſſus, Alexander ſtopped his chariot and aſked, why he had firſt put in chains
and afterwards murdered his Sovereign, who was alſo his friend and benefactor.
The villainy of courtiers is equalled only by their meanneſs. " It was not my act
merely, replied the culprit: all who were about Darius were concerned. We
hoped by this means to make our peace with Alexander." (Arrian. B. III.)
By ſuch a defence he paſſed ſentence upon himſelf.—On repaſſing the mountains,
Alexander moved directly eaſtward. During his progreſs along the ſkirts of India,
he had gathered ſuch information as probably revived many pleaſing ideas that were
ſlumbering in his breaſt. It is reaſonable to conjecture that his mind had dwelled
upon thoſe remote regions with peculiar complacency from his earlieſt youth;
for the reports at this period current among the Greeks concerning India, conſiſted
of ſome genuine information mixed with a large proportion of fable and unauthori-
zed tradition. Tales of this romantic caſt are admirably calculated to inflame a ſuf-
ceptible imagination. In every age the effect of ſuch a miſty and magnified view
of diſtant objects has been powerfully felt. We may recollect in what golden colours the unexplored countries of America exhibited themſelves to European imaginations about the time of Raleigh's expedition: and we may thus conceive ſome

A thou-

A thoufand fails attendant catch the wind,   5

And yet a thoufand prefs the wave behind;

Two Veteran hofts, outftretched on either hand,

Wide wave their wings and fweep the trembling land.

faint idea of the feelings and expectations with which fuch a man as Alexander muft have entered India. Strabo (B. XV.) confirms thefe reflections.

V. 2. *Fierce Hydafpes.* The five great rivers of the PANJAB or province of LA-HORE are precipitated from different parts of the lofty and extenfive ridge of Himmaleh, Imäus, or the *fnowy* mountains. They foon attain a confiderable bulk: their vaft rapidity fhews the great declivity of the countries at the foot of this chain. The natives demolifhed a bridge of boats, thrown by Nadir Shah acrofs the Acefines, by rolling large trees into the ftream. (Abdul-Kurreem, Memoirs p. 3.) The fame writer compares the Sinde (Indus) to a deadly fnake, on account both of its winding courfe and rapid current. Mr. Forfter, July 10th, 1783, found this river very rapid and turbulent, though it was not agitated by any wind: It was three quarters of a mile broad 20 miles above Attock. The water was extremely cold and turbid; it was therefore affected by the rains and melted fnows. The Hydafpes and Acefines as we fhall find below, rufh together with prodigious impetuofity, and with fuch danger to navigators that fome of Alexander's large fhips were loft, many veffels damaged and the whole fleet thrown into confternation. The Hydafpes becomes navigable a few miles below its moft remote fource. After traverfing the happy valley of Cafhmere, it cuts its way through deep ranges of mountains: where it hurries along with fuch rapidity that the ftouteft elephant cannot preferve his footing in it. (Rennel, Memoir 2nd ed. p. 99.)

V. 3—8. The troops had fo feverely fuffered from the rains that all the influence of their general could not prevail upon them to advance beyond the Hyphafis, the

      The

The ferried Phalanx TERROR ftalks befide,
And fhakes o'er blazing helms his crefted pride;   10
While VICTORY, ftill companion of his way,
Sounds her loud trump and flaunts her banners gay.

By mofs-grown cliffs, where infant fountains weep;
Where cataracts thunder down the fhattered fteep;

moft eafterly river of the Panjab.   On the farther bank of this river he erected
12 large altars to mark the limit of his expedition.   His enterprizing genius, after
this difappointment, was obliged to direct itfelf towards a new object.   He had already ftationed a body of troops on the Hydafpes with orders to provide a fleet.
This fleet he deftined to explore, firft the rivers and afterwards the coafts of the Indian Ocean weftward from the mouth of the Indus to the Perfian gulph.   On his
return to the banks of the Hydafpes he found that about 2,000 veffels had been
built or collected.   One third of the army, which altogether confifted of 120,000
men, was placed on board this fleet.   Another third was directed to attend the
movements of the fleet on the right, and the remainder on the left hand of the
river.   " The conduct of this expedition (Robertfon's Antient India p. 17.) was
committed to Nearchus, an Officer equal to that important truft.   But as Alexander
was ambitious of fame of every kind, and fond of engaging in new and fplendid
undertakings, he himfelf accompanied Nearchus in his navigation down the river.
This armament was indeed fo great and magnificent as deferved to be commanded
by the Conqueror of Afia."   In a modern hiftorian the phrafe " *Conqueror of Afia*"
will appear fomewhat ftrong.   To the motives of Alexander Dr. Robertfon might
fafely have added ardent curiofity.   He ftands honourably diftinguifhed among
Conquerors by his eager thirft as well as liberal encouragement of fcience; and in
his character " the romantic traveller is blended with the adventurous foldier."

Where

Where from the rocky pier and ftream-worn cave   15

Umbrageous forefts fpan the lurid wave,

Swift-gliding galleys trace the mazy way,

Their clamours mingle, and their ftate difplay.

Forth from their fecret glooms and rugged foil,

The voice of Uproar calls the Sons of fpoil;   20

V. 13 &c. Arrian's account of this extraordinary naval proceffion is as follows. "Orders were given as to the diftances which the baggage and horfe tranfports and the war-veffels were to obferve, left they fhould run foul of each other. The quickeft failors were not allowed to outftrip the reft. And the noife of the rowing exceeded any thing ever heard before, partly from the multitude of veffels propelled together, partly from the number of boatfwains (keleuftai) who gave the word for the ftroke and the paufe, and partly from the fhouts uttered by the rowers the inftant they ftruck the ftream. And the banks being frequently higher than the fhips and confining the found, returned it from fide to fide greatly increafed: which effect was enhanced, wherever there were woods on each fide, both by the folitude and echoes. And the barbarous fpectators were fo furprized at the fight of horfes on board, for no fuch fight had ever been beheld in the country of the Indians, that they followed to a great diftance. And wherever the fhouts of the rowers and the found of the oars reached the Indians, that had fubmitted to Alexander, thefe alfo crowded to the banks of the river and followed, finging in concert after their barbarous manner.". .
.. "Where the Hydafpes and the Acefines meet, they form one very narrow river in place of two; and the current becomes rapid from its confinement, and there are prodigious whirlpools from the recoil of the ftream; and the water foams and roars exceedingly, fo that the found is heard to a great diftance." He adds, that though they were apprized of thefe particulars, the rowers fufpended their oars, and the keleuftai were ftruck dumb by aftonifhment; many veffels were damaged, two funk &c. B. VI.

Far

Far o'er acclaiming shores the bounding throngs
Attend the triumph with barbaric songs,
Or, spent with haste, on wreathes of prostrate grass
Recumbent, watch the long procession pass;
Admiring much, as varied barks succeed,   25
But most the wonder of the wafted steed.
—The line flows on, by many a palmy isle,
Round jutting capes, down many a deep defile,
Where rifted mountains o'er the lost array
Fling their vast shadows, and exclude the day: 30
While Echo, listening from her dripping cave,
Mocks the shrill cry, dashed oar, and rippling wave.
—Now, quick emerging, o'er the wondering vale
Peeps the proud beak, and gleams the illumined sail—
—Now sudden horror chills the jocund course—   35
Impetuous rivers clash with headlong force—
Dire seeths the foam, and loud the surges roar;
The deafened Bands suspend the uplifted oar;

Back

Back reels the flood—devouring eddies curl—
And foundering keels revolve with dizzy whirl.   40

From diftant heights, the Shepherd's awe-ftruck gaze
War's pomp terrific, pacing flow, furveys;
O'er his ftrained bofom, billowy paffions roll
Their adverfe tides, and poife his ftruggling foul.
" Quick, quick avert thy fafcinated fight;   45
" To fafer climes oh fpeed thy inftant flight."
Thus Danger warns—in vain—the potent charm
Roots his fixed foot and grafps his rigid arm.
—So when dark volumes of the labouring ftorm
Sail flow o'er earth, and day's bright arch deform,   50
Swift floods of flame when fkies unfolding pour,
And onward rolls the long explofive roar,
Pale, fad, transfixed, the gafping Wanderer ftands,
Refigns his fwimming head and powerlefs hands:

                                        Yet,

Yet, ere he finks, with mild reviving glow   55

Back to the feats of fenfe his fpirits flow;

Then breaks thy gloom, Defpair; Hope's ftreaming light

Scares the gaunt forms that crofs thy troubled night;

And Fancy, fallying mid the wild career,

Bids Wonder ope the clofe-preffed lids of Fear.   60

Wɪᴛʜ deep-felt tread the founding march difturbs

The dark receffes of the matted herbs;

Uncoiling Serpents rear the towery creft,

Point the dire hifs, and fwell the fpeckled breaft;

V. 63—67. The Serpents of this diftrict were accounted very formidable. Ariftotle (on Animals. Francofurti p. 255.) mentions one fpecies fo venomous, that for his bite alone there is no remedy. The fame author (p. 254.) lays it down as a general character of the wild beafts of Afia, that they are more favage than in any other quarter of the globe. Modern experience of the dauntlefs ferocity of the Ty- ger of Bengal feems to give fome countenance to this opinion. The number of thefe animals and the depredations they commit, will perhaps appear incredible. In one year in Dinagepour* alone 10,000 rupees were paid for tygers; the Compa- ny's reward for deftroying a tyger is 10 rupees. I can add on the authority of two Gentlemen, well qualified to judge, that probably not fewer than 5 or 6,000 na- tives are annually deftroyed in Bengal by tygers. The bite of ferpents proves fatal to a great number.——Arrian (Amft. 1668. p. 538—9.) having mentioned

Through

*One of the 8 diftricts of Bengal and Bahar.

Swift, Terror's arm lays low the hideous heads,   65

The venomed monſters dart to diſtant beds;

Aghaſt the Tyger and the Lion quake,

Shrink from their bulk and crouch within the brake

Through quivering foliage ſteely luſtres glance;

With kindling eye-ball from his holy trance,   70

Behold! the ſoul-abſtracted FAQUIR ſtart,

And human feelings touch his palſied heart.

the ſize, ſwiftneſs, and variegated colours of the ſerpents, adds that the Greek Phyſicians had not diſcovered any remedy for their bite; the Indians however knew a
remedy; Alexander therefore retained about him the beſt Indian Phyſicians; and
cauſed it to be proclaimed through the camp, that whoever was bitten by a ſerpent,
ſhould repair to the King's tent.

V 71. *Faquir*. The Faquirs or devotees of India rank under ſeveral different
claſſes, each diſtinguiſhed by its peculiar title and object: as the Sinaſſee or Brami-
nical pilgrim, who cuts and ſhaves all the hair from his head, burns his *braminical*
thread, and clothing himſelf in two red cloths, and taking a bamboo ſtaff of his own
height in his right hand and an earthen pot in his left, forſakes his wife and children; the Ban Peruſt is one who after 50 years of age devotes himſelf to the ſervice
of God in the deſert. The Catry-Patry-Pandarams do not fly the face of man, but
by engaging to maintain a perpetual ſilence, they at once renounce the great cha-

—And you, mild tenants of the peaceful shore,

Which ne'er Invader's step profaned before,

racteriflic attribute of rational nature, and the beft comfort of life—the mutual interchange of fentiment. Their mode of foliciting alms is by flriking together the palms of their hands at the doors of houfes. But voluntary tortures, far exceeding in feverity thefe examples of mortification, are among the moft familiar fpectacles to the obfervers of Hindoo manners, nor has any of the various modes of fuperflition given rife to fufferings fo horrible to conceive as thofe, which fome of thefe fanatics inflict upon themfelves; fuch as keeping the eyes all day long fixed upon the Sun—an Eaft Indian Sun!—Clafping the hands over the head, till the arms wither, and the mufcles and joints are become incapable of motion: clenching the fift till the nails grow through the back of the hands. Sometimes they embrace the opportunity of being crufhed to death under the wheels of the chariots of their idols, when thefe enormous ftructures are moved along by hundreds of hands at their feftivals. One of thefe victims of fanaticifm burned himfelf to death in the prefence of Alexander and his officers. ——Mr. Sonnerat has figured one, whofe cheeks are perforated with a rod of iron, which alfo paffes through his tongue; on the projecting ends is fixed another piece of iron, bent like an horfe-fhoe, and hanging down under his chin. Has the emulation of vanity or elegance in Europe contrived more variations of drefs, or this brutal fpirit of devotion, of practices at once ridiculous and horrible? I will add, from the fame Mr. Sonnerat, a fpecimen of occafional piety, which may vie with the habitual penances of the Faquir. When an Hindoo defires to fhew his fenfe of gratitude towards the Goddefs Mariatala, two hooks are paffed through the fkin and mufcles of his back. The hooks are appended to one end of a lever, which refts upon an upright piece about 20 feet high. The votary is hoifted up into the air by depreffing the oppofite end of the lever. In general he bears in one hand a fabre and in the other a fhield; during his elevation he imitates the geftures of a man engaged in combat. Whatever may be his feelings, he muft ap-

Who

Who bask secure amid your sunny glades,   75

Or ply the loom beneath your scented shades,

pear chearful and alert, under penalty of expulsion from his caft, which is a very uncommon event. This edifying exercise is, as doubtlefs it ought to be, performed before an admiring concourfe of fpectators, principally compofed of ladies, who in all countries difpute the palm of devotion with the rougher fex, and in moft, for very obvious reafons, bear it away. (See Sonnerat Voyage aux Indes l. 244. pl. 66.) See alfo at the end fome reflections on the torpid indolence *(faineantife)* of the Afiatics.

V. 74. The expeditions of Hercules and Bacchus into India are to be ranked among thofe fables, with which nations fill up the void of their early hiftory. They were accordingly long fince rejected by the good fenfe of Strabo as fabulous. Under Darius Hyftafpes a naval expedition down the Indus—not by way of the Hydafpes—is faid by Herodotus to have been accomplifhed by Scylax. This expedition, however, is not mentioned by Nearchus, Ariftobulus, Arrian or Ptolemy (Robertfon p. 187.) In a fpeech in which Alexander vehemently reproaches the Macedonians, he afferts that no one ever croffed the Indus before except Bacchus, and that no one had ever led an army through the defert Gedrofia (Arrian. B. VII). Though the filence of the writers abovementioned may appear remarkable, yet there does not feem to be any contradiction between them and Herodotus. Scylax did not crofs, he only navigated the Indus. He had no defign of conqueft; and I do not fee any reafon for imagining that the fubfequent conquefts of Darius extended beyond, or to the Eaft of, that river. (Compare Rennel Introd. p. 22. 23.)

V. 76. In Hindoftan the weaver early in the morning fets up his loom under the fhadow of a tree, and takes it down in the evening. The fine muflins are wrought within doors; the thread, of which they are made, is too delicate to be expofed to

C 2

How

How throbbed each gentle breaſt with wild alarms,

As o'er you burſt the ſtartling blaze of arms?—

the agitation of the air. But near manufacturing villages, it is not uncommon to
ſee groves, full of looms employed in the weaving of coarſer cloths.—(See Sketches
relating to the Hindoos. p. 32.)

V. 77. *gentle breaſts.*   In the whole courſe of his marches in India, from Caucaſus
to Moultan, Alexander experienced the natives to be a brave and hardy race; all
we know concerning them at preſent impreſſes the ſame idea. A ſpirit of rapine,
which civilization gradually ſoftens into independance, is natural to men inhabiting
countries rugged with mountains and abounding in faſtneſſes. I venture here to
ſuppoſe that in the Delta of the Indus, as in that of the Ganges, the character of the
natives is ſoft and gentle. Moſt authors, tranſcribing one another with ſcrupulous
fidelity, give us to underſtand that this wildneſs of character co-extends with the religion of Brimha, and is its effect. This repreſentation betrays ignorance both of
hiſtory and of human nature. Chriſtians themſelves are not more bloodthirſty and
rapacious, than the Raipoots, Mahrattas, and other Gentoo tribes. The compariſon
of religious codes, with the hiſtory of nations profeſſing obedience to them, will de-
monſtrate that till the mind is prepared, precepts are of ſmall avail; and ſurely their
value has at all times been exceſſively over-rated. The art of humanizing the mind
doubtleſs in great meaſure conſiſts in making it feel the full force of moral obligation; but precepts are little calculated to produce this ſalutary effect; and I hardly
know any thing but arithmetic that can be tolerably taught by dry rules. Thoſe
who undertake to educate children and convert *heathens* are ſeldom ſenſible of this
important truth.   If well apprehended, it will induce the philoſopher to look out for
more efficacious cauſes of the unoffending manners of ſome Hindoo tribes than precepts however juſt, and ſentiments however beautiful, contained in their ſacred books.
I leave the reflecting reader to develope theſe ideas and to apply the principle to

—Rouſed

—Roufed mid the filence of their lone retreats,

Your RAJAHS hafte from foreft-cinctured feats,   80

other cafes.   Let him alfo confider if it would not be prudent to afcertain the effect
compleatly, before we attempt to fpecify the caufe?   Does this gentlenefs of manners
flow from equity or imbecillity of mind?   Depravity, we know, does not always walk
with the dagger in her hand: and it is almoft a reproach to the abject flaves of
defpotifm that they are incapable of a courageous crime.   I fee as deep flains of
guilt upon the Gentoo rulers as upon our European potentates and flatefmen.
I have learned with forrow but without furprize, that too many of the poorer clafs in
Bengal are fraudulent, falfe and venal—Gentoos as well as Mahometans.   In every
climate alike a dependant differs little from a corrupted foul.   It by no means, however, follows that we fhould withdraw our pity from an unhappy people, degraded
by oppreffion; but rather that every one contribute his utmoft to banifh flavery and
defpotifm of every fpecies from the face of the earth.   The moral character of the
Hindoos can never begin to improve, if it needs improvement, till the laft hour of
their mercilefs tyrants from Europe fhall arrive.   And then perhaps they will only
experience a change of tyrants.

   V. 80. *foreft-cinctured feats.*   In the part of India, fo improperly called the
Peninfula, the refidence of thofe Rajahs or feudal Chiefs, whofe poffeffions are fituated in woody or hilly tracts, is frequently encompaffed by an impenetrable thicket
of bamboos and other thorny plants.   This ring is fometimes not lefs than 4 miles
in breadth.   The roads are flanked on each fide with plantations, from which the
enemy may be annoyed during his approach: thus Bufh-fighting is not peculiar to
the new continent.   Man is every where what circumftances make him.   The roads
are traced in a very ferpentine direction and are interfected with many barriers.
How much every thing is calculated in this manner for defence, the following quota-
tion may ferve to fhew.

                                                                    Spice

Spice, gold, and gems, and fine-wrought fabrics bring,

And foothe with gifts out-fpread the Stranger-King.

"On our arrival before the town of Shevigerry, the Polygar Rajah retired to the thickets, near 4 miles deep, in front of his *Comby*, which they cover and defend. He manned the whole extent of a ftrong embarkment, that feparates the wood and open country,..........and muftered 8 or 9,000 men in arms........Finding that they *trifled with our propofals*, the line was ordered under arms on the morning following.......It commenced by the Europeans and 4 battalions of Seapoys, moving againft the embarkment which covers the wood. The Polygars, in full force, oppofed us, but our troops remained with their firelocks fhouldered under an heavy fire, until they approached the embarkment; where they gave a general difcharge and rufhed upon the enemy. By the vigour of this advance, we got poffeffion of the fummit, and the Polygars took poft on the verge of the adjoining wood, difputing every ftep with great lofs on both fides. As we found the *Comby* could not be penetrated in front, we proceeded to cut a road through impenetrable thickets for 3 miles to the bafe of the hill that bounds the Comby on the weft. We continued to cut our way under an unabating fire from 8,000 Polygars" (did thofe who were killed and wounded during the *great lofs* rife like Falftaff, and fall to again?)......
...."Before funfet we had opened a paffage entirely to the mountain; it is extremely high, rocky and in many places perpendicular." Sometimes within the circular thicket there is an area many miles in circumference, in the centre of which is the town. [See Fullarton's View of the Englifh Interefts in India, a book which ought to bear a very different title p. 128. &c. and Sketches p. 102. &c.]

V. 81. At Tatta or Pattala, at the head of the Delta, the antients purchafed fpices, gems, filks, cottons, black-pepper—More eafterly emporiums furnifhed pearls, ivory and a few articles befide. *Sindon*, fine linen, is fuppofed to have derived its name from Sindus or Indus. Arrian, whom one always quotes in preference to the undiftinguifhing compiler, Diodorus, or the exaggerating rhetorician,

THE

(15)

The glowing Hero—while responsive shores
Ring to the labour of unnumbered oars,
While with slow pace, his long-protracted train   85
Toils up the steep, expands along the plain;
While Tribes of tawnier hue and lighter dress
Submissive awe, by suppliant signs express,
And Patriarchs hoar, and Chiefs of manly prime
Bend to the Warrior of the Western clime;   90
From the scared groves as plumes unknown arise,
Strange notes resound, and glance more vivid dies;

Curtius, speaks of the extreme whiteness of the Indian *linen*, as he calls it, unless as
he very properly adds, the blackness of complexion of the Indians makes it appear
whiter than it really is. (p. 530.)—As to Gold, of the 20 Persian Satrapies under
Darius Hystaspes, India alone paid its tribute in this metal, the rest in silver—the
rivers of the Panjab were auriferous, particularly the Eastern branches of the Indus
(Rennel XXV.)—There was an antient fable, that ants as big as foxes threw up gold,
along with the soil. Nearchus seems to have given some countenance to this account,
and Megasthenes still more. Arrian laughs at it as well as Strabo, who adds, that
the ants were reported to defend the treasure with great resolution, and sometimes to
kill both men and horses in the contest. But what if some curious piece of Natural
History should be thus disguised? Nearchus *saw* the skins of these ants ; a testimoy
too express, and a witness too respectable, to be slightly rejected.

V. 82—86. *Tribes*. Historians inform us that as the armament advanced, the
tribes on either side were compelled or persuaded to submit.

As

As ſtems of ranker growth and gaudier flowers

Entwine wild fragrance round unfading bowers,

And Giant trunks outſtretch their mightier ſhoots,   95

Spread ampler leaves, and tempt with fairer fruits;

As to their dark pavilions, terror-chaced,

Grim tyrants of the foreſt, growling, haſte;

In ſwift ſucceſſion as before his eyes

A new Creation's crowded wonders riſe—   100

—And now, his nodding prows triumphant dance

O'er ſwelling waves, on Indus' broad expanſe;

V. 101. *Tide and Bore.* The Bore is " the ſudden influx of the tide, in a body
of water, elevated above the common ſurface of the ſea" (Rennel XXV). Alexander and his troops, ſays Arrian, were not a little aſtoniſhed, when the ebb left
their veſſels aground; but they were ſtill much more aſtoniſhed, when they were lifted again by the waves, ruſhing upon them in a great body. *This affection of the great
ſea,* as that hiſtorian terms it, equally ſurprized and terrified Cæſar and his troops, to
whom it was unknown; and ſurely nothing could be more capable of inſpiring terror, till the law of the reciprocation of the tide was diſcovered. It belongs to philoſophy to diſarm Nature as well as Superſtition of her terrors. The reader will recollect that in the Mediteranean the tides are ſcarce perceptible, and for a long time
were actually not perceived. On account of their ſmall proficiency in phyſiological
knowledge, the ancients were incapable of perceiving phænomena much more ſtrik-

With

With eye aftonifhed now he marks the tide

Propel its curly foam, now flow fubfide;

Now lifts, with ftartled ear, the angry Bore   105

His whelming wave urge on, and boifterous roar——

——Long mute, long fixed by Extacy's controul,

Pours forth at laft the fervour of his foul.

     " Hail, Thou unnamed of Greece! Thou fportive

            God!

" Controller of the flood! whofe changeful nod   110

" Now rolls thy living liquids o'er the ftrand,

" Now calls them refluent from thy lawns of fand,

" Who now, with arm upreared and murmurs hoarfe,

" Full in mid ftream impelleft their furious courfe;

ing than thefe inconfiderable movements of the waters. In many refpects the ancients had not much more ufe of their fenfes, than infants have of their mufcles. Phyfical fcience, by exercifing and directing the fenfes, never fails to render
them more acute. (For the Tides and Bore fee Robertfon p. 188. and Rennel ub. fup.)

D" Thee

" Thee I invoke! thy name, thy nature fay: 115
" Oh! grant thy prefence to the eye of Day!
" So fhall thy cenfors blaze, thy temples rife,
" And Nations offer rightful facrifice.
" Our Weftern Main thou fcorneft—Benumbing Sleep
" With leaden fceptre quells that fluggifh Deep." 120
So fpake the Monarch, and with arms outfpread,
Bowed to the Power unknown his radiant head;
Mufing he bends, as though beneath the wave
He faw revealed the Godhead's chryftal cave;
Then, flow with fweeping eye, from fhore to fhore 125
The twinkling mafs of waters meafures o'er;
Now, with uplifted brow, purfues the gale,
Whofe playful pinion fans the panting vale;
Marks giant harvefts wave, or graffy dells
Wind their foft lap around the copfe-crowned fwells; 130
Now o'er the foreft's clofely-tufted head
He longs with airy ftep aloft to tread;

O'er

O'er cheequered shades where whispering branches play,

On Nature's yielding couch his limbs to lay:

Now starts, with infant eagerness, to chace   135

The bright-plumed rivals of the insect race.

—Soft, soothing scenes! you lulled to short repose

An heart, where ever-restless ardour glows,

The calm you breathe could still the Victor's mind,

Though soaring hopes perturb, and wreaths fresh-twined:

—On the green sod, awhile his eye-balls rest;   141

Joy's genial tide pervades his rising breast;

And hark! his tongue the bland emotions owns,

And warbles Gratulation's dulcet tones.

" Ye Fields for ever fair, Thou, mighty stream! 145

" Bright Regions! blest beyond the Muse's dream!

V. 145. &c. " In every step of his progress, says Dr. Robertson, objects no less
striking than new presented themselves to Alexander. The magnitude of the Indus,
even after he had seen the Nile, the Euphrates, and the Tigris, must have filled him

D 2   " Thou

" Thou, fruitful womb of ever-teeming Earth!

" Ye foftering fkies, that rear each beauteous birth!

" Trees, that aloft uprear your ftately height!

" Whofe fombrous branches fhed a noontide night! 150

" Groves, that for ever wear the fmile of fpring!

" Gay birds, that wave the many-tinted wing!

" Of Reptiles, Fifhes, Brutes ftupendous forms!

" And Ye, of namelefs Infects glittering fwarms!

—" Sons of foft toil, whofe fhuttle Beauty throws, 155

" Whofe tints the Graces' earneft hands difpofe,

" Whofe guilelefs bofom Care avoids and Crime,

" Gay as your groves and cloudlefs as your clime!

" Primæval Piles, that rofe in maffive pride,

" Ere Weftern Art her firft, faint effort tried!   160

with furprize. No Country he had hitherto vifited was fo populous and well cultivated, or abounded in fo many valuable productions of Art and Nature." The
Panjab produces wine, fugars, and cotton, which laft fupplied the manufactures of
the province. It has alfo wonderfully productive falt mines. Arrian tells us that
the Indus is the only river befides the Nile that produces Crocodiles; the ancient
writers infift upon its abundance of fifhes.

Ye

(21)

" Ye Brachmans old, whom purer æras bore,

" Ere Weſtern Science liſped her infant lore !

" How will your wonders fluſh the Athenian Sage?

" How ray with glory my hiſtoric page?

" Ne'er—though the ſeries of my martial toils   165

" Has led my footſteps o'er a thouſand ſoils—

" Ne'er through my breaſt has equal tranſport ſtreamed,

" Ne'er on theſe eyes ſuch pure effulgence beamed.

" How mean thy vale, O Tempe! ah how vain

" The boaſt, Euphrates, of thy boundleſs plain!   170

" How fade the glories of the favoured tide,

" Whoſe waves beneath my riſing bulwarks glide !

" Nor Fancy now, with lingering fondneſs ſtrays

" O'er thoſe fair fields, where ſparkling Pharphar plays;

V. 159—62. See obſervations at the end on the antiquity of the Hindoos &c.

" Where his fmooth ftate reflects Damafcus' towers, 175

" Or pleafed Orontes, mid his whifpering bowers,

" Hears Syrian Virgins pour the thrilling ftrain,

" Breathe the warm figh, and foothe the tender pain."

" Ye blooms, that proud difplay the glowing hue,

" And fip the beverage of ambrofial dew !

" Skies, that the Seafons bind in lafting peace,

" And bid the difcord of the rivals ceafe,

V. 175—8. The foftnefs of Syrian manners; and the beauty and fertility of many diftricts in Syria are univerfally known. The environs of Antioch, particularly
————— —————that fweet grove
Of Daphne by Orontes—— ————
did not acquire their full celebrity, till afterwards, during the reign of the Macedonian kings of Syria. One may however fairly prefume, that not only the permanent beauties of fituation, but thofe more perifhable productions of nature, which fo richly adorned it, exifted in the time of Alexander. Mr. Gibbon will give the reader an idea of this fpot and of the fables belonging to it; for this, like every other fpot, in any way remarkably diftinguifhed by Nature had its appropriate fables, and the mythology of the Greeks is almoft always of an agreeable caft.

Save

" Save Winters ruthlefs foul—He drives afar

" O'er blafted realms his tempeft-fhaken car—

" And you, where Dayfpring's frefheft glances fhine,

" Fair Gardens, planted by an hand divine !   186

" She, at whofe call the clime remote appears,

" Who fpreads Exiftence through departed years—

" Oft fhall her hand before my charmed fight,

" Your fmiling femblance hold, and colours bright;   190

" And Fancy ftill, mid Night's infpiring fhades,

" With fond illufion rove among your glades.

—" Paufe ! vagrant Airs, whofe wings afar diffufe

" The floating fragrance of your balmy dews,

" A moment paufe ! then, gently flitting, bear   195

" Wide o'er Elyfian lands the vow I fwear.

—" When every clime fhall fee my flag unfurled,

" And boundlefs Commerce mix a cultured world,

V. 197. &c. Several of the moft popular modern writers, as Pope in England

" From mad mifrule reclaimed, and brutal ftrife,

" Trained to the foft civilities of life,   200

and Boileau in France, have amufed themfelves with reprefenting Alexander as a mere madman. And without doubt it was much more obvious, confidering only his military expeditions and paffionate excelfes, to bring the matter to this fimple iffue, than to enter into his extenfive fchemes and difcern the policy of his arrangements.   Montefquieu has contributed towards the vindication of his character. " Alexander, fays he, formed the defign of uniting the Indies to the Weftern nations by a maritime commerce, as he had already united them by the colonies he eftablifhed by land." (B. XXI. ch. 7.)   Montefquieu however denies that he built Alexandria with commercial views; as Lucretius denies the eye to be made for feeing.   Full juftice has fince been done to Alexander by one endowed with all the talents Montefquieu poffeffed, and all he wanted, towards forming a compleat philofopher.   " When you have reflected that Alexander in the fiery feafon of pleafure, and in the very delirium of victory, built more cities than all the other Conquerors of Afia have deftroyed, when you confider that it is a young man who changes the commerce of the world, you will be furprized to find Boileau treating him, firft as a madman and then as an highwayman, and propofing to La Reine, as lieutenant of the police, fometimes to confine and fometimes to hang him. This propofal could not have been admitted either according to the cuftom of Paris or the law of nations.   Alexander would have pleaded that, having been elected, at Corinth, Captain General of Greece, and in this capacity having it in charge to avenge his country of all the invafions of the Perfians, he did no more than his duty in deftroying their empire: and that having always joined magnanimity to the moft fignal courage, having refpected the wife and daughters of Darius, who were his prifoners, he did not on any account deferve confinement or the gallows, and that at all events he appealed from the faid Monfieur La Reinie's fentence to the tribunal of the whole world.

When

" When Home's dear ties fhall fix each roaming horde,

" And Earth fhall kneel before her Grecian Lord,

" Here fhall my arms be hung—in this retreat

" My age repofe—here fix it's filent feat."

Here clofed his lips—ftill fpake his gliftening eye, 205

Still Admiration heaved her deep-drawn figh;

Rollin pretends that Alexander took the famous city of Tyre purely to ferve the Jews, who did not love the Tyrians. It is neverthelefs probable that he had fome other reafons, as it was by no means the part of a wife general to leave Tyre, miftrefs of the fea, when he was about to attack Egypt." See other paffages (*art. Alexandre Dict. Philofophique*) of Voltaire, who has written hiftory with the fagacity of Locke and the humanity of Fenelon, and been calumniated accordingly. Diodorus Siculus fpeaks of memorandums of Alexander, found after his death, for confolidating the union of his fubjects. He built cities, fays Montefquieu, and would not fuffer the Ichthyophagi to live upon fifh, being defirous that the maritime countries fhould be inhabited by civilized nations. His liberal policy in the treatment of his conquered fubjects, in oppofition to the advice of Ariftotle, is juftly commended by Dr. Robertfon.—Now confider that the ancients were fcarce fo far advanced in political œconomy as in natural philofophy; remember alfo that the Greeks looked upon the barbarians, that is, all but themfelves, juft as Slave-merchants and Weft-India planters look upon Negroes; and then determine what muft have been the originality of Alexander's genius, the enlargement of his conceptions, and the equity of his mind, whenever ambition did not interfere with the latter quality.

E

Around

Around the foul-wrapt Chief—in crowded rings
His kindling warriors prefs—the deftined Kings,
Of mighty ftates—They catch the Monarch's fire:
Their geftures, foon, the train remote infpire;   210
From foul to foul triumphant ardours run,
And all partake the blifs of Philip's fon;
At firft low murmurs creep; at length the bands
Ope their glad lips and fmite their joyous hands,
The land and waters pour exulting cries,   215
And pealing fhouts affail the Indian Skies—
—HE, from applauding myriads loud acclaim,
Accepts the omen of immortal fame,
And feels affuaged, in that enraptured hour,
His ardent thirft of Glory and of Power.   220

V. 208. *deftined kings.* The names and hiftory of thofe chiefs, whofe ambition
and abilities the premature death of Alexander brought into action, are abundantly
known. Several of them were prefent on this expedition.

And

And now the Hofts, on India's fultry verge,

See fmooth-fpread fhores receive the failing Surge;

Hoarfe round his finuous fweep of marfhy bounds

Hear Ocean murmur ftorm-portending founds,

Or roar, impatient, from his wave-worn cells, 225

Loud o'er the lands, where liftening Plenty dwells.

V. 223. *marfhy bounds.* At the lower extremity both of the Ganges and Indus we find a labyrinth of rivers and creeks, curioufly interfecting confiderable tracts of low land. The breadth of the Bengal *Sunderbunds* is 180 miles. Major Rennel has laid down this fingular affemblage of wood and water on a large fcale in his Bengal Atlas No. XX. The paffages through the Sunderbunds, obferves the fame excellent geographer (p. 363.), afford both a grand and a curious fpectacle; a navigation of more than 200 miles through a foreft, divided into numberlefs iflands by a continued labyrinth of channels, fo various in point of width, that a veffel has at one time her mafts almoft entangled in the trees; and at another, fails uninterruptedly on a capacious river, beautifully fkirt with woods, and affording a vifta of many miles each way. The water is every where falt; and the whole extent of the foreft abandoned to wild beafts, fo that the fhore is feldom vifited, but in cafes of neceffity. In thefe forefts, the wood-cutters and falt-makers exercife their " dreadful trade" at the perpetual rifque of life; for the tygers not only appear on the margin in queft of prey, but often, in the night time, fwim to the boats that lie at anchor in the middle of the channel. The procefs of nature, in the formation of land by alluvion, does not feem to have gone fo far at the mouth of the Indus. The dry parts of the iflands are covered only with brufh-wood, the remainder, by much the largeft portion, confifts of noifome fwamps, and muddy lakes.

E 2

To

To HER scared eye, as Fate's dark leaves disclose

The ghastly characters of India's woes,

Thy parting fail, O King, the pensive Muse

With many a sigh, down Indus' stream, pursues.　230

—Large was thy thought, and liberal was thy soul,

Nor stooped thy glance beneath bright Honour's goal;

Beyond the Sage's ampleft grasp, thy mind

Embraced the mighty mass of human kind,

And spurned, with firm disdain, the barbarous rule,　235

Framed by the Founder of the subtle School.—

Where awful History, mid the dome of Fame,

Awards the Tyrant's and the Conqueror's shame,

Humanity's mild voice, still raised for THEE,

Abates the rigour of her stern decree.　　240

For Sympathy could melt that feeling breast,

And vanquished realms thy healing mercy blest;

On agonizing woe and captive fear,

Thy pity dropped the warm balsamic tear:—

Thy

And each soft deed, through many a distant age,   245
Shall swell the canvas, and bedew the Stage.

Lo! in redundant current, Commerce pours,
Obedient to thy call, her Eastern stores;
And still, though Plague and Rapine range the land,
Her spicy bale perfumes thy chosen strand.   250
And oh! had years matured the fair design,
Of which thy Genius traced the wondrous line;
Had GENERAL CONCORD, from her finished fane,
Shed her pure light, and breathed her strains humane,
Man's varied race, from far-dissevered lands,   255
Her courts had thronged, and pledged discoloured hands;
Her shrines had witnessed varying voices blend
The vow, and in the stranger hail the friend;
Stern Scythia's clans had cast their rage aside,
Unsocial Greece renounced her scornful pride;   260

V. 260. *Unsocial Greece.* If the reader has not conceived a proper detestation of the

And long, beneath thy ftar's protecting ray,

Had bloomed the regions of the rifing day;

With keen awakened fenfe, the liftening child

Still on his mother's fearlefs bofom fmiled,

As, deep concealed o'er-arching fhades among,   265

Content had caroled blithe his chearing fong.

And ftill, from far, the fwarm of plunderers loured,

Eyed the fair fruits, and but in thought devoured.

brutal inftitutions of Sparta, let him read the ingenious Mr. De Pau's *recherches fur les Grecs*, or even the ftrictures upon thefe refearches by the candid Heyne, who has the learning, without the narrownefs, of pedantry (Comment. Gottingens. Vol. ix. if my memory does not fail me.) Athens had philofophers, and was very little the better. Their difdain of barbarians and their inhuman ideas, particularly thofe of Ariftotle, on flavery are well known. Their contentious philofophy however only produced a wafte of genius with fome illiberality of fentiment. Had wealth, power, and titles been unhappily annexed to the doctrines of any fect, the hiftory of thefe fubtleties might have rivalled the horrors of our dogmatical theology. When to its ordinary objects of defire, ambition affociates the tempting claim of authority over opinion, it becomes capable, we fee, of converting the moft incomprehenfible nonfenfe into the moft deadly of weapons.

And

But Earth's fond Hopes, how blafted in their bloom!

How feels a World convulfed thy fated doom!   270

What mingling founds of woe and outrage rife!

How wild the eddying duft of Ruin flies!

See frantic Chiefs the Mafter's pile deface,

Dafh down his walls, and fhake the deep-laid bafe!

V. 269. Immediately upon Alexander's death, fociety was thrown into the moft dreadful convulfions; the moft bloody diffenfions broke out among his generals. The Macedonians have been compared to thofe fwarms of emigrating rats, the peft of the North, which, after ravaging whole countries, at laft for want of fubfiftance fall upon and devour one another. The face of the known world was covered with confufion. The republics preferved only a vain appearance of liberty, which left the inconveniences without the advantages of that form of government. Turbulence took the place of ftrength, factions multiplied, and became irreconcileable. But the whole contention was for the choice of tyrants. Whether the Seleucidæ, the Lagidæ &c. fhould have the preference. " To whom fhall garlands be decreed, and whofe ftatues fhall be demolifhed?" Such was the fubject of every deliberation. And fo bufy was Servility, one moment in erecting, and the next in demolifhing ftatues, that it became the practice to faw off an old head, and place upon the trunk the effigies of a new tyrant. Nor was the world ravaged only by a Ptolemy, a Caffander, an Antigonus, an Eumenes, characters which ftill fhone with a luftre borrowed from Alexander, but a crowd of petty ufurpers perpetually fprung up, and different countries became the prey of the firft adventurer, who invaded them. See the admirable treatife, *De la felicite publique*, Bouillon, 1776. T. I. ch. 8.

Mourn,

Mourn, India, mourn—the womb of future Time   275
Teems with the fruit of each portentous crime.
The Crefcent onward leads confuming hofts,
And Carnage dogs the Crofs along thy coafts;
From Chriftian ftrands, the Rage accurfed of gain
Wafts all the Furies in her baleful train: 280
Their eye-ball ftrained, impatient of the way,
They fnuff, with noftril broad, the diftant prey.
—And now, the Rout pollutes the hallowed fhore,
That nurfed young Art, and infant Science bore.
Fierce, in the van, her firebrand Warfare waves,   285
Dire, at her heels, the cry of hell-hounds raves;
Roufed by the yell, the Greedy and the Bold
Start to the favage chace of blood and gold.

In vain fteep Gwalior rears his towers on high,
In vain thy walls, dread Nature, touch the Sky.   290

V. 289. *Gwalior*. This aftonifhing fortrefs is fituated on a rock of about 4 miles

O'er

(33)

O'er towers and mountains Slaughter's torrent rolls

No force refifts it, and no mound controuls.

in length, but narrow, and unequal in breadth: the area at top is nearly flat.
The fides are fo fteep as to appear almoft perpendicular, for the rock has been
fcarped away, where it was not naturally fo fteep. The height above the plain is
from 200 to 300 feet. The rampart follows the edge of the precipice. The only
approach is by fteps winding along the fide of the rock; and this is guarded as well
by a wall and baftions as by feven ftone gate-ways, placed at certain diftances from
each other. The area contains noble buildings, refervoirs of water, wells and cultivated fields, fo that it is a little diftrict within itfelf. (Rennel. 234). It was
taken by the Englifh in 1780. The rock Aornus, defcribed by Alexander's hiftorians, is another of thefe ftrong Afiatic holds. The fituation of Dellam-cotta, of which
a flight view is fubjoined to the advertifement, is thus defcribed.—The Southern-
moft ridge of the Bootan mountains, rifes near a mile and half perpendicular above
the plains of Bengal; it attains this elevation within 15 miles of horizontal diftance.
From the fummit, the aftonifhed traveller looks back on the plains, as on an extenfive Ocean beneath him. There are not many paffes through this ridge: Dellam-
cotta, which commands the principal, was taken by ftorm by Capt. I. Jones in
1773, an exploit which induced the natives of Thibet to fue for peace. The road
between Bengal and Taffafudon lies chiefly over the fummits of ftupendous mountains, or craggy precipices. Between Taffafudon and Paridrong, is a chain of
mountains ftill higher. They are vifible from the plains of Bengal, at the diftance
of 150 miles, and are generally covered with fnow (Rennel 302. and Bengal
Atlas No. 17. Hodges Views in India Nos. I. II. and III.)

V. 291. &c. In confequence of the difference of colour, cuftoms, religious creed
or rather title of their religion, the European Soldiers have little or no fellow-feeling
with the natives of thefe regions; and they will, of courfe, take every opportunity

F

Alike

Alike on proftrate foes and plighted friends

The ceafelefs fury of the blade defcends.

of giving a loofe to their rapacity, cruelty and caprice. Of this a late Madras newfpaper affords a recent inftance of unqueftionable authenticity; here are the words in which Gen. Abercrombie exprefles his juft indignation at fome fhocking enormities of this nature:

" Since the Commander in Chief has had the honour of being at the head of the
" Bombay army, there is nothing which has given him fo much uneafinefs, and that
" he has fo much reafon to be difpleafed at, as the reports that have been made of
" the licentious behaviour of fome of the foldiers and followers of the advanced
" corps."

" Plundering the women and children of defencelefs villages muft in every coun-
" try be a difcredit to the Commander, and difhonour to the troops; but in the
" prefent inftance he feels it materially injurious to himfelf and difgraceful to his
" army.

" The villages that have been plundered and burnt belonging to one of the moft
" active, gallant and fteady allies the Company have" (the Corgar Rajab?) " an ally
" who has invited us to his Country, without whofe aid we could not have ad-
" vanced fo far, or proceed any farther.

" The villages that have been deftroyed too were left defencelefs, from a confi-
" dence of fecurity in our protection, and from a zeal in the owners to advance and
" engage the common enemy.

" The General is forry to remark that at the time they were rejoicing at the bril-
" liant victory which they gained, the news muft have reached them that their ha-
" bitations were in flames and their families difperfed, and that the outrage had
" been committed, not by the enemy, but by thofe whom they invited into their
" country and confidered as their friends.——March 2, 1791." See obfervations
at the end.

—One

—One heap unites the subject and the king.—— 295

On female helplessness the ruffians spring;

The still Zenana's sacred glooms profane;

The shrieking inmates clasp their seats in vain;

No rescuer hears the shrill, distressful cry

And Death's cold hand has closed each pitying eye; 300

Whelmed by Despair's deep wave, the quivering throngs

Endure all Rapine's and all Insult's wrongs.

On the meek race each plague of guilt is poured;

Gaunt Famine gleans the relics of the sword:

V. 304. *Famine.* " When the effects of the scarcity became more and more visi-
" ble, the natives complained to the Nabob....that the English had engrossed all
" the rice......This complaint was laid before the president and council by the
" Nabob's minister who resides in Calcutta; but the interest of the Gentlemen con-
" cerned was too powerful at the board; so that the complaint was only laughed at
" and thrown out." It is probable these gentlemen were thorougly convinced of the
futility of the principle, that the consent of the people governed is necessary to constitute a just government, and therefore very consistently disregarded their complaints

" By the time the famine had been about a fortnight over the land, we were
" greatly affected at Calcutta; many thousands falling daily in the streets and fields,
" who'e bodies, mangled by jackalls, dogs and vultures, in that hot season when at
" best the air is very infectious, made us dread the consequences of a plague. We

For

For food their fruitlefs cries thy infants raife,   305

The gafping parents choak thy fpacious ways:

" had 100 people employed upon the Cutchevry lift. on the company's account,
" with doolys, fledges and bearers, to carry the dead, and throw them into the
" river Ganges. I have counted from my bed-chamber window in the Morning
" when I got up, forty dead bodies lying within twenty yards of the wall, befides
" many hundreds lying in the agonies of death for want, bending double, with their
" ftomachs quite clofe contracted to their back bones. I have fent my fervant to
" defire thofe who had ftrength to remove farther off: whilft the poor creatures look-
" ing up with arms extended, have cried out, Baba, Baba, my father, my father, this
" affliction comes from the hand of your countrymen, and I am come here to die, if
" it pleafe God, in your prefence. I cannot move, do what you will with me."

 " At this time we could not touch fifh, the river was fo full of carcafes.".........

....." After one had fucked the bones quite dry, and thrown them away, I have
" feen another take them up, fand and all upon them, and do the fame, and fo by a
" third, and fo on.

........I cannot help, although with the greateft reverence, enquiring from our
nobility and gentry who are fo ftrenuous for punifhing the perfidious French, till
they have amply atoned for all their crimes, particularly from the R. H. L. North,
who has expatiated upon that idea with fo much energy and eloquence, whether
thefe facts are true? and if true, what atonement either the Britifh nation, or the
Britifh government have offered to the manes of thefe victims, or to their furviving
friends and relations? The marked paffages are from Ann. Regift. 1771. p. 205.
the others from Thomas Day, the premature lofs of whofe genius, fpirit and virtue
the friends of mankind will long lament.—A remark, fimilar to the laft, is fuggefted by obvious circumftances. We have heard loud exclamations againft
Tippoo Sultan. And affuredly Humanity muft fhudder at fome of his actions.
But how few have been the defpots to whom this reflection will not apply;
and if a wife and juft tribunal were to decide between the Myforean Tyrant

Wan,

Wan, fhrivelled fhapes, in lifelefs langour laid,

Nor Morning's ray they blefs, nor Evening's fhade!

Where filent heaps abide their lingering fate,

And Pride difgufted fpurns them from her gate,   310

" Oh, Father, grant," the unmurmuring victims cry,

" 'Tis all we afk—this little fpace to die."—

Meanwhile the Buryer, with unheeding tread,

Crufhes the dying, as he drags the dead.

—E'en now, inflamed with ravenous thirft of fpoil,   315

Wide-wafting legions fcour thy haplefs foil.

I hear, I hear the ravaged nations groan,

Their figh unpitied, and defpairing moan.

I fee the fufferers ope their failing eyes,

And feek the bolt of Juftice in the fkies.   320

In quivering gore his beak the Vulture dips,

The glutted Panther licks his blood-ftained lips,

and the perfon who has declaimed moft vehemently againft him, which would be
condemned as the moft atrocious enemy of his fpecies? But now as of old—
Clodius accufat mœchos, Catilina Cethegos.

O'er

Wide o'er thy realms funereal horror reigns,

And bones unburied whiten o'er thy plains.

O Thou! whofe magic tones of burfting fong   325

Rude Nature hufh'd, and charmed the favage throng——

——But ah! the Warrior raifed thy youthful flame,

For him thy hand unbarred the gates of Fame:

V 324. *Martial poetry.* 325. The fpirit of antient poetry muft undoubtedly have contributed to pervert the moral fentiments of mankind, by eftablifhing a falfe ftandard of excellence. The fafcinating power of the Iliad, we are told, induced Alexander to regard Achilles as a model; and the choice could not but debafe his own fuperior character. It may be worth while to confider whether, in confequence of the prefent abfurd mode of education, a fimilar pernicious influence is not ftill exerted upon the ardour of the youthful mind. We know what impreffions the Roman poets and hiftorians leave in favour of the Roman people, who furely are not more amiable, though they were more audacious and fuccefsful, deprædators than the people of Algiers. For my part I conceive that *liberal* education, as we fee it conducted, pretty much refembles a practice common among fportfmen, who, by way of encouraging them to the chace, befmear the dewlaps of young hounds with the blood of the firft animal they affift in running down.

Whenever, therefore, it fhall become the bufinefs of inftruction to inculcate juft fentiments, the fpirit of a great part of the antient poetry will become difgufting: juft as we read fome antient tragedies, at prefent, with worfe than indifference, on account of their abfurd and perverted morality.

Each

Each foftening Art and gentler Virtue pined;
Vain were their charms; nor moved the martial mind.

    Again from Night ere radiant Science broke,   331
While Nature groaned beneath her feudal yoke,
Thy fires revive; thy foul-impelling breath,
With zeal mifguided, fwells the trump of death.
Dire howls the din along the wafte of life,   225
As fpurious Honour wakes infatiate Strife,
And Madnefs bellows o'er his mangled foe,
And Folly hails the Tourney's brutal fhow.
—With oozing wounds all faint, by toils oppreffed,
At length the nations fink to fervile reft;   340
High o'er the ruins Giant Robbers tower,
And grafp, with crimfon hand, tyrannic power;
For them thy lyre was ftrung to venal praife,
Soft toned the chords, but abject flowed the lays:

Bland.

Bland from thy lips, the vocal poiſon ſtole,   345

Lulled Guilt's ſharp pangs, benumbed the freeborn ſoul:

No more dread viſions haunt the Oppreſſor's night;

Inebriate crowds adore his ſacred right,

Kiſs the red ſcourge, outſtretch their willing hands,

In torture ſmile, and bleſs the galling bands.— 350

Now—while on high a purer morning breaks,

Gleams with mild light, and rays its ruddy ſtreaks,

Through torpid minds while kindling ardours dart,

And Terror vibrates to the Tyrant's heart;

—Oh ſkilled to win! adorn a worthier theme, 355

And bid the tear for harraſſed myriads ſtream;

Redeem the miſchiefs of thy thoughtleſs youth,

And tune to thy ſweet notes the lore of truth.—

With Freedom's crayon, on the patriot ſcroll,

Pourtray the paſſions of the Deſpot's ſoul: 360

V 360. _the Deſpot's ſoul._ It would well become poetry, philoſophy, and all the powers propitious to mankind, to correct the prevailing ideas reſpecting the

O'er

O'er War's wild fury, Empire's fatal thirst,

Of grief indignant pour the warning burst—

So shall the Nations' long delusions end,

So Peace o'er Earth her fostering wing extend—

" First o'er HIS breast dark fumes of vengeance rise,   365

" Foul as the Typhon's terrors blot the skies;

" As dread Contagion, from her bone-strewed cell,

" Aims the keen arrow, dipt in poison fell,

" So, deep immured, amid his dark divan,

" Devising evil, sits the Foe of Man;   370

powerful. We may be sure that the world will ever continue to be, as it has been heretofore, wasted by the unbridled passions of its rulers, till they are judged according to the plain rules and feelings of morality. As long as Nations shall indiscriminately offer to every Sovereign the richest incense of flattery, they must expect to be frequently and severely admonished, how wantonly they toss out of their hands the most effectual, yet the gentlest, curb upon propensities, so apt to arise in the minds of individuals, whose crimes and follies are visited upon guiltless millions. And, indeed, what motive or restraint is left to him, who is taught to believe, that Public Opinion will obsequiously attend upon his footsteps, whatever path he pursues, and in whose ears *Regum Optime!* is for ever ringing? Perpetual abuse, one might have hoped, would have brought this, as it has done so many other cant phrases, into disrepute. And if it be true that Sovereigns have seldom had heart or head to desire the applause, or dread the tardy vengeance, of history, this will be a strong additional reason, why men should think, before they shout.

G

" The

" The mandate iffues, and unchained by Hate,

" Commiffioned Murder moves in guilty State,

" And ftrews, with impious arm, the human wreck

" O'er heaven-loved realms, which Peace and Plenty deck.

" With courtier glance, meanwhile, a fawning ring 375

" Of Priefts and Nobles eyes the vengeful king,

" Lifts the fhrill horn proclaim the fpreading ill,

" And hymns, to Flattery's harp, his SOVEREIGN WILL.

" Secure the Coward, on his diftant throne,

" Smiles as the fmitten fink, the tortured groan.   380

" As when of old, prophetic rage poffeffed

" The facred Maid, and ftruggled in her breaft

" With foamy lip awhile, and fiery glare,

" With vifage flufhed, and wild diverging hair,

" She owns the fury of the o'er-powering God,   385

" Then finks, exhaufted, on the clay-cold fod:

" Such

" Such the fierce toffings of Ambition's dream,

" Thy fever, Glory, Conqueſt's frantic ſcheme;

" So war-ſpent Nations pine in ſcorned decay,

" Or fall Invaſion's unrefiſting prey." 390

Thus clear the gathered films of mortal fight,

Thus ſhed, benignant Muſe, thy kindly light.—

And fee! Philanthropy unfolds her charms,

And wooes thy footſteps to her tender arms?

Oh fly, embrace the heaven-defcended gueſt, 395

And in the union let mankind be bleſt.

—Yet, ere the ſplendours of the dawning Age,

A dearer theme, thy fond regard engage,

A little on the Greek's bold progreſs trace,

And bid the ſtrain refpire thy winning grace. 400

Now, from the Indian Main, returning flow,

His white-winged galleys upwards point the prow,

G 2

Thy

Thy scenes, Futurity, before him lie,

Tinge his warm cheek, and fill his musing eye;

And, quick intruding, many a mingling scheme   405

Plays o'er his thought, and weaves his wakeful dream;

" With idle wing no more," he deems, " the breeze

" Shall brush yon lone expanse of desert seas;

" Soon crossing barks shall gleam with sidelong sail,

" Mount the broad billow, and perfume the gale."   410

Thus o'er untraversed waves and trackless sands

As on she bears with ever-bounteous hands

Thy treasures, Ganges, to the strands of Nile,

Delighted Fancy prompts the unconscious smile;

Poured from her urn, soft streams of feeling flow,   415

Diffusing purer bliss than palms bestow.

From the broad deck the placid Chief descends,

To Persia's plains his course triumphant bends;

And

And oft with joy-illumined mien furveys

Their fair extent, and oft the march delays;   420

And dreadlefs now of force or ambufhed wile,

Relaxing hofts the weary way beguile;

Sweet breathes the Dorian mood, and Grecian fongs

Rehearfe the heartfelt tale of Grecia's wrongs: 424

" At Eve's calm hour" they tell, " how favage yells

" Her hallowed groves alarmed, and peaceful dells;

" With ruffian gripe how Afian rovers tore

" The ftruggling virgin from her natal fhore;

" Stripped the rich mantle from her funny rocks,

" Strewed o'er the thymy turf her browfing flocks,   430

" In fpires afcending through the wafte of night

" From fhrieking hamlets reared the ghaftly light;

V. 422—423. *Relaxing files and Grecian fongs.* According to an account quoted by Arrian (p. 432.), Alexander caufed two cars to be joined together, upon which he with his friends reclined to the found of Mufic during the march through Carmania: the army, crowned with garlands and fporting, followed, the Carmanians every where offering by the way both provifions and luxuries.

" Stamped

" Stamped with wild foot o'er Autumn's amber pride,

" Her powerlefs Gods and paffive States defied;

" Paffive too long, till Infult's maddening fting   435

" Tranfpierced the bofom of the Spartan King.

" Then keen Revenge, and Honour breathing high,

" Lift every breaft, and flafh from every eye,

" The willing matron gives her youth to bleed,

" The plighted virgin prompts her lover's fpeed;   440

" Through wafte difpeopled realms till Silence reigns

" And flighted Ceres flies the forrowing plains.

" Yet what avails, that armed in Virtue's caufe,

" Valour's ftrong arm the blade of Juftice draws?

" That Grecia's galleys, o'er the darkened Main,   445

" Her thronging nations waft, and Hero-train?

" That fiery Youth combines with wily Age,

" And Neftor's counfels guide Pelides' rage?

" Too

" Too long, thou darling of the Muse, in vain

" Thy prowefs thundered o'er Scamander's plain;   450

" With Fate in vain maternal fondnefs ftrove;

" In vain the Goddefs feeks the throne of Jove,

" In fuppliant woe outfpreads her foftened charms,

" And fheaths her Boy in heavenly-tempered arms.

" Lo! Coward Fraud confpires thy early doom,   455

" And yon unfhaken turrets mock thy tomb.

" Each mightieft comrade lays his helmet low,

" And falling Troy inflicts the deadlier blow.

" Twice with a whirlwind's rage the Eaftern World

" Againft the fhores of fhrinking Greece is hurled:—

" Swoln with the Defpot's fcorn of human kind,   361

" From power obdurate, and from flattery blind;

—" While boundlefs Empires bend the adoring knee,

—" Shall you infulting corner dare be free?"

" Darius

" Darius cries, convokes his gorgeous bands,   465

" Equips his navies, and exhausts his lands.

" His courtier-bards preluding praises breathe,

" And for his brows prepare the Victor's wreathe:

—" Those reeking brows, thou baffled Tyrant, hide;

" Rise, silken Satraps, soothe his wounded pride;   470

" For Freedom's spear has gored his vaunting hosts,

" And Havoc dogs them to his slave-trod coasts.

—" With grim delight the Power of carnage mounts

" His scythed car, his gaudy victims counts;   474

" Wide o'er rude steeps, fair plains and plashy meads,

" His spreading swarms as furious Xerxes leads,

" And bids his streamers to the Skies displayed,

" O'er Earth and Ocean wave their awful shade.

" Then shares the haughtier Son the Sire's disgrace,

" And decks with richer palms an hated race.   480

" The rock unmoved of SPARTA's SAVIOUR-BAND

" Checks the rude storm on Malea's narrow strand;

" Thy

" Thy Genius, Greece, wide o'er Platœa's plain

" Spreads his bright plumes, and numbers o'er the flain,

" Then lifts his wreathed front, and fmites his fhield,

" And calls his Heroes to the foreign field: 486

" No Hero heard; no Patriot Chieftain rofe

" To roll fwift Vengeance o'er his country's foes;

—" Her torch o'er Greece infernal Difcord fhakes,

" Strains her wild eye, and roufes all her fnakes;   490

" In vain joint Honour binds, joint toils endear!

" Their hoftile banners kindred Nations rear;

" Nor Prudence checks, nor Nature's cry withftands;

" Each in a Sifter's blood embrues her hands,

" Far round her venomed breath the Fury fpreads,   495

" And rears a direr creft of Hydra-heads.

" What new-born glory, from the brightening fky

" Defcends ferene, and clears the clouded eye!

H*

" And

" And hark! with muttered curfes Difcord flies,

" Scared Peace returns, and guilty Rancour dies;   500

" He comes! the Youth! deputed from above,

" Rejoins the wide-rent bonds of Grecian love,

" With pious arms appeafes yon fad ghofts,

" Whofe pale troops flit along her moaning coafts.

" The new Pelides Perfia's pride o'erwhelms!   505

" And Afia trembles through her thoufand realms!

" Bards of my Country! wake the flumbering lyre,

" And wing the fong with his own Homer's fire;

" Behold! his bright-eyed dawn of martial days

" Of old renown obfcures the noon-tide blaze."   510

So ftreamed the ftrains, till high imperial towers
Spring from the bofom of enclafping bowers.

Then

Then to the clamours of barbarian tongues
Yields the glad fymphony, and choral fongs;
With zeal impatient as they hail from far,   515
High towering mid the hofts, the Conqueror's car.
Still from her crowded gates the City-train
Gufh ftruggling on, and deluge o'er the plain,
Where ftreamers chequer o'er the martial blaze
With wildly-devions eye at firft they gaze,   520
And Joy and Wonder mix their throbbing tides;
At length the tumult of the foul fubfides;
Then with collected thought, and fteadier glance,
They mark the leaders of the war advance,
With reverent awe furvey the fons of fame,   525
And bufy whifpers buzz each honoured name.
As nearer now the car-imperial draws,
Hufhed Expectation holds her ftilleft paufe;
And, as the world's young Victor paffes by,
The pageant kindles Hope's prophetic eye;   530

                                              Fair

Fair mid the funny plain of future years

The glittering ftructure of his Fame appears,

In bright gradation loftier fplendours rife

Till the proud Summit pierce his kindred fkies.

Its penfile garlands now the ringing arch   535

Shakes o'er the footfteps of the clofing march.

With long refounding tones and waving hands

The Chiefs difmifs the quick fucceeding bands;

And crowds officious lead each weary gueft ,

Where Silence guards the fhadowy bowers of Reft; 540

On turgid filk his limbs the Veteran throws,

And owns the grateful numbnefs of repofe ;

Or, mid the luxury of parting pain,

With unfelt ardours fires the liftening train.

Flufhed

Flufhed by the tale, they hail the Soldier bleft,   545
Spurn daftard floth, and hate ignoble reft,
Fierce burns the rapture; quick the warrior-flame
Darts through each throbbing heart and glowing frame;
And nerves unftrung the ponderous faulchion wield,
And trembling arms effay the maffive fhield,   550
And little bofoms pant for martial toils,
Pierce the ftern foe, and ftrip his blood-ftained fpoils.

The feaft refounds in Sufa's ftately halls,
And gorgeous trophies deck her echoing walls;
From horns reverfed as Plenty pours her hoard,   555
And piles his bleffings on the Vintage board:
With mellow luftre, on each feftive mien,
The light of Pleafure's fparkling glance is feen;

To

To kindled breafts applauding hymns reftore

Each high defign that fwelled the foul before,   560

And Beauty's fmile, the Warrior's deareft meed,

Repays the paft, and prompts the future deed.

1. Observations on the Hindoo austerieslies and on ceremonious devotion; and
2. On the indolence of the Asiatic character.

THE antient historians have preserved an anecdote, which seems to me extremely well calculated to shew the spirit of the Hindoo devotees. Poaus, king, as
he styled himself, of six hundred kings, was induced by the reputation of the Roman name, to send an Embassy to Augustus Cæsar. To prevent misapprehension,
the reader must observe that the Hindoos did not, at this period, live to the age of
100,000 years as in the Suttee Yogue, when their stature also reached 21 cubits;
nor of 10,000 years, as during the Tirtah Yogue, nor so long as in the Dwapaav
Yogue, when the duration of life was almost contracted to the paltry span of Me-
thusalem. They were now—for it was the Collee Yogue, or iron age—reduced to
the ordinary dimensions of life and stature. Hence the reader will conclude, that

H

this

this King Porus was not the celebrated adversary of Alexander, though he might be one of his descendants. The Monarch of the East professes for the Monarch of the West that tender regard, which potentates, perfect strangers to each other, so naturally felt and so warmly avowed, as well in ancient as in modern times. After exhibiting their presents, which consisted of an Hermes, or a man born without arms, whom Strabo, the geographer saw, several snakes, a serpent 10 cubits long, a fresh-water tortoise of 3 cubits, a partridge larger than a vulture and some tygers, an animal which the Romans are then said to have beheld for the first time; the ambassadors, we may suppose, took their leave in good order, charged with many fair professions from the Emperor to his swarthy brother. On their way home they passed through Athens, even then, perhaps, the brightest eye of the world, however tarnished might be its lustre. Here one of the train caused a tall and handsome funeral pile to be erected, upon which, being first duly anointed and otherwise properly equipped, he took his seat with great composure. We may conclude, since the contrary is not related, that as long as the smoke suffered him to be seen, he betrayed no symptom of human frailty. On his monument there was engraved this inscription. HERE LIES ZARMENOCHEGAS, THE INDIAN, WHO PUT HIMSELF TO DEATH ACCORDING TO THE CUSTOM OF HIS COUNTRY.(a).

Now, What could be the motive that prompted this action? What ideas occupied the mind of this volunteer victim? He might, equally, one would suppose, have enjoyed at home the simple satisfaction of broiling alive, either before his departure or after his return. Was it to barter his temporal sufferings for an eternal recompense? could he really suppose that an all-wise Being was to be duped into so disadvantageous a bargain? or, according to the candour of Strabo's stoical interpretation, had he in view to prevent a reverse of prosperous fortune, or to escape from present afflictions? But why then pitch upon this theatre of elegance and philosophy? Why, but to be conspicuous? For my part, I cannot help fancying Saint Zarmenochegas looking around from his combustible throne, in a firm persuasion that the public eye was intent upon an example of fortitude, unprecedented in the Western world. This is a comfortable idea, and has sustained many a martyr in the hour of his extremity. In every kind of theatre, as much depends on the spectators as upon the actors.

(a)Strabo (p. 1084. B. XV). Dion Cassius calls him Zarmarus. The modern geographer and historian has every day to lament the inaccuracy of the ancients with regard to barbarous names.

Such

Such is, I suppose, the original principle of the austerities of Faquirs, Bonzes, Talapoins, Pillar-saints, Flagellants, Monks and public Penitents of all denominations. That exemplary tormentor of himself, Simeon Stylites I dare say, acknowledged the full recompense of his weather-beaten existence, in the summons which called him to be the arbitrator between an Emperor and a Patriarch. If our ladies were grosly superstitious enough to offer the premium of their respect and attendance, I doubt not but their irresistable influence would very soon people our woods and wastes with Faquirs and Pillar-saints. The different forts of devotees may, perhaps, be discriminated in some degree by the livery of the climate, and their numbers may depend on the productive powers of the soil ; otherwise their practices are purely the effect of moral causes ; and when these causes operate, it is pretty much a matter of chance what particular form the practices assume.

It is, I think, easy to trace these wild extravagances gradually dwindling, into the common manœuvres of devotion. And, if there are cases to which this supposition does not apply, still both the one and the other are the offspring of a common parent—vanity recommending herself to the admiration of minds, that entertain unworthy notions of the Supreme Being. It has been said that a law which should oblige the Gentoo widows to burn themselves in the presence of their chambermaid alone, could the knowledge of the fact at the same time be confined to the witness, would effectually check these demonstrations of conjugal tenderness. Few persons, I suppose, by themselves would go through the various postures of what is called, but is not piety, as few would pronounce an animated oration, unless for exercise, to the walls of an apartment. It is not therefore to the eye of heaven, but of the world that these ceremonies are addressed. " Yes, and very properly for the fake of example." I am much afraid this vague phrase will shelter every absurdity alike. The various genuflexions, inclinations, prostrations, supinations, which any man or set of men may choose to recommend as indications of proper respect to the deity, are just as much the result of taste or caprice as the varieties of dress: And do we not daily see the pageantry which attracted the veneration of a savage or superstitious age, degenerating into a contemptible farce? The processions of guilds, monks, and universities were once respectable shows. Besides, it is not easy to conceive, only I ought to recommend to my neighbour by hypocritical grimace what I feel, in my own case, to be insignificant   And such is the narrowness of human capacity, that in any matter it refuses to admit more than one or a few points as essential. The whole stress, therefore, of example and precept ought to be directed to points

really

really essential. Hence superstitious observances as well as dogmas weaken or destroy the sense of moral obligation; it is so easy and often so convenient to substitute the phrases of a creed, and the manœuvres of a rubrick in the place of heartfelt piety and active virtue! In religions overloaded with priests, there is another abundant source of forms and ceremonies; for, unless they cut out work for themselves, the profane sagacity of the laity will soon discover, that there can be no reason for maintaining a numerous order in idleness, though it be even for the glory of God. The Priesthood, for the sake of sustaining the credit of their functions, necessarily insist upon the importance of ceremonies and dogmas. To establish a multiplicity of observances, that many hands may seem requisite to perform the labour of the Lord, is indeed the great secret of Priest-craft. As it is more and more divulged, it will, like the publication of other secrets, lessen the credit of the performance; and it may not, perhaps, be long before it is generally perceived that the interests of virtue and piety no more enjoin states to maintain a set of men for the purpose of reading prolix prayers and practising fanciful ceremonies, than for that of howling at midnight for the souls of the departed. As to the great object of public instruction, it must be attempted, if we would effectually attain it, by means very different from church establishments. The wheat of morality will otherwise be in danger of suffocation from the tares of theology.

So ostentatious is the spirit of devotion, and so strongly do these other principles co-operate with it, that neither evident propriety, nor injunctions, expressly laid down by the very founders of religion, have been able to prevent or correct vain repetitions and pharisaical length of liturgies. And yet, if it be asked, which is it that you distrust in the Deity whom you address, his equity, or his intelligence, that you cry to him so long and so loud? a satisfactory answer does not seem extremely obvious.

This train of thought naturally terminates in a melancholy reflection. I know not whether it be for millions, or only for tens of thousands of years, that pious Brachmans and Brahmins have been commenting the Bedes of the Shaster. Go into a public library in Europe, you will see innumerable volumes, from the gigantic Folio to the dwarfish duodecimo, marshalled under the Banner of Theology. Theology means the science of God, or of things appertaining to God. Now what has been the fruit of these immense labours? what knowledge of God have they either produced or disseminated? Observe the practice, and attend to the conversation of mankind. You will not find one in many thousands, who entertains for the

Supreme

Supreme Being so rational a respect as for a mere mortal of sense and virtue. A man of understanding, should he be able to refrain from laughter, would be offended at any application similar to our ordinary modes of propitiating and supplicating the Omniscient Deity, as at an insult offered to his judgment or integrity. And they are, in fact, derived from those times, when the imagination of men had placed in heaven a phantom revengeful, capricious, and unprincipled, like themselves. Were it possible to doubt the infallibility of our Doctors, one might suspect that the study of divine things has hitherto been conducted as preposterously as that of human things before Bacon. It is scarce for want of sermons and dissertations, that men entertain these degrading notions. Is it then that the masses of theology contain nothing luminous? and that they partake of the nature of clouds rather than stars, and intercept instead of giving light? for I will not suppose that lay minds are incapable of receiving the divine light. For I cannot consent to give up the greater part of our species, as incurably stupid, till every different mode of instruction shall have been essayed in vain: and it is easy to imagine modes that have not yet been tried.

In all moral disquisitions it must carefully be remembered, that human actions may be compared to bodies propelled by an infinite variety of forces, operating in all directions; of these forces it is sufficient to trace the principal and prevailing; otherwise I might have mentioned indolence among the generating causes of Monks and Faquirs. There have always in every country existed numbers who prefer penury and idleness to industry with her horn of plenty. Numbers also would assume the tonsure or the staff, from mere blind imitation. Numbers also, in the simplicity of their heart, would believe their mortification and penance to be really acceptable to God. The reader may, if he chooses, apply these considerations to religious forms also; but should it suit his inclination or interest more, he may indulge his indignation at an attempt however weak, to expel from the consciences of men, those vile intruders, which have usurped the place of universal charity of thought and action; and he may point the artillery of heaven at that temerity, which dares to question the sanctifying virtue of forms and phrases.—" *Ces hommes sont donc bien devots,*" *dira le lecteur! Oni, sans etre meilleurs.* Says a late philosophical traveller of the natives of Syria and Egypt. Did these Orientals attach any sort of merit to their observances, I should have thought it very high praise, if he could have remarked of them generally.—*Oni, sans en etre plus mechans.* I know indeed, and God forbid that I should insinuate any thing to the contrary, that in all countries

there

there are individuals, who scrupulously observe, whatever their priests have prescribed under the title of devotion, without any apparent diminution of their social
virtues. But the comprehension of mind and general justness of intellect, necessary
to this equal association of discordant qualities, are far from being common; and
then devotion stands partly or altogether in the place of the social virtues.

2. Few, perhaps, of the austerities, which the Hindoo devotees endure, will present themselves to our imaginations in such forbidding colours, as the continued
torpor of mind and body in which they seem to wear away their wearisome existence. Nor is there any thing in the contrast, which the character of the Asiatic,
compared with that of the European exhibits, and which may be traced through all
the minutiæ of dress and behaviour, so striking as the habitual indolence and indifference of the former. It is perhaps superfluous to illustrate a point so generally
admitted by examples; but I have two or three before me which are not likely to
occur to every reader, though they appear to be worthy of notice.—

During the residence of Mr. Nichbuhr at Beit-el-Fakih in Arabia Felix, almost the
whole town was destroyed by fire. In that hot climate, during the season of
drought, the houses or huts burned with the violence of dried furze. Yet no out-
cry or lamentation was heard in the streets; " when we condoled with them on
their calamity, they replied; " it is the will of God." A poor man of letters
(Fakih), after he had put his scanty furniture in a place of safety, came to us, and,
with the greatest unconcern, pointed out, when the conflagration reached his own
house. What an Arab loses on such occasions is indeed a trifle, compared with the
loss of an European. He can secure his furniture by taking it on his back: and
his hut is replaced with little cost and trouble. Nevertheless to a poor man the
loss is still considerable." (Nichbuhr Reise, I. p. 355.) ——The term " *Opadhee*"
in the Shanscrit language has no European Synonym. It expresses " a kind of
obstinately stupid lethargy, or perverse absence of mind, in which the will is not
altogether passive. *It seems to be a weakness peculiar to Asia:* for we cannot find a
term by which to express the precise idea in the European languages; it operates
somewhat like the violent impulse of fear, under which men will utter falsehoods
totally incompatible with each other, and utterly contrary to their own opinion,
knowledge, and conviction; and it may be added also, their inclination and intention. A very remarkable instance of this temporary frenzy happened lately at Calcutta, where a man, not an idiot, swore upon a trial, that he was no kind of relation to his own brother who was then in court, and who had constantly supported

him

him from his infancy; and that he lived in a houſe by himſelf, for which he paid the rent from his own pocket, when it was proved that he was not worth a rupee, and when the perſon, in whoſe houſe he had always reſided, ſtood at the bar cloſe to him." See the obſervations of Mr. Halhed, or perhaps, as one may infer from Mr. Halhed's, the modeſt inſinuations of Mr. Haſtings, in the elegant and philoſophical preface to the code of Gentoo laws (p. xlix).

As far as one may judge from this account, it would have been better to tranſlate ORADILEE *infatuation* than *folly*.—It appears from the conciſe view of the Hindoo Cyclopædia, for which the world is indebted to the ſame gentlemen, that their pſychology enumerates three modes of exiſtence, 1. to be awake. 2. to be aſleep. 3. to be abſorbed in a ſtate of unconſciouſneſs—in a kind of trance, as if the human mind was as liable to this mixed and middle condition, as to either of the others. (ib. p. xxxiv).

Monteſquieu imputes this habitual liſtleſſneſs to the relaxing power of an hot climate. And his ſhallow, but ſpecious theory, has been eagerly adopted; for there are multitudes who deſire to poſſeſs, or to be thought to poſſeſs, an inſight into human nature without the trouble of obſervation and reflection. The theory of Monteſquieu has indeed been amply refuted both by Voltaire and Volney. But ſuperſtition has laid her interdict upon the immortal works of Voltaire; and ſhe cannot but regard thoſe of Volney with an evil eye. Beſides theſe philoſophers have by no means exhauſted the ſubject, and attention is, on every account, due to the opinions and facts of ſuch writers as Mr. Halhed and Mr. Haſtings: nor is it a matter of ſmall conſequence to entertain juſt ideas on this point.

It may, in the firſt place, be obſerved, that the courts of Great Britain preſent inſtances of infatuation, as remarkable as that of Bengal. There occurred one in particular at the ſpring aſſizes of 1792, for the county of Salop, which perhaps deſerves to be preſerved as a document towards the hiſtory of the human underſtanding, and as a problem for the ſolution of philoſophers. A woman accuſed a perſon of throwing her maliciouſly into the river Severn, from a great height. Her own evidence moſt completely acquitted him. For ſhe either atteſted glaring falſehoods and contradictions, or elſe a ſucceſſion of miracles had been wrought in her favour, a ſuppoſition, according to which a court of juſtice ought ſeldom to decide. What deſerves attention is, that you could not eaſily refer her conduct or her evidence to any denomination of ordinary motives. It was not confuſion or terror; it was not idiotiſm, or inſanity under any common ſhape. She was cool, collected, and ſeem-

ed

ed to have full poſſeſſion of her mind. A falſe accuſation implies malice undoubtedly; but it was allied with a ſpecies of infatuation or wrongheadedneſs, equal at
leaſt to the Aſiatic example; ſimilar in its operation to another cauſe, which, according to the Italian poet, fa traudir and traveder ciaſcuno; as if the organs were moved by a foreign agent and the will of the individual ſuperſeded, as in witch-craft or
enchantment.

By taking into the account what we may daily ſee at home, it will be evident that
the Aſiatic *faineantiſe* is at moſt but a higher term in the general ſeries of human indolence; and this is perhaps too large a conceſſion. Even in the flouriſhing countries of Europe, where there is ſo much to ſtimulate, and ſo little to check activity,
we ſee inſtances of that torpid indolence, which takes no concern in the affairs of
this world; and which ſometimes, without actual incapacity, borrowing ſomething
from infanity and ſomething from idiotiſm, conſtitutes an unhappy compound of
inert perverſeneſs; ſuch characters ſeldom move but at the ſuggeſtion of malice, entertain no ſuſpicion of their own inferiority and ignorance, adopt the moſt circuitous
means to attain the ſimpleſt ends, feel no charm in Art or Nature, no obligation in
truth or virtue, and are whatever an Hindoo deprecates, when he entreats Brama the
Supreme God, his Son Burmha or Brimha, Narrayna the ſpirit of God, or Brimha,
and Sheevah, Viſſnou, the Three in One, to deliver him from Opadhee.

If we enlarge our views to more extenſive conſiderations, we ſhall find that a ſul-
try climate is by no means an efficient cauſe of indolence. From Japan to Syria, in
Phœnicia, in Egypt, in Arabia, in Aſſyria, in Perſia, in Hindoſtan, in China, and
in the Japaneſe iſlands, where Thunberg, the ſucceſſor of Linneus, could hardly dif-
cover a weed in the corn fields—ſuch is the induſtry of the cultivators of the land—
human activity either has been, or is practiſed under every form of ſudden effort, or
continued labour. Mr. Townſhend, a traveller ſo judicious in every thing that concerns political œconomy, alone furniſhes facts enough to ſhew the futility of this
opinion. I will content myſelf with referring to his account of Catalonian induſtry;
but a paſſage relating to a more torrid region, deſerves to be quoted. " When it
is conſidered that thoſe vineyards (thoſe near Malaga) are on the declivity of hills,
inclined towards the ſcorching ſun, it may be readily conceived that the labour is
ſevere;........the peaſants of no country upon earth are more patient of heat, of
hunger, and of thirſt, or capable of greater exertions, than this very people who
have been accuſed of indolence. For my part, from what I have obſerved, and
have been able to collect, I am ſatiſfied, that if the Spaniards of the interior pro-

vinces are unemployed, it is to be attributed neither to the climate, nor to their conftitutions, but either to the *neglects*" (*neglect* is not the proper term) " of government, or to other accidental caufes already noticed and explained" (Journey through Spain, III, 28,). Warmth is indeed the great animating principle of nature; and we may borrow even from our own climate fome illuftration of this important doctrine, for the warmeft part of our year is the period, during which not only moft labour is actually performed, but that in which there is the greateft difpofition to labour. If the reader find a refutation of this latter affertion in his own feelings during the dog days, let him paufe a moment, and confider whether his own effeminacy or debauchery be not the caufe of his oppreffion, rather than the temperature of the atmofphere. If he fhould object that no conclufion will hold from the temperate to the torrid zone, let him recollect that our feelings depend upon habit, and not upon any pofitive temperature. A native of Africa can bafk in the fun upon the fands of the defert of Barca. Laft of all, let him confider whether an order of things which fhould have eftablifhed, in the relation between the temperature of the faireft regions of the globe, and the conftitution of the human frame, a degradation of the human character, would have been entitled either to his admiration or his gratitude.

What then are the real caufes of an indifputable phænomenon? 1. The ready fupply of the moft urgent neceffities in the fertility of the countries in queftion. Doubtlefs, energy of character both in nations and individuals is originally determined by their wants, and the urgency of the feelings arifing from them. Could we ftretch forth our hands and grafp every thing we defire, we fhould not often change our place, and but feldom perhaps our pofture. We fhould pafs our lives with few defires and as little enjoyment.

Left there fhould feem here any thing inconfiftent with the conclufion of the paragraph before the laft, it will be neceffary to offer a confideration of fome importance in the hiftory of mankind. Our moft antient hiftorical documents agree in placing the original flock of the human race in thofe countries, where our neceffities are feweft and moft eafily fupplied. The helplefs condition of man, before he could have acquired power from knowledge, and prudence from experience, required fuch a nurfery. Here the fpecies would go on increafing, till it equalled the natural and fpontaneous refources of the foil. Very fimple arts would afford new fupplies in great abundance. By degrees focieties would be formed, and great empires eftablifhed. This order of things would have fecured all the happinefs of which man

I

feems

feems capable, a perpetual and unlimited extenfion of defires and gratifications, a boundlefs activity of mind and body: But in this promifing progrefs he was arrefted by the rife of monarchies and hierarchies: and it appears that he is every where doomed to learn the value of his natural rights by long experience of the fufferings which attend their privation or infringement. The energy of human nature being repreffed on all fides by the tyranny of priefts and defpots, the primitive nations funk into langour; *that* activity, which had arifen in the progrefs of fociety, conti-nued from habit, rather than from any generous impulfe of the mind; and it could find no field of exertion, but in the arts of frivolity and corruption. In the mean time, other nations were more flowly formed in lefs fortunate climates; and then the former, having endured all the evils of domeftic fervitude, became fubject to the relentlefs oppreffion of foreign tyrants. One reflection confoles us, while we con-template the paft or prefent calamities of Afia. The pofterity of the oppreffed will at laft, receive from the pofterity of their oppreffors the doctrines and the example of freedom; Faquirs and Bramins, indolence and fervitude, whether of mind or bo-dy, will at length difappear from the face of Hindoftan.

In thefe reflections I have anticipated the other comprehenfive caufes of Afiatic indolence, viz. temporal and ecclefiaftical defpotifm. The great fource of activity lies in the mind: the idiots, the faineans, and the favages of every quarter of the globe equally exemplify this truth. It is indifferent whether the organs of thought be imperfect, the habit not acquired, or the faculty fuppreffed. Thefe caufes will only be more or lefs extenfive in their operation.

II.

Obfervations on the manufactures of the Hindoos.

THE reafoning of Dr. Robertfon in the caufe, which has carried the ornamental wares of India to fo great a degree of perfection, does not feem better calcu-lated, than his palliative flatement of the conduct of the Spaniards towards the na-tive Americans, to confole the friends of humanity. Fortunately, however, the principle on which he proceeds, as well as his inference, are liable to weighty ob-jections. He deduces the proficiency of the Hindoos in weaving, embroidery and fuch arts, from a particular regulation in their laws. In deducing this inference, he advances a fingular opinion on the fpirit of thofe laws: " The object, he tells us, " of the firft Indian legiflators, was to employ the moft effectual means of providing

" for

" for the subsistence, the security, and *happiness* of all the members of the communi-
" ty, over which they presided. *With this view* they set apart certain races of men
" for each of the professions and arts necessary in a well-ordered society, and ap-
" pointed the exercise of them to be transmitted from father to son in successi-
" on (p. 260)." He adds, that this system will be found more effectually to attain
the end in view than may at first sight be supposed. He allows, indeed, that such a
regulation must, at times, check genius and repress talents. He has, however, a
saving clause. For, says he, the arrangements of civil government are made, not
for what is extraordinary, but what is common; not for the few, but the many.
Notwithstanding our boasted advances in the science of politics, the author of these
discoveries might reasonably expect that they would astonish us. Why did he not
propose the introduction of regulations in the same spirit here? Since the majority
of every nation consists not of what is extraordinary, but what is common, not of
the few, but the many, one would think the analogy ought to hold in some degree
throughout: especially as we are told (p. 261,) that " the early distribution of
" the people into classes attached to particular kinds of labour, secured such abun-
" dance of the more common and useful commodities, as not only supplied their
" own wants, but ministered to the countries around them." I know not what
more a nation can want as the basis of its prosperity. Perhaps, however, the double and triple crops, which the soil is capable of producing in the same year, may
claim a small share of what is here exclusively ascribed to political regulations.
Perhaps, there is an energy in nature and in man, which Despotism itself finds it
difficult to stifle. Where has Dr. Robertson discovered the indications of those
pure motives, which he ascribes to the Hindoo legislators? The high authority,
for instance, and exclusive privileges of the Brahmins—which do they betray? the
liberal spirit of legislators holding in view the happiness of a whole community, or
selfish craft, abusing the pernicious influence of superstition? Is it to attain the sacred end of general felicity, that no individual of this cast can be put to death for
any, the most enormous crime? that the property of a Brahmin is considered as too
sacred to fall into profane hands? that a sovereign is liable to be deposed for slight-
ing the remonstrances of a Brahmin? was it humanity that dictated such laws as
these? " If a Sooder (such is the denomination of the lowest and most numerous
of the 4 casts) give much and frequent molestation to a Brahmin, the magistrate
shall instantly put him to death.—If a Sooder sits upon the carpet of a Brahmin, in
that case, the magistrate, having thrust a hot iron into his buttock, shall banish him

I 2

the

the kingdom; or elfe, he fhall cut off his buttock (Gentoo Code, p. 207.)." Was it a defire of promoting the welfare of fociety, or of rendering Brahmins of importance, that life was condemned by the Indian laws to be harraffed by a conftant fucceffion of minute fuperftitious obfervances? Is not this the perpetual burden of their odious fong " there are now frefh ceremonies to be performed, and prefents given to the Brahmins—(Sketches, p. 257)." Of the many fimilar fyftems of prieft-craft, which Hiftory prefents to our indignation, if no memorials relative to their fabrication had been preferved, their fpirit would have betrayed their origin. Nor let the morality of the Hindoo fyftem be adduced in praife or in excufe of the framers of its laws. The founder of every fuperftition has invariably attempted to ennoble that bafe material, by the addition of the beft morality he could make or find.

I cannot but conjecture that Dr. Robertfon, who does not often write from the fund of his own reflections, has followed the tranflator of the Gentoo code, pp. 54, 55, and 63. And, acute and ingenious as the writer of that preface moft affuredly is, his remarks fometimes betray the weaknefs, to which tranflators are liable. He praifes the Brahmins for moderation in refigning the executive power to another caft; but it is natural for a prieftbood, to feek to inveft itfelf in this manner with an air of greater fanctity.

It has been a very common practice with the priefthood to withdraw themfelves from worldly affairs; juft as according to Milton

————————————" Oft amidft
" Thick clouds and dark, doth Heaven's all-ruling Sire
" Choofe to refide, his glory unobfcured,
" And with the Majefty of darknefs round
" Covers his throne"——

Nor is there a fhadow of moderation in this conduct, fince they retain the power of cenfuring and even of depofing the civil magiftrate.

" Whatever order the Brahmins fhall iffue, conformably to the Shafter, the ma-" giftrate fhall take his meafures accordingly." (Code, p. cxv.i). Obferve that the Brahmins are the depofitaries and interpreters of the Shafter, that a Sooder is liable to a very fevere punifhment for reading or liftening to the Beids; and to death, for getting them by heart. (p. 261—2). A Brahmin is polluted by eating with his Sovereign! exemplary felf-denial! that of the Chief Druid in his conteft with Caractacus, is not more praife-worthy;——

" I am

   " I am a Prieſt, a ſervant of the Gods,
   " Thou art a King, a Sovereign o'er frail man,
   " Such Service is above ſuch Sovereignity."

The tranſlator thinks, the penalties for theft committed by the Brahmin tribe leave them but a ſlender ſatisfaction in their exemption from capital puniſhment. But who does not perceive that ſuch ſeverities are an immediate conſequence of their corporation ſpirit, which will always rage againſt crimes derogatory to the body? Mr. Halhed even believes that the exemption from capital puniſhment itſelf " is really founded upon a *reverential regard to the ſanctity of their function and character*, rather than upon the *unjuſt preference of ſelf-intereſted partiality*." I ſee not wherein the meaning of theſe two phraſes differs.—The ſubject would ſupply many more obſervations; but theſe would be too many, if to expoſe wolves, whenever they appear in ſheep's cloathing, were not a duty more ſacred than the functions of the Brahmins: if there were not danger, left the falſe views, preſented by a popular writer ſhould ſpread or perpetuate pernicious prejudices. Dr. Robertſon, having, as we have ſeen, paſſed his ſentence of unmerited panegyric upon the general tenour of the Hindoo laws, and endeavoured to defend that particular proviſion, by which the ſon is devoted to the occupation of the father, proceeds to the application of his principle. " The human mind bends to the law of neceſſity, and acquieſces in eſtabliſhed inſtitutions." A moſt encouraging maxim for oppreſſors! Provided their vexations do not produce a general mortality or ſuicide, they may it ſeems, be continued without any great harm. But do the fetters of Indian policy impede the operations of the hands and of the underſtanding? and in proportion as they ſhackle induſtry, diminiſh happineſs? This is the only queſtion worth conſideration. Let us hear how our hiſtorian goes on to illuſtrate it. " An Indian knows the functions, to which he is deſtined by his birth, ...; from his earlieſt years, he is trained to the habit of doing with eaſe and pleaſure that which he muſt continue to do through life. To this may be aſcribed that high degree of perfection, conſpicuous in many of the Indian manufactures." Now, in order to ſhew the imperfection of this account, it is neceſſary to obſerve, that beyond the mere neceſſity of procuring ſuſtenance, men are impelled by two diſtinct general motives to employ themſelves. One is the eager deſire of fame or wealth: this motive is felt in commercial ſtates; it is felt alſo powerfully by the philoſopher as well as the merchant; and it adds to mere preſent occupation the animating ardour of hope. This only deſerves the title of activity and exertion. The other motive is of a much more languid

guid and fluggifh complexion, and afforts very well with that lethargic indolence, which is fuppofed to characterize the Afiatic difpofition. Thofe who are under its in-dependant influence are confcious of none of thofe fenfations, which the Italians defign, when they fay a purfuit is followed *con amore*. They look not beyond the prefent moment. They wifh only to efcape from the vacancy of their own minds. They employ themfelves upon toys of nice and difficult execution. Almoft every mufeum has to exhibit fome device of ufelefs curiofity, fabricated by the hand of the criminal or the captive. Nuns and monks, who properly rank under the deno-mination of prifoners, and who have no object of exiftence, nothing to do but *kill time*, excel in fuch devices and in the manufacture of frivolous ornaments. This *labor ineptiarum*, this fort of trifling dexterity, if favoured by circumftances, will na-turally flourifh moft in countries where but a comparatively fmall portion of labour is neceffary to fecure fubfiftence. Here much leifure will be enjoyed, and the hands will be at liberty to execute the fuggeftions of the fancy. In fuch countries either a defpot may erect fepulchral pyramids, that his corpfe may enjoy the diftinction of putrifying in ftate, a fanatical people may be led to confecrate the moft ftupendous monuments to fuperftition, or individuals may apply themfelves to the moft exqui-fite works of the loom or the needle, taking but little note of the time they employ. The firft known invaders of India found the natives in poffeffion of their elegant arts; and among the Greeks and Romans, as Dr. Robertfon has acutely obferved, there could be no extenfive demand for cotton cloths. The manufactures were not therefore originally, nor very early in any confiderable degree, encouraged by ex-ternal traffick : nor was there, perhaps, any great activity of internal barter.

This kind of elegant induftry will arife, in certain fituations, where thefe caufes have little operation ;—for I do not pretend to fay that they never had any fort of in-fluence in India—The iflands in the Southern Hemifphere afford a remarkable example in point. Every perfon muft have feen articles, conceived and executed with the utmoft elegance, by the natives of thofe iflands. Some of their female ornaments, to fay nothing of their canoes, nets, cordage, would do honour to the tafte of the moft ingenious of our European Belles. We are frequently aftonifhed at the labour beftowed by our forefathers on their carvings, and on the conftruction and decorations of their maffive monkifh piles. This is univerfal where there is an excefs of manual power above the demands of neceffary labour, during the period which precedes the activity of profitable commerce. The Indian manufactures, therefore, when we afcend to their ultimate caufe, appear to have

been

been the fruit of plenty, leifure and a fportive fancy. Their Induftry it is true, has been limited in its objects by the inftitution of cafts and the perpetuation of trades in families; and this reftriction may have operated like the divifion of labour in conferring dexterity. But if the legiflators had not exerted that wifdom and bene-ficence, for which the hiftorian gives them fo much unneceffary credit, they would ftill have fabricated delicate wares in equal abundance, and by virtue of a freer exertion of genius, their manufactures would have extended to a thoufand elegant and ufeful articles befides.

Should the exhaufted patience of afflicted millions at laft demand of their brami-nical legiflators; " why deprive us of thofe fenfations, which the felf-applaufe of " fuccefsful genius infpires? why rob us of hope, the common patrimony of man? " why, by arrefting us in the childhood of fociety, deliver us over, defencelefs, to " an uninterrupted fucceffion of oppreffors, who had not even a Defpot's, who had " but a plunderer's intereft in us?"

Dr. Robertfon will perhaps kindly attempt to confole them, by faying, that " the human mind bends to the law of neceffity." I know not, if they would be more benefited by his attentions than a man about to be fufpended at the gallows, or ftretched upon the wheel. But I know that it is grateful to oppofe writers, who are led, by whatever motives, to palliate the crimes of the moft cruel enemies of mankind; and I feel it difficult altogether to reprefs the warmth which fo great an intereft infpires.

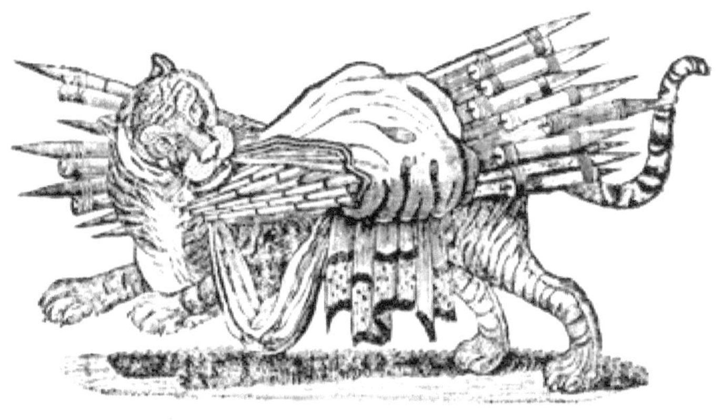

III.

Conjectures on explosive compositions.

" IT will no doubt strike the reader with wonder, to find a prohibition of fire-
" arms in records of such unfathomable antiquity; and he will probably from
" hence renew the suspicion which has been deemed absurd, that Alexander the
" Great did absolutely meet with some weapons of that kind in India, as a passage
" in Quintus Curtius seems to ascertain. Gunpowder has been known in China
" as well as in Hindostan, far beyond all periods of investigation.—The word fire-
" arms is literally in Shanscrit *Agnee-aster*, a weapon of fire : they describe the first
" species of it to have been a kind of dart or arrow tipt with fire, and discharged
" upon the enemy from a bamboo. Among several extraordinary properties of
" this weapon, one was, that after it had taken its flight, it divided into several
" darts or streams of flame, each of which took effect, and which, when once kind-
" led, could not be extinguished (b). But this kind of Agnee-aster is now lost.—
" Cannon in the Shanscrit idiom is called *Shet Agnee*, or the weapon that kills an

---

(b)" It seems exactly to agree with the Feu Gregeois of the Crusades."

" hundred-

" hundred men at once.......... The Pooran Shasters," (the historical part of
their scriptures) " ascribe the invention of these destructive weapons to Bee-
" shookerma, who is related to have forged all the weapons for the war which was
" maintained in the Sutte Jogue between Dewta and Ossoor, or the good and bad
" spirits, for the space of one hundred years." Such is the translator's commentary
upon a passage of the Gentoo code which prohibits war from being waged " with
" any deceitful machine, or with poisoned weapons, or with cannon and guns, or
" any other kind of fire-arms.

The circumstance in the history of the middle ages, which, as the translator justly
observes, bears some resemblance to this passage, must, I should suppose, solicit the
curiosity of every reader; though no writer will afford him any considerable gratification. Yet, by the application of modern science, the principal circumstances,
relating to this curious invention, may perhaps be elucidated with some degree of
precision, and all regret on account of our ignorance of the rest be dissipated. The
authorities, which have been collected by the industry of Ducange, if criticized with
minuteness, would furnish a treatise of some bulk: The following observations are
all that seem to me to be essential, and, all of course that can be properly introduced into a popular essay.

The liquid, inextinguishable, maritime, Greek fire is said to have delayed the
fate of the Greek empire; and from the latter end of the seventh to the middle of
the fourteenth century, great effects are ascribed to it by the writers, who have recorded the transactions of those dark and calamitous ages.

We cannot however reasonably expect genuine information from any quarter.
The Byzantine receipts are justly suspected of deliberate falsehood. The Greeks
had a very strong interest in preserving the secret, and this interest was strengthened
by superstitious motives. In the relation of the most obvious phænomena, by terrified spectators, circumstances are introduced which cannot possibly be admitted as
matters of fact. These and other such considerations afford a strong inducement to
prefer the probabilities arising from our present knowledge of chemistry to the testimony of fear and interest, of which the former inevitably would be confused and
exaggerated, while the latter was partial and calculated to mislead.

From the concurrence of the witnesses, which so far there is nothing to invalidate,
we may conclude, that it could burn without the access of atmospheric air and was
occasionally explosive, and that it had a power of motion within itself. It is said
to have traversed the air with the report of thunder, and is sometimes compared to a

K

whirlwind

whirlwind on account of its violence. Oil, bitumens, wax, pitch entered into its compofition. But no combination of mere inflammable materials can poffibly produce effects, nearly refembling the pieces in fome of our artificial fire-works, and which amount, as I imagine, to an hiffing noife, with occafional explofions and reports. But though fand, vinegar and other faline liquids would extinguifh it, it is related to have burned under water. Here utter ignorance renders me fceptical, or elfe I muft impute to the ancients the want of power to obferve the moft evident phœnomena; and indeed perfons unacquainted as they were with natural philofophy, even fo much as in our time, has imperceptibly made its way even to thofe who never profeffedly paid any attention to it, will always be found incompetent reporters of fuch phœnomena. I fhall therefore embrace that alternative which is moft flattering to my vanity, and believe in oppofition to teftimony, that, all circumftances being alike, the Greek fire would no more burn under water, than under vinegar or fand. The error in the obfervation may, I think, be accounted for. From the oilinefs of its compofition one may infer, that it was at once lighter than water and immixable with that liquid. It was very much ufed in fea engagements. It is therefore obvious to fuppofe that it might have floated and continued to burn for a time on the furface of fo denfe a medium. As to any paticular contrivance for enabling it to burn under water, fuch as we fee in water-rockets, I conceive this to be entirely out of the queftion.

One may therefore venture confidently to affert that, befides oils and refins, mentioned by Anna Comena and other writers, the Greek fire muft have contained nitre, or fome equivalent ingredient. I am much inclined to fuppofe that the whole fecret confifted in the admixture of this material. We know from the Roman hiftory that the Alchemifts had been extremely bufy long before this period. They perhaps had become acquainted with this remarkable fubftance, and with fome of its effects in mixture. I find no indication of the time or the manner, in which nitre became an article of commerce or of experiment: whether it was firft imported from the Eaft, or difcovered within the precinfts of the Roman world.

Calliurcus, according to one hiftorian, a native of Heliopolis in Syria, and according to another, in Heliopolis in Egypt, is faid to have taught the Greeks how to compound and manage this fpecies of fire-arms. It is however utterly incredible that one man fhould both have difcovered the compofition and conceived the application. So many combinations exceed the powers of any fingle mind, how-

ever

ever ſtimulated. Where our information is both ſo ſcanty and inconſiſtent, it is ſurely allowable to hazard a conjecture. It may be ſuppoſed that the rapid progreſs of the Arabian arms, ſharpened the ingenuity of the Greeks; and that in the urgency of need, a lucky thought drew forth this compound from the caverns of Alchemy, where it had perhaps long been known as exhibiting a ſpectacle to idle admiration. It is poſſible that, during this eventful period, when the moſt diſtant things and perſons were thrown into colliſion, the natives of Conſtantinople might acquire abundant ſupplies of nitre, or become acquainted with the Indian mixtures of nitre and combuſtibles. When Amrou had added Egypt to the provinces of the Caliph Omar, the commerce between Europe and India was obliged to ſeek a different channel. The ſilks of China were tranſported by a tedious journey of 100 days to the Oxus, and after traverſing the Caſpian ſea, aſcended the river Cyrus. From the Cyrus the cargo was conveyed to the Phaſis, and then along the Euxine, by Conſtantinople. The wares of India were alſo conveyed over land to the Oxus or the Caſpian. One may ſuſpect that the merchants, having their attention awakened to theſe objects, would eagerly convey to their trembling countrymen, any new means of defence. In the interval that took place between the conqueſt of Egypt and the two ſieges of Conſtantinople, it is probable that ſeveral inhabitants of the latter city muſt have traverſed the interior parts of Aſia for the ſake of exploring or arranging the new route. But it would be imprudent to lay any ſtreſs upon a conjecture that has no other foundation than poſſibility ariſing from the commercial relations between ſuch remote countries.

The exiſtence of rockets and fire-works in India long before Alexander, ſeems perfectly well eſtabliſhed; and yet that neither he nor Megaſthenes, who penetrated ſo much further eaſtward, ſhould have introduced ſo ſtriking an invention into Europe. Had the younger Porus known that the Weſtern world was unacquainted with phœnomena, which are amuſing, when no longer new, and ſo much aſtoniſh thoſe who behold them for the firſt time, he would have thought a bundle of ſky-rockets the moſt acceptable preſent he could have offered to Auguſtus. It is remarkable that the vanity of the ambaſſadors did not impart to the Romans ſome idea of this wonder of India.

Upon the whole, I conſider it as probable, that the Greek fire was an invention originally due to the Grecian Alchemiſts: and as certain, ſince it burned independantly of the atmoſphere, that it contained oxygene, or that ſubſtance which in the ſtate of an elaſtic fluid, has been called *dephlogiſticated air*. Competent judges will,

I think,

I think, admit this principle muſt have been ſupplied by nitre. For what equivalent ſubſtance was ſo likely to be known? Or, ſhall we give them credit for having poſſeſſed ſome ſalt or calx, with which we are unacquainted?

Thus the invention of gunpowder is reduced to the common law of human diſcoveries, which are always progreſſive, and generally ſlowly progreſſive. It is not extraordinary that between the end of the ſeventh and the middle of the fourteenth century nitre, if frequently compounded with other inflammable ſubſtances, ſhould at laſt be mixed in ſuch proportions with ſulphur and charcoal as to be capable of exploding ſuddenly; nor that an accident in the fiery workſhops of the Alchemiſts, ſhould produce the exploſion. Then the Greek fire retreated before a ſuperior engine of deſtruction, and the receipt for its compoſition, being diſuſed, was at length loſt. The invention of gunpowder, whatever is its preciſe date, was not long poſterior to the laſt cruſade, when the Greek fire was in the hands of the Saracens, and its effects proved ſo terrible to the ſenſes, or the imagination, of thoſe Weſtern Barbarians, who invaded the Holy Land, as that barren and rocky diſtrict of Syria is called. After this period, it obtains but little, if any, notice from hiſtory.

IV.

Antiquity of the Hindoos.

THE Hindoos, Chineſe and Tartars lay claim to an antiquity, which equally ſurprizes and ſcandalizes the followers of the Jewiſh mythology. By a very natural, but pernicious error, all theſe nations aſcribe to their remote anceſtors long life, uninterrupted happineſs, and unſullied innocence. According to the fabulous doctrine of Hindoſtan, the Principle of truth, or ſole omnipotent God, produced a being called Burmha for the creation of all beings. He had, firſt, himſelf formed the earth, heavens, water, fire and air. Then Burmha, the agent of Supreme Power, created the Brahmin(c), from his mouth—the Chehterce, or magiſtrate and ſoldier, from his arms,—the Bice, or merchant and huſbandman, from his belly,—

(c) All Prieſts are Brahmins, but all Brahmins are not Prieſts. The Brahmin Caſt, being allowed to marry, multiplied beyond the demands of their ſuperſtition, however encumbered with ceremonies.

and

and the Sooder, or fervile caft, from his feet. For fome time after the creation of the world, there was neither magiftrate nor punifhment; and no man was guilty of injuftice or oppreffion, or of any other crime. The fucceffive degeneration of mankind took place, as follows:

The Suttee Jogue, or pure age, lafted - - -	3, 200, 000 years.
Human life - - - - - - -	100, 000
Human ftature was - - - - - -	21 cubits
The Tirtah Jogue, when $\frac{1}{3}$ of men were depraved -	2, 400, 000
Human life - - - - - - -	10, 000
The Dwapaar Jogue, when $\frac{1}{4}$ of men were depraved	1, 600, 000
Human life - - - - - - -	1, 000
The Collee Jogue, when all men are *leffened*, will laft	400, 000
Human life does not exceed - - - - -	100

At the expiration of the Collee Jogue, another Suttee Jogue is to commence and fo on——

Magnus ab integro fæclorum nafcitur ordo:

O—Redit et Virgo, redeunt Saturnia regna—

The happieft, furely, and moft philofophical turn, ever given to a fable of this fort! For, it fhould be obferved that retribution is not forgotten, though Burmha has not been fo inexorable, as to damn finners everlaftingly.

According to the Chinefe 130 millions of years elapfed before the firft dynafty, I neglect fome fractions, which do not affect the fum total, more than fo many miles do the diftance between the earth and the fun.

Tien-hoam-ti (auguft family of heaven) reigned -	1, 800, 000 years
Ti-hoam-chi (auguft family of earth) - -	1, 800, 000 alfo

Yu or Tigu, the founder of the firft dynafty, reigned 2198 years before our æra. One day as his mother was walking out, fhe was ftruck by a ftar and became pregnant. Prodigies always attend the birth or conception of all the remarkable Chinefe characters; but this fort of credulity by no means diftinguifhes this people from the reft of the world. To diffeminate the knowledge of their traditions may, however, have a very happy moral effect, if Chinefe, Hindoos and Europeans, by comparing their feveral mythologies, fhould trace them to their common parent, the human imagination, or if they fhould refpectfully allow each other to cherifh their feveral creeds undifturbed by the rage of perfecution, or the ambition of profelytifm, a fpecies of humanity which indeed, the Afiatics both profefs and practice.

Dr. Pallas.

Dr. Pallas, whofe obfervations take in a wider range of phyfical and moral objects than thofe of perhaps any other traveller, and whofe travels it is a reproach to our language not to poffefs, gives a curious account of the mythology and religious ceremonies of the Calmuck Tartars. Thefe Tartars acknowledge the fupremacy of the Dulai Lama. According to their doctrine, there originally exifted a fpace or chaos extending in breadth and depth 6,116,000 of their miles. In this fpace clouds of the colour of gold collected, and difcharged rain enough to form a boundlefs ocean. There arofe, by degrees, upon this fea, a fcum, like cream upon milk; out of which men and all living creatures, as alfo their inferior divinities were produced. Then ftorms burft from ten quarters of the fky over the fea, by which there was formed a pillar in the firmament above, that defcended below the bottom of the primitive fea. They eftimate the circumference of the pillar at feveral thoufand miles. All the inhabited worlds, as alfo the fun revolve round this pillar . . . . which has 4 fides, one of the colour of filver, another azure blue, a third of gold, and a fourth of a dark red. When the filver fide is illuminated, we have day-break, when the blue, it is towards mid-day, when the golden, it is high noon, when the fun moves towards the dark-red fide, we have the red evening fky, till at laft it difappears behind this pillar, and then night comes on.

Immediately after the origin of our world, men lived to be 80,000 years old. They were full of righteoufnefs, nourifhed with invifible gifts of grace, and had the wonderful talent of afcending up into heaven. In this age the metempfychofis was general; at prefent it is a privilege confined to the priefts and the ariftocracy. The thoufand Burchans, or faints adored by the Kalmucks, afcended to heaven during this age.

An unhappy period followed. The earth brought forth a certain herb, that had the tafte of honey: and there came a gluttonous man, and tafted of this herb, and made it known to others. Hence all their ancient fanctity and the power of rifing up to heaven difappeared from among men: the duration of life began to fhorten, and their gigantic fize to diminifh. . . . . . .

After men had long fed upon this plant, it began to fail; then they took to a fort of butter of the earth; and then of a kind of flag; which at laft alfo difappeared, and now all the virtues took their departure from the earth, and all manner of crimes were introduced. They began to cultivate the ground; and fet over them the moft prudent to divide the land and other goods, and at laft became Chan.

During this long period of degradation, many of their Burchans have appeared upon the earth, in order to mend mankind; their kind intentions were however of fmall avail. The obftinate race gradually became more and more wicked and fhort-lived: When the fpan was contracted to 100 years, *Shadfhimmuni*, the laft and greateft Burchan and founder of the prefent religion of the Lama, came down from heaven, and preached to fixty-one nations. Unfortunately each nation heard the doctrine with different organs and underftood it in a different fenfe: Hence the variety of religions and languages.

I pafs over their doctrine of a future ftate, of the Devil who is an extremely re-fpectable perfonage, and of the privileges enjoyed by the fouls of the priefts over thofe of the laity. But I think it worth while to tranflate Dr. Pallas's account of their fabbatical inftitution.

" The Kalmucks celebrate three days every month, the 8th, 15th, and 30th, after the full moon. No devout Kalmuck eats any thing either of thefe three days, except milk and preparations of milk. They fpend moft of the day at the tent of their prieft, whither they are fummoned in the morning by drums and trumpets. The principal only and the learned enter the tent. The undiftinguifhed multitude fits on the outfide; the men and women drop a bead from their rofary, every time they pronounce certain fix words with their eyes clofed and repeat to themfelves another fhort formula, which they have got by rote without underftanding it. The priefts perform their part in a very obftreperous manner. They befides hoift ftrips of cotton upon tall poles. On the ftrips are infcribed prayers in the Tangut language: it is their opinion that the fluttering of thefe prayers in the wind, is juft as efficacious as the repetition of them would be" (Pallas Reife, I. 334. &c.).

It is remarkable that they have a fpiritual language, not underftood by the common people, as every priefthood has had, or would defire to have.

The comparifon of thefe and other fyftems of mythology affords one general reflection. Their refemblance fhews them to have been derived from that vanity, and thofe hopes, fears, and moral fentiments, which are common to all mankind; while their differences warrant us in concluding that they were not copied from one another. Refervoirs, hidden within the bowels of the earth, fupply alike in every region of the globe, fources of frefh water to the neceffities of man, though each particular water may receive a flight impregnation from the minerals with which it has come in contact: In like manner the imagination univerfally fupplies fables to affuage the thirft of credulity. The happinefs of our progenitors, of which thefe fables prefent fo romantic an idea, charms our prefent wretchednefs, as poverty

and

and neglect fuftain themfelves by looking back upon the fplendor of an illuftrious anceftor: we eafily learn to derive a better confolation from the time to come than the paft, by oppofing to the difquieting confcioufnefs of a frail and perifhable exiftence here, the profpect of an immortal futurity. But in both thefe pictures though the outlines be fimilar, a difference of colouring will arife from a difference of climate, of furrounding objects, of accidents that have occurred to different tribes.

If we enquire for a moment concerning the fubjects of the facred writings of thefe ancient nations, we fhall find them to be very mifcellaneous: befides fables, they confift of laws, precepts, chronicles, and poetry or prophecy. Where there was a regular priefthood, as among the Hindoos, Chinefe, Tartars, Egyptians and Jews, who exercifed fo horrible a tyranny over opinion, and in order to maintain their authority, guarded what knowledge they puffeffed with all the vigilance of jealoufy, that fentiment of reverence, which the term *facred* expreffes, would attach itfelf to literature and fcience of every fpecies. The firft imperfect opinions concerning natural appearances, which are never true, and frequently directly oppofite to the truth, would be fanctioned. Succeeding priefts would neither dare nor defire to correct them. The mind would remain in eternal infancy; all accumulation of national as well as individual power would ceafe, for collective can only be the fum of fingle ability; and the ftate would be perpetually liable to all thofe dreadful evils, which hang over political imbecillity. The great reafon why the genius of Greece foared fo high and fo rapidly was the abfence of controul over thought; and the fame caufe muft have effentially contributed to the vigour of Rome. Exactly in proportion to the exiftence of fuch controul, exactly in that proportion will man fall fhort of his capability, and fail to fulfil his high deftination.

There is no occafion to refute thefe fables in any other way than to fhew the ftrong tendency of the imagination to fabricate them. Nor indeed have we any other means of refuting them, unlefs we choofe to oppofe other fables to them. Neverthelefs, the claim of the Hindoos to a very remote, though indefinite antiquity, remain unimpeached. In the firft place, the fyftem of fubterranean Nature, which is beginning to be underftood, and which exhibits, as well as the fyftem of the heavens, an arrangement highly worthy of admiration, proves the earth to have exifted for millions of years, perhaps of ages. For I cannot fcruple to apply a rule, fimilar to one of Newton's rules for philofophifing, to this fubject and to take it for granted that the fame caufes operate in the fame manner and in the fame time now, as they ever did. Secondly, nothing in art oppofes this refult from nature. It has indeed

been

been pretended that the small progress of mankind in arts and sciences argues the recent origin of the species. But where is the certain or even probable standard of this progress? How is it shewn that we must advance so far in such a time? It will cost us a considerable effort of abstraction to conceive the extreme slowness of the first steps. Some writers endeavour to escape from the insuperable objection to the system of a recent origin, which arises from the difficult formation of language, by the contrivance which clumsy poets employ to bring an ill-constructed plot to a conclusion; as if it were not a more worthy supposition to conceive that his Creator endowed man with a capacity to invent the means of conveying his thoughts by sounds, and as if language did not bear certain signs of its human origin and gradual advancement. But was man taught to write as well as to speak? If even the hardiness of orthodoxy will not maintain this assertion, what period shall we allow for an attainment which the most civilized states in America had not reached?

The enquiries of the moderns have produced a particular proof of the great antiquity of Indian science; and this proof is of the most precise and determinate nature. It appears from the researches of the celebrated philosophical patriot, Mr. Bailly, that, 4894 years ago, the Hindoo astronomers had attained a degree of perfection in calculation, at which the European philosophers have but just arrived. The strictest scrutiny has served but to confirm the pretensions of the tables to this antiquity. There exists no reason to suppose that these tables could have been forged at any recent period, or at any period posterior to their date. Science has so much declined among the Brahmins in consequence of the evils attending foreign dominion, that they now are only able to use the tables empirically, and without understanding the principles on which they are constructed: and so perfect is their accuracy, that only the modern European astronomers would be equal to their fabrication(d).—How many thousands or tens of thousands of years will the reader allow a native of Christmas Sound, or even of Otaheite to make such an advance in science? He must either suppose the Hindoos to have been inspired astronomers, or else he must allow them time to invent language and letters, to make astronomical observations, cultivate the science of quantity, and combine the two

---

(d) How does this proficiency in a laborious science agree with the indolence supposed to be natural to an hot climate?

L

latter

latter materials into this perfect aftronomical edifice. Then let him add the period he may choofe to affign for thefe purpofes to almoft 5000 years.

It deferves to be remarked that Mr. Bailly, having compared the Hindoo with the Tartar, Perfian, and Greek fyftems, has found that the one could not be copied from the other. This independence of their fcience would afford a very ftrong prefumption of the independence of their mythology, even if Sir W. Jones had offered any tolerable evidence of his hypothefis of the derivation of the Gods of Greece from the Gods of India.

Dr. Robertfon fpeaks at large of the " early and high civilization" of the natives of India; and the writer of the preface to the Gentoo Code fays " It is certain that thefe two nations (the Hindoos and Chinefe) have been acquainted with letters from the *very earlieft* period." Thefe phrafes are ufed with relation to other ftates, whofe merchants from the firft dawn of Weftern Hiftory are found importing the natural and artificial productions of India. All the obfervations, to which either commerce or conqueft gave occafion, tend to confirm the pretenfions of the Hindoos themfelves. A fociety thoroughly regulated, the inftitution of cafts, the minutenefs of the provifions of their laws, which could only have arifen from long experience and multiplied relations, their public works, and their literature, have extorted from the hiftorian whom I have fo often quoted, this confeffion, " What now is in India, always was there;" an exaggeration undoubtedly, but at the fame time one that is abundantly expreffive. All thefe confiderations afford as ftrong evidence as can be defired, and more precife than could be expected of the great antiquity of the Hindoos, and of the human race in general. We may be fure that the period, preceding monuments, muft very far exceed the time that has elapfed fince. The infancy of the fpecies would very much furpafs in proportional duration the infancy of the individual. And how diftant is even yet the maturity of any part of the fpecies?

It has been remarked that the number of Gentoo converts to Chriftianity has been too trifling to be noticed; and that the few profelytes have been almoft univerfally *outcafts*, Chandalas, Parias, or men expelled from one of the 4 cafts and held in a degree of contempt, of which nothing but the deadly animofity of rival fects in Europe can fuggeft to us an adequate conception. If miffionaries and their employers had been capable of a fhort procefs of liberal reafoning, they muft have anticipated the difappointment of their endeavours. In traditions of an age of innocence, of a fall, of incarnate deities, of a divine founder of their fyftem, in the

doctrine

doctrine of future retribution, in metaphysical dogmas, in pure maxims of morality, they already possess all that can be offered them. Pride, faith, and reason conspire to rear round their creed a Rampart impregnable to the attacks of a rival religion. Nor is there any appearance that the slower operations of philosophy will speedily undermine its authority, and the despotism of the Brahmins of India, the ultimate cause of all the calamities of a country so favoured by Nature.

The following quotations will furnish an idea of the Hindoo doctrines, relative to the Deity, to piety and morality. They may be agreeable, and they may be useful as a lesson of diffidence and moderation to many readers. I know of nothing that would so much contribute to soften the hard heart of blind credulity, and to diffuse peace and good will among mankind, as a work which should exhibit an impartial comparison of the religious dogmas and morality of different nations; and we have lately acquired some precious materials for such a work.

The Supreme Being says: " I am the creator of all things, and all things pro-
" ceed from me. Those who are endued with spiritual wisdom know this, and
" worship me."

" I am the soul, which is in the bodies of all things. I am the beginning and
" the end. I am time; I am all-grasping death; and I am the resurrection. I am
" the seed of all things in nature, and there is not any thing animate or inanimate
" without me.

" I am the mystic figure Oom, the Reek, the Sam, and the Yayoor Veds. I am
" the witness, the comforter, the asylum, the friend. I am generation, and disso-
" lution : in me all things are reposited.

" The whole universe was spread abroad by me.

" The foolish are unacquainted with my supreme and divine nature. They are
" of vain hope, of vain endeavours, and void of reason; whilst those of true wisdom
" serve me in their hearts, undiverted by other gods.

" Those who worship other gods, worship me. I am in the sacrifice, in the
" spices, in the invocation, in the fire, and in the victim."

It is said to the Supreme Being: " Thou art the prime Creator—Eternal God!
" Thou art the Supreme! By thee the universe was spread abroad! Thou art
" Vayoo, the god of the winds; Agnee, the god of fire; Varoon, the god of the
" oceans, &c.

" Reverence be unto thee; again and again reverence, O thou, who art all in
" all! Great is thy power, and great thy glory! Thou art the father of all things;

L 2

" wherefore

" wherefore I bow down, and with my body proſtrate on the ground, crave thy
" mercy. Lord, worthy to be adored! bear with me as a father with a ſon; a
" friend with a friend; a lover with the beloved."

Of piety the Deity ſays: " They who delighting in the welfare of all nature,
" ſerve me in my incorruptible, ineffable, and inviſible form; omnipotent, incom-
" prehenſible, ſtanding on high, fixed, and immoveable, with ſubdued paſſions, and
" who are the ſame in all things, ſhall come unto me.

" Thoſe whoſe minds are attached to my inviſible nature, have the greater la-
" bour, becauſe an inviſible path is difficult to corporeal beings. Place thy heart
" on me, and penetrate me with thy underſtanding, and thou ſhalt hereafter enter
" unto me. But if thou ſhouldſt be unable at once ſtedfaſtly to fix thy mind on
" me, endeavour to find me by means of conſtant practice.

" He, my ſervant, is dear to me, who is free from enmity; merciful, and exempt
" from pride and ſelfiſhneſs; who is the ſame in pain and in pleaſure; patient of
" wrongs; contented; and whoſe mind is fixed on me alone.

" He is my beloved, of whom mankind is not afraid, and who is not afraid of
" mankind; who is unſolicitous about events; to whom praiſe and blame are as
" one; who is of little ſpeech; who is pleaſed with whatever cometh to paſs; who
" has no particular home, and is of a ſteady mind."

Of good works, he ſays: " Both the deſertion and practice of works, are the
" means of happineſs. But of the two, the practice is to be diſtinguiſhed above
" the deſertion.

" The man, who, performing the duties of life, and quitting all intereſt in them,
" placeth them upon Brahm, the ſupreme, is not tainted with ſin, but remaineth
" like the leaf of the lotus unaffected by the waters.

" Let not the motive be in the event: be not one of thoſe, whoſe motive for
" action is in the hope of reward.

" Let not thy life be ſpent in inaction: perform thy duty, and abandon all
" thoughts of the conſequence. The miſerable and unhappy are ſo about the
" event of things; but men, who are endued with true wiſdom, are unmindful
" of them."

Of benevolent maxims this may ſerve as a ſpecimen: " Hoſpitality is command-
" ed to be exerciſed even towards an enemy, when he cometh into thine houſe:
" the tree doth not withdraw its ſhade even from the wood-cutter.

" Good

" Good men extend their charity unto the vileſt animals. The moon doth not
" withhold her light even from the cottage of the Chandala.

" Is this one of us or is he a ſtranger ?—Such is the reaſoning of the ungenerous:
" but to thoſe, by whom liberality is practiſed, the whole world is but as one
" family."

Taken from the Baghvat-Geeta, an epiſode in an ancient Epic Poem, called Mahah-
barat; See Mr. Wilkins's tranſlation of this epiſode: it is highly worthy of curioſity.

V.

On the complexion of the natives of hot countries, and the varieties of the human races.

IT is ſaid either by Arrian or Strabo, that the Indians are the blackeſt of all men
except the Ethiopians. And, from other expreſſions of the former writer, we
may collect that the ancients had made this obſervation upon the natives of Sindy,
as well as upon thoſe of the more eaſterly diſtricts of Hindoſtan.

The queſtion concerning the varieties of mankind has ſeldom been approached
without prejudice. It has generally been treated as ſubordinate to another queſtion,
which was already decided in a different manner in the minds of the diſputants,
who had therefore no other view than to obtain ſome confirmation of their pre-
conceived opinions.

If it be conſidered purely and ſimply as a point of Natural Hiſtory, we ſhall perhaps find ourſelves enabled, by the modern progreſs of ſcience to add ſomething to
former analogies and probabilities: but we ſhall fall ſo far ſhort of cogent proof,
that thoſe whoſe views are not limited to the deciſion of this one queſtion, may continue to accumulate words, on which ever ſide they ſhall judge moſt convenient.

Much depends on the ideas, of which the term *ſpecies* is made the ſign. If thoſe
animals be ſaid to belong to the ſame ſpecies, of which the progeny is fertile, experience has decided this once in favour of orthodoxy. But this definition is little
better than an aſſumption of the diſputed point: nor will Natural Hiſtory ever in-
ſtruct us, whether in hating, oppreſſing or butchering the inhabitants of another
zone or hemiſphere, the ſin is committed againſt aliens or kindred. Though a
colony of Negroes had been tranſported to Circaſſia, and a number of Circaſſians
had

had been brought to occupy the place they had left, and though it had been found after a thousand generations, that a reciprocal change had taken place, this would prove nothing in favour of a common origin, but to thofe who had previoufly yielded to authority. Others might fay; " It is true; man is every where the fame, " allowing for circumſtances, but as we muſt judge of the paſt from the prefent, and " fuppofe that he was always equally expofed to the power of accident, it would be " neceffary to plant many individuals of fo tender a fpecies, leſt it ſhould have be- " come extinct before it had borne fruit; befides, if the earth was to be repleniſhed, " why choofe precifely the moſt tedious method of effecting this purpofe?" To confiderations fuch as thefe, it might be anfwered that the guardian care of him who produced, could protect, his helplefs creatures; and that an almighty arm could conduct them either over extenfive oceans, or by way of thofe iſlands which are placed like fo many ſtepping ſtones between the old and the new continents; and that the plan of unerring wifdom could never have been to people the earth as foon as poffible, otherwife it would have been accomplifhed by the firſt effort of creative power. To this the objector might oppofe a reply equally vague and inconclufive with the anfwer.

The naturaliſt, meanwhile difcovers few direct probabilities on either fide. Obfervation has certainly not afcertained any adequate power in climate to convert the varieties mutually; but if we confider how much more flowly the generations of men fucceed each other than thofe of moſt other animals, we may reafonably fufpect time to have been wanting to effect any confiderable change, even if our nature were equally plaſtic. As to any inftances of change, for certain changes are mentioned, it is either fo flight and fuperficial, or the circumſtances are fo ambiguous, that no perfon accuſtomed accurately to compare conclufions with facts, can draw any inference from them.

The Hindoo offers to the phyfiologiſt a much more fimple problem than the African. The former is but a difcoloured European; and thofe naturaliſts who have attempted to reduce the human race to a few varieties, place them together(e). The Negro has many different external characters befides the colour; and his internal differences, as we fhall foon fee, are perhaps more important than the external.

The colour of the Hindoo feems fimply to depend on the heat and light of the climate. This appears not only, (as I have been informed by perfons that have re-

---

(e) As Blumenbach de generis humani varietate nativa. Ed. 2nda. Goetting. 1781.

ſided in India) from the compariſon of thoſe who are carefully ſecluded from the direct rays of the ſun with others; but a very probable cauſe may be aſſigned for the phœnomenon. It has long been known that heat and light have ſeparately and jointly the power of cauſing an extrication of elaſtic fluids from many different bodies. There are no experiments more curious in themſelves or more important in their conſequences, than thoſe by which the effect of light in ſlowly diſengaging oxygen air from vegetables has been diſcovered. Light has the ſame effect on other ſubſtances; it turns the combination of nitrous acid and ſilver black by diſengaging oxygen air; and we need not wonder that an alteration of the compoſition of any body ſhould change the relation of its particles to the particles of light, and conſequently alter its colour.

Theſe conſiderations led me to conjecture that the black complexion of certain races of men is owing to the diſcharge of the elaſtic fluid abovementioned, an operation I ſuppoſe owing to the power of the Sun in the countries they inhabit. I have ſought for an opportunity of trying this conjecture by its proper teſt, but in ſome ſituations it is not eaſy to procure a Negro, who will ſubmit to become the ſubject of experiment; and I have not ſucceeded to my wiſh. Something however I have attempted; and I relate it here that others more favourably ſituated may confirm or correct my opinion.

I put a lock of Negro's hair recently cut from his head, into a bottle full of oxygenated marine acid air, a ſubſtance which is well known to natural philoſophers to have the power of diſcharging a great variety of colours. The hair in a ſhort time became white with ſcarce any tinge of yellow.

At another time I prevailed upon a Negro to introduce his arm into a large jar full of the ſame elaſtic fluid, at the bottom of which there lay a ſmall quantity of water impregnated with it. The back of the fore finger and part of the ſecond lay in this water. Knowing the prodigious efficacy of this air, I deſired the man to withdraw his arm as ſoon as he ſhould be ſenſible of any pain. The ſkin was broken in ſeveral parts; and in about 12 minutes he complained that the ſore places ſmarted. The arm being now withdrawn and examined, there appeared over its whole ſurface ſomething of a greyiſh caſt, like the colour of ointment of quickſilver. But the two fingers, where they had lain in the water, were remarkably changed. They had acquired very much the colour of white lead paint, but they did not retain this colour for many days. Some inflammation enſued, but it ſoon abated. It was however ſufficiently evident that this would not have been the

caſe,

cafe, if the fkin had been entire before the experiment. The man did not choofe to rifque any more pain.

If fuch experiments were to be repeated, it might be prudent to give the impregnated water a full trial, before the air is employed, which fhould be done with the utmoft caution; and perhaps the water, from its action on the epidermis, will be more efficacious.

Thefe experiments proceed upon this fuppofition; if the Negro's complexion be black, becaufe the *rete mucofum* has too fmall a proportion of oxygen, it may be whitened by combining with it an additional quantity of this principle. It remains to be decided 1. how far this is true, and 2. whether if the fkin can be bleached, whether it will retain the oxygen or continue in the habit of difcharging it. It is not fo obvious to make the converfe of this experiment, but a careful confideration of the refources of chemiftry would, I believe, furnifh the European with the means of turning his fkin black; and we know that by keeping the light excluded, it may be rendered more delicately white. It is poffible that a profecution of thefe ideas might found the *cofmetic art* upon fixed principles. In the mean time I may recall an analogous fact to the reader's memory. There are fome animals, born black or dark-coloured, which afterwards, when they come to be covered with clofe hair, acquire a fkin of the moft delicate whitenefs. Could an infant Negro be prevented from changing colour by any application to his fkin?—May the extricated oxygen contribute to the fætor of the Negro's perfpiration, as phofphorus, fulphur and other acidifiable bafes acquire a ftrong fmell from a certain proportion of oxygen?

By applying oxygenated muriatic gas to his fkin, without much care or precaution, the European will find it to be turned yellower. This feems to be the effect of oxygen applied to moft animal fubftances in large quantities; nitrous acid produces a deep yellow upon the fkin and blood; (when mixed with blood, the tafte alfo becomes intenfely bitter; a fact which perhaps may afford fome illuftration of the biliary fecretion.) It is no wonder that it fhould produce difcolouration either in excefs or defect.

CAMPER, who united tafte and philofophy to nice anatomical fkill, obferves that the great painters have delineated black European men inftead of negroes. Several anatomifts on the continent, have beftowed much attention on the differences between the African and European. Dr. Soemmerring, one of the moft accurate, has diffected a great number of Negroes; his obfervations have been extended even to the Fetus, and both in the hard and foft parts, he has pointed out many important

diftinctions.

diftinctions. The angle, formed by a line drawn from the projection of the frontal bone above the nofe, to the moft projecting part of the upper jaw-bone, (Bonn expreffes it, *a fronte ad nafi mucronem, aut ad commiffuram labiorum,*) and another line, drawn through the meatus auditorius externus to the bottom of the nofe, *(fundus nafi)* is much lefs in the Negro Skeleton, viz as 70° to 80°;—in the antient ideal heads it is 100°; and this is Campers teft of beauty. The heads muft be viewed in profile. There is lefs room for brain, not only on account of the truncation of the forehead, but alfo of the hind-head, and the compreffion of the fides, the parietal bones being fmaller.—In the Afiatic, the cavity of the Cranium is ftill larger than in the European.—In and about the Eye, there are feveral little circumftances, in which the negro approaches more to the ape-kind: the choroid coat is covered with a darker and tougher mucus; the retina is firmer; the nofe flatt, even in the fetus; yet the noftrils being broader, receive more odoriferous particles, and as they come almoft over the mouth, this conformation indicates a clofer connection between the organs of fmell and tafte. The ethmoidal bone is fo conftructed, as to afford the olfactory nerve greater expanfion.—The bony compages, deftined for the maftication of food, as well as for the protection of the organs of fenfe, is more firmly put together, and each feparate bone is ftronger. The temporal mufcle makes a deeper impreffion on the fide of the fkull, and reaches higher up towards the fagittal future. " The orbits," fays Bonn, fpeaking of a negrefs, " lie in the fame vertical plane, *quod fimiis proprium*." The well known protuberance of the jaws, is the moft obvious, and perhaps the moft effential character of the negro's head. Dr. Soemmerring was ftruck in three inftances, by the ftrength of the lower jaw-bone, and by the fmallnefs of its angle, which is occafioned by the breadth of that part, to which the prodigioufly powerful maffeter mufcle is attached; " *fere ut in fimus*" fays he: yet he adds, that in a negro fkeleton belonging to Dr. Blumenbach, the angle is 130°, i. e. about the ufual fize.—The nerves of fmell and fight, as alfo the fifth pair, feemed to Dr. S. exceedingly large.——Man he moreover obferves, has not (as fo often fuppofed) the largeft brain, in proportion to the weight of his body; birds, apes, and fome fmall quadrupeds much exceed him; but in proportion to the fize of his nerves, he has the largeft brain. He adds, that probably, only a fmall portion of brain is neceffary to maintain the animal functions; confequently, where there is moft excefs above this neceffary quantity, there will be moft intellectual power; thus fuppofe the optic nerve in any animal to contain fix hundred fibres, and in another animal of half the fize, three hundred equal fibres; let

M

the

the brain in the larger, weigh feven, and in the fmaller five ounces; now reckon one ounce of brain to every hundred fibres, and the fmaller animal will have twice as much fuperfluous brain to retain and combine ideas. The anatomift obferves, that in this point of view, the negro's brain is fmaller than that of the European. None of the negro fubjects exhibited the fmalleft veftige of the Os intermaxillare, a bone occurring in all animals, man excepted.

I extract thefe particulars, folely for the fake of the curious and the fpeculative. I hope it is unneceffary to proteft againft all attempts to wreft them to a palliation of that criminal commerce, which is as difgraceful to a nation, as robbery and murder to an individual. At the time I am writing, it has been fentenced to abolition by one branch of our legiflature; and another will not furely refufe to an innocent and oppreffed people, that juftice, which it is accuftomed fo impartially to adminifter in the laft refort, to the natives of Great Britain. At all events, to whatever differences of conformation, moral and phyfical caufes may have given rife, they can never repeal the great law of fympathy, nor confer upon us the right of doing, that which we fhould be unwilling under the fame circumftances to fuffer.

<h2 style="text-align:center">VI.</h2>

On the poffeffions of the Britifh in Hindoftan.

THE very phrafe " OUR FOREIGN POSSESSIONS IN THE EAST," by appealing at once to our pride and avarice, prejudges a queftion which involves too great an intereft both at home and abroad to be flightly difmiffed. The influence of falfe analogy, which has mifled mankind in every age and on every fubject, is alfo clearly difcernible here. We are ready to imagine that Bahar, Bengal, and Oriffa are to the Nation at large, what an eftate, fituated in a diftant county, is to an individual. It would be much nearer the truth, if we were to confider ourfelves as mere nominal proprietors of an eftate, which yields no rent, but of which we are obliged to keep the buildings and fences in repair.

Thefe poffeffions undoubtedly enable minifters to enlift more recruits under the banners of Corruption; and they have enriched a number of private adventurers. Thefe queftionable advantages are all that feem to belong to the favourable fide of

the

the account. If we reckon up the difadvantages, we fhall find them to prefs fenfibly upon this country; already we fhall fee reafon to apprehend a perpetually increafing burden; and upon India we fhall find them weighing with a load that bears
down prefent happinefs and virtue; and together with indigenous oppreffion, totally crufhing thofe powers, which his Maker implanted in Man, in order that he
might gradually exalt himfelf towards the perfection of Superior Natures.

L The commerce and manufactures of this country are not benefited by thefe
poffeffions. This truth has been fo amply demonftrated in general by the modern
political philofophers, particularly by Dr. Adam Smith, that it muft very foon be
placed among thofe univerfally received maxims, which feem the felf-evident dictates
of common fenfe. The cafe of America, one would think, muft inftantly decide
the queftion even for thofe, who are unwilling or unable to enter into fpeculations
of any extent. From that country our traders derive their full profits: nor is there
any demand upon the nation for keeping poffeffion. Indirectly foreign territory
is injurious to our trade, and will every day render us lefs able to ftand the competi-
tion of other manufacturing countries: and it is capable of creating rivals in
branches of trade, where none exifted before.

II. For perpetual wars muft increafe our taxes perpetually.—Since the Englifh
have gained any confiderable footing in India, there has been no fecure or permanent peace. Thofe who are beft acquainted with the country give us plainly to
underftand that there is no profpect of any fuch peace in India. Mr. Haftings, in
his laft fpeech before the Lords, infifts upon the neceffity of keeping an army in
readinefs to march at a moment's warning; and he adds that the refources in India
can never be equal to the expences of a war in India. Captain Broome, whofe
opinion feems to be entitled to the higheft refpect, confirms this encouraging profpect. Speaking of the extreme diftrefs of the Calcutta Prefidency during the laft
war, he fays, " I fee but one way of avoiding fimilar cafes of difficulty, nor am I
" quite certain whether it would anfwer or not. It is that of permitting the go-
" vernment of India to draw bills on the Company in time of war and real diftrefs,
" for the payment of which the BRITISH PARLIAMENT fhould become fecurity."
(Broome's *Elucidations of the charges againft Mr. Haftings*). That is, I fuppofe, upon
a fair interpretation, that the Prefidency fhould have unlimited credit upon the
purfe of every man in Britain.

If we confider the character of the furrounding people, a fucceffion of wars with
little interruption will appear inevitable. Polifhed ftates are ready enough to take
advantage

advantage of the diſtreſs of their neighbours. But the *levis Barbarorum fides* ought to have become long ſince proverbial. And the Mahrattas neither want cunning to perceive an advantage, nor pretexts to begin a quarrel. Perhaps however we ſhall go on exterminating nation after nation, till our victorious banners wave over the banks of the Indus, or, if neceſſary, even of the Euphrates. Another comfortable proſpect for politicians and for men of humanity.

Poſſibly however, before we get quite ſo far, Fortune will ſerve us as ſhe has ſerved all the commercial Conquerors, our predeceſſors. And with Portugal, Spain and Holland, we may exhibit another melancholy example of that imbecillity, to which diſtant poſſeſſions and diſtant wars muſt inevitably reduce every ſtate. Poſſibly in that forlorn condition, ſome future maritime power may conſpire with ſome future military Deſpot, to dragoon us into proper ſubmiſſion to our ſuperiors.

That the Nation muſt pay the future and even the preſent expences of war in India, is I fear, too melancholy a truth. Nor is it probable, as was once hoped in the diſpatches, that plunder enough will be found to pay the enormous charges of the campaigns. The opinion of Engliſh invincibility which Capt. Broome tells us, " is every day growing weaker," and conſidering our efforts, allies, and the tedious progreſs of the war, final ſucceſs cannot again impreſs the natives with any great awe of us.

III. " But we ſhall derive a revenue from India ſoon." Doubtleſs, if a total revolution ſhould take place in human nature, and if the ſame cauſes ſhould ceaſe to produce the ſame effects, together with a few other equally probable contingencies. If we are not ſhocked at the horrible injuſtice of ſuch a project, we ought to be warned by the fate of the ſame prediction reſpecting America. I am ſure our paſt experience of the Prophet ought not to inſpire us with any confidence in the oracles he delivers.

IV. The late general interpoſitions in behalf of the Africans, beſpeak the diffuſion of a liberality, to which the people of every country have too long been ſtrangers, and afford an example of diſintereſted virtue, that has hitherto been wanting to the annals of mankind. No ſuch idea ever originated in a conclave or a cabinet; and it is entirely to be aſcribed to the humane principles of the modern political philoſophers, diffuſed partly by their writings, and partly by converſation(f). And one

---

(f) Dr. Smith's treatiſe on the Wealth of Nations will alone convince any man, that it is not leſs the intereſt than the duty of every people to do as they would be done by.

may augur, that if ever a LAS CASAS or a CLARKSON shall arise in behalf of the Hindoos, his appeal to humanity will not be in vain: Though whatever might be the eloquence or the zeal of their advocate, he would never be able to discover and delineate all the evils that necessarily flow from subjection to so distant a state.

The deplorable condition of the human species has never more forcibly struck me than in reading various publications relative to the state of a considerable portion of Hindostan for some years past. The sufferings of Africans may have been as acute, but such numbers have not suffered. I wish I could excite the reader to reflect upon this subject by a few of the passages which have left this general impression upon my mind; and I wish still more earnestly that some person of wider information would offer to the public a summary view of all the facts, of which we have obtained possession, and apply to them the plain principles of morality.

The spirit of the Government is exactly stated in this passage. " Here I cannot " help commenting a little upon one striking absurdity which exists in the Bengal " government. The Company require two millions sterling annually to be drawn " from Bengal by way of investment, or to be sent to Madrass and Bombay: Yet " after all these exactions, they expect the country to flourish and wonder it does " not. Neither the Directors nor the Managers seem to consider the difference that " must unavoidably take place in the state of two countries governed on diametri- " cally opposite principles. This kingdom is governed with an eye to its own " prosperity and advantage. But Bengal is governed with an eye not to its own " prosperity, but to the prosperity and advantage of Great Britain. It is in my " opinion extremely absurd to expect the same effect from two causes so totally " different." (Broome, p. 120). Let the intelligent or humane reader reflect upon this passage; he cannot have a more prolific text. I find in the same writer a distinct account of a transaction where injustice and oppression alternately put on the appearance of ridicule and horror. The company's servants interfered to pre- vent Sujah Dowla from enforcing a demand of five lacks of rupees upon the cele- brated Cheyt Sing, his vassal. The interference of the company, observes the author, was unconstitutional, not in one instance only, but in every stage of the business. It is, he adds, reconcileable only to the *jus fortioris:* Their policy he proceeds, was not to serve Cheyt Sing, but to weaken the power of Sujah Dowla … ……their idea was *divide et impera;* and in effecting their views, they considered not the legality of the means. One is surprized to find him representing this con- duct as justifiable, because " perfectly reconcileable to what they thought their duty, " namely,

" namely to advance the interest of their masters." I hope the reader's morality will resist this doctrine of advancing a Master's interest *per fas et nefas*. But this is a trifle in comparison with the remainder of the Oude transaction. The supreme council demanded, soon after the accession of Asoph Ul Dowla, the cession of Benares and Gazipour: upon what grounds Mr. Broome could never learn. Mr. Hastings remonstrated against the measure as a flagrant violation of a late treaty. The Council persisted and obtained the cession. The Court of Directors thought it a violation of the treaty too, but as they obtained 23 lacks of rupees additional revenue, they did not express much dissatisfaction; nor did they order restitution to be made. " Their demand," says Mr. B. to whose narrative I scrupulously adhere, " is not justifiable by the law of nations, nor by the laws of the empire, " nor by the plea of necessity.........Asoph Ul Dowla was robbed of provinces " worth 400,000l. a year." This is not all; the Company, as Superior, make the demand which they had prevented the Superior immediately proceeding from enforcing. They demand from Cheyt Sing an increase of rent or tribute, for the nature of his tenure is doubted. Disputes, bloodshed and the expulsion of Cheyt Sing are the consequences. And having thus disposed of Cheyt Sing, Asoph Ul Dowla has gradually been reduced to dependance, for an army of the Company's is maintained at his expence in his own dominions. Mr. Broome, p. 134. compares the encroachments on A. U. Dowla's authority to the partition of Poland; and if it be condemned as immoral, he thinks the accusation will be against human nature, " as there is not, nor ever was, nor probably ever will be that state which " would not take advantage of a weaker one" (p. 135). Would it not be much more accurate to say there is not, nor ever was, nor probably ever will be a Despot or a small governing Junto, who would not sacrifice the people of their own, or any other country to their avarice and ambition? I believe however this holds more universally of Juntos, as far as their power extends, than even of Despots, as the Triumvirs were more bloody than the Emperors. Mr. B.'s observation then is either not generally true of states where the will of the people has a preponderating influence, or it will not long be so.

Acts of gross injustice, involving provinces and states, do not affect the mind so sensibly as the recital of the sufferings of individuals; yet they must generally involve the ruin and distress of multitudes.—Of the famines that so frequently sweep thousands and tens of thousands from the face of India, I shall only say, that if not occasioned, it should seem they must be commonly aggravated by the European

Strangers;

Strangers; fince they will confume much, and produce nothing. If Mr. Haftings, by his exertions and forefight, once alleviated this calamity, his merit is probably as fingular, as his talents.

Thofe who referve their fympathy for the great, will read, with deep concern, Mr. B.'s account (p. 161. 162.) of the harfh treatment experienced by a lady of the higheft rank in Bengal. She was not fufpected or accufed of any crime or mif-conduct. An inquifitor was fent to extort from her, an account of the fum fhe had expended in entertaining Mr. Haftings. "She hinted that there were courts of "Juftice at Calcutta to redrefs the injured, upon which the agent propofes to the "board that the confinement of her fervants fhould be in the Nabob's name, in "order that he might avoid perfonal refponfibility for the oppreffions he was "about to commit." One may imagine the tendernefs with which the bulk of the people are treated, where authority to imprifon the fervants, and "abfolute "power over the perfon of a lady of the firft rank," is delegated (as it would appear) contrary to the laws.

Mr. Bolts and Colonel Dow concur in their reprefentation of the treatment the manufacturers frequently experience. "The affent of the poor weaver (Bolts "India Affairs, 1772. p. 193. 194.) is in general not deemed neceffary (to the "bargain), for the Gomaftahs (or agents), when employed in the Company's in-"veftment, frequently make them fign what they pleafe, and upon the weavers "refufing to take the money offered, it has been known that they have had it tied "in their girdles, and they have been fent away with a flogging........A number "of thefe weavers are alfo generally regiftered in the books of the Company's "Gomaftahs, and not permitted to work for any others, being transferred from "one to another like fo many flaves, and fubject to the roguery of every fucceed-"ing Gomaftah.... .... The winders of raw filk have been treated alfo "with fuch injuftice, that inftances have been known of their cutting off their "thumbs, to prevent their being forced to wind filk." Verelft, the very unfatis-factory anfwerer of Bolts, admits (View. p. 38. 1772.) the exiftence of the oppref-fion, but charges Bolts with endeavouring to "prevent any effectual protection from being given to the natives." The protection on both fides, is fuch as con-tending wolves afford to the lamb. Mr. Dow (p. 113.) afferts that the fruit of their labours is taken from the filk-winders, fpinners and weavers at an arbitrary price.

I will

I will only add to thefe examples of horrors, from which I have fo often turned away in forrow and difguft, that Colonel Fullarton (g) draws a moft melancholy picture of the famine, and of the cruel method of collecting rents in the Carnatic; and I have been affured by perfons acquainted with the manufacturing parts of the country that this oppreffion in detail has continued. And it cannot well be otherwife. It is in human nature that the infolence of office fhould be moft feverely exerted by thofe, whofe difcretionary power is confined to a few.

A people under a foreign commercial tyranny, can leaft of all people, attain an erect and independant mind, that bafe of all excellence. It is no more poffible for them to advance in fcience or in virtue, than for the brutes who draw our ploughs and carts, to become rational. Some individuals will indeed be lefs feverely flogged and more plentifully fed than others. And in this will confift the whole difference. It is ftrange, but it is true, that men are but juft beginning to feel that the natives of other countries and climates are human beings.

Nor, when we fee that Tyburn and Newgate have not repreffed crimes here, can we hope that any dread of diftant and uncertain punifhment, will deter the wholefale or retail oppreffors of the Hindoos.—It has been difputed whether the European or Mahometan governments were moft favourable to the natives. If the queftion be concerning fome Emperors, fuch as Acbar, or men much inferior to Acbar, there can exift no doubt: and it affords but little edification to difpute whether the Indians have fuffered as feverely under Europeans as under the worft of their domeftic tyrants.

Poffibly if we had a fair and full defcription of the adminiftration of Tippoo Saib, it might appear that Afia will have to lament in him the lofs of a great benefactor. We cannot found any fafe judgment upon the facts reported by fear and hatred, and circulated for no other purpofe than to render him odious. By fuch a felection, a Peter or a Frederic might be made to rank with the Neros or Caracallas. The imperfect relations we fometimes receive of his inftitutions, give us a glimpfe

---

(g) It would be rendering a great fervice to humanity, to extricate the more recent facts relating to the treatment of the natives from the mafs of parliamentary inveftigations. Rhetorical exaggeration has done much mifchief during thefe difcuffions. For it is a very common fallacy with the defenders of abufes to take advantage from fome flight inaccuracy, or the too high flights of an Orator's imagination. If they can make it probable that oppreffion has not been exactly carried on, according to the ftatement, they infer that the whole account is falfe.

of a Defpot, who being deeply fenfible of the infeparable connection between his own intereft and the improvement of his people, has the will and the ability to introduce unknown arts among them, and to animate them to induftry. In the prefent moft unequal conteft, there has appeared none of that difaffection, which when fuch an opportunity was afforded, would be fhewn by an oppreffed people againft one of thofe inhuman monfters, that have at times been the fcourge of the Eaft and of the Weft. In the eftimation of a Defpot it is true, the life of a man is of fmall eftimation; and if this obfervation is more particularly true of Afiatic Defpots, it is only becaufe their power is more uncontrolled. Let us therefore join in execrating defpotifm in all its forms and degrees, whether mercantile or monarchical, but if we would be at all equitable, we cannot wonder, that an Afiatic defpot fhould as little refpect the lives and perfons of Europeans as of Afiatics: though doubtlefs every ftate ought to protect its citizens againft his capricious or deliberate cruelties.

Both as a Man and as an Englifhman one may therefore lament the extenfion of territory in India as an heavy calamity. The infane fhouts of a deluded populace foon ceafe, and the burlefque gravity of a gazette is fpeedily forgotten. Nor do I fee what the fplendid victories of an Alboquerque or an Olive leave behind them but weaknefs or ruin to their refpective countries. And indeed as to bold enterprizes and fuccefsful ftratagems in war, every nation can equally boaft of them: and none therefore derive from them any credit to itfelf. Should the promifed revenue ever arrive, and that without wringing out the blood of the natives, the example of Spain affords no favourable omen of its effects. The melancholy decline of Portugal, and Holland as well as of Spain, has at leaft been principally effected by the drain of foreign poffeffions, and the debilitating efforts occafioned by diftant wars; muft not England, if fhe treads in their footfteps, arrive at the fame fate? Or fhall we vainly flatter ourfelves that Commerce can be fo doatingly fond of one particular country, that no outrage fhall expel her? She and her attendant Profperity have never yet fixed their refidence long in the tents of the rapacious and the bloodthirfty. There would have been an inexcufable blemifh in the conftitution of the things of this world, if they could long have remained in fuch a fituation.

Nor let the caufe of a few individuals, in place and out of place, be confounded with the caufe of the people at large. However contrary to the general welfare, *they* will continue their efforts to retain and extend foreign poffeffions, until avarice and ambition fhall ceafe to be infatiable paffions.

N

It

It would be curious to investigate, how far the sudden fortunes imported from India into England differ, and how far they agree, in their operation with that sudden influx of wealth which ruined Spain. One visible effect is the great increase of menial servants, which is not only pernicious as it augments the unproductive proportion of the community; but inasmuch as the conversation, idleness, and gaudy finery tends powerfully to corrupt the lower orders of citizens. And however rapidly their numbers have increased, the increase of their profligacy has I am afraid, been much more rapid.

OWEN of CARRON:

A

POEM.

BY DR. LANGHORNE.

(PRICE THREE SHILLINGS.)

THIS POEM

IS INSCRIBED TO A

L A D Y,

WHOSE ELEGANT TASTE,

WHOSE AMIABLE SENSIBILITY,

AND

WHOSE UNAFFECTED FRIENDSHIP,

HAVE LONG CONTRIBUTED TO THE

PLEASURE AND HAPPINESS

OF

THE AUTHOR.

ADVERTISEMENT.

THERE is fomething Romantic in the Story of the following POEM; but the Author has his Reafons for believing that there is fomething, likewife, authentic. On the fimple Circumftances of the ancient Narrative, from which He firft borrowed his Idea, thofe Reafons are principally founded, and they are fupported by others, with which, in a Work of this Kind, to trouble his Readers would be fuperfluous.

OWEN OF CARRON.

ON CARRON's Side the Primrose pale,
    Why does it wear a purple Hue?
Ye Maidens fair of MARLIVALE,
    Why stream your Eyes with Pity's Dew?

'Tis all with gentle OWEN's Blood
    That purple grows the Primrose pale;
That Pity pours the tender Flood
    From each fair Eye in MARLIVALE.

B

The

(10)

The Evening Star fate in his Eye,
  The Sun his golden Treffes gave,
The North's pure Morn her Orient Dye,
  To Him who refts in yonder Grave!

Beneath no high, hiftoric Stone,
  Tho' nobly born, is OWEN laid,
Stretch'd on the green Wood's Lap alone,
  He fleeps beneath the waving Shade.

There many a flowery Race hath fprung,
  And fled before the Mountain Gale,
Since firft his fimple Dirge ye fung;
  Ye Maidens fair of MARLIVALE!

Yet ftill, when MAY with fragrant Feet
  Hath wander'd o'er your Meads of Gold,
That Dirge I hear fo fimply fweet
  Far echoed from each Evening Fold.

'Twas

II.

'Twas in the Pride of WILLIAM's * Day,
　　When SCOTLAND's Honours flourished ſtill,
That MORAY's Earl, with mighty Sway,
　　Bore Rule o'er many a Highland Hill.

And far for Him their fruitful Store
　　The fairer Plains of CARRON ſpread;
In Fortune rich, in Offspring poor,
　　An only Daughter crown'd his Bed.

Oh! write not poor—the Wealth that flows
　　In Waves of Gold round INDIA's Throne,
All in her ſhining Breaſt that glows,
　　To ELLEN's † Charms, were Earth and Stone.

* William the Lyon, King of Scotland.

+ The Lady Ellen, only Daughter of John Earl of Moray, betrothed to the Earl of Nithiſdale, and afterwards to the Earl Barnard, was eſteemed one of the fineſt Women in Europe, inſomuch that ſhe had ſeveral Suitors and Admirers from Foreign Courts.

B 2

For

For Her the Youth of SCOTLAND figh'd,
   The FRENCHMAN gay, the SPANIARD grave,
And fmoother ITALY applied,
   And many an ENGLISH Baron brave.

In Vain by foreign Arts affail'd,
   No foreign Loves her Breaft beguile,
And ENGLAND's honeft Valour fail'd,
   Paid with a cold, but courteous Smile.

" Ah! Woe to Thee, young NITHISDALE,
   " That o'er thy Cheek thofe Rofes ftray'd,
" Thy Breath, the Violet of the Vale,
   " Thy Voice, the Mufic of the Shade!

" Ah! Woe to Thee, that ELLEN's Love
   " Alone to thy foft Tale would yield!
" For foon thofe gentle Arms fhall prove
   " The Conflict of a ruder Field."

4

'Twas

'Twas thus a wayward Sifter fpoke,
   And caft a rueful Glance behind,
As from her dimwood Glen fhe broke,
   And mounted on the moaning Wind.

She fpoke and vanifh'd,—more unmov'd
   Than MORAY's Rocks, when Storms inveft,
The valiant Youth by ELLEN lov'd
   With aught that Fear, or Fate fuggeft.

For Love, methinks, hath Power to raife
   The Soul beyond a vulgar State;
Th' unconquer'd Banners He difplays
   Control our Fears, and fix our Fate.

III.

III.

'Twas when, on Summer's softest Eve,
    Of Clouds that wander'd West away,
Twilight with gentle Hand did weave
    Her Fairy Robe of Night and Day.

When all the Mountain Gales were still,
    And the Wave slept against the Shore,
And the Sun, sunk beneath the Hill,
    Left his last Smile on LEMMERMORE *.

Led by those waking Dreams of Thought
    That warm the young unpractis'd Breast,
Her wonted Bower sweet ELLEN sought,
    And CARRON murmur'd near, and footh'd her into Rest.

* A Chain of Mountains running through Scotland from East to West.

IV.

IV.

There is fome kind and courtly Sprite
   That o'er the Realm of Fancy reigns,
Throws Sunfhine on the Mafk of Night,
   And fmiles at Slumber's powerlefs Chains;

'Tis told, and I believe the Tale,
   At this foft Hour that Sprite was there,
And fpread with fairer Flowers the Vale,
   And fill'd with fweeter founds the Air.

A Bower he fram'd (for He could frame
   What long might weary mortal Wight:
Swift as the Lightning's rapid Flame
   Darts on the unfufpecting Sight).

Such

Such Bower he fram'd with magic Hand,
   As well that Wizard Bard hath wove,
In Scenes where fair ARMIDA's Wand
   Wav'd all the Witcheries of Love.

Yet was it wrought in fimple Shew;
   Nor Indian Mines nor Orient Shores
Had lent their Glories here to glow,
   Or yielded here their fhining Stores.

All round a Poplar's trembling Arms
   The Wild Rofe wound her Damafk Flower;
The Woodbine lent her fpicy Charms,
   That loves to weave the Lover's Bower.

The Afh, that courts the Mountain-Air,
   In all her painted Blooms array'd,
The Wilding's Bloffom blufhing fair,
   Combin'd to form the flowery Shade.

With

With Thyme that loves the brown Hill's Breast,
  The Cowslip's sweet, reclining Head,
The Violet of sky-woven Vest,
  Was all the Fairy Ground bespread.

But, who is He, whose Locks so fair
  Adown his manly Shoulders flow?
Beside Him lies the Hunter's Spear,
  Beside Him sleeps the Warrior's Bow.

He bends to ELLEN—(gentle Sprite,
  Thy sweet seductive Arts forbear)
He courts her Arms with fond Delight,
  And instant vanishes in Air.

C

V.

V.

Haſt Thou not found at early Dawn
    Some ſoft Ideas melt away,
If o'er ſweet Vale, or flowery Lawn,
    The Sprite of Dreams hath bid Thee ſtray?

Haſt Thou not ſome fair Object ſeen,
    And, when the fleeting Form was paſt,
Still on Thy Memory found its Mien,
    And felt the fond Idea laſt?

Thou haſt—and oft the pictur'd View,
    Seen in ſome Viſion counted vain,
Haſt ſtruck thy wondering Eye anew,
    And brought the long-loſt Dream again.

With

With Warrior-Bow, with Hunter's Spear,
   With Locks adown his Shoulder ſpread,
Young Nithisdale is ranging near—
   He's ranging near yon mountain's head.

Scarce had one pale Moon paſs'd away,
   And fill'd her ſilver Urn again,
When in the devious Chace to ſtray,
   Afar from all his Woodland Train,

To Carron's Banks his Fate conſign'd,
   And, all to ſhun the fervid Hour,
He ſought ſome friendly Shade to find,
   And found the viſionary Bower.

Led

VI.

Led by the golden Star of Love,
  Sweet ELLEN took her wonted Way,
And in the deep-defending Grove
  Sought Refuge from the fervid Day—

Oh!—Who is He whofe Ringlets fair
  Diforder'd o'er his green Veft flow,
Reclin'd in Reft—whofe funny Hair
  Half hides the fair Cheek's ardent Glow?

'Tis He, that Sprite's illufive Gueft,
  (Ah Me! that Sprites can Fate control!)
That lives ftill imag'd on her Breaft,
  That lives ftill pictur'd in her Soul.

As

As when some gentle Spirit fled
   From Earth to breathe Elysian Air,
And, in the Train whom we call dead,
   Perceives its long-lov'd Partner there;

Soft, sudden Pleasure rushes o'er,
   Resistless, o'er it's airy Frame,
To find it's future Fate restore
   The Object of it's former Flame.

So ELLEN stood—less Power to move
   Had He, who, bound in Slumber's Chain,
Seem'd haply, o'er his Hills to rove,
   And wind his Woodland Chace again.

She stood, but trembled—mingled Fear,
   And fond Delight and melting Love
Seiz'd all her Soul; she came not near,
   She came not near that fated Grove.

4

She

She strives to fly—from Wizzard's Wand
  As well might powerless Captive fly—
The new cropt Flower falls from her Hand—
  Ah! fall not with that Flower to die!

VII.

She strives to fly—from Wizzard's Wand
  As well might powerless Captive fly—
The new cropt Flower falls from her Hand—

VII.

Haſt Thou not ſeen ſome azure Gleam
   Smile in the Morning's Orient Eye,
And ſkirt the reddening Cloud's ſoft Beam
   What Time the Sun was haſting nigh?

Thou haſt—and Thou canſt fancy well
   As any Muſe that meets thine Ear,
The Soul-ſet Eye of NITHISDALE,
   When wak'd, it fix'd on ELLEN near.

Silent they gaz'd—that Silence broke;
   ' Hail Goddeſs of theſe Groves, He cry'd,
' O let me wear thy gentle Yoke!
   ' O let me in thy Service bide!

4' For

' For Thee I'll climb the Mountain steep,
   ' Unwearied chase the destin'd Prey,
' For Thee I'll pierce the Wild-wood deep,
   ' And part the Sprays that vex thy Way,'

For Thee —' O Stranger, cease,' she said,
   And swift away, like DAPHNE, flew,
But DAPHNE's Flight was not delay'd
   By aught that to her Bosom grew.

'Twas ATALANTA's golden Fruit,
   The fond IDEA that confin'd
Fair ELLEN's Steps, and bless'd his Suit,
   Who was not far, not far behind.

VIII.

VIII.

O Love! within thofe golden Vales,
  Thofe genial Airs where Thou waft born,
Where Nature, liftening thy foft Tales,
  Leans on the rofy Breaft of Morn.

Where the fweet SMILES, the GRACES dwell,
  And tender Sighs the Heart emove,
In filent Eloquence to tell
  Thy Tale, O Soul-fubduing Love!

Ah! wherefore fhould grim Rage be nigh,
  And dark Diftruft, with changeful Face,
And Jealoufy's reverted Eye
  Be near thy fair, thy favour'd Place?

D

IX.

(26)

IX.

Earl Barnard was of high Degree,
 And Lord of many a Lowland Hind,
And long for Ellen Love had He,
 Had Love, but not of gentle Kind.

From Moray's Halls her abfent Hour
 He watch'd with all a Mifer's Care;
The wide Domain, the princely Dower
 Made Ellen more than Ellen fair.

Ah Wretch! to think the liberal Soul
 May thus with fair Affection part!
Though Lothian's Vales thy Sway controul,
 Know, Lothian is not worth one Heart.

Studious

Studious he marks her abfent Hour,
    And, winding far where Carron flows,
Sudden he fees the fated Bower,
    And red Rage on his dark Brow glows.

For who is He?—'Tis Nithisdale!
    And that fair Form with Arm reclin'd
On His?—'Tis Ellen of the Vale,
    'Tis She (O Powers of Vengeance!) kind.

Should He that Vengeance fwift purfue?
    No—that would all his Hopes deftroy;
Moray would vanifh from his view,
    And rob Him of a Mifer's Joy.

Unfeen

Unseen to MORAY's Halls He hies—
  He calls his Slaves, his Ruffian Band,
‘ And, Hafte to yonder Groves,’ He cries,
  ‘ And ambufh'd lie by CARRON's Strand.’

‘ What Time ye mark from Bower or Glen
  ‘ A gentle Lady take her Way,
‘ To Diftance due, and far from Ken,
  ‘ Allow her Length of Time to ftray.

‘ Then ranfack ftraight that Range of Groves.—
  ‘ With Hunter's Spear, and Veft of Green,
‘ If chance, a rofy Stripling roves,—
  ‘ Ye well can aim your Arrows keen.’

And now the Ruffian Slaves are nigh,
  And ELLEN takes her homeward Way:
Though ftay'd by many a tender Sigh,
  She can no longer, longer ftay.

Penfive,

Penſive, againſt yon Poplar pale
   The Lover leans his gentle Heart,
Revolving many a tender Tale,
   And wondering ſtill how They could part.

Three Arrow's pierc'd the deſert Air,
   Ere yet his tender Dreams depart;
And One ſtruck deep his Forehead fair,
   And One went through his gentle Heart.

Love's waking Dream is loſt in Sleep—
   He lies beneath yon Poplar pale;
Ah! could we marvel Ye ſhould weep;
   Ye Maidens fair of MARLIVALE!

X.

When all the Mountain Gales were ſtill,
   And the Wave ſlept againſt the Shore,
And the Sun, ſunk b'eneath the Hill,
   Left his laſt Smile on LEMMERMORE;

Sweet ELLEN takes her wonted Way
   Along the fairy-featur'd Vale:
Bright o'er his Wave does CARRON play,
   And ſoon ſhe'll meet her NITHISDALE.

She'll meet Him ſoon—for at her Sight
   Swift as the Mountain Deer He ſped;
The Evening Shades will ſink in Night,—
   Where art Thou, loitering Lover, fled?

O! She

O ! She will chide thy trifling Stay,
   E'en now the foft Reproach She frames :
‘ Can Lovers brook fuch long Delay ?
   ‘ Lovers that boaft of ardent Flames !’

He comes not—weary with the Chace,
   Soft Slumber o'er his Eyelids throws
Her Veil—we 'll fteal one dear Embrace,
   We 'll gently fteal on his Repofe.

This is the Bower—we 'll foftly tread—
   He fleeps beneath yon Poplar pale—
Lover, if e'er thy Heart has bled,
   Thy Heart will far forego my Tale !

XI.

XI.

ELLEN is not in princely Bower,
    She's not in MORAY's fplendid Train;
Their Miftrefs dear, at Midnight Hour,
    Her weeping Maidens feek in vain.

Her Pillow fwells not deep with Down;
    For Her no Balms their Sweets exhale:
Her Limbs are on the pale Turf thrown,
    Prefs'd by Her lovely Cheek as pale.

On that fair Cheek, that flowing Hair,
    The Broom it's yellow Leaf hath fhed,
And the chill Mountain's early Air
    Blows wildly o'er her beauteous Head.

As

As the foft Star of Orient Day,
   When Clouds involve his rofy Light,
Darts thro' the Gloom a tranfient Ray,
   And leaves the World once more to Night ;

Returning Life illumes her Eye,
   And flow it's languid Orb unfolds—
What are thofe bloody Arrows nigh ?
   Sure, bloody Arrows fhe beholds !

What was that Form fo ghaftly pale,
   That low beneath the Poplar lay ?—
' Twas fome poor Youth—' Ah NITHISDALE !'
   She faid, and filent funk away.

F.

XII.

The Morn is on the Mountains fpread,
   The Wood-lark trills his liquid Strain—
Can Morn's fweet Mufic roufe the dead?
   Give the fet Eye it's Soul again?

A Shepherd of that gentler Mind
   Which Nature not profufely yields,
Seeks in thefe lonely Shades to find
   Some Wanderer from his little Fields.

Aghaft He ftands—and fimple Fear
   O'er all his paly Vifage glides—
   Ah Me! what means this Mifery here?
   " What Fate this Lady fair betides?"

He

He bears Her to his friendly Home,
   When Life, He finds, has but retir'd ;—
With Hafte He frames the Lover's Tomb,
   For his is quite, is quite expir'd !

XIII.

XII.

'' O hide Me in thy humble Bower'
   Returning late to Life she said;
' I 'll bind thy Crook with many a Flower;
   ' With many a rofy Wreath thy Head.

' Good Shepherd, hafte to yonder Grove,
   ' And, if my Love afleep is laid,
' Oh! wake Him not; but foftly move
   ' Some Pillow to that gentle Head.

' Sure, Thou wil't know Him, Shepherd Swain,
   ' Thou know'ft the Sun rife o'er the Sea—
' But Oh! no Lamb in all thy Train
   ' Was e'er fo mild, fo mild as He.'

' His

‘ His Head is on the Wood-Mofs laid;
  ‘ I did not wake his Slumber deep—
‘ Sweet fings the Redbreaft o'er the Shade—
  ‘ Why, gentle Lady, would you weep?’

As Flowers that fade in burning Day,
  At Evening find the Dew-drop dear,
But fiercer feel the Noon-tide Ray,
  When foften'd by the nightly Tear;

Returning in the flowing Tear,
  This lovely Flower, more fweet than They,
Found her fair Soul, and, wandering near,
  The Stranger, Reafon, crofs'd her Way.

Found her fair Soul—Ah! fo to find
  Was but more dreadful Grief to know :
Ah! fure, the Privilege of Mind
  Can not be worth the Wifh of Woe.

XIV.

XIV.

On Melancholy's filent Urn
  A fofter Shade of Sorrow falls,
But ELLEN can no more return,
  No more return to MORAY's Halls.

Beneath the low and lonely Shade
  The flow-confuming Hour fhe'll weep,
Till Nature feeks her laft-left Aid,
  In the fad, fombrous Arms of Sleep.

' Thefe Jewels, all unmeet for Me,
  ' Shalt Thou.' fhe faid, ' good Shepherd, take;
' Thefe Gems will purchafe Gold for Thee,
  ' And thefe be Thine for ELLEN's Sake.

' So

‘ So fail Thou not, at Eve and Morn,

  ‘ The Rofemary’s pale Bough to bring—

‘ Thou know’ft where I was found forlorn—

  ‘ Where Thou haft heard the Redbreaft fing.

‘ Heedful I’ll tend thy Flocks the while,

  ‘ Or aid thy Shepherdefs’s Care,

‘ For I will fhare her humble Toil,

  ‘ And I her friendly Roof will fhare.’

XV.

XV.

And now two longsome Years are past
  In Luxury of lonely Pain—
The lovely Mourner, found at last,
  To Moray's Halls is borne again.

Yet has She left one Object dear,
  That wears Love's funny Eye of joy—
Is Nithisdale reviving here?
  Or is it but a Shepherd's Boy?

By Carron's Side, a Shepherd's Boy,
  He binds his Vale-flowers with the Reed;
He wears Love's funny Eye of Joy,
  And Birth he little seems to heed.

XVI.

XVI.

But ah ! no more his Infant Sleep
  Clofes beneath a Mother's Smile,
Who, only when it clos'd, would weep,
  And yield to tender Woe the While.

No more, with fond Attention dear,
  She feeks th' unfpoken Wifh to find;
No more fhall She, with Pleafure's Tear,
  See the Soul waxing into Mind.

XVII.

XVII.

Does Nature bear a Tyrant's Breaft?
   Is She the Friend of ftern Controul?
Wears She the Defpot's purple Veft?
   Or fetters She the free-born Soul?

Where, worft of Tyrants, is thy Claim
   In Chains thy Childrens' Breafts to bind?
Gav'ft Thou the Promethéan Flame?
   The incommunicable Mind?

Thy Offspring are great NATURE's,—free,
   And of her fair Dominion Heirs;
Each Privilege She gives to Thee;
   Know, that each Privilege is theirs.

They

They have thy Feature, wear thine Eye,
   Perhaps fome Feelings of thy Heart;
And wilt Thou their lov'd Hearts deny
   To act their fair, their proper Part?

XVIII.

XVIII.

The Lord of LOTHIAN's fertile Vale,
   Ill-fated ELLEN, claims thy Hand;
Thou know'ft not that thy NITHISDALE
   Was low laid by his Ruffian-Band.

And MORAY, with unfather'd Eyes,
   Fix'd on fair LOTHIAN's fertile Dale,
Attends his human Sacrifice,
   Without the Grecian Painter's Veil.

O married Love! thy Bard fhall own,
   Where two congenial Souls unite,
Thy golden Chain inlaid with Down,
   Thy Lamp with Heaven's own Splendor bright.

But

But if no radiant Star of Love,
   O Hymen! fmile on thy fair Rite,
Thy Chain a wretched Weight fhall prove,
   Thy Lamp a fad fepulchral Light.

XIX.

XIX.

And now has Time's flow wandering Wing
  Borne many a Year unmark'd with Speed—
Where is the Boy by CARRON's Spring,
  Who bound his Vale-Flowers with the Reed?

Ah Me! thofe Flowers He binds no more;
  No EARLY Charm returns again;
The Parent, Nature keeps in Store
  Her beft Joys for her little Train.

No longer heed the Sun-beam bright
  That plays on CARRON's Breaft He can,
Reafon has lent HER quivering Light,
  And fhewn the checquer'd Field of Man.

XIX.

XX.

As the firft human Heir of Earth
    With penfive Eye Himfelf furvey'd,
And, all unconfcious of his Birth,
    Sate thoughtful oft in EDEN's Shade;

In penfive Thought fo OWEN ftray'd
    Wild CARRON's lonely Woods among,
And once, within their greeneft Glade,
    He fondly fram'd this fimple Song:

XXI.

XXI.

Why is this Crook adorn'd with Gold?
Why am I Tales of Ladies told?
Why does no Labour Me employ,
If I am but a Shepherd's Boy?

A filken Vest like mine fo green
In Shepherd's Hut I have not feen—
Why fhould I in fuch Vefture joy,
If I am but a Shepherd's Boy?

I know it is no Shepherd's Art
His WRITTEN Meaning to impart—
They teach Me, fure, an idle Toy,
If I am but a Shepherd's Boy.

This

This Bracelet bright that binds my Arm—
It could not come from Shepherd's Farm ;
It only would that Arm annoy,
If I were but a Shepherd's Boy.

And, O Thou filent Picture fair,
That lov'ft to fmile upon me there,
O fay, and fill my Heart with Joy,
That I am NOT a Shepherd's Boy.

G

XXII.

Ah lovely Youth! thy tender Lay
   May not thy gentle Life prolong :
See'ft Thou yon Nightingale a Prey ?
   The fierce Hawk hovering o'er his Song ?

His little Heart is large with Love :
   He fweetly hails his Evening Star,
And Fate's more pointed Arrows move,
   Infidious, from his Eye afar.

XXIII.

XXIII.

The Shepherdefs, whofe kindly Care
   Had watch'd o'er Owen's Infant Breath,
Muft now THEIR filent Manfions fhare,
   Whom Time leads calmly down to Death.

' O tell me, Parent if Thou art,
   ' What is this lovely Picture dear?
' Why wounds its mournful Eye my Heart,
   ' Why flows from mine th' unbidden Tear?

' Ah! Youth! to leave Thee loth am I,
   ' Tho' I be not thy Parent dear;
' And would'ft Thou wifh, or ere I die,
   ' The Story of thy Birth to hear?

G 2

But,

‘ But it will make Thee much bewail,
  ‘ And it will make thy fair Eye fwell—’
She faid, and told the woefome Tale,
  As footh as Sheperdefs might tell.

XXIV.

XXIV.

The Heart, that Sorrow doom'd to ſhare,
   Has worn the frequent Seal of Woe,
Its ſad Impreſſions learns to bear,
   And finds full oft, its Ruin ſlow.

But when that Seal is firſt impreſt,
   When the young Heart its Pain ſhall try,
From the ſoft, yielding, trembling Breaſt,
   Oft ſeems the ſtartled Soul to fly.

Yet fled not OWEN's—wild Amaze
   In Paleneſs cloath'd, and lifted Hands,
And Horror's Dread, unmeaning gaze,
   Mark the poor Statue, as it ſtands.

The

The fimple Guardian of his Life
    Look'd wiftful for the Tear to glide;
But, when fhe faw his tearlefs Strife,
    Silent, fhe lent him one,—and died.

XXV.

XXV.

' No, I am not a Shepherd's Boy,'
   Awaking from his Dream, He faid,
' Ah where is now the promis'd Joy
    ' Of this ?—for ever, ever fled !

' O Picture dear !—for her lov'd Sake
    ' How fonly could my Heart bewail !
' My friendly Shepherdefs, O wake,
    ' And tell me more of this fad Tale.

' O tell me more of this fad Tale—
    ' No ; Thou enjoy thy gentle Sleep !
' And I will go to LOTHIAN's Vale,
    ' And more than all her Waters weep.'

XXVI.

XXVI.

Owen to Lothian's Vale is fled—
    Earl Barnard's lofty Towers appear—
' O! art Thou there,' the full Heart said,
    ' O! art Thou there, my Parent dear?'

Yes, She is there: From idle State
    Oft has she stole her Hour to weep;
Think how she ' by thy Cradle sate,'
    And how she ' fondly saw Thee sleep *.'

Now tries his trembling Hand to frame
    Full many a tender Line of Love;
And still He blots the Parent's Name,
    For that, He fears, might fatal prove.

---

* See the ancient Scottish Ballad, called Gill Morrice.

XXVII.

XXVII.

O'er a fair Fountain's smiling Side
    Reclin'd a dim Tower, clad with Mofs,
Where every Bird was wont to bide,
    That languifh'd for it's Partner's Lofs.

This Scene He chofe, this Scene affign'd
    A Parent's firft Embrace to wait,
And many a foft Fear fill'd his Mind,
    Anxious for his fond Letter's Fate.

The Hand that bore thofe Lines of Love,
    The well-informing Bracelet bore—
Ah! may They not unprofperous prove!
    Ah! fafely pafs yon dangerous Door!

H

XXVIII.

XXVIII.

‘ She comes not ;—can She then delay ?
　‘ Cried the fair Youth, and dropt a Tear—
　Whatever filial Love could fay,
　‘ To Her I faid, and call'd her dear.

‘ She comes—Oh ! No—encircled round
　‘ Tis fome rude Chief with many a Spear.
‘ My haplefs Tale that Earl has found—
　‘ Ah Me ! my Heart !—for Her I fear.’

His tender Tale that Earl had read,
　Or ere it reach'd his Lady's Eye,
His dark Brow wears a Cloud of red,
　In Rage He deems a Rival nigh.

XXIX.

XXIX.

'Tis o'er—thofe Locks that wav'd in Gold,
   That wav'd adown thofe Cheeks fo fair,
Wreath'd in the gloomy Tyrant's Hold,
   Hang from the fever'd Head in Air,

That ftreaming Head He joys to bear
   In horrid Guife to LOTHIAN's Halls;
Bids his grim Ruffians place it there,
   Erect upon the frowning Walls.

The fatal Tokens forth He drew—
   ' Know'ft thou thefe—ELLEN of the Vale ?'
The pictur'd Bracelet foon She knew,
   And foon her lovely Cheek grew pale.—

The

'The trembling Victim, straight He led,
    Ere yet Her Soul's first Fear was o'er:
He pointed to the ghastly Head—
    She saw—and sunk, to rise no more.

T H E   E N D

SLAVERY,

A POEM.

BY

HANNAH MORE.

O great defign!
Ye Sons of Mercy! O complete your work;
Wrench from Oppreffion's hand the iron rod,
And bid the cruel feel the pains they give.
THOMPSON'S LIBERTY.

LONDON:

PRINTED FOR T. CADELL, IN THE STRAND.

M.DCC.LXXXVIII.

S L A V E R Y,

A P O E M.

IF Heaven has into being deign'd to call
    Thy light, O LIBERTY! to ſhine on all;
Bright intellectual Sun! why does thy ray
To earth diſtribute only partial day?
Since no reſiſting cauſe from ſpirit flows   5
Thy penetrating eſſence to oppoſe;
No obſtacles by Nature's hand impreſt,
Thy ſubtle and ethereal beams arreſt;
Nor motion's laws can ſpeed thy active courſe,
Nor ſtrong repulſion's pow'rs obſtruct thy force;   10
Since there is no convexity in MIND,
Why are thy genial beams to parts confin'd?

B

While

While the chill North with thy bright ray is bleſt,

Why ſhould fell darkneſs half the South inveſt?

Was it decreed, fair Freedom! at thy birth, 15

'That thou ſhou'd'ſt ne'er irradiate *all* the earth?

While Britain baſks in thy full blaze of light,

Why lies ſad Afric quench'd in total night?

   Thee only, ſober Goddeſs! I atteſt,

In ſmiles chaſtis'd, and decent graces dreſt. 20

Not that unlicens'd monſter of the crowd,

Whoſe roar terrific burſts in peals ſo loud,

Deaf'ning the ear of Peace: fierce Faction's tool;

Of raſh Sedition born, and mad Miſrule;

Whoſe ſtubborn mouth, rejecting Reaſon's rein, 25

No ſtrength can govern, and no ſkill reſtrain;

Whoſe magic cries the frantic vulgar draw

To ſpurn at Order, and to outrage Law;

3

To

To tread on grave Authority and Pow'r,

And fhake the work of ages in an hour: 30

Convuls'd her voice, and peftilent her breath,

She raves of mercy, while fhe deals out death :

Each blaft is fate ; fhe darts from either hand

Red conflagration o'er th' aftonifh'd land ;

Clamouring for peace, fhe rends the air with noife,   35

And to reform a part, the whole deftroys.

O, plaintive Southerne ! * whofe impaffion'd ftrain

So oft has wak'd my languid Mufe in vain !

Now, when congenial themes her cares engage,

She burns to emulate thy glowing page ;   40

Her failing efforts mock her fond defires,

She fhares thy feelings, not partakes thy fires.

Strange pow'r of fong ! the ftrain that warms the heart

Seems the fame infpiration to impart ;

Touch'd

* Author of the Tragedy of Oronoko.

Touch'd by the kindling energy alone,   45

We think the flame which melts us is our own;

Deceiv'd, for genius we miſtake delight,

Charm'd as we read, we fancy we can write.

   Tho' not to me, ſweet Bard, thy pow'rs belong,

Fair Truth, a hallow'd guide! inſpires my ſong.   50

Here Art wou'd weave her gayeſt flow'rs in vain,

For Truth the bright invention wou'd diſdain.

For no fictitious ills theſe numbers flow,

But living anguiſh, and ſubſtantial woe;

No individual griefs my boſom melt,   55

For millions feel what Oronoko felt:

Fir'd by no ſingle wrongs, the countleſs hoſt

I mourn, by rapine dragg'd from Afric's coaſt.

   Periſh th' illiberal thought which wou'd debaſe

The native genius of the ſable race!   60

Periſh

Perish the proud philosophy, which sought

To rob them of the pow'rs of equal thought!

Does then th' immortal principle within

Change with the casual colour of a skin?

Does matter govern spirit? or is mind   65

Degraded by the form to which 'tis join'd?

   No: they have heads to think, and hearts to feel,

And souls to act, with firm, tho' erring zeal;

For they have keen affections, kind desires,

Love strong as death, and active patriot fires;   70

All the rude energy, the fervid flame,

Of high-soul'd passion, and ingenuous shame:

Strong, but luxuriant virtues boldly shoot

From the wild vigour of a savage root.

   Nor weak their sense of honour's proud control,   75

For pride is virtue in a Pagan soul;

C

A sense

A fenfe of worth, a confcience of defert,

A high, unbroken haughtinefs of heart;

That felf-fame ftuff which erft proud empires fway'd,

Of which the conquerors of the world were made.   80

Capricious fate of man! that very pride

In Afric fcourg'd, in Rome was deify'd.

   No Mufe, O * Qua-fhi! fhall thy deeds relate,

No ftatue fnatch thee from oblivious fate!

For

   * It is a point of honour among negroes of a high fpirit to die rather than to fuffer their gloffy fkin to bear the mark of the whip.   Qua-fhi had fomehow offended his mafter, a young planter with whom he had been bred up in the endearing intimacy of a play-fellow.   His fervices had been faithful; his attachment affectionate.   The mafter refolved to punifh him, and purfued him for that purpofe.   In trying to efcape Qua-fhi ftumbled and fell; the mafter fell upon him: they wreftled long with doubtful victory; at length Qua-fhi got uppermoft, and, being firmly feated on his mafter's breaft, he fecured his legs with one hand, and with the other drew a fharp knife; then faid, " Mafter, I " have been bred up with you from a child; I have loved you as myfelf: in

" return,

For thou waft born where never gentle Mufe   85

On Valour's grave the flow'rs of Genius ftrews;

And thou waft born where no recording page

Plucks the fair deed from Time's devouring rage.

Had Fortune plac'd thee on fome happier coaft,

Where polifh'd fouls heroic virtue boaft,   90

To thee, who fought'ft a voluntary grave,

Th' uninjur'd honours of thy name to fave,

Whofe generous arm thy barbarous Mafter fpar'd,

Altars had fmok'd, and temples had been rear'd.

   Whene'er to Afric's fhores I turn my eyes,   95

Horrors of deepeft, deadlieft guilt arife;

"return, you have condemned me to a punifhment of which I muft ever have
"borne the marks: thus only I can avoid them;" fo faying, he drew the knife
with all his ftrength acrofs his own throat, and fell down dead, without a groan,
on his mafter's body.

Ramfay's Effay on the Treatment of African Slaves.

I fee,

I see, by more than Fancy's mirror shewn,

The burning village, and the blazing town:

See the dire victim torn from social life,

The shrieking babe, the agonizing wife!   100

She, wretch forlorn! is dragg'd by hostile hands,

To distant tyrants sold, in distant lands!

Transmitted miseries, and successive chains,

The sole sad heritage her child obtains!

Ev'n this last wretched boon their foes deny,   105

To weep together, or together die.

By felon hands, by one relentless stroke,

See the fond links of feeling Nature broke!

The fibres twisting round a parent's heart,

Torn from their grasp, and bleeding as they part.   110

   Hold, murderers, hold! nor aggravate distress;

Respect the passions you yourselves possess;

7

Ev'n

Ev'n you, of ruffian heart, and ruthlefs hand,

Love your own offspring, love your native land.

Ah! leave them holy Freedom's cheering fmile,   115

The heav'n-taught fondnefs for the parent foil;

Revere affections mingled with our frame,

In every nature, every clime the fame;

In all, thefe feelings equal fway maintain;

In all the love of Home and Freedom reign: 120

And Tempe's vale, and parch'd Angola's fand,

One equal fondnefs of their fons command.

Th' unconquer'd Savage laughs at pain and toil,

Bafking in Freedom's beams which gild his native foil.

Does thirft of empire, does defire of fame,   125

(For thefe are fpecious crimes) our rage inflame?

No: fordid luft of gold their fate controls,

The bafeft appetite of bafeft fouls;

DGold,

Gold, Letter gain'd, by what their ripening fky,

Their fertile fields, their arts * and mines fupply.   130

   What wrongs, what injuries does Oppreffion plead

To fmooth the horror of th' unnatural deed?

What ftrange offence, what aggravated fin?

They ftand convicted—of a darker fkin!

Barbarians, hold! th' opprobrious commerce fpare,   135

Refpect *his* facred image which they bear:

Tho' dark and favage, ignorant and blind,

They claim the common privilege of kind;

Let Malice ftrip them of each other plea,

They ftill are men, and men fhou'd ftill be free.   140

Infulted Reafon loaths th' inverted trade—

Dire change! the agent is the purchafe made!

   Befides many valuable productions of the foil, cloths and carpets of exquifite manufacture are brought from the coaft of Guinea.

Perplex'd,

Perplex'd, the baffled Mufe involves the tale ;

Nature confounded, well may language fail !

The outrag'd Goddefs with abhorrent eyes   145

Sees MAN the traffic, SOULS the merchandize !

　　Plead not, in reafon's palpable abufe,

Their fenfe of * feeling callous and obtufe :

From heads to hearts lies Nature's plain appeal,

Tho' few can reafon, all mankind can feel.   150

Tho' wit may boaft a livelier dread of fhame,

A loftier fenfe of wrong refinement claim ;

Tho' polifh'd manners may frefh wants invent,

And nice diftinctions nicer fouls torment ;

Tho' thefe on finer fpirits heavier fall,   155

Yet natural evils are the fame to all.

---

* Nothing is more frequent than this cruel and ftupid argument, that they do not *feel* the miferies inflicted on them as Europeans would do.

7

Tho'

Tho' wounds there are which reafon's force may heal,

There needs no logic fure to make us feel.

The nerve, howe'er untutor'd, can fuftain

A fharp, unutterable fenfe of pain;   160

As exquifitely fafhion'd in a flave,

As where unequal fate a fceptre gave.

Senfe is as keen where Congo's fons prefide,

As where proud Tiber rolls his claffic tide.

Rhetoric or verfe may point the feeling line,   165

They do not whet fenfation, but define.

Did ever flave lefs feel the galling chain,

When Zeno prov'd there was no ill in pain?

Their miferies philofophic quirks deride,

Slaves groan in pangs difown'd by Stoic pride.   170

    When the fierce Sun darts vertical his beams,

 And thirft and hunger mix their wild extremes;

                                              When

When the sharp iron * wounds his inmoft foul,

And his ftrain'd eyes in burning anguifh roll;

Will the parch'd negro find, ere he expire,   175

No pain in hunger, and no heat in fire?

  For him, when fate his tortur'd frame deftroys,

What hope of prefent fame, or future joys?

For *this*, have heroes fhorten'd nature's date;

For *that*, have martyrs gladly met their fate;   180

But him, forlorn, no hero's pride fuftains,

No martyr's blifsful vifions footh his pains;

Sullen, he mingles with his kindred duft,

For he has learn'd to dread the Chriftian's truft;

---

* This is not faid figuratively. The writer of thefe lines has feen a complete fet of chains, fitted to every feparate limb of thefe unhappy, innocent men, together with inftruments for wrenching open the jaws, contrived with fuch ingenious cruelty as would fhock the humanity of an inquifitor.

E   To

To him what mercy can that Pow'r difplay,   185

Whofe fervants murder, and whofe fons betray?

Savage! thy venial error I deplore,

They are *not* Chriftians who infeft thy fhore.

    O thou fad fpirit, whofe prepofterous yoke

The great deliverer Death, at length, has broke!   190

Releas'd from mifery, and efcap'd from care,

Go, meet that mercy man deny'd thee here.

In thy dark home, fure refuge of th' opprefs'd,

The wicked vex not, and the weary reft.

And, if fome notions, vague and undefin'd,   195

Of future terrors have affail'd thy mind;

If fuch thy mafters have prefum'd to teach,

As terrors only they are prone to preach;

(For fhou'd they paint eternal Mercy's reign,

Where were th' oppreffor's rod, the captive's chain?)   200

If,

If, then, thy troubled foul has learn'd to dread

The dark unknown thy trembling footfteps tread ;

On HIM, who made thee what thou art, depend ;

HE, who withholds the means, accepts the end.

Not *thine* the reckoning dire of LIGHT abus'd,   205

KNOWLEDGE difgrac'd, and LIBERTY mifus'd ;

On *thee* no awful judge incens'd fhall fit

For parts perverted, and difhonour'd wit.

Where ignorance will be found the fureft plea,

How many learn'd and wife fhall envy *thee* !   210

    And thou, WHITE SAVAGE ! whether luft of gold,

Or luft of conqueft, rule thee uncontrol'd !

Hero, or robber !—by whatever name

Thou plead thy impious claim to wealth or fame ;

Whether inferior mifchiefs be thy boaft,   215

A petty tyrant rifling Gambia's coaft :

Or

Or bolder carnage track thy crimson way,

Kings difpoffefs'd, and Provinces thy prey;

Panting to tame wide earth's remoteft bound;

All Cortez murder'd, all Columbus found;   220

O'er plunder'd realms to reign, detefted Lord,

Make millions wretched, and thyfelf abhorr'd;——

In Reafon's eye, in Wifdom's fair account,

Your fum of glory boafts a like amount;

The means may differ, but the end's the fame;   225

Conqueft is pillage with a nobler name.

Who makes the fum of human bleffings lefs,

Or finks the flock of general happinefs,

No folid fame fhall grace, no true renown,

His life fhall blazon, or his memory crown.   230

   Had thofe advent'rous fpirits who explore

Thro' ocean's tracklefs waftes, the far-fought fhore;

Whether of wealth infatiate, or of pow'r,

Conquerors who wafte, or ruffians who devour :

Had thefe poffefs'd, O Cook! thy gentle mind,   235

Thy love of arts, thy love of humankind ;

Had thefe purfued thy mild and liberal plan,

Discoverers had not been a curfe to man !

Then, blefs'd Philanthropy! thy focial hands

Had link'd diffever'd worlds in brothers bands;   240

Carelefs, if colour, or if clime divide ;

Then, lov'd, and loving, man had liv'd, and died.

  The pureft wreaths which hang on glory's fhrine,

For empires founded, peaceful Penn ! are thine ;

No blood-ftain'd laurels crown'd thy virtuous toil,   245

No flaughter'd natives drench'd thy fair-earn'd foil.

Still thy meek fpirit in thy * flock furvives,

Confiftent ftill, *their* doctrines rule their lives ;

F

Thy

* The Quakers have emancipated all their flaves throughout America.

Thy followers only have effac'd the shame

Inscrib'd by SLAVERY on the Christian name.   250

   Shall Britain, where the soul of Freedom reigns,

Forge chains for others she herself disdains?

Forbid it, Heaven! O let the nations know

The liberty she loves she will bestow;

Not to herself the glorious gift confin'd,   255

She spreads the blessing wide as humankind;

And, scorning narrow views of time and place,

Bids all be free in earth's extended space.

   What page of human annals can record

A deed so bright as human rights restor'd?   260

O may that god-like deed, that shining page,

Redeem our fame, and consecrate our age!

   And see, the cherub Mercy from above,

Descending softly, quits the sphere of love!

On

On feeling hearts fhe fheds celeftial dew,   265

And breathes her fpirit o'er th' enlighten'd few ;

From foul to foul the fpreading influence fteals,

Till every breaft the foft contagion feels.

She bears, exulting, to the burning fhore

The lovelieft office Angel ever bore ;   270

To vindicate the pow'r in Heaven ador'd,

To ftill the clank of chains, and fheathe the fword ;

To cheer the mourner, and with foothing hands

From burfting hearts unbind th' Oppreffor's bands ;

To raife the luftre of the Chriftian name,   275

And clear the fouleft blot that dims its fame.

   As the mild Spirit hovers o'er the coaft,

A frefher hue the wither'd landfcapes boaft ;

Her healing fmiles the ruin'd fcenes repair,

And blafted Nature wears a joyous air.   280

She

She spreads her blest commission from above,

Stamp'd with the sacred characters of love;

She tears the banner stain'd with blood and tears,

And, LIBERTY! thy shining standard rears!

As the bright ensign's glory she displays,   285

See pale OPPRESSION faints beneath the blaze!

The giant dies! no more his frown appals,

The chain untouch'd, drops off; the fetter falls.

Astonish'd echo tells the vocal shore,

Oppression's fall'n, and Slavery is no more!   290

The dusky myriads crowd the sultry plain,

And hail that mercy long invok'd in vain.

Victorious Pow'r! she bursts their two-fold bands,

And FAITH and FREEDOM spring from Mercy's hands.

F I N I S.

THE

FABLES OF FLORA.

BY DR. LANGHORNE.

———SYLVAS, SALTUSQUE SEQUAMUR
INTACTOS——— ———   VIRG.

THE FIFTH EDITION.

LONDON:
PRINTED FOR T. BECKET, IN THE STRAND.
MDCCLXXIII.

THE COUNTESS

O F

HERTFORD.

M A D A M,

THERE is a tax upon the Name of the Countefs of HERTFORD, an heredi-tary obligation to patronize the Mufes; and in times like thefe, when their influence, I will not fay their reputation, is on the de-cline, they can by no means difpenfe with fo effential a privilege. I intreat you, Madam, to take the following poems under your pro-

B   tection.

DEDICATION.

tection.　They were written with an unaffected wish to promote the love of Nature
and the interests of Humanity.　On the
credit of such motives I lay them at your
feet, and beg to be esteemed,

MADAM,

Your most devoted and

most obedient servant,

JOHN LANGHORNE.

*I*N the following Poems, the plan of Fable is somewhat enlarged, and the province so far extended, that the original NARRATIVE and MORAL may be accompanied with imagery, description, and sentiment. The scenery is formed in a department of Nature adapted to the genius and disposition of POETRY; where she finds new objects, interests, and connexions, to exercise her fancy and her powers. If the execution, therefore, be unsuccessful, it is not the fault of the Plan, but of the Poet.

FABLES of FLORA.

FABLE I.

The SUNFLOWER and the IVY.

A S duteous to the place of prayer,
   Within the convent's lonely walls,
The holy sisters still repair,
   What time the rosy morning calls:

So fair, each morn, so full of grace,
   Within their little garden reared,
The flower of PHOEBUS turned her face
   To meet the POWER she loved and feared.

C   And

And where, along the rifing fky,
  Her God in brighter glory burned,
Still there her fond obfervant eye,
  And there her golden breaft fhe turned.

When calling from their weary height
  On weftern waves his beams to reft,
Still there fhe fought the parting fight,
  And there fhe turned her golden breaft.

But foon as night's invidious fhade
  Afar his lovely looks had borne,
With folded leaves and drooping head,
  Full fore fhe grieved, as one forlorn.

Such duty in a flower difplayed
  The holy fifters fmiled to fee,
Forgave the pagan rites it paid,
  And loved its fond idolatry.

But

But painful ſtill, though meant for kind,
  The praiſe that falls on Envy's ear !
O'er the dim window's arch entwined,
  The cankered I v y chanced to hear.

And " See, ſhe cried, that ſpecious flower,
  " Whoſe flattering boſom courts the ſun,
" The pageant of a gilded hour,
  " The convent's ſimple hearts hath won !

" Obſequious meanneſs ! ever prone
  " To watch the patron's turning eye ;
" No will, no motion of its own !
  " 'Tis this they love, for this they ſigh :

" Go, ſplendid ſycophant ! no more
  " Diſplay thy ſoft ſeductive arts !
" The flattering clime of courts explore,
  " Nor ſpoil the convent's ſimple hearts.

" To

" To me their praife more juftly due,

   " Of longer bloom, and happier grace !

" Whom changing months unaltered view,

   " And find them in my fond embrace."

" How well," the modeft flower replied,

   " Can ENVY's wrefted eye elude

" The obvious bounds that ftill divide

   " Foul FLATTERY from fair GRATITUDE.

" My duteous praife each hour I pay,

   " For few the hours that I muft live ;

" And give to him my little day,

   " Whofe grace another day may give.

" When low this golden form fhall fall

   " And fpread with duft its parent plain ;

" That duft fhall hear his genial call,

   " And rife, to glory rife again.

2

" To

" To thee, my gracious power, to thee
  " My love, my heart, my life are due !
" Thy goodnefs gave that life to be ;
  " Thy goodnefs fhall that life renew.

" Ah me ! one moment from thy fight
  " That thus my truant-eye fhould ftray !
" The God of glory fets in night ;
  " His faithlefs flower has loft a day."

Sore grieved the flower, and drooped her head ;
  And fudden tears her breaft bedewed :
Confenting tears the fifters fhed,
  And, wrapt in holy wonder, viewed.

With joy, with pious pride elate,
  " Behold," the aged abbefs cries,
" An emblem of that happier fate
  " Which heaven to all but us denies.

D" Our

" Our hearts no fears but duteous fears,

   " No charm but duty's charm can move ;

" We fhed no tears but holy tears

   " Of tender penitence and love.

" See there the envious world pourtrayed

   " In that dark look, that creeping pace !

" No flower can bear the Ivy's fhade ;

   " No tree fupport its cold embrace.

" The oak that rears it from the ground,

   " And bears its tendrils to the fkies,

" Feels at his heart the rankling wound,

   " And in its poifonous arms he dies."

Her moral thus the matron read,

   Studious to teach her children dear,

And they by love, or duty led,

   With pleafure heard, or feemed to hear.

Yet

Yet one lefs duteous, not lefs fair,
 (In convents ftill the tale is known)
The fable heard with filent care,
 But found a moral of her own.

The flower that fmiled along the day,
 And drooped in tears at evening's fall ;
Too well fhe found her life difplay,
 Too well her fatal lot recall.

The treacherous Ivy's gloomy fhade,
 That murdered what it moft embraced,
Too well that cruel fcene conveyed
 Which all her fairer hopes effaced.

Her heart with filent horror fhook ;
 With fighs fhe fought her lonely cell :
To the dim light fhe caft *one* look ;
 And bade *once more* the world *farewell*.

FABLE   II.

The Evening Primrose.

THERE are that love the shades of life,
　　And shun the splendid walks of fame ;
There are that hold it rueful strife
　　To risque Ambition's losing game :

That far from Envy's lurid eye
　　The fairest fruits of Genius rear,
Content to see them bloom and die
　　In Friendship's small but kindly sphere.

Than vainer flowers tho' sweeter far,
　　The Evening Primrose shuns the day ;
Blooms only to the western star,
　　And loves its solitary ray,

In

In Eden's vale an aged hind,
   At the dim twilight's clofing hour,
On his time-fmoothed ftaff reclined,
   With wonder viewed the opening flower.

" Ill-fated flower, at eve to blow,"
   In pity's fimple thought he cries,
" Thy bofom muft not feel the glow
   " Of fplendid funs, or fmiling fkies.

" Nor thee, the vagrants of the field,
   " The hamlet's little train behold ;
" Their eyes to fweet oppreffion yield,
   " When thine the falling fhades unfold.

" Nor thee the hafty fhepherd heeds,
   " When love has filled his heart with cares,
" For flowers he rifles all the meads,
   " For waking flowers—but thine forbears.

E   " Ah !

" Ah ! wafte no more that beauteous bloom
    " On night's chill fhade, that fragrant breath,
" Let fmiling funs thofe gems illume !
    " Fair flower, to live unfeen is death."

Soft as the voice of vernal gales
    That o'er the bending meadow blow,
Or ftreams that fteal thro' even vales,
    And murmur that they move fo flow :

Deep in her unfrequented bower,
    Sweet Philomela poured her ftrain ;
The bird of eve approved her flower,
    And anfwered thus the anxious fwain.

Live unfeen !
By moonlight fhades, in valleys green,
    Lovely flower, we'll live unfeen.

Of

Of our pleafures deem not lightly,
Laughing day may look more fprightly,
    But I love the modeft mien,
    Still I love the modeft mien
Of gentle evening fair, and her ftar-trained queen.

    Didft thou, fhepherd, never find,
    Pleafure is of penfive kind ?
    Has thy cottage never known
    That fhe loves to live alone ?
    Doft thou not at evening hour
    Feel fome foft and fecret power,
    Gliding o'er thy yielding mind,
    Leave fweet ferenity behind ;
    While all difarmed, the cares of day
    Steal thro' the falling gloom away ?
    Love to think thy lot was laid
    In this undiftinguifhed fhade.

Far

Far from the world's infectious view,
Thy little virtues safely blew.
Go, and in day's more dangerous hour,
Guard thy emblematic flower.

FABLE III.

The LAUREL and the REED.

THE * Reed that once the shepherd blew
   On old CEPHISUS' hallowed side,
   To SYLLA's cruel bow applied,
Its inoffensive master slew.

Stay, bloody soldier, stay thy hand,
   Nor take the shepherd's gentle breath :
Thy rage let innocence withstand ;
   Let music soothe the thirst of death.

He frowned—He bade the arrow fly—
   The arrow smote the tuneful swain ;
No more its tone his lip shall try,
   Nor wake its vocal soul again.

* The reeds on the banks of the Cephisus, of which the shepherds
made their pipes, Sylla's soldiers used for arrows.

F   CEPHISUS,

CEPHISUS, from his fedgy urn,
  With woe beheld the fanguine deed :
He mourned, and, as they heard him mourn,
  Affenting fighed each trembling Reed.

" Fair offspring of my waves, he cried ;
  " That bind my brows, my banks adorn,
" Pride of the plains, the rivers' pride,
  " For mufic, peace, and beauty born !

" Ah ! what, unheedful have we done ?
  " What dæmons here in death delight ?
" What fiends that curfe the focial fun ?
  " What furies of infernal night ?

" See, fee my peaceful fhepherds bleed !
  " Each heart in harmony that vyed,
" Smote by its own melodious Reed,
  " Lies cold, along my blufhing fide.

" Back

" Back to your urn, my waters, fly ;
    " Or find in earth fome fecret way ;
" For horrour dims yon confcious fky,
    " And hell has iffued into day."

Thro' DELPHI's holy depth of fhade
    The fympathetic forrows ran ;
While in his dim and mournful glade
    The genius of her groves began.

" In vain CEPHISUS fighs to fave
    " The fwain that loves his watry mead,
" And weeps to fee his reddening wave,
    " And mourns for his perverted Reed :

" In vain my violated groves
    " Muft I with equal grief bewail,
" While defolation fternly roves,
    " And bids the fanguine hand affail.

                                    " God

" God of the genial ſtream, behold
    " My laurel ſhades of leaves ſo bare!
" Thoſe leaves no poet's brows enfold,
    " Nor bind APOLLO's golden hair.

" Like thy fair offspring, miſapplied,
    " Far other purpoſe they ſupply ;
" The murderer's burning cheek to hide,
    " And on his frownful temples die.

" Yet deem not theſe of PLUTO's race,
    " Whom wounded NATURE ſues in vain ;
" Pluto diſclaims the dire diſgrace,
    " And cries, indignant, " They are men."

FABLE IV.

The GARDEN ROSE and the WILD ROSE.

AS DEE, whofe current, free from ftain,
    Glides fair o'er MERIONETH's plain,
By mountains forced his way to fteer
Along the lake of PIMBLE MERE,
Darts fwiftly thro' the ftagnant mafs,
His waters trembling as they pafs,
And leads his lucid waves below,
Unmixed, unfullied as they flow—
So clear thro' life's tumultuous tide,
So free could THOUGHT and FANCY glide;
Could HOPE as fprightly hold her courfe,
As firft fhe left her native fource,
Unfought in her romantic cell
The keeper of her dreams might dwell.

G

But

But ah ! they will not, will not laft—
When life's firft fairy ftage is paft,
The glowing hand of HOPE is cold ;
And FANCY lives not to be old.
Darker, and darker all before ;
We turn the former profpect o'er ;
And find in MEMORY's faithful eye
Our little ftock of pleafures lie.

    Come, then ; thy kind recefles ope !
Fair keeper of the dreams of HOPE !
Come with thy vifionary train ;
And bring my morning fcenes again !

    To ENON's wild and filent fhade,
Where oft my lonely youth was laid ;
What time the *woodland* GENIUS came,
And touched me with his holy flame.—

                                    Or,

Or, where the hermit, BELA, leads
Her waves thro' solitary meads;
And only feeds the desart-flower,
Where once she soothed my slumbering hour:
Or roused by STAINMORE's wintry sky,
She wearies echo with her cry;
And oft, what storms her bosom tear,
Her deeply-wounded banks declare.——

Where EDEN's fairer waters flow,
By MILTON's bower, or OSTY's brow,
Or BROCKLEY's alder-shaded cave,
Or, winding round the Druid's grave,
Silently glide, with pious fear
To found his holy slumbers near.——

To these fair scenes of FANCY's reign,
O MEMORY! bear me once again:
For, when life's varied scenes are past,
'Tis simple Nature charms at last.

'Twas thus of old a poet prayed ;
    Th' indulgent power his prayer approved,
And, ere the gathered Rofe could fade,
    Reftored him to the fcenes he loved.

A Rofe, the poet's favourite flower,
    From FLORA's cultured walks he bore ;
No fairer bloomed in ESHER's bower,
    Nor PRIOR's charming CHLOE wore.

No fairer flowers could FANCY twine
    To hide ANACREON's fnowy hair ;
For there ALMERIA's bloom divine,
    And ELLIOT's fweeteft blufh was there.

When fhe, the pride of courts, retires,
    And leaves for fhades, a nation's love,
With awe the village maid admires,
    How WALDEGRAVE looks, how WALDEGRAVE moves.

So

So marvelled much in Enon's fhade
    The flowers that all uncultured grew;
When there the fplendid Rofe difplayed
    Her fwelling breaft, and fhining hue.

Yet one, that oft adorned the place
    Where now her gaudy rival reigned,
Of fimpler bloom, but kindred race,
    The penfive Eglantine complained.—

" Miftaken youth," with fighs fhe faid,
    " From nature and from me to ftray !
" The bard, by fplendid forms betrayed,
    " No more fhall frame the purer lay.

" Luxuriant, like the flaunting Rofe,
    " And gay the brilliant ftrains may be,
" But far, in beauty, far from thofe,
    " That flowed to nature and to me."

H   The

The poet felt, with fond furprize,
  The truths the fylvan critic told ;
And " though this courtly Rofe," he cries,
  " Is gay, is beauteous to behold ;

" Yet, lovely flower, I find in thee
  " Wild fweetnefs which no words exprefs,
" And charms in thy fimplicity,
  " That dwell not in the pride of drefs."

FABLE V.

The VIOLET and the PANSY.

SHEPHERD, if near thy artlefs breaft
 The god of fond defires repair;
Implore him for a gentle gueft,
 Implore him with unwearied prayer.

Should beauty's foul-enchanting fmile,
 Love-kindling looks, and features gay,
Should thefe thy wandering eye beguile,
 And fteal thy warelefs heart away;

That heart fhall foon with forrow fwell,
 And foon the erring eye deplore,
If in the beauteous bofom dwell
 No gentle virtue's genial ftore.

Far from his hive one summer-day,
 A young and yet unpractifed bee,
Borne on his tender wings away,
 Went forth the flowery world to fee.

The morn, the noon in play he paffed,
 But when the fhades of evening came,
No parent brought the due repaft,
 And faintnefs feized his little frame.

By nature urged, by inftinct led,
 The bofom of a flower he fought,
Where ftreams mourned round a moffy bed,
 And violets all the bank enwrought.

Of kindred race, but brighter dies,
 On that fair bank a Panfy grew,
That borrowed from indulgent fkies
 A velvet fhade and purple hue.

The

The tints that ſtreamed with gloſſy gold,
  The velvet ſhade, the purple hue,
The ſtranger wondered to behold,
  And to its beauteous boſom flew.

Not fonder haſte the lover ſpeeds,
  At evening's fall, his fair to meet,
When o'er the hardly-bending meads
  He ſprings on more than mortal feet.

Nor glows his eye with brighter glee,
  When ſtealing near her orient breaſt,
Than felt the fond enamoured bee,
  When firſt the golden bloom he preſt.

Ah! pity much his youth untried,
  His heart in beauty's magic ſpell!
So never paſſion thee betide,
  But where the genial virtues dwell.

I

In vain he seeks those virtues there;
    No soul-sustaining charms abound:
No honeyed sweetness to repair
    The languid waste of life is found.

An aged bee, whose labours led
    Thro' those fair springs, and meads of gold,
His feeble wing, his drooping head
    Beheld, and pitied to behold.

" Fly, fond adventurer, fly the art
    " That courts thine eye with fair attire;
" Who smiles to win the heedless heart,
    " Will smile to see that heart expire.

" This modest flower of humbler hue,
    " That boasts no depth of glowing dyes,
" Arrayed in unbespangled blue,
    " The simple cloathing of the skies——

2

" This

" This flower, with balmy fweetnefs bleft,

  " May yet thy languid life renew :"

He faid, and to the Violet's breaft

  The little vagrant faintly flew.

FABLE   VI.

The QUEEN OF THE MEADOW and the CROWN IMPERIAL.

FROM BACTRIA's vales, where beauty blows
    Luxuriant in the genial ray ;
Where flowers a bolder gem difclofe,
    And deeper drink the golden day :

From BACTRIA's vales to BRITAIN's fhore
    What time the CROWN IMPERIAL came,
Full high the ftately ftranger bore
    The honours of his birth and name.

In all the pomp of eaftern ftate,
    In all the eaftern glory gay,
He bade, with native pride elate,
    Each flower of humbler birth obey.

O, that

O, that the child unborn might hear,
   Nor hold it ſtrange in diſtant time,
That freedom even to flowers was dear,
   'To flowers that bloomed in Britain's clime !

Thro' purple meads, and ſpicy gales,
   Where STRYMON's * ſilver waters play,
While far from hence their goddeſs dwells,
   She rules with delegated ſway.

That ſway the CROWN IMPERIAL ſought,
   With high demand and haughty mien :
But equal claim a rival brought,
   A rival called the MEADOW's QUEEN.

" In climes of orient glory born,
   " Where beauty firſt and empire grew ;
" Where firſt unfolds the golden morn,
   " Where richer falls the fragrant dew :

* The Ionian Strymon.

K   " In

" In light's ethereal beauty dreſt,
  " Behold," he cried, " the favoured flower,
" Which FLORA's high commands inveſt
  " With enſigns of imperial power !

" Where proſtrate vales, and bluſhing meads,
  " And bending mountains own his ſway,
" While PERSIA's lord his empire leads,
  " And bids the trembling world obey ;

" While blood bedews the ſtraining bow,
  " And conqueſt rends the ſcattered air,
" 'Tis mine to bind the victor's brow,
  " And reign in envied glory there.

" Then lowly bow, ye Britiſh flowers !
  " Confeſs your monarch's mighty ſway,
" And own the only glory yours,
  " When fear flies trembling to obey."

He

He faid, and fudden o'er the plain,
　　From flower to flower a murmur ran,
With modeſt air, and milder ſtrain,
　　When thus the MEADOW's QUEEN began.

" If vain of birth, of glory vain,
　　" Or fond to bear a regal name,
" The pride of folly brings difdain,
　　" And bids me urge a tyrant's claim :

" If war my peaceful realms aſſail,
　　" And then, unmoved by pity's call,
" I fmile to fee the bleeding vale,
　　" Or feel one joy in nature's fall,

" Then may each juſtly vengeful flower
　　" Purfue her Queen with generous ſtrife,
" Nor leave the hand of lawlefs power
　　" Such compafs on the fcale of life.

" One

" One fimple virtue all my pride !

    " The wifh that flies to mifery's aid ;

" The balm that ftops the crimfon tide *,

    " And heals the wounds that war has made."

Their free confent by Zephyrs borne,

    The flowers their MEADOW's QUEEN obey ;

And fairer blufhes crowned the morn,

    And fweeter fragrance filled the day.

* The property of that flower.

FABLE VII.

The WALL-FLOWER.

" WHY loves my flower, the sweetest flower
  " That swells the golden breast of May,
" Thrown rudely o'er this ruined tower,
 " To waste her solitary day?

" Why, when the mead, the spicy vale,
 " The grove and genial garden call,
" Will she her fragrant soul exhale,
 " Unheeded on the lonely wall?

" For never sure was beauty born
 " To live in death's deserted shade!
" Come, lovely flower, my banks adorn,
 " My banks for life and beauty made."

L

Thus

Thus Pity waked the tender thought,
  And by her sweet persuasion led,
To seize the hermit-flower I sought,
  And bear her from her stony bed.

I sought—but sudden on mine ear
  A voice in hollow murmurs broke,
And smote my heart with holy fear—
  The Genius *of the Ruin* spoke.

" From thee be far th' ungentle deed,
  " The honours of the dead to spoil,
" Or take the sole remaining meed,
  " The flower that crowns their former toil!

" Nor deem that flower the garden's foe,
  " Or fond to grace this barren shade ;
" 'Tis Nature tells her to bestow
  " Her honours on the lonely dead.

" For

" For this, obedient Zephyrs bear
  " Her light feeds round yon turret's mold,
" And undifperfed by tempefts there,
  " They rife in vegetable gold.

" Nor fhall thy wonder wake to fee
  " Such defart fcenes diftinction crave ;
" Oft have they been, and oft fhall be
  " Truth's, Honour's, Valour's, Beauty's grave.

" Where longs to fall that rifted fpire,
  " As weary of th' infulting air ;
" The poet's thought, the warrior's fire,
  " The lover's fighs are fleeping there.

" When that too fhakes the trembling ground,
  " Borne down by fome tempeftuous fky,
" And many a flumbering cottage round
  " Startles—how ftill their hearts will lie !

" Of

" Of them who, wrapt in earth fo cold,
     " No more the fmiling day fhall view,
" Should many a tender tale be told ;
     " For many a tender thought is due.

" Haft thou not feen fome lover pale,
     " When evening brought the penfive hour,
" Step flowly o'er the fhadowy vale,
     " And ftop to pluck the frequent flower ?

" Thofe flowers he furely meant to ftrew
     " On loft affection's lowly cell ;
" Tho' there, as fond remembrance grew,
     " Forgotten, from his hand they fell.

" Has not for thee the fragrant thorn
     " Been taught her firft rofe to refign ?
" With vain but pious fondnefs borne
     " To deck thy Nancy's honoured fhrine !

                                    " 'Tis

" 'Tis NATURE pleading in the breaſt,

  " Fair memory of her works to find ;

" And when to fate ſhe yields the reſt,

  " She claims the monumental mind.

" Why, elſe, the o'ergrown paths of time

  " Would thus the lettered ſage explore,

" With pain theſe crumbling ruins climb,

  " And on the doubtful ſculpture pore ?

" Why ſeeks he with unwearied toil

  " Thro' death's dim walks to urge his way,

" Reclaim his long-aſſerted ſpoil,

  " And lead OBLIVION into day ?

" 'Tis NATURE prompts, by toil or fear

  " Unmoved, to range thro' death's domain :

" The tender parent loves to hear

  " Her childrens' ſtory told again.

M   " Treat

" Treat not with fcorn his thoughtful hours,
    " If haply near thefe haunts he ftray ;
" Nor take the fair enlivening flowers
    " That bloom to cheer his lonely way."

FABLE   VIII.

The Tulip and the Myrtle*.

'TWAS on the border of a ftream
   A gayly-painted Tulip ftood,
And, gilded by the morning beam,
   Surveyed her beauties in the flood.

And fure, more lovely to behold,
   Might nothing meet the wiftful eye,
Than crimfon fading into gold,
   In ftreaks of faireft fymmetry.

The beauteous flower, with pride elate,
   Ah me! that pride with beauty dwells!
Vainly affects fuperior ftate,
   And thus in empty fancy fwells.

* This Fable was firft publifhed in a Collection of Letters, fuppofed to have paffed between St. Evremond and Waller.

2   " O luftre

" O luſtre of unrivalled bloom !

    " Fair painting of a hand divine !

" Superior far to mortal doom,

    " The hues of heaven alone are mine !

" Away, ye worthleſs, formleſs race !

    " Ye weeds, that boaſt the name of flowers !

" No more my native bed diſgrace,

    " Unmeet for tribes ſo mean as yours !

" Shall the bright daughter of the ſun

    " Aſſociate with the ſhrubs of earth ?

" Ye ſlaves, your ſovereign's preſence ſhun !

    " Reſpect her beauties and her birth.

" And thou, dull, ſullen ever-green !

    " Shalt thou my ſhining ſphere invade ?

" My noon-day beauties beam unſeen,

    " Obſcured beneath thy duſky ſhade !"

" Deluded

" Deluded flower !" the Myrtle cries,

  " Shall we thy moment's bloom adore ?

" The meaneft fhrub that you defpife,

  " The meaneft flower has merit more.

" That daify, in its fimple bloom,

  " Shall laft along the changing year ;

" Blufh on the fnow of winter's gloom,

  " And bid the fmiling fpring appear.

" The violet, that, thofe banks beneath,

  " Hides from thy fcorn its modeft head,

" Shall fill the air with fragrant breath,

  " When thou art in thy dufty bed.

" Even I, who boaft no golden fhade,

  " Am of no fhining tints poffefs'd,

" When low thy lucid form is laid,

  " Shall bloom on many a lovely breaft.

N

" And

" And he, whofe kind and foftering care
  " To thee, to me, our beings gave,
" Shall near his breaft my flowrets wear,
  " And walk regardlefs o'er thy grave.

" Deluded flower, the friendly fcreen
  " That hides thee from the noon-tide ray,
" And mocks thy paffion to be feen,
  " Prolongs thy tranfitory day.

" But kindly deeds with fcorn repaid,
  " No more by virtue need be done :
" I now withdraw my dufky fhade,
  " And yield thee to thy darling fun."

Fierce on the flower the fcorching beam
  With all its weight of glory fell ;
The flower exulting caught the gleam,
  And lent its leaves a bolder fwell.

2

Expanded

Expanded by the fearching fire,
  The curling leaves the breaft difclofed ;
The mantling bloom was painted higher,
  And every latent charm expofed.

But when the fun was fliding low,
  And evening came, with dews fo cold ;
The wanton beauty ceafed to blow,
  And fought her bending leaves to fold.

Thofe leaves, alas ! no more would clofe ;
  Relaxed, exhaufted, fickening, pale ;
They left her to a parent's woes,
  And fled before the rifing gale.

FABLE IX.

The BEE-FLOWER *.

COME, let us leave this painted plain ;
    This waste of flowers that palls the eye :
The walks of NATURE's wilder reign
    Shall please in plainer majesty.

Thro' those fair scenes, where yet she owes
    Superior charms to BROCKMAN's art,
Where, crowned with elegant repose,
    He cherishes the social heart—

---

* This is a species of the Orchis, which is found in the barren and
mountainous parts of Lincolnshire, Worcestershire, Kent, and Hertford-
shire.   Nature has formed a Bee apparently feeding on the breast of the
flower with so much exactness, that it is impossible at a very small distance
to distinguish the imposition.   For this purpose she has observed an
œconomy different from what is found in most other flowers, and has laid
the petals horizontally.   The genus of the Orchis, or Satyrion, she seems
professedly to have made use of for her paintings, and on the different
species has drawn the perfect forms of different insects, such as Bees,
Flies, Butterflies, &c.

Thro'

Thro' thofe fair fcenes we'll wander wild,
     And on yon paftured mountains reft ;
Come, brother dear ! come, Nature's child !
     With all her fimple virtues bleft.

The fun far-feen on diftant towers,
     And clouding groves and peopled feas,
And ruins pale of princely bowers
     On BEACHBOROUGH's airy heights fhall pleafe.

Nor lifelefs there the lonely fcene ;
     The little labourer of the hive,
From flower to flower, from green to green,
     Murmurs, and makes the wild alive.

See, on that flowret's velvet breaft
     How clofe the bufy vagrant lies !
His thin-wrought plume, his downy breaft,
     Th' ambrofial gold that fwells his thighs !

O   Regardlefs,

Regardlefs, whilſt we wander near,
   Thrifty of time, his taſk he plies ;
Or ſees he no intruder near ?
   And reſt in ſleep his weary eyes ?

Perhaps his fragrant load may bind
   His limbs ;—we'll ſet the captive free—
I ſought the living Bee to find,
   And found the picture of a Bee.

Attentive to our trifling ſelves,
   From thence we plan the rule of all ;
Thus NATURE with the fabled elves
   We rank, and theſe her *Sports* we call.

Be far, my friends, from you, from me,
   Th' unhallowed term, the thought profane,
That LIFE'S MAJESTIC SOURCE may be
   In idle fancy's trifling vein.

2

Remember

Remember ftill, 'tis NATURE's plan
    Religion in your love to find ;
And know, for this, fhe firft in man
    Infpired the imitative mind.

As confcious that affection grows,
    Pleafed with the pencil's mimic power * ;
That power with leading hand fhe fhews,
    And paints a Bee upon a flower.

Mark, how that rooted mandrake wears
    His human feet, his human hands !
Oft, as his fhapely form he tears,
    Aghaft the frighted plowman ftands.

* The well known Fables of the Painter and the Statuary that fell in
love with objects of their own creation, plainly arofe from the idea of
that attachment, which follows the imitation of agreeable objects, to the
objects imitated.

See

See where, in yonder orient ftone,
    She feems ev'n with herfelf at ftrife,
While fairer from her hand is fhewn
    The pictured, than the native life.

HELVETIA's rocks, SABRINA's waves,
    Still many a fhining pebble bear,
Where oft her ftudious hand engraves
    The perfect form, and leaves it there.

O long, my PAXTON *, boaft her art ;
    And long her laws of love fulfil :
To thee fhe gave her hand and heart,
    To thee, her kindnefs and her fkill !

* An ingenious Portrait Painter in Rathbone Place.

FABLE X.

The WILDING and the BROOM.

IN yonder green wood blows the Broom;
   Shepherds, we'll truft our flocks to ftray,
Court nature in her fweeteft bloom,
   And fteal from care one fummer-day.

From Him * whofe gay and graceful brow
   Fair-handed HUME with rofes binds,
We'll learn to breathe the tender vow,
   Where flow the fairy FORTHA winds.

* WILLIAM HAMILTON of Bangour.

P

And

And oh ! that He * whofe gentle breaft
   In nature's fofteft mould was made,
Who left her fmiling works impreft
   In characters that cannot fade.

That He might leave his lowly fhrine,
   Tho' fofter there the Seafons fall—
They come, the fons of verfe divine,
   They come to fancy's magic call.

—————————" What airy founds invite
" My fteps not unreluctant, from the depth
" Of SHENE's delightful groves ? Repofing there
" No more I hear the bufy voice of men
" Far-toiling o'er the globe—fave to the call
" Of foul-exalting poetry, the ear
" Of death denies attention. Rouzed by her,

* THOMSON.

" The

" The genius of sepulchral silence opes

" His drowsy cells, and yields us to the day.

" For thee, whose hand, whatever paints the spring

" Or swells on summer's breast, or loads the lap

" Of autumn, gathers heedful—Thee whose rites

" At nature's shrine with holy care are paid

" Daily and nightly, boughs of brightest green,

" And every fairest rose, the god of groves,

" The queen of flowers, shall sweeter save for thee.

" Yet not if beauty only claim thy lay,

" Tunefully trifling. Fair philosophy,

" And nature's love, and every moral charm

" That leads in sweet captivity the mind

" To virtue—ever in thy nearest cares

" Be these, and animate thy living page

" With truth resistless, beaming from the source

" Of perfect light immortal—Vainly boasts

" That golden Broom its sunny robe of flowers :

" Fair are the sunny flowers ; but, fading soon

2   " And

" And fruitlefs, yield the forefter's regard

" To the well-loaded Wilding—Shepherd, there

" Behold the fate of fong, and lightly deem

" Of all but moral beauty."

————————————" Not in vain"——

I hear my HAMILTON reply,

(The torch of fancy in his eye)

" 'Tis not in vain," I hear him fay,

" That nature paints her works fo gay ;

" For, fruitlefs tho' that fairy broom,

" Yet ftill we love her lavifh bloom.

" Cheered with that bloom, yon defart wild

" Its native horrors loft, and fmiled.

" And oft we mark her golden ray

" Along the dark wood fcatter day.

" Of moral ufes take the ftrife ;

" Leave me the elegance of life.

" Whatever

" Whatever charms the ear or eye,

" All beauty and all harmony ;

" If fweet fenfations thefe produce,

" I know they have their moral ufe.

" I know that NATURE's charms can move

" The fprings that ftrike to VIRTUE's love."

Q   FABLE

F A B L E   XI.

The MISLETOE and the PASSION-FLOWER.

IN this dim cave a druid sleeps,
　　Where stops the passing gale to moan;
The rock he hollowed o'er him weeps,
　　And cold drops wear the fretted stone.

In this dim cave, of different creed,
　　An hermit's holy ashes rest:
The school-boy finds the frequent bead,
　　Which many a formal matin blest.

That truant-time full well I know,
　　When here I brought, in stolen hour,
The druid's magic Misletoe,
　　The holy hermit's Passion-flower.

2

The

The offerings on the myſtic ſtone
　　Penſive I laid, in thought profound,
When from the cave a deepening groan
　　Iſſued, and froze me to the ground.

I hear it ſtill—Doſt thou not hear ?
　　Does not thy haunted fancy ſtart ?
The ſound ſtill vibrates thro’ mine ear—
　　The horror ruſhes on my heart.

Unlike to living ſounds it came,
　　Unmixed, unmelodized with breath ;
But, grinding thro’ ſome ſcrannel frame,
　　Creaked from the bony lungs of death.

I hear it ſtill—“ Depart,” it cries ;
　　“ No tribute bear to ſhades unbleſt :
“ Know, here a bloody druid lies,
　　“ Who was not nurſed at Nature’s breaſt.

　　　　　　　　　　“ Aſſociate

" Aſſociate he with dæmons dire,

   " O'er human victims held the knife,

" And pleaſed to ſee the babe expire,

   " Smiled grimly o'er its quivering life.

" Behold his crimſon-ſtreaming hand

   " Erect !—his dark, fixed, murderous eye !"

In the dim cave I ſaw him ſtand ;

   And my heart died—I felt it die.

I ſee him ſtill—Doſt thou not ſee

   The haggard eye-ball's hollow glare ?

And gleams of wild ferocity

   Dart thro' the ſable ſhade of hair ?

What meagre form behind him moves,

   With eye that rues th' invading day ;

And wrinkled aſpect wan, that proves

   The mind to pale remorſe a prey ?

What

What wretched—Hark—the voice replies,
    " Boy, bear thefe idle honours hence !
" For, here a guilty hermit lies,
    " Untrue to Nature, Virtue, Senfe.

" Tho' Nature lent him powers to aid
    " The moral caufe, the mutual weal ;
" Thofe powers he funk in this dim fhade,
    " The defperate fuicide of zeal.

" Go, teach the drone of faintly haunts,
    " Whofe cell's the fepulchre of time ;
" Tho' many a holy hymn he chaunts,
    " His life is one continued crime.

" And bear them hence, the plant, the flower ;
    " No fymbols thofe of fyftems vain !
" They have the duties of their hour ;
    " Some bird, fome infect to fuftain."

THE END.

AN

ESSAY

ON

HISTORY;

IN THREE EPISTLES

To EDWARD GIBBON, Esq.

WITH

NOTES.

Της ιστορίας οικειον αμα και χρησιμον εξεταζεσθω.
POLYBIUS, Lib. ii.

By WILLIAM HAYLEY, Esq.

LONDON:
PRINTED FOR J. DODSLEY IN PALL-MALL.
M.DCC.LXXX.

EPISTLE

THE FIRST.

B

ARGUMENT

OF THE FIRST EPISTLE.

*Introduction.—Relation between History and Poetry—Decline of the latter.—Subject of the present Poem slightly touched by the Ancients.—*DIONYSIUS—LUCIAN.—*Importance and advantage of History—its origin—subsequent to that of Poetry—disguised in its infancy by Priestcraft and Superstition—brought from* EGYPT *into* GREECE.—*Scarcity of great Historians—Perfect composition not to be expected.—Address to History, and Characters of many ancient Historians—*HERODOTUS—THUCYDIDES—XENOPHON—POLYBIUS—SALLUST—LIVY—TACITUS.—*Biography—*PLUTARCH.—*Baleful influence of despotic power —* AMMIANUS MARCELLINUS—ANNA COMNENA.

EPISTLE I.

HIGH in the world of Letters, and of Wit,
   Enthron'd like Jove, behold Opinion fit!
As fymbols of her fway, on either hand
Th' unfailing urns of Praife and Cenfure ftand *;
Their mingled ftreams her motley fervants fhed   5
On each bold Author's felf-devoted head.

  On thee, O Gibbon! in whofe fplendid page
Rome fhines majeftic 'mid the woes of age,
Miftaken Zeal, wrapt in a prieftly pall,
Has from the bafer urn pour'd darkeft gall: 10
Thefe ftains to Learning would a Bard efface
With tides of glory from the golden vafe,

* Ver. 4. See NOTE I.

But

But that he feels this nobler tafk require
A fpirit glowing with congenial fire—
A Virgil only may uncenfur'd aim   15
To fing in equal verfe a Livy's fame :
Yet while Polemics, in fierce league combin'd,
With favage difcord vex thy feeling mind ;
And with a pure Religion's juft defence,
Blend grofs detraction and perverted fenfe ;   20
Thy wounded ear may haply not refufe
The foothing accents of an humbler Mufe.

   The lovely Science, whofe attractive air
Derives new charms from thy devoted care,
Is near ally'd to that bewitching Art,   25
Which reigns the idol of the Poet's heart.
'Tho' fifter Goddeffes, thy guardian maid
Shines in the robe of frefher youth array'd,
Like Pallas recent from the brain of Jove,
When Strength with Beauty in her features ftrove ; 30
While elder Poefy, in every clime
The flower of earlieft fall, has paft her prime :

The

The bloom, which her autumnal cheeks fupply,
Palls on the Public's philofophic eye.
But tho' no more with Fancy's ftrong controul   35
Her Epic wonders fafcinate the foul;
With humbler hopes, fhe wifhes ftill to pleafe
By moral elegance, and labour'd eafe:
Like other Prudes, leaves Beauty's loft pretence,
And ftrives to charm by Sentiment and Senfe.   40
Yet deaf to Envy's voice, and Pride's alarms,
She loves the rival, who eclips'd her charms;
Safe in thy favour, fhe would fondly ftray
Round the wide realm, which owns that Sifter's fway,
Sing the juft fav'rites of hiftoric fame,   45
And mark their pureft laws and nobleft aim.

  My eyes with joy this pathlefs field explore,
Crofs'd by no ROMAN Bard, no GREEKS of yore.
Thofe mighty Lords of literary fway
Have pafs'd this province with a flight furvey: 50
E'en He, whofe bold and comprehenfive mind
Immortal rules to Poefy affign'd,

High

[6]

High Prieſt of Learning! has not fix'd apart
The laws and limits of hiſtoric Art:
Yet one excelling † GREEK in later days,   55
The happy teacher of harmonious phraſe,
Whoſe patient fingers all the threads untwine,
Which in the myſtic chain of Muſic join;
Strict DIONYSIUS, of ſevereſt Taſte,
Has juſtly ſome hiſtoric duties trac'd,   60
And ſome pure precepts into practice brought,
Th' Hiſtorian proving what the Critic taught.
And ‡ LUCIAN! thou, of Humour's ſons ſupreme!
Haſt touch'd with livelieſt art this tempting theme.
When in the ROMAN world, corrupt and vain,   65
Hiſtoric Fury madden'd every brain;
When each baſe GREEK indulg'd his frantic dream,
And roſe a § XENOPHON in ſelf-eſteem;
Thy Genius ſatyriz'd the ſcribbling ſlave,
And to the liberal pen juſt leſſons gave: 70

† Ver. 55. See NOTE II.
‡ Ver. 63. See NOTE III.
§ Ver. 68. See NOTE IV.

O ſkill'd

O ſkill'd to ſeaſon, in proportion fit,
Severer wiſdom with thy ſportive wit!
Breathe thy ſtrong power! thy ſprightly grace infuſe
In the bold efforts of no ſervile Muſe,
If ſhe tranſplant ſome lively flower, that throws   75
Immortal ſweetneſs o'er thy Attic Proſe!

   In Egypt * once a dread tribunal ſtood;
Offspring of Wiſdom! ſource of Public Good!
Before this Seat, by holy Juſtice rear'd,
The mighty Dead, in ſolemn pomp, appear'd;   80
For 'till its ſentence had their rights expos'd,
The hallow'd portals of the tomb were clos'd;
A ſculptur'd form of Truth the Judges wore,
A ſacred emblem of the charge they bore!
The claims of Virtue their pure voice expreſt,   85
And bade the opening grave receive its honor'd gueſt.
In ſuch a court, array'd in Judgment's robe,
With powers extenſive as the peopled Globe;

* Ver. 77 See NOTE V.

To

'To her juſt bar impartial Hiſt'ry brings
The gorgeous group of Stateſmen, Heroes, Kings ;   90
With all whoſe minds, out-ſhining ſplendid birth,
Attract the notice of th' enlighten'd earth.
From artful Pomp ſhe ſtrips the proud diſguiſe
That flaſh'd deluſion in admiring eyes ;
To injur'd Worth gives Glory's wiſh'd reward,   95
And blazons Virtue in her bright record :
Nature's clear Mirror ! Life's inſtructive Guide !
Her Wiſdom four'd by no preceptive Pride !
Age from her leſſon forms its wifeſt aim,
And youthful Emulation ſprings to Fame.   100
    Yet thus adorn'd with nobleſt powers, deſign'd
To charm, correct, and elevate mankind,
From darkeſt Time her humble Birth ſhe drew,
And ſlowly into Strength and Beauty grew ;
As mighty ſtreams, that roll with gather'd force,   105
Spring feebly forth from ſome ſequeſter'd ſource.
    The fond deſire to paſs the nameleſs crowd,
Swept from the earth in dark Oblivion's cloud ;

Of

Of tranfient life to leave fome little trace,
And win remembrance from the rifing race ,   110
Led early Chiefs to make their prowefs known
By the rude fymbol on the artlefs ftone :
And, long ere man the wondrous fecret found
To paint the voice, and fix the fleeting found,
The infant Mufe, ambitious at her birth, *   115
Rofe the young herald of heroic worth.
The tuneful record of her oral praife,
The Sire's atchievements to the Son conveys :
Keen Emulation, wrapt in trance fublime,
Drinks with retentive ear the potent rhyme ;   120
And faithful Memory, from affection ftrong,
Spreads the rich torrent of her martial fong.
Letters at length arife ; but envious Night
Conceals their bleft Inventor from our fight.
O'er the wide earth his fpreading bounty flew,   125
And fwift thofe precious feeds of Science grew ;

* Ver. 115. See N O T E VI.

C

Thence

Thence quickly fprung the Annal's artlefs frame,

Time its chief boaft ! and brevity its aim !

The Temple-wall preferv'd a fimple date,

And mark'd in plaineft form the Monarch's fate.　130

But in the center of thofe vaft abodes, *

Whofe mighty mafs the land of Egypt loads;

Where, in rude triumph over years unknown,

Gigantic Grandeur, from his fpiry throne,

Seems to look down difdainful, and deride　135

The poor, the pigmy toils of modern Pride;

In the clofe covert of thofe gloomy cells,

Where early Magic fram'd her venal fpells,

Combining priefts, from many an ancient tale,

Wove for their hallow'd ufe Religion's veil;　140

A wondrous texture ! fupple, rich, and broad,

To dazzle Folly, and to fhelter Fraud !

This, as her cæftus, Superftition wore;

And faw th' enchanted world its powers adore:

* Ver. 131. See N O T E VII.

For in the myſtic web was every charm   145
To lure the timid, and the bold diſarm;
To win from eaſy Faith a blind eſteem,
And lull Devotion in a laſting dream.
The Sorcereſs, to ſpread her empire, dreſt
Hiſtory's young form in this illuſive veſt,   150
Whoſe infant voice repeated, as ſhe taught,
The motley fables on her mantle wrought;
Till Attic Freedom brought the Foundling home
From the dark cells of her Egyptian dome;
Drew by degrees th' oppreſſive veil aſide,   155
And, ſhewing the fair Nymph in nature's pride,
Taught her to ſpeak, with all the fire of youth,
The words of Wiſdom in the tone of Truth;
To catch the paſſing ſhew of public life,
And paint immortal ſcenes of Grecian ſtrife.   160
Inchanting Athens! oft as Learning calls
Our fond attention to thy foſt'ring walls,
Still with freſh joy thy glories we explore,
With new idolatry thy charms adore.

C 2

Bred

Bred in thy bofom, the Hiftorian caught   165
The warmeft glow of elevated thought.
Yet while thy triumphs to his eye difplay,
The nobleft fcene his pencil can portray ;
While thy rich language, grac'd by every Mufe,
Supplies the brighteft tints, his hand can ufe ;   170
How few, O Athens ! can thy genius raife
To the bright fummit of hiftoric praife !
But fuch hard fortunes human hopes attend :
Tho' to each Science many myriads bend,
Each gives, and with a coy, reluctant hand,   175
Her badge of honor to a chofen band.

   Pure, faultlefs writing, like tranfmuted gold,
Mortals may wifh, but never fhall behold :
Let Genius ftill this glorious object own,
And feek Perfection's philofophic ftone !   180
For while the mind, in ftudy's toilfome hours,
Tries on the long refearch her latent powers,
New wonders rife, to pay her patient thought,
Inferior only to the prize fhe fought.

But

But idle Pride no arduous labor fees,   185
And deems th' Hiftorian's toil a tafk of eafe :
Yet, if furvey'd by Judgment's fteady lamp,
How few are juftly grac'd with Glory's ftamp !
Tho' more thefe volumes, than the ruthlefs mind
Of the fierce Omar to the flames confign'd,*   190
When Learning faw the favage with a fmile
Devote her offspring to the blazing pile !

O Hiftory ! whofe pregnant mines impart
Unfailing treafures to poetic art ;
The Epic gem, and thofe of darker hues,   195
Whofe trembling luftre decks the tragic Mufe ;
If, juftly confcious of thy powers, I raife
A votive tablet to record thy praife,
That ancient temple to my view unfold,
Where thy firft Sons, on Glory's lift enroll'd,   200
To Fancy's eye, in living forms, appear,
And fill with Freedom's notes the raptur'd ear !—

* Ver. 190. See NOTE VIII.

The dome expands !—Behold th' Hiſtoric Sire !*

Ionic roſes mark his ſoft attire ;

Bold in his air, but graceful in his mien   205

As the fair figure of his favour'd Queen, †

When her proud galley ſham'd the Perſian van,

And grateful Xerxes own'd her more than man !

  Soft as the ſtream, whoſe dimpling waters play, ‡

And wind in lucid lapſe their pleaſurable way,   210

His rich, Homeric elocution flows,

For all the Muſes modulate his proſe :

Tho' blind Credulity his ſtep miſleads

Thro' the dark miſt of her Egyptian meads,

Yet when return'd, with patriot paſſions warm,   215

He paints the progreſs of the Perſian ſtorm,

In Truth's illumin'd field, his labours rear

A trophy worthy of the Spartan ſpear :

His eager country, in th' Olympic vale,

Throngs with proud joy to catch the martial tale.   220

* Ver. 203. See N O T E IX.
† Ver. 206. See N O T E X.
‡ Ver. 209. See N O T E XI.

                                          Behold !

Behold ! where Valour, refting on his lance,

Drinks the fweet found in rapture's filent trance,

Then, with a grateful fhout of fond acclaim,

Hails the juft herald of his country's fame !—

But mark the Youth, in dumb delight immers'd !*   225

See the proud tear of emulation burft !

O faithful fign of a fuperior foul !

Thy prayer is heard :—'tis thine to reach the goal.

See ! bleft OLORUS ! fee the palm is won !

Sublimity and Wifdom crown thy Son :   230

His the rich prize, that caught his early gaze,

Th' eternal treafure of increafing praife !

Pure from the ftain of favor, or of hate,

His nervous line unfolds the deep Debate ;

Explores the feeds of War ; with matchlefs force   235

Draws Difcord, fpringing from Ambition's fource,

With all her Demagogues, who murder Peace,

In the fierce ftruggles of contentious Greece.

Ver. 225. See N O T E XII.

Stript by Ingratitude of juſt command—
Above reſentment to a thankleſs land,					240
Above all envy, rancour, pride, and ſpleen,
In exile patient, in diſgrace ſerene,
And proud to celebrate, as Truth inſpires,
Each patriot Hero, that his ſoul admires—
The deep-ton'd trumpet of renown he blows,			245
In ſage retirement 'mid the Thracian ſnows.
But to untimely ſilence Fate devotes
Thoſe lips, yet trembling with imperfect notes,
And baſe Oblivion threatens to devour
Ev'n this firſt offspring of hiſtoric power.				250
A generous guardian of a rival's fame,*
Mars the dark Fiend in this malignant aim :
Accompliſh'd Xenophon ! thy truth has ſhewn
A brother's glory ſacred as thy own :
O rich in all the blended gifts, that grace				255
Minerva's darling ſons of Attic race !

* Ver. 251. See N O T E XIII.

The

The Sage's olive, the Historian's palm,
The Victor's laurel, all thy name embalm!
Thy simple diction, free from glaring art,
With sweet allurement steals upon the heart,   260
Pure, as the rill, that Nature's hand refines;
Clear, as thy harmony of soul, it shines.
Two passions there by soft contention please,
The love of martial Fame, and learned Ease:
These friendly colours, exquisitely join'd,   265
Form the inchanting picture of thy mind.
Thine was the praise, bright models to afford
To Cæsar's rival pen, and rival sword:
Blest, had Ambition not destroy'd his claim
To the mild lustre of thy purer fame!   270
Thou pride of Greece! in thee her triumphs end:
And Roman chiefs in borrow'd pomp ascend.
Rome's haughty genius, who enslav'd the Greek, *
In Grecian language deigns at first to speak:
By slow degrees her ruder tongue she taught   275
To tell the wonders that her valour wrought;

* Ver. 273. See NOTE XIV.

D   And

And her hiftoric hoft, with envious eye,

View in their glittering van a Greek ally.

Thou Friend of Scipio ! vers'd in War's alarms ! *

Torn from thy wounded country's ftruggling arms ! 280

And doom'd in Latian bofoms to inftill

Thy moral virtue, and thy martial fkill !

Pleas'd, in refearches of elaborate length,

To trace the fibres of the Roman ftrength !

O highly perfect in each nobler part,   285

The Sage's wifdom, and the Soldier's art !

This richer half of Grecian praife is thine :

But o'er thy ftyle the flighted Graces pine,

And tir'd Attention toils thro' many a maze,

To reach the purport of thy doubtful phrafe :   290

Yet large are his rewards, whofe toils engage

To clear the fpirit of thy cloudy page ;

Like Indian fruit, its rugged rind contains

Thofe milky fweets that pay the fearcher's pains.

But Rome's proud Genius, with exulting claim,   295
Points to her rivals of the Grecian name !

* Ver. 279. See N O T E XV.

Sententious

Sententious SALLUST leads her lofty train ; *

Clear, tho' concise, elaborately plain,

Poifing his fcale of words with frugal care,

Nor leaving one fuperfluous atom there !　　　300

Yet well difplaying, in a narrow fpace,

Truth's native ftrength, and Nature's eafy grace ;

Skill'd to detect, in tracing Action's courfe,

The hidden motive, and the human fource.

His lucid brevity the palm has won,　　　305

By Rome's decifion, from OLORUS' Son.

　　Of mightier fpirit, of majeftic frame,

With powers proportion'd to the Roman fame,

When Rome's fierce Eagle his broad wings unfurl'd,

And fhadow'd with his plumes the fubject world,　　310

In bright pre-eminence, that Greece might own,

Sublimer LIVY claims th' Hiftoric throne ; +

With that rich Eloquence, whofe golden light

Brings the full fcene diftinctly to the fight ;

* Ver. 297.　See N O T E XVI.
‡ Ver. 312.　See N O T E XVII.

　　　　　　That

That Zeal for Truth, which Intereſt cannot bend,   315
That Fire, which Freedom ever gives her friend.
Immortal artiſt of a work ſupreme !
Delighted Rome beheld, with proud eſteem,
Her own bright image, of Coloſſal ſize,
From thy long toils in pureſt marble riſe.   320
But envious Time, with a malignant ſtroke,
This ſacred ſtatue into fragments broke ;
In Lethe's ſtream its nobler portions ſunk,
And left Futurity the wounded trunk.
Yet, like the matchleſs, mutilated frame, *   325
To which great Angelo bequeath'd his name,
This glorious ruin, in whoſe ſtrength we find
The ſplendid vigour of the Sculptor's mind,
In the fond eye of Admiration ſtill
Rivals the finiſh'd forms of modern ſkill.   330
    Next, but, O Livy ! as unlike to thee,
As the pent river to th' expanding ſea,

' Ver. 325. See NOTE XVIII.

Sarcaſtic

Sarcastic Tacitus, abrupt and dark, *

In moral anger forms the keen remark ;

Searching the soul with microscopic power,　　　335

To mark the latent worm that mars the flower.

His Roman voice, in base degenerate days,

Spoke to Imperial Pride in Freedom's praise ;

And with indignant hate, severely warm,

Shew'd to gigantic Guilt his ghastly form !　　　340

There are, whose censures to his Style assign

A subtle spirit, rigid and malign ;

Which magnified each monster that he drew,

And gave the darkest vice a deeper hue :

Yet his strong pencil shews the gentlest heart,　　　345

In one sweet sketch of Biographic art,

Whose softest tints, by filial love combin'd,

Form the pure image of his Father's mind.

O blest Biography ! thy charms of yore

Historic Truth to strong Affection bore,　　　350

* Ver. 333. See NOTE XIX.

And

And foft'ring Virtue gave thee as thy dower,

Of both thy Parents the attractive power;

To win the heart, the wavering thought to fix,

And fond delight with wife inftruction mix.

Firft of thy votaries, peerlefs, and alone,   355

Thy PLUTARCH fhines, by moral beauty known : *

Enchanting Sage ! whofe living leffons teach,

What heights of Virtue human efforts reach.

Tho' oft thy Pen, eccentrically wild,

Ramble, in Learning's various maze beguil'd ;   360

Tho' in thy Style no brilliant graces fhine,

Nor the clear conduct of correct Defign,

Thy every page is uniformly bright

With mild Philanthropy's diviner light.

Of gentleft manners, as of mind elate,   365

Thy happy Genius had the glorious fate

To regulate, with Wifdom's foft controul,

The ftrong ambition of a TRAJAN's foul.

* Ver. 356. See N O T E XX.

But

But O ! how rare benignant Virtue fprings,

In the blank bofom of defpotic kings!   370

   Thou bane of liberal Knowledge ! Nature's curfe !

Parent of Mifery ! pamper'd Vice's nurfe !

Plunging, by thy annihilating breath,

The foul of Genius in the trance of death !

Unbounded Power ! beneath thy baleful fway,   375

The voice of Hift'ry finks in dumb decay.

   Still in thy gloomy reign one martial Greek,

In Rome's corrupted language dares to fpeak ;

Mild Marcellinus ! free from fervile awe !*

A faithful painter of the woes he faw ;   380

Forc'd by the meannefs of his age to join

Adulterate Colours with his juft Defign !

The flighted Attic Mufe no more fupplies

Her pencil, dipt in Nature's pureft dies ;

And Roman Emulation, at a ftand,   385

Drops the blurr'd pallet from her palfy'd hand.

* Ver. 379. See NOTE XXI.

But

But while Monaftic Night, with gathering fhades,

The ruin'd realm of Hiftory invades;

While, pent in CONSTANTINE's ill-fated walls,

The mangled form of Roman Grandeur falls ;   390

And, like a Gladiator on the fand,

Props his faint body with a dying hand ;

While favage Turks, or the fierce Sons of Thor,

Wage on the Arts a wild Titanian war ;

While manly Knowledge hides his radiant head,   395

As Jove in terror from the Titans fled ;

See ! in the lovely charms of female youth,

A fecond Pallas guards the throne of Truth !

And, with COMNENA's royal name impreft, *

The zone of Beauty binds her Attic veft !   400

Fair ftar of Wifdom ! whofe unrival'd light

Breaks thro' the ftormy cloud of thickeft night ;

Tho' in the purple of proud mifery nurft,

From thofe oppreffive bands thy fpirit burft ;

* Ver. 399. See N O T E XXII.

Pleas'd

Pleas'd, in thy public labours, to forget   405
The keen domeſtic pangs of fond regret !
Pleas'd to preſerve, from Time's deſtructive rage,
A Father's virtues in thy faithful page !
Too pure of ſoul to violate, or hide
Th' Hiſtorian's duty in the Daughter's pride !   410
Tho' baſe Oblivion long with envious hand
Hid the fair volume which thy virtue plann'd,
It ſhines, redeem'd from Ruin's darkeſt hour,
A wond'rous monument of Female power ;
While conſcious Hiſt'ry, careful of thy fame,   415
Ranks in her Attic band thy filial name,
And ſees, on Glory's ſtage, thy graceful mien
Cloſe the long triumph of her ancient ſcene !

END OF THE FIRST EPISTLE.

                      EPISTLE

E P I S T L E

T H E   S E C O N D.

Sunt et alii Scriptores boni: fed nos genera deguftamus, non bibliothecas excutimus.　　　　QUINTIL. Lib. x.

A R G U M E N T

OF THE SECOND EPISTLE.

Defects of the Monkiſh Hiſtorians — our obligations to the beſt of them.—Contraſt between two of the moſt fabulous, and two of the moſt rational.—Indulgence due to Writers of the dark Ages.—Slow Progreſs of the human Mind.— Chivalry. — FROISSART. *— Revival of ancient Learning under* LEO X.*—Hiſtorians in Italy,* MACHIAVEL, GUICCIARDIN, DAVILA, *and Father* PAUL *— in Portugal,* OSORIUS*—in Spain,* MARIANA*—in France,* THUANUS. *—Praiſe of Toleration.—*VOLTAIRE.*—Addreſs to England.—*CLARENDON—BURNET—RAPIN—HUME—LYTTELTON. *— Reaſon for not attempting to deſcribe any living Hiſtorian.*

EPISTLE II.

AS eager Foſſiliſts with ardour pore
    On the flat margin of the pebbled ſhore,
Hoping ſome curious Shell, or Coral-root,
May pay the labours of their long purſuit;
And yield their hand the pleaſure to diſplay   5
Nature's neglected Gems in nice array:
So, GIBBON! toils the mind, whoſe labour wades
Thro' the dull Chronicle's monaſtic ſhades,
To pick from that drear coaſt, with learned care,
New ſhells of Knowledge, thinly ſcatter'd there;   10
Who patient hears, while cloiſter'd Dullneſs tells
The lying legend of her murky cells;

Or

Or stranger mingles, in her phrase uncouth,

Difgufting Lies with unimportant Truth :

How Bifhops give (each tort'ring Fiend o'ercome)   15

Life to the faint, and language to the dumb :

How fainted Kings renounce, with holy dread, *

The chafte endearments of their marriage-bed :

How Nuns, entranc'd, to joys celeftial mount, †

Made drunk with rapture from a facred fount :   20

How cunning Priefts their dying Lord cajole,

And take his riches to enfure his foul :

While he endows them, in his pious will,

With thofe dear gifts, the Meadow, and the Mill, ‡

They wifely chronicle his Spirit's health,   25

And give him Virtue in return for Wealth.

So Hift'ry finks, by Hypocrites depreft,

In the coarfe habit of the cloifter dreft ;

While her weak Sons that noxious air imbibe,

Such are the tales of their monaftic tribe !   30

* Ver. 17.   See N O T E I.
† Ver. 19.   See N O T E II.
‡ Ver. 24.   See N O T E III.

But

But let not Pride, with blind contempt, arraign
Each early Writer in that humble train !
No ! let the Muse, a friend to every claim,
That marks the Candidate for honeſt fame,
Be juſt to patient Worth, ſeverely ſunk,   35
And paint the merits of the modeſt Monk !

Ye purer minds ! who ſtopt, with native force,
Barbaric Ignorance's brutal courſe ;
Who, in the field of Hiſt'ry, dark and waſte,
Your ſimple path with ſteady patience trac'd ;   40
Bleſt be your labours ! and your virtues bleſt !
Tho' paid with inſult, and with ſcorn oppreſt,
Ye reſcu'd Learning's lamp from total night,
And ſav'd with anxious toil the trembling light,
In the wild ſtorm of that tempeſtuous time,   45
When Superſtition cheriſh'd every crime ;
When meaner Prieſts pronounc'd with falt'ring tongue,
Nor knew to read the jargon which they ſung ;
When Nobles, train'd like blood-hounds to deſtroy,
In ruthleſs rapine plac'd their ſavage joy ;   50

And

And Monarchs wanted ev'n the skill to frame
The letters that compos'd their mighty name.
How strong the mind, that, try'd by ills like these,
Could write untainted with the Time's disease !
That, free from Folly's lie, and Fraud's pretence,   55
Could rise to simple Truth, and sober Sense !
Such minds existed in the darkest hour
Of blind Barbarity's debasing power.

   If mitred Turpin told, in wildest strain, *
Of giant-feats atchiev'd by Charlemain ;   60
Of spears, that blossom'd like the flowery thorn,
Of Roland's magic sword, and ivory horn,
Whose sound was wafted by an angel's wing,
In notes of anguish, to his distant king ;
Yet modest Æginhard, with grateful care, +   65
In purer colours, and with Nature's air,
Has drawn distinctly, in his clear record,
A juster portrait of this mighty Lord,

* Ver. 59. See N O T E IV.
+ Ver. 65. See N O T E V.

Whose

Whose forceful lance, against the Pagan hurl'd,
Shone the bright terror of a barbarous world.   70
Nor on his master does he idly shower
The priestly gifts of supernat'ral Power:
This candid Scribe of Gratitude and Truth,
Correctly paints the Patron of his youth,
Th' imperial Savage, whose unletter'd mind   75
Was active, strong, beneficent, and kind;
Who, tho' he lov'd the Learned to requite,
Knew not that simplest art, the art to write.

If British GEFFREY fill'd his motley page *
With MERLIN's spells, and UTHER's amorous rage;   80
With fables from the field of Magic glean'd,
Giant and Dragon, Incubus and Fiend;
Yet Life's great drama, and the Deeds of men,
Sage Monk of Malm'sbury! engag'd thy pen. †
Nor vainly dost thou plead, in modest phrase,   85
Thy manly passion for ingenuous praise:

* Ver. 79.   See N O T E VI.
† Ver. 84.   See N O T E VII.

F

'Twas

'Twas thine the labours of thy Sires to clear
From Fiction's harden'd fpots, with toil fevere;
To form, with eyes intent on public life,
Thy bolder fketches of internal ftrife;   90
And warmly celebrate, with love refin'd,
The rich endowments of thy GLO'STER's mind;
May this, thy Praife, the Monkifh pen exempt
From the ungenerous blame of blind Contempt!

   Tho' Truth appear to make thy works her care,   95
The lurking Prodigy ftill lingers there:
But let not cenfure on thy name be thrown
For errors, fpringing from thy age alone!
Shame on the Critic! who, with idle fcorn,
Depreciates Authors, in dark periods born,   100
Becaufe they want, irregularly bright,
That equal Knowledge, and that fteadier Light,
Which Learning, in its wide meridian blaze,
Has haply lavifh'd on his luckier days!

   In all its various paths, the human Mind   105
Feels the firft efforts of its ftrength confin'd;

And in the field, where Hiſtory's laurels grow,

Winds its long march ſuperlatively ſlow :

Like Fruit, whoſe taſte to ſweet luxuriance runs

By conſtant ſuccour from autumnal ſuns,   110

This lovely Science ripens by degrees,

And late is faſhion'd into graceful eaſe.

In thoſe enlivening days, when Europe roſe

From the long preſſure of lethargic woes ;

When the Provençal lyre, with roſes dreſt,   115

By ardent Love's extatic fingers preſt,

Wak'd into life the Genius of the Weſt ;

When Chivalry, her banners all unfurl'd

Fill'd with heroic fire the ſplendid world ;

In high-plum'd grandeur held her gorgeous reign,   120

And rank'd each brilliant Virtue in her train ;

When ſhe imparted, by her magic glove,

To Honour ſtrength, and purity to Love ;

New-moulded Nature on her nobleſt plan,

And gave freſh ſinews to the ſoul of man :   125

When the chief model of her forming hand,

Our ſable EDWARD, on the Gallic ſtrand,

                              Diſplay'd

Difplay'd that fpirit which her laws beftow,

And fhone the idol of his captive foe:

Unbleft with Arts, th' unletter'd age could yield   130

No fkilful hand, to paint from Glory's field

Scenes, that Humanity with pride muft hear,

And Admiration honour with a tear.

    Yet Courtefy, with generous Valour join'd,

Fair Twins of Chivalry I rejoic'd to find   135

A faithful Chronicler in plain FROISSART ; *

As rich in honefty as void of art.

As the young Peafant, led by fpirits keen

To fome great city's gay and gorgeous fcene,

Returning, with increafe of proud delight,   140

Dwells on the various fplendor of the fight ;

And gives his tale, tho' told in terms uncouth,

The charm of Nature, and the force of Truth,

Tho' rude engaging ; fuch thy fimple page

Seems, O FROISSART ! to this enlighten'd age.   145

Proud of their fpirit, in thy writings fhewn,

Fair Faith and Honour mark thee for their own ;

* Ver. 136. See NOTE VIII.

Tho'

Tho' oft the dupe of thofe delufive times,
Thy Genius, fofter'd with romantic rhymes,
Appears to play the legendary Bard,   150
And trefpafs on the Truth it meant to guard.
Still fhall thy Name, with lafting glory, ftand
High on the lift of that advent'rous band,
Who, bidding Hiftory fpeak a modern Tongue,
From her cramp'd hand the Monkifh fetters flung,   155
While yet deprefs'd in Gothic night fhe lay,
Nor faw th' approaching dawn of Attic day.

On the bleft banks of Tiber's honour'd ftream
Shone the firft glance of that reviving beam ;
Enlighten'd Pontiffs, on the very fpot   160
Where Science was profcrib'd, and Senfe forgot ;
Bade Learning ftart from out her mould'ring tomb,
And taught new laurels on her brow to bloom ;
Their Magic voice invok'd all Arts, and all
Sprung into glory at the potent call.   165

As in Arabia's wafte, where Horror reigns,
Gigantic tyrant of the burning plains !

The

The glorious bounty of some Royal mind,

By Heaven infpir'd, and friend to human kind,

Bids the rich Structure of refreshment rise,   170

To chear the Traveller's defpairing eyes ;

Who fees with rapture the new fountains burft,

And, as he flakes his foul-fubduing thirft,

Bleffes the hand which all his pains beguil'd,

And rais'd an Eden in the dreary wild :   175

Such praifes, Leo ! to thy name are due,

From all, who Learning's cultur'd field review,

And to its Fountain, in thy liberal heart,

Trace the diffufive Stream of modern Art.

'Twas not thy praife to animate alone   180

The fpeaking Canvafs, and the breathing Stone,

Or tides of Bounty round Parnaffus roll,

To quicken Genius in the Poet's foul ;

Thy Favour, like the Sun's prolific ray,

Brought the keen Scribe of Florence into Day ;*   185

* Ver. 185. See NOTE IX.

Whofe

Whose subtle Wit discharg'd a dubious shaft,
Call'd both the Friend and Foe of Kingly Craft.
Tho', in his maze of Politics perplext,
Great Names have differ'd on that doubtful text;
Here crown'd with praise, as true to Virtue's side,   190
There view'd with horror, as th' Assassin's guide;
High in a purer sphere, he shines afar,
And Hist'ry hails him as her Morning-star.

    Nor less, O Leo! was it thine to raise
The great Historic Chief of modern days, *   195
The solemn Guicciardin, whose pen severe,
Unsway'd by favour, nor restrain'd by fear,
Mark'd in his close of life, with keen disdain,
Each fatal blemish in thy motley reign;
Who, like Olorus' Son, of spirit chaste,   200
And form'd to martial toils, minutely trac'd
The woes he saw his bleeding country bear,
And wars, in which he claim'd no trivial share.

* Ver. 195. See NOTE X.

With equal wreaths let DAVILA be crown'd, *

Alike in letters and in arms renown'd !   205

Who, from his country driv'n by dire mifchance,

Plung'd in the civil broils of bleeding France,

Maintaining ftill, in Party's raging fea,

His judgment fteady, and his fpirit free ;

Save when the fierce religion of his Sires   210

Drown'd the foft zeal Humanity infpires :

Who boldly wrote, with fuch a faithful hand,

The tragic ftory of that foreign land,

The hoary Gallic Chief, whofe tranquil age

Liften'd with joy to his recording page,   215

Tracing the fcenes familiar to his youth,

Gave his ftrong fanction to th' Hiftorian's truth.

 Oh Italy ! tho' drench'd with civil blood,

Tho' drown'd in Bigotry's foul-quenching flood,

Hiftoric Genius, in thy troubles nurft,   220

Ev'n from the darknefs of the Convent burft.

* Ver. 204. See NOTE XI.

Venice

Venice may boaſt eternal Honour, won

By the bright labours of her dauntleſs Son,

Whoſe hand the curtains of the Conclave drew,

And gave each prieſtly art to public view.   225

   Sarpi, bleſt name ! from every foible clear, *

Not more to Science than to Virtue dear.

Thy pen, thy life, of equal praiſe ſecure !

Both wiſely bold, and both ſublimely pure !

That Freedom bids me on thy merits dwell,   230

Whoſe radiant form illum'd thy letter'd cell ;

Who to thy hand the nobleſt taſk aſſign'd,

That earth can offer to a heavenly mind :

With Reaſon's arms to guard invaded laws,

And guide the pen of Truth in Freedom's cauſe.   235

Too firm of heart at Danger's cry to ſtoop,

Nor Lucre's ſlave, nor vain Ambition's dupe,

Thro' length of days invariably the ſame,

Thy Country's liberty thy conſtant aim !

* Ver. 226. See N O T E XII.

G   For

For this thy fpirit dar'd th' Affaffin's knife,   240
That with repeated guilt purfu'd thy life ;
For this thy fervent and unweary'd care
Form'd, ev'n in death, thy patriotic prayer,
And, while his fhadows on thine eye-lids hung,
" Be it immortal !" trembled on thy tongue.   245

 But not reftricted, by the partial Fates,
To the bright clufter of Italian States,
The light of Learning, and of liberal Tafte,
Diffufely fhone o'er Europe's Gothic wafte.

 On Tagus' fhore, from whofe admiring ftrand   250
Great GAMA fail'd, when his advent'rous hand
The flag of glorious enterprize unfurl'd,
To purchafe with his toils the Eaftern world,
The clear OSORIUS, in his claffic phrafe, *
Portray'd the Heroes of thofe happier days,   255
When Lufitania, once a mighty name,
Outftripp'd each rival in the chace of Fame :

* Ver. 254. See N O T E XIII.

Mild

Mild and majeftic, her Hiftorian's page
Shares in the glory of her brighteft age.
Iberia's Genius bids juft Fame allow   260
An equal wreath to MARIANA's brow : *
Skill'd to illuminate the diftant fcene,
In diction graceful, and of fpirit keen,
His labour, by his country's love endear'd,
The gloomy chaos of her Story clear'd.   265
He firft afpir'd its fcatter'd parts to clafs,
And bring to jufter form the mighty mafs ;
As the nice hand of Geographic art
Draws the vaft globe on a contracted chart,
Where Truth uninjur'd fees, with glad furprize,   270
Her fhape ftill perfect, tho' of fmaller fize.
Exalted Mind ! who felt the People's right,
In climes, where fouls are crufh'd by Kingly might ;
And dar'd, unaw'd before a tyrant's throne,
To make the fanctity of Freedom known !   275

* Ver. 261. See N O T E XIV.

                                                     But

But fhort, O Genius! is thy tranfient hour,

In the dark regions of defpotic Power.

As the faint ftruggle of the folar beam,

When vapours intercept the golden ftream,

Pouring thro' parted clouds a glancing fire,   280

Plays, in fhort triumph, on fome glittering fpire;

But while the eye admires the partial ray,

The pale and watery luftre melts away:

Thus gleams of literary fplendor play'd,

And thus on Spain's o'erclouded realm decay'd :   285

While happier France, with longer glory bright,

Caught richer flafhes of the flying light.

There, with the dignity of virtuous Pride,

Thro' painful fcenes of public fervice try'd,

And keenly confcious of his Country's woes,   290

The liberal fpirit of Thuanus rofe : *

O'er Earth's wide ftage a curious eye he caft,

And caught the living pageant as it paft :

* Ver. 291. See N O T E XV.

With

With patriot care moſt eager to advance
The rights of Nature, and the weal of France !   295
His language noble, as his temper clear
From Faction's rage, and Superſtition's fear !
In Wealth laborious ! amid Wrongs ſedate !
His Virtue lovely, as his Genius great !
Ting'd with ſome marks, that from his climate ſpring,
He priz'd his Country, but ador'd his King ;   301
Yet with a zeal from ſlaviſh awe refin'd,
Shone the clear model of a Gallic mind.
Thou friend of Science ! 'twas thy ſignal praiſe,
A juſt memorial of her Sons to raiſe ;   305
To blazon firſt, on Hiſt'ry's brighter leaf,
The laurel'd Writer with the laurel'd Chief !

 But O ! pure Spirit ! what a fate was thine !
How Truth and Reaſon at thy wrongs repine !
How blame thy King, tho' rob'd in Honour's ray,   310
Who left thy Fame to ſubtle Prieſts a prey,
And tamely ſaw their murky wiles o'erwhelm
Thy works, the light of his reviving realm !

The

Tho' Pontiffs execrate, and Kings betray,
Let not this fate your generous warmth allay,　　315
Ye kindred Worthies ! who still dare to wield
Reafon's keen fword, and Toleration's fhield,
In climes where Perfecution's iron mace
Is rais'd to maffacre the human race !
The heart of Nature will your virtue feel,　　320
And her immortal voice reward your zeal :
Firft in her praife her fearlefs champions live,
Crown'd with the nobleft palms that earth can give.
Firm in this band, who to her aid advance,
And high amid th' Hiftoric fons of France,　　325
Delighted Nature faw, with partial care,
The lively vigour of the gay VOLTAIRE;
And fondly gave him, with ANACREON's fire,
To throw the hand of Age acrofs the lyre :
But mute that vary'd voice, which pleas'd fo long !　330
Th' Hiftorian's tale is clos'd, the Poet's fong !
Within the narrow tomb behold him lie,
Who fill'd fo large a fpace in Learning's eye !

Thou

Thou Mind unweary'd! thy long toils are o'er;
Cenfure and Praife can touch thy ear no more :   335
Still let me breathe with juft regret thy name,
Lament thy foibles, and thy powers proclaim!

   On the wide fea of Letters 'twas thy boaft
To croud each fail, and touch at every coaft :
From that rich deep how often haft thou brought   340
The pure and precious pearls of fplendid Thought!
How didft thou triumph on that fubject-tide,
Till Vanity's wild guft, and ftormy Pride,
Drove thy ftrong bark, in evil hour, to fplit
Upon the fatal rock of impious Wit !   345
But be thy failings cover'd by thy tomb!
And guardian laurels o'er thy afhes bloom!

   From the long annals of the world thy art,
With chemic procefs, drew the richer part :
To Hift'ry gave a philofophic air,   350
And made the intereft of mankind her care ;
Pleas'd her grave brow with garlands to adorn,
And from the rofe of Knowledge ftrip the thorn.

Thy lively Eloquence, in profe, in verfe,

Still keenly bright, and elegantly terfe,   355

Flames with bold fpirit ; yet is idly rafh :

Thy promis'd light is oft a dazzling flafh ;

Thy Wifdom verges to farcaftic fport,

Satire thy joy ! and ridicule thy *fort !*

But the gay Genius of the Gallic foil,   360

Shrinking from folemn tafks of ferious toil,

Thro' every fcene his playful air maintains,

And in the light Memoir unrival'd reigns.

Thy Wits, O France ! (as e'en thy Critics own) *

Support not Hiftory's majeftic tone ;   365

They, like thy Soldiers, want, in feats of length,

The perfevering foul of Britifh ftrength.

 Hail to thee, Britain ! hail ! delightful land !

I fpring with filial joy to reach thy ftrand :

And thou ! bleft nourifher of Souls, fublime   370

As e'er immortaliz'd their native clime,

* Ver. 364. See N O T E XVI.

Rich

Rich in Poetic treasures, yet excuse

The trivial offering of an humble Muse,

Who pants to add, with fears by love o'ercome,

Her mite of Glory to thy countless sum !   375

With vary'd colours, of the richest die,

Fame's brilliant banners o'er thy Offspring fly :

In native Vigour bold, by Freedom led,

No path of Honour have they fail'd to tread :

But while they wisely plan, and bravely dare,   380

Their own atchievements are their latest care.

Tho' CAMDEN, rich in Learning's various store,

Sought in Tradition's mine Truth's genuine ore,

The waste of Hist'ry lay in lifeless shade,

Tho' RAWLEIGH's piercing eye that world survey'd.   385

Tho' mightier Names there cast a casual glance,

They seem'd to saunter round the field by chance,

Till CLARENDON arose, and in the hour

When civil Discord wak'd each mental Power,

With brave desire to reach this distant Goal,   390

Strain'd all the vigour of his manly soul.

H

Nor

Nor Truth, nor Freedom's injur'd Powers, allow

A wreath unfpotted to his haughty brow :

Friendfhip's firm fpirit ftill his fame exalts,

With fweet atonement for his leffer faults.   395

His Pomp of Phrafe, his Period of a mile,

And all the maze of his bewilder'd Style,

Illum'd by Warmth of Heart, no more offend :

What cannot Tafte forgive, in FALKLAND's friend ?

Nor flow his praifes from this fingle fource ;   400

One province of his art difplays his force :

His Portraits boaft, with features ftrongly like,

The foft precifion of the clear VANDYKE :

Tho', like the Painter, his faint talents yield,

And fink embarrafs'd in the Epic field.   405

Yet fhall his labours long adorn our Ifle,

Like the proud glories of fome Gothic pile :

They, tho' conftructed by a Bigot's hand,

Nor nicely finifh'd, nor correctly plan'd,

With folemn Majefty, and pious Gloom,   410

An awful influence o'er the mind affume ;

And

And from the alien eyes of every Sect
Attract obfervance, and command refpect.

In following years, when thy great name, NASSAU !
Stampt the bleft deed of Liberty and Law ;   415
When clear, and guiltlefs of Oppreffion's rage,
There rofe in Britain an Auguftan age,
And clufter'd Wits, by emulation bright,
Diffus'd o'er ANNA's reign their mental light ;
That Conftellation feem'd, tho' ftrong its flame,   420
To want the fplendor of Hiftoric fame :
Yet BURNET's page may lafting glory hope,
Howe'er infulted by the fpleen of POPE.
Tho' his rough Language hafte and warmth denote,
With ardent Honefty of Soul he wrote ;   425
Tho' critic cenfures on his work may fhower,
Like Faith, his Freedom has a faving power.

Nor fhalt thou want, RAPIN ! thy well-earn'd praife ;
The fage POLYBIUS thou of modern days !
Thy Sword, thy Pen, have both thy name endear'd ; 430
This join'd our Arms, and that our Story clear'd :

                                                    Thy

Thy foreign hand difcharg'd th' Hiftorian's truft,

Unfway'd by Party, and to Freedom juft.

To letter'd Fame we own thy fair pretence,

From patient Labour, and from candid Senfe.   435

Yet Public Favour, ever hard to fix,

Flew from thy page, as heavy and prolix.

For foon, emerging from the Sophifts' fchool,

With Spirit eager, yet with Judgment cool,

With fubtle fkill to fteal upon applaufe,   440

And give falfe vigour to the weaker caufe;

To paint a fpecious fcene with niceft art,

Retouch the whole, and varnifh every part;

Graceful in Style, in Argument acute;

Mafter of every trick in keen Difpute!   445

With thefe ftrong powers to form a winning tale,

And hide Deceit in Moderation's veil,

High on the pinnacle of Fafhion plac'd,

HUME fhone the idol of Hiftoric Tafte.

Already, pierc'd by Freedom's fearching rays,   450

The waxen fabric of his fame decays.—

Think not, keen Spirit ! that thefe hands prefume
To tear each leaf of laurel from thy tomb !
Thefe hands ! which, if a heart of human frame
Could ftoop to harbour that ungenerous aim,   455
Would fhield thy Grave, and give, with guardian care,
Each type of Eloquence to flourifh there !
But Public Love commands the painful tafk,
From the pretended Sage to ftrip the mafk,
When his falfe tongue, averfe to Freedom's caufe,   460
Profanes the fpirit of her antient laws.
As Afia's foothing opiate Drugs, by ftealth,
Shake every flacken'd nerve, and fap the health ;
Thy Writings thus, with noxious charms refin'd,
Seeming to foothe its ills, unnerve the Mind.   465
While the keen cunning of thy hand pretends
To ftrike alone at Party's abject ends,
Our hearts more free from Faction's Weeds we feel,
But they have loft the Flower of Patriot Zeal.

Wild

Wild as thy feeble Metaphyfic page, 470

Thy Hift'ry rambles into Sceptic rage;

Whofe giddy and fantaftic dreams abufe

A HAMPDEN's Virtue, and a SHAKESPEAR's Mufe.

   With purer Spirit, free from Party ftrife,

To foothe his evening hour of honour'd life, 475

See candid LYTTELTON at length unfold

The deeds of Liberty in days of old !

Fond of the theme, and narrative with age,

He winds the lengthen'd tale thro' many a page;

But there the beams of Patriot Virtue fhine; 480

There Truth and Freedom fanctify the line,

And laurels, due to Civil Wifdom, fhield

This noble Neftor of th' Hiftoric field.

   The living Names, who there difplay their power,

And give its glory to the prefent hour, 485

I pafs with mute regard; in fear to fail,

Weighing their worth in a fufpected fcale:

Thy

Thy right, Pofterity ! I facred hold,

To fix the ftamp on literary Gold ;

Bleft ! if this lighter Ore, which I prepare   490

For thy fupreme Affay, with anxious care,

Thy current fanction unimpeach'd enjoy,

As only tinctur'd with a flight alloy !

END OF THE SECOND EPISTLE.

EPISTLE

THE THIRD.

Ventum eft ad partem operis deftinati longe graviffimam - - - - nunc
quoque, licet major quam unquam moles premat, tamen profpi-
cienti finem mihi conftitutum eft vel deficere potius, quam def-
perare - - - - noftra temeritas etiam mores ci conabitur dare, et
affignabit officia. QUINTIL. Lib. xii.

ARGUMENT

OF THE THIRD EPISTLE.

The sources of the chief defects in History — Vanity National and private, Flattery, and her various arts—Party-spirit, Superstition, and false Philosophy. — Character of the accomplish'd Historian.—The Laws of History—Style—Importance of the subject—Failure of KNOLLES from a subject ill chosen—Danger of dwelling on the distant and minute parts of a subject really interesting—Failure of MILTON in this particular.—The worst defect of an Historian, a system of Tyranny — Instance in BRADY. — Want of a General History of England: Wish for its accomplishment.—Use and Delight of other Histories —of Rome. —Labour of the Historian—Cavils against him.—Concern for GIBBON's irreligious spirit — The idle censure of his passion for Fame—Defence of that passion.—Conclusion.

E P I S T L E   III.

S AY thou! whofe eye has, like the Lynx's beam,
    Pierc'd the deep windings of this mazy ftream,
Say, from what fource the various Poifons glide,
That darken Hiftory's difcolour'd tide ;
Whofe purer waters to the mind difpenfe   5
The wealth of Virtue, and the fruits of Senfe !
Thefe Poifons flow, collective and apart,
From Public Vanity, and Private Art.
At firft Delufion built her fafe retreat
On the broad bafe of National Conceit :   10
Nations, like Men, in Flattery confide,
The flaves of Fancy, and the dupes of Pride.

I 2

Each

Each petty region of the peopled earth,

Howe'er debas'd by intellectual dearth,

Still proudly boafted of her claims to fhare   15

The richeft portion of celeftial care :

For her fhe faw the rival Gods engage,

And Heaven convuls'd with elemental rage.

To her the thunder's roar, the lightning's fire,

Confirm'd their favour, or denounc'd their ire.   20

To feize this foible, daring Hift'ry threw

Illufive terrors o'er each fcene fhe drew ;

Nor would her fpirit, in the heat of youth,

Watch, with a Veftal's care, the lamp of Truth ;

But, wildly mounting in a Witch's form,   25

Her voice delighted to condenfe the ftorm ;

With fhowers of blood th' aftonifh'd earth to drench,

The frame of Nature from its bafe to wrench ;

In Horror's veil involve her plain events,

And fhake th' affrighted world with dire portents. *   30

* Ver. 30.   See N O T E I.

Still softer arts her subtle spirit try'd,

To win the easy faith of Public Pride:

She told what Powers, in times of early date,

Gave confecration to the infant State;

Mark'd the bleft spot by facred Founders trod,   35

And all th' atchievements of the guardian God.

Thus while, like Fame, fhe refts upon the land,

Her figure grows; her magic limbs expand;

Her tow'ring head, towards Olympus toft,

Pierces the fky, and in that blaze is loft.   40

    Yet bold Philofophy at length deftroy'd

The brilliant phantoms of th' Hiftoric void;

Her fcrutinizing eye, whofe fearch fevere

Rivals the preffure of Ithuriel's fpear,

Lets neither dark nor fplendid Fraud efcape,   45

But turns each Marvel to its real fhape.

The blazing meteors fall from Hift'ry's fphere;

Her darling Demi-gods no more appear;

No more the Nations, with heroic joy,

Boaft their defcent from Heaven-defcended Troy: 50

On

On FRANCIO now the Gallic page is mute, *

And Britifh Story drops the name of BRUTE.

What other failings from this fountain flow'd,

Ill-meafur'd fame on martial feats beftow'd,

And heaps, enlarg'd to mountains of the flain,   55

The miracles of valour, ftill remain.

But of all faults, that injur'd Truth may blame,

Thofe proud miftakes the firft indulgence claim,

Where Public Zeal the ardent Pen betrays,

And Patriot Paffions fwell the partial praife.   60

Ev'n private Vanity may pardon find,

When built on Worth, and with Inftruction join'd :

In Britifh Annalifts moft rarely found,

This venial foible fprings on foreign ground ;

'Tis theirs, who fcribble near the Seine or Loire,   65

Thofe lively Heroes of the light Memoir !

   Defects more hateful to ingenuous eyes,

In Adulation's fervile arts arife :

* Ver. 51. See NOTE II.

Mean

Mean Child of Int'reft ! as her Parent bafe !
Her charms Deformity ! her wealth Difgrace !   70
Dimm'd by her breath, the light of Learning fades ;
Her breath the wifeft of mankind degrades,
And Bacon's felf, for mental glory born, *
Meets, as her flave, our pity, or our fcorn.
Unhappy Genius ! in whofe wond'rous mind   75
The fordid Reptile and the Seraph join'd ;
  ow traverfing the world on Wifdom's wings,
Now bafely crouching to the laft of Kings :
Thy fault, which Freedom with regret furveys,
This ufeful Truth, in ftrongeft light, difplays ;   80
That not fufficient are thofe fhining parts,
Which fhed new radiance o'er concenter'd arts ;
To reach with glory the Hiftoric goal
Demands a firm, an independent foul,
An eagle-eye, that with undazzled gaze   85
Can look on Majefty's meridian blaze.

* Ver. 73. See N O T E III.

But Adulation, in the worft of times,

Throws her broad mantle o'er imperial crimes;

In Hift'ry's field, her abject toils delight

To fhut the fcenes of Nature from our fight,   90

Each human Virtue in one mafs to fling,

And of that mountain make the ftatue of a King. *

Yet oft her labours, flighted or abhorr'd,

Receive in prefent fcorn their juft reward;

Scorn from that Idol, at whofe feet fhe lays   95

The fordid offering of her venal praife.

As crown'd with Indian laurels, nobly won, †

His conqueft ended, Philip's warlike Son

Sail'd down th' Hydafpes in a voyage of fport,

The chief Hiftorian of his fumptuous court   100

Read his defcription of the fingle fight,

Where Porus yielded to young Ammon's might ;

And, like a Scribe in courtly arts adroit,

Moft largely magnify'd his Lord's exploit:

* Ver. 92. See NOTE IV
† Ver. 97. See NOTE V.

7

Tho'

Tho' ever on the ftretch to Glory's goal,   105

Fame the firft paffion of his fiery foul !

Fierce from his feat the indignant Hero fprung,

And o'er the veffel's fide the volume flung ;

Then, as he faw the fawning Scribler fhrink,

" Thus fhould the Author with his Writing fink,   110

" Who ftifles Truth in Flattery's difguife,

" And buries honeft Fame beneath a load of Lies."

  But modern Princes, having lefs to lofe,

Rarely thefe infults on their name accufe :

In Dedications quietly inurn'd,*   115

They take more lying Praife than Ammon fpurn'd ;

And Learning's pliant Sons, to flattery prone,

Bend with fuch blind obeifance to the throne,

The bafeft King that ever curft the earth,

Finds many a witnefs to atteft his worth :   120

Tho' dead, ftill flatter'd by fome abject flave,

He fpreads contagious poifon from his grave,

* Ver. 115. See NOTE VI.

K   While

While fordid hopes th' Hiftorian's hand entice
To varnifh ev'n the tomb of Royal Vice.

   Tho' Nature wept with defolated Spain,   125
In tears of blood, the fecond Philip's reign;
Tho' fuch deep fins deform'd his fullen mind,
As merit execration from mankind :
A mighty empire by his crimes undone ;
A people maffacred ; a murder'd fon :   130
Tho' Heaven's difpleafure ftopt his parting breath,
To bear long loathfome pangs of hideous death ;
Flattery can ftill the Ruffian's praife repeat,
And call this Wafter of the earth difcreet :
Still can HERRERA, mourning o'er his urn, *   135
His dying pangs to blifsful rapture turn,
And paint the King, from earth by curfes driven,
A Saint, accepted by approving Heaven !

   But arts of deeper guile, and bafer wrong,
To Adulation's fubtle Scribes belong :   140

---

* Ver. 135. See NOTE VII.

              They

They oft, their prefent idols to exalt,

Profanely burft the confecrated vault;

Steal from the buried Chief bright Honour's plume,

Or ftain with Slander's gall the Statefman's tomb :

Stay, facrilegious flaves! with reverence tread   145

O'er the bleft afhes of the worthy dead!

See! where, uninjur'd by the charnel's damp,

The Veftal, Virtue, with undying lamp,

Fond of her toil, and jealous of her truft,

Sits the keen Guardian of their facred duft,   150

And thus indignant, from the depth of earth,

Checks your vile aim, and vindicates their worth :

" Hence ye! who buried excellence belied,

" To footh the fordid fpleen of living Pride ;

" Go! gild with Adulation's feeble ray   155

" Th' imperial pageant of your paffing day!

" Nor hope to ftain, on bafe Detraction's fcroll,

" A TULLY's morals, or a SIDNEY's foul!"— *

* Ver. 158. See NOTE VIII.

                    Juft

Juſt Nature will abhor, and Virtue ſcorn,

That Pen, tho' eloquence its page adorn,   160

Which, brib'd by Intereſt, or from vain pretence

To ſubtler Wit, and deep-diſcerning Senſe,

Would blot the praiſe on public toils beſtow'd,

And Patriot paſſions, as a jeſt, explode.

   Leſs abjeſt failings ſpring from Party-rage,   165

The peſt moſt frequent in th' Hiſtoric page ;

That common jaundice of the turbid brain,

Which leaves the heart unconſcious of a ſtain,

Yet ſuffers not the clouded mind to view

Or men, or aſtions, in their native hue :   170

For Party mingles, in her feveriſh dreams,

Credulity and Doubt's moſt wild extremes :

She gazes thro' a glaſs, whoſe different ends

Reduce her foes, and magnify her friends :

Deluſion ever on her ſpirit dwells ;   175

And to the worſt exceſs its fury ſwells,

When Superſtition's raging paſſions roll

Their ſavage frenzy thro' the Bigot's ſoul.

Nor

Nor lefs the blemifh, tho' of different kind, *

From falfe Philofophy's conceits refin'd !　　　　180

Her fubtle influence, on Hiftory fhed,

Strikes the fine nerve of Admiration dead,

(That nerve defpis'd by fceptic fons of earth,

Yet ftill a vital fpring of human worth.)

This artful juggler, with a fkill fo nice,　　　　185

Shifts the light forms of Virtue and of Vice,

That, ere this wakens fcorn, or that delight,

Behold ! they both are vanifh'd from the fight ;

And Nature's warm affections, thus deftroy'd,

Leave in the puzzled mind a lifelefs void.　　　　190

　Far other views the liberal Genius fire,

Whofe toils to pure Hiftoric praife afpire ;

Nor Moderation's dupe, nor Faction's brave,

Nor Guilt's apologift, nor Flattery's flave :

Wife, but not cunning ; temperate, not cold ;　　　　195

Servant of Truth, and in that fervice bold ;

* Ver. 179.　See N O T E IX.

Free from all biafs, fave that juft controul

By which mild Nature fways the manly foul,

And Reafon's philanthropic fpirit draws

To Virtue's intereft, and Freedom's caufe ;   200

Thofe great ennoblers of the human name,

Pure fprings of Power, of Happinefs, and Fame !

To teach their influence, and fpread their fway,

The juft Hiftorian winds his toilfome way ;

From filent darknefs, creeping o'er the earth,   205

Redeems the finking trace of ufeful worth ;

In Vice's bofom marks the latent thorn,

And brands that public peft with public fcorn.

A lively teacher in a moral fchool !

In that great office fteady, clear, and cool !   210

Pleas'd to promote the welfare of mankind,

And by informing meliorate the mind !

Such the bright tafk committed to his care !

Boundlefs its ufe ; but its completion rare.

   Critics have faid " Tho' high th' Hiftorian's charge, 215

His Law's as fimple as his Province large ;

Two

Two obvious rules enfure his full fuccefs—
To fpeak no Falfehood; and no Truth fupprefs: *
Art muft to other works a luftre lend,
But Hiftory pleafes, howfoe'er it's penn'd."   220

It may in ruder periods; but in thofe,
Where all the luxury of Learning flows,
To Truth's plain fare no palate will fubmit,
Each reader grows an Epicure in Wit;
And Knowledge muft his nicer tafte beguile   225
With all the poignant charms of Attic ftyle.
The curious Scholar, in his judgment choice,
Expects no common Notes from Hiftory's voice;
But all the tones, that all the paffions fuit,
From the bold Trumpet to the tender Lute: 230
Yet if thro' Mufic's fcale her voice fhould range,
Now high, now low, with many a pleafing change,
Grace muft thro' every variation glide,
In every movement Majefty prefide:

* Ver. 218. See NOTE X.

With

With eafe not carelefs, tho' correct not cold ;   235
Soft without languor, without harfhnefs bold.

  'Tho' Affectation can all works debafe,
In Language, as in Life, the bane of Grace !
Regarded ever with a fcornful fmile,
She moft is cenfur'd in th' Hiftoric ftyle :   240
Yet her infinuating power is fuch,
Not ev'n the Greeks efcap'd her baleful touch ;
And hence th' unutter'd Speech, and long Harangue,
Too oft, like weights, on ancient Story hang.
Lefs fond of labour, modern Pens devife   245
Affected beauties of inferior fize :
They in a narrower compafs boldly ftrike
The fancied Portrait, with no feature like ;
And Nature's fimple colouring vainly quit,
To boaft the brilliant glare of fading Wit.   250
Thofe works alone may that bleft fate expect
To live thro' time, unconfcious of neglect,
That catch, in fpringing from no fordid fource,
The eafe of Nature, and of Truth the force.

                But

But not ev'n Truth, with bright Expreſſion grac'd, 255

Nor all Deſcription's powers, in lucid order plac'd,

Not even theſe a fond regard engage,

Or bind attention to th' Hiſtoric page,

If diſtant tribes compoſe th' ill-choſen Theme,

Whoſe ſavage virtues wake no warm eſteem;   260

Where Faith and Valour ſpring from Honour's grave,

Only to form th' Aſſaſſin and the Slave.

From Turkiſh tyrants, ſtain'd with ſervile gore,

Enquiry turns; and Learning's ſighs deplore,

While o'er his name Neglect's cold ſhadow rolls,   265

A waſte of Genius in the toil of KNOLLES. *

There are, we own, whoſe magic power is ſuch,

Their hands embelliſh whatſoe'er they touch:

Their bright Moſaic ſo enchants our eyes,

By nice Arrangement, and contraſted Dies,   270

What mean materials in the texture lurk,

Serve but to raiſe the wonder of the work.

* Ver. 266. See NOTE X.

L   Yet

[74]

Yet from th' Hiſtorian (as ſuch power is rare)
The choice of Matter claims no trifling care.

  'Tis not alone collected Wealth's diſplay,   275
Nor the proud fabric of extended Sway,
That mark (tho' both the eye of Wonder fill)
The happy Subject for Hiſtoric ſkill :
Wherever Nature, tho' in narrow ſpace,
Foſters, by Freedom's aid, a liberal race ;   280
Sees Virtue ſave them from Oppreſſion's den,
And cries, with exultation, " Theſe are Men ;"
Tho' in Bœotia or Batavia born,
Their deeds the Story of the World adorn.

  The Subject fix'd, with force and beauty fraught, 285
Juſt Diſpoſition claims yet deeper thought ;
To caſt enlivening Order's lucid grace
O'er all the crouded fields of Time and Space ;
To ſhew each wheel of Power in all its force,
And trace the ſtreams of Action from their ſource ; 290
To catch, with ſpirit and preciſion join'd,
The varying features of the human Mind ;

The

The Grace, the Strength, that Nature's children draw
From Arts, from Science, Policy, and Law ;
Opinion's fafhion, Wifdom's firmer plan,   295
And all that marks the character of Man.
Of all the parts, that Hiftory's volume fill,
The juft Digreffion claims the niceft fkill ;
As the fwift Hero, in the Olympic race,
Ran with lefs toil along the open fpace ;   300
But round the Goal to form the narrow curve,
Call'd forth his utmoft ftrength from every nerve.

The Subject's various powers let Study tell !
And teach th' Hiftorian on what points to dwell !
How in due fhades to fink each meaner part,   305
And pour on nobler forms the radiance of his art !
Tho' Patriot Love the curious fpirit fires
With thirft to hear th' atchievements of his Sires ;
And Britifh ftory wins the Britifh mind
With all the charms that fond attention bind ;   310
Its early periods, barbarous and remote,
Pleafe not, tho' drawn by Pens of nobleft note :

L 2

O'er

O'er thofe rude fcenes Confufion's fhadows dwell,

Beyond the power of Genius to difpell ;

Mifts ! which ev'n MILTON's fplendid mind enfhroud ;

Loft in the darknefs of the Saxon cloud!   316

    Neglect alone repays their flight offence,

Whofe wand'ring wearies our bewilder'd fenfe :

But juft Abhorrence brands his guilty name,

Who dares to vilify his Country's fame ;   320

With Slander's rage the pen of Hiftory grafp,

And pour from thence the poifon of the Afp ;

The murd'rous falfehood, ftifling Honour's breath !

The flavifh tenet, Public Virtue's death !

With all that undermines a Nation's health,   325

And robs the People of their richeft wealth !

Ye tools of Tyranny ! whofe fervile guile

Would thus pollute the records of our ifle,

Behold your Leader curft with public hate,

And read your juft reward in BRADY's fate ! *   330

* Ver. 330. See N O T E XII.

O facred

O facred Liberty ! fhall Faction's train
Pervert the reverend archives of thy reign ?
Shall flaves traduce the blood thy votaries fpilt,
Blafpheming Glory with the name of Guilt ?
And fhall no Son of thine their wiles o'erwhelm,   335
And clear the ftory of thy injur'd realm ?
To this bright tafk fome Britifh fpirit raife,
With powers furpaffing ev'n a LIVY's praife !
Thro' this long wildernefs his march infpire,
And make thy temperate flame his leading fire !   340
Teach his keen eye, and comprehenfive foul,
To pierce each darker part, and grafp the whole !
Let Truth's undoubted fignet feal his page,
And Glory guard the work from age to age !
That Britifh minds from this pure fource may draw 345
Senfe of thy Rights, and paffion for thy Law,
Wifdom to prize, and Honour, that afpires
To reach that virtue which adorn'd our Sires !

But not alone our native land attracts ;
Far different Nations boaft their fplendid facts :   350

                                        In

In ancient Story the rich fruits unite
Of civil Wifdom and fublime Delight :
At Rome's proud name Attention's fpirits rife,
Rome, the firft idol of our infant eyes !
Ufe and Importance mark the vaft defign,   355
Clearly to trace her periods of Decline.
Yet here, O GIBBON ! what long toils enfue ?
How winds the labyrinth ? how fails the clue ?
Tho' rude materials Time's deep trenches fill,
A radiant ftructure rifes from thy fkill ;   360
Whofe fplendor, fpringing from a dreary wafte,
Enchants the wondering eye of Public Tafte.
Thus to the ancient traveller, whofe way
Acrofs the hideous fands of Syria lay,
The Defart blaz'd with fudden glory bright ;   365
And rich Palmyra rufh'd upon his fight.

   But O ! what foes befet each honour'd Name,
Advancing in the path of letter'd fame !
To ftop thy progrefs, and infult thy pen,
The fierce Polemic iffues from his den.   370

Think

Think not my Verfe means blindly to engage

In rafh defence of thy profaner page !

Tho' keen her fpirit, her attachment fond,

Bafe fervice cannot fuit with Friendfhip's bond ;

Too firm from Duty's facred path to turn, 375

She breathes an honeft figh of deep concern,

And pities Genius, when his wild career

Gives Faith a wound, or Innocence a fear.

Humility herfelf, divinely mild,

Sublime Religion's meek and modeft child, 380

Like the dumb Son of CROESUS, in the ftrife, *

Where Force affail'd his Father's facred life,

Breaks filence, and, with filial duty warm,

Bids thee revere her Parent's hallow'd form !

Far other founds the ear of Learning ftun, 385

From proud Theology's contentious Son ;

Lefs eager to correct, than to revile, †

Rage in his voice ! and Rancour in his ftyle !

* Ver. 381. See N O T E XIII.
† Ver. 387. See N O T E XIV.

His

His idle scoffs with coarse reproof deride
Thy generous thirst of Praise, and liberal Pride ;   390
Because thy spirit dares that wish avow,
Which Reason owns, and Wisdom must allow!
The noble Instinct, Love of lasting Fame,*
Was wisely planted in the human frame :
From hence the brightest rays of History flow ;   395
To this their Vigour and their Use they owe.
Nor scorns fair Virtue this untainted source,
From hence she often draws her lovely force :
For Heaven this passion with our life combin'd,
Which, like a central power, impels the languid mind. 400
When, clear from Envy's cloud, that general pest !
It burns most brightly in the Author's breast,
Its soothing hopes his various pains beguile,
And give to Learning's face her sweetest smile :
What joy, to think his Genius may create   405
Existence far beyond the common date !

* Ver. 393. See NOTE XV.

His Wealth of Mind to lateſt ages give,

And in Futurity's affection live!

From unborn Beauty, ſtill to Fancy dear,

Draw with ſoft magic the delightful tear ;   410

Or thro' the boſom of far diſtant Youth,

Spread the warm glow of Liberty and Truth!

  O GIBBON ! by thy frank ambition taught,

Let me like thee maintain th' enlivening thought,

That, from Oblivion's killing cloud ſecure,   415

My Hope may proſper, and my Verſe endure :

While thy bright Name, on Hiſtory's car ſublime,

Rolls in juſt triumph o'er the field of Time,

May I, unfaltering, thy long march attend,

No flattering Slave ! but an applauding Friend !   420

Diſplay th' imperfect ſketch I fondly drew,

Of that wide province, where thy laurels grew ;

And, honour'd with a wreath of humbler bays,

Join the loud Pæan of thy laſting praiſe !

M

NOTES

N O T E S.

Indocti difcant et ament meminiffe periti.

NOTES

TO THE

FIRST EPISTLE,

NOTE I. VERSE 4.

TH' unfailing urns of Praise and Censure stand.]

Δοιοὶ γάρ τε πίθοι κατακείαται ἐν Διὸς οὔδει
Δώρων, οἷα δίδωσι, κακῶν· ἕτερος δὲ ἑάων·

Two urns by Jove's high throne have ever stood,
The source of evil one, and one of good.

POPE's Iliad xxiv. v. 663.

NOTE II. VERSE 55.

Yet one excelling Greek, &c.] Dionysius of Halicarnassus, the celebrated historian and critic of the Augustan age, who settled in Italy, as he himself informs us, on the close of the civil war. He has addressed a little treatise, containing a critique on the elder historians, to his friend Cnæus Pompeius, whom the French critics

tics suppose to be Pompey the Great; but Reiske, the last editor of Dionysius, has sunk him into a petty Greek grammarian, the client or freedman of that illustrious Roman.

In this treatise of Dionysius, and in one still longer, on the character of Thucydides, there are some excellent historical precepts, which Mr. Spelman has judiciously thrown together in the preface to his admirable translation of the Roman Antiquities.— He introduces them by the following observation, which may serve perhaps to recommend the subject of the present poem.— " So much has been said, both by the antients and the moderns, in praise of the advantages resulting from the study of History, particularly by Diodorus Siculus among the former, in the noble preface to his Historical Collections; and by the late Lord Bolingbroke, among the moderns, in his admirable letter on that subject; that I am astonished no treatise has ever yet appeared in any age, or any language, professedly written to prescribe rules for writing History; a work allowed to be of the greatest advantage of all others to mankind, the repository of truth, fraught with lessons both of public and private virtue, and enforced by stronger motives than precepts—by examples. Rules for Poetry and Rhetoric have been written by many authors, both antient and modern, as if delight and eloquence were of greater consequence than instruction : however, Rhetoric was a part of History, as treated by the antients; not the principal part indeed, but subservient to the principal; and calculated to apply the facts exhibited by the narration. I know it may be said, that many antient histories are still preserved, and that these models are sufficient guides for modern Historians, without particular rules : so had the Greeks Poets of all denominations in their hands, and yet Aristotle thought it necessary to prescribe particular rules to his countrymen for applying those examples to every branch of Poetry : I wish he had done the same in History; if he had, it is very probable that his precepts would have rendered

2

the

the beſt of our modern Hiſtories more perfect, and the worſt, leſs
abominable.—Since the reſurrection of letters, the want of ſuch a
guide has been complained of by many authors, and particularly
by Rapin, in the preface to his Hiſtory of England."—Spelman,
page 15.   But this ingenious and learned writer ſpeaks a little too
ſtrongly, in ſaying no treatiſe has ever appeared in any age or language, containing rules for Hiſtory.   There is one in Latin by the
celebrated Voſſius, entitled Ars Hiſtorica; another by Hubertus
Folieta, an elegant Latin writer, of the 16th century, on whom
Thuanus beſtows the higheſt commendation; and Maſcardi, an
Italian critic, patroniſed by Cardinal Mazarine, has written alſo
dell Arte Hiſtorica.   The curious reader may find a ſingular anecdote relating to the publication of this work in Bayle, under the
article Maſcardi.   But to return to Dionyſius, in comparing Herodotus and Thucydides,   He cenſures the latter with a degree of
ſeverity unwarranted by truth and reaſon : indeed this ſeverity appeared ſo ſtriking to the learned Fabricius, that he ſeems to conſider it as a kind of proof, that the critical works of Dionyſius were
compoſed in the haſty fervor of youth.   They are however in general, to uſe the words of the ſame ingenuous author, eximia & lectu
digna; and a valuable critic of our own country, who reſembles
Dionyſius in elegance of compoſition, and perhaps in ſeverity of
judgment, has ſpoken yet more warmly in their favour.—See
Warton's Eſſay on Pope, 3d edit. page 175.

NOTE III. Verse 63.

And Lucian! thou, of Humour's ſons ſupreme!] The little treatiſe of
Lucian " How Hiſtory ſhould be written," may be conſidered as
one of the moſt valuable productions of that lively author; it is
not only written with great vivacity and wit, but is entitled to the
ſuperior

superior praise of breathing most exalted sentiments of liberty and virtue. There is a peculiar kind of sublimity in his description of an accomplished Historian.

Τοιουτος ουν μοι ο συγγραφευς εστω, αφοβος, αδεκαστος, ελευθερος, παρρησιας και αληθειας φιλος, ως ο Κωμικος φησι, τα συκα, συκα, την σκαφην δε σκαφην ονομαζων, ου μισει, ουδε φιλια νεμων, ουδε φειδομενος, η ελεων, η αισχυνομενος, η δυσωπουμενος· ισος δικαστης, ευνης απασιν, αχρι του μη θατερω τι απονειμαι πλειον τη δεοντος· ξενος εν τοις βιβλιοις, και απολις, αυτονομος, αβασιλευτος, ου τι τωδε, η τωδε δοξει λογιζομενος, αλλα τι πεπρακται λεγων.

It is a piece of justice due to our own country to remark, that in the 3d volume of the World, there is a ludicrous essay on History by Mr. Cambridge, which is written with all the spirit and all the humour of Lucian.

NOTE IV.   VERSE 68.

And rose a Xenophon in self-esteem.] Ουδεις δε τις ουχ ιστοριαν συγγραφει· μαλλον δε Θουκυδιδαι, και Ηροδοτοι, και Ξενοφωντες ημιν απαντες.

LUCIAN. edit. Riollay, p. 6.

NOTE V.   VERSE 77.

In Egypt once a dread tribunal stood.] This singular institution, which is alluded to by many of our late authors, is related at large in the First Book of Diodorus Siculus; and as the passage is curious, the following free translation of it may afford entertainment to the English reader—" Those who prepare to bury a relation, give notice of the day intended for the ceremony to the judges, and to all the friends of the deceased; informing them, that the body will pass over the lake of that district to which the dead be-

longed:

5

longed : when, on the judges being affembled, to the number of
more than forty, and ranging themfelves in a femicircle on the
farther fide of the lake, the veffel is fet afloat, which thofe who
fuperintend the funeral have prepared for this purpofe. This veffel
is managed by a pilot, called in the Egyptian language Charon ; and
hence they fay, that Orpheus, travelling in old times into Egypt,
and feeing this ceremony, formed his fable of the infernal regions,
partly from what he faw, and partly from invention. The veffel
being launched on the lake, before the coffin which contains the
body is put on board, the law permits all, who are fo inclined, to
produce an accufation againft it.—If any one fteps forth, and proves
that the deceafed has led an evil life, the judges pronounce fentence,
and the body is precluded from burial ; but if the accufer is convicted of injuftice in his charge, he falls himfelf under a confiderable penalty. When no accufer appears, or when the accufer is
proved to be an unfair one, the relations, who are affembled,
change their expreffions of forrow into encomiums on the dead :
yet they do not, like the Greeks, fpeak in honour of his family,
becaufe they confider all Egyptians as equally well-born ; but they
fet forth the education and manners of his youth, his piety and
juftice in maturer life, his moderation and every virtue by which
he was diftinguifhed ; and they fupplicate the infernal Deities to
receive him as an affociate among the bleft. The multitude join
their acclamations of applaufe in this celebration of the dead, whom
they confider as going to pafs an eternity among the juft below * "—
Such is the defcription which Diodorus gives of this funereal
judicature, to which even the kings of Egypt were fubject. The
fame author afferts, that many fovereigns had been thus judi-cially
deprived of the honours of burial by the indignation of their people : and that the terrors of fuch a fate had a moft falutary influence
on the virtue of their kings.

* Diodor. Siculi Lib. i. Τις δὲ μελλόντων ταφησομένων —

The Abbè Terrasson has drawn a sublime picture of this sepulchral procefs, and indeed of many Egyptian Myfteries, in his
very learned and ingenious romance, The Life of Sethos.

NOTE VI.   Verse 115.

The infant Mufe, ambitious at her birth,
Rofe the young herald of heroic worth.]   " Not only the Greek
writers give a concurrent teftimony concerning the priority of
hiftorical Verfe to Profe; but the records of all nations unite
in confirming it.   The oldeft compofitions among the Arabs
are in Rythm or rude Verfe; and are often cited as proofs of the
truth of their fubfequent Hiftory.   The accounts we have of
the Peruvian ftory confirm the fame fact; for Garcilaffo tells us,
that he compiled a part of his Commentaries from the antient
fongs of the country—Nay all the American tribes, who have
any compofitions, are found to eftablifh the fame truth—Northern
Europe contributes its fhare of teftimony : for there too we find
the Scythian or Runic fongs (many of them hiftorical) to be the
oldeft compofitions among thefe barbarous nations."

BROWNE'S Differtation on Poetry, &c. Page 50.

NOTE VII.   Verse 131.

But in the center of thofe vaft abodes,
Whofe mighty mafs the land of Egypt loads.]   This account of the
Pyramids I have adopted from the very learned Mr Bryant, part
of whofe ingenious obfervation upon them I fhall here prefent
to the reader.—

One great purpofe in all eminent and expenfive ftructures is to
pleafe the ftranger and traveller, and to win their admiration. This

is

is effected fometimes by a mixture of magnificence and beauty:
at other times folely by immenfity and grandeur. The latter
feems to have been the object in the erecting of thofe celebrated
buildings in Egypt : and they certainly have anfwered the defign.
For not only the vaftnefs of their ftructure, and the area which they
occupy, but the ages they have endured, and the very uncertainty
of their hiftory, which runs fo far back into the depths of antiquity,
produce altogether a wonderful veneration ; to which buildings
more exquifite and embellifhed are feldom entitled. Many have
fuppofed, that they were defigned for places of fepulture : and it
has been affirmed by Herodotus, and other ancient writers. But
they fpoke by guefs : and I have fhewn by many inftances, how
ufual it was for the Grecians to miftake temples for tombs. If the
chief Pyramid, were defigned for a place of burial, what occafion
was there for a well, and for paffages of communication which led
to other buildings? Near the Pyramids are apartments of a wonderful fabric, which extend in length one thoufand four hundred feet,
and about thirty in depth. They have been cut out of the hard rock,
and brought to a perpendicular by the artift's chizel ; and through
dint of labour fafhioned as they now appear. They were undoubtedly defigned for the reception of priefts ; and confequently were
not appendages to a tomb, but to a temple of the Deity . . ..
The priefts of Egypt delighted in obfcurity ; and they probably
came by the fubterraneous paffages of the building to the dark
chambers within ; where they performed their luftrations, and other
nocturnal rites. Many of the ancient temples in this country were
caverns in the rock, enlarged by art, and cut out into numberlefs
dreary apartments : for no nation upon earth was fo addicted to
gloom and melancholy as the Egyptians.

Bryant's Analyfis, Vol. III. Page 529.

N 2 N O T E

NOTE VIII.   Verse 190.

Of the fierce Omar, &c.]   The number of volumes deftroyed
in the plunder of Alexandria is faid to have been fo great, that although they were diftributed to heat four thoufand baths in that
city, it was fix months before they were confumed.   When a pe-
tition was fent to the Chaliph Omar for the prefervation of this
magnificent library, he replied, in the true fpirit of bigotry, " What
is contained in thefe books you mention, is either agreeable to what
is written in the book of God (meaning the Alcoran) or it is not:
if it be, then the Alcoran is fufficient without them : if otherwife,
'tis fit they fhould be deftroyed."

Ockley's Hiftory of the Saracens, Vol. I. Page 313.

NOTE IX.   Verse 203.

The dome expands!—Behold th' Hiftoric Sire!]   Herodotus, to
whom Cicero has given the honourable appellation of The Father
of Hiftory, was born in Halicarnaffus, a city of Caria, four years
before the invafion of Xerxes, in the year 484 before Chrift.   The
time and place of his death are uncertain ; but his countryman
Dionyfius informs us, that he lived to the beginning of the Pelo-
ponnefian war ; and Marcellinus, the Greek author who wrote a
life of Thucydides, affirms there was a monument erected to thefe
two great Hiftorians in a burial-place belonging to the family of
Miltiades.

There is hardly any author, antient or modern, who has been
more warmly commended, or more vehemently cenfured, than this
eminent Hiftorian.   But even the fevere Dionyfius declares, he is
one of thofe enchanting writers, whom you perufe to the laft fyl-
lable with pleafure, and ftill wifh for more.—Plutarch himfelf, who
has made the moft violent attack on his veracity, allows him all
the

the merit of beautiful compofition.   From the heavy charges
brought againſt him by the antients, the famous Henry Stephens,
and his learned friend Camerarius, have defended their favourite Hiſtorian with great ſpirit.   But Herodotus has found a more formidable antagoniſt in a learned and animated writer of our own
times, to whom the public have been lately indebted for his having
opened to them new mines of Oriental learning.—If the ingenious
Mr. Richardſon could effectually ſupport his Perſian ſyſtem, the
great Father of the Grecian ſtory muſt ſink into a fabuliſt as low in
point of veracity as Geoffrey of Monmouth.   It muſt be owned,
that ſeveral eminent Writers of our country have treated him as
ſuch.   Another Orientaliſt, who, in his elegant Preface to the Life of
Nader Shaw, has drawn a ſpirited and judicious ſketch of many capital Hiſtorians, declares, in paſſing judgment on Herodotus, that
" his accounts of the Perſian affairs are at leaſt doubtful, if not
fabulous."—Hume, I think, goes ſtill farther, and ſays, in one of
his eſſays—" The firſt page of Thucydides is, in my opinion, the
commencement of real Hiſtory."   For my own part, I confeſs myſelf more credulous : the relation, which Herodotus has given of
the repulſe of Xerxes from Greece, is ſo delightful to the mind,
and ſo animating to public virtue, that I ſhould be ſorry to number it among the Grecian fables.

———Et madidis cantat quæ Soſtratus alis.

N O T E X.   VERSE 206.

As the fair figure of his favour'd Queen.] Artemiſia of Halicar-
naſſus, who commanded in perſon the five veſſels, which ſhe contributed to the expedition of Xerxes.   On hearing that ſhe had
funk a Grecian galley in the ſea-fight at Salamis, he exclaimed,
that his men had proved women, and his women men.

HEROD. Lib. VIII. p. 660.   Edit. Weſſ.

7   N O T E

NOTE XI.   VERSE 209.

Soft as the stream, whose dimpling waters play.] Sine ullis sale-
bris quafi fedatus amnis fluit.

CICERO in Oratore.

NOTE XII.   VERSE 225.

But mark the Youth, in dumb delight immers'd.] Thucydides,
the fon of Olorus, was born at Athens in the year 471 before
Chrift, and is faid, at the age of 15, to have heard Herodotus
recite his Hiftory at the Olympic games.—The generous youth
was charmed even to tears, and the Hiftorian congratulated
Olorus on thefe marks of genius, which he difcovered in his fon.
—Being invefted with a military command, he was banifhed from
Athens at the age of 48, by the injuftice of faction, becaufe he
had unfortunately failed in the defence of Amphipolis.—He retired
into Thrace, and is reported to have married a Thracian lady poffeffed of valuable mines in that country.—At the end of 20 years
his fentence of banifhment was revoked. Some authors affirm
that he returned to Athens, and was treacheroufly killed in that
city. But others affert that he died in Thrace, at the advanced age
of 80, leaving his Hiftory unfinifhed.

MARCELLINUS; and DODWELL. Annales Thucydid.

NOTE XIII.   VERSE 251.

A generous guardian of a rival's fame.] It is faid by Diogenes
Laertius, that Xenophon firft brought the Hiftory of Thucydides
10   into

into public reputation, though he had it in his power to affume to himfelf all the glory of that work. This amiable
Philofopher and Hiftorian was born at Athens, and became
early a difciple of Socrates, who is faid by Strabo to have faved
his life in battle. About the 50th year of his age, according to
the conjecture of his admirable tranflator Mr. Spelman, he engaged
in the expedition of Cyrus, and accomplifhed his immortal retreat
in the fpace of 15 months.—The jealoufy of the Athenians banifhed him from his native city, for engaging in the fervice of
Sparta and of Cyrus.—On his return therefore he retired to Scillus,
a town of Elis, where he built a temple to Diana, which he mentions in his Epiftles, and devoted his leifure to philofophy and
rural fports.—But commotions arifing in that country, he removed
to Corinth, where he is fuppofed to have written his Grecian
Hiftory, and to have died at the age of ninety, in the year 360
before Chrift. By his wife Philefia he had two fons, Diodorus and
Gryllus. The latter rendered himfelf immortal by killing Epa-
minondas in the famous battle of Mantinea, but perifhed in that
exploit, which his father lived to record.

NOTE XIV.   VERSE 273.

Rome's haughty genius, who enflav'd the Greek,

In Grecian language deigns at firft to fpeak.] Some of the
moft illuftrious Romans are known to have written Hiftories
in Greek. The luxuriant Lucullus, when he was very young,
compofed in that language a Hiftory of the Marfi, which, Plutarch fays, was extant in his time—Cicero wrote a Greek Commentary on his own confulfhip—and the elegant Atticus produced
a fimilar work on the fame fubject, that did not perfectly fatisfy
the nice ear of his friend, as we learn from the following curious

paffage

paſſage in a letter concerning the Hiſtory in queſtion :—" Quanquam tua illa (legi enim libenter) horridula mihi atque incompta viſa ſunt : ſed tamen erant ornata hoc ipſo, quod ornamenta neglexerant, et ut mulieres, ideo bene olere, quia nihil olebant, videbantur."   Epiſt. ad ATTICUM. Lib. II. Ep. 1.

NOTE XV.   VERSE 279.

Thou friend of Scipio! vers'd in War's alarms.] Polybius, born at Megalopolis in Arcadia, 205 years before Chriſt.—He was trained to arms under the celebrated Philopœmen, and is deſcribed by Plutarch carrying the urn of that great but unfortunate General in his funeral proceſſion. He aroſe to conſiderable honours in his own country, but was compelled to viſit Rome with other principal Achæans, who were detained there as pledges for the ſubmiſſion of their ſtate.—From hence he became intimate with the ſecond Scipio Africanus, and was preſent with him at the demolition of Carthage.—He ſaw Corinth alſo plundered by Mummius, and thence paſſing through the cities of Achaia, reconciled them to Rome.—He extended his travels into Egypt, France, and Spain, that he might avoid ſuch geographical errors as he has cenſured in other writers of Hiſtory. He lived to the age of 82, and died of an illneſs occaſioned by a fall from his horſe.   FABRICIUS, Bibliotheca Græca.

In cloſing this conciſe account of the capital Greek Hiſtorians, I cannot help obſerving, that our language has been greatly enriched, in the courſe of the preſent century, by ſuch tranſlations of theſe Authors as do great honour to our country, and are at leaſt equal to any which other nations have produced.

In the chief Roman Hiſtorians we ſeem to have been leſs fortunate; but from the ſpecimen which Mr. Aikin has lately given

the

the public in the fmaller pieces of Tacitus, we may hope to fee
an excellent verfion of that valuable author, who has been hitherto
ill treated in our language, and among all the antients there is
none perhaps whom it is more difficult to tranflate with fidelity and
fpirit.

NOTE XVI. VERSE 297.

Sententious Salluft leads her lofty train.] This celebrated Hiftorian, who from the irregularity of his life, and the beauty of
his writings, has been called, not unhappily, the Bolingbroke
of Rome, was born at Amiternum, a town of the Sabines.——
For the profligacy of his early life he was expelled the fenate, but reftored by the intereft of Julius Cæfar, who gave him
the command of Numidia, which province he is faid to have plundered by the moft infamous extortion, purchafing with part of this
treafure thofe rich and extenfive poffeffions on the Quirinal Hill,
fo celebrated by the name of the Horti Salluftiani.——He died in
the 70th year of his age, four years before the battle of Actium,
and 35 before the Chriftian æra. His enmity to Cicero is well
known, and perhaps it had fome influence on the peculiarity of his
diction—perfonal animofity might make him endeavour to form a
ftyle as remote as poffible from the redundant language of the immortal Orator, whofe turbulent wife, Terentia, he is faid to have
married after her divorce. This extraordinary woman is reported
to have lived to the age of 103, to have married Meffala, her third
hufband, and Vibius Rufus her fourth.——The latter boafted, with
the joy of an Antiquarian, that he poffeffed two of the greateft cu-
riofities in the world, namely Terentia, who had been Cicero's wife,
and the chair in which Cæfar was killed.——St. JEROM ; and DIO
CASSIUS, quoted by Middleton in his life of Cicero.——But to re-

O

turn

turn to Salluſt.—His Roman Hiſtory, in ſix books, from the death of
Sylla to the conſpiracy of Catiline, the great work from which he
chiefly derived his glory among the Antients, is unfortunately loſt,
excepting a few fragments;—but his two detached pieces of
Hiſtory, which happily remain entire, are ſufficient to juſtify the
great encomiums he has received as a writer.—He has had the ſingular honour to be twice tranſlated by a royal hand—firſt by our
Elizabeth, according to Camden; and ſecondly by the preſent Infant of Spain, whoſe verſion of this elegant Hiſtorian, lately
printed in folio, is one of the moſt beautiful books that any country has produced ſince the invention of printing.

N O T E XVII.   VERSE 311.

In bright pre-eminence, that Greece might own,
Sublimer Livy claims th' Hiſtoric throne.] All the little per-
ſonal account, that can be collected of Livy, amounts only
to this—that he was born at Patavium, the modern Padua;
that he was choſen by Auguſtus to ſuperintend the education
of the ſtupid Claudius; that he was rallied by the Emperor
for his attachment to the cauſe of the Republic; and that he died
in his own country in the 4th year of Tiberius, at the age of 76.—
There is a paſſage in one of Pliny's letters, which, as it ſhews the
high and extenſive reputation of our Hiſtorian during his life, I
ſhall preſent to the reader in the words of Pliny's moſt elegant
tranſlator.—" Do you remember to have read of a certain inhabi-
tant of the city of Cadiz, who was ſo ſtruck with the illuſtrious
character of Livy, that he travelled to Rome on purpoſe to ſee that
great Genius; and as ſoon as he had ſatisfied his curioſity, returned
home again?"—MELMOTH's Pliny, Vol. I. Page 71.——A veneration
ſtill more extraordinary was paid to this great author by Alphonſo

King

King of Naples, who in 1451 fent Panormita as his Ambaffador to
the Venetians, in whofe dominion the bones of Livy had been
lately difcovered, to beg a relic of this celebrated Hiftorian.—
They prefented him with an arm-bone, and the Prefent is recorded
in an infcription preferved at Padua, which the curious reader may
find in Voffius de Hiftoricis Latinis. This fingular anecdote is
alfo related in Bayle, under the article Panormita.——Learning perhaps never fuftained a greater lofs, in any fingle author, than by
the deftruction of the latter and more interefting part of Livy.—
Several eminent moderns have indulged the pleafing expectation that
the entire work of this noble Hiftorian might yet be recovered.—
It has been faid to exift in an Arabic verfion: and even a compleat
copy of the original is fuppofed to have been extant as late as the
year 1631, and to have perifhed at that time in the plunder of Mag-
deburgh.—That munificent patron of learning, Leo the Xth, exerted the moft generous zeal to refcue from oblivion the valuable
treafure, which one of his moft bigotted predeceffors, Gregory the
Great, had expelled from every Chriftian library.—Bayle has preferved, under the article Leo, two curious original letters of that
Pontiff, concerning his hopes of recovering Livy; which afford
moft honourable proofs of his liberality in the caufe of letters.

NOTE XVIII. VERSE 325.

Yet, like the matchlefs, mutilated frame,

To which great Angelo bequeath'd his name.] The trunk of a
ftatue of Hercules by Apollonius the Athenian, univerfally
called the Torfo of Michael Angelo, from its having been the
favourite ftudy of that divine Artift.—He is faid to have made
out the compleat figure in a little model of wax, ftill preferved at Florence, and reprefenting Hercules repofing after his
O 2

labours.—

labours.—The figure is fitting in a penfive pofture, with an elbow refting on the knee.

NOTE XIX.   VERSE 333.

Sarcaftic Tacitus, abrupt and dark.] Tacitus was born, according to the conjecture of Lipfius, in the clofe of the reign of Claudius: paffing through various public honours, he rofe at length to the confular dignity, under Nerva, in the year of Chrift 97. The date of his death is unknown, but he is faid to have lived happily to an advanced age with his wife, the amiable daughter of the virtuous Agricola, whofe life he has fo beautifully written. By this lady he is fuppofed to have left children; and the emperor Tacitus is conjectured to have been a remote defcendant from the Hiftorian, to whofe works and memory he paid the higheft regard.—It is reported by Sidonius Apollinaris, that Tacitus recommended the province of writing Hiftory to Pliny the Younger, and that he did not himfelf engage in that employment, till his friend had declined it. This is not mentioned, indeed, in any of the beautiful letters ftill remaining from Pliny to Tacitus; but it is an inftance of delicacy not unparallel'd among the Antients, as will appear from the following remark by one of the moft elegant and liberal of modern critics.—" The Roman Poet, who was not more eminent by his genius than amiable in his moral character, affords perhaps the moft remarkable inftance that any where occurs, of the conceffions which a mind ftrongly impregnated with fentiments of genuine amity, is capable of making. Virgil's fuperior talents rendered him qualified to excel in all the nobler fpecies of poetical compofition: neverthelefs, from the moft uncommon delicacy of friendfhip, he facrificed to his intimacy with Horace, the unrivall'd reputation he might have acquired by indulging his lyric vein; as from the fame refined motive he forbore to exercife his dramatic

powers,

powers, that he might not obfcure the glory of his friend Va-
rius.

> Aurum et opes et rura, frequens donabit amicus :
>   Qui velit *ingenio cedere,* rarus erit."
>
> MART. VIII. 18.

MELMOTH's Remarks on LÆLIUS, Page 292:

As to Tacitus, it is clear, I think, from the Letters of Pliny,
as well as from his own moft pleafing Life of Agricola, that he poffeffed all the refined and affectionate feelings of the heart in a very
high degree, though the general caft of his hiftorical works might
lead us to imagine, that aufterity was his chief characteriftic.—It
would be eafy to fill a volume in tranfcribing the great encomiums,
and the violent cenfures, which have been lavifhed by modern
writers of almoft every country on this profound Hiftorian.—The
laft critic of eminence, who has written againft him, in Britain, is,
I believe, the learned Author of The Origin and Progrefs of Language ; who, in his 3d volume of that work, has made many curious remarks on the compofition of the antient Hiftorians, and is
particularly fevere on the diction of Tacitus. He reprefents him
as the defective model, from which modern writers have copied,
what he is pleafed to call, " *the fhort and priggifh cut of ftyle fo
much in ufe now.*"

NOTE XX. VERSE 356.

Thy Plutarch fhines, by moral beauty known.] It is to be wifhed,
that this moft amiable Moralift and Biographer had added a Life of
himfelf, to thofe which he has given to the world: as the particulars, which other Writers have preferved of his perfonal Hiftory,
are very doubtful and imperfect. According to the learned Fabri-

cius.

cius, he was born under Claudius, 50 years after the Christian æra, raised to the consular dignity under Trajan, whose preceptor he is said to have been, and made Procurator of Greece in his old age by the Emperor Adrian—in the 5th year of whose reign he is supposed to have died, at the age of 70. He was married to a most amiable woman of his own native town Chæronea, whose name was Timoxena, and to whose sense and virtue he has borne the most affectionate testimony in his moral works; of which it may be regretted that we have no elegant translation. Indeed even the Lives of Plutarch, the most popular of all the antient historical compositions, were chiefly known to the English reader by a motley and miserable version, till a new one, executed with fidelity and spirit, was presented to the public by the Langhornes in 1770.

NOTE XXI.   Verse 379.

Mild Marcellinus! free from servile awe!] Ammianus Marcellinus, a Grecian and a Soldier, as he calls himself, flourished under Constantius and the succeeding emperors, as late as Theodosius. He served under Julian in the East, and wrote a History from the reign of Nerva to the death of Valens, in 31 books, of which 18 only remain.—The time and circumstances of his own death are unknown.—Bayle has an article on Marcellinus, in which he observes, that he has introduced a most bitter invective against the Practitioners of Law into his History.—He should have added, that the Historian bestows great encomiums on some illustrious characters of that profession, and even mentions the peculiar hardship to which Advocates are themselves exposed.—The curious reader may find this passage, Lib. xxx. Cap. 4.

NOTE

NOTE XXII.   VERSE 399.

And, with Comnena's royal name impreſt.] Anna Comnena was the eldeſt daughter of the emperor Alexius Comnenus, and the empreſs Irene, born 1083.—She wrote the Hiſtory of her father, in 15 books, firſt publiſhed, very imperfectly, by Hæſchelius, in 1610, and ſince printed in the collection of the Byzantine Hiſtorians, with a diffuſe and incorrect Latin verſion by the Jeſuit Poſſinus, but with excellent notes by the learned Du Freſne.

Conſidering the miſeries of the time in which ſhe lived, and the merits of her work—which ſome Critics have declared ſuperior to every other in that voluminous collection—this Lady may be juſtly regarded as a ſingular phænomenon in the literary world; and, as this mention of her may poſſibly excite the curioſity of my fair Readers, I ſhall cloſe the Notes to this Epiſtle with preſenting to them a Tranſlation of the Preface to her Hiſtory, as I believe no part of her Works have yet appeared in any modern language. I found that I could not abridge it without injuring its beauty, and though long, I flatter myſelf it will eſcape the cenſure of being tedious, as ſhe feelingly diſplays in it the misfortunes of her life, and the character of her mind.

THE PREFACE OF THE PRINCESS ANNA COMNENA,

FROM THE GREEK,

Prefixed to her ALEXIAD, or Hiſtory of her Father
the Emperor ALEXIUS.

TIME, which flows irreſiſtibly, ever encroaching, and ſtealing ſomething from human life, ſeems to bear away all that is mortal into a gulph of darkneſs; ſometimes deſtroying ſuch things as

10   deſerve

deſerve not utterly to be forgotten, and ſometimes, ſuch as are moſt noble, and moſt worthy of remembrance.   Now (to uſe the words of the tragic poet *)

> Diſcovering things inviſible; and now
> Sweeping each preſent object from our ſight.

But Hiſtory forms the ſtrongeſt barrier againſt this tide of Time: it withſtands, in ſome meaſure, the violence of the torrent, and, by collecting and cementing ſuch things as appear worthy of preſervation, while they are hurried along the ſtream, it allows them not to ſink into the abyſs of oblivion.

On this conſideration, I Anna, the daughter of the emperor Alexius, and his conſort Irene, born and educated in imperial ſplendor—not utterly void of literature, and ſolicitous to diſtinguiſh myſelf by that Grecian characteriſtic—as I have already applied myſelf to Rhetoric, and having thoroughly ſtudied the Principles of Ariſtotle and the Dialogues of Plato, have endeavoured to adorn my mind with the † four uſual branches of education (for I think it incumbent on me, even at the riſque of appearing vain, to declare what qualifications for the preſent taſk I have received from nature, or gained by application; what Providence has beſtowed upon me, or time and opportunity ſupplied.) On theſe accounts, I am deſirous of commemorating, in my preſent work, the actions of my father, as they deſerve not to be buried in ſilence, or to be plunged, as it were, by the tide of Time, into the ocean of Oblivion: both thoſe actions which he performed after he obtained the diadem, and thoſe before that period, while he was himſelf a ſubject of other Princes.   I engage in this narration, not ſo much to diſplay any little talent for compoſition,

---

* Sophocles.   † Aſtrology, Geometry, Arithmetic, and Muſic.

3   as

as to prevent tranfactions of fuch importance from perifhing unre-
corded: fince even the brighteft of human atchievements, if not
configned to memory under the guard of writing, are extinguifhed,
as it were, by the Darknefs of Silence.

My father was a man, who knew both how to govern, and to
pay to governors a becoming obedience: but in chufing his actions
for my fubject, I am apprehenfive, in the very outfet of my work,
left I may be cenfured as the Panegyrift of my own family for
writing of my father; that if I fpeak of him with admiration, my
whole Hiftory will be confidered as a falfe and flattering encomium; and if any circumftance, I may have occafion to mention,
leads me, as it were by force, to difapprove fome part even of his
conduct, I am apprehenfive, on the other hand, not from the character of my father, but from the very nature of things, that fome
malignant cenfurers may compare me to Cham, the fon of Noah;
fince there are many, whom envy and malevolence will not fuffer
to form a fair judgment, and who, to fpeak in the words of
Homer,

Are keen to cenfure, where no blame is due.

For whoever engages in the province of Hiftory, is bound to forget all fentiments both of favour and averfion; and often to adorn
his enemies with the higheft commendations, when their actions
are entitled to fuch reward; and often to cenfure his moft intimate
friends, when the failings of their life and manners require it.—
Thefe are duties equally incumbent on the Hiftorian, which he
cannot decline. As to myfelf, with regard to thofe who may be
affected either by my cenfure or my praife, I would wifh to affure
them, that I fpeak both of them, and their conduct, according to
the evidence of their actions themfelves, or the report of thofe
who beheld them; for either the fathers, or the grandfathers, of
many perfons now living were ocular witneffes of what I fhall
P   record.

record.   I have been chiefly led to engage in this History of my
father by the following circumstance :—It was my fortune to marry
Cæsar Nicephorus, of the Bryennian family, a man far superior to
all his cotemporaries, not only in personal beauty, but in sublimity
of understanding, and all the charms of eloquence ! for he was
equally the admiration of those who saw, and those who heard
him.   But that my discourse may not wander from its present purpose, let me proceed in my narration !—He was then, among all
men, the most distinguished ; and when he marched with the
emperor John Comnenus, my brother, on his expedition against
Antioch, and other places in possession of the Barbarians, still unable to abstain from literary pursuits, even in those scenes of labour
and fatigue, he wrote various compositions worthy of remembrance
and of honour.   But he chiefly applied himself to the writing an
account of what related to my father Alexius, emperor of the
Romans, at the request of the empress ; reducing into proper form
the transactions of his reign, whenever the times would allow him
to devote short intervals of leisure from arms and battle to works
of literature, and the labour of composition.   In forming this
History, he deduced his accounts from an early period, being directed in this point also by the instruction of our royal mistress ;
beginning from the emperor Diogenes, and descending to the person, whom he had chosen for the Hero of his Drama—for this
person first shewed my father to be a youth of expectation.   Before this period he was a mere infant ; and of course performed
nothing worthy of being recorded : unless even the occurrences of
his childhood should be thought a fit subject for History.   Such
then was the design and scope of Cæsar's composition: but he fail'd
in the hope he had entertained, of bringing his History to its
conclusion : for having brought it to the times of the emperor
Nicephorus Botoniates, he there broke off, having no future opportunity allowed him of continuing his narration : a circum-
                                                     stance,

ftance, which has proved a fevere lofs to Literature, and robbed his readers of delight!—On this account I have undertaken to record the actions of my father, that fuch atchievements may not efcape pofterity. What degree of harmony and grace the writings of Cæfar poffeffed, all perfons know, who have been fortunate enough to fee his compofitions. But having executed his work to the period I have mentioned, in the midft of hurry and fatigue, and bringing it to us half finifhed from his expedition, he brought home, alas! at the fame time, a diforder that proved mortal, contracted perhaps from the hardfhips of his paffage, or perhaps from that harraffing fcene of perpetual action, and poffibly indeed from his infinite anxiety on my account; for anxiety was natural to his affectionate heart, and his labours were without intermiffion. Moreover the change and badnefs of climates might prepare for him this draught of death. For notwithftanding the dreadful ftate of his health, he perfevered in the campaign againft the Syrians and Cilicians, till at length he was conveyed out of Syria in a moft infirm ftate, and was brought through Cilicia, Pamphylia, Lydia, and Bithynia, home to the metropolis of the empire, and to his family. But his vitals were now affected by his infinite fatigue.— Even in this ftate of weaknefs he was defirous of difplaying the events of his expedition: but this his diforder rendered him unable to execute, and indeed we enjoined him not to attempt it, left by the effort of fuch a narration he fhould burft open his wound.— But in the recollection of thefe things, my whole foul is darkened, and my eyes are covered with a flood of tears.—O what a director of the Roman counfels was then torn from us! O what an end was there to all the treafures of clear, of various, and of ufeful knowledge, which he had collected from obfervation and experience, both in regard to foreign affairs, and the internal bufinefs of the empire! —O what a form was then deftroyed!—Beauty, that feemed not only entitled to dominion, but bearing even the

P 2

femblance

semblance of divinity!—I indeed have been conversant with every calamity; and have found, even from the imperial cradle, an unpropitious fortune: some perhaps might esteem that fortune not unpropitious, which seemed to smile upon my birth, in giving me sovereigns for my parents, and nursing me in the imperial purple: but for the other circumstances of my life, alas, what tempests! alas, what perturbations! The melody of Orpheus affected even inanimate nature; and Timotheus, in playing the Orthic song to Alexander, made the Macedon start to arms.

The relation of my miseries would not, indeed, produce such effects; but it would move every auditor to tears; it would force not only beings endued with sensibility, but even inanimate nature to sympathize in my sorrow.—This remembrance of Cæsar, and his unexpected death, tears open the deepest wound of my soul: Indeed, I consider all my former misfortunes, if compared to this immeasureable calamity, but as a drop of water to the Atlantic sea: or rather, my earlier afflictions were a kind of prelude to this: they first involved me, as it were, like a smoke preceding this raging fire: they were a kind of heat, that portended a conflagration, which no words can describe. O thou fire, that blazest without fuel, preying on my heart without destroying its existence; piercing through my very bones, and shrinking up my soul!— But I perceive myself hurried away from my subject: this mention of Cæsar, and what I suffer in his loss, has led me into the prolixity of grief: wiping therefore the tear from my eyes, and restraining myself from this indulgence of sorrow, I will proceed in order; yet, as the * tragic Poet says,

Still adding tear to tear,

as recollecting misfortune after misfortune: for the entering on the History of such a king, so eminent for his virtues, revives

* Euripides.

in

in my mind all the wonders he performed, which move me to
frefh tears : and thefe I fhare in common with all the world; for
the remembrance of him, and the recital of his reign, fupplies to
me a new fubject of lamentation, and muft remind others of the
lofs they have fuftained.

But let me at length begin the Hiftory of my father, from
the period moft proper :—now the moft proper period is that,
which will give to my narration the cleareft, and moft hiftorical
appearance.——

END OF THE NOTES TO THE FIRST EPISTLE.

N O T E S

r o t h e

S E C O N D   E P I S T L E.

NOTE I.   VERSE 17.

H O W saintly Kings renounce, with holy dread,
   The chaste endearments of their marriage-bed.] It is well known
how Edward the Confessor is celebrated for his inviolable chas-
tity by the Monkish Historians—one of them, in particular, is so
solicitous to vindicate the piety of Edward in this article, that he
passes a severe censure on those, who had imputed his singular con-
tinence to a principle of resentment against the father of his queen
—Hanc quoque Rex ut conjugem tali arte tractavit; quod nec
thoro removit; nec eam virili more carnaliter cognovit: quod
utrum patris illius, qui proditor convictus erat, et familiæ ejus
odio quod prudenter pro tempore dissimulabat; an amore castitatis
id fecerit, incertum est aliquibus, qui in dubiis sinistra interpre-
tantur.   Veruntamen non benevoli, et veritati, ut videtur, dissoni
dicere præsumunt.   Quod Rex charitatis et pacis munere ditatus,
de genere proditoris hæredes, qui sibi succederent, corrupto semine
                  2   noluerit

noluerit procreare. Sciebat enim rex pacificus quod filia nihil
criminis commifit cum patre proditore, & ideo non refpuit thorum
virginis ; fed ambo unanimi affenfu caftitatem voverunt, parilique
voluntate   THOMÆ RUDBORNE, Hift. major. in Anglia Sacra.
Tom. I. p. 241.

The very high degree of merit, which the writers of the dark
ages attributed to this matrimonial mortification, is ftill more forcibly difplayed in a miraculous ftory related by Gregory of Tours,
which the curious reader may find in the Firft Book and 42d
chapter of that celebrated Hiftorian.

N O T E II.   VERSE 19.

How Nuns, entranc'd, to joys celeftial mount,
Made drunk with rapture from a facred fount.] The Monkifh Hiftorians feem to have confidered a vifion as the moft engaging embellifhment that Hiftory could receive—Even the fage Matthew
Paris delights in thefe heavenly digreffions. But the vifions, to
which the preceding verfes particularly allude, are thofe of the
Virgin Flotilda, printed in the 2d volume of the Hiftoriæ Franco-
rum Scriptores, by the learned Du Chefne: A very fhort fpecimen
may fatisfy the curiofity of the Reader—Videbatur Canis candidus
eidem adgaudere, quem tamen illa timens pertranfiit, & ad quen-
dam locum in medium decentium clericorum pervenit, qui eam
gratanter excipiebant, et potum ei in vafe pulcherrimo quafi aquam
clariffimam offerebant.——P. 624.

N O T E III.   VERSE 24.

With thofe dear gifts, the Meadow, and the Mill.] The ufual
legacy of the old Barons to their monaftic dependants.

N O T E

NOTE IV.   VERSE 59.

If mitred Turpin told, in wildest strain.] It is now generally agreed, that the History which bears the name of Turpin, Archbishop of Rheims, was the forgery of a Monk, at the time of the Crusades, though Pope Calixtus the Second declared it to be authentic.—But, as it was certainly intended to pass as genuine History, whenever it was composed, and actually did so for some ages, this poetical mention of it appeared not improper. For the entertainment of the curious reader, I shall transcribe the two miraculous passages alluded to in the poem :—Ante diem belli, castris et arietibus & turmis præparatis in pratis, scilicet quæ sunt inter castrum, quod dicitur Talaburgum, & urbem, juxta fluvium Caranta, infixerunt Christiani quidam hastas suas erectas in terra ante castra, crastina vero die hastas suas corticibus & frondibus decoratas invenerunt ; hi scilicet qui in bello præsenti accepturi erant martyrii palmam pro Christi fide.—Qui etiam tanto miraculo Dei gavisi, abscissis hastis suis de terra, simul coaduniti primitus in bello perierunt, & multos Saracenos occiderunt, sed tandem Martyrio coronantur. Cap. X.

After the soliloquy of Roland, addressed to his sword, which most readers have seen quoted in Mr. Warton s excellent Observations on Spenser, the Historian proceeds thus :—Timens ne in manus Saracenorum deveniret, percussit spata lapidem marmoreum trino ictu; a summo usque deorsum lapis dividitur, & gladius biceps illæsus educitur.——Deinde tuba sua cœpit altisona tonitruare, si forte aliqui ex Christianis, qui per nemora Saracenorum timore latitabant, ad se venirent. Vel si illi, qui portus jam transierant, forte ad se redirent, suoque funeri adessent, spatamque suam & equum acciperent, et Saracenos persequerentur. Tunc tanta virtute tuba sua eburnea insonuit, quod flatu omnis ejus tuba per

3   medium

medium fciffa, & venæ colli ejus & nervi rupti fuiffe feruntur,
cujus vox ad aures Caroli, qui in valle quæ Caroli dicitur, cum
exercitu fuo tentoria fixerat, loco fcilicet, qui diftabat a Carolo
octo milliaribus verfus Gafconiam, Angelico ductu pervenit.

Cap. xxii. & xxiii.

NOTE V.   VERSE 65.

Yet modeft Æginhard, with grateful care.] The celebrated Secretary
and fuppofed Son-in-law of Charlemain; who is faid to have been
carried through the fnow on the fhoulders of the affectionate and
ingenious Imma, to prevent his being tracked from her apartment
by the Emperor her father: a ftory which the elegant pen of
Addifon has copied and embellifhed from an old German Chronicle, and inferted in the 3d volume of the Spectator.—This happy
lover (fuppofing the ftory to be true) feems to have poffeffed a
heart not unworthy of fo enchanting a miftrefs, and to have returned her affection with the moft faithful attachment; for there
is a letter of Æginhard's ftill extant, lamenting the death of his
wife, which is written in the tendereft ftrain of connubial affliction—it does not however exprefs that this lady was the affectionate Princefs, and indeed fome late critics have proved, that
Imma was not the daughter of Charlemain.——But to return to our
Hiftorian.—He was a native of Germany, and educated by the munificence of his imperial mafter, of which he has left the moft
grateful teftimony in his Preface to the Life of that Monarch—
the paffage may ferve to fhew both the amiable mind of the
Hiftorian, and the elegance of his ftyle, confidering the age in
which he wrote:—Suberat & alia non irrationabilis, ut opinor
caufa, quæ vel fola fufficere poffet, ut me ad hæc fcribenda com-
pelleret; nutrimentum videlicet in me impenfum, & perpetua,
poftquam in aula ejus converfari cœpi, cum ipfo ac liberis ejus
amicitia, qua me ita fibi devinxit, debitoremque tam vivo quam

Q

mortuo

mortuo conftituit ; ut merito ingratus videri & judicari poffem, fi
tot beneficiorum in me collatorum immemor clariffima & illuftrif-
fima hominis optime de me meriti gefta filentio præterirem : pate-
rerque vitam ejus quafi qui nunquam vixerit fine literis ac debita
laude manere ; cui fcribendæ atque explicandæ non meum ingenio-
lum, quod exile & parvum imo nullum pene eft, fed Tullianam
par erat defudare facundiam.—The terms in which he fpeaks of
Charlemain's being unable to write are as follow :—Tentabat & fcribere fabulafque & codicellos ad hoc in lectulo fub cervicalibus
circumferre folebat, ut cum vacuum tempus effet, manum effigiun-
dis literis affuefaceret. Sed parum profperè fucceffit labor præ-
pofterus, ac ferò inchoatus.—Æginhard, after the lofs of his lamented wife, is fuppofed to have paffed the remainder of his days
in religious retirement, and to have died foon after the year 840.—
His Life of Charlemain, his Annals from 741 to 829, and his Letters, are all inferted in the 2d volume of Duchefne's Scriptores Fran-
corum. But there is an improved edition of this valuable Hiftorian, with the Annotations of Hermann Schmincke, in Quarto
1711.

NOTE VI. VERSE 79.

If Britifh Geoffrey fill'd his motley page
With Merlin's fpells and Uther's amorous rage.] The firft of the
two excellent differtations prefixed to Mr. Warton's Hiftory of
Englifh Poetry, gives the moft perfect account of this famous old
Chronicler and his whimfical performance.—" About the year
1100, Gualter, Archdeacon of Oxford, a learned man, and a dili-
gent collector of Hiftories, travelling through France, procured
in Armorica an antient Chronicle, written in the Britifh or Armo-
rican language, entitled, *Brut-y-Brenhined*, or the Hiftory of the
Kings of Britain. This book he brought into England, and communicated it to Geoffrey of Monmouth, a Welfh Benedictine
Monk,

Monk, an elegant writer of Latin, and admirably fkilled in the Britifh tongue. Geoffrey, at the requeft and recommendation of Gualter the Archdeacon, tranflated this Britifh Chronicle into Latin, executing the Tranflation with a tolerable degree of purity, and great fidelity, yet not without fome interpolations.—It was probably finifhed after the year 1138."- - - "The fimple fubject of this Chronicle, divefted of its romantic embellifhments, is a deduction of the Welfh Princes from the Trojan Brutus to Cadwallader, who reigned in the feventh century." To this extract from Mr. Warton, it may be proper to add a concife account of that romantic embellifhment, to which I have particularly alluded :—Uther Pendragon, at the feftival of his coronation, falls in love with Igerna, the wife of Gorlois, Duke of Cornwall ; and being prevented from purfuing his addreffes by the vigilance of the hufband, he applies to the magical power of Merlin for the completion of his defire.—This he obtains by being transformed into the perfon of Gorlois, and thus introducing himfelf to the deluded Igerna, as Jupiter vifited Alcmena, he gives birth to the celebrated Arthur.—Manfit itaque rex ea nocte cum Igerna & fefe defiderata venere refecit. Deceperat namque illam falfa fpecies quam affumpferat : deceperat etiam fictitiis fermonibus, quos ornate componebat . . . unde ipfa credula nihil quod pofcebatur abnegavit. Concepit itaque eadem nocte celeberrimum illum Arthurum, qui poftmodum ut celebris effet, mira probitate promeruit.

GALFRIDUS Mon. Lib. vi. cap. 2.

NOTE VII. VERSE 83.

Yet Life's great drama, and the Deeds of men,
Sage Monk of Malm'fbury ! engag'd thy pen.] William, furnamed of Malmefbury from being a member of that church, was a native of Somerfetfhire, and is fuppofed to have received his education at Oxford. He is juftly called, by almoft every writer on Englifh

 History,

Hiſtory, the moſt liberal and judicious of all our monaſtic Hiſtorians. His principal work is a Hiſtory of our Kings, from the arrival of the Saxons to the 20th year of Henry the Firſt. This was followed by two books of later Hiſtory, which cloſe with the celebrated eſcape of the Empreſs Matilda from the Caſtle of Oxford, 1142. Theſe works are both addreſſed to that munificent patron of merit, Robert Earl of Glouceſter, natural ſon of Henry the Firſt, who was perhaps the moſt exalted and accompliſhed character, that ever flouriſhed in ſo barbarous an age. The Hiſtorian ſpeaks of his noble friend with all the ſimplicity of truth, and all the warmth of virtuous admiration. He died, according to Pitts, in 1143, three years before his generous patron ; and this is probable, from his not purſuing his Hiſtory, which he intimates a deſign of reſuming.—Yet there is a paſſage preſerved in Tanner, from the Preface to his Comments on Jeremiah, which ſeems to prove, that he lived to a later period, ſince he mentions his hiſtorical works as the production of his younger days, and ſpeaks of his age as devoted to religious compoſition. Beſides his four books de geſtis Pontificum Anglorum, he wrote many works of the ſame pious turn, which the curious reader may ſee enumerated in Tanner's Bibliotheca.

NOTE VIII. VERSE 136.

A faithful Chronicler in plain Froiſſart.] John Froiſſart, Canon and Treaſurer of the collegiate church of Chimay, in Henault, was born at Valenciennes, a city of that province, in 1337, according to the conjecture of that elaborate and ingenious antiquarian Mr de St. Palaye ; who has amply illuſtrated the Life and Writings of this engaging Hiſtorian, in a ſeries of diſſertations among the Memoirs of the French Academy, Vol. X. XIII. XIV.—St. Palaye imagines, from a paſſage in the MS Poems of Froiſſart, that his father was a painter of Armories :—and it is certain the Hiſtorian diſcovers a

paſſion

passion for all the pomp and all the minutiæ of heraldry, of that martial age; and Froiffart, more the prieft of gallantry than of religion, devoted himfelf entirely to the celebration of love and war. —At the age of 20, he began to write Hiftory, at the requeft *de fon cher Seigneur & Maitre Meffire* Robert de Namur, Chevalier Seigneur de Beaufort.—The anguifh of unfuccefsful love drove him early into England, and his firft voyage feems a kind of emblem of his future life; for he failed hither in a ftorm, yet continued writing a rondeau in fpite of the tempeft, till he found himfelf on that coaft, ou l'on aime mieux la guerre, que la paix, & ou les eftrangers font très-bien venus, as he faid of our country *in his verfes*, and happily experienced in his kind reception at court, where Philippa of Henault, the Queen of Edward the Third, and a Patronefs of learning, diftinguifhed the young Hiftorian, her countryman, by the kindeft protection; and, finding that love had rendered him unhappy, fupplied him with money and with horfes, that he might prefent himfelf with every advantage before the object of his paffion.—Love foon efcorted him to his miftrefs—but his addreffes were again unfuccefsful; and, taking a fecond voyage to England, he became Secretary to his royal patronefs Philippa, in 1361, after having prefented to her fome portion of his Hiftory.—He continued five years in her fervice, entertaining her majefty *de beaux dictiez & traictez amoureux:* in this period he paid a vifit to Scotland, and was entertained 15 days by William Earl Douglas.—In 1366, when Edward the Black Prince was preparing for the war in Spain, Froiffart was with him in Gafcony, and hoped to attend him during the whole courfe of that important expedition:—but the Prince fent him back to the Queen his mother.—He continued not long in England, as he vifited many of the Italian courts in the following year, and during his travels fuftained the irreparable lofs of that patronefs, to whofe bounty he had been fo much indebted.—Philippa died 1369, and Froiffart is reported to have

2

written

written the life of his amiable protectress; but of this performance the researches of St. Palaye could discover no trace.

After this event, he retired to his own country, and obtained the benefice of Lestines, in the diocese of Cambray.—But the cure of souls was an office little suited to the gay and gallant Froissart.— His genius led him still to travel from castle to castle, and from court to court, to use the words of Mr. Warton, who has made occasional mention of our author, in his elegant History of English Poetry.—Froissart now entered into the service of the Duke of Brabant; and, as that Prince was himself a poet, Froissart collected all the compositions of his master, and adding some of his own, formed a kind of romance, which he calls

> Un Livre de Meliador
> Le Chevalier au soleil d'or,

and of which, in one of his later poems, he gives the following account:

> Dedans ce Romant sont encloses
> Toutes les chançons que jadis,
> Dont l'ame soit en paradis,
> Que fit le bon Duc de Braibant,
> Wincelaus, dont on parla tant;
> Car un prince fu amorous,
> Gracious & chevalerous,
> Et le livre me fit ja faire,
> Par très grant amoureus à faire,
> Coment qu'il ne le veist onecques.

The Duke died in 1384, before this work was completed; and Froissart soon found a new patron in Guy earl of Blois, on the marriage of whose Son he wrote a Pastoral, entitled Le Temple d'Honneur.—The earl having requested him to resume his History,

he travelled for that purpofe to the celebrated court of Gafton earl
of Foix, whofe high reputation for every knightly virtue attracted
to his refidence at Orlaix, thofe martial adventurers, from whofe
mouth it was the delight of Froiffart to collect the materials of his
Hiftory.—The courteous Gafton gave him the moft flattering reception : he faid to him with a fmile (& en bon François) "qu'il le
connoiffoit bien, quoyqu'il ne l'euft jamais veu, mais qu'il avoit
bien oui parler de luy, & le retint de fon hoftel."—It became a favourite amufement of the Earl, to hear Froiffart read his Romance
of Meliador after fupper.—He attended in the caftle every night at
12, when the Earl fate down to table, liftened to him with extreme attention, and never difmiffed him, till he had made him
vuider tout ce qui eftoit refté du vin de fa bouche.—Froiffart
gained much information here, not only from his patron, who was
himfelf very communicative, but from various Knights of Arragon
and England, in the retinue of the Duke of Lancafter, who then
refided at Bordeaux.—After a long refidence in this brilliant court,
and after receiving a prefent from the liberal Gafton, which he
mentions in the following verfes :

> Je pris congé & li bons Contes
> Me fit par fa chambre des comptes
> Delivrer quatrevins florins
> D'Arragon, tous pefans & fins
> Et mon iivre, qu'il m'ot laiffé.

Froiffart departed in the train of the Countefs of Boulogne, related
to the earl of Foix, and juft leaving him, to join her new hufband
the Duke of Berry.—In this expedition our Hiftorian was robbed
near Avignon, and laments the unlucky adventure in a very long
poem, from which Mr. de St. Palaye has drawn many particulars
of his life. The ground-work of this poem (which is not in the
lift of our Author's poetical pieces, that Mr. Warton has given us
from Pafquier) feems to have a ftrong vein of humour.—It is a
dialogue

dialogue between the Poet and the single Florin that he has left
out of the many which he had either spent, or been obliged to sur-
render to the robbers.—He reprefents himfelf as a man of the moſt
expenfive turn: in 25 years he had fquandered two thoufand franks,
befides his ecclefiaſtical revenues. The compofition of his works
had coſt him 700 ; but he regretted not this fum, as he expected to
be amply repaid for it by the praife of poſterity.

After having attended all the feſtivals on the marriage of the
Duke of Berry, having traverfed many parts of France, and paid a
vifit to Zeland, he returned to his own country in 1390, to continue
his Hiſtory from the various materials he had collected.—But not
fatisfied with the relations he had heard of the war in Spain, he
went to Middlebourgh in Zeland, in purfuit of a Portugueze Knight,
Jean Ferrand Portelet, vaillant homme & fage, & du Confeil du Roy
de Portugal. From this accomplifhed foldier Froiffart expected
the moſt perfect information, as an ocular witnefs of thofe fcenes,
which he now wifhed to record.—The courteous Portelet received
our indefatigable Hiſtorian with all the kindnefs which his en-
thufiafm deferved, and in fix days, which they paffed together, gave
him all the intelligence he defired.—Froiffart now returned home,
and finifhed the third book of his Hiſtory.—Many years had paſt
fince he had bid adieu to England : taking advantage of the truce
then eſtablifhed between France and that country, he paid it another vifit in 1395, with letters of recommendation to the King and
his uncles.—From Dover he proceeded to Canterbury, to pay his
devoirs at the fhrine of Thomas of Becket, and to the memory of
the Black Prince.—Here he happened to find the fon of that hero,
the young King Richard, whom devotion had alfo brought to make
his offerings to the fafhionable Saint, and return thanks to Heaven
for his fuccefles in Ireland.—Froiffart fpeaks of this adventure,
and his own feelings on the great change of fcene that had taken
place fince his laſt vifit to England, in the following natural and
lively terms :—Le Roy .. vint .. a trez grant arroy, et bien accom-
paigne

paigne de feignneurs, de dames et demoifelles, et me mis entre eulx, & entre elles, et tout me fembla nouvel, ne je ny congnoiffoye perfonne ; car le tems eftoit bien change en Angleterre depuis le tems de vingt & huyt ans : et en la compagnie du roy n'avoit nuls de fes oncles . . . . fi fus du premier ainfi que tout efbahy . . . Tho' Froiffart was thus embarraffed in not finding one of his old friends in the retinue of the King, he foon gained a new Patron in Thomas Percy, Mafter of the Houfehold, who offered to prefent him and his letters to Richard ; but this offer happening on the eve of the King's departure, it proved too late for the ceremony— Le Roy eftoit retrait pour aller dormir.—And on the morrow, when the impatient Hiftorian attended early at the Archbifhop's palace, where the King flept, his friend Percy advifed him to wait a more convenient feafon for being introduced to Richard.—Froiffart ac- quiefced in this advice, and was confoled for his difappointment by falling into company with an Englifh Knight, who had attended the King in Ireland, and was very willing to gratify the curiofity of the Hiftorian by a relation of his adventures.—This was Wil- liam de Lifle, who entertained him, as they rode along together, with the marvels of St. Patrick's Cave, in which he affured him he had paffed a night, and feen wonderful vifions.—Though our ho- neft Chronicler is commonly accufed of a paffion for the marvel- lous, with an excefs of credulity, he fays very fenfibly on this oc- cafion, de cette matiere je ne luy parlay plus avant, et m'en ceffay, car voulentiers je luy euffe demande du voyage d'Irlande, et luy eu voulaye parler, et mettre en voye.—It appears plainly from this paffage, that our Hiftorian was more anxious to gain information concerning the fcenes of real action, than to liften to the extrava- gant fictions of a popular legend.—But here he was again difap- pointed.—New companions joined them on the road, and their hiftorical conference was thus interrupted.—Thefe mortifications were foon repaid by the kind reception he met with from the Duke of York, who faid to him, when he received the recom-

mendatory

R

mendatory letter from the Earl of Henault, " Maiftre Jehan tenez vous toujours deles nous, & nos gens, nous vous ferons tout amour & courtoifie, nous y fommes tenus pour l'amour du tems paffé & de notre dame de mere à qui vous futes ; nous en avons bien la fouvenance."—With thefe flattering marks of remembrance and favour the Duke prefented him to the King, lequel me receut joyeufement et doulcement (continues Froiffart) . et ne dift que je fuffe le bien venus et fi j'avoye efte de l'hoftel du Roy fon Ayeul & de Madame fon Ayeule encores eftoys je de l'hoftel d'Angleterre. ——Some time however elapfed, before he had an opportunity of prefenting his romance of Meliador, which he had prepared for the King.—The Duke of York and his other friends at length obtained for him this honour : He gives the following curious and particular account of the ceremony : et voulut veoir le Roy mon livre, que je luy avoye apporte. Si le vit en fa chambre : car tout pourveu je l'avoye, et luy mis fur fon lict. Et lors il l'ouvrit et regarda dedans, et luy pleut tres grandement. Et plaire bien luy devoit : car il eftoit enlumine, efcrit et Hiftorie, & couvert de vermeil veloux a dix cloux d'argent dorez d'or et rofes d'or ou meillieu a deux gros fermaulx dorez et richement ouvrez ou meillieu rofiers d'or. Adonc me demanda le Roy de quoy il traictoit : et je luy dis d'amours. De cefte refponce fut tout resjouy, et regarda dedans le livre en plufieurs lieux, et y lyfit, car moult bien parloit et lyfoit Françoys, et puis le fift prendre par ung fien Chevalier, qui fe nomme Meffire Richard Credon, et porter en fa chambre de retrait dont il me fift bonne chere.

After paffing three months in this court, Froiffart took his leave of the munificent but ill-fated Richard. In the laft chapter of his Hiftory, where he mentions the unfortunate end of this Monarch, he fpeaks with an honeft and affecting gratitude of the liberal prefent he received from him on his departure from England.—It was a goblet of filver gilt, weighing two marks, and filled with a hundred nobles.

5

On

On leaving England, he retired to his own country, and is fuppofed to have ended his days at his benefice of Chimay, but the
year of his death is uncertain.—There is an antient tradition in
the country, fays Mr. de Saint Palaye, that he was buried in the
chapel of St. Anne, belonging to his own church.—That ingenious antiquarian produces an extract from its archives, in which the
death of Froiffart is recorded, but without naming the year, in the
moft honourable terms.—His obit bears the date of October, and
is followed by 20 Latin verfes, from which I felect fuch as appear
to me the moft worth tranfcribing.

> Gallorum fublimis honos, & fama tuorum,
>   Hic Froiffarde jaces, fi modo forte jaces.
> Hiftorie vivus ftuduifti reddere vitam,
>   Defuncto vitam reddet at illa tibi.
> Proxima dum propriis florebit Francia fcriptis,
>   * Famia dum ramos, * Blancaque fundet aquas,
> Urbis ut hujus honos, templi fic fama vigebis,
>   Teque ducem Hiftorie Gallia tota colet,
> Belgica tota colet, Cymeaque vallis amabit,
>   Dum rapidus proprios Scaldis obibit agros.

As I have never met with any fatisfactory account of Froiffart's
life in our language, I have been tempted to fwell this Note to an
inordinate length; yet it feems to me ftill neceffary to add a few
lines more concerning the character both of the Hiftorian and the
Poet.—A long feries of French Critics, to whom even the judicious
Bayle has been tempted to give credit, have feverely cenfured Froiffart,
as the venal partizan of the Englifh, and they have accufed his laft
Editor, Sauvage, of mutilating his author, becaufe they could find
in his edition no proofs of their charge.—The amiable St. Palaye
has defended le bon Froiffart, as he is called by honeft Montaigne,

* * A foreft and a river near Chimay.

from this unjust accusation, and done full justice at the same time to the injured reputation of his exact and laborious editor.

It may serve as a kind of memento mori to poetical vanity to reflect, that Froissart is hardly known as a Poet, though his fertile pen produced 30,000 verses, which were once the delight of Princes, and the favourite study of the gallant and the fair.—How far he deserved the oblivion, into which his poetical compositions have fallen, the reader may conceive from the following judgment of his French Critic ; with whose ingenious reflection on the imperfections attending the early state both of Poetry and Painting, I shall terminate this Note.

On peut dire en général au sujet des Poesies de Froissart, que l'invention pour les sujets lui manquoit autant que l'imagination pour les ornemens ; du reste le style qu'il employe, moins abondant que diffus, offre souvent la répétition ennuyeuse des mêmes tours, & des mêmes phrases, pour rendre des idées assez communes : cependant la simplicité et la liberté de sa versification ne font pas toûjours dépourvûes de graces, on y rencontre de tems en tems quelques images & plusieurs vers de suite dont l'expression est assez heureuse.

Tel étoit alors l'état de notre Poesie Françoise, et le sort de la Peinture étoit à peu près le meme. Ces deux arts que l'on a toujours comparez ensemble paroissent avoir eu une marche presqu' uniforme dans leur progrès. Les Peintres au sortir de la plus grossiére barbarie, saisissant d'abord en détail tous les petits objets que la nature leur presentoit, s'attachérent aux insectes, aux fleurs, aux oiseaux, les parérent des couleurs les plus vives, les dessinérent avec une exactitude que nous admirons encore dans les vignettes & dans les miniatures des manuscrits ; lorsqu'ils vinrent à représenter des figures humaines, ils s'étudiérent bien plus à terminer les contours & à exprimer jusqu' aux cheveux les plus fins, qu'à donner de l'ame aux visages & du mouvement aux corps ; et ces figures dont la nature la plus commune fournissoit toujours les

3

modelles,

modelles, étoient jettées enfemble au hazard, fans choix, fans or-
donnance, fans aucun goût de compofition.

Les Poetes auffi ftériles que les Peintres, bornoient toute leur in-
duftrie à fcavoir amener des defcriptions proportionnées à leur ta-
lens, et ils ne les quittoient qu'après les avoir épuifées ; ils ne fça-
vent guéres parler que d'un beau printems, de la verdure des cam-
pagnes, de l'émail des prairies, du ramage de mille efpeces d'oi-
feaux, de la clarté et de la vivacité d'une belle fontaine ou d'un
ruiffeau qui murmure ; quelquefois cependant ils rendent avec
naïveté les amufemens enfantins des amans, leurs ris, leurs jeux,
les palpitations ou la joie d'un cœur amoreux ; ils n'imaginent rien
au delà, incapable d'ailleurs de donner de la fuite et de la liaifon à
leurs idées.

Notice des Poefies de Froiffart ; Memoires de l'Academie,

Tom. xiv. p. 225.

NOTE IX. VERSE 184.

Thy Favour, like the Sun's prolific ray,

Brought the keen Scribe of Florence into Day.] Nicholas Machiavel,
the celebrated Florentine, was firft patronized by Leo, who caufed
one of his comedies to be acted with great magnificence at Rome,
and engaged him to write a private Treatife de Reformatione Rei-
publicæ Florentinæ. His famous political Effay, entitled, " The
Prince," was publifhed in 1515, and dedicated to the Nephew of
that Pontiff. The various judgments that have been paffed on this
fingular performance are a ftriking proof of the incertitude of human opinion.—In England it has received applaufe from the great
names of Bacon and Clarendon, who fuppofe it intended to promote the intereft of liberty and virtue. In Italy, after many years
of approbation, it was publicly condemned by Clement the VIIIth,
at the inftigation of a Jefuit, who had not read the book. In
France it has even been fuppofed inftrumental to the horrid

maffacre

maſſacre of St. Bartholomew, as the favourite ſtudy of Catherine
of Medicis and her Sons, and as teaching the bloody leſſons of ex-
tirpation, which they ſo fatally put in practice. Yet one of his
French Tranſlators has gone ſo far as to ſay, that " Machiavel,
who paſſes among all the world for a teacher of Tyranny, deteſted
it more than any man of the age, in which he lived." It muſt
however be owned, that there is a great mixture of good and evil in
his political precepts. For the latter many plauſible apologies have
been made; and it ſhould be remembered to his honour, that his
great aim was to promote the welfare of his country, in exciting
the Houſe of Medicis to deliver Italy from the invaſion of fo-
reigners.

He is ſaid to have been made Hiſtoriographer of Florence, as a
reward for having ſuffered the torture on ſuſpicion of conſpiring
againſt the government of that city, having ſupported the ſevere
trial with unfailing reſolution. His Hiſtory of that republic he
wrote at the requeſt of Clement the VIIth, as we are informed in
his Dedication of it to that Pontiff. The ſtyle of this work is much
celebrated, and the firſt Book may be regarded as a model of
Hiſtorical abridgment.—He died, according to Paul Jovius, in
1530.

NOTE X. VERSE 194.

Nor leſs, O Leo, was it thine to raiſe
The great Hiſtoric Chief of modern days.] Francis Guicciardin,
born at Florence 1482, of an antient and noble family, was appointed a Profeſſor of Civil Law in that city at the age of 23. In
1512 he was ſent Embaſſador to Ferdinand King of Arragon;
and ſoon after his return deputed by the Republic to meet Leo
the Xth at Cortona, and attend him on his public entry into Florence.—That diſcerning Pontiff immediately became his Patron,
and raiſed him to the government of Modena and Reggio. He

ſucceeded

succeeded to that of Parma, which he defended with great fpirit againft the French, on the death of Leo.—He rofe to the higheft honours under Clement the VIIth, having the command of all the ecclefiaftical forces, and being Governor of Romagna, and laftly of Bologna, in which city he is faid to have received the moft flattering compliments from the Emperor Charles V.—Having gained much reputation, both civil and military, in various fcenes of active life, he paffed his latter days in retirement, at his villa near Florence, where he died foon after completing his Hiftory, in the 59th year of his age, 1540.   Notwithftanding the high reputation of Guicciardin, his Hiftory has been violently attacked, both as to matter and ftyle.—The honeft Montaigne inveighs with great warmth againft the malignant turn of its author ; and his own countryman Boccalini, in whofe whimfical but lively work there are many excellent remarks on Hiftory and Hiftorians, fuppofes a Lacedæmonian thrown into agonies by a fingle page of Guicciardin, whom he is condemned to read, for having himfelf been guilty of ufing three words inftead of two.   The poor Spartan cries for mercy, and declares that any tortures are preferable to the prolixity of fuch a Writer.—This celebrated Hiftorian was alfo a Poet.   The three following verfes are the beginning of an Epiftle, which he entitled Supplicazione d'Italia al Chriftianiffimo Rè Francefco I.

> Italia afflitta, nuda, e miferanda,
> Ch' or de Principi fuoi ftanca fi lagna
> A Te, Francefco, quefta Carta manda.

They are preferved in Crefcimbeni della volgar Poefia.   Vol. v. p. 132.

NOTE XI.   Verse 204.

With equal wreaths let Davila be crown'd.] Henry Catherine Davila was the youngeft fon of Antonio Davila, Grand Conftable of Cyprus.

prus, who had been obliged to retire into Spain on the taking of that ifland by the Turks in 1570. From Spain Antonio repaired to the court of France, and fettled his fon Lewis and two daughters under the patronage of Catherine of Medicis, whofe name he afterwards gave to the young Hiftorian, born 1576, at an antient caftle in the territories of Padua, though generally called a native of Cyprus. The little Davila was brought early into France;—at the age of 18 he fignalized himfelf in the military fcenes of that country. His laft exploit there was at the fiege of Amiens, where he fought under Henry IV, and received a wound in the knee, as he relates himfelf in his Hiftory.——After peace was eftablifhed in France, he withdrew into Italy, and ferved the Republic of Venice with great reputation till a moft unfortunate adventure put an end to his life in 1631.——Paffing through Verona with his wife and family, on his way to Crema, which he was appointed to defend, and demanding, according to the ufual cuftom of perfons in his ftation, a fupply of horfes and carriages for his retinue, a brutal Veronefe, called il Turco, entered the room where he and his family were at fupper, and being mildly reprimanded for his intrufion by Davila, difcharged a piftol at the Hiftorian, and fhot him dead on the inftant.—His accomplices alfo killed the Chaplain of Davila, and wounded many of his attendants. But his eldeft fon Antonio, a noble youth of eighteen, revenged the death of his father by killing his murderer on the fpot. All the confederates were fecured the next morning, and publicly executed at Verona.—Memoire Iftoriche, prefixed to the London edition of Davila, 4to, 1755.——It is very remarkable, that Davila paffes no cenfure on the Maffacre of St. Bartholomew.—His character of the Queen Mother has that partiality, which it was natural for him to fhew to the Patronefs of his family; but his general veracity is confirmed by the great authority of the firft Duke of Epernon, who, (to ufe the words of Lord Bolingbroke) " had been an actor, and a principal actor too, in many of the fcenes that Davila recites."

Girard,

Girard, Secretary to this Duke, and no contemptible Biographer, relates, that this Hiſtory came down to the place where the old man reſided, in Gaſcony, a little before his death ; that he read it to him ; that the Duke confirmed the truth of the narrations in it : and ſeemed only ſurpriſed by what means the author could be ſo well informed of the moſt ſecret councils and meaſures of thoſe times."——Letters on Hiſtory.

NOTE XII.   VERSE 226.

Sarpi, bleſſ name! from every foible clear.] Father Paul, the moſt amiable and exalted character that was ever formed in monaſtic retirement, was the ſon of Franceſco Sarpi, a merchant of Venice, and born in that city, 1552. He took the religious habit in the monaſtery of the Servites, 1565. After receiving prieſt's orders in 1574, he paſſed four years in Mantua, being appointed to read Lectures on Divinity and Canon Law, by the Biſhop of that dioceſe ; and in this early part of his life, he is conjectured to have conceived the firſt idea of writing his celebrated Hiſtory, as he formed an intimate friendſhip, during his reſidence in Mantua, with Camillo d'Oliva, who had been Secretary to Cardinal Gonzaga at the Council of Trent, and excited the learned Venetian to the arduous taſk, which he ſo happily accompliſhed in a future period. He was recalled from Mantua, to read Lectures on Philoſophy in his own convent at Venice, which he did with great reputation, during the years 1575, 1576, and 1577.——He went to Rome as Procurator General in 1585. Paſſing from thence to Naples, he there formed an acquaintance with the famous Baptiſta Porta, who has left this honourable teſtimony of his univerſal knowledge : ——Eo doctiorem, ſubtiliorem, quotquot adhuc videre contigerit, neminem cognovimus ; natum ad Encyclopediam, &c. Nor is this an exaggerated compliment, as there is hardly any ſcience which eſcaped his active mind. His diſcoveries in Optics and Anatomy would be alone ſufficient to immortalize his name, had he not

S

gained

gained immortality by a still nobler exertion of his mental powers, in defending the liberties of his country against the tyranny of Rome. On the first attack of Pope Paul V. on two laws of Venice, very wisely framed to correct the abuses of the clergy, Father Paul arose as the literary champion of the Republic, and defended its cause with great spirit and temper, in various compositions; though he is said not to be Author of the Treatise generally ascribed to him on the occasion, and entitled, *The Rights of Sovereigns*, &c.—His chief performance on the subject was *Considerazioni sopra le Censure di Paolo V.* The Venetians shewed a just admiration of the sublime virtue of a Monk, who defended so nobly the civil rights of his country against the separate interest of the church. In 1606 the Council passed a decree in his favour; which I shall transcribe in this note, because it is not found in the common Lives of Father Paul, and because there is hardly any object more pleasing to the mind, than the contemplation of a free state rewarding one of its most virtuous servants with liberality and esteem.——Continuando il R. P. M. Paolo da Venezia dell ordine de Serviti a prestare alla Signoria Nostra con singolar Valore quell ottimo servigio, ch' è ben conosciuto, potendosi dire, ch' egli fra tutti con le sue scritture piene di profonda dottrina sostenti con validissimi fondamenti le potentissime e validissime ragioni nostre nella causa, che ha di presente la Repubblica con la corte di Roma, anteponendo il servigio e la soddisfazione nostra a qualsivoglia suo particolare ed importante rispetto. E perciò cosa giusta e ragionevole, e degna dell ordinaria munificenza di questo Consiglio, il dargli modo, con che possa assicurare la sua Vita da ogni pericolo, che gli potesse soprastare, e sovvenire insieme alli suoi bisogni, bench, egli non ne faccia alcuna istanza, ma piutosto si mostri alieno da qualsivoglia ricognizione, che si abbia intenzione di usargli. Tal è la sua modestia, e così grande il desiderio, che ha di far conoscere, che nessuna pretensione di premio, ma la sola divozione sua verso la Repubblica, e la giustizia della Causa lo muo-

vano

vano adoperarſi con tanto ſtudio e con tante fatiche alli ſervizi noſtri. Percio anderà parte, che allo ſtipendio, il quale a' 28 del Meſe di Gennaio paſſato fu aſſegnato al ſopradetto R. P. M. Paolo da Venezia di Ducati duecento all anno, ſiano accreſciuti altri ducati duecento, ſicchè in avvenire abbia ducati quattrocento, acciòchè reſtando conſolato per queſta ſpontanea e benigna dimoſtrazione pubblica, con maggior ardore abbia a continuare nel ſuo buono e divoto ſervizio, e poſſa con queſto aſſequamento provvedere maggiormente alla ſicurezza della ſua Vita.——The generous care of the Republic to reward and preſerve ſo valuable a ſervant, could not ſecure him from the baſe attempts of that enemy, whom his virtue had provoked.   In 1607, after Venice had adjuſted her diſputes with Rome, by the mediation of France, the firſt attack was made on the life of Father Paul.   He was beſet near his convent, in the evening, by five aſſaſſins, who ſtabbed him in many places, and left him for dead.   He recovered, under the care of the celebrated Acquapendente, appointed to attend him at the public charge; to whom, as he was ſpeaking on the depth of the principal wound, his patient ſaid pleaſantly, that the world imputed it ſtylo Romanæ Curiæ.—The crime is generally ſuppoſed to have proceeded from the Jeſuits; but the ſecret authors of it were never clearly diſcovered, though the five ruffians were traced by the Venetian Ambaſſador in Rome, where they are ſaid to have been well received at firſt, but failing afterwards in their expected reward, to have periſhed in miſery and want.   The Senate of Venice paid ſuch attention to Father Paul, as expreſſed the higheſt ſenſe of his merit, and the moſt affectionate ſolicitude for his ſafety.   They not only doubled his ſtipend a ſecond time, but entreated him to chuſe a public reſidence, for the greater ſecurity of his perſon.   The munificence and care of the Republic was equalled by the modeſty and. fortitude of their ſervant.   He choſe not to relinquiſh his cell; and, though warned of various machinations againſt his life, he continued to ſerve his country with unabating zeal; diſcovering, in his private letters to

S 2

his

his friends, the moſt heroic calmneſs of mind, and ſaying, in anſwer to their admonitions, that " no man lives well, who is too anxious for the preſervation of life."——Yet the apprehenſions of his friends had too juſt a foundation. In 1609 another conſpiracy was formed, to murder him in his ſleep, by ſome perſons of his own convent—but their treachery was happily diſcovered.—From this time he lived in more cautious retirement, ſtill devoting himſelf to the ſervice of the Republic on various occaſions, and acquiring new reputation by many compoſitions. At length the world was ſurprized by his Hiſtory of the Council of Trent, firſt publiſhed at London, 1619; with the fictitious name of Pietro Soave Polano; and dedicated to James the Iſt, by Antonio de Dominis, the celebrated Archbiſhop of Spalatro, who ſpeaks of the concealed Author as his intimate friend, who had entruſted him with a manuſcript, on which his modeſty ſet a trifling value, but which it ſeemed proper to beſtow upon the world even without his conſent.—The myſtery concerning the publication of this noble work has never been thoroughly cleared up, and various falſities concerning it have been reported by authors of conſiderable reputation.—It has even been ſaid that James the Iſt had ſome ſhare in the compoſition of the book—if he had, it was probably in forming the name Pietro Soave Polano, which is an anagram of Paolo Sarpi Veneziano, and the only part of the book which bears any relation to the ſtyle or taſte of that Monarch.——Father Paul was ſoon ſuppoſed to be the real Author of the work in queſtion. The Prince of Condé, on a viſit to his cloyſter, expreſſly aſked him, if he was ſo—to which he modeſtly replied, that at Rome it was well known who had written it.—He enjoyed not many years the reputation ariſing from this maſterly production—in 1623 a fever occaſioned his death, which was even more exemplary and ſublime than his life itſelf. —He prepared himſelf for approaching diſſolution with the moſt devout compoſure; and, as the liberty of his country was the darling object of his exalted mind, he prayed for its preſervation

with

with his laft breath, in the two celebrated words Efto Perpetua.

There is a fingular beauty in the character of Father Paul,
which is not only uncommon in his profeffion, but is rarely found
in human nature.—Though he paffed a long life in controverfy of
the moft exafperating kind, and was continually attacked in every
manner that malignity could fuggeft, both his writings and his
heart appeared perfectly free from a vindictive fpirit—devoting all
the powers of his mind to the defence of the public caufe, he
feemed entirely to forget the injuries that were perpetually offered
to his own perfon and reputation.

His conftitution was extremely delicate, and his intenfe application expofed him to very frequent and violent diforders: thefe he
greatly remedied by his fingular temperance, living chiefly on
bread, fruits, and water.—This imperfect account of a character
deferving the nobleft elogium, is principally extracted from an oc-
tavo volume, entitled, Memoire Anedote fpettanti a F Paolo da
Francefco Grifelini Veneziano, &c. edit. 2d, 1760.   The author of
this elaborate work has pointed out feveral miftakes in the French
and Englifh accounts of Father Paul; particularly in the anecdotes
related of him by Burnet, in his Life of Bifhop Bedell, and by
Mr. Brent, the fon of his Englifh Tranflator.—Some of thefe
had indeed been obferved before by Writers of our own.—See the
General Dictionary under the article Father Paul.——For the
length and for the deficiencies of this Note, I am tempted to apo-
logize with a fentence borrowed from the great Hiftorian who is
the fubject of it: – Chi mi offerverà in alcuni tempi abondare, in
altri andar riftretto, fi ricordi che non tutti i campi fono di ugnal
fertilità, ne tutti li grani meritano d'effer confervati, e di quelli
che il mietitore vorrebbe tenerne conto, qualche fpica anco sfugge
la prefa della mano, o il filo della falce, cofi comportando la con-
ditione d'ogni mietitura che refti anco parte per rifpigolare.

N O T E

NOTE XIII. Verse 254.

The clear Oforius, in his claffic phrafe.] Jerom Oforius was born of a noble family at Lifbon, 1506. He was educated at the univerfity of Salamanca, and afterwards ftudied at Paris and Bologna. On his return to Portugal, he gradually rofe to the Bifhopric of Sylves, to which he was appointed by Catherine of Auftria, Regent of the kingdom in the minority of Sebaftian. At the requeft of Cardinal Henry of Portugal, he wrote his Hiftory of King Emanuel, and the expedition of Gama—which his great contemporary Camoens made at the fame time the fubject of his immortal Lufiad; a poem which has at length appeared with due luftre in our language, being tranflated with great fpirit and elegance by Mr. Mickle. It is remarkable, that the Hiftory of Oforius, and the Epic Poem of Camoens, were publifhed in the fame year, 1572: but the fate of thefe two great Authors was very different; the Poet was fuffered to perifh in poverty, under the reign of that Henry, who patronized the Hiftorian: yet, allowing for the difference of their profeffions, I am inclined to think they poffeffed a fimilarity of mind. There appear many traces of that high heroic fpirit, even in the Prieft Oforius, which animated the Soldier Camoens: particularly in the pleafure, with which he feems to defcribe the martial manners of his countrymen, under the reign of Emanuel.—Illius ætate (fays the Hiftorian, in the clofe of his manly work) inopia in exilium pulfa videbatur: mæftitiæ locus non erat: querimoniæ filebant: omnia choreis & cantibus perfonabant: ejufmodi ludis aula regia frequenter oblectabatur. Nobiles adolefcentes cum virginibus regiis in aulâ fine ulla libidinis fignificatione faltabant, et quamvis honeftiffimis amoribus indulgerent, virginibus erat infitum, neminem ad familiaritatem admittere, nifi illum qui aliquid fortiter & animofe bellicis in rebus effeciffet. Pueris enim nobilibus, qui in aula regia verfabantur, non erat licitum pallium virile fumere,

5

antequam

antequam in Africam trajicerent & aliquod inde decus egregium reportarent. Et his quidem moribus erat illius temporis nobilitas inftituta, ut multi ex illius domo viri omni laude cumulati prodirent.—This is a ftriking picture of the manners of chivalry, to which Portugal owed much of its glory in that fplendid period. There is one particular in the character of Oforius, which, confidering his age and country, deferves the higheft encomium; I mean his tolerating fpirit. In the firft book of his Hiftory, he fpeaks of Emanuel's cruel perfecution of the Jews in the following generous and exalted language :—Fuit quidem hoc nec ex lege nec ex religione factum. Quid enim? Tu rebelles animos nullaque ad id fufcepta religione conftrictos, adigas ad credendum ea, quæ fumma contentione afpernantur & refpuunt? Idque tibi affumas, ut libertatem voluntatis impedias, & vincula mentibus effrænatis injicias? at id neque fieri poteft, neque Chrifti fanctiffimum numen approbat. Voluntarium enim facrificium, non vi et malo coactum ab hominibus expetit, neque vim mentibus inferri fed voluntates ad ftudium veræ religionis allici & invitari jubet. . . . . . Poftremo quis non videt. . . . . et ita religionem per religionis fimulationem indigniffime violari?—Oforius is faid to have ufed many arguments to diffuade Sebaftian from his unfortunate expedition into Africa, and to have felt fo deeply the miferies which befell the Portugueze after that fatal event, that his grief was fuppofed to accelerate his death.— He expired in 1580, happy, fays De Thou (who celebrates him as a model of Chriftian virtue) that he died juft before the Spanifh army entered Portugal, and thus efcaped being a witnefs to the defolation of his country.—His various works were publifhed at Rome in 1592, by his nephew Oforius, in four volumes folio, with a Life of their Author. Among thefe are two remarkable productions; the firft, an admonition to our Queen Elizabeth, exhorting her to return into the Church of Rome: the fecond, an Effay on Glory, written with fuch claffical purity, as to give

birth

birth to a report, that it was not the compofition of Oforius, but
the loft work of Cicero on that fubject.

NOTE XIV.   VERSE 260.

Iberia's Genius bids juft Fame allow

An equal wreath to Mariana's brow.] John Mariana was born
1537, at Talavera (a town in the diocefe of Toledo) as he himfelf
informs us in his famous Effay *de Rege*, which opens with a beautiful romantic defcription of a fequeftered fpot in that neighbourhood, where he enjoyed the pleafures of literary retirement with
his friend Calderon, a Minifter of Toledo; whofe death he mentions
in the fame Effay, commemorating his learning and his virtues in
the moft pleafing terms of affectionate admiration.—Mariana was
admitted into the order of Jefuits at the age of 17. He travelled
afterwards into Italy and France, and returning into Spain in 1574,
fettled at Toledo, and died there in the 87th year of his age, 1624.
—Hearing it frequently regretted, in the courfe of his travels, that
there was no General Hiftory of his country, he engaged in that
great work on his return; and publifhed it in Latin at Toledo,
1592, with a dedication to Philip the IId; where he fpeaks of his
own performance with modefty and manly freedom, and perhaps
with as little flattery as ever appeared in any addrefs of that nature, to a Monarch continually fed with the groffeft adulation. ——
This elaborate work he tranflated into Spanifh, but, as he himfelf
declares, with all the freedom of an original author. He publifhed
his Verfion in 1601, with an addrefs to Philip the IIId, in which
he laments the decline of Learning in his country, and declares
he had himfelf executed that work from his apprehenfion of its
being mangled by an ignorant Tranflator. He had clofed his Hiftory (which begins with the firft peopling of Spain) with the
death of Ferdinand, in 1516; but in a fubfequent edition, in 1617,

he added to it a short summary of events to the year 1612: but in the year before he first published the Spanish Version of his History, he addressed also, to the young Monarch Philip the IIId, his famous Essay, which I have mentioned, and which was publicly burnt at Paris, about 20 years after its publication, on the supposition that it had excited Ravaillac to the murder of Henry the IVth; though it was asserted, with great probability, by the Jesuits, that the Assassin had never seen the book.—It is true, indeed, that Mariana, in this Essay, occasionally defends Clement the Monk, who stabbed Henry the IIId; and it is very remarkable, that he grounds this defence, not on the bigotted tenets of a Priest, who thinks every thing lawful for the interest of his church, but on those sublime principles of civil liberty, with which an antient Roman would have vindicated the dagger of Brutus. Indeed, this Essay contains some passages on Government, which would not have dishonoured even Cicero himself; but, it must be owned, they are grievously disgraced by the last chapter of the Work, which breathes a furious spirit of ecclesiastical intolerance, and yet closes with these mild and modest expressions: Nostrum de regno et Regis institutione judicium fortasse non omnibus placeat; qui volet sequatur, aut suo potius stet, si potioribus argumentis nitatur, de quibus rebus tantopere asseveravi in his libris, eas nunquam veriores quam alienam sententiam affirmabo. Potest enim non solum mihi aliud, aliud aliis videri, sed et mihi ipsi alio tempore. Suam quisque sententiam per me sequatur . . . et . . qui nostra leget . . . memor conditionis humanæ, si quid erratum est, pio studio rempublicam juvandi veniam benignus concedat et facilis.——This is not the only work of Mariana which fell under a public proscription; he was himself persecuted, and suffered a year's imprisonment, for a treatise, which seems to have been dictated by the purest love to his country; it was against the pernicious practice of debasing the public coin, and as it was supposed to reflect on the Duke of Lerma, called the Sejanus of Spain, it exposed the Author, about the

T

year

year 1609, to the perfecution of that vindictive Minifter; from which it does not appear how he efcaped.—Indeed the accounts of Mariana's life are very imperfect : Bayle, whom I have chiefly followed, mentions a life of him by De Vargas, which he could not procure. I have fought after this Biographer with the fame ill fuccefs, as I wifhed to give a more perfect account of this great Author, whofe perfonal Hiftory is little known among us, though it is far from being unworthy of attention.

NOTE XV. VERSE 291.

The liberal fpirit of Thuanus rofe.] James Auguftus De Thou was the youngeft fon of Chriftopher De Thou, Firft Prefident of the Parliament of Paris, and born in that city, 1553. His own Memoirs give a pleafing account of the early activity of his mind.— As his health, during his childhood, was fo tender and infirm, that his parents rather reftrained him from the ufual ftudies of his age, he devoted much of his time to drawing, and copied with a pen the engravings of Albert Durer, before he was ten years old. At that age he was fettled in the college of Burgundy ; but this plan of his education was foon interrupted by a fever, in which his life was defpaired of, and in which the mother of his future friend, the Duke of Montpenfier, watched him with an attention fingularly happy, after his phyficians and his parents had confidered him as dead. In a few years after his recovery, he repaired to Orleans to ftudy the civil law ; from thence he was drawn to Valence in Dauphiny, by the reputation of Cujacius, who was then reading lectures there ; on his road he embraced an opportunity of hearing Hotoman, the celebrated author of Franco-Gallia, who was reading lectures alfo at Bourges.——During his refidence at Valence, he contracted a friendfhip with Jofeph Scaliger, which he cultivated through life.—In 1572, his father recalled him to Paris, juft before the maffacre of St. Bartholomew.—He mentions in his Memoirs

3

moirs

moirs the horrors which he felt in feeing a very fmall part of that bloody fcene.—He refided in the houfe of his uncle Nicholas De Thou, promoted to the bifhopric of Chartres: he was then defigned himfelf for the church; and, beginning to collect his celebrated library, applied himfelf particularly to the Civil Law, and to Grecian literature.

He travelled into Italy in 1573, with Paul De Foix, going on an embaffy to the Pope and the Italian Princes. Of De Foix, he gives the moft engaging character, and fpeaks with great pleafure of the literary entertainment and advantages which he derived from this expedition.—He returned to Paris, and devoted himfelf again to his ftudies, in the following year.—On the diffentions in the Court of France, in 1576, he was employed to negotiate with the Marefchal Montmorency, and engage him to interpofe his good offices to prevent the civil war; which he for fome time effected.——The fame year he vifited the Low Countries, and on his return was appointed to a public office, on which he entered with that extreme diffidence which is fo natural to a delicate mind.

In 1579 he travelled again, with his elder brother, who was fent by his phyficians to the baths of Plombieres in Lorrain: from hence he made a fhort excurfion into Germany, and was received there with the jovial hofpitality of that country, which he defcribes in a very lively manner.—But affection foon recalled him to Plombieres, to attend his infirm brother to Paris, who died there in a few months after their return.

In 1580, on the plague's appearing in the capital, our Hiftorian retired into Touraine, and after vifiting the principal places in Normandy, returned to Paris in the winter.—In the following year, he was of the number chofen from the Parliament of Paris to adminifter juftice in Guienne, as two ecclefiaftics were included in that commiffion.—In this expedition he embraced every opportunity of preparing the materials of his Hiftory, feeking, as he ever did, the fociety of all perfons eminent for their talents, or

T 2

capable

capable of giving him any ufeful information. He fpeaks with great pleafure of a vifit which he paid at this time to the celebrated Montaigne, whom he calls a man of a moft liberal mind, and totally uninfected with the fpirit of party.—After various excurfions, he was now returning to Paris, when he received the unexpected news of his father's death, an event which affected him moft deeply, as filial affection was one of the ftriking characteriftics of his amiable mind.—He confoled himfelf under the affliction of having been unable to pay his duty to his dying parent, by erecting a magnificent monument to his memory, expreffive of the high veneration in which he ever held his virtues.—He engaged again in public bufinefs, devoting his intervals of leifure to mathematical ftudies, and to the compofition of Latin verfe, which feems to have been his favourite amufement. In 1584, he publifhed his Poem, de re Accipitraria, which, though much celebrated by the critics of his age, has fallen, like the fubject of which it treats, into univerfal neglect.——In 1585, he bid adieu to the Court, on finding himfelf treated with fuch a degree of coldnefs, as his ingenuous nature could not fubmit to ; and being eager to advance in his great work, which he had already brought down to the reign of Francis II.—In 1587, having been often preffed to marry by his family, and being abfolved from his ecclefiaftical engagements for that purpofe, he made choice of Marie Barbanfon, of an antient and noble family ; but as her parents were fufpected of a fecret inclination to the reformed religion, it was thought proper that the lady fhould undergo a kind of expiation in a private conference with two Catholic Divines ; a circumftance of which the great Hiftorian fpeaks with an air of triumph in his Memoirs, as a proof of his own inviolable attachment to the faith of his fathers. In 1588, he loft his affectionate mother; who is defcribed, by her fon, as meeting death with the fame gentlenefs and tranquillity of mind, by which her life was diftinguifhed. When the violence of the league had reduced Henry the IIId to abandon Paris, our Hiftorian was fent

into

into Normandy to confirm the magiſtrates of that province in their
adherence to the King.—He afterwards met Henry at Blois, and
while he was receiving from him in private ſome commiſſions to
execute at Paris, the King preſſed his hand, and ſeemed preparing
to impart to him ſome important ſecret; but after a long pauſe dif-
miſſed him without revealing it.—This ſecret was afterwards ſuppoſed to have been the projected aſſaſſination of the Duke of Gùiſe:
the ſuppoſition is probable, and it is alſo probable, that if Henry
had then revealed his deſign, the manly virtue and eloquence of
De Thou might have led him to relinquiſh that infamous and fatal
meaſure.—He was, however, ſo far from ſuſpecting the intended
crime of the King, that when he firſt heard at Paris, that Guiſe
was aſſaſſinated, he believed it a falſe rumour, only ſpread by that
faction, to introduce, what he ſuppoſed had really happened, the
murder of the King.—In the commotions which the death of Guiſe
produced in Paris, many inſults were offered to the family of De
Thou : his wife was impriſoned for a day in the Baſtile; but obtaining her liberty, ſhe eſcaped from the city in a mean habit, attended by her huſband, diſguiſed alſo in the dreſs of a ſoldier. Having ſent his wife in ſafety into Picardy, he repaired to the King,
who was almoſt deſerted, at Blois; and was greatly inſtrumental in
perſuading his maſter to his coalition with Henry of Navarre.—
The King determined to eſtabliſh a Parliament at Tours, and De
Thou was conſidered as the moſt proper perſon to be the Preſident
of this aſſembly; but with his uſual modeſty he declined this
honour, and choſe rather to engage with his friend Mr. de Schomberg, in an expedition to Germany for the ſervice of the King.—
He was at firſt deſigned for the embaſſy to Elizàbeth, but at the
requeſt of Schomberg declined the appointment, and accompanied
his friend.

He firſt received intelligence of the King's death at Venice,
where he had formed an intimacy with the celebrated Arnauld
d'Oſſat, at that time Secretary to the Cardinal Joyeuſe.—In con-

ſequence

sequence of their converfation on this event, and the calamities of France, De Thou addreffed a Latin Poem to his friend, which he afterwards printed at Tours.

In leaving Italy, he paffed a few days at Padua, with his friend Vicenzio Pinelli; from whom he collected many particulars concerning the moft eminent Italian and Spanifh Authors, whom he determined to celebrate in his Hiftory, in the hope, as he honeftly confeffes, that his liberal attention to foreign merit might entitle his own Works to the favour both of Italy and Spain; but he was difappointed in this fair expectation, and laments the ingratitude which he experienced from both.

On his return to France, he was gracioufly received by Henry the IVth; and in giving that Prince an account of Italy, fuggefted to him the idea of a connexion with Mary of Medicis. After the battle of Ivry, he complimented the King in a fhort Poem, which clofes with the following lines:

> Aufpiciis vulgo peraguntur prælia regum,
>   Perque duces illis gloria multa venit:
> Tu vincis virtute tua, nec militis hæc eft;
>   Ifta tibi propria laurea parta manu.

As he was travelling, foon afterwards, with his wife and family, which he defigned to fettle at Tours, his party was intercepted by the enemy, and he was obliged to abandon his wife and her attendants, being prevailed on by their intreaties to fecure his own efcape by the fwiftnefs of his horfe.—He repaired to the King at Gifors, and foon obtained the reftitution of his family.—On the death of Amyot, Bifhop of Auxerre, well known by his various Tranflations from the Greek language, the King appointed De Thou his Principal Librarian. In 1592, our Hiftorian was very near falling a victim to the plague, but happily ftruggled through that dangerous diftemper by the affiftance of two fkilful phyficians, who

attended

attended him at Tours.—In 1593, he began the moſt important part
of his Hiſtory; and under this year he introduces in his Memoirs a
long and ſpirited Poem addreſſed to Poſterity, in which he enters
into a juſtification of himſelf againſt the malignant attacks, which
the manly and virtuous freedom of his writings had drawn upon
him. It concludes with the following animated appeal to the ſpirit of his father:

> Vos O majorum Cineres, teque optime longis
> Soliciti genitor defuncte laboribus ævi,
> Teſtor, pro patria nullas regnique ſalute
> Vitaviſſe vices, veſtra virtute meaque
> Indignum nil feciſſe, et ſi fata tuliſſent,
> Prodeſſem ut patriæ, patriæ ſuccurrere, livor
> Abſiſtat, pietate mea meruiſſe petenti.
> Pura ad vos anima atque hodiernæ neſcia culpæ
> Deſcendam, quandoque noviſſima venerit hora,
> Noſtraque ſub tacitos ibit fama integra manes.

In 1594, he ſucceeded his uncle Auguſtin as Preſident a Mor-
tier.—In 1596, he loſt his valuable and learned friend Pithou, who
firſt ſolicited him to undertake his Hiſtory, and had greatly aſſiſted
him in the proſecution of that laborious work.—How deeply the
affectionate mind of De Thou was wounded by this event, appears
from his long letter to Caſaubon on the occaſion.—In 1597, he began to be engaged in thoſe negotiations, which happily terminated
in the famous edict of Nantes.—It may be proper to obſerve here,
that De Thou was accuſed of being a Calviniſt, in conſequence of
the part he acted in this buſineſs, as well as from the moderate
tenor of his Hiſtory; and it is remarkable, that Sully ſeems in his
Memoirs to countenance the accuſation.

In 1601, our Hiſtorian ſuffered a ſevere domeſtic affliction in
the loſs of his wife.—He celebrated her virtues, and his own con-

nubial

nubial affection, in a Latin Poem : with this, and a Greek epitaph
on the same lady, written by Cafaubon, he terminates the Commentary of his own Life, of which the preceding account is an
imperfect abridgment.——His first wife leaving him no children,
he married, in 1603, Gafparde de la Chaftre, an accomplished lady
of a noble family ; who having brought him three fons and three
daughters, died at the age of 39, 1616.—There is a fine letter of
Daniel Heinfius, addreffed to our author on this occafion, exhorting
him to fortitude : but this unexpected domeftic calamity, and the
miferies which befel his country on the murder of Henry the
Great, are faid to have wounded his feeling mind fo deeply, as to
occafion his death, which happened in May 1617.—Under the re-
gency of Mary of Medicis, he had been one of the Directors general of the finances, maintaining the fame reputation for integrity
in that department, which he had ever preferved in his judicial
capacity.

The firft part of his Hiftory appeared in 1604, with a Preface
addreffed to Henry IV, juftly celebrated for its liberal and manly
fpirit.—But I muft obferve, that the following compliment to the
King—Quicquid de ea ftatueris jufferifve, pro divinæ vocis oraculo
mihi erit — was more than even that moft amiable of Monarchs deferved, as he ungratefully deferted the caufe of our Hiftorian, in
fuffering his work to be profcribed by the public cenfure of Rome
in 1609, as De Thou plainly intimates, in the following paffage
from one of his letters, written 1611 :—Publicata prima parte [Hif-
toriæ meæ] immane quam commoti funt plerique, five invidi, five
factiofi, qui mox proceres quofdam, qui per fe in talibus rebus nihil
vident, per calumnias artificiofe confictas, ut fcis, in me concita-
verunt, remque e veftigio Romam detulerunt, et auctore maligne
exagitato, facile pervicerunt, ut morofi illi cenfores omnia mea
finiftre interpretarentur, et præjudicio perfonæ opus integrum,
cujus ne tertiam quidem partem legerant, præcipitato ordine
damnarent. Rex caufam meam initio quidem tuebatur, quamdiu

proceres in aula infestos habui. Sed paulatim ipfe eorundem aftu infractus eft; cognitoque Romæ per emiffarios labare regem, poft Offati et Serafini Cardinalium mihi amiciffimorum obitum, et illuftriffimi Perronii ex urbe difceffum, ictus poftremo in me directus eft, qui facile vitari potuit, fi qui circa regem erant, tantæ injuriæ fenfum ad fe ac regni dignitatem pertinere vel minima fignificatione præ fe tuliffent. Ita in aula omni ope deftitutus, facile Romæ oppreffus fum.——De Thou was preparing a new edition of his Hiftory at the time of his death.—His paffion for Latin verfe appears never to have forfaken him, as the lateft effufion of his pen was a little poem defcriptive of his laft illnefs, and an epitaph in which he draws the following juft character of himfelf:

> Mihi veritatis cura vitæ commodis
> Antiquiorque charitatibus fuit,
> Nullique facto, voce nulli injurius,
> Injurias patienter aliorum tuli.
> Tu quifquis es, qualifque, quantufque, O bone,
> Si cura veri eft ulla, fi pietas movet,
> A me meifque injuriam, quæfo, abftine.

The pious paternal prayer in the laft line was very far from being crowned with fuccefs. Francis, the eldeft fon of De Thou, fell a victim to the refentment which Cardinal Richelieu is faid to have conceived againft him, from a paffage in the great Hiftorian, reflecting on the Richelieu family.—He was beheaded at Lyons, 1642, for having been privy to a confpiracy againft the Cardinal. —Voltaire, with his ufual philanthropy and fpirit, inveighs againft the iniquity of this execution, in his Melanges, tom. iii.—The curious reader may find a particular account of this tragical event in the laft volume of that noble edition of Thuanus, which was publifhed under the aufpices of Dr. Mead, and does great honour to

U

our

our country.—I fhall clofe this Note by tranfcribing from it the following fpirited epitaph on the unfortunate victim.

Hiftoriam quifquis vult fcribere, fcribere veram
    Nunc vetat Exitium, magne Thuane, tuum.
Richeliæ ftirpis proavos læfiffe, Paterni
    Crimen erat calami, quo tibi vita perit.
Sanguine delentur nati monumenta parentis :
    Quæ nomen dederant fcripta, dedere necem.
Tanti morte viri fic eft fancita Tyrannis :
    Vera loqui fi vis, difce cruenta pati.

NOTE XVI. VERSE 364.

Thy Wits, O France! (as ev'n thy Critics own)
Support not Hiftory's majeftic tone.] To avoid every appearance of national prejudice, I fhall quote on this occafion fome paffages from a very liberal French Critic, who has paffed the fame judgment on the Hiftorians of his country. The Marquis d'Argenfon, in a memoir read before the French Academy, 1755, not only confeffes that the French Writers have failed in Hiftory, but even ventures to explain the caufe of their ill fuccefs.

Nous avons, fays he, quelques morceaux, ou l'on trouve tout à la fois la fidelité, le gout, et le vrai ton de l'Hiftoire; mais outre qu'ils font en petit nombre, et tres-courts, les auteurs, à qui nous en fommes redevables, fe font defié de leurs forces; ils ont craint de manquer d'haleine dans des ouvrages de plus longue étendue.

Pourquoi les anciens ont-ils eu des Thucydides, des Xenophons, des Polybes, & des Tacites ? pourquoi ne pouvons nous leur comparer que des St. Réals, des Vertots, des Sarrafins ? nous ne devons point attribuer cette difette à la decadence de l'Efprit humain. Il

faut

.faut en chercher, ſi j'oſe m'exprimer ainſi, quelque raiſon nationale, quelque cauſe, qui ſoit particuliere aux François . . . . .

Quatre qualités principales ſont néceſſaires aux Hiſtoriens.

1. Une critique exaƈte & ſavante, fondée ſur des recherches laborieuſes, pour la colleƈtion des faits.

2. Une grande profondeur en morale & en politique.

3. Une imagination ſage, & fleurie, qui peigne les aƈtions, qui deduiſe les cauſes, & qui preſente les reflexions avec clarté & ſimplicité ; quelquefois avec feu, mais toujours avec gout & élégance.

4. Il faut de plus la conſtance dans le travail, un ſtyle égal & ſoutenu, & une exaƈtitude infatigable, qui ne montre jamais l'impatience d'avancer, ni de laſſitude pendant le cours d'une longue carrière.

Qu'on ſepare ces qualités, on trouvera des chefs-d'œuvres parmi nous, des Critiques, des Moraliſtes, des Politiques, des Peintres, & des literateurs laborieux, dont le produit nous ſurprend. Mais qu'on cherche ces qualités raſſemblées, on manquera d'exemples à citer entre nos Auteurs.——The critic then takes a rapid review of the French Hiſtorians, and proceeds to make the following lively remarks on the difficulty of writing Hiſtory in France, and the volatile charaƈter of his countrymen—J'ai dejà prévenu l'une des plus grandes difficultés pour les auteurs ; ils devroient etre en meme tems hommes de cabinet & hommes du monde. Par l'etude on ne connoit que les anciens, & les mœurs bourgeoiſes ; & dans la bonne compagnie, on perd ſon tems, l'on ecrit peu, et l'on penſe encore moins. . ..

L'haleine manque à un écrivain François faute de conſtance ; il entrepend légèrement de grands ouvrages, il les continue avec nonchalance, il les finit avec dégôut : s'il les abandonne quelque tems, il ne les reprend plus, & nous voyons que tous nos continuateurs ont échoué. La laſſitude du ſoir ſe reſſent de l'ardeur

U 2

du

du matin. C'eſt delà qu'il nous arrive de n'avoir de bon, que de petits morceaux, ſoit en poeſie, ſoit en proſe . . . . . nous n'avons que . . . . . des morceaux Hiſtoriques, & preſque pas une Hiſtoire générale digne de louange.

Choix des Memoires de l'Academie, &c.
Londres, 1777, tom. iii. p. 627.

END OF THE NOTES TO THE SECOND EPISTLE.

NOTES

N O T E S

TO THE

THIRD EPISTLE.

NOTE I. VERSE 30.

AND shake th' affrighted world with dire portents.] There is a curious treatise of Dr. Warburton's on this subject, which is become very scarce; it is entitled, " A critical and philosophical Enquiry into the causes of prodigies and miracles, as related by Historians, with an Essay towards restoring a method and purity in History." It contains, like most of the compositions of this dogmatical Writer, a strange mixture of judicious criticism and entertaining absurdity, in a style so extraordinary, that I think the following specimens of it may amuse a reader, who has not happened to meet with this singular book.—Having celebrated Rawleigh and Hyde, as writers of true historic genius, he adds : "almost all the rest of our Histories want Life, Soul, Shape, and Body: a mere hodgepodge of abortive embryos and rotten carcases, kept in an unnatural ferment (which the vulgar mistake for real life) by the rank leven of prodigies and portents. Which can't but afford good

diversion

diverfion to the Critic, while he obferves how naturally one of their own fables is here mythologiz'd and explain'd, *of a church-yard carcafe, raifed and fet a ftrutting by the inflation of fome hellifh fuc-cubus within.*" He then paffes a heavy cenfure on the antiqua-rian publications of Thomas Hearne; in the clofe of which he ex-claims—" Wonder not, reader, at the view of thefe extravagancies. The Hiftoric Mufe, after much vain longing for a vigorous adorer, is now fallen under that indifpofition of her fex, fo well known by a depraved appetite for trafh and cinders."—Having quoted two paffages from this fingular Critic, in which his metaphorical lan-guage is exceedingly grofs, candour obliges me to tranfcribe ano-ther, which is no lefs remarkable for elegance and beauty of ex-preffion. In defcribing Salluft, at one time the loud advocate of public fpirit, and afterwards fharing in the robberies of Cæfar, he expreffes this variation of character by the following imagery:— " No fooner did the warm afpect of good fortune fhine out again, but all thofe exalted ideas of virtue and honour, raifed like a beau-tiful kind of froft-work, in the cold feafon of adverfity, diffolved and difappeared."

Enquiry, &c. London, 1727, page 17.

N O T E II. V E R S E 51.

On Francio now the Gallic page is mute,

And Britifh Story drops the name of Brute.] The origin of the French nation was afcribed by one of the Monkifh Hiftorians to Francio, a fon of Priam : Mr. Warton, who mentions this circum-ftance in his Differtation on the origin of romantic fiction in Europe, fuppofes that the revival of Virgil's Æneid, about the fixth or fe-venth century, infpired many nations with this chimerical idea of tracing their defcent from the family of Priam. There is a very remarkable proof in the Hiftorian Matthew of Weftminfter, how fond the Englifh were of confidering themfelves as the defcendants

of

of the Trojan Brutus. In a letter from Edward the First to Pope Boniface, concerning the affairs of Scotland, the King boasts of his Trojan predeceffor in the following terms :—Sub temporibus itaque Ely & Samuelis prophetarum, vir quidam ftrenuus et infignis, Brutus nomine, de genere Trojanorum, poft excidium urbis Trojanæ cum multis nobilibus Trojanorum applicuit in quandam Infulam tunc Albion vocatam, a gigantibus inhabitatam, quibus fua et fuorum feductis potentia et occifis, eam nomine fuo Britanniam fociofque fuos Britannos appellavit, & ædificavit civitatem quam Trinovantum nuncupavit, quæ modo Londinum nuncupatur.

MATT. WESTMON. p. 439.

NOTE III.   VERSE 73.

And Bacon's felf, for mental glory born,

Meets, as her flave, our pity, or our fcorn.] I wifh not to dwell invidioufly on the failings of this immortal Genius; but it may be ufeful to remark, that no Hiftorical work, though executed by a man of the higheft mental abilities, can obtain a lafting reputation, if it be planned and written with a fervility of fpirit.—This was evidently the cafe in Bacon's Hiftory of Henry the VIIth: it was the firft work he engaged in after his difgrace, and laid as a peace-offering at the feet of his mafter, the defpicable James, who affected to confider his great grandfather, the abject and avaricious Henry, as the model of a King. It was therefore the aim of the unfortunate Hiftorian to flatter this phantafy of the royal pedant, for whom he wrote, and he accordingly formed a coloffal ftatue to reprefent a pigmy.—It is matter of aftonifhment that Lord Bolingbroke, who in his political works has written on the vices of this very King, with a force and beauty fo fuperior to the Hiftory in queftion, fhould fpeak of it as a work poffeffing merit fufficient to bear a comparifon with the antients: on the contrary, the extreme awk-

wardnefs

2

wardnefs of the tafk, which the Hiftorian impofed upon himfelf, gave a weaknefs and embarraffment to his ftyle, which in his nobler works is clear, nervous, and manly. This will particularly appear from a few lines in his character of Henry.—" This King, to fpeak of him in terms equal to his deferving, was one of the beft fort of wonders, a wonder for wife men. He had parts, both in his virtues and his fortune, not fo fit for a common-place as for obfervation. . . . . His worth may bear a tale or two, that may put upon him fomewhat, that may feem divine."—He then relates a dream of Henry's mother, the Lady Margaret: but the quotations I have made may be fufficient to juftify my remark; and, as Dr. Johnfon fays happily of Milton, " What Englifhman can take delight in tranfcribing paffages, which, if they leffen the reputation of Bacon, diminifh in fome degree the honour of our country ?"

NOTE IV. Verse 92.

And of that mountain make the ftatue of a King.] An allufion to the Architect Dinocrates, who offered to cut Mount Athos into a ftatue of Alexander the Great.

NOTE V. Verse 97.

As crown'd with Indian laurels, nobly won, &c.] This ftory is told on a fimilar occafion by Lucian. Having afferted that hiftorical flatterers often meet with the indignation they deferve, he proceeds to this example : ὥσπερ Ἀριστοβούλου μονομαχιαν γραψαντος Ἀλεξανδρῳ και Πωρου, και αναγνοντος αυτω τυτο μαλιστα το χωριον της γραφης· (ᾠετο γαρ χαριεισθαι τα μεγιστα τω βασιλει, επιψευδομενος αριστειας τινας αυτω, και αναπλαττων εργα μειζω της αληθειας) λαβων εκεινος το βιβλιον (πλεοντες δ᾽ ετυγχανον εν τω ποταμω τω Ὑδασπει) ερριψεν επι κεφαλην ες το ὕδωρ, υδωρ, επειπων " Και σε δε ουτως εχρην, ω Αριϛοϐυλε, τοιαυτα υπερ εμε μονομαχηντα, και ελεφαντας εν ακοντιω Φονευοντα."

Lucian Edit. Riollay, p. 28.

The Critics are much divided on this paſſage : I have followed an interpretation very different from that adopted by a learned and judicious author, who has lately entered into a thorough diſcuſſion of all the anecdotes relating to this celebrated Conqueror, in a very elaborate and ſpirited diſſertation, entitled, " Examen critique des Hiſtoriens d'Alexandre," Paris, 4to, 1775. But there is great probability in his conjecture, that the name of Ariſtobulus has ſlipt into the ſtory by ſome miſtake ; and that the ſycophant ſo juſtly reprimanded was Oneſicritus, who attended the hero of Macedon in quality of Hiſtoriographer, and is cenſured by the judicious Strabo as the moſt fabulous of all the Writers who have engaged in his Hiſtory. For the reaſons which ſupport this conjecture, ſee the book I have mentioned, page 19.

NOTE VI. Verse 115.

In Dedications quietly inurn'd,

They take more lying Praiſe than Ammon ſpurn'd.] As Hiſtory is the compoſition moſt frequently addreſſed to Princes, modern Hiſtorians have been peculiarly tempted to this kind of adulation.— Indeed Dedications in general are but too commonly a diſgrace to letters. Perhaps a conciſe Hiſtory of this ſpecies of writing, and the fate of ſome remarkable Dedicators, might have a good influence towards correcting that proſtitution of talents, which is ſo often obſerved in productions of this nature ; and ſuch a work might be very amuſing to the lovers of literary anecdote.—The two moſt unfortunate Dedications that occur to my remembrance, were written by Joſhua Barnes, and Dr. Pearce, late Biſhop of Rocheſter : The firſt dedicated his Hiſtory of Edward the IIId, to James the IId, and unluckily compared that Monarch to the moſt valiant of his

X
predeceſſors,

predeceffors, juft before his timidity led him to abdicate the throne: the fecond dedicated his edition of Tully de Oratore to Lord Macclesfield, and as unluckily celebrated his patron as a model of public virtue, not many years before he was impeached in parliament, and fin.d £ 30,000 for the iniquity of his conduct in the office of Cha..eilor.

NOTE VII. VERSE 135.

Still can Herrera, mourning o'er his urn,

His dying pangs to blissful rapture turn.] Antonio de Herrera, a Spanifh Hiftorian of great reputation, defcribes the death of Philip II. in the following terms:—" Y fue cofa de notar, que aviendo dos, o tres horas antes que efpiraffe, tenido un paraxifmo tan violento, que le tuvieron por acabado, cubriendole el roftro con un panno, abrio los ojos con gran efpiritu, y tomò el crucifixo de mano de Don Hernando de Toledo, y con gran devocion, y ternura le besò muchas vozes, y a la imagen de nuefira Sennora de Monferrate, que eftava en la candela. Pareciò al Arçobifpo de Toledo, a los confeffores, y a quantos fe hallaron prefentes, que era impoffible, que naturalmente huvieffe podido bolver tan prefto, y con tan vivo efpiritu, fino que devio de tener en aquel punto alguna vifion y favor del cielo, y que mas fue rapto que paraxifmo: luego bolviò al agonia, y fe fue acabando poco a poco, y con pequenno movimiento fe le arrancò el alma, domingo a treze de Setiembre a las cinco horas de la mannana, fiendo fus ultimas palabras, que moria como Catolico en la Fè y obediencia de la fanta Iglefia Romana; y affi acabò efte gran Monarca con la mifma prudencia con que vivio: por lo qual (meritamente) fe le dio el atributo de prudente.

Hift. General del Mundo, por Ant. Herrera, Madrid 1612.
Tom. iii. f. 777.

After fpeaking fo freely on the vices of this Monarch, it is but juft to obferve, that Philip, who poffeffed all the fedate cruelty

of

of the cold-blooded Octavius, refembled him alfo in one amiable quality, and was fo much a friend to letters, that his reign may be confidered as the Auguftan age of Spanifh literature.—His moft bloody minifter, the mercilefs Alva, was the Mæcenas of that wonderful and voluminous Poet, Lope de Vega. I cannot help regretting that the two eminent Writers, who have lately delineated the reigns of Charles the Vth, and his Son Philip, fo happily in our language, have entered fo little into the literary Hiftory of thofe times.

N O T E VIII. VERSE 158.

Nor hope to ftain, on bafe Detraction's fcroll,

A Tully's morals, or a Sidney's foul !] Dion Caffius, the fordid advocate of defpotifm, endeavoured to depreciate the character of Cicero, by inferting in his Hiftory the moft indecent Oration that ever difgraced the page of an Hiftorian.—In the opening of his 46th book, he introduces Q. Fufius Calenus haranguing the Roman fenate againft the great ornament of that affembly, calling Cicero a magician, and accufing him of proftituting his wife, and committing inceft with his daughter. Some late hiftorical attempts to fink the reputation of the great Algernon Sidney, are fo recent, that they will occur to the remembrance of almoft every Reader.

N O T E IX. VERSE 179.

Nor lefs the blemifh, tho' of different kind,

From falfe Philofophy's conceits refin'd ! &c.] The ideas in this paffage are chiefly borrowed from the excellent obfervations on Hiftory in Dr. Gregory's *Comparative View.* As that engaging little volume is fo generally known, I fhall not lengthen thefe Notes by tranfcribing any part of it; but I thought it juft to acknowledge my

X 2

obligations

obligations to an Author, whose sentiments I am proud to adopt, as he united the noblest affections of the heart to great elegance of mind, and is justly ranked among the most amiable of moral writers.

N O T E X.   Verse 218.

To speak no Falsehood; and no Truth suppress.] Quis nescit, primam esse Historiæ legem ne quid falsi dicere audeat? deinde, ne quid veri non audeat.   De Oratore, Lib. ii.

Voltaire has made a few just remarks on the second part of this famous Historical maxim; and it certainly is to be understood with some degree of limitation. The sentence of the amiable Pliny, so often quoted—Historia quoquo modo scripta delectat—is liable, I apprehend, to still more objections.

N O T E XI.   Verse 266.

A waste of Genius in the toil of Knolles.] Richard Knolles, a native of Northamptonshire, educated at Oxford, published, in 1610, a History of the Turks. An Author of our age, to whom both criticism and morality have very high obligations, has bestowed a liberal encomium on this neglected Historian; whose character he closes with the following just observation:

" Nothing could have sunk this Author in obscurity, but the remoteness and barbarity of the people whose story he relates. It seldom happens, that all circumstances concur to happiness or fame. The nation which produced this great Historian, has the grief of seeing his genius employed upon a foreign and uninteresting subject; and that Writer, who might have secured perpetuity to his name, by a History of his own country, has exposed himself to the

10   danger

danger of oblivion, by recounting enterprizes and revolutions, of which none defire to be informed."

RAMBLER, Vol. III. N° 122.

NOTE XII.   VERSE 330.

And read your juft reward in Brady's fate!] Robert Brady, born in Norfolk, was Profeffor of Phyfic in the Univerfity of Cambridge, which he reprefented in Parliament.—He was Mafter of Caius College, and Phyfician in ordinary to James II. He publifhed, in 1684, a Hiftory of England, from the invafion of Julius Cæfar to the death of Richard the Second, in three volumes folio: and died in 1700.—His character cannot be more juftly or more forcibly expreffed, than in the words of a living Author, who has lately vindicated the antient conftitution of our country with great depth of learning, and with all the energy of genius infpirited by freedom.

" Of Dr. Brady it ought to be remembered, that he was the flave of a faction, and that he meanly proftituted an excellent underftanding, and admirable quicknefs, to vindicate tyranny, and to deftroy the rights of his nation."

STUART's View of Society in Europe.
Notes, page 327.

NOTE XIII.   VERSE 381.

Like the dumb Son of Crœfus, in the ftrife.] Herodotus relates, that a Perfian foldier, in the ftorming of Sardis, was preparing to kill Crœfus, whofe perfon he did not know, and who, giving up all as loft, neglected to defend his own life; a fon of the unfortunate Monarch, who had been dumb from his infancy, and who never

fpake

spake afterwards, found utterance in that trying moment, and preserved his father, by exclaiming " O kill not Crœsus."

NOTE XIV. VERSE 387.

Less eager to correct, than to revile.] This is perhaps a just description of *The polemical Divine*, as a general character: but there are some authors of that class, to whom it can never be applied. —Dr. Watson, in particular, will be ever mentioned with honour, as one of the happy few, who have preserved the purity of justice and good manners in a zealous defence of religion; who have given elegance and spirit to controversial writing, by that liberal elevation of mind, which is equally removed from the meanness of flattery and the insolence of detraction.

NOTE XV. VERSE 393.

The noble instinct, Love of lasting Fame.] There is a most animated and judicious defence of this passion in Fitzosborne's Letters.—But I must content myself with barely referring my Reader to that amiable Moralist, as I fear I have already extended these Notes to such a length, as will expose me to the severity of criticism. Indeed I tremble in reviewing the size of this Comment: which I cannot close without entreating my Reader to believe, that its bulk has arisen from no vain ideas of the value of my own Poem, but from a desire to throw collected light on a subject, which appeared to me of importance, and to do all the justice in my power to many valuable writers, whom I wished to celebrate.—Those who are inclined to censure, will perhaps think this apology insufficient; and I foresee

         that

that some hasty Critics will compare the length of the Poem with that of the Annotations, and then laying down the book without perusing either, they will apply perhaps (not unhappily) to the Author the following lively couplet of Dr. Young:

> Sure, next to writing, the most idle thing
> Is gravely to harangue on what we sing.

F I N I S.

E R R A T A.

Pag 9. end of Ver. 110, the Semicolon should be a Comma.
   58. 1st Line of the Argument, should read thus, *Vanity, national and private—*
   7. l. 15. *after* Thucydides—the Full Stop should be a Comma.
   1. l. 7. from the bottom, *for* adgandere, *read* adgaudere.
   1. l. 3. from the bottom, *for* 13, 14. read XIII. XIV.
   1. l. 1. *after* heraldry, *add* it was indeed the favourite study.